BEHIND THE GLAMOUR
AND THE FAME
ARE THE SECRETS THAT
COULD BREAK HER HEART . . .

Glitter Baby

"Next to Tracy and Hepburn,
nobody does romantic comedy better than
Susan Elizabeth Phillips."
Minneapolis Star Tribune

"Phillips's characters are full of heart,
and you'll have no trouble seeing the chemistry
between them . . . steam rises from the pages."
Richmond Times-Dispatch

"Simply irresistible."
Booklist

"[Susan Elizabeth Phillips is]
a natural-born storyteller who has a wicked way with words."
Library Journal

* * *

"Engaging and funny. "
The State (Columbia, MD)

"Funny, smart, satisfying read."
Contra Costa Times

* * *

"Phillips not only plucks at heartstrings, she plays a full concert."
Romantic Times BOOKreviews

* * *

"Delightful, funny, and quirky."
Columbus Dispatch

"She makes you laugh, makes you cry—
makes you feel good."
JAYNE ANN KRENTZ

* * *

"Susan Elizabeth Phillips's bestselling novels have
helped to give romance fiction something
it long deserved—respectability."
Chicago Sun-Times

* * *

"Romance fans should check out
Susan Elizabeth Phillips."
Omaha World Herald

"A dazzling voice in
contemporary woman's fiction."
LINDA BARLOW

* * *

"Susan Elizabeth Phillips writes a story that wraps
around your heart and doesn't let go."
Oakland Press

* * *

"If you can read Susan Elizabeth Phillips
without laughing out loud,
check for a pulse!"
ELIZABETH LOWELL

By Susan Elizabeth Phillips

GLITTER BABY
NATURAL BORN CHARMER
MATCH ME IF YOU CAN
AIN'T SHE SWEET?
BREATHING ROOM
THIS HEART OF MINE
JUST IMAGINE
FIRST LADY
LADY BE GOOD
DREAM A LITTLE DREAM
NOBODY'S BABY BUT MINE
KISS AN ANGEL
HEAVEN, TEXAS
IT HAD TO BE YOU

And in Hardcover
WHAT I DID FOR LOVE

Susan Elizabeth Phillips

Glitter Baby

AVON
An Imprint of HarperCollins*Publishers*

This book was originally published in mass market January 1987 in a slightly altered form by Dell Publishing, a division of Random House.

AVON BOOKS
An Imprint of HarperCollins*Publishers*
10 East 53rd Street
New York, New York 10022-5299

ISBN 978-0-06-143856-1
www.avonbooks.com

First Avon Books paperback printing: January 2009

Printed in the U.S.A.

10 9 8 7 6 5 4 3 2 1

To Lydia, with love

Sisters forever

* * *

Chapter 1

The Glitter Baby was back. She paused inside the arched entrance to the Orlani Gallery so the opening night guests would have time to recognize her. The low buzz of polite party conversation mixed with the street noises outside as the patrons pretended to view the African primitives hanging on the walls. The air carried the scent of Joy, imported pâté de foie gras, and money. Six years had passed since hers was one of the most famous faces in America. The Glitter Baby wondered if they'd still remember . . . and what she would do if they didn't.

She gazed straight ahead with studied ennui, her lips slightly parted and her hands, bare of rings, relaxed at her sides. In ankle-strap stilettos she stood more than six feet tall, a beautiful Amazon with a thick mane of hair that fell past her shoulders. It used to be a game among New York's one-name hairdressers to try to identify the color with only a single word. They offered up "champagne," "butterscotch," "taffy," but never got it quite right because her hair was all those colors, interwoven threads of every shade of blond that changed hue with the light.

It wasn't just her hair that inspired the poetic. Everything about the Glitter Baby encouraged superlatives. Years earlier, a temperamental fashion editor had famously fired an assistant editor who made the mistake of referring to the celebrated eyes as "hazel." The editor herself rewrote the copy, describing the irises of Fleur Savagar's eyes as being "marbled with gold, tortoise, and startling sluices of emerald-green."

On this September evening in 1982, the Glitter Baby looked more beautiful than ever as she gazed at the crowd. A trace of hauteur shone in her not-quite-hazel eyes, and her sculpted chin held an almost arrogant tilt, but inside, Fleur Savagar was terrified. She took a deep, steadying breath and reminded herself that the Glitter Baby had grown up, and she wouldn't ever let them hurt her again.

She watched the crowd. Diana Vreeland, impeccably dressed in an Yves Saint Laurent evening cape and black silk pants, studied a bronze Benin head, while Mikhail Baryshnikov, all cheeks and dimples, stood at the center of a group of women more interested in Russian charm than African primitives. In one corner a television anchorman and his socialite wife chatted with a fortyish French actress making her first public appearance since a not so hush-hush face-lift, while across from them, the pretty showpiece wife of a notoriously homosexual Broadway producer stood alone in a Mollie Parnis she had foolishly left unbuttoned to the waist.

Fleur's dress was different from everyone else's. Her designer had seen to that. *You must be elegant, Fleur. Elegance, elegance, elegance in the Era of the Tacky.* He'd cut bronze stretch satin on the bias and constructed a cleanly sculpted gown with a high neck and bare arms. At mid-thigh, he'd slashed the skirt in a long diagonal to the opposite ankle, then filled in the space with a waterfall flounce of the thinnest black *point d'esprit.* He'd teased her about the flounce, saying he'd been forced to design it as camouflage for her size-ten feet.

Heads began to turn, and she saw the exact instant when the crowd's curiosity changed to recognition. She slowly let out her breath. A hush fell over the gallery. A bearded photographer turned his Hasselblad from the French actress to Fleur and caught the picture that would take up the entire front page of the next morning's *Women's Wear Daily*.

Across the room, Adelaide Abrams, New York's most widely read gossip columnist, squinted toward the arched doorway. It couldn't be! Had the real Fleur Savagar finally been flushed out? Adelaide took a quick step forward and bumped into a multimillionaire real estate developer. She glanced wildly about for her own photographer, only to see that *nafka* from *Harper's Bazaar* already bearing down. Adelaide plunged past two startled socialites, and, like Secretariat going for the Triple Crown, made the final dash to Fleur Savagar's side.

Fleur had been watching the race between *Harper's* and Adelaide Abrams, and she didn't know whether she was relieved or not to see Adelaide winning. The columnist was a shrewd old bird, and it wouldn't be easy to put her off with half-truths and vague answers. On the other hand, Fleur needed her.

"Fleur my God it really is you I can't believe what I see with my very own eyes my God you look wonderful!"

"So do you, Adelaide." Fleur had a vaguely Midwestern accent, pleasant and slightly musical. No one listening would have guessed that English wasn't her first language. The bottom of her chin met the top of Adelaide's hennaed hair, and she had to lean down for their air kiss. Adelaide pulled her toward the back corner of the room, effectively cutting her off from the other members of the press.

"Nineteen seventy-six was a bad year for me, Fleur," she said. "I went through menopause. God forbid you should ever go through the hell I did. It would have lifted my spirits if you'd given me the story. But I guess you had too much on your mind to spare me a thought. Then, when you finally show up again in New York . . ." She shook her finger at Fleur's chin. "Let's just say you've disappointed me."

"Everything in its proper time."

"That's all you have to say?"

Fleur gave what she hoped was an inscrutable smile and took a glass of champagne from a passing waiter.

Adelaide grabbed a glass of her own. "I'll never forget your first *Vogue* cover if I live to be a hundred. Those bones of yours . . . and those great, big hands. No rings, no nail polish. They shot you in furs and a Harry Winston diamond choker that had to cost a quarter of a million."

"I remember."

"No one could believe it when you disappeared. Then Belinda . . ." A calculating expression crossed her face. "Have you seen her lately?"

Fleur wouldn't talk about Belinda. "I was in Europe most of the time. I needed to sort out some things."

"Sorting out I can understand. You were a young girl. It was your first movie, and you'd hardly had a normal childhood. Hollywood people aren't always sensitive, not like us New Yorkers. Six years, then you come back, and you're not yourself. What kind of sorting takes six years?"

"Things got complicated." She gazed across the room to signal the subject was closed.

Adelaide switched direction. "So tell me, mystery lady, what's your secret? Hard to believe, but you look even better now than you did at nineteen."

The compliment interested Fleur. Sometimes when she looked at her photographs, she could glimpse the beauty others saw in her, but only in a detached way, as if the image belonged to someone else. Although she wanted to believe the years had brought greater strength and maturity to her face, she hadn't known how others would view the changes.

Fleur had no personal vanity, simply because she'd never been able to see what all the fuss was about. She found her face too strong. The bones that photographers and fashion editors raved about looked masculine to her. As for her height, her large hands, her long feet . . . They were simply impossible.

"You're the one with secrets," she said. "Your skin is amazing."

Adelaide allowed herself to be flattered for only a moment before she waved off the compliment. "Tell me about that gown. Nobody's worn anything like it in years. It reminds me of what fashion used to be about . . ." She tilted her head toward the unzipped producer's wife. " . . . before vulgarity replaced style."

"The man who designed it will be here later tonight. He's extraordinary. You have to meet him." Fleur smiled. "I'd better go talk to *Harper's* before she burns a hole in your back."

Adelaide caught her arm, and Fleur saw what looked like genuine concern on her face. "Wait. Before you turn around, you should know that Belinda just walked in."

A queer, dizzy sensation swept through Fleur. She hadn't expected this. How stupid of her. She should have realized . . . Even without looking, she knew every eye in the room would be watching them. She turned slowly.

Belinda was loosening the scarf that lay just inside the collar of her golden sable coat. She froze when she saw Fleur, then her unforgettable hyacinth-blue eyes widened.

Belinda was forty-five, blond, and lovely. Her jawline remained firm, and her knee-high soft leather boots clung to small, shapely calves. She'd worn the same hairstyle since the fifties—Grace Kelly's sophisticated *Dial M for Murder* side-parted bob—and it still looked fashionable.

Without even a glance at the people standing around her, she walked straight toward Fleur. On her way, she pulled off her gloves and stuffed them in her pockets. She didn't notice when one of her gloves fell to the floor. She was conscious only of her daughter. The Glitter Baby.

Belinda had invented the name. So perfect for her beautiful Fleur. She touched the small spinning charm that she'd begun to wear again on a chain under her dress. Flynn had given it to her during those golden days at the Garden of Allah. But that hadn't really been the beginning.

The beginning . . . She remembered so clearly the day it had all started. That September Thursday in 1955 had been hot for Southern California. It was the day she'd met James Dean . . .

The Baron's Baby

Chapter 2

Belinda Britton lifted a copy of *Modern Screen* from the magazine rack at Schwab's Sunset Boulevard drugstore. She couldn't wait to see Marilyn Monroe's new movie, *The Seven Year Itch*, although she wished Marilyn weren't making it with Tom Ewell. He wasn't very handsome. She'd rather see her with Bob Mitchum again, like in *River of No Return*, or Rock Hudson, or, even better, Burt Lancaster.

A year ago Belinda had a terrible crush on Burt Lancaster. When she'd seen *From Here to Eternity*, she'd felt as if it were her body, not Deborah Kerr's, that he'd embraced as the waves crashed around them, and her lips he'd kissed. She wondered if Deborah Kerr had opened her mouth when Burt kissed her. Deborah didn't seem the type, but if Belinda had been playing the part, she would have opened her mouth for Burt Lancaster's tongue, you could bet on that.

In her fantasy, the light wasn't right or the director had gotten distracted. For some reason the camera wouldn't stop and neither would Burt. He'd peel down the top of her sandy one-piece bathing suit, stroke her, and call her "Karen" because that was her name in the movie. But Burt would know it was really Belinda, and when he bent his head to her breasts . . .

"Excuse me, miss, but could you hand me a copy of *Reader's Digest*?"

Fade to waves pounding, just like in the movies.

Belinda passed over the magazine, then traded her *Modern Screen* for a *Photoplay* with Kim Novak on the cover. It had been six months since she'd daydreamed about Burt Lancaster or Tony Curtis or any of the rest. Six months since she'd seen the face that had made all the other handsome faces fade away. She wondered if her parents ever missed her, but suspected they were glad to have her gone. Every month, they sent her one hundred dollars so she didn't have to work at a menial job that would embarrass them if their Indianapolis society friends ever found out about it. Her well-to-do parents had both been forty when she was born. They'd named her Edna Cornelia Britton. She was a terrible inconvenience. Although they weren't cruel, they were cold, and she grew up with a faint sense of panic stemming from a feeling that she was somehow invisible. Other people told her she was pretty, her teachers told her she was smart, but their compliments meant nothing. How could someone who was invisible be special?

When she was nine, Belinda discovered that all the bad feelings went away when she sat in the Palace Theater and pretended she was one of the dazzling goddesses who shone on the screen. Beautiful creatures with faces and bodies a hundred times bigger than life. These women were the chosen ones, and she vowed that she, too, would someday take her place among them on that same screen, that she would be magnified as they were until she never again felt invisible.

"That'll be twenty-five cents, beautiful." The cashier was a handsome, Chiclet-toothed blond, too obviously an unemployed actor. His gaze slid over Belinda's figure, fashionably clad in a pencil-slim navy cotton sheath trimmed in white and cinched at the waist with a poppy-red patent leather belt. The dress reminded her of something Audrey Hepburn would wear, although Belinda thought of herself more as the Grace Kelly type. People told her she looked like Grace. She'd even had her hair cut to make the resemblance more pronounced.

The style complemented her small, fine features, meticulously enhanced with Tangee's Red Majesty lipstick. She'd blended a few dabs of Revlon's newest cream rouge just below her cheekbones to emphasize their contour, a trick she'd learned in a *Movie Mirror* article by Bud Westmore, makeup man to the stars. She kept her pale lashes touched up with dark brown mascara, which highlighted her very best feature, a pair of exceptionally startling hyacinth-blue eyes, saturated with color and innocence.

The Chiclet-toothed blond leaned over the counter. "I get off work in an hour. How about waiting around for me? *Not as a Stranger*'s playing down the street."

"No, thank you." Belinda picked up one of the Bavarian chocolate mint bars that Schwab's kept displayed on the counter and handed over a dollar bill. They were her special treat, along with a new movie magazine, on her twice-weekly trips to the Sunset Boulevard drugstore. So far, she'd seen Rhonda Fleming at the counter buying a bottle of Lustre-Creme shampoo and Victor Mature walking out the door.

"How about this weekend?" the cashier persisted.

"I'm afraid not." Belinda took her change and gave him a sad, regretful smile that made him feel as if she would remember him forever with faint, bittersweet regret. She liked the effect she had on men. She assumed it came from her uncommon looks, but it sprang from something quite different. Belinda made men feel stronger, more intelligent, more masculine than they were. Other women would have turned this power to their advantage, but Belinda thought too little of herself.

Her gaze fell on a young man sitting in a back booth, shoulders hunched over a book and a cup of coffee. Her heart flipped, even as she told herself she would only be disappointed again. She thought about him so much that she imagined she saw him everywhere. Once she'd followed a man for nearly a mile only to discover he had a big, ugly nose that didn't belong on the face of her dreams.

She walked slowly toward the back booth, excitement, anticipation, and almost certain disappointment churning inside her. As he reached for a pack of Chesterfields, she saw fingernails bitten to the quick. He tapped out a cigarette. Belinda held her breath, waiting for him to look up. Everything around her faded. Everything except the man in the booth.

He turned a page of his book, the cigarette dangling unlit from the corner of his mouth, and thumbed open a match pack. She'd nearly reached the booth when he struck the match and looked up. Just like that, Belinda found herself staring through a cloud of gray smoke into the cool blue eyes of James Dean.

In that instant she was back in Indianapolis at the Palace Theater. The movie was *East of Eden.* She'd been sitting in the last row when this same face had exploded on the screen. With his high, intelligent forehead and restless blue eyes, he'd roared into her life larger than all the other larger-than-life faces she'd ever seen. Fireworks exploded inside her and Catherine wheels spun, and she'd felt as if all the air had been punched from her body.

Bad Boy James Dean, with the smoldering eyes and crooked grin. Bad Boy Jimmy, who snapped his fingers at the world and laughed when he told it to go to hell. From the moment she saw him on the Palace Theater screen, he meant everything to her. He was the rebel . . . the lure . . . the shining beacon . . . The tilt of his head and slouch of his shoulders proclaimed that a man is his own creation. She'd transformed that message within herself and walked out of the theater her own woman. A month before her high school graduation, she lost her virginity in the backseat of an Olds 88 to a boy whose sulky mouth reminded her of

Jimmy's. Afterward, she packed her suitcase, slipped out of the house, and headed for the Indianapolis bus station. By the time she reached Hollywood, she'd changed her name to Belinda and put Edna Cornelia behind her forever.

She stood in front of him, her heart thumping in a crazy dance. She wanted to be wearing her tight black pedal pushers instead of this prim, navy-blue cotton dress. She wanted dark glasses, her highest heels, her blond hair pulled back on one side with a tortoiseshell comb.

"I—I loved your movie, Jimmy." Her voice quivered like a violin string drawn too tight. "*East of Eden.* I loved it." *And I love you. More than you can imagine.*

The cigarette formed an exclamation point to his sulky lips. His heavy-lidded eyes squinted against the smoke. "Yeah?"

He was speaking to her! She couldn't believe it. "I'm your biggest fan," she stammered. "I've lost count of how many times I've seen *East of Eden.*" *Jimmy, you're everything to me! You're all I have.* "It was wonderful. You were wonderful." She stared worshipfully at him, her hyacinth-blue eyes luminous with love and adoration.

Dean shrugged his fine, narrow shoulders.

"I can't wait for *Rebel Without a Cause.* It opens next month, doesn't it?" *Get up and take me home with you, Jimmy. Please. Take me home and make love to me.*

"Yeah."

Her heart was racing so fast she felt dizzy. No one understood him like she did. "I heard *Giant*'s really going to be something." *Love me, Jimmy. I'll give everything to you.*

Success had made him immune to hyacinth-eyed blondes with star-worship emblazoned across their pretty faces. He grunted and hunched back over his book. She didn't consider his behavior rude. He was a giant, a god. Rules that applied to others didn't apply to him. "Thank you," she murmured, as she backed away. And then, in a whisper, "I love you, Jimmy."

Dean didn't hear. Or if he had, he didn't care. He'd heard those words too many other times.

Belinda spent the rest of the week reliving the magical encounter. His location shooting in Texas was over, so he was sure to be at Schwab's again, and she'd go there every day until he reappeared. She wouldn't stammer, either. Men had always liked her, and Jimmy would be no different. She'd wear her sexiest outfit, and he'd have to fall in love with her.

But it was the respectable navy-blue sheath she wore the following Friday evening when she walked out of the shabby apartment she shared with two other girls and went off with her date. Billy Greenway was an acne-scarred sex fiend, but he was also the head messenger for Paramount's casting department. A month ago, she'd gotten an audition at Paramount. She thought she'd been one of the prettiest girls in the waiting room, but she didn't know if the assistant casting director had liked her. As she left the building, she'd met Billy, and by their third date she made him promise to get her a copy of the casting director's memo if she'd let him touch her titties. Yesterday he'd called to tell her he finally had it.

They'd nearly reached his car when he pulled her against him for a long kiss. She heard the rustle of paper in the pocket of his checked sports shirt and pushed him away. "Is that the memo, Billy?"

He kissed her neck, his heavy breathing reminding her of all the raw Indiana boys she'd left behind. "I told you I'd bring it, didn't I?"

"Let me see."

"Later, babe." His hands moved to her hips.

"You're going out with a lady, and I don't appreciate being mauled." She gave him her coldest look and got in the car, but she knew she wouldn't see the paper until she'd paid his price. "Where are you taking me tonight?" she asked as they drove away from her apartment.

"How'd you like to go to a little blast at the Garden of Allah?"

"The Garden of Allah?" Belinda's head came up. During

the forties, the Garden had been one of the most famous hotels in Hollywood. Some of the stars still stayed there. "How did you get an invitation to a party at the Garden?"

"I got my ways."

He drove with one hand on the steering wheel and the other draped over her shoulder. As she expected, he didn't take her directly to the Garden. Instead he wound through the side streets off Laurel Canyon until he found a secluded spot. He turned off the ignition and flicked the key over so they could hear the radio. Pérez Prado playing "Cherry Pink and Apple Blossom White." "Belinda, you know I'm real crazy about you." He nuzzled her neck.

She wished he would just give her the memo, then take her to the party at the Garden without making her go through this. Still, it hadn't been too bad last time, not once she'd closed her eyes and pretended he was Jimmy.

He thrust his tongue in her mouth before she caught her breath. She made a soft, gagging sound, then imprinted Jimmy's face on the backs of her eyelids. *Bad Boy Jimmy, taking what you want without asking.* A small moan escaped at the feel of the rough, invading tongue. *Bad Boy Jimmy, tongue so sweet.*

He began tugging at the buttons of her navy sheath, his tongue stuck deep in her mouth. Cold air brushed her back and shoulders as he peeled the dress down to her waist and pushed her bra away. She pressed her eyes more tightly shut and pretended Jimmy was looking at her. *Am I beautiful for you, Jimmy? I like it when you look at me. I like it when you touch me.*

His hand slid up her stocking and over her garter onto bare flesh. He touched the inside of her thigh, and she eased her legs open for him. *Touch me, Jimmy. Touch me there. Beautiful Jimmy. Oh yes.*

He pressed her hand into his lap and rubbed it against him. Her eyes flew open. "No!" She pulled herself away and began straightening her clothes. "I'm not a tramp."

"I know that, babe," he said tightly. "You got a lot of

class. But it's not right the way you get me all worked up and then turn off."

"You got yourself all worked up. And if it bothers you, stop dating me."

He didn't like that, and he peeled out onto the dark street. All the way down Laurel Canyon, he sulked in silence, and he was still sulking as he swung onto Sunset Boulevard. Only when he'd eased the car into the parking space at the Garden of Allah did he reach into his pocket and pull out the paper she wanted. "You're not going to like this."

The pit of her stomach lurched. She snatched the paper from him and ran her eyes down the typed list. She had to scan the page twice before she found her name. A comment was printed next to it. She stared at it, tried to make sense of what she was seeing. Gradually she absorbed the words.

Belinda Britton, she read. *Great eyes, great tits, no talent.*

★

The Garden of Allah was once Hollywood's favorite playground. Originally the home of Alla Nazimova, the great Russian film star, it had been turned into a hotel in the late twenties. Unlike the Beverly Hills and the Bel Air, the Garden had never been completely respectable, and even when it first opened, there'd been something slightly seedy about it. But still the stars came, drawn like silvery moths to the twenty-five Spanish bungalows and the party that never seemed to stop.

Tallulah Bankhead cavorted naked around the pool, which was shaped like Nazimova's Black Sea. Scott Fitzgerald met Sheilah Graham in one of the bungalows. The men lived there between marriages: Ronald Reagan when it was over with Jane Wyman, Fernando Lamas after Arlene Dahl. During the Golden Age, they could all be found at the Garden: Bogart and his Baby, Ty Power, Ava Gardner. Sinatra was there, and Ginger Rogers. Screenwriters sat on white slat chairs by their front doors and typed during the day. Rachmaninoff rehearsed in one bungalow, Benny Goodman in another. And always, there was a party.

By that September night in 1955, the Garden was in its death throes. Dirt and rust streaked the white stucco walls, the furniture in the bungalows was shabby, and just the day before, a dead mouse had been found floating in the pool. Ironically, it still cost the same to rent a bungalow there as it did at the Beverly Hills, although within four years the place would fall to the wrecker's ball. But on that September night, the Garden was still the Garden, and some of the stars were still around.

Billy opened the car door for Belinda. "Come on, babe. The party will cheer you up. A few of the guys from Paramount will be here. I'll introduce you around. You'll knock 'em dead yet."

Her hands curled into fists on the paper in her lap. "Leave me alone for a little bit, will you? I'll meet you inside."

"Okay, babe." His footsteps crunched in the gravel as he moved away. She wadded the memo into a ball, then sagged against the seat. What if it was true that she had no talent? When she'd dreamed about being a movie star she'd never thought much about acting. She'd imagined they would give her lessons or something.

A car pulled into the space next to her with the radio blaring. The couple didn't bother to turn off the engine before they started necking. High school kids, hiding out in the parking lot at the Garden of Allah.

And then the music was over and the news came on.

It was the first story.

The announcer repeated the information calmly, as if it were an everyday occurrence, as if it were not an outrage, not the end of Belinda's life, not the end of everything. She screamed, a terrible, long cry, all the more horrible because it happened inside her head.

James Dean was dead.

She threw open the door and stumbled across the parking lot, not looking where she was going, not caring. She tore through the shrubbery and down one of the paths, trying to outrace her suffocating anguish. She ran past the swimming pool shaped like Azimova's Black Sea, past a big oak at the end of the pool that held a telephone box with a sign, FOR CENTRAL CASTING ONLY. She ran until she came to a long stucco wall beside one of the bungalows. In the dark, she sagged against the wall and cried over the death of her dreams.

Jimmy was from Indiana, just like her, and now he was dead. Killed on the road to Salinas driving a silver Porsche he called "Little Bastard." He'd said anything was possible. A man was his own man; a woman her own woman. Without Jimmy, her dreams seemed childish and impossible.

"My dear, you're making a frightful noise. Would you mind terribly taking your troubles somewhere else? Unless, of course, you're very pretty, in which case you're invited to come through the gate and have a drink with me." The voice, deep and faintly British, drifted over the top of the stucco wall.

Belinda's head jerked up. "Who are you?"

"An interesting question." There was a short silence, punctuated by the distant sound of music from the party. "Let's say I'm a man of contradictions. A lover of adventure, women, and vodka. Not necessarily in that order."

There was something about the voice . . . Belinda wiped her tears with the back of her hand and looked for the gate. When she found it, she stepped inside, drawn by his voice and the possibility of distraction from her awful pain.

A pool of pale yellow light washed the center of the patio. She gazed toward the dark figure of a man sitting in the night shadows just beyond. "James Dean is dead," she said. "He was killed in a car accident."

"Dean?" Ice cubes clicked against his glass. "Ah, yes. Undisciplined sort of chap. Always raising a ruckus. Not that I hold that against him, mind you. I've raised a few in my time. Sit down, my dear, and have a drink."

She didn't move. "I loved him."

"Love, I've discovered, is a transient emotion best satisfied by a good fuck."

She was deeply shocked. No one had ever used that word in her presence, and she said the first thing that came to mind. "I didn't even get that."

He laughed. "Now there, my dear, is the real tragedy." She heard a soft creak, and then he stood and walked toward her. He was tall, probably over six feet, a little thick around the middle, with wide shoulders and a straight carriage. He wore white duck trousers and a pale yellow shirt filled in at the neck with a loosely knotted ascot. She took in the small details—a pair of canvas deck shoes, a watch with a leather band, a webbed khaki belt. And then her gaze lifted, and she found herself looking into the world-weary eyes of Errol Flynn.

Chapter 3

* * * * * * * *

By the time Belinda met him, Flynn had gone through three wives and several fortunes. He was forty-six but looked twenty years older. The famous mustache was grizzled; the handsome face, with its chiseled bones and sculpted nose, had grown jowly and lined from vodka, drugs, and cynicism. His face formed a road map of his life. In four years he'd be dead, falling victim to a long list of ailments that would have killed other men much earlier. But most men weren't Flynn.

He'd swashbuckled his way across the screen for two decades, fighting villains, winning wars, and saving damsels. Captain Blood, Robin Hood, Don Juan—Flynn had played them all. Sometimes, if the mood struck him, he'd even played them well.

Long before he came to Hollywood, Errol Flynn had taken part in adventures every bit as dangerous as those he'd played on screen. He'd been an explorer, a sailor, a gold prospector. He'd traded for slaves in New Guinea. The scar on his heel came from a shot fired by a party of head-hunters, another scar on his abdomen from a scuffle with a rickshaw driver in India. At least that's what he said. With Flynn, no one could ever be sure.

Always, there were women. They couldn't get enough of him, and Flynn felt the same about them. He especially liked them young. The younger the better. Looking into a fresh young face and plunging into a fresh young body gave him the illusion of recovering his lost innocence. It also brought him trouble.

In 1942 he was put on trial for statutory rape. Although the girls were willing, California law made it illegal to have sexual intercourse with anyone under the age of eighteen, willing or not. Nine women served on the jury, however, and Flynn was acquitted. Afterward, he perpetuated the myth of his prowess even as he hated becoming a phallic joke.

The trial didn't end his fascination with young girls, and even though he was forty-six, alcoholic, and dissipated, they still found him irresistible.

"Come over here, my dear, and sit next to me."

He touched her arm, and Belinda felt as if the earth had spun out of its orbit. She sank into the chair he led her to just as she thought her knees would give out. Her hand shook as she took the glass he pressed toward her. This wasn't a dream. It was real. She and Errol Flynn were alone together. He smiled at her, a crooked smile, roguish, urbane, the famous left eyebrow slightly higher than the right. "How old are you, my dear?"

It took her a moment to find her voice. "Eighteen."

"Eighteen . . ." His left eyebrow rose a little higher. "I don't suppose—no, of course not." He tugged on the corner of his mustache and gave her an apologetic chuckle, both charming and disarming. "You wouldn't happen to have your birth certificate on you?"

"My birth certificate?" She looked at him quizzically. Such a strange question. And then the old stories about the trial clicked into place, and she laughed. "I'm not carrying my birth certificate, Mr. Flynn, but I truly am eighteen." Her laughter turned daringly mischievous. "Would it make any difference if I weren't?"

His response was vintage Flynn. "Of course not."

For the next hour they observed the amenities. Flynn told her a story about John Barrymore and gossiped about his leading ladies. She confided what had happened with Paramount. He asked her to call him "Baron," his favorite nickname. She said she would, but she called him "Mr. Flynn" just the same. At the end of the hour, he took her by the hand and led her inside.

With some embarrassment, she asked to use the bathroom. After she had flushed the toilet and washed her hands, she sneaked a peak at the contents of his medicine cabinet. Errol Flynn's toothbrush. Errol Flynn's razor. Her eyes skipped over the pills and Errol Flynn's suppositories. When she shut the cabinet, her face in the mirror was flushed and her eyes bright with excitement. She'd wandered into the presence of a great star.

He waited for her in the bedroom. He wore a burgundy-colored dressing gown and smoked a cigarette in a short amber holder. A fresh bottle of vodka sat on the table at his side. She smiled tentatively, not sure what she should do next. He seemed both amused and pleased. "Contrary to what you may have read, my dear, I am not a ravisher of young women."

"I didn't think you were, Mr. Flynn . . . Baron."

"Are you absolutely certain you know what you're doing here?"

"Oh yes."

"Good." He took a last drag on the cigarette, then set the holder in the ashtray. "Perhaps you'd like to undress for me."

She swallowed hard. She'd never been completely naked with a man. She'd had her panties off or her dress unbuttoned, like tonight with Billy, but the boys had always done that. She'd never personally gotten undressed for anybody. Of course, Errol Flynn wasn't just anybody.

Reaching behind her, she fumbled with the buttons. When she finally had them unfastened, she slipped the dress over her hips. She didn't dare look at him, so she thought of his wonderful movies: *The Dawn Patrol, Objective, Burma!, The Charge of the Light Brigade.* She'd seen that one on television. She looked nervously for someplace to put her dress and spotted a closet on the far side of the room. After she'd hung it up, she stepped out of her shoes, then tried to think what she should take off next.

Darting a quick glance at him, she felt a little shiver of pleasure. Her eyes lovingly erased his wrinkles and jowls until he looked the same as he did on-screen. She remembered how handsome he'd been in *Against All Flags.* He'd played a British naval officer, and Maureen O'Hara had been a pirate named Spitfire. Reaching beneath the lace hem of her slip, Belinda unfastened her garters, drew off her stockings, and folded them neatly. After that, she took off her garter belt. *Santa Fe Trail* had been on television not long ago. He and Olivia de Havilland were wonderful together. He was so masculine, and Olivia was always such a lady.

Belinda wore only a slip, her bra and panties, and her charm bracelet. She unfastened the small gold clasp. Her hands shook, but she finally got it off and set it next to her stockings. She wished he'd get up and do the rest, but he showed no signs of moving. Slowly she pulled her slip over her head.

She remembered he was married. He'd met Patrice Wymore, his current wife, when they were filming *Rocky Mountain.* Patrice was so lucky to be married to a man like Errol Flynn, but the rumors of their breakup must be true, or he'd be with Patrice instead of her. It was hard to make a marriage work in Hollywood.

When she was finally naked, she saw by the direction of Flynn's gaze that he liked what she'd revealed. "Come here, my dear."

Embarrassed but excited, she walked toward him. He stood and touched her chin. She nearly fainted from excitement. She waited for him to kiss her. His hands slipped to her shoulders. She wanted the same kiss he'd given Olivia de Havilland, and Maureen O'Hara, and all the other beautiful women he'd loved on the screen, but he opened his robe instead. He was naked underneath. Her eyes denied the looseness of his suntanned skin.

"I'm afraid you'll have to give me a bit of help, my dear," he said. "Vodka and lovemaking aren't always the best of companions."

She looked up into his eyes. It would be her privilege to help him, except she wasn't exactly sure what he wanted her to do.

Not being a stranger to the minds of young girls, he understood her hesitation and offered a specific suggestion. She was shocked, but at the same time fascinated. So this was the way famous men made love. It was strange, but somehow it seemed appropriate.

She lowered herself to her knees.

It took a long time, and she got tired, but eventually he pulled her up and laid her on the bed. The mattress sagged as he rolled on top of her. Surely he'd kiss her now, but to her disappointment, he didn't.

He nudged her legs, and she quickly parted them for him. His eyes were closed, but she kept hers open so she could treasure every moment. Errol Flynn was going to do it to her. Errol Flynn. A chorus sang in her heart. She felt a probe. A push. It was really Errol Flynn!

Her body exploded.

★

Later that night he asked her what her name was and offered her a cigarette. She didn't really smoke, so she took short drags. Leaning next to him against the headboard with a cigarette thrilled her. For the first time in hours she remembered about Jimmy. Poor Jimmy, to have died so young. Life could be cruel. How lucky she was to be here alive and happy.

Flynn told her about his yacht, the *Zaca*, and about his

recent travels. Belinda didn't want to pry, but she was curious about his wife. "Patrice is very beautiful."

"A wonderful woman. I've treated her badly." He drained his glass, then reached across her for a refill from the bottle on the nightstand. As he poured, his shoulder dug into her breast. "It's a habit I have with women. I don't mean to hurt them, but I wasn't made for marriage."

"Will you get a divorce?" She self-consciously tapped the ash from her cigarette.

"Probably. Although, God knows, I can't afford it. The IRS wants me for almost a million, and I'm so far behind on alimony I've lost track."

Belinda's eyes filled with sympathetic tears. "It doesn't seem fair that a man like you should have to worry about such things. Not with all the pleasure you've given so many people."

Flynn patted her knee. "You're a sweet girl, Belinda. And a beautiful one. There's something in your eyes that makes me forget how old I'm getting to be."

She took the liberty of resting her cheek against his shoulder. "You mustn't talk that way. You're not old."

He smiled and kissed the top of her head. "Sweet girl."

★

By the end of the week Belinda had moved into Flynn's bungalow at the Garden of Allah. A month flew by. At the end of October, he gave her a gold charm, a small disk suspended from a wishbone frame with "LUV" engraved in the center of one side and the letters "I" and "U" on the other. When she flicked the charm with the tip of her finger, it spun and the message "I LUV U" came together. She knew he didn't mean it, but she treasured the charm and wore it with pride as a symbol to the world that she belonged to Errol Flynn.

In the reflected glow of his fame, her old feelings of invisibility vanished. Never had she felt so pretty, so smart, so important. They slept late and spent their days either on the *Zaca* or alongside the pool. They marked their nights in clubs and restaurants. She learned to smoke and drink, she learned not to stare when she met famous people, no matter how excited she felt inside, and she learned that famous people seemed to like her. An actor who was a friend of Flynn's told her it was because she offered no judgment, only adoration. The remark puzzled her. How could she judge? It wasn't up to ordinary people to pass judgment on the stars.

Sometimes at night she and Flynn made love, but more often they talked. It hurt her to see how sad and troubled he was beneath his devil-may-care facade. She devoted herself to making him happy.

She saw *Rebel Without a Cause* and thought that maybe her dream hadn't died after all. She was meeting studio executives now instead of lowly assistant casting directors. She needed to take advantage of those contacts and prepare for the inevitable time when Flynn moved on to another woman. She had no delusions about that. She wasn't important enough to hold him for long.

Flynn bought her a daring lipstick-red French bikini and sat by the side of the pool sipping his vodka while he watched her play. No one else at the Garden was adventurous enough to wear one of the new bikinis, but Belinda didn't feel embarrassed. She loved watching Flynn watch her. She loved emerging from the water to be wrapped in the towel he held for her. She felt sheltered, protected, and adored.

Late one morning while Flynn was still sleeping, Belinda donned the red bikini and dived into the deserted pool. She swam several easy laps, opening her eyes under water to look at the initials of Alla Nazimova carved into the concrete just below the water line. When she came to the surface, she found herself staring at a pair of highly polished leather shoes.

"*Tiens!* A mermaid has taken over the pool at the Garden of Allah. A mermaid with eyes bluer than the sky."

Treading water, Belinda squinted against the morning sun to see the man standing over her. He was distinctly European. His oyster-white suit had the sheen of silk and the immaculate press of a man who kept a valet. He was of medium height, slim and aristocratic, with dark hair that had been skillfully cut to disguise its thinning. Small, slanted eyes sat above a broad nose with a slight hook at the end. He wasn't handsome, but he was imposing. The smell of money and power clung to him as tenaciously as his expensive cologne. She judged him to be in his mid-to-late thirties, French by his accent, although his features were more exotic. Maybe he was a European filmmaker.

She gave him a saucy grin. "No mermaid, monsieur. Just a very ordinary girl."

"*Ordinaire?* I would hardly say so. *Três extraordinaire*, in fact."

She accepted his compliment graciously, and in her best accented high school French replied, "*Merci beaucoup, monsieur. Vous êtes trop gentil.*"

"Tell me, *ma petite* mermaid. Is there a tail beneath that *charmant* red bikini?"

Amusement glinted in his eyes, but Belinda sensed something calculated about his audaciousness. This man did nothing, said nothing, by accident. "*Mais non, monsieur,*" she replied evenly. "Only two ordinary legs."

He raised an eyebrow. "Perhaps, mademoiselle, you will let me be the judge?"

She gazed at him for a moment, then dived under and swam in long, clean strokes for the ladder at the opposite end of the pool. But when she climbed out, he'd disappeared. Half an hour later, she walked into the bungalow and found him talking to Flynn over Bloody Marys.

Mornings weren't Flynn's best time, and next to the immaculately groomed stranger he looked rumpled and old. Still, he was by far the more handsome. She sat on the arm of his chair and placed her hand on his shoulder. She wished she had the courage to plant a casual good-morning kiss on his cheek, but the sporadic nighttime intimacies that passed between them didn't make her feel entitled to that kind of informality. He looped his arm around her waist. "Good morning, my dear. I understand the two of you met by the pool."

The stranger's eyes slid down the long suntanned legs extending beneath the terry wrap she'd tossed on over her bikini. "Not a tail after all." He rose gracefully to his feet. "Alexi Savagar, mademoiselle."

"He's being modest, my dear. Our visitor is actually Count Alexi Nikolai Vasily Savagarin. Did I get it right, old sport?"

"My family left the title behind in St. Petersburg, *mon ami*, as you very well know." Although Alexi sounded faintly reproachful, Belinda sensed he was pleased by Flynn's use of his title. "We're now hopelessly French."

"And bloody rich. Your family didn't leave their rubles behind in Mother Russia, did they, old sport? Not by a long shot." Flynn turned toward Belinda. "Alexi is in California buying a few old cars to ship back to Paris for his collection."

"What a peasant you are, *mon ami*. A 1927 Alfa Romeo is hardly just an 'old car.' Besides, I'm here on business."

"Alexi is adding to the family fortune by meddling in electronics. What's that gadget you were telling me about? Has something to do with vacuum tubes?"

"The transistor. It's going to replace the vacuum tube."

"Transistor. That's it. And if it'll make money, you can bet Alexi's sitting on a truckload of the little buggers. You'd think he'd be willing to lend me some of his profits so I could produce my next picture." Although he was looking at her, Belinda had the feeling he was really talking to Alexi.

Alexi regarded him with amusement. "I haven't made my fortune by throwing good money after bad. Unless, of course, you're willing to part with the *Zaca*. Now that would be quite a different story."

"You'll get the *Zaca* over my dead body," Flynn replied, an edge to his voice.

"From the looks of things, *mon ami*, I may not have long to wait."

"Spare me your lectures. Belinda, fix us two more Bloodys."

"Of course." She took their glasses and went into the kitchenette that opened off the living room. Neither man made an effort to lower his voice, and she could hear their conversation as she refilled their glasses from a fresh can of tomato juice. At first they talked about the transistors and Alexi's business, but before long, the conversation became more personal.

"Belinda is an improvement over the last one, *mon ami*," she heard Alexi say. "Those eyes are quite *extraordinaire*, A little old, though, isn't she? Past sixteen."

"Casting stones, Alexi?" Flynn laughed. "Don't get any ideas of your own about her. You'll only be wasting your time. Belinda is my joy. Rather like a faithful dog, but housebroken and beautiful. She only gives adoration. No nagging, no lectures about my drinking. She puts up with my moods, and she's surprisingly intelligent. If more women were like Belinda, there'd be more happy men."

"*Mon Dieu*, you sound as if you're ready for another trip to the altar. Are you sure you can afford it?"

"She's merely a diversion," Flynn replied with a trace of belligerence. "And a damned pleasant one."

Belinda's cheeks were flushed as she brought their drinks to them. She didn't like what he'd said about the dog, but the other things he'd said about her were nice.

"There you are, darling. I was just telling Alexi about you."

She sensed a subtle tension between the two men she hadn't noticed before.

"You're a paragon, mademoiselle, if I am to believe the Baron here. Intelligent, adoring, beautiful—although my views of your beauty have been somewhat limited, so he may be lying."

Flynn took a careful sip from the drink she handed him. "I thought you met her at the pool."

"She was under water. And now, as you see . . ." He nodded dismissively toward the terry-cloth wrap.

A long look passed between the men. Was it challenge she saw in Alexi's eyes? Belinda felt as though she were witnessing an old, familiar game between them, a game she didn't understand.

"Belinda, darling, take that off, would you?" Flynn crumpled an empty cigarette pack.

"What?"

"Your wrap, my dear. Take it off, there's a good girl."

She looked from one man to the other. Flynn was putting a fresh cigarette in the amber holder, but Alexi watched her, a trace of something that might have been sympathy underlying his amusement. "You've embarrassed her, *mon ami.*"

"Nonsense. Belinda doesn't mind." Flynn rose and walked over to her. He tilted up her chin just as she'd seen him do so often to Olivia de Havilland. "She'll do anything I ask. Won't you, darling?" He leaned down and brushed a kiss over her lips.

She hesitated only a moment before she dropped her fingers to the sash on her wrap. Flynn touched her cheek with the back of his hand. Slowly she loosened the knot and let the sash fall away. Turning her body toward Flynn, she allowed the wrap to drop to the floor.

"Let Alexi see, if you don't mind, my dear. I want him to have a good view of what his money can't buy."

She regarded Flynn unhappily, but his eyes were on Alexi, and his expression seemed vaguely triumphant. Slowly she pivoted toward the Frenchman. The chilly air brushed her skin, and her bikini halter felt clammy against her breasts. She told herself it was childish to feel embarrassed. This was no different from standing at the edge of the pool. But she still couldn't bring herself to meet the slanted, Russian eyes of Alexi Savagar.

"Her body is lovely, *mon ami,*" he said. "I congratulate you. But your beauty is wasted on this faded matinee idol. I think I shall steal you away." His tone was light, but something in his expression told her his words hadn't been spoken casually.

"I think not." She tried to sound cool and sophisticated, like Grace Kelly in *To Catch a Thief*. Something about him frightened her. Perhaps it was his air of power, the impression of authority he wore every bit as easily as the oyster-white suit. She bent to retrieve her wrap, but as she straightened, Flynn's hand cupped her bare shoulder, preventing her from covering herself.

"Take no notice of Alexi, Belinda. Our rivalry is an old one." His hand moved down the length of her arm and splayed possessively across her bare midriff. His little finger slipped in the hollow of her navel. "He can't abide seeing me with a woman he can't have. It goes back to our younger days when I stole them all away from him. My friend is still a very bad loser."

"You didn't steal all of them away. I remember a few who were more attracted to my money than to your pretty face."

Belinda sucked in her breath as Flynn's hand, warm and possessive, dipped lower and settled over the lipstick-red crotch of her tiny bikini. "But they were old. Not our type at all."

Against her will she looked up and saw Alexi leaning back in his chair, a portrait of aristocratic indolence with one immaculately trousered leg crossed over the other. He lifted his eyes to hers, and for a fraction of a moment, she forgot Flynn was in the room.

Chapter 4

Alexi cruised with them on the *Zaca* and took them out to dinner at the best restaurants in Southern California. Sometimes he bought Belinda gifts of jewelry, dainty and expensive. She kept them in their boxes and wore only Flynn's small spinning charm on a chain around her neck.

Alexi berated Flynn for the charm. "What a vulgar bauble. Surely Belinda deserves better."

"Oh, much better," Flynn replied. "But I couldn't afford it, old chap. Not all of us were born with your silver spoon."

The two men had met on the private yacht of the Shah of Iran nearly a decade earlier, but over the years, their friendship had developed an edge. Alexi's presence reminded Flynn of past mistakes and lost opportunities. Still, he never stopped hoping to divert some of Alexi's wealth in his own direction, and, in the end, Alexi felt the rivalry more keenly.

Beneath his charm Alexi Savagar was a man who took life seriously. As an aristocrat, he disdained Flynn's inferior breeding and lack of formal education. As a businessman, he scorned his playboy lifestyle and contempt for self-discipline. But at thirty-eight—his fortune secure and his power unquestioned—amusement had become a precious commodity. Besides, Flynn had never posed a serious threat to him. Not until the moment Alexi had gazed at the mermaid swimming in the pool at the Garden of Allah.

Their tastes were similar—young girls with the bloom of innocence still on their flushed cheeks. Flynn's fame and sexual magnetism seemed to give him an advantage, but Alexi's wealth and carefully executed charm were a formidable aphrodisiac. Flynn saw Belinda as a new pawn in the game the men had played over the years. He had no way of knowing Alexi viewed her differently.

Alexi's visceral reaction to Belinda Britton had taken him by surprise. She was a silly child absurdly obsessed with movie stars. Except for her youth, she had little to recommend her. Although she was intelligent, she'd been badly educated. She was undeniably beautiful, but so were other women he'd known. Still, next to Belinda's air of tainted innocence, his more sophisticated female companions seemed old and weary. Belinda was the perfect combination of child and whore, her mind untouched, her body lush and experienced.

But his attraction to Belinda went deeper than sexual desire. She was a bright-eyed child, eager for life to begin and full of trust in the future. He wanted to be the one to introduce her to the world, to shelter and protect her, to mold her into the ideal woman she could become. As the days passed, the accumulated years of his cynicism peeled away. He felt like a boy again with his life stretching before him, full of promise.

Toward the end of November, Flynn announced he was going to Mexico for a week and asked Alexi to watch after her. Alexi gave Belinda a slow smile, then turned to Flynn. "You might wish to think twice about deserting the field."

Flynn laughed. "Belinda won't even wear the trinkets you give her, will you, my dear? I don't believe I have much need to worry."

Belinda laughed as if it were all a wonderful joke, but

Alexi Savagar made her uneasy. No one had ever treated her with so much courtesy. Her feelings confused her. He was an important man, but he wasn't a movie star—he wasn't Errol Flynn—so why should she be so disturbed by him?

For the next week, Alexi became her constant companion. They drove everywhere at breakneck speed in a red Ferrari that seemed like an extension of Alexi's well-tuned body. She watched his hands on the controls, observed the sureness of his touch, the steady grip of his fingers. What would it be like to have such self-confidence? As they roared through the streets of Beverly Hills, she felt the surge of the car's engine through her thighs. She imagined everyone speculating about her. Who was this blond-haired woman who'd managed to capture the interest of two such important men?

In the evening they went to Ciro's or Chasen's. Sometimes they spoke French, with Alexi keeping his vocabulary simple so she could follow it. He described his classic car collection, he detailed the beauties of Paris, and one night, with the Ferrari parked on a hill and the city lights spread at her feet, he spoke more personally.

"My father was a Russian aristocrat wise enough to leave for Paris before the First World War broke out. He met my mother there. She convinced him to shorten his name from Savagarin to Savagar so he'd fit into Parisian society. I was born a year before the war ended, and a week before my father died. I've received my love of fine things from my French mother. But do not fool yourself. Beneath it all, I remain relentlessly Russian."

Alexi's ruthlessness both fascinated and frightened Belinda. She told him about herself, describing her parents and the loneliness of her early life. He listened with flattering intensity as she shared her dreams of stardom and confided things she'd never told anyone. He spoke to her about Flynn. "He will leave you, *ma chère*. You must understand that."

"I know. He probably sent me off with you so he could be with other women. Maybe even his wife." She looked imploringly at him. "Please don't tell me if you know. He can't help himself. I understand that."

"Such adoration." Alexi's mouth gave a slight twist. "As always, my friend is a lucky man. It's a pity he doesn't appreciate you. Perhaps you'll be luckier next time in your choice of companions."

"You make me sound like some sort of tramp," Belinda snapped. "I don't like it."

Alexi's strange, slanted eyes pierced through her clothing, through her skin, into a place so secret that only he knew it existed. "A woman like you, *ma chère*, will always need a man." He picked up her hand and played with her fingertips, sending a little shiver through her. "You are not one of those fierce, modern women. You need to be sheltered and protected, molded into something precious and fine." For a moment she thought she saw pain in his eyes, but the impression faded as his voice grew harsh. "You sell yourself too cheaply."

She snatched her hand away. He didn't understand. There was nothing cheap about giving herself to Flynn.

Everything came to a crashing end shortly after Christmas when Flynn tired of the game they were playing. As they all sat at a banquette in Romanoff's, he slipped a cigarette into his amber holder and said he'd be leaving to spend a few months in Europe. From the way he avoided looking at her, Belinda understood she wasn't invited to go along.

A great, suffocating mass expanded in her chest, and her eyes flooded with tears. Just as the last vestige of control slipped from her, a sharp pain gripped her thigh. Alexi's hand squeezed her under the table, forbidding her to humiliate herself. His strength flowed through her, and she managed to endure the rest of the evening. When Flynn left on New Year's Day, Alexi took her in his arms and let her cry. Later, she read in the newspaper that Flynn's new traveling companion was fifteen years old.

Although Alexi had finished his business in California long ago, he made no move to return to Paris. The rental on the bungalow had been paid through the end of January—not, she suspected, by Flynn—and, for the next few weeks, they spent nearly every evening together. One night, unexpectedly, he leaned over and kissed her lightly on the lips.

"Don't!" She jumped up, angry with him for the intimacy. Alexi wasn't Flynn, and she wasn't a tramp. She rushed through the patio doors into the living room and snatched a cigarette from the china holder that sat on the coffee table.

Outside on the patio, years of iron control and self-discipline shattered inside Alexi Savagar. He jumped up and strode into the room. "You stupid little bitch."

She spun around, stunned by his venom. The well-polished Gallic mask had dropped away, baring the naked, atavistic product of countless generations of noble Russian breeding.

"How dare you think you can refuse me," he said on a snarl. "You're just another whore. But instead of fucking a man for his money, you fuck him for his fame."

She let out a muffled cry as he advanced on her. He caught her by the shoulders and jammed her against the wall. His hand grabbed her jaw, but before she could scream again, he'd covered her mouth with his own. He bit at her lips, forcing them open. She tried to clamp down on the tongue he thrust into her, but his fingers closed tightly around her throat, their message clear. He was Count Alexi Nikolai Vasily Savagarin, omnipotent overlord of serfs, entitled by birth to take possession of whatever he desired, and she must subjugate herself to him.

When his rape of her mouth was complete, he pulled back. "I am worthy of respect. Flynn is a fool, a court jester. He lives on charm and then whines when things go badly. But you are too stupid to see that, so I must teach you."

She gave a strangled sob as he reached under her skirt. He pulled at her panties and separated her legs with his knee. Ignoring her sobs, he possessed her with his aristocratic fingers, invading each place he imagined Flynn had claimed. Through her horror she felt his arousal hard against her thigh. His assault was an act of possession, a living out of the divine right of czars, an indelible reaffirmation of the proper social order in which the nobility outranked any movie star.

She was crying when he opened her blouse, so she didn't notice his gentler touch. Her tears fell on his hands as he pushed her bra aside and caressed her breasts, kissing them with a tenderness Flynn had never displayed, murmuring to her in French, perhaps even Russian, words she didn't understand.

Slowly he soothed her. "I am sorry, my little one. I am sorry to have frightened you." He turned off the lights, picked her up, and cradled her in his lap. "I have done a terrible thing to you," he whispered, "and you must forgive me—for your own sake as well as mine." His lips touched her hair. "I am your only hope, *chérie.* Without me, your promise as a woman will never be realized. Without me, you will drift through your days trying to see your reflection in the eyes of men who are unworthy of you."

He stroked her hair until her body relaxed.

As Belinda fell asleep in his arms, Alexi stared into the quiet darkness. How could he have let himself fall so foolishly in love? This woman, whose hyacinth-blue eyes worshipped men with anthems of adoration, stirred feelings in him he hadn't known he possessed. He'd been raised to live his life only from a position of strength, and for the first time in years he was uncertain what to do. He didn't doubt his ability to win her love—such a task was trivial, and she already cared far more than she was willing to admit. No, winning her love didn't frighten him. It was the power she'd gained over him that was so terrifying.

He'd been taught self-discipline at an early age. He remembered as a small boy being ill with some childhood disease that left him burning with fever. His mother had come into his bedroom, a composition book dangling from her ringed fingers, her eyes hard. Was it true that he had not finished his Latin translation? He explained he was sick.

Only peasants find excuses to shirk their responsibilities. His mother pulled him from his bed and set him at his desk. Eyes bright with fever, hand shaking, he worked until the translation was done while she stood at the window, ruby bracelets glittering in the sunlight, and smoked one cigarette after another.

Spartan boarding schools shaped the heirs to France's great fortunes into men worthy of their family names. That was where the last remnants of childhood had been stripped from him. At eighteen, he began gaining control of the Savagar fortune—first wresting power from the aging trustees who'd grown fat and lazy on his money, then from his mother. He'd become one of the most powerful men in France, with homes on two continents, a priceless collection of European masterpieces, and a string of teenage mistresses who catered to his every whim. Until he'd met Belinda Britton, with her untainted optimism and child's bright view of the world, he hadn't realized anything was missing from his life.

Belinda awakened the next morning, still dressed in her clothes from the night before, the thin chenille spread thrown over her. Her eyes fell on a piece of hotel stationery propped against the pillow. Quickly she read the few lines of spidery handwriting:

Ma chére,

I am flying to New York today. I have already neglected business far too long. Perhaps I will return, perhaps not.

Alexi

She crumpled the note and pitched it to the floor. Damn him! After what he'd done to her last night, she was glad he was gone. He was a monster. She swung her feet over the edge of the bed, only to feel her stomach pitch. As she fell back on the pillow, she closed her eyes and admitted to herself that she was afraid. Alexi had been taking care of her, and without him, she didn't know what to do.

Throwing her forearm across her eyes, she tried to reason away her fears by reconstructing James Dean's face in her mind—the disobedient hair, the sulky eyes and rebellious mouth. Gradually she grew calmer. *A man is his own man, a woman her own woman.* She'd let her ambitions drift while she was with Flynn. It was time to take charge of her life again.

She spent the rest of January trying to reach her contacts. She placed telephone calls, wrote notes to the studio executives she'd met through Flynn, and began making the rounds again, but nothing happened. The rent came due on the bungalow at the Garden of Allah, and she was forced to return to her old apartment, where she fought with her roommates until they told her to move out. She ignored them. Stupid cows, content with so little.

Disaster arrived in a pale blue envelope. A letter from her mother informed Belinda her parents would no longer support her foolishness. Enclosed was their last check.

She made a halfhearted attempt to get a job, but she'd been feeling sick, plagued by mysterious headaches and a perpetual upset stomach, like a case of the flu that wouldn't quite take hold. She began hoarding what little money she had left, going without the meals she didn't want to eat anyway, eliminating her trips to Schwab's, and wondering how such horrible things could be happening to the woman Errol Flynn had once adored.

The knowledge that she was pregnant with Flynn's child finally hit her the morning she couldn't force herself to get dressed. For two days she lay in her rickety bed, staring at the stained ceiling, trying to comprehend what had happened. She remembered horrified whispers about Indianapolis girls who'd gone too far, rumors of shotgun weddings or, even worse, no weddings at all. But those were girls from the wrong side of the tracks, not Dr. Britton's daughter, Edna Cornelia. Girls like her got married first and then had babies. To do it the other way around was unimaginable.

She thought about trying to contact Flynn, but she didn't know how to locate him. Besides, she couldn't imagine him helping her. And then she thought about Alexi Savagar.

It took her two days to locate him. He was staying at the Beverly Hills Hotel. She left a message.

Miss Britton will be waiting for Mr. Savagar in the Polo Lounge this evening at five o'clock.

The late February afternoon was cool, and she dressed carefully in a butterscotch velvet suit and a white nylon blouse that hinted at the lacy detail of her slip beneath. She wore pearl button earrings and a string of cultured pearls she'd received for her sixteenth birthday because her parents didn't want to bother with a party. Her hat was a butterscotch tam, jaunty and carefree perched on the side of her head. With the addition of proper white cotton gloves and slightly improper needle-pointed heels, she was ready for the drive to Schwab's, where she left her battered Studebaker and called a taxi to deliver her to the elegant porte-cochere that marked the entrance of the Beverly Hills Hotel.

Flynn had taken her to the Polo Lounge several times, but she still felt a thrill as she stepped inside. She gave the maître d' Alexi's name, and followed him to a curved banquette facing the door, priority seating in the most famous cocktail lounge in the country. Even though she didn't like martinis, she ordered one because it was sophisticated, and she wanted Alexi to see her with it.

While she waited for him, she tried to calm herself by studying the other patrons. Van Heflin sat with a tiny blonde. She spotted Greer Garson and Ethel Merman at separate tables, and, across the room, one of the studio executives she had met when she was with Flynn. A page dressed in a brass-buttoned jacket came through. "Call for Mis-tuh Heflin. Call for Mis-tuh Heflin." Van Heflin lifted his hand, and a pink telephone appeared at his table.

As she toyed with the long, cool stem of her glass, she tried not to notice that her hands were trembling. Alexi wouldn't arrive at five o'clock. She'd damaged his pride the last time they were together. But would he come at all? She couldn't imagine what she'd do if he didn't.

Gregory Peck and his new French wife, Veronique, arrived. Veronique was a former newspaperwoman, dark-haired and beautiful, and envy coiled inside Belinda. Veronique's famous husband gave her a private smile and said something only she could hear. Veronique laughed and placed her hand over his, the gesture tender and proprietary. In that instant Belinda hated Veronique Peck as she had never hated another human being.

At six o'clock Alexi walked into the Polo Lounge. He paused in the doorway to exchange a few words with the maître d' before he moved toward her banquette. He was dressed in a pearl-gray silk suit, immaculate as always, and several people greeted him as he passed their tables. She had forgotten how much attention Alexi attracted. Flynn had said it was because Alexi had the uncanny ability to turn old money into new.

He slid wordlessly into the banquette, bringing with him the expensive scent of his cologne. His expression was unfathomable, and a small shiver slid down her spine.

"Château Haut-Brion, 1952," he said to the waiter. He gestured toward her half-finished martini. "Take that away. Mademoiselle will have wine with me."

As the waiter disappeared, Alexi lifted her hand to his lips and gently kissed it. She tried not to think about the last time they were together when his kiss hadn't been gentle at all.

"You seem nervous, *ma chère.*"

The small collection of cells relentlessly multiplying inside her made doubts impossible, and she lifted her shoulders in a casual shrug. "It's been a long time. I—I missed you." Her sense of injustice sprang to the surface. "How could you go off like that? Without calling me or anything."

He looked amused. "You needed time to think, *chérie.* To see how you liked being alone."

"I didn't like it at all," she retorted.

"I didn't think you would." He studied her as if she'd been mounted between glass slides and pushed under a microscope. "Tell me what you learned during your time of introspection."

"I learned that I've grown to depend on you," she replied carefully. "Everything fell apart after you left, and you weren't around to help me put it back together. I guess I'm not as independent as I thought."

The waiter appeared with the wine. Alexi took a sip, gave a distracted nod, and waited until they were alone before returning his attention to her. She told him what had taken place in the past month: her failure to capture the interest of a single producer, the fact that her parents would no longer support her. She told him all her miseries except the most important one.

"I see," he said. "So much to have happened in such a

short time. Are there any more disasters you need to lay at my feet?"

She swallowed hard. "No, nothing else. But I'm out of money, and I need you to help me make some decisions."

"Why don't you go to your former lover? Surely he'll help you. I'm certain he'll rush to your side on his white charger, sword flashing, slaying your villains. Why don't you go to Flynn, Belinda?"

She bit down on the inside of her cheek to keep her tongue in check. Alexi didn't understand Flynn—he never had—but she couldn't say that. Somehow she needed to ease his bitterness, even if it meant lying. "Those days at the Garden . . . They were like nothing that had ever happened to me. I mixed the two of you together in my mind. I made myself believe all my feelings were coming from Flynn, but after you left, I realized they were coming from you." She'd rehearsed exactly what she needed to say. "I need help, and I don't know where else to turn."

"I see."

But he didn't see, not at all. She began pleating her napkin to avoid looking at him. "I—I'm out of money, and I can't go back to Indianapolis. I—I'd like you to give me a loan—just for a year or so until I get the studios to notice me." She took a sip of the wine she didn't want. With Alexi's money, she could go away, find someplace where no one knew her, and have her baby.

He didn't say anything, and her nervousness grew. "I don't know where else to turn. I'll die if I have to go back to Indianapolis. I know I will."

"Death before Indianapolis." His voice carried a note of amusement. "How childishly poetic, and how like you, my sweet Belinda. But if I loan you this money, what would I receive in return?"

The page brushed by their table, brass buttons glinting. "Call for Mis-tuh Peck. Call for Mis-tuh Peck."

"Whatever you want," Belinda said.

The moment she spoke, she knew she'd made a horrible mistake.

"I see." The words were a hiss. "You're selling yourself again. Tell me, Belinda, what sets you apart from those overdressed young women the maître d' is turning away at the door? What sets you apart from the whores?"

Her eyes clouded at the injustice of his attack. He wasn't going to help her. What had made her think he would? She stood and snatched up her purse so she could get away before she humiliated herself by committing the unpardonable sin of crying in the public glare of the Polo Lounge. But before she could move, Alexi caught her arm and pulled her gently back into her seat. "I'm sorry, *chérie.* Once again I have hurt you. But if you keep throwing these knives at me, sooner or later you must expect me to bleed."

She bent her head to hide the tears spilling down her cheeks. One of them made a dark smear on the skirt of her butterscotch suit. "Maybe you can take from someone without giving anything in return, but I can't." She fumbled with the clasp of her purse, trying to open it to get a handkerchief. "If that makes me a whore in your eyes, then I wish I'd never come to you for help."

"Don't cry, *chérie.* You make me feel like a monster." A handkerchief, folded into a precise rectangle, dropped in front of her.

She closed her hand around it, lowered her head, and dabbed at her eyes. She made the motion as inconspicuous as possible, terrified that Van Heflin might be watching her, or the tiny blonde with him, or Veronique Peck. But when she raised her head, no one seemed to have noticed her at all.

Alexi leaned into the banquette and regarded her intently. "Everything is simple for you, isn't it?" His voice grew husky. "Will you put away your fantasies, *chérie*? Will you give me your adoration?"

He made it seem so simple, but it wasn't. He fascinated her. He even excited her, and she loved the way people looked at her when they were together. But his face had never been magnified on a silver screen until it was big enough for all the world to see.

He pulled a cigarette from a silver case. She thought his fingers trembled on the lighter, but the flame held steady. "I will help you, *chérie*, even though I know I shouldn't. When I have finished my business here, we will go to Washington and be married in the French embassy."

"Married?" She couldn't believe she'd heard him right. "You're not going to marry me."

The harsh lines around his mouth softened, and his eyes filled with emotion. "Am I not, *chérie*? I want you, not as my mistress but as my wife. Foolish of me, *non*?"

"But I already told you—"

"*Ça suffit!* Do not make your offer again."

Frightened by his intensity, she drew back from him.

"As a businessman, I never gamble foolishly, and there are no guarantees with you, are there, *chérie*?" He traced the stem of his wineglass with his finger. "*Hélas*, I am also a Russian. A film career is not what you want, although you don't understand that yet. In Paris you will take your place as my wife. It will be a new life for you. Unfamiliar, but I will guide you, and you will become the talk of the city—Alexi Savagar's child bride." He smiled. "You will love the attention."

Her mind raced. She couldn't imagine herself as Alexi's wife, always under the scrutiny of those strange, slanted eyes. Alexi was rich and important, famous in his world. He'd said she'd be the talk of Paris. But she couldn't give up her dreams of being a star.

"I don't know, Alexi. I haven't thought—"

The planes of his face grew harsh. She felt him withdraw. If she refused him now—if she hesitated for even a moment—his pride would never allow him to forgive her again. She had only this one chance.

"Yes!" Her laughter was high-pitched and strained. The baby! She had to tell him about the baby. "Yes. Yes, of course, Alexi. I'll marry you. I want to marry you."

For a moment he didn't move, and then he lifted her hand to his mouth. With a smile, he turned her wrist and covered the pulse that beat there with his lips. She ignored the pounding of her heart, the fearful rush of blood that asked her what she'd done.

He ordered a bottle of Dom Perignon. "To the end of fantasy." He lifted his glass.

She licked her dry lips. "To us."

At the next banquette, Veronique Peck's soft laughter chimed like a string of silver bells.

Chapter 5

To Belinda's surprise, her wedding night didn't occur until the night of her wedding, a week after her meeting with Alexi in the Polo Lounge. They were married in the French embassy in Washington and left immediately after the ceremony to honeymoon at the ambassador's summer home.

Belinda's nervousness grew as she stepped from the ambassador's tub and dried herself with a thick, nutmeg-brown towel. She hadn't told Alexi about the baby. If she was lucky and the baby small, he might believe the child was his, born prematurely. If he didn't believe it, then he'd probably divorce her, but the baby would still have his name, and she wouldn't have to live with the stigma of being an unwed mother. She could go back to California and start all over again, but this time with Alexi's money.

Every day she saw surprising new evidence of the depth of Alexi's feelings, not only in the gifts he lavished on her, but in his patience with her silly mistakes as she entered his world. Nothing she did made him angry. The thought brought her comfort.

She gazed at the dress box wrapped in silver paper sitting on the basin. He wanted her to wear what was inside for her wedding night. She hoped it was a peignoir set, black and lacy like something Kim Novak would own.

But when she opened the dress box, she nearly cried with disappointment. The long white cotton garment nestled in the cloud of tissue paper looked more like a child's nightgown than the peignoir of her fantasies. Although the fabric was sheer and fine, the high neck had the barest edging of lace while a row of pink bows held the bodice modestly closed. As she pulled the garment from its box, something fell at her feet. She leaned over and picked up matching white cotton underpants with little ruffs of lace at the leg openings. She remembered Alexi's pride and the fact that she wasn't coming to him as a virgin.

It was past midnight when she entered the elegant jade-green bedroom. The brocade drapes had been drawn, and the polished teak furniture glowed in the warm light filtering through the cream silk lampshades. The room couldn't have been more different from the wonderfully tawdry interior of the Spanish bungalow at the Garden of Allah. Alexi wore a pale gold dressing gown. With his small eyes and dark, thinning hair, he could only play a villain on screen. But a powerful villain. He gazed at her until the room's silence grew oppressive. Finally he spoke. "You're wearing lipstick, *chérie*?"

"Is something wrong?"

He pulled a handkerchief from the pocket of his dressing gown. "Come near the light." She padded across the carpet on bare feet instead of the high-heeled black satin mules of her imagination. He took her chin in his hand and gently wiped at her mouth with his white linen handkerchief. "No lipstick in the bedroom, *mon amour.* You are beautiful enough without it." Stepping back, he slowly raked his eyes over her body and stopped at her scarlet-painted toenails. "Sit on the bed."

She did as he asked. He rummaged through her cosmetic case until he found a bottle of nail polish remover. He knelt before her and began removing the polish from each of her toes with his handkerchief. When he was done, he lightly bit her instep, then touched it with his tongue. "Are you wearing the panties I gave you?"

Embarrassed, she dropped her eyes to the collar of his dressing gown and nodded.

"*Bon.* You are my sweet bride, then, come to please me. You are shy, inexperienced, a little frightened perhaps. That is as it should be."

She *was* frightened. His soft words, the virginal nightgown . . . He was treating her as if she were an innocent, but that wouldn't erase her time with Flynn. The memory of the night Alexi had assaulted her wormed its way into her thoughts. She shook it off. He'd been jealous of Flynn, but now she was his wife, and he would never hurt her.

He rose and held out his hand. "Come to me, *chérie.* I've waited so long to make love to you."

Alexi eased her onto the bed. When she was lying down, he brushed his mouth over her lips. She told herself to imagine he was Flynn. "Put your arms around me, *chérie,*" he murmured. "I am your husband now."

She did as he asked, and as his face drew near, she tried to pretend, but Flynn had seldom kissed her and never with Alexi's intensity. "You kiss like a child." Alexi's lips moved against hers. "Open your mouth for me. Be gracious with your tongue."

Cautiously she parted her lips. This was Flynn kissing her. Flynn's mouth covering hers. But the great star's face refused to take shape.

Her body grew lax and warm. She pulled Alexi closer, her tongue growing bold in his mouth. She moaned softly when he moved away from her. "Open your eyes, Belinda. You must watch me make love to you." Cool air brushed her skin as he tugged on the bows holding the nightgown together and separated the bodice. "Watch my hands on your breasts, *chérie.*"

She opened her eyes to the burning intensity of his gaze, the searing eyes that could pierce flesh and bone to uncover even the smallest seed of deception. Panic mixed with her excitement. She tried to pull the nightgown back together.

He chuckled, the sound deep and low in his throat, and she realized he'd mistaken her fear for shyness. Before she could stop him, he peeled the nightgown over her hips. She lay on the bed, clad only in the lace-trimmed cotton underpants. He grasped her arms and placed them at her sides. "Let me look." His hands moved to her breasts, handling them gently, tracing light, feathery circles until her nipples hardened into tiny bells. He touched each tip. "I'm going to suckle you," he whispered.

Waves of heat shot through her as his head dipped. He drew her nipple into his mouth, sculpting it with his tongue and then drawing on it as if he were taking his nourishment. Excitement spread through her body like a betrayal, burning hotter and fiercer as he began stroking the insides of her thighs. His fingers moved beneath the lacy leg band of the panties just as Billy Greenway's had done so many lifetimes ago, and then slid inside her with a practiced touch so different from the awkward fumbles of her past.

"You're tight," he whispered, withdrawing from her. He pulled the underpants down over her hips, separated her legs, and began doing something to her with his mouth that was so forbidden, so thrilling, she couldn't believe it was happening. At first she fought against it, but her resistance was no match for his skill. He took control of her body, and she surrendered to him. She cried out as he brought her to an orgasm so exquisite she felt as if she were shattering into a thousand pieces.

After it was over, he lay beside her. What he had done was dirty, and she couldn't bear to look at him.

"That has never happened to you before, has it?" She heard the satisfaction in his voice and turned her back to him. "What a dear little prude you are, ashamed of yourself for enjoying something so natural." He leaned over to kiss her, but she turned her head away. Nothing would make her kiss a mouth that had been where his had.

He laughed, imprisoned her head between his palms, and brought his lips to hers. "See how sweet you are." Only then did he desert her long enough to open his dressing gown and let it fall to the floor. His body was lean and swarthy, covered in dark hair, and fully aroused. "Now I will explore you for my pleasure," he said.

He touched every part of her, leaving the mark of Alexi Savagar behind and once again setting her afire with desire. When he finally entered her, she wrapped her legs around him and dug her fingers into his buttocks and silently begged him to go faster. Just before his orgasm, he muttered thickly in her ear, "You are mine, Belinda. I am going to give you the world."

In the morning there was a smear of blood on the sheet from a long, thin scratch he'd made on her hip.

Paris was everything Belinda had imagined, and Alexi took her to all the places tourists adore. At the top of the Eiffel Tower exactly an hour before sunset, he kissed her until she thought her body would float. They sailed a toy boat in the *bassin* at the Luxembourg Gardens and wandered through Versailles in a thunderstorm. In the Louvre he found a deserted corner where he felt her breasts to see if they were as plump as those of the Renaissance Madonnas. He showed her the Seine at dawn near the Pont St.-Michel when the newborn sun struck the windows of the old buildings and set the city on fire. They visited Montmartre at night, and the wicked, smoky cafés of Pigalle, where he titillated her with whispered sex talk that left her breathless. They dined on trout and truffles in the Bois de Boulogne beneath chandeliers that hung from the chestnut trees, and they sipped Château Lafite in a café where tulips bloomed in the window. As each day passed, Alexi's step grew lighter and his laugh easier until he almost seemed like a boy again.

At night, he sealed them away in the great bedroom of his gray stone mansion on the Rue de la Bienfaisance and took her again and again until her body ceased to exist separate from his. She began to resent the demands of the job that stole him away from her each morning. Mornings left her with too much time to think about the baby she was carrying. Flynn's baby. The baby Alexi didn't know existed.

Life on the Rue de la Bienfaisance without Alexi was nearly unbearable. She hadn't been prepared for the grandeur of the gray stone mansion with its salons and apartments and dining room that could seat fifty. At first she'd been giddy at the idea of living amid so much splendor, but the huge house quickly oppressed her. She felt small and defenseless as she stood on the red and green veined marble in the oval foyer and surveyed the gruesome tapestries of martyrdom and crucifixion hanging on the walls. In the main salon, allegorical figures clad in capes and armor battled giant serpents on the ceiling. Friezes stretched over the heavily draped windows; pilasters flanked them. And all of it was ruled by Alexi's mother, Solange Savagar.

Solange was tall and thin, with dyed black hair cut close to her head, a large nose, and papery wrinkles. Each morning at ten o'clock she dressed in one of an endless number of white wool suits designed for her by Norell before the war, slipped on her rubies, and took her place on a Louis Quinze chair at the center of the main salon, where she began her daily rule over the house and its inhabitants. The possibility that Belinda, the unforgivably young American who had somehow managed to bewitch her son, would take Solange's place was unthinkable. The mansion on the Rue de la Bienfaisance was Solange's domain alone.

Alexi made it clear that his mother was to be respected, but Solange made companionship impossible. She refused to speak English except to criticize, and she took delight in laying out each *gaucherie* Belinda committed for Alexi's later inspection. Every evening at seven o'clock they gathered in the main salon, where Solange would sip white vermouth and smoke one lipstick-tipped Gauloise after another while she chattered at her son in staccato French.

Alexi kissed away Belinda's complaints. "My mother is a bitter old woman who has lost much. This house is all the kingdom she has left." His kisses strayed to her breasts. "Humor her, *chérie*. For my sake."

And then, abruptly, everything changed.

One night in mid April, six weeks after their wedding, she decided to surprise Alexi by modeling a transparent black negligee she'd bought that afternoon. As she pirouetted next to the bed, his face grew pale and he stalked from the room. She waited in the dark, angry with herself for not realizing how much he'd hate seeing her in anything but the simple white gowns he selected. The hours dragged by and he didn't return. By morning, she'd exhausted herself with her tears.

The next night she went to her mother-in-law. "Alexi has disappeared. I want to know where he is."

An ancient ruby on Solange's twisted finger winked like an evil eye. "My son tells me only what he wishes me to know."

He returned two weeks later. Belinda stood on the marble staircase in a Balmain dress that was too tight at the waist and watched him hand his briefcase to the butler. He seemed to have aged ten years. When he saw her, his mouth curled in the cynical twist she hadn't witnessed since they'd first met. "My dear wife. You look beautiful as always."

The next few days confused her. He treated her with deference in public, but in private he tormented her with his lovemaking. He abandoned tenderness for conquest and kept her poised on the brink of fulfillment for so long that her pleasure crossed the boundary into pain. During the last week of April, he announced that they were going on a trip but wouldn't tell her where.

He drove the 1933 Hispano-Suiza from his antique car collection with utter concentration. She was glad to be spared the effort of making conversation. Out the window, the land near Paris gradually gave way to the bare, chalky hillsides of Champagne. She couldn't make herself relax. She was nearly four months pregnant, and the effort of deceiving him was sapping her strength. She pretended to have menstrual periods that never came, secretly adjusted the buttons on the waists of her new skirts, and plotted to keep her naked body away from the light. She did everything she could to postpone the time when she'd be forced to tell him about the baby.

As the vineyards turned lavender in the lengthening afternoon shadows, they reached Burgundy. Their inn had a red-tiled roof and charming pots of geraniums in the windows, but she was too tired to enjoy the simple, well-cooked meal that was set before them.

The next day Alexi drove her out into the Burgundian countryside. They ate a silent picnic lunch on a hilltop covered with wildflowers, dining on a *potée* filled with fresh chervil, tarragon, and chives that Alexi had purchased in the neighboring village. They ate it with bread crusted in poppy seeds, a runny Saint Nectaire cheese, and a raw young country wine. Belinda picked at her food, then tied her cardigan around her shoulders and walked along the hilltop to escape Alexi's oppressive silence.

"Enjoying the view, my sweet?" She hadn't heard him come up behind her, and she jumped as he put his hands on her shoulders.

"It's pretty."

"Are you enjoying being with your husband?"

She curled her fingers over the knot she'd made in the sweater. "I always enjoy being with you."

"Especially in bed, *n'est-ce pas*?" He didn't wait for her answer but pointed out a vineyard and told her which grapes it produced. He began to seem like the Alexi who had shown her the sights of Paris, and she gradually relaxed.

"Over there, *chérie.* Do you see that collection of gray stone buildings? That is the Couvent de l'Annonciation. The nuns there run one of the best schools in France."

Belinda was more interested in the vineyards.

"Some of the finest families in Europe send their children to the nuns to be educated," he went on. "The sisters even take babies, although the male children are sent to the brothers near Langres when they are five."

Belinda was shocked. "Why would a rich family send away its babies?"

"It is necessary if the daughter is unmarried and a proper husband cannot be found. The sisters keep the babies until a discreet adoption can take place."

The talk of babies was making her nervous, and she tried to change the subject, but Alexi wasn't ready to be distracted. "The sisters take good care of them," he said. "They're not abandoned to spend their days in cribs. They have the best food and attention."

"I can't imagine a mother turning over her baby to someone else's care." She untied her sweater and slipped it on. "Let's go. I'm getting cold."

"You can't imagine it because you still think like the bourgeoisie," he said without moving. "You will have to think differently now that you are my wife. Now that you are a Savagar."

Her hands closed involuntarily over her abdomen, and she turned slowly. "I don't understand. Why are you telling me this?"

"So you know what will happen to your bastard child. As soon as it's born, it will go to the sisters at the Couvent de l'Annonciation to be raised."

"You know," she whispered.

"Of course I know."

The sun drained from the day as all her nightmares sprang to life.

"Your belly is swollen," he said, his voice laden with

contempt, "and the veins of your breasts show through your skin. The night I looked at you standing in our bedroom in that black nightgown . . . It was as if someone had ripped the blinders from my eyes. How long did you think you could deceive me?"

"No!" Suddenly it was all more than she could bear, and she did what she'd sworn she never would. "No! The baby's not a bastard! It's your baby! It's your—"

He slapped her hard across the face. "Do not humiliate yourself with lies that you know I will never believe!" She tried to pull away from him, but he held her tight. "How you must have been laughing at me that day at the Polo Lounge. You trapped me into marriage just as if I were a schoolboy. You made a fool of me!"

She began to cry. "I know I should have told you. But you wouldn't have helped me, and I didn't know what else to do. I'll go away. After our divorce. You'll never have to see me again."

"Our divorce? Oh no, *ma petite*. There will be no divorce. Did you not understand what I was telling you about the Couvent de l'Annonciation? Did you not understand that you are the one who has been trapped?"

Fear gripped her as she remembered what he'd said. "No! I'll never let you take away my baby." Her baby. Flynn's baby! She had to make her dreams come true. She'd start her life again in California. She and a little boy, as handsome as his father, or a little girl, more beautiful than any child born.

The expression on his face turned fierce, and all the foolish dream castles she'd built crumbled. "There will be no divorce," he said. "If you try to run away, you will never have a sou from me. You are not good at surviving without other people's money, are you, Belinda?"

"You can't take my baby away!"

"I can do anything I want." His voice grew deadly quiet. "You do not know French law, my dear. Your bastard child will be legally mine. In this country, the father has complete authority over his children. And, I warn you, if you ever tell anyone of your foolishness, I will ruin you. Do you understand me? You will be left with nothing."

"Alexi, don't do this to me," she whimpered.

But he was already walking away from her.

They drove silently back to Paris. As Alexi pulled the Hispano-Suiza through the gate and into the drive, Belinda looked up at the house she had grown to hate. It loomed over her, like a great, gray tombstone. She fumbled blindly for the door handle and jumped from the car.

Alexi was at her side almost immediately. "Enter the house with dignity, Belinda, for your own sake."

Her eyes filled with tears. "Why did you marry me?"

He gazed at her, the seconds ticking away like lost promises. His mouth tightened with bitterness. "Because I loved you."

She stared at him, and a lock of hair whipped her cheek. "I'll hate you forever for this." She pulled away and ran blindly down the drive toward the Rue de la Bienfaisance, her misery stark against the sunny beauty of the spring afternoon.

She fled into the leafy shadows near the gate where the old chestnut trees hung heavy with white blossoms. Petals dripped onto the pavement and lay in great snowy drifts at the curb. As she turned onto the street, a gust of wind from a passing car swept up the fallen petals from the sidewalk and enveloped her in a cloud of white. Alexi stood unmoving and watched. Belinda, captured for one heartbreaking beat of time in a swirling cloud of chestnut blossoms.

It was a moment he would remember for the rest of his life. Belinda in blossoms—silly and shallow, agonizingly young. Heartbroken.

Belinda's Baby

Chapter 6

The man cracked an ugly black whip over his head, and the younger girls squealed. Even the older students, who had just last night agreed they were much too sophisticated to be frightened by the *fouettard*, felt their throats go dry. He was ferociously ugly, with a filthy, matted beard and a long, dirt-stained robe. Every December 4 the *fouettard* singled out the very worst girl at the Couvent de l'Annonciation to receive his bundle of birch twigs.

For once the convent's dining room was free of its customary morning chatter, delivered in as many as five different languages. The girls pressed more closely together, and delicious quivers of fear shot through their stomachs.

Please, Blessed Mother, don't let it be me. Their prayers came more from habit than any real fear since they already knew whom he would chose.

She stood slightly apart from them, near a plastic Christmas wreath that hung alongside construction paper snowflakes and a poster of Mick Jagger the sisters hadn't yet spotted. Even though she was dressed in the same white blouse, blue plaid skirt, and dark kneesocks as her classmates, she looked different from the rest. Although she was only fourteen, she towered over all of them. She had huge hands, paddleboat feet, and a face too big for her body. An unruly ponytail contained the streaky blond hair that fell well past her shoulders. Her pale hair contrasted with a set of thick, dark eyebrows that almost met in the middle and looked as if they'd been painted on her face with a blunt-tipped marking pen. Her mouth, complete with a full set of silver braces, spread across the bottom of her face. Her arms and legs were long and ungainly, all pointy elbows and knobby knees, one of which bore a scab and the dirty outline of a Band-Aid. While the other girls wore slim Swiss wristwatches, she wore a man's chronometer, the black leather strap fitting her so loosely that the face of the watch hung to the side of her bony adolescent wrist.

It wasn't only her size that set her apart, but also the way she stood, her chin thrust forward, her funny green eyes glaring defiantly at anything she didn't like—in this case the *fouettard.* Her rebellious expression dared him to touch her with the whip. No one but Fleur Savagar could have managed that look.

By that winter of 1970, the more progressive areas of France had outlawed the *fouettard*, the wicked "whipper" who threatened to give badly behaved French schoolchildren birch sticks instead of presents for Christmas. But at the Couvent de l'Annonciation changes weren't made lightly, and the sisters hoped the shameful notoriety of being singled out as the worst-behaved girl at the *couvent* would breed reform. Unfortunately it hadn't worked out that way.

For the second time the *fouettard* cracked his whip, and for the second time Fleur Savagar refused to move, even though she had good reason to be worried. In January she'd stolen the keys to the mother superior's old Citroën. After bragging to everyone that she knew how to drive, she'd run the car straight through the toolshed. In March she'd broken her arm doing bareback acrobatics on the *couvent*'s bedraggled pony, then stubbornly refused to tell anyone she'd hurt herself until the nuns had spotted her badly swollen arm. An unfortunate incident with fireworks had led to the destruction of the garage roof, but that was a mild transgression compared to the unforgettable day all the *couvent*'s six-year-olds had disappeared.

The *fouettard* pulled the hated handful of birch twigs from an old gunnysack and let his eyes slide over the girls before they finally came to rest on Fleur. With a baleful stare, he placed the twigs at the toes of her scuffed brown oxfords. Sister Marguerite, who found the custom barbaric, looked away, but the other nuns clucked their tongues and shook their heads. They tried so hard with Fleur, but she was like quicksilver running through their disciplined days—changeable, impulsive, aching for her life to begin. They secretly loved her the best because she'd been with them the longest and because it was impossible not to love her. But they worried about what would happen when she was no longer under their firm control.

They watched for signs of remorse as she picked up the twigs. *Hélas!* Her head came up, and she flashed them a mischievous grin before she clamped the twigs into the crook of her arm like a bouquet of long-stemmed roses. All the girls giggled as she blew kisses and made mock bows.

★

As soon as Fleur was certain everybody understood how little she cared about the stupid *fouettard* and his stupid twigs, she slipped out the side door, grabbed her old wool coat from the row of hooks in the hallway, and raced outside. The morning was cold, and her breath formed a frosty cloud as she raced across the hard-packed earth away from the gray stone buildings. In her coat pocket, she found her beloved blue New York Yankees hat. It pulled at the rubber band on her ponytail, but she didn't care. Belinda had bought the hat for her last summer.

Fleur could only see her mother twice a year—during the Christmas holidays and for a month in August. In exactly fourteen days they'd be together in Antibes, where they spent every Christmas. Fleur had been marking off the days on her calendar since last August. She loved being with Belinda more than anything in the world. Her mother never scolded her for talking too loud, or upsetting a glass of milk, or even for swearing. Belinda loved her more than anybody in the whole world.

Fleur had never seen her father. He'd brought her to the *couvent* when she was only one week old and never come back. She'd never seen the house on the Rue de la Bienfaisance where all of them lived without her—her mother, her father, her grandmother . . . and her brother, Michel. It wasn't her fault, her mother said.

Fleur gave a shrill whistle as she reached the fence that marked the edge of the *couvent* property. Before she got her braces, she'd whistled a lot better. Before she got her braces, she hadn't believed anything could make her uglier. Now she knew she'd been wrong.

The chestnut whickered as he came up to the edge of the fence and stuck his head over the post to nuzzle her shoulder. He was a *Selle Français*, a French saddle horse owned by the neighboring vintner, and Fleur thought he was the most beautiful creature in the world. She'd give anything to ride him, but the nuns wouldn't let her, even though the vintner had given his permission. She wanted to disobey them and ride him anyway, but she was afraid they'd punish her by telling Belinda not to come.

Fleur planned to be a great horsewoman someday, despite her current status as the clumsiest girl at the *couvent*. She tripped over her big feet a dozen times a day, sending serving platters crashing to the floor, flower vases wobbling off tabletops, and the nuns scurrying into the nursery to safeguard whatever baby she might have taken it into her head to cuddle. Only when it came to sports did she forget her self-consciousness over her big feet, towering height, and oversized hands. She could run faster, swim farther, and score more goals at field hockey than anyone else. She was as good as a boy, and being as good as a boy was important to her. Fathers liked boys, and maybe if she was the bravest, the fastest, and the strongest, just like a boy, her father would let her come home.

★

The days before the Christmas holiday dragged endlessly until the afternoon arrived for her mother to pick her up. Fleur was packed hours in advance, and as she waited, the nuns passed through the chilly front hallway one by one.

"Do not forget, Fleur, to keep a sweater with you. Even in the South, it can be cool in December."

"Yes, Sister Dominique."

"Remember that you're not in Châtillon-sur-Seine where you know everyone. You mustn't talk to strangers."

"Yes, Sister Marguerite."

"Promise me you'll go to Mass every day."

She crossed her fingers in the folds of her skirt. "I promise, Sister Thérèse."

Fleur's heart burst with pride when her beautiful mother finally swept into their midst. She looked like a bird of paradise descending into a flock of chimney swifts. Beneath a snow-white mink coat, Belinda wore a yellow silk top over indigo trousers belted at the waist with braided orange vinyl. Platinum and Lucite bangles clicked at her wrists, and matching disks swung from her ears. Everything about her was colorfully mod, stylish, and expensive.

At thirty-three, Belinda had become a costly gem, cut to perfection by Alexi Savagar and polished by the luxuries of the Faubourg St.-Honoré. She was thinner, more prone to small, quick gestures, but the eyes that drank in her daughter's face had not changed at all. They were the same innocent hyacinth-blue as they'd been the day she'd met Errol Flynn.

Fleur bounded across the hallway like a Saint Bernard

pup and threw herself in her mother's arms. Belinda took a small step backward to steady herself. "Let's hurry," she whispered into Fleur's ear.

Fleur waved a hasty good-bye to the nuns, grabbed her mother's hand, and pulled her toward the door before the sisters could bombard Belinda with an account of Fleur's latest misdeeds. Not that Belinda paid any attention. "Those old bats," she'd said to Fleur the last time. "You have a wild, free spirit, and I don't want them to change one thing about you.' "

Fleur loved when her mother talked like that. Belinda said wildness was in Fleur's blood.

A silver Lamborghini stood at the bottom of the front steps. As Fleur slid into the passenger seat, she gulped in the sweet, familiar scent of her mother's Shalimar.

"Hello, baby."

She slipped into Belinda's arms with a small sob and cuddled into the mink, the Shalimar, and everything that was her mother. She was too old to cry, but she couldn't help herself. It felt so good to be Belinda's baby again.

*

Belinda and Fleur loved the Côte d'Azur. The day after they arrived, they drove from their pink stucco hotel near Antibes into Monaco along the famous Corniche du Littoral, the serpentine road that twisted around the cliffs of the coastline. "You wouldn't get carsick if you'd look straight ahead instead of out the sides," Belinda said, just as she'd said the year before.

"But then I'd miss too many things."

They stopped first at the market at the foot of Monte Carlo's palace hill. Fleur's stomach quickly recovered, and she bounded from one food stall to another pointing at everything that caught her eye. The weather was warm, and she wore khaki camp shorts, her favorite T-shirt, which said, "Draft beer, not students," and a new pair of Jesus sandals Belinda had bought her the day before. Belinda wasn't like the nuns about clothes. "Wear what makes you happy, baby," she said. "Develop your own style. There's plenty of time for high fashion later."

Belinda was wearing Pucci.

After Fleur made her selections for lunch, she dragged her mother up the steep path from the Monte Carlo market to the palace, eating a ham and poppy seed roll as she walked. Fleur spoke four languages, but she was proudest of her English, which was flawlessly American. She'd learned it from the American students who attended the *couvent*—daughters of diplomats, bankers, and the bureau chiefs of the American newspapers. By adopting their slang and their attitudes, she'd gradually stopped thinking of herself as French.

Someday she and Belinda were going to live in California. She wished they could go now, but Belinda wouldn't have any money if she divorced Alexi. Besides, Alexi wouldn't let her get a divorce. Fleur wanted to go to America more than anything in the world.

"I wish I had an American name." She scratched a bug bite on her thigh and tore off another bite of sandwich with her teeth. "I hate my name. I really do. Fleur is a stupid name for somebody as big as me. I wish you'd named me Frankie."

"Frankie is a hideous name." Belinda collapsed on a bench and tried to catch her breath. "Fleur was the closest I could get to the female version of a man I cared about. Fleur Deanna. It's a beautiful name for a beautiful girl."

Belinda always told Fleur she was beautiful, even though it wasn't true. Her thoughts flew in another direction. "I hate having my period. It's disgusting."

Belinda delved into her purse for a cigarette. "It's part of being a woman, baby."

Fleur made a face to show Belinda exactly what she thought of that, and her mother laughed. Fleur pointed up the path toward the palace. "I wonder if she's happy?"

"Of course she's happy. She's a princess. One of the

most famous women in the world." Belinda lit her cigarette and pushed her sunglasses on top of her head. "You should have seen her in *The Swan*, with Alec Guinness and Louis Jourdan. God, she was beautiful."

Fleur stretched out her legs. They were covered with fine, pale hair, and pink with sunburn. "He's kind of old, don't you think?"

"Men like Rainier are ageless. He's quite distinguished, you know. Very charming."

"You've met him?"

"Last fall. He came for dinner." Belinda pulled her sunglasses back over her eyes.

Fleur dug the heel of her sandal into the dirt. "Was *he* there?"

"Hand me some of those olives, darling." Belinda gestured toward one of the paper cartons with an almond-shaped fingernail painted the color of ripe raspberries.

Fleur handed her the carton. "Was he?"

"Alexi owns property in Monaco. Of course he was there."

"Not him." Fleur's sandwich had lost its taste, and she pulled off a piece to toss to the ducks across the path. "I didn't mean Alexi. I meant Michel." She used the French pronunciation of her thirteen-year-old brother's name, which was a girl's name in America.

"Michel was there. He had a school recess."

"I hate him. I really do."

Belinda set aside the olive carton without opening it and took a drag on her cigarette.

"I don't care if it's a sin," Fleur said. "I hate him even more than Alexi. Michel has everything. It's not fair."

"He doesn't have *me*, honey. Just remember that."

"And I don't have a father. But it's still not even. At least Michel gets to go home when he's not in school. He gets to be with you."

"We're here to have a good time, baby. Let's not get so serious."

Fleur wouldn't be sidetracked. "I can't understand Alexi. How could anybody hate a baby so much? Maybe now that I'm grown up . . . But not when I was one week old."

Belinda sighed. "We've been through this so many times. It's not you. It's just the way he is. God, I wish I had a drink."

Even though Belinda had explained it dozens of times, Fleur still didn't understand. How could a father want to have sons so much that he would send his only daughter away and never see her again? Belinda said Fleur was a reminder of his failure and Alexi couldn't stand failure. But even when Michel was born a year after Fleur, he hadn't changed. Belinda said it was because she couldn't have any more children.

Fleur had cut pictures of her father out of the newspapers, and she kept them in a manila envelope in the back of her closet. She used to pretend Mother Superior called her to the office and that Alexi was there waiting to tell her he'd made a terrible mistake and he'd come to take her home. Then he'd hug her and call her "baby" the way her mother did.

She tossed another piece of bread at the ducks. "I hate him. I hate them both." And then, for good measure, "I hate my braces, too. Josie and Celine Sicard hate me because I'm ugly."

"You're just feeling sorry for yourself. Remember what I've been telling you. In a few years, every girl at the *couvent* will want to look just like you. You need to grow up a little more, that's all."

Fleur's bad mood slipped away. She loved her mother.

The palace of the Grimaldi family was a sprawling stone and stucco edifice with ugly square turrets and candy cane guard boxes. As Belinda watched her daughter dart through the crowd of tourists to climb on top of a cannon that overlooked the Monaco yacht basin, she felt a lump form in her throat. Fleur had Flynn's wildness, his restless zest for living.

Belinda had wanted to blurt out the truth so many times. She wanted to tell Fleur that a man like Alexi Savagar could never have been her father. That Fleur was Errol Flynn's daughter. But fear kept her silent. She'd learned long ago not to cross Alexi. Only once had she beaten him. Only once had he been the helpless one. When Michel was born.

After dinner that night, Belinda and Fleur went to see an American Western with French subtitles. The film was half over when Belinda saw him for the first time. She must have made some sort of sound because Fleur looked over at her. "What's wrong?"

"Nothing," Belinda managed. "It's . . . That man . . ."

Belinda studied the cowboy who'd just sauntered into the saloon where Paul Newman was playing poker. The cowboy was very young and far from movie star handsome. The camera moved in for a close-up and Belinda forgot to breathe. It didn't seem possible. And yet. . .

The lost years dropped away. James Dean had come back.

The man was tall and lean with legs that didn't stop. His long, narrow face looked as if it had been chipped from flint by a rebellious hand, and his irregular features projected a confidence that went beyond arrogance. He had straight brown hair; a long, narrow nose with a bump at the bridge; and a sulky mouth. His slightly crooked front tooth had the tiniest chip at one corner. And his eyes . . . Restless and bitter blue.

He didn't look at all like Jimmie—she saw that now. He was taller, not as handsome. But he was another rebel—she felt it in her bones—another man who lived life on his own terms.

The film ended, but she stayed in her seat, clutching Fleur's impatient hand and watching the credits roll. His name flashed on the screen. Excitement welled inside her.

Jake Koranda.

After all these years, Jimmie had sent her a sign. He was telling her she mustn't lose hope. *A man is his own man. A woman her own woman.* Jake Koranda, the man behind that off-kilter face, had given her hope. Somehow she could still make her dreams come true.

★

The boys of Châtillon-sur-Seine discovered Fleur the summer before her sixteenth birthday. "*Salut, poupée!*" they called out as she emerged from the *boulangerie.*

She looked up, a smear of chocolate dotting her chin, and saw three boys lounging in the doorway of the *pharmacie* next door. They were smoking cigarettes and listening to "Crocodile Rock" on a portable radio. One boy stubbed out his cigarette. "*Hé poupée, irons voir par ici.*" He made a beckoning gesture with his head.

Fleur glanced around to see which of her classmates he was talking to.

The boys laughed. One nudged his friend and pointed at her legs. "*Regardez-moi ces jambes!*"

Fleur looked down to see what was wrong, and another dab of chocolate from her éclair dripped onto the blue leather strap of her Dr. Scholl's sandals. The taller of the boys winked, and she realized they were admiring her legs. *Hers!*

"*Qu'est-ce que tu dirais d'un rendezvous?*"

A date. He was asking her for a date! She dropped the éclair and ran up the street to the bridge where the girls were meeting. Her streaky blond hair flew behind her like a horse's mane. The boys laughed and whistled.

When she got back to the *couvent*, she dashed to her room and stared at herself in the mirror. Those same boys used to call her *l'épouvantail*, the scarecrow. What had happened? Her face looked the same: thick, marking-pen eyebrows, green eyes set too far apart, mouth spread all over. She'd finally stopped growing, but not until she'd reached five feet, eleven and a half inches. The braces were gone now. Maybe that was it.

By the time August arrived, Fleur was nearly sick with excitement. A whole month to be with her mother. And on Mykonos, her favorite of all the Greek islands. The first morning as they walked along the beach in the dazzling white sunlight, she couldn't stop talking about everything she'd been saving up.

"It's creepy the way those boys keep calling out at me. Why would they do something like that? I think it's because I got rid of my braces." Fleur tugged on the oversized T-shirt she'd pulled on top of the apple-green bikini Belinda had bought to surprise her. She loved the color, but its skimpy cut embarrassed her. Belinda wore an oatmeal striped tunic and a chrome Galanos slave bracelet. Both of them had bare feet, but Belinda's toenails were painted burnt umber.

Her mother sipped from the Bloody Mary she'd brought along. Belinda drank a lot more than she should, but Fleur didn't know how to get her to stop.

"Poor baby," Belinda said, "it's hard not being the ugly duckling anymore. Especially when you've been so dedicated to the idea." She slipped her free arm around Fleur's waist, and her hipbone brushed the top of her daughter's thigh. "I've been telling you for years the only problem with your face is that you hadn't grown into it, but you're stubborn."

The way Belinda said it made Fleur feel as though that was something to be proud of. She hugged her mother, then flopped down on the sand. "I couldn't ever have sex. I mean it, Belinda. I am *never* getting married. I don't even like men."

"You don't *know* any men, darling," Belinda said dryly. "Once you've gotten away from that godforsaken convent, you'll feel differently."

"I won't. Can I have a cigarette?"

"No. And men are wonderful, baby. The right men, of

course. Powerful ones. When you walk into a restaurant on the arm of an important man, everyone looks at you, and you see admiration in their eyes. They know you're very special."

Fleur frowned and picked at the bandage on her toe. "Is that why you won't get divorced from Alexi? Because he's important?"

Belinda sighed and tilted her face into the sun. "I've told you, baby. It's money. I don't have the skills to support us."

But Fleur would have the skills. She already excelled in math. She spoke French, English, Italian, and German, even a little Spanish. She knew history and literature, she could type, and when she went to the university, she'd learn even more. Before long, she'd be able to support them both. Then she and Belinda could live together forever and never be separated again.

Two days later, one of Belinda's Parisian acquaintances arrived on Mykonos. Belinda introduced Fleur as her niece, something she always did on the rare occasions when they ran into a person she knew. Each time it happened, Fleur felt sick inside, but Belinda said she had to do it or Alexi would cancel their trips.

The woman was Madame Phillipe Jacques Duverge, but Belinda said she'd once been Bunny Groben, from White Plains, New York. She'd also been a famous model during the sixties, and she kept pointing her camera at Fleur. "Just for fun," she said,

Fleur hated having her picture taken, and she kept running into the water.

Madame Duverge followed, clicking away.

As one white-hot Mykonos day gave way to another, Fleur discovered the young men who roamed the sandy Greek beaches were no different from the boys of Châtillon-sur-Seine. She told Belinda they were making her so nervous she couldn't enjoy her new snorkeling mask. "Why do they have to act so stupid?"

Belinda took a sip of her gin and tonic. "Ignore them. They're not important."

When Fleur returned to the *couvent* for her final year, she had no way of knowing her life was about to change forever. In October, shortly after her sixteenth birthday, a fire broke out in the dormitory, and all the girls were forced to evacuate. A photographer for the local newspaper rushed out and caught the daughters of France's most exclusive families standing by the blazing building in their pajamas. Although the dormitory was badly damaged, no one was hurt, but because of the notoriety of the families involved, several of the photos made their way into *Le Monde*, including a close-up of the nearly forgotten daughter of Alexi Savagar.

Alexi was too intelligent to keep Fleur's existence a secret. Instead he'd simply look pensive whenever her name was mentioned, and people assumed his daughter was handicapped, perhaps mentally retarded. But the astonishingly beautiful young woman with the wide mouth and startled eyes could never be mistaken for anybody's closet skeleton.

Alexi was furious that the newspaper had identified her, but it was too late. People began asking questions. To make it worse, Solange Savagar picked that particular time to die. Alexi couldn't tolerate the vulgar speculation that would grow even worse if the obviously healthy granddaughter who'd been so recently photographed was absent from her grandmother's funeral.

He ordered Belinda to send for her bastard.

Chapter 7

I'm going to meet my father today. The words tumbled through Fleur's head as she followed a maid down the silent, forbidding hallway of the gray stone mansion on the Rue de la Bienfaisance. When they reached a small salon with a pilaster-framed doorway, the maid turned the knob, then slipped away.

"Baby!" Liquor splashed over the edge of Belinda's glass as she shot up from the silk damask couch. She abandoned her glass and held out her arms.

Fleur rushed forward, only to stumble on the Persian carpet and nearly fall. They hugged each other, and, as she inhaled her mother's Shalimar, Fleur felt a little better.

Belinda looked pale and elegant in a black Dior suit and low-heeled pumps with pear-shaped openings at the toes. Fleur couldn't bear having *him* think she was trying to impress, so she'd dressed in her black wool slacks, cowl-necked sweater, and an old tweed blazer with a black velvet collar. Her friends Jen and Helene had told her to put up her hair so she'd look more sophisticated, but she'd refused. The barrettes on each side of her head weren't an exact match, but they were close enough. Finally she'd tucked her silver horseshoe stickpin in her lapel for confidence. So far, it wasn't working.

Belinda cupped Fleur's cheek. "I'm so glad you're here."

Fleur saw the shadows under her mother's eyes, the drink on the table, and hugged her more tightly. "I missed you so much."

Belinda grasped her shoulders. "It's not going to be easy, baby. Stay out of Alexi's way, and we'll hope for the best."

"I'm not afraid of him."

Belinda waved off Fleur's bravado with a trembling hand. "He's been impossible ever since Solange got sick. I'm glad the old bitch is dead. She was getting to be a trial, even for him. Michel is the only one who's sorry to see her go."

Michel. Her brother was fifteen now, a year younger than she. She'd known he'd be here, but she hadn't let herself think about it.

The door behind them gave a soft click. "Belinda, did you telephone the Baron de Chambray as I asked? He was especially fond of Mother."

His voice was low and deep, filled with authority. The kind of voice that never had to be raised to be obeyed.

He can't do anything more to me, Fleur thought. *Nothing.* Slowly she turned to face her father.

He was surgically well groomed, his hands and fingernails immaculate, his thin, steel-gray hair impeccably neat. He wore a necktie the color of old sherry and a dark vested suit. Next to Pompidou, he was said to be the most powerful man in France. He gave a short, elegant snort as she saw her. "So, Belinda, this is your daughter. She dresses like a peasant."

Fleur wanted to cry, but somehow she managed to lift her chin and look down at him. She spoke English deliberately. American English. Strong and clear. "The nuns taught me that good manners are more important than clothes. I guess things are different in Paris."

She heard Belinda's quick intake of breath, but the only

reaction Alexi showed to Fleur's impertinence was in his eyes. They drifted slowly over her, searching for the flaws she knew he'd find in abundance. She'd never felt bigger, uglier, more awkward, but she matched him stare for stare.

Standing off to the side, Belinda watched the duel taking place between Alexi and Fleur. A rush of pride swelled inside her. This was her daughter—strong, full of spirit, achingly beautiful. Let Alexi compare Fleur with his weakling son. Belinda sensed the exact moment when he saw the resemblance, and for the first time in longer than she could remember, she felt calm in his presence. When he finally looked her way, she gave him a small, triumphant smile.

It was Flynn's face Alexi saw in Fleur, the young, unblemished Flynn, with his features softened and transformed, made beautiful for his daughter. Fleur's face had the same strong nose and wide, elegant mouth, the same high forehead. Even her eyes bore his mark in their shape and generous spacing. Only the green-gold irises were Fleur's own.

Alexi turned on his heel and left the salon.

Fleur stood at the window of her mother's bedroom while Belinda napped. She watched Alexi pull away from the house in a chauffeured Rolls. The silver car glided down the drive and through the great iron gates onto the Rue de la Bienfaisance. The Street of Charity. What a stupid name. There was no charity in this house, just a horrible man who hated his own flesh and blood. Maybe if she'd been tiny and pretty . . . But weren't fathers supposed to love their daughters no matter how they looked?

She was too old for the baby tears she wanted to shed, so she slipped into her loafers and set out to explore. She found a back staircase leading into a garden where mathematically straight paths delineated geometric beds of ugly shrubbery. She told herself she was lucky to have been sent away from this horrible place. At the *couvent*, petunias flopped over the borders and cats could sleep in the flower beds.

She swiped her eyes with the sleeve of her sweater. Some small, stupid part of her had wanted to believe her father would have a change of heart when he saw her. That he'd realize how wrong he'd been to abandon her. Stupid. Stupid.

She took in a T-shaped, one-story building sitting at the back of the grounds. Like the house, it was constructed of gray stone, but it had no windows. When she found the side door unlocked, she turned the knob and stepped into a jewel box.

Black watered silk covered the walls, and gleaming ebony marble floors stretched before her. Small, recessed spotlights shone down from the ceiling in starry clusters like a Van Gogh night sky, each cluster lighting an antique automobile. Their polished finishes reminded her of gemstones—rubies, emeralds, amethysts, and sapphires. Some of the automobiles rested on the marble floor, but many sat on platforms, so they seemed to be suspended in the air like a handful of jewels flung into the night.

Slim columns bearing engraved silver plaques sat next to each car. The heel plates of her loafers clicked on the hard marble floor as she investigated. Isotta-Fraschini Type 8, 1932. Stutz Bearcat, 1917. Rolls-Royce Phantom I, 1925. Bugatti Brescia, 1921. Bugatti Type 13, 1912. Bugatti Type 59, 1935. Bugatti Type 35.

All the automobiles grouped in the shorter wing of the L-shaped room bore the distinctive red oval of the Bugatti. Positioned in the exact center, a brightly illuminated platform, larger than all the others, sat empty. The label at the corner of the platform had been printed in big, bold script.

BUGATTI TYPE 41 ROYALE

"Does he know you're here?"

She spun around and found herself gazing at the most

beautiful boy she'd ever seen. He had hair like fine yellow silk and small, delicately formed features. Dressed in a faded green pullover and rumpled chinos fastened at the waist with an oversized cowboy belt, he was much shorter than she and as small-boned as a woman. His long, tapered fingers had nails bitten to the quick. His chin was pointed, and pale eyebrows arched over eyes that were exactly the same brilliant shade of blue as the first spring hyacinths.

Belinda's face looked back at her from the form of a young man. Her old bitterness rose like bile in her throat.

He looked younger than his fifteen years as he nibbled on the remnants of a thumbnail. "I'm Michel. I didn't mean to spy." He gave her a sad, sweet smile that suddenly made him look older. "You're mad, aren't you?"

"I don't like people sneaking up on me."

"I wasn't really sneaking, but I guess that doesn't matter. Neither of us is supposed to be here. He'd be pissed if he found out."

His English was as American as hers, and that made her hate him even more. "He doesn't scare me," she said belligerently.

"That's because you don't know him."

"I guess some of us are lucky." She made the words as nasty as she could.

"I guess." He walked over to the door and began flicking off the ceiling lights from a panel of switches. "You'd better go now. I have to lock up before he finds out we've been in here."

She hated him for being so tiny and pretty. A puff of air could blow him away. "I'll bet you do everything he tells you to. Like a scared rabbit."

He shrugged.

She couldn't face him a moment longer. She dashed through the door and rushed out into the garden. All those years she'd worked so hard to win her father's love by being the bravest, the fastest, and the strongest. The joke was on her.

⁂

Michel gazed at the door his sister had disappeared through. He shouldn't have let himself hope they'd be friends, but he'd wanted it so much. He'd needed something, someone, to help fill the aching chasm left by the death of the grandmother who'd raised him. Solange had said he was her chance to make up for past mistakes.

It was his grandmother who'd overheard his mother screaming the news to his father that she was pregnant with Michel. Belinda had told Alexi she wouldn't give any more love to the child she was carrying than he'd given to the baby abandoned at the Couvent de l'Annonciation. His grandmother said his father had laughed at Belinda's threats. He'd said Belinda couldn't resist loving her own flesh and blood. That this baby would make her forget the other one.

But his father had been wrong. Solange was the one who'd held him, and played with him, and comforted him when he was hurt. Michel should be glad she was finally free from her suffering, but he wanted her back, puffing away on her lipstick-stained Gauloise, stroking his hair as he knelt in front of her, offering all the love that the others in the house on the Rue de la Bienfaisance denied him.

She was the one who'd negotiated the uneasy truce between his parents. Belinda had agreed to be seen in public with Michel in return for twice-yearly visits with her daughter. But the truce hadn't changed the fact that his mother didn't love him. She said he was his father's child. But Alexi didn't want him, either, not when he'd seen that Michel couldn't be like him.

All the trouble in his family had happened because of his sister, the mysterious Fleur. Not even his grandmother knew why Fleur had been sent away.

He left the garage and made his way back to his rooms in the attic. He'd gradually transported his belongings up there until no one remembered exactly how it was that the heir to the Savagar fortune came to be living in the old servants' quarters.

He lay on his bed and locked his hands behind his head. A white parachute hung as a canopy over his small iron bed. He'd bought it in an army surplus store not far from the Boston prep school he attended. He liked the way the parachute rippled in the moving air currents and sheltered him like a great, silken womb.

On the whitewashed walls he'd hung his precious collection of photographs. Lauren Bacall in Helen Rose's classic red sheath from *Designing Woman.* Carroll Baker swinging from a chandelier in *The Carpetbaggers*, clad in Edith Head's gaudy sprinkle of beads and ostrich plumes. Above his desk, Rita Hayworth wore Jean Louis's famous Gilda gown, and, by her side, Shirley Jones struck a pose in the deliciously tawdry pink slip she'd worn in *Elmer Gantry.* The women and their wonderful costumes enchanted him.

He picked up his sketch pad and began drawing a tall, thin girl, with bold slashes for eyebrows and a wide mouth. His telephone rang. It was André. Michel's fingers began to tremble around the receiver.

"I just heard the wretched news about your grandmother," André said. "I'm so sorry. This is very difficult for you."

Michel's throat constricted at the warm show of sympathy.

"Is it possible for you to slip out this evening? I—I want to see you. I want to comfort you, *chéri.*"

"I'd like that," Michel said softly. "I've missed you."

"And I've missed you. England was beastly, but Danielle insisted on staying through the weekend."

Michel didn't like being reminded of André's wife, but soon André would leave her, and the two of them would move to the south of Spain and live in a fishing cottage. In the mornings Michel would sweep the terra-cotta floors, plump the cushions, and set out earthenware pitchers filled with flowers and wicker bowls piled with ripe fruit. In the afternoons, while André read him poetry, Michel would create beautiful clothes on the sewing machine he'd taught himself to use. At night they would love each other to the music of the Gulf of Cadiz lapping at the sandy shore outside their window. That's the way Michel dreamed it.

"I could meet you in an hour," he said softly.

"An hour it is." André's voice dropped in pitch. "*Je t'adore, Michel.*"

Michel choked back his tears. "*Je t'adore, André.*"

★

Fleur had never worn such an elegant dress, a long-sleeved black sheath, with small, overlapping leaves picked out in tiny black beads at one shoulder. Belinda put Fleur's hair up in a loose chignon and fastened polished onyx drops at her ears. "There," her mother said as she stepped back to observe her handiwork. "Let him call you a peasant now."

Fleur could see that she looked older and more sophisticated than sixteen, but she felt weird, as if she'd dressed up in Belinda's clothes.

Fleur took her place at the center of the long, silent dinner table with Belinda sitting at one end and Alexi at the other. Everything was white. White linen, white candles, heavy alabaster vases holding dozens of full-blown white roses. Even the food was white—a cream soup, white asparagus, and pale scallops whose smell mixed with the cloying fragrance of the white roses. The three of them dressed in black looked like ravens perched around a funeral bier, with Belinda's blood-red fingernails the only spot of color. Even Michel's absence didn't make the awful meal bearable.

Fleur wished her mother would stop drinking, but Belinda consumed one glass of wine after another while only toying with her food. When her mother ground out a cigarette on her dinner plate, a servant whisked it away. Alexi's voice penetrated the silence. "I will take you to view your grandmother now."

Wine sloshed over the rim of Belinda's glass. "For God's sake, Alexi. Fleur didn't even know her. There's no need for this."

Fleur couldn't bear the twisted, frightened expression on her mother's face. "It's okay. I'm not afraid." A servant pulled back Fleur's chair while Belinda sat frozen, her skin as pale as the white roses in front of her.

Fleur followed Alexi into the hallway. Their footsteps echoed off a vaulted ceiling, with violent frescoes of women in breastplates and men stabbing each other. They reached the gilded doors that marked the entrance to the main salon. He opened one of them and gestured for her to enter.

The room held only a shiny black casket banked in white roses and a small ebony chair. Fleur tried to act as though she saw corpses all the time, but the only dead body she'd seen had belonged to Sister Madeleine, and that had only been a glimpse. Solange Savagar's wrinkled face looked as if it had been molded from old candle wax.

"Kiss your grandmother's lips as a sign of respect."

"You're not serious." She nearly laughed, but then she looked at him, and the expression on his face stopped her cold. He didn't care about Fleur showing respect. He was testing her courage. This was a dare, *un defi*. And he didn't believe for one moment she could meet it.

"Oh, but I'm very serious," he said.

She locked her knees so they didn't tremble. "I've been facing bullies all my life."

His mouth curled unpleasantly. "Is that what you think I am? A bully?"

"No." She forced her own mouth to form the same unpleasant sneer. "I think you're a monster."

"You are such a child."

She'd never imagined she could hate anyone so much. Slowly she took a step, and then another. She moved across the polished floor toward the casket, and as she came closer, she fought the urge to run from this silent house, run from the Street of Charity, run from Alexi Savagar back to the safe, suffocating comfort of the nuns. But she couldn't run. Not until she showed him what he'd tossed away.

She reached the casket and sucked in her breath. Then she bent forward and touched her lips to the cold, still ones of her grandmother.

She heard a sudden, sharp hiss. For one horrifying moment, she thought it was coming from the corpse, but then Alexi grabbed her shoulders and pulled her back from the coffin.

"*Sale garce!*" He uttered a vicious curse and shook her. "You're just like him. You'll do anything to save your pride!" Her hair came loose and tumbled down her back. He shoved her into the small black chair next to the casket. "Nothing is too vile when your pride is at stake." He wiped away the kiss with his bare hand, smearing her lipstick across her cheek.

She tried to push his arm away. "Don't touch me! I hate you. Don't ever touch me."

His grip loosened on her arm. He said something so softly she almost missed it.

"*Pur sang.*"

She stopped struggling.

He stroked her mouth with his fingers, his touch gentle. He traced the line where her lips came together. And then, unexpectedly, his finger slid inside her mouth and moved gently along the barrier of her teeth.

"*Enfant. Pauvre enfant.*"

She sat there stunned, spellbound, mesmerized. He crooned as if he were singing her a lullaby. "You have been caught in something you don't understand. *Pauvre enfant.*"

His touch was so tender. Was this the way fathers treated daughters they loved?

"You are extraordinary," he murmured. "The photograph in the newspaper didn't prepare me." He gently tangled his fingers in the tendril of hair that had fallen over her cheek. "I've always loved beautiful things. Clothing.

Women. Automobiles." He brushed his thumb over her jawline. She smelled his cologne, faintly spicy. "At first I loved indiscriminately, but I've learned better."

She didn't know what he was talking about.

He touched her chin. "Now I have only one obsession. The Bugatti. Do you know the Bugatti?"

Why was he talking about a car? She remembered what she'd seen in the garage, but she shook her head.

"Ettore Bugatti called his cars *pur sang*, pure blood, like a Thoroughbred horse." The tips of his fingers brushed the polished onyx drops in her earlobes and pulled gently. "I have the finest collection of *pur sang* Bugattis in the world, all but the crown jewel—the Bugatti Royale." His voice was soft, loving . . . hypnotic. She felt as if he'd cast a spell over her. "He built only six of them. During the war, one Royale was left in Paris. Three of us hid it from the Germans in the sewers beneath the city. That car has become a legend, and I'm determined to own it. I must own it because it is the very best. *Pur sang*, do you understand me, *enfant*? Not to possess the best is unthinkable." He stroked her cheek.

She nodded, although she didn't understand at all. Why was he talking about this now? But his voice was so loving, and the old fantasies rose up inside her. Her eyes drifted shut. Her father had seen her, and after all these years, he finally wanted her.

"You remind me of that car," he whispered. "Except you are not *pur sang*, are you?"

At first she thought she felt his finger on her mouth. Then she realized it was his lips. Her father was kissing her.

"Alexi!" The shriek of a wounded animal penetrated the room. Fleur's eyes flew open.

Belinda stood at the door, her face twisted with anguish. "Get your hands off her! I'll kill you if you touch her again! Get away from him, Fleur. You mustn't ever let him touch you!"

Fleur rose awkwardly from the chair. Her faltering words were unplanned. "But . . . He's . . . He's my father . . ."

Belinda looked as if she'd been slapped. Fleur felt sick. She rushed to her mother. "It's all right. I'm sorry!"

"How could you?" Belinda's voice was almost a whisper. "Does one meeting with him make you forget everything?"

Fleur shook her head miserably. "No. No, I haven't forgotten anything."

"Come upstairs with me," Belinda said stonily. "Now."

"Go with your mother, *chérie*." His voice slid between them like silk. "We will have time to talk after the funeral tomorrow and make plans for your future."

His words gave her a sweet, fluttery sensation that felt like a betrayal.

Belinda stood at her bedroom window looking through the trees at the headlights flickering past on the Rue de la Bienfaisance. Muddy mascara tears trickled down her cheeks and dripped onto the lapels of her ice-blue robe. In the next room, Fleur slept. Flynn had died without ever knowing about her.

Belinda was only thirty-five, but she felt like an old woman. She wouldn't let Alexi steal her beautiful baby away. No matter what she had to do. She stumbled over to the stereo. An hour ago, she'd made a phone call. She couldn't think what else to do. As she looked around for her drink, she knew that, after tonight, there couldn't be any more.

Her glass sat on the floor next to the pile of record albums. She crouched in the midst of them and picked up the album that lay on top. The soundtrack from the Western *Devil Slaughter*. She stared at the picture on the cover.

Jake Koranda. Actor and playwright. *Devil Slaughter* was the second of his Bird Dog Caliber movies. She loved them both, even if the critics didn't. They said Jake was prostituting his talent by appearing in junk, but she didn't feel that way.

The cover photo depicted the movie's opening scene. Jake, as Bird Dog Caliber, stared into the camera, his face dirt-creased and weary; his soft, sulky mouth slack, almost ugly. Pearl-handled Colt revolvers gleamed at his sides. She leaned back, shut her eyes, and reached for the fantasies that made her feel better. Gradually the sounds of the distant cars slipped away until she could only hear his breathing and feel his hands on her breasts.

Yes, Jake. Oh yes. Oh yes, my darling, Jimmy.

The record album slipped from her fingers, jarring her back to reality. She reached for her crumpled pack of cigarettes, but it was empty. She'd meant to send someone out after dinner, but she'd forgotten. Everything was slipping away from her. Everything except the daughter she'd never let go.

She heard the sound she'd been waiting for, Alexi's footsteps on the stairs. She splashed more scotch in her glass and carried it out into the hallway. Alexi's face looked drawn. His newest teenage mistress must have worn him out. She walked toward him, her robe slipping over one naked shoulder.

"You're drunk," he said.

"Just a little." An ice cube clinked dully against the side of her glass. "Just enough so I can talk to you."

"Go to bed, Belinda. I'm too tired to satisfy you tonight."

"I only want a cigarette."

Watching her carefully, he drew out his silver case and opened it. She took her time pulling one out, then stepped past him into his bedroom. Alexi followed her. "I don't remember inviting you in."

"Pardon me for entering kiddieland," she retorted.

"Go away, Belinda. Unlike my mistresses, you're old and ugly. You've become a desperate woman who knows she has nothing fresh to bargain with."

She couldn't let his words hurt her. She had to concentrate on the awful obscenity of his mouth covering Fleur's lips. "I won't let you have my daughter."

"*Your* daughter?" He took off his jacket and tossed it over a chair. "Don't you mean *our* daughter?"

"I'll kill you if you touch her."

"*Bon Dieu, chérie.* Your drinking has finally driven you over the edge." His cuff links clanked on the bureau as he discarded them. "For years you have begged me to include her in our family."

Even though he had no way of knowing about the phone call she'd made, she had to fight to sound calm. "I wouldn't be too confident. Now that Fleur's older, you don't have many holds left on me."

His fingers paused on his shirt studs.

She forced herself to go on. "I have plans for her, and I don't care any longer who knows that you've been raising another man's daughter." It wasn't true. She did care. She couldn't bear the idea of her daughter's love turning to hatred. If Fleur discovered Alexi wasn't her father, she wouldn't understand how Belinda could have lied to her. Even worse, she wouldn't understand why Belinda had stayed with him.

Alexi seemed amused. "Is this blackmail, *chérie*? Have you forgotten how much you love your luxuries? If anyone learns the truth about Fleur, I'll cut you off without a penny, and you know you can't survive without money. How would you keep yourself in scotch?"

Belinda walked slowly toward him. "Maybe you don't know me as well as you think."

"Oh, I know you, *chérie*." His fingers trailed a path down her arm. "I know you better than you know yourself."

She gazed into his face, searching for some softness there. But she could only see the mouth that had crushed her daughter's lips.

6★

The morning after Solange's funeral, Fleur woke up before dawn to the sound of someone in her room. As she eased her eyes open, she saw Belinda throwing clothes in her suitcase. "Get up, baby," she whispered. "I have your things all packed. Don't make any noise."

Belinda wouldn't explain where they were going until they'd reached the outskirts of Paris. "We're staying with Bunny Duverge for a while at her estate in Fontainebleau." Her eyes darted nervously to the rearview mirror, and lines of strain pulled at the corners of her mouth. "You met her when we were on Mykonos this summer, remember? The woman who kept taking your picture."

"I asked her not to. I hate having my picture taken." Fleur couldn't smell any liquor, but she wondered if Belinda had been drinking. It wasn't even seven o'clock. The idea upset her nearly as much as being awakened at dawn and dragged away from the house without an explanation.

"Fortunately Bunny ignored you." Once again, Belinda's eyes darted to the rearview mirror. "She called me a couple of times after I got back to Paris. She thought you were my niece, remember? All she could talk about was how striking you were and how you should be a model. She wanted your phone number."

"A model!" Fleur leaned forward in her seat and stared at Belinda. "That's crazy."

"She says you have exactly the face and body designers want."

"I'm six feet tall!"

"Bunny used to be a famous model, so she should know." Belinda dug into her purse with one hand and pulled out her cigarette case. "When she saw that photo of you in *Le Monde* after the fire, she realized you weren't my niece. At first she was angry, but two days ago she called and admitted she'd sent the Mykonos pictures to Gretchen Casimir, the woman who owns one of the most exclusive modeling agencies in New York."

"Modeling agency! Why?"

"Gretchen loved the photos, and she wants Bunny to get some proper test shots of you."

"I don't believe it. She's putting you on."

"I told her the truth. That Alexi would never permit you to model." She pulled the cigarette lighter from the dashboard. "But after what's happened . . ." She filled her lungs with smoke. "We have to be able to support ourselves. And we need to get as far away from him as we can, which means New York. This is going to be our ticket out, baby. I just know it."

"I can't be a model! I don't look anything like one." She planted her loafers against the dash and drew her knees to her chest, hoping the pressure would ease the knots in her stomach. "I—I don't understand why we have to go right now. I need to finish school." She clasped her knees tighter. "And . . . Alexi doesn't . . . He doesn't seem to hate me so much anymore."

Belinda's knuckles turned white as she gripped the steering wheel, and Fleur knew she'd said the wrong thing. "I only mean—"

"He's a snake. You've been begging me for years to leave him. Now I've finally done it, and I don't want to hear another word. If those test shots are good, you'll make more than enough to support us."

Fleur had always intended to support them, but not like this. She wanted to use her math and language skills in business, or maybe be a translator at NATO. Belinda's plan was a fantasy. Fashion models were beautiful women, not clumsy, too-tall sixteen-year-olds.

She rested her chin on her knees. Why did they have to leave now? Why did they have to leave just when her father had started to like her?

⁂

Bunny Duverge lectured Fleur on makeup, on how to walk, on who was who in New York fashion, as if Fleur cared about any of it. She clucked over Fleur's ragged fingernails, her lack of interest in clothes, and her habit of bumping into furniture.

"I can't help it," Fleur said at the end of her first miserable week at the Duverge Fontainebleau estate. "I'm a lot more graceful on a horse."

Bunny rolled her eyes and complained to Belinda about Fleur's American accent. "A French accent is so much more appealing."

But despite all that, Bunny swore to Belinda that Fleur had *it*. When Fleur asked what *it* was, Bunny waved her hands and said *it* was elusive. "One simply knows."

For all her faults, Bunny knew how to keep a secret, and she was as determined as Belinda to prevent Alexi from finding them. Instead of choosing a Parisian coiffeur, Bunny flew in a famous London hairdresser who began snipping at Fleur's hair, a quarter of an inch here, a half inch there. When he was done, Fleur thought her hair looked pretty much the same, but Bunny had tears in her eyes and called him "maestro."

One good thing happened. Belinda stopped drinking. Fleur was glad, even though it made her mother a lot jumpier. "If Alexi finds out about Casimir, he'll put a stop to it. You don't know him like I do, baby. We have to be established in New York before he finds us. If this goes wrong, he'll come up with a way to separate us forever."

Knowing Belinda was resting all her hopes on this made Fleur sick at her stomach. She tried to pay attention to everything Bunny told her. She practiced her walk. Though the halls. Up and down the stairs. Across the lawn. Sometimes Bunny made her walk with her hips leading. Other times with what Bunny called a "New York street stride." Fleur worked on makeup and posture. She struck poses and practiced different facial expressions.

Finally Bunny called in her favorite fashion photographer.

*

Gretchen Casimir's pampered pedicured toes curled in her pumps as she pulled the latest photos Bunny had sent from the envelope. She owed Bunny for this one. God, did she ever. The girl was breathtaking. Hers was the kind of face that appeared once every ten years, like Suzy Parker's, or Jean Shrimpton's, or Twiggy's. She reminded Gretchen of both Shrimpton and the great Verushka. This girl's face would shape the look of a decade.

She stared into the camera, her bold, almost masculine features surrounded by that great mane of streaky blond hair. Every woman in the world would want to look like this. In Gretchen's favorite shot, Fleur stood barefoot, her hair in a single braid like a mountain girl, her big hands hanging slack at her sides. She wore a water-soaked cotton shift. The hem hung heavy and uneven around her knees. Her nipples were erect, and the wet material defined the endless line of hip and leg more clearly than if she'd been nude. *Vogue* would be in raptures.

Gretchen Casimir had built Casimir Models from a one-room office into an organization nearly as prestigious as the powerful Ford agency. But "nearly" wasn't good enough. It was time to make Eileen Ford eat her dust.

Fleur Savagar would make that happen.

Fleur gazed out the window as the taxi jockeyed for position in the Manhattan traffic. It was a cold, crisp early December afternoon. Everything was dirty and beautiful and wonderful. If she wasn't so terrified, New York City would have felt just right to her.

Belinda stubbed out her third cigarette since they'd gotten in the cab. "I can't believe it, baby. I can't believe we got away. Alexi's going to be furious. His daughter, a model. But since we won't need his money, he can't do one thing to stop us. Ouch! Be careful, baby."

"Sorry." Fleur pulled her elbow in. Knowing that

Belinda was pinning their futures on Fleur having a modeling career made her sick at her stomach.

Gretchen was supposed to have rented a modest apartment for them, but the cab pulled up in front of a luxury high-rise with the address cut into the glass above the door. The doorman wheeled their suitcases into an elevator whose last occupant had been wearing Joy.

Fleur's stomach jumped as the elevator shot upward. She couldn't do this. She'd seen the test shots, and they were ugly. Her feet sank into thick celery-green carpeting as they got out. She followed Belinda and the doorman down a short hallway to a paneled door. He unlocked it and set their suitcases inside. Belinda entered the apartment first. As Fleur followed her, she noticed a weird smell. Familiar, but she couldn't identify it. Sort of like—

She looked past Belinda and saw them. They were everywhere. Vase after vase of full-blown white roses. She sucked in her breath. Belinda made a soft, muffled cry. Alexi Savagar stepped out of the shadows.

"Welcome to New York, my darlings."

The Glitter Baby

Chapter 8

"What are you doing here?" Belinda's voice was little more than a whisper.

"*Quelle question.* My wife and daughter strike out for the New World. Should I not at least be here to greet them?" He gave Fleur a disarming smile, inviting her to share the joke.

Fleur started to smile in response, but caught herself as she saw how pale her mother had become. She moved closer to Belinda's side. "I won't go back. And you can't make me."

She sounded like a baby, and he seemed amused. "Whatever makes you think I would want you to? My attorneys have examined the contract Gretchen Casimir has offered you, and it seems quite fair."

All the secrecy Belinda had imposed was for nothing. Fleur breathed in the scent of roses. "You know about Casimir?"

"I do not mean to sound immodest, but little escapes my notice when it comes to the welfare of my only daughter."

Belinda seemed to come out of a trance. "Don't believe him, Fleur! This is a trick."

Alexi sighed. "Please, Belinda, do not inflict your paranoia on our daughter." He made an elegant gesture. "Let me show you the apartment. If you don't like it, I will find you something else."

"You found this apartment for us?" Fleur said.

"A father's gift to his daughter." His smile made her feel soft inside. "It is past time for me to begin to make amends. This is a small token of my best wishes for her future career."

A small, inarticulate sound escaped Belinda's lips. She reached out to pull Fleur to her side, but she was a moment too late. Fleur had already gone off with Alexi.

Alexi took a suite at the Carlyle for the month of December. During the day, Fleur spent countless hours being primped and polished by Gretchen Casimir's team. She met with movement coaches and dance teachers, ran every day in Central Park, and studied with the tutors Alexi hired so she could complete her education.

In the evening, he showed up at the apartment with theater or ballet tickets, sometimes with an invitation to a restaurant where the food was simply too wonderful to miss. He took her on a trip to Connecticut to track down the rumor that a 1939 Bugatti was hidden away on a Fairfield estate. Belinda sat in the backseat and chain-smoked. She never let Fleur go anywhere alone with him. If Fleur laughed at one of his jokes or sampled some tidbit he fed her from his fork, Belinda stared at her with an expression of such deep betrayal that Fleur felt sick. She hadn't forgotten what he'd done to her, but he sounded so sorry about it.

"It was childish jealousy," he told her when Belinda slipped off to the restroom during one of their meals together. "The pathetic insecurity of a middle-aged husband deeply in love with a bride twenty years his junior. I was afraid you would take my place in her affections, so after you were born, I simply made you disappear. The power of money, *chérie*. Do not ever underestimate it."

She had to blink back tears. "But I was just a baby."

"Unconscionable. I knew it at the time. Also ironic, *non*? What I did drove your mother away far more than one small child could ever have done. By the time Michel arrived, it made no difference."

His explanation confused her, but he kissed the palm of her hand. "I don't ask you to forgive me, *chérie*. Some things are not possible. I merely ask that you give me some small place in your life before it is too late for both of us."

"I—I want to forgive you."

"But you can't. Your mother would never allow it. I understand."

In January, Alexi returned to Paris and Fleur had her first shoot—a shampoo print ad. Belinda stayed with her the whole time. Fleur was petrified, but everybody was nice, even when she tripped on a tripod and knocked over the art director's coffee. The photographer played the Rolling Stones, and a really nice stylist made Fleur dance with her. After a while, Fleur forgot about her height, her shovel hands, tugboat feet, and great big face.

Gretchen said the photos were "historic." Fleur was just glad to have the first experience behind her.

She shot another ad two days later, and a third the next week. "I never thought it would happen this fast," she told Alexi during one of their frequent telephone conversations.

"Now the entire world will see how beautiful you are and fall under your spell, just as I have."

Fleur smiled. She missed him, but she wasn't so foolish as to mention that to Belinda. With Alexi back in Paris, Belinda had started to laugh again, and she hadn't taken a single drink.

The buzz began to build. In March, Fleur did her first fashion spread, and Gretchen's press agent started referring to her as the "Face of the Decade." No one except Fleur objected.

Suddenly it seemed everyone wanted her. In April, she got a Revlon contract. In May, she shot a six-page fashion spread for *Glamour. Vogue* sent her to Istanbul to shoot caftans, then to Abu Dhabi for resort wear. She celebrated her seventeenth birthday at a resort in the Bahamas shooting swimwear while Belinda flirted with a former soap opera star vacationing there.

She continued to have various tutors, but it wasn't the same as being in a classroom. She missed her schoolmates. Fortunately Belinda went everywhere with her. They were more than mother and daughter. They were best friends.

Fleur began earning bigger sums of money that needed to be invested, but Belinda didn't understand finance, so Fleur started asking Alexi questions during their phone calls. His answers were so helpful that she and Belinda grew to rely on him and eventually dumped the entire matter into his capable hands.

Fleur's first cover appeared. Belinda bought two dozen copies and propped them all over the apartment. The magazine sold more issues than any in its history, and Fleur's career exploded. She was grateful that her success had come so easily, but it also made her uncomfortable. Every time she looked in a mirror, she wondered what all the fuss was about.

People magazine asked for an interview. "My baby doesn't just shine," Belinda told the reporter. "She glitters." That was all *People* needed.

GLITTER BABY FLEUR SAVAGAR
SIX FEET OF SOLID GOLD

When Fleur saw the cover, she told Belinda she was never *ever* going out in public again.

"Too late." Belinda laughed. "Gretchen's press agent is making sure the nickname sticks."

*

Fleur had been in New York for a year when the first movie offer rolled in. The script was trash, and Gretchen advised Belinda to turn it down. Belinda did, but she was depressed for days afterward. "I've been dreaming about us going to Hollywood, but Gretchen's right. Your first movie has to be special."

Hollywood? It was all happening too quickly. Fleur took a deep breath and tried to hold on.

The *New York Times* did a feature story. "The Glitter Baby Is Big, Beautiful, and Rich."

"I mean it this time." Fleur moaned. "I'm never, never going out again."

Belinda laughed and poured herself a Tab.

★

Belinda gradually got rid of the antiques in their apartment and decorated it in a starkly contemporary style, as different from the house on the Rue de la Bienfaisance as she could make it. Buff suede covered the living room walls. A chrome and glass Mies van der Rohe table sat in front of the pit sofa, which had black and brown graphic pillows. Fleur didn't tell Belinda she liked the antiques better. She especially hated the long living room wall decorated with window-sized enlargements of her own face. Looking at them made her feel creepy. It was as if someone else had taken up residence in her body, and the makeup and clothes formed a thick shell hiding the real person beneath. Except she didn't know who that person was.

Alexi promised he'd come to New York in February. He'd canceled two other trips to the city, but this time he swore nothing would keep him away. As the day approached, she struggled to hide her excitement from Belinda, but just hours before his plane was supposed to land, the phone rang in the apartment.

"*Chérie*," Alexi said, as foreboding curled in her stomach. "I've had an emergency. It's impossible for me to leave Paris now."

"But you promised! It's been more than a year."

"Once again I have failed you. If only . . ." She knew what he was going to say. "If only your mother would let you come to Paris. But we both know she will forbid it, and I won't go against her wishes. *Hélas*, she uses you to hurt me."

Fleur wouldn't betray Belinda by agreeing. As she tried to swallow her disappointment, she heard high heels tapping down the hallway. A moment later, Belinda's bedroom door clicked shut.

Belinda settled on the edge of her bed and closed her eyes. He was canceling on Fleur again, just as he'd done twice before. Fleur would be heartbroken and resentful, not at Alexi but at her. His strategy was brilliant. Make it Belinda's fault that father and daughter couldn't be together.

Fleur had held out against Alexi's charms longer than Belinda had expected, and even now, she maintained at least a trace of reserve with him. Alexi didn't like that, which was why he called her several times a week, why he sent lavish gifts calculated to make her feel his presence, and why he'd stayed away for the past year. Any moment now, Fleur would knock on her bedroom door and beg for permission to fly to Paris to see him. Belinda would refuse. Fleur would be resentful and withdraw into herself. Although she wouldn't say it out loud, she saw her mother as neurotic and jealous. But Belinda had to keep Fleur in New York where she could protect her. If only she could explain why it was so necessary without offering up the truth.

Your father—who, by the way, isn't your father—is seducing you.

Fleur would never believe it.

"Further to the right, sweetheart."

Fleur tipped her head and smiled into the camera.

Her neck hurt, and she had cramps, but Cinderella hadn't whined at the ball just because her glass slippers pinched.

"That's beautiful, honey. Perfect. A little more teeth. Amazing."

She sat on a stool in front of a small table with a mirrored top, which was elevated like an easel to reflect the light. The open neck of her champagne silk blouse revealed a magnificent string of square-cut emeralds. Summer had arrived, and it was a blistering hot New York afternoon. Out of camera range, she wore cutoffs and pink rubber shower thongs.

"Fix her eyebrows," the photographer said.

The makeup man handed her a tiny comb, then dabbed at her nose with a small, clean sponge. She leaned over her reflection and combed her thick brows back into place. She used to regard things like eyebrow combs as weird, but she no longer thought about it.

Out of the corner of her eye, she watched Chris Malino, the photographer's assistant. With his shaggy, sandy hair and open, friendly face, he wasn't nearly as good-looking as the male models she worked with, but she liked him a lot better. He was taking filmmaking classes at NYU, and the last time they'd worked together, he'd talked to her about Russian films. She wished he'd ask her out, but none of the guys she liked ever got up the nerve. Her only dates were with older men, celebrities in their twenties that Belinda and Gretchen wanted her to be seen with at some important event. She was eighteen years old, and she'd never had a real date.

Nancy, the stylist on the shoot, adjusted one of the clothespins on the back of Fleur's blouse so it better fit her smaller breasts. Then she checked the piece of Scotch Tape she'd stuck to Fleur's neck to raise the height of the emerald necklace. Fleur had come to think of the beautiful clothes on magazine pages as false-fronted buildings on a movie set.

"I've got three rolls on the emeralds," the photographer said not long after. "Let's take a break."

Fleur stepped around Nancy's ironing board and changed into her own open-necked gauze shirt. Chris was shifting the backdrop. She poured a cup of coffee and wandered over to Belinda, who was studying a magazine ad.

Her mother had changed so much since they'd come to New York a little over two and a half years ago. The quiet, nervous gestures had disappeared. She was more confident. Prettier, too—tan and healthy from weekends at the Long Island beach house they rented. Today she wore a Gatsby white tank top and matching skirt with mulberry kid sandals and a slim gold ankle bracelet.

"Look at her skin." Belinda tapped her fingernail against the page. "She doesn't have pores. Photos like this make me feel forty breathing hard down my neck."

Fleur gazed more closely at model in the ad for an expensive cosmetics line. "That's Annie Holman. Remember the Bill Blass layout Annie and I did together a couple of months ago?"

Belinda had trouble remembering anyone who wasn't already famous, and she shook her head.

"Mother, Annie Holman is thirteen years old!"

Belinda gave a weak laugh. "It's no wonder every woman in this country over thirty is depressed. We're competing with children."

Fleur hoped women didn't feel that way when they looked at her photographs. She hated the idea that she was earning eight hundred dollars an hour making people feel bad.

Belinda went off to the bathroom. Fleur got up her nerve and approached Chris, who'd just finished hanging the backdrop. "So . . . How's school going?" *Smile, stupid. And don't be so big.*

"Same old stuff."

She could tell he was trying to act casual, as if she were just another girl in one of his classes and not the Glitter Baby. She liked that.

"I'm working on a new film, though," he said.

"Really? Tell me about it." She eased herself into a folding chair. It creaked as she sat.

He started to talk, and before long, he got so caught up in what he was saying that he forgot to be intimidated by her.

"It's so interesting," she said.

He stuck his thumb into the pocket of his jeans, then pulled it back out again. His Adam's apple bobbed a couple of times. "Do you want to . . . I mean, I'll understand if you've got other things going on. I know you have a lot of guys asking you out, and—"

"I don't." She hopped up from the chair. "I know everybody thinks I do—that everybody's asking me out. But it's not true."

He picked up a light meter and toyed with it. "I see your picture in the paper with movie stars and Kennedys and everybody."

"Those aren't real dates. They're . . . sort of for publicity."

"Does that mean you'd like to go out with me? Maybe Saturday night. We could go down to the Village."

Fleur grinned. "I'd love to."

He beamed at her.

"You'd love to what, baby?" Belinda came up behind her.

"I asked Fleur to go to the Village with me on Saturday night, Mrs. Savagar," Chris said, looking nervous again. "There's this restaurant where they have Middle Eastern food."

Fleur curled her toes in her shower thongs. "I said I'd go."

"Did you, baby?" Belinda's forehead puckered. "I'm afraid that won't work. You already have plans, remember? The premiere of the new Altman picture. You're going with Shawn Howell."

Fleur had forgotten about the premiere, and she definitely wanted to forget about Shawn Howell, who was a twenty-two-year-old film star with an IQ that matched his age. On their first date he'd spent the evening complaining that everybody was "out to screw him," and he'd told her he'd dropped out of high school because all the teachers were creeps and faggots. She'd begged Gretchen not to arrange any more dates with him, but Gretchen said Shawn was hot now, and business was business. When she'd tried to talk to her mother about it, Belinda had been incredulous.

"But, baby, Shawn Howell's a star. Being seen with him makes you twice as important." When Fleur complained that he kept trying to put his hand under her skirt, Belinda had pinched her cheek. "Celebrities are different from ordinary people. They don't follow the same rules. I know you can handle him."

"That's okay," Chris said, disappointment written all over his face. "I understand. Some other time."

But Fleur knew there wouldn't be another time. It had taken all of Chris's courage to ask her out once, and he'd never do it again.

*

Fleur tried to talk to Belinda about Chris in the cab on the way home, but Belinda refused to understand. "Chris is a nobody. Why on earth would you want to go out with him?"

"Because I like him. You shouldn't have . . ." Fleur pulled on the fringe of her cutoffs. "I wish you hadn't put him off like that. It made me feel like I was twelve."

"I see." Belinda's voice grew chilly. "You're telling me that I embarrassed you."

Fleur felt a little flutter of panic. "Of course not. No. How could you embarrass me?" Belinda had withdrawn from her, and Fleur touched her arm. "Forget I said anything. It's not important." Except it was important, but she didn't want to hurt Belinda's feelings. When that happened, Fleur always felt as though she was standing in front of the Couvent de l'Annonciation watching her mother's car disappear.

Belinda didn't say anything for a while, and Fleur's misery deepened

"You have to trust me, baby. I know what's best for you." Belinda cupped Fleur's wrist, and Fleur felt as if she'd been about to fall off a precipice, only to be snatched back to safety.

*

That night after Fleur had gone to bed, Belinda stared at her daughter's photographs on the wall. Her determination grew stronger than ever. Somehow she had to protect Fleur from all of them—from Alexi, from nobodies like Chris, from anyone who stood in their way. It would be the hardest things she'd ever done, and on days like today, she wasn't sure how she'd manage.

The blanket of depression began to settle over her. She pushed it away by reaching for the telephone and quickly dialing a number.

A sleepy male voice answered. "Yeah."

"It's me. Did I wake you?"

"Yeah. What do you want?"

"I'd like to see you tonight."

He yawned. "When you coming?"

"I'll be there in twenty minutes."

As she began to pull the phone away from her ear, she heard his voice on the other end. "Hey, Belinda? How 'bout you leave your panties at home."

"Shawn Howell, you're a devil." She hung up the phone, grabbed her purse, and left the apartment.

Chapter 9

Hollywood wanted Jake Koranda smart-ass and mean. They wanted him staring at a piece of street scum over the barrel of a .44 Magnum. They wanted him using pearl-handled Colts on a band of desperados and then kissing a busty broad good-bye before he walked out the saloon doors. Koranda might only be twenty-eight years old, but he was a real man, not one of those pansies who carried a hair dryer in his hip pocket.

Jake had hit it big right from the start playing a drifter named Bird Dog Caliber in a low-budget Western that grossed six times what it had cost to make. Despite his youth, he had the rough, outlaw image that men liked as much as women, the same as Eastwood did. Two more Caliber pictures immediately followed the first, each one bloodier. After that, he made a couple of modern action-adventure movies. His career rise was meteoric. Then Koranda got stubborn. He said he needed more time to *write his plays.*

What was Hollywood supposed to do about that? The best action actor to come along since Eastwood, and he wrote shit that ended up in college anthologies instead of staying in front of a camera where he belonged. The fuckin' Pulitzer Prize had ruined him.

And it got worse . . . Koranda decided he wanted to try writing for film instead of the theater. He called his screenplay *Sunday Morning Eclipse*, and there wasn't a single car chase in the whole damned thing. "That highbrow shit is okay for the stage, kid," the Hollywood brass told him when he started shopping it around, "but the American public wants tits and guns on screen."

Koranda eventually ended up with Dick Spano, a small-time producer who agreed to do *Sunday Morning Eclipse* on two conditions: Jake had to take the leading role, and he had to give Spano a big-budget cops-and-robbers afterward.

On a Tuesday night in early March, three men sat in a smoke-filled projection room. "Run Savagar's screen test again," Dick Spano called out around one of the fat Cuban cigars he loved to smoke.

Johnny Guy Kelly, the film's legendary silver-haired director, popped the lid on a can of Orange Crush and spoke over his shoulder to the lone figure sitting in the shadows at the back. "Jako, boy, we don't want you unhappy, but I think you left those genius brains of yours in bed with your latest lady friend."

Jake Koranda pulled his long legs from the back of the seat in front of him. "Savagar's wrong for Lizzie. I can feel it in my gut."

"You take a long, hard look at Cupcake up there and tell me you don't feel something someplace other than in your gut." Johnny Guy pointed his Orange Crush toward the screen. "The camera loves her, Jako. And she's also been taking acting lessons, so she's real serious about this."

Koranda slouched deeper into his seat. "She's a model. One more ditzy glamour girl who wants a movie career. I went through this with what's-her-name last year, and I swore I'd never do it again. Especially not on this picture. Did you check Amy Irving again?"

"Irving is tied up," Spano said, "and even if she wasn't, I gotta tell you I'd go with Savagar right now. She's hot. You can't pick up a magazine without seeing her face on the cover. Everybody's been waiting to see what she chooses for her first film. It's built-in publicity."

"Screw the publicity," Koranda said.

Dick Spano and Johnny Guy Kelly exchanged glances. They liked Jake, but he had strong opinions, and he could be a stubborn son of a bitch when he believed in something. "It's not that easy," Johnny Guy said. "She's got some smart people behind her. They'd been waiting a long time to find exactly the right picture."

"Bullshit," Jake retorted. "All they want is a leading man tall enough to play with their little girl. It doesn't go any deeper than that."

"I think you're underestimating them."

Cold silence drifted their way from the back of the room.

"Sorry, Jake," Spano finally said, not without some trepidation, "but we're going to overrule you on this one. We're making her an offer tomorrow."

Behind them, Koranda uncoiled from his seat. "Do what you have to, but don't expect me to roll out the welcome mat."

Johnny Guy shook his head as Jake disappeared, then once again looked at the screen. "Let's hope Cupcake up there knows how to take some heat."

Belinda had dragged Fleur to all of Jake Koranda's pictures, and Fleur had hated every one of them. He was always shooting someone in the head, knifing him in the belly, or terrorizing a woman. And he seemed to enjoy it! Now she had to work with him, and she knew from her agent exactly how dead set he'd been against casting her. Part of her couldn't exactly blame him. No matter what Belinda believed, Fleur was no actress.

"Stop worrying," Belinda said, whenever Fleur tried to

talk to her about it. "The minute he sees you, he'll fall in love."

Fleur couldn't imagine that happening.

The white stretch limousine the studio had sent to pick her up at LAX delivered her to the two-story Spanish-style Beverly Hills house Belinda had rented for them. It was early May, unseasonably cold when she'd left New York, but warm and sunny in Southern California. When she'd come over from France three years ago, she'd never imagined her life taking such a strange direction. She tried to be grateful, but lately that had been hard.

A housekeeper who looked like she was at least a hundred years old let her into a foyer with white walls, dark beams, a wrought-iron chandelier, and a terra-cotta floor. Fleur took the suitcases away from her when she started to carry them upstairs. She chose a back bedroom that looked down over the pool and left the master bedroom for Belinda. The house seemed even larger than the photos. With six bedrooms, four decks, and a couple of Jacuzzis, it had more space than two people needed, something she'd made the mistake of mentioning to Alexi during one of their phone conversations that substituted for visits.

"In Southern California, lack of ostentation is vulgar," he'd said. "Follow your mother's lead, and you will be a wonderful success."

She'd let the dig pass. The problems between Alexi and Belinda were too complicated for her to solve, especially since she'd never been able to understand why two people who hated each other so much didn't get a divorce. She kicked off her shoes and gazed around the room with its warm wooden pieces and earth-toned fabrics. A collection of Mexican crosses hanging on the wall gave her a pang of homesickness for the nuns. Never once had she imagined making this particular trip alone.

She sat on the side of the bed and called New York. "Are you feeling any better?" she asked when Belinda answered.

"I'm miserable. And humiliated. How can a woman my age get chicken pox?" Belinda blew her nose. "My baby is going to star in the most talked-about film of the year, and here I am stuck in New York with this ridiculous disease. If I get scars . . ."

"You'll be fine in a week or so."

"I'm not coming out there until I look my best. I want them to see what they passed up all those years ago." Another nose blow. "Call me the moment you meet him. Don't worry about the time difference."

Fleur didn't have to ask whom Belinda was talking about. She braced herself, and—sure enough. . .

"My baby's going to be doing love scenes with Jake Koranda."

"If you say that one more time, I'm going to throw up."

Belinda managed a laugh through her misery. "Lucky, lucky, baby."

"I'm hanging up now."

But Belinda had beaten her to it.

Fleur walked over to the window and gazed down at the pool. She'd started to hate modeling, another thing Belinda would never understand. And she definitely didn't want to be an actress. But since she had no idea what she wanted to do instead, she could hardly complain. She had gobs of money, a fabulous career, and a great part in a prestigious film. She was the luckiest girl in the world, and she was going to stop acting like a spoiled brat. So what if she never felt completely comfortable in front of the camera? She did a darned good job of faking it, and that's exactly what she'd do with this movie. She'd fake it.

She changed into shorts, twisted her hair on top of her head, and carried the script of *Sunday Morning Eclipse* out to the patio. She settled into one of the cushioned chaises along with a glass of fresh orange juice and gazed down at the script.

Jake Koranda was playing Matt, the lead, a soldier returning home to Iowa from Vietnam. Matt is tortured by memories of a My Lai–type massacre he witnessed. When he gets home, he finds his wife pregnant with another man's child and his brother caught up in a local scandal. Matt is drawn to Lizzie, his wife's kid sister, who's grown up in his absence. Fleur was playing Lizzie. She thumbed to the script notes.

Untouched by the smell of napalm and the corruption in Matt's own family, Lizzie makes Matt feel innocent again.

The two of them get into a playful argument over the best place to find a great hamburger, and after a traumatic scene with his wife, Matt takes Lizzie on a week-long odyssey through Iowa in search of an old-fashioned root beer stand. The root beer stand served as both a tragic and comic symbol of the country's lost innocence. At the end of the journey, Matt discovers that Lizzie is neither as guileless nor as virginal as she acts.

Despite the movie's cynical view of women, Fleur liked the script a lot better than the Bird Dog Caliber pictures. But even after two months of acting lessons, she didn't see how she'd ever play a character as complex as Lizzie. She wished she was doing some kind of romantic comedy.

At least she wouldn't have to do the movie's nude love scene. This was the only battle with Belinda that she'd won. Her mother said Fleur was being a prude and that her attitude was hypocritical after all the swimsuit ads she'd done, but swimsuits were swimsuits, and naked was naked. Fleur wouldn't budge.

She'd always refused to pose nude, even for the world's most respected photographers. Belinda said it was because she was still a virgin, but that wasn't it. Fleur had to keep some part of herself private.

The housekeeper interrupted and told her she needed to look outside. Fleur went to the front door. In the center of the driveway sat a shiny new red Porsche topped with a giant silver bow.

She raced to the phone and caught Alexi just as he was getting ready for bed. "It's beautiful," she cried. "I'm going to be scared to death to drive it."

"Nonsense. It is you who control the car, *chérie*, not the other way around."

"I've got the wrong number. I want to speak with the man who's invested a fortune trying to find the Bugatti Royale that spent the war in the sewers of Paris."

"That, my dear, is different."

Fleur smiled. They chatted for a few minutes, then she rushed outside to drive her new car. She wished she could thank Alexi in person, but he'd never come back to see her.

Some of her pleasure in the gift faded. She'd become a pawn in the battle between her parents, and she hated that. But as important as her new relationship was with her father, and as much as she appreciated this beautiful car, her first loyalty would always be with Belinda.

The next morning, she drove the Porsche through the studio gates to the soundstage where *Sunday Morning Eclipse* was shooting. Fleur Savagar was too scared to show up on the set herself, so she'd sent the Glitter Baby instead. As she'd gotten dressed, she'd taken extra care with her makeup and pulled her hair away from her face with a set of enameled combs so that it fell long and straight down her back. Her peony-colored Sonia Rykiel body sweater complemented a pair of strappy lizard sandals with three-inch heels. Jake Koranda was tall, but those heels should just about even them out.

She found the parking lot the guard had directed her to. The toast she'd eaten for breakfast clumped in her stomach. Although filming on *Sunday Morning Eclipse* had been under way for several weeks, she didn't have to report for another few days, but she'd decided that checking things out before she had to go in front of the camera would build her confidence. So far, it wasn't working.

This was silly. She'd made television commercials, so she understood the process. She knew how to hit her marks and take direction. But her anxiety refused to ease. Belinda should have been the movie star. Not her.

The guard had phoned ahead, and Dick Spano, the producer, met her inside the soundstage door. "Fleur, sweetheart! It's good to see you." He welcomed her with a cheek kiss and an admiring look at the leggy expanse that the body sweater put on display. Fleur had liked Spano when they'd met in New York, especially when she'd found out how much he loved horses. He led her toward a pair of heavy doors. "They're getting ready to shoot. I'll take you in."

Fleur recognized the brightly lit set on the soundstage as the kitchen of Matt's house in Iowa. Standing in the middle of it, she saw Johnny Guy Kelly deep in conversation with Lynn David, the tiny, auburn-haired actress who was playing Matt's wife, DeeDee. Dick Spano gestured Fleur toward a canvas director's chair. She resisted the urge to peek at the back and see if her name was stenciled there.

"You ready, Jako?"

Jake Koranda stepped out of the shadows.

The first thing Fleur noticed was his impossible mouth, soft and sulky as a baby's. But that was the only thing babylike about him. His walk was loose-jointed with a rolling, slouch-shouldered gait that made him look more like a range-weary cowboy than a playwright–movie star. His straight brown hair had been cut shorter than he wore it in the Caliber pictures, making him look both taller and thinner than his screen image. Offscreen, she decided, he didn't look any friendlier than he did onscreen.

Thanks to Belinda, Fleur knew more about him than she wanted to. Although he was notoriously reticent with the press and seldom gave interviews, certain facts had emerged. He'd been born John Joseph Koranda and raised in the worst part of Cleveland, Ohio, by a mother who cleaned houses during the day and offices at night. He had a juvenile police record. Petty theft, shoplifting, hot-wiring a car when he was thirteen. When reporters tried to get him to open up about how he'd turned his life around, he referred to a college athletic scholarship. "Just a punk who got lucky with a basketball," he said. He refused to talk about why he'd left college during his sophomore year, his short-lived marriage, or his military service in Vietnam. He said his life was his own.

Johnny Guy called out for quiet, and the set grew still. Lynn David stood with her head down, not looking at Jake, who was all sulky mouth and hard blue eyes. Johnny Guy called for action.

Jake leaned a shoulder against the doorframe. "You can't help being a tramp, can you?"

Fleur clutched her hands in her lap. They were filming one of the uglier scenes in the movie, where Jake's character, Matt, had just found out about DeeDee's infidelity. In the editing room, the scene would be interspersed with quick cuts of the village massacre Matt had witnessed in Vietnam, shadow images that make him lose control until he lashes out at DeeDee in a macabre duplication of the violence he'd witnessed.

Matt began walking across the kitchen floor, every muscle in his body taut with menace. In a small, helpless gesture, DeeDee closed her fingers around a necklace he'd given her. She was so tiny next to him, a fragile little Kewpie doll about to be broken. "It wasn't like that, Matt. It wasn't."

Without warning, his hand shot out and ripped off her necklace. She screamed and tried to get away from him, but he was too fast. He shook her, and she started to cry. Fleur's mouth went dry. She hated this scene. Hated everything about it.

"Cut!" Johnny Guy called out. "We've got a shadow by the window."

Jake's angry voice ripped through the set. "I thought we were going to try to do this in one take!"

Fleur couldn't have picked a worse day to show up. She wasn't ready to do a movie. She especially wasn't ready to do a movie with Jake Koranda. Why couldn't it have been with Robert Redford or Burt Reynolds? Somebody nice. At least she didn't have any scenes where Jake beat her up. But that wasn't any consolation when she thought about the scenes she did have with him.

Johnny Guy called for quiet. Someone from wardrobe replaced Lynn's necklace. Fleur's palms started to sweat.

"You can't help being a tramp, can you?" Matt said in the same ugly voice. He bore down on DeeDee and yanked off the necklace. DeeDee screamed and struggled with him. He shook her harder, his expression so vicious that Fleur had to remind herself he was acting. God, she hoped he was acting.

He pushed DeeDee against the wall, and then he slapped her. Fleur couldn't watch any more. She closed her eyes and wished she was anywhere but here.

"Cut!"

Lynn David's crying didn't stop with the end of the scene. Jake pulled Lynn into his arms and tucked her head under his chin.

Johnny Guy ambled forward. "You okay, Lynnie?"

Jake rounded on him. "Leave us alone!"

Johnny Guy nodded and moved away. A moment later he spotted Fleur. She stood half a head taller, but that didn't stop him from enveloping her in a bear hug. "Aren't you just what the doctor ordered? Pretty as a Texas sunset after a spring rain."

Johnny Guy was one of the best directors in the business, despite his good ol' boy manner. When they'd met in New York, he'd been sensitive to her inexperience and promised he'd do everything he could to make her comfortable. "Come on over here with me. I want you to meet everybody."

He began introducing her to the crew, telling her something personal about each one. The names and faces flew past her too quickly to remember, but she smiled at everyone. "Where's that pretty mother of yours?" he asked. "I thought she'd come with you today."

"She had some business to take care of." Fleur didn't mention the business involved cotton swabs and calamine lotion. "She'll be here in a week or so."

"I remember her from the fifties," he said. "I was working as a grip then. I saw her once at the Garden of Allah when she was with Errol Flynn."

Fleur tripped over a cable she hadn't noticed. Johnny Guy caught her arm. Belinda had chronicled every movie star she had ever met, but she'd never mentioned Errol Flynn. He must be mistaken.

Johnny Guy suddenly looked uncomfortable. "Come on, darlin'. Let me take you over to meet Jake."

Exactly what she most didn't want to do, but Johnny Guy was already steering her toward him. Her discomfort increased at the sight of a teary Lynn David still tucked against Jake's side. Fleur whispered to Johnny Guy. "Why don't we wait—"

"Jako, Lynnie. I've got somebody here I want you to meet." He propelled her forward and introduced her.

Lynn managed a weak smile of acknowledgment. Jake looked at her with Bird Dog Caliber's eyes and gave her a brusque nod. Fleur's three-inch lizard strap sandals let her eye him dead on, and somehow she managed not to flinch.

An awkward silence followed, broken finally by a stubble-faced young man. "We have to do it again, Johnny Guy," he said. "We picked up some noise."

Koranda pushed past Fleur and stalked toward the center of the set. "What the hell is wrong with all of you?" The set grew instantly quiet. "Get your act together. How many times do we have to go through this for you?"

A long silence followed. Finally an anonymous voice filled the tense stillness. "Sorry, Jake. It couldn't be helped."

"The hell it couldn't!" Fleur waited for him to pull out the pearl-handled Colts. "Get your shit together! We're only doing it once more."

"Easy, boy," Johnny Guy said. "Last time I checked, I was the director around here."

"Then do your job," Koranda shot back.

Johnny Guy scratched his head. "I'm gonna pretend I didn't hear that, Jako, and chalk this up to a full moon. Let's get back to work."

Temper tantrums weren't new to Fleur—she'd seen some doozies in the last few years—but this one made the butterflies in her stomach do nosedives. She looked down at her fat runner's watch and yawned. It was a technique she'd developed when she got uncomfortable—looking at her watch and yawning. It made people think they couldn't get to her, even when they could.

She imagined what Belinda would say if she'd seen her idol's obnoxious behavior. *Celebrities are different from ordinary people, baby. They don't have to follow the same rules.*

Not in Fleur's book. Rude was rude no matter how famous you were.

The scene began again. Fleur stole back into the shadows where she didn't have to watch, but she couldn't block out the sounds of violence. It seemed like forever before it was over.

A woman Johnny Guy had introduced earlier as a production assistant appeared at Fleur's side and asked if she'd go to wardrobe. Fleur could have kissed her. By the time she returned, the crew was taking a lunch break. Lynn and Jake sat eating sandwiches off to the side by themselves, and Lynn immediately spotted her. "Come over and join us."

All Fleur wanted to do was get away, but she couldn't think of a polite way to refuse. The heels of her lizard strap sandals tapped on the concrete floor as she made her way across the set. They'd changed into jeans, which made her feel like an overdressed outsider. She picked up her chin and pulled back her shoulders.

"Have a seat." Lynn gestured toward a folding chair. "Sorry we didn't get a chance to talk earlier."

"That's okay. You were busy."

Jake stood and balled his sandwich in the wrapper. Fleur was used to looking down at men, not looking up, and he was so intimidating she had to force herself not to step back. She stared at that impossible mouth and saw his famous front tooth with the tiny chip at the corner. He gave her another short nod, then turned to Lynn. "I'm going out to shoot some baskets. I'll see you later."

As he disappeared, Lynn held out half her sandwich. "Eat this so I don't gain any more weight. It's salmon with low-cal mayonnaise."

Fleur took the friendship offering and sat down. Lynn was in her mid-twenties and delicate, with tiny hands and wispy auburn hair. A thousand magazine covers wouldn't change the way being around such a petite woman made Fleur feel like the Jolly Green Giant.

Lynn was returning the inspection. "You don't look like you have to worry about your weight."

Fleur swallowed a bite of sandwich. "I do. Working in front of a camera, I can't go above one thirty-five. That's hard with my height, especially for somebody who loves bread and ice cream."

"Good, then we can be friends." Lynn's smile showed a row of small, straight teeth. "I hate women who can eat anything."

"Me, too." Fleur smiled, and they talked for a while about the injustices of being female. Eventually the subject shifted to *Sunday Morning Eclipse*.

"Playing DeeDee is the break I've been waiting for after the soaps." Lynn picked a flake of salmon from her jeans. "Critics say Jake's women aren't as well-written as his men, but I think DeeDee's an exception. She's foolish, but she's vulnerable. Everybody has a little DeeDee in them."

"It's a really great part," Fleur said. "More straightforward than Lizzie. I'm . . . nervous about playing her. I guess . . . I'm not too sure of myself." She flushed. This was hardly the way to inspire confidence in a coworker.

But Lynn nodded. "Once you get into the part, you'll be more confident. Talk to Jake about Lizzie. He's good about that kind of thing."

Fleur picked at a loop of yarn on her sweater. "I don't think Jake's going to be too interested in talking to me about anything. It's no secret he didn't want me in the picture."

Lynn gave her a sympathetic smile. "When he sees you're committed, he'll come around. Give him time."

"And space," Fleur said. "The more the better."

Lynn settled back into the chair. "Jake's the last of the good guys, Fleur."

She retrenched. "I'm sure you're right."

"No. I mean it."

"Well . . . You know him a lot better than I do."

"You're thinking about what you saw today."

"He was . . . sort of rough on the crew."

Lynn picked up her purse and began rummaging through it. "Jake and I were an item a couple of years ago. Nothing serious, but we got to know each other pretty well, and once we stopped sleeping together, we became good friends." She pulled out a pack of breath mints. "I confided in him a lot, and Jake drew on something that happened to me when he wrote that scene. He knew it would bring back bad memories, and he wanted to get it over with for my sake."

Fleur pulled her legs tighter again the chair. "I'm not . . . too comfortable with men like him."

The corner of Lynn's mouth curled. "That's what makes men like him irresistible."

It wasn't the word Fleur would have picked, but she'd already said more than she should.

★

For the next few days, Fleur kept out of Jake Koranda's way. At the same time, she found herself watching him. He and Johnny Guy sparred constantly, frequently going out of their way to disagree. Their arguments made her uncomfortable until she saw how much they enjoyed their spats. Considering his outburst that first day, she was surprised to see how popular Jake was with the crew. In fact, he seemed easy with everybody except her. Other than a brief nod in the morning, he acted as though she didn't exist.

Fortunately her first scene was with Lynn. On Thursday night before the shoot, she studied her lines until she was letter-perfect and got ready to go to bed early so she'd be fresh for her seven o'clock makeup call. But just before she turned off the light, the phone rang. She expected to hear Belinda's voice, but it was Barry, the assistant director.

"Fleur, we had to change the schedule for tomorrow. We're shooting the opening scene with Matt and Lizzie."

Her stomach dropped. She couldn't stand the idea of working with Jake, not on her first day.

After that, sleep was impossible. She kept turning the light on to review her lines, and she didn't drift off until it was nearly dawn, only to be awakened by her alarm an hour later. Her makeup artist grumbled about the dark circles under her eyes. Fleur apologized and said it wouldn't happen again. She was a ball of nerves by the time Johnny Guy appeared in the makeup trailer to discuss the opening scene.

"We're working on the back lot today. You'll be sitting in the swing on the farmhouse porch."

Fleur had seen the exterior of the Iowa farmhouse they'd built, and she was glad they'd be working outside today. "You look up and see Matt standing by the road. You call out his name, jump out of the swing, and run across the yard to get to him. Throw yourself right at him. An easy scene."

And Fleur was going to blow it. A few months of acting classes didn't make her an actress. She'd seen what a perfectionist Jake was. He already hated her. Just wait till he saw how incompetent she was.

Her spirits dipped lower when she got into costume. The movie was set in August, and she was wearing a skimpy white bikini embossed with little red hearts and cut high at the thigh to make her legs look even longer. A man's blue work shirt tied in a knot at the waist left her stomach bare, and they'd arranged her hair in a loose braid down her back. The stylist had wanted to tie a red bow on the end to emphasize Lizzie's false innocence, but Fleur told him to forget it. She didn't wear bows in her hair, and neither would Lizzie.

Just as she made her fourth trip to the bathroom, the assistant director called for her. Fleur took her place on the porch swing and reviewed what she had to do. Lizzie was expecting to see Matt, but she couldn't show it. Lizzie couldn't show a lot of things—how much she resented her sister, how much she lusted after her sister's husband. Jake stood near one of the trailers. He wore the soldier's uniform that was his costume at the beginning of the film. How could she lust after him when she didn't even like him? She yawned and looked at her watch only to realize she wasn't wearing one.

He stuffed one hand in his pocket. As he leaned against the trailer, he planted the sole of his shoe against the tire in a sexy, slouchy kind of posture that reminded her of his publicity photographs. All he needed was a squint and a cigarette to make Bird Dog come to life.

"Showtime, boys and girls," Johnny Guy called out. "You ready, Fleur honey? Let's walk it through."

She followed his directions, carefully noting the path he wanted her to run. Finally she returned to the swing and waited nervously while the crew made the final adjustments. Excitement . . . she had to think excitement. But not too soon. *Don't anticipate. Wait until you see him before you let it show on your face. Don't think about anything but Matt. Matt, not Jake.*

Johnny Guy called for action. She lifted her head. Spotted Matt. *Matt!* He was back! Jumping up, she ran across the porch. She took the wooden steps in one leap. Her braid slapped the back of her neck. She had to get to him. Touch him. He was hers, not DeeDee's. She ran across the yard. There he was, just ahead of her. "Matt!" She called out his name again and catapulted into his arms.

He stumbled backward, and they both crashed to the ground.

There was an explosion of laughter from the crew. Fleur lay sprawled on top of Jake Koranda, pinning him down with her half-naked body. She wanted to crawl into a corner and die. She was an elephant. A big, clumsy giant of an elephant, and this was the most humiliating moment of her life.

"Anybody hurt here?" Johnny Guy chuckled as he came over and helped her up.

"No, I—I'm all right." She kept her head down and concentrated on brushing the dirt from her legs. One of the makeup people ran over with a wet cloth, and she wiped herself off without looking up at Jake. If he needed any more proof that she wasn't right for the part, she'd just given it to him. She wanted to go back to New York. And she wanted her mother!

"How 'bout you, Jako?"

"I'm okay."

Johnny Guy patted her arm. "That was real nice, honey." He grinned. "Too bad this boy's so puny he can't stand up to a real woman."

Johnny Guy was trying to make her feel better, but he was making it worse. She felt big and clumsy and ugly. Everybody was staring at her. If only she could shrink-wrap herself. "I—I'm sorry," she said stiffly. "I think I've ruined this suit. The dirt doesn't want to come out."

"That's why we have spares. Go on and get changed."

In too short a time, she was back in the porch swing, and they were ready to go again. As the cameras rolled, she tried to recreate the feeling of excitement she'd experienced during the first take. She saw Matt, jumped up, ran down the steps and across the yard. *Please God, don't let me knock him over again.* She checked herself ever so slightly and slid into his arms.

Johnny Guy hated it.

They did it again, and she stumbled going down the steps. The fourth time the porch swing bumped against the backs of her legs. The fifth time she made it all the way to Jake, but again she checked herself at the last moment. Her misery was growing by the minute.

"You're not relating to him, honey," Johnny Guy said as Jake released her. "You're not connecting. Don't worry so much about where you're putting your feet. Do it the way you did it the first time."

"I'll try." She had to endure more humiliation as wardrobe noticed she'd sweated through the work shirt and had to bring her a new one without half-moons under the arms. As she headed back for the porch swing, she knew no power on earth could make her throw her body full force at Jake Koranda again. Her chest tightened, and she swallowed hard.

"Hey, wait up."

Slowly she turned and watched Jake walk up to her. "I was off balance the first time," he said curtly. "It was my fault, not yours. I'll catch you the next time."

Sure he would. She nodded and started to walk away.

"You don't believe me, do you?"

She turned back to him. "I'm not exactly a lightweight."

His mouth curved in a cocky grin that looked strange on Bird Dog Caliber's face. "Hey, Johnny Guy!" he called over his shoulder. "Give us a few minutes, will you? Flower Power here thinks she's got me beat."

"Flower Power!"

He grabbed her arm and propelled her none-too-gently around the side of the house away from the crew. When they were ankle-deep in weeds, he let her go. "I've got ten bucks says you can't knock me over again."

She shoved a hand on her bare hip and tried to look like she wasn't nineteen and scared to death. "I'm not getting into a wrestling match with you."

"Glitter Baby worried about messing up her hair? Or are you afraid you'll knock me down again and win the bet?"

"I know I'll win the bet," she shot back.

"We'll have to see about that. Ten bucks, Flower. Put up or shut up."

He was baiting her on purpose, but she didn't care. All she wanted to do was wipe that stupid smirk off his stupid mouth. "Make it twenty."

"I'm scared, Flower. Real scared." He moved back and braced himself. A lot of good it would do him.

She glared at him. "I hope you have a good doctor."

"So far all you've got is talk."

"Don't you think this is just a little juvenile?"

"Glitter Baby's chickening out. She's afraid she's going to hurt herself."

"That's it!" She dug her feet into the sandy ground, pumped her arms, and charged him.

It was like hitting a wall.

The impact would have sent her to the ground if he hadn't caught her. Instead he held her tightly against him. A few seconds ticked by as she tried to catch her breath, then she jerked away. Her chin hurt where she'd bumped it against his shoulder, and her shoulder throbbed. "This is stupid." She started to stomp away.

"Hey, Flower." He ambled forward with his worn-out cowboy gait and reined in next to her. "Is that really the best you can do? Or are you afraid of getting that skimpy white bikini dirty again?"

She looked at him incredulously. Her ribs ached, her

chin was killing her, and she couldn't seem to catch her breath. "You're crazy."

"Double or nothing. And this time get farther back."

She rubbed her shoulder. "I think I'll pass."

He laughed. It was almost a nice sound. "Okay, I'll let you off. But you owe me twenty bucks."

He looked so smug that she actually opened her mouth to take him up on his challenge. Fortunately her common sense kicked in. Whether she wanted to admit it or not, he'd done a nice thing for her. They began walking back around the house together. "You think you're pretty smart, don't you," she said.

"Hey, I'm a boy genius. Read the critics. Any of them. They'll tell you."

She looked up at him and curled her mouth in a fake-sweet smile. "Glamour girls don't know how to read. We just look at the pictures."

He laughed and walked away.

★

They did the scene in the next take, and Johnny Guy said it was exactly what he wanted, but Fleur's brief moment of satisfaction disappeared as he rehearsed them for the following scene. While Lizzie was still in Matt's arms, she was supposed to give him a sisterly kiss. They exchanged a few lines of dialogue, then Lizzie kissed him again, but this time it wasn't supposed to be sisterly. Matt would pull away confused while the camera showed him trying to take in the changes since he had last seen her.

Jake continued joking around with her, refusing to go to work until she'd handed over twenty bucks. He made her laugh, and she handled the sisterly kiss without a problem. But her dialogue delivery was stiff and required too many takes. Still, Lizzie couldn't have been all that comfortable, either, and it wasn't a complete disaster. When they broke for lunch, Jake pulled on her braid as if she were ten years old and told her not to beat up anybody while he was gone.

After lunch, they shot some close-ups, and by the time they were done, she'd perspired through her third shirt. The wardrobe people started sewing in dress shields.

The second kiss was up next, and she knew she was going to have trouble. She'd kissed men on camera and a few of them off camera, too, but she didn't want to kiss Jake Koranda, not because he was being a hard-ass—he was going out of his way to be friendly—but because something weird had started happening to her when she got too close to him.

The assistant director called for her. Jake was already in place talking to Johnny Guy. While Johnny Guy explained the shot, she stared at Jake's mouth, that soft, sulky, baby's pout. He caught her at it and looked at her funny. She yawned and gazed at her bare wrist.

"Does the Glitter Baby have a hot date waiting?" he asked.

"Always," she said.

Johnny Guy turned to her. "What we need here, honey lamb, is a real open-mouth tonsil bouncer. Lizzie's got to wake Matt up."

She gave him a grin and a thumbs-up. "Gotcha." The butterflies in her stomach started a war dance. She wasn't the greatest kisser in the world. But how could she be when she hardly ever got to go out with someone she actually liked?

Jake put his arms around her. She felt his hands flatten against the bare skin just above her bikini bottom and realized she'd spent most of the day crawling over his body in one way or another.

"Your feet, honey," Johnny Guy said.

She looked down. They were as big as ever.

"A little closer, baby lamb."

That's when she saw what she'd done. Although her chest was pressed against Jake's, she'd pulled her bottom half as far away as she could. She quickly adjusted herself.

With his shoes and her bare feet, he was about four inches taller. That was weird, and she didn't like it.

This is Matt, she told herself, as Johnny Guy moved behind the cameras. *You've been with other men, but Matt is the one you want.*

Johnny Guy called for action and she ran her fingers over the front of Matt's uniform. Closing her eyes, she touched her lips to his soft, warm ones. She held them there, trying to think about Matt and Lizzie.

Johnny Guy was less than impressed. "You didn't put too much into that one, honey. Let's try it again."

During the next take, she moved her hands up and down the sleeves of Matt's uniform. Jake yawned when the scene was over and looked at his watch. Something told her it wasn't because he was nervous.

Johnny Guy took her aside. "Forget about the people watching you. All they're thinking about is getting home for dinner. Relax. Lean into him a little more."

She talked to herself all the way back to her mark. This was nothing more than a technical piece of business, just like opening a door. She had to relax. Relax, damn it!

She thought the next kiss was better, but apparently she was the only one. "Do you think you could open your mouth a little, honey lamb?" Johnny Guy said.

Muttering to herself, she stepped back into Jake's arms and then glanced up to see if he'd overheard her. "Sorry, kiddo, but I can't help you out," he said. "I'm the passive party here."

"I don't need help."

"My mistake."

"Like I'd need help."

"Whatever you say."

Johnny Guy called for action. She did her best, but when the kiss was over, Jake rubbed the back of his neck. "You're putting me to sleep, Flower Power. Want me to ask Johnny Guy for a break so we can go behind the house and practice?"

"I'm a little nervous, that's all. It's my first day. And I'm not doing another practice session with you without a helmet and knee pads."

He grinned and then, unexpectedly, leaned down to whisper in her ear. "I got a twenty-dollar bill says you can't wake me up, Flower."

It was the sexiest, most devastating, bedroomiest whisper she'd ever heard.

The next take was better, and Johnny Guy said to print it, but Jake told her she owed him another twenty bucks.

Chapter 10

* * * * * * * * *Belinda was waiting* on the patio when Fleur got home from the studio. She hadn't seen her in almost two weeks. Belinda looked fresh and pretty in a sleeveless red and yellow batik print top and belted linen slacks. Fleur gave her a bear hug, then inspected her face. "No pox marks."

"Do I look good enough to make them wish they'd noticed me when I was eighteen?"

"You're going to break their hearts."

Belinda shuddered. "Chicken pox was a horrible experience. I don't recommend it." She kissed Fleur again. "I missed you so much, baby."

"Me, too."

They ate by the pool on pottery plates generously heaped with Fleur's favorite salad, a tangy mixture of shrimp, pineapple, and fresh watercress. Fleur filled Belinda in on most of the events of the last week, but, even though she normally told her mother everything, she held back when the subject turned to Jake. By the end of their second day of shooting, which was Monday, she'd decided she'd misjudged him. He teased her and called her "Flower Power," but he also seemed to be looking out for her. By Tuesday, she'd decided she sort of liked him. By Wednesday, she knew for sure she liked him, and by lunchtime today, she'd realized she had a tiny little crush on him, something she had to make sure Belinda didn't discover or she'd never hear the end of it. So when her mother pressed her about him, Fleur only told the story of how she'd knocked him over the first day and how great he'd been about it.

Belinda reacted predictably. "I knew he'd be like that. He's one of the biggest names in film, but he understood how embarrassed you were. He's like Jimmy, all rough on the outside, but sweet and sensitive inside."

Belinda's conviction that Jake embodied all the qualities of her beloved James Dean irritated Fleur. "He's a lot taller. And they don't look anything alike."

"They have the same quality, baby. Jake Koranda is a rebel, too."

"You haven't even *met* him. He's not like anybody else. At least he's not like anybody I've ever known." Belinda gave her a funny, fishy look, and she shut up.

Mrs. Jurado, the housekeeper, who'd turned out to be sixty and loved showing off her double-jointed thumb, stepped out on the patio and plugged in the phone she was carrying. "It's Mr. Savagar." Fleur reached over to take it, but Mrs. Jurado shook her head. "For Mrs. Savagar."

Belinda gave Fleur a puzzled shrug, tugged off her earring, and picked up the receiver. "What is it, Alexi?" She tapped her fingernails on the glass tabletop. "What do you expect me to do about it? No, of course he hasn't called me. Yes. Yes, all right. Yes, I'll let you know if I hear anything."

"What's wrong?" Fleur asked after Belinda had hung up.

"Michel disappeared from the clinic. Alexi wanted to know if he'd contacted me." Belinda clipped her earring back on. "It must be obvious, even to your father, that he gave away the wrong child. My daughter is beautiful and successful. His son is a homosexual weakling."

Michel was Belinda's son, too, and Fleur lost her appetite. As much as she still resented him, Belinda's attitude felt wrong.

Several months ago, gossip had surfaced that Michel was engaged in a long-term affair with a married man who was well-known in Parisian society. The man had suffered a fatal heart attack after the disclosure, and Michel attempted suicide. Fleur was accustomed to the open homosexuality of the fashion world and couldn't believe the fuss everybody was making. Alexi refused to let Michel return to his Massachusetts school and locked him away in a private clinic in Switzerland. Fleur tried to feel sorry for Michel—she did feel sorry for him—but some ugly, unforgiving part of her found a terrible justice in Michel finally being the outcast.

"Aren't you going to eat the rest of your salad?" Belinda asked.

"I'm not hungry anymore."

*

The stench of Dick Spano's cigar filled the projection room, along with a lingering onion odor from the rubble of fast-food containers. Tonight Jake was watching two weeks' worth of rushes from the back row. As an actor, he never did this, but as a fledgling screenwriter he knew he had to see how his dialogue was working so he could think about what might need to be rewritten.

"You nailed it there, Jako," Johnny Guy said in response to the first exchange of dialogue between Matt and Lizzie. "You're one hell of a writer. Don't know why you waste your time with those New York theater types."

"They feed my ego." Jake kept his eyes on the screen as Lizzie began to kiss Matt. "Damn."

The men watched one cut after another of the kiss.

"It's not bad," Dick Spano offered at the end.

"She's on the right track," Johnny Guy said.

"It sucks." Jake finished his Mexican beer and set the

bottle on the floor. "She's okay up to the kiss, but she's never going to be able to handle the heavier stuff."

"Stop being so negative. She'll do fine."

"It's not in her to handle Lizzie. Fleur's feisty, and she puts up a hell of a good front, but she grew up in a convent, for God's sake."

"It wasn't a convent," Dick said. "It was a convent school. There's a difference."

"It's more than that. She's sophisticated, but she isn't worldly. She's traveled all over the world, and I've never met a kid her age who's so well-read—she talks about philosophy and politics like a European. But she seems to have been living her life inside some kind of glass bubble. Her handlers have kept a tight rein on her. She doesn't have any ordinary life experience, and she's not a good enough actress to hide that."

Johnny Guy peeled the wrapper from a Milky Way. "She'll come through. She's a hard worker, and the camera loves her."

Jake slumped in his seat and watched. Johnny Guy was right about one thing. The camera did love her. That big face illuminated the screen, along with those knockout chorus-girl legs. She wasn't conventionally graceful, but he found something appealing about her long, strong stride.

Still, her odd naïveté was a far cry from Lizzie's manipulative sexuality. In the final love scene, Lizzie had to dominate Matt so that his last illusions about her innocence are ripped away. Fleur went through the motions, but he'd seen women go through the motions all his life, and this kid didn't ring true.

It had been a long day, and he rubbed his eyes. This film's success was more important to him than anything he'd done. He'd written a couple of screenplays, but they'd ended up in the wastebasket. With *Sunday Morning Eclipse*, he was finally satisfied. Not only did he believe an audience existed for thoughtful films, but he also wanted to play a part where he could use more than two facial expressions, although he doubted he'd ever win any awards for his acting.

It had happened so fast. He'd written his first play in Vietnam when he was twenty. He'd worked on it in secret and finished it not long before he was shipped home. After he'd been released from a San Diego military hospital, he rewrote it, then mailed it to New York the day he was discharged. Forty-eight hours later, an L.A. casting agent spotted him and asked him to read for a small part in a Paul Newman Western. He'd been signed the next day, and a month later, a New York impresario called to talk about producing the play he'd sent off. Jake had finished the film and caught a red-eye east.

That experience marked the beginning of his hectic double life. The producer staged his play. Jake received little money, but a lot of glory. The studio liked his screen performance and offered him a bigger part. The money was too good for a kid from the wrong side of Cleveland to turn down. He began to juggle. West Coast for money, East Coast for love.

He signed on for the first Caliber picture and began a new play. Bird Dog buried the studio under an avalanche of fan mail, and the play won the Pulitzer. He thought about quitting Hollywood, but the play had earned less than half of what he could get for his next picture. He made the picture, and he'd been making them ever since, one after the other. No regrets—or at least not very many.

He returned his concentration to the screen. Despite the way he teased Flower Power about being a glamour girl, she didn't seem to care much about her appearance. She didn't look into a mirror unless she had to, and even then she never spent an extra second admiring herself. Fleur Savagar was more complicated than he'd expected.

Part of his problem with her was that she didn't look anything like the real Liz, who'd been petite and brunette. When he and Liz had walked across campus, she'd needed to take two steps to his one. He remembered looking up into the stands when he was playing basketball and seeing her shiny dark hair caught back with the silver clip he'd bought her. All that naïve, romantic bullshit.

He couldn't handle any more memories or he'd start hearing Creedence Clearwater and smelling napalm. He headed for the door. On the way, his foot caught the empty beer bottle, and he sent it crashing into the wall.

★

The morning after her arrival in L.A., Belinda waited at the back of the soundstage while Fleur was in makeup. Finally she heard his footsteps. The years slipped away. She was eighteen again, standing at the counter of Schwab's drugstore. She half expected him to pull a crumpled pack of Chesterfields from the pocket of his uniform jacket. Her heart began to pound. The slouch of his shoulders, the dip of his head—a man is his own man. Bad Boy James Dean.

"I love your movies." She stepped forward, neatly blocking his path. "Especially the Caliber pictures."

He gave her a crooked smile. "Thanks."

"I'm Belinda Savagar, Fleur's mother." She extended her hand. As he took it, she felt dizzy.

"Mrs. Savagar. It's nice to meet you."

"Please. Call me Belinda. I want to thank you for being so nice to Fleur. She told me how you've helped her."

"It's hard at first."

"But not everyone is kind enough to ease the way."

"She's a good kid."

He was getting ready to move away, so she set the tips of her manicured fingers on his sleeve. "Forgive me if I'm being presumptuous, but Fleur and I would like to thank you properly. We're tossing some steaks on the grill Sunday afternoon. Nothing fancy. Strictly Indiana backyard cookout."

His eyes skimmed over her navy Yves Saint Laurent tunic and white gabardine trousers. She could see he liked what he saw. "You don't look like you're from Indiana."

"Hoosier born and bred." She favored him with a mischievous look. "We're lighting the charcoal around three."

"I'm afraid I'm tied up Sunday," he said, with what sounded like genuine regret. "Could you hold that charcoal for a week?"

"I just might be able to do that."

As he smiled and walked away, she knew she'd done it exactly right, the same way she'd have done it for Jimmy. Cold beer, potato chips served in the bag, and hide the Perrier. God, she missed real men.

The following weekend, Fleur glared down at her mother. Belinda lay on a lounge at the side of the pool, her white bikini and gold ankle bracelet glimmering against her oiled body, her eyes closed beneath oversized tortoiseshell sunglasses. It was five minutes past three on Sunday afternoon. "I can't believe you did this. I really can't! I haven't been able to look him in the eye since you told me. You put him in a horrible position, not to mention me. The last thing he wants to do on his only day off is come here."

Belinda spread her fingers so she could tan between them. "Don't be silly, baby. He's going to have a wonderful time. We'll see to it."

Exactly what Belinda had been saying ever since she told Fleur she'd invited Jake for a Sunday cookout. Fleur grabbed the leaf net and marched to the edge of the pool. It was bad enough she had to watch how she behaved around Jake all week. Now she had to do it on Sunday, too. If he ever suspected she had this dumb crush on him . . .

She began skimming the pool for leaves. What had started as a tiny crush was getting bigger by the day. Fortunately she was smart enough to know this didn't have anything to do with two hearts beating as one. What it had to do with was sex. She'd finally met a man who made her go weak-kneed with lust. But why did it have to be *this* man?

No matter what, she wouldn't act stupid today. She

wouldn't stare at him, or talk too much, or laugh too loud. She'd ignore him, that's what she'd do. Belinda had invited him, and Belinda could entertain him.

Her mother tilted up her sunglasses and eyed the snagged seat of Fleur's oldest black tank. "I wish you'd change into one of your bikinis. That suit is dreadful."

Jake stepped through the open French doors onto the patio. "Looks good to me."

Fleur dropped the net and dived into the water. She'd worn her old black tank so Jake couldn't lump her in with all those other women who drooled over him. Lynn called it the "Koranda Sex Effect."

She touched the bottom, then came to the surface. He was sitting on the chaise next to Belinda. He wore baggy navy swim trunks, a gray athletic T-shirt, and a pair of running shoes that had seen better days. She'd already discovered he was only neat when was in costume. Otherwise he wore more ragged jeans and faded T-shirts than any man should own.

And he looked great in every one of them.

As he tilted back his head and laughed at something Belinda said, Fleur felt a flash of jealousy. Belinda knew exactly how to talk to a man. Fleur wished she could be like that, but the only men she found it easy to talk to were the ones she didn't care about, like the actors and wealthy playboys Belinda and Gretchen wanted her to be seen with. She had almost no practice talking to a man she wanted to impress. She dived under again. If only she could have had her first lust-crush when she was sixteen like other girls. Why was she always such a late bloomer? And why did her first crush have to be on a famous playwright–movie star who had women hanging all over him?

She surfaced again in time to see Belinda swing her legs over the side of the chaise. "Fleur, come entertain Jake while I get a cover-up. I'm starting to burn."

"Stay where you are, Flower. I'm coming in." He pulled his T-shirt over his head, kicked off his shoes, and dived into the pool. As he surfaced at the far end and swam toward her, she watched the play of muscles in his arms, the way the water streamed over his face and neck. He put his feet down next to her. His crooked-tooth grin was irresistible, and something inside her ached.

"You got your hair wet," he said. "I thought New York glamour girls only looked at the water."

"Shows how much you know about New York glamour girls." She dived under, but before she could get away, a hand grabbed her ankle and pulled her back. She sputtered to the surface.

"Hey!" he said with fake outrage. "I'm a hotshot movie star? Girls don't swim away from me."

"Maybe not ordinary girls, but hotshot glamour girls can do a lot better than an egghead screenwriter."

He laughed, and she made it to the ladder before he could stop her.

"Not fair," he called out. "You're a better swimmer than I am."

"I noticed. Your form stinks."

But it didn't stink bad enough to keep him from climbing up the ladder right after her. "Correct me if I'm wrong, Flower Power, but you don't seem all that happy to see me today."

Maybe she was a better actress than she thought. She picked up a towel from a chair and wrapped herself in it. "Nothing personal," she said. "I had a late night." Because she'd stayed up reading his plays. "I'm also a little worried about the scene I have with you and Lynn tomorrow." More than a little. She was panicked.

"Let's go for a run and talk about it."

She'd been running nearly every day since she came to L.A., and he couldn't have suggested a better way for her to work off some of her nervous energy. "Good idea."

"Mind if I steal your little girl for a while?" Jake called out to Belinda, who'd just returned to the patio wearing her lacy cover-up. "I need to make room for those steaks."

"Go ahead," Belinda replied with a gay wave. "And don't hurry back. I've got a new Jackie Collins I'm dying to cuddle up with."

Jake made a face. Fleur smiled and hurried inside to change into shorts and running shoes. As she sat on the side of the bed to tie her laces, the book she'd been reading dropped to the floor. She looked down at the page she'd marked just that morning.

> Koranda holds his personal mirror up to the faces of the American working class. His characters are the men and women who love beer and contact sports, who believe in an honest day's work for an honest day's wage. In language that is frequently raw and often funny, he shows us the best and the worst of the American spirit.

A critic in the next paragraph said it more plainly:

> Ultimately Koranda's work is successful because he grabs the country by the balls and squeezes hard.

She'd been reading Jake's plays as well as a few scholarly articles about his work. She'd also done some research on his social life, which wasn't as easy because of his obsession with privacy. Still, she'd discovered he seldom dated the same woman more than a few times.

She met him at the end of the driveway where he was stretching his hamstrings. "Think you can keep up, Flower, or should I get a stroller for you?"

"That's so weird. I was getting ready to bring out a wheelchair."

"Ouch."

She grinned, and they took off at an easy trot. Since it was Sunday, the army of gardeners who kept the unused front lawns of Beverly Hills immaculate was absent, and the street looked even more deserted than usual. She tried to think of something interesting to say. "I've seen you shooting baskets by the parking lot. Lynn told me you played in college."

"I play a couple of times a week now. It helps clear my head to write."

"Aren't playwrights supposed to be intellectuals instead of jocks?"

"Playwrights are poets, Flower, and that's what basketball is. Poetry."

And that's what you are, she thought. *A dark and complicated piece of erotic poetry.* She had to be careful not to trip over her feet. "I like basketball, but it doesn't exactly fit my idea of poetry."

"You ever hear of a guy named Julius Erving?"

She shook her head and picked up the pace so he couldn't accuse her of holding him back.

He altered his rhythm. "They call Erving 'The Doctor.' He's a young player with the New York Nets, and he's going to be one of the best. Not just good, you understand—but one of the best basketball players who ever lived."

Fleur mentally added Julius Erving to her reading list.

"Everything the Doc does on the court is poetry. Laws of gravity disappear when he moves. He flies, Flower. Men aren't supposed to fly, but Julius Erving does. That's poetry, kiddo, and that's what makes me write."

He suddenly looked uncomfortable, as if he'd revealed too much about himself. Out of the corners of her eyes, she saw the shutters slam over his face. "Let's pick up the pace," he said with a growl. "We might as well be walking."

Not because of her. She shot ahead of him and cut over to a paved bike path, stretching her legs and pushing herself. He caught up with her, and before long, patches of sweat had broken out on both their T-shirts. "Tell me about your problem with the scene tomorrow," he finally said.

"It's kind of . . . hard to explain." She was out of breath, and she sucked in more air. "Lizzie . . . seems so calculating."

He slowed the pace for her. "She is. A calculating bitch."

"But even though she resents DeeDee, she loves her . . . and she knows how DeeDee feels about Matt." She filled her lungs. "I can understand why she's attracted to him—why she wants to . . . go to bed with him—but I don't understand her being so calculating about it."

"It's the history of womankind. Nothing like a man to break up the friendship of two women."

"That's crap." She thought of her earlier stab of jealousy toward Belinda and didn't like herself for it. "Women have better things to do than fight over some guy who probably isn't worth anything in the first place."

"Hey, I'm the one who's defining reality around here. You're only the mouthpiece."

"Writers."

He smiled, and she fortified herself with more air. "DeeDee seems more . . . complete than Lizzie. She has strengths and weaknesses. You want to comfort her and shake her at the same time." She stopped just short of saying that DeeDee was better written, even though it was true.

"Very good. You read the script."

"Don't patronize me. I have to play the part, and I don't understand her. She bothers me."

Jake picked up the pace again. "She's supposed to bother you. Look, Flower, from what I understand you led a pretty sheltered life until a couple of years ago. Maybe you've never experienced anyone like Lizzie, but a woman like that leaves tooth marks in a man."

"Why?"

"Who cares? It's the end effect that matters."

Her lust-crush didn't keep her from getting angry with him. "You don't say 'who cares' about your other characters. Why do you say it about Lizzie?"

"I guess you'll have to trust me." He pulled ahead of her.

"Why should I trust you?" she called out after him. "Because you've got a big Pulitzer, and all I have are *Cosmo* covers!"

He slowed his stride. "I didn't say that." They'd reached a small park as empty as the rest of the neighborhood. "Let's walk for a while."

"You don't have to babysit me." She hated the sulky note in her voice.

"Let's have it out," he said, as he slowed. "Are you pissed about Lizzie or about the fact that you know I didn't want to cast you?"

"You're the one defining reality. Take your pick."

"Let's talk about casting, then." He picked up the tail of his T-shirt and wiped his face. "You're beautiful on screen, Flower. Your face is magic, and you've got knockout legs. Johnny Guy's been adjusting the shooting script every night to add more close-ups. The man gets tears in his eyes watching you in the rushes." He smiled at her, and she could feel some of her anger dissolving. "You're also a great kid."

A *kid*. That hurt.

"You listen to other people's opinions, you work hard, and I'll bet you don't have a malicious bone in your body."

She thought about Michel and knew that wasn't true.

"That's why I had misgivings about you playing Lizzie. She's a carnivore. The whole concept is foreign to your nature."

"I'm an actress, Jake. Part of acting is playing a role different from yoursef." She felt like a hypocrite. She wasn't an actress. She was a fake, a girl whose freak-show body was mysteriously transformed by the camera into something beautiful.

He ran his fingers through his hair, making it stand up in little spikes along one side. "Lizzie is a hard character for me to talk about. She's based on a girl I used to know. We were married a long time ago."

Was Jake, the Greta Garbo of male actors, going to confide in her? Not willingly. He looked angry at having revealed even that small amount of personal history. "What was she like?" she asked.

A muscle in his jaw ticked. "It's not important."

"I want to know."

He took a few steps, then stopped. "She was a maneater. Ground me up between her pretty little teeth and spit me out."

The stubbornness that had caused her so much trouble in the past took over. "But there had to have been something that made you fall in love with her."

He started walking again. "Lay off."

"I need to know."

"I said lay off. She was a great fuck, okay?"

"Is that all?"

He stopped and spun on her. "That's all. Thousands of satisfied customers found happiness between her legs, but the Slovak kid from Cleveland was too ignorant to figure that out, and he lapped her up like a puppy dog!"

His pain hit her like a slap. She touched his arm. "I'm sorry. Really." He pulled his arm away, and as they ran back to the house in silence, Fleur wondered what kind of person his former wife had been.

Jake's thoughts were following a similar path. He'd met Liz at the beginning of his freshman year in college. He'd been on the way home from basketball practice when he'd wandered into a rehearsal at the university theater building. She was onstage, the most beautiful girl he'd ever seen, a tiny, dark-haired kitten. He asked her out that same night, but she told him she didn't date jocks. Her resistance made her even more appealing, and he began hanging out at the theater building between practices. She continued to ignore him. He discovered she was taking a playwriting class the next semester, and he fast-talked his way past the prerequisites into the same class. It changed his life.

He wrote about the men he'd met when he was doing odd jobs in Cleveland's blue-collar bars. The Petes and Vinnies who'd gradually taken the place of the father he didn't have, the men who asked him about his schoolwork, and laid into him for cutting class, and one night, when they found out he'd been picked up by the police for trying to steal a car, took him into the alley behind the bar and taught him the meaning of tough love.

The words poured out of him, and the professor was impressed. Even more important, he'd finally drawn Liz's attention. Because her family was wealthy, his poverty fascinated her. They read Gibran together and made love. He began letting down the walls he'd built around himself. Before he knew it, they'd decided to get married, even though he was only nineteen, and she was twenty. Her father threatened to cut off her allowance, so she told him she was pregnant. Daddy whisked them to Youngstown for a fast ceremony, but when he found out the pregnancy was a sham, he stopped the checks. Jake lengthened his hours working at the town diner when he wasn't in class or at basketball practice.

A new graduate student enrolled in the theater department, and when Jake came home, he found him sitting with Liz at the gray Formica kitchen table talking about the meaning of life. One night he walked in on them in bed. Liz cried and begged Jake to forgive her. She'd said she was lonely and not used to being poor. Jake forgave her.

Two weeks later he found her down on her knees working over one of his teammates. Her innocence, he discovered, had been shared with legions. He took the keys to her Mustang, headed for Columbus, and enlisted. The divorce papers reached him near Da Nang. Vietnam, coming so soon after Liz's betrayal, had changed him forever.

When he'd written *Sunday Morning Eclipse*, Liz's ghost had come back to haunt him. She'd sat on his shoulder whispering words of innocence and corruption. She'd become Lizzie. Lizzie with her open, innocent face and the heart of a harlot. Lizzie, who bore no resemblance to the beautiful giant of a kid running beside him.

"I was wrong about you. You're going to be a great Lizzie," he said, not meaning it. "All you need is a little faith in yourself."

"Do you really think so?"

"Absolutely." He reached out and gave her hair a quick tug. "You're a good kid, Flower Power. If I had a sister, I'd want her to be just like you. Except not such a smart-ass."

Chapter 11

Jake watched as Belinda gradually won over every male on the set, from the lowliest crew member to Dick Spano to Jake himself. She was always there if someone needed her. She ran lines with the actors, joked with the grips, and rubbed away Johnny Guy's stiff neck. She brought them all coffee, teased them about their wives and girlfriends, and pumped up their egos.

"The changes you made in DeeDee's monologue were pure genius," she told Jake in June, during the second month of shooting. "You dug deep."

"Shucks, ma'am, it weren't nothing."

She regarded him earnestly. "I mean it, Jake. You nailed it. When she said, 'I give up, Matt. I give up.' I started to cry. You're going to win an Oscar. I just know it."

What touched him about Belinda's enthusiasm was that she meant every overly effusive word. After a few moments with her, whatever bad mood he might have been carrying around vanished. She flirted shamelessly with him, soothed him, and made him laugh. Beneath the balm of her hyacinth-eyed adoration, he felt like a better actor, a better writer, and a less cynical man. She was fascinating, a worldly sophisticate with a child's eager passion for everything bright and shiny. She helped make *Eclipse* one of the best sets he'd ever worked on.

"Years from now," she proclaimed, "everyone here will be proud to tell the world they worked on *Eclipse*."

No one disagreed.

Fleur dreaded going to work more each day. She hated hearing Jake and Belinda laugh. Why couldn't she entertain him like her mother did? Being on the set was torture, and not just because of Jake. She hated acting even more than modeling. Maybe if she were better in her part, she wouldn't feel so dispirited. Not that she was awful or anything, but she was the weak link in a great cast, and she'd never been satisfied with being anything but the bravest, the fastest, and the strongest.

Belinda predictably pushed aside her concerns. "You're being way too hard on yourself, baby. It's those awful nuns. They gave you overachiever's syndrome."

Fleur gazed across the set at Jake. He mussed her hair, dragged her out to shoot baskets with him, yelled at her if she argued with him, and treated her exactly like a kid sister. She wished she could talk to Belinda about her feelings for him, but her mother was the last person she could ever confide in about this.

Of course you've fallen in love with him, Belinda would say. *How could you help it? He's a great man, baby. Just like Jimmy.*

She told herself she hadn't exactly fallen in love, not eternal love, anyway. That had to work two ways, didn't it? But her feelings had grown more complex than a lust-crush. Maybe she simply had an advanced case of puppy love. Unfortunately she'd directed it toward a man who treated her as though she were twelve.

One Friday evening, Dick Spano had a party catered to the set. Fleur put on three-inch heels and a crepe de chine sarong that she tied at the bust. Every man on the set noticed except for Jake. He was too busy talking to Belinda. Belinda never gave him a hard time, never challenged him. No wonder he loved being with her.

Fleur started counting the days until they left for location in Iowa. The sooner this picture was over, the sooner she could return to New York and forget about Jake Koranda. If only she could come up with a plan for what she wanted to do with her life once this was all behind her.

Dick Spano rented out a motel not far from Iowa City to house the actors and crew and to serve as the production's command post. Fleur's room had a pair of ugly lamps, worn orange carpeting, and a reproduction of *Sunday Afternoon on the Island of La Grande Jatte* bolted to the wall. The painting's cardboard center curled in like a potato chip. Belinda wrinkled her nose as she studied it. "Lucky you. I got fake Van Gogh sunflowers."

"You didn't have to come with me," Fleur said more sharply than she should have.

"Don't be cranky, darling. You know I couldn't stay behind. After all those miserable years in Paris with nothing to do but drink, this had been a dream come true."

Fleur gazed up from the stack of bras she was putting away in the bureau. Even in this drab hotel room, Belinda looked happy. And why shouldn't she? Belinda was living out her dream. But this wasn't Fleur's dream. She fixed her eyes on the bras. "I've been . . . sort of thinking about what I want to do when this is over."

"Don't think too hard, darling. That's what we pay Gretchen and your agent for." Belinda rummaged through Fleur's cosmetic case and pulled out a hairbrush. "We're going to have to make a decision soon, though, about the Paramount project. It really is tempting. Parker's sure it's right for you, but Gretchen hates the script. One way or another, we need to close the Estee Lauder deal first."

Fleur took a pair of running shoes from her suitcase and

tried to sound casual. "Maybe . . . we should wait awhile before we do anything. I wouldn't mind taking some time off. We could travel, just the two of us. It'd be fun."

"Don't be silly, baby." Belinda eyed her reflection in the mirror and fingered a lock of hair. "Maybe I should go lighter? What do you think?"

Fleur abandoned all pretense of unpacking. "I'd really like some time off. I've been working hard for three years, and I need a vacation. A chance to think some things over."

She finally had Belinda's complete attention. "Absolutely not." Belinda slapped down the hairbrush. "Dropping out of sight now would be career suicide."

"But . . . I want to take a break. It's all happened so quickly. I mean, it's been wonderful and everything, but . . ." Her words came out in a rush. "How do I know this is what I really want to do with my life?"

Belinda looked at her as if she'd gone crazy. "What more could you possibly want?"

Fleur couldn't jump into another movie right away, and she hated the idea of more modeling, but she felt herself faltering. "I—I don't know. I'm not sure."

"You're not sure? I guess it's a little difficult to find something else to do when you're already sitting on top of the world."

"I'm not saying I want another career. I just . . . I just need some time to think about my choices. To make sure this is really what I want."

Belinda turned into a cold, distant stranger. "Do you have something more exciting in mind than being the most famous model in the world? Something more glamorous than being a film star? What are you thinking about doing, Fleur? Do you want to be a secretary? Or a store clerk? Or how about a nurse's aide? You could clean up vomit and scrub out bedpans. Is that good enough for you?"

"No, I—"

"Then what? What do you want?"

"I don't know!" She sank down on the edge of the bed.

Her mother punished her with silence.

Misery welled inside her. "I'm just . . . confused," she said in a small voice.

"You're not confused. You're spoiled." Belinda's scorn scraped her skin like rough steel wool. "You've had everything you could possibly want handed to you, and you haven't had to work for any of it. Do you realize how immature you sound? It might be different if you had a goal, but you don't even have that. When I was your age, I knew exactly what I wanted out of life, and I was willing to do anything to get it."

Fleur felt herself wilt. "Maybe . . . Maybe you're right."

Belinda was angry, and she wouldn't let her off so easily. "I never thought I'd say this, but I'm disappointed in you." She crossed the sad orange carpet. "Think about what you're planning to throw away, and when you're ready to talk sensibly, come find me." Without another word, she walked out.

Suddenly Fleur was a child again, back at the Couvent de l'Annonciation watching her mother disappear. She came up off the bed and rushed out into the hallway, but Belinda had vanished. Her palms got sweaty and her heart raced. She turned down the corridor and made her way to her mother's room. No one answered when she knocked. She went back to her own room, but she couldn't sit still.

She headed for the lobby and found it deserted except for a couple of crew members. Maybe Belinda had gone out to swim. But the only person around the small motel pool was a workman emptying the trash can. She went back into the lobby and spotted Johnny Guy. "Have you seen Belinda?"

He shook his head. "Maybe she's in the bar."

Her mother didn't drink anymore, but Fleur had no place else to look.

Her eyes needed a moment to adjust to the dim light. She saw Belinda sitting at the corner table by herself, twirling a swizzle stick in what looked like a tumbler of scotch. All the blood rushed from her head. After three years of sobriety, her mother had fallen off the wagon, and Fleur was responsible.

She dashed over to her. "What are you doing? Please don't do this. I'm sorry."

Belinda stabbed the swizzle stick toward the bottom of the glass. "I'm not feeling like the best of company right now. Maybe you'd better leave me alone."

Fleur fell into the chair across from her. "You've been doing so great. Just because you have an ungrateful daughter doesn't mean you should punish yourself. I need you too much."

Belinda gazed into her drink. "You don't need me, baby. Apparently I've been pushing you into things you don't want."

"That's not true."

Belinda looked up, and her eyes were awash in tears. "I love you so much. I only want what's best for you."

Fleur grabbed her mother's hand. "It's like you've always said. There's a bond between us, as if we're one person, not two." Her voice grew choked. "Whatever makes you happy makes me happy. I've just been confused, that's all." She tried to smile. "Let's go for a ride. We can make up our mind about Paramount."

Belinda dipped her head. "Don't resent me, baby. I couldn't stand it if you resented me."

"That'll never happen. Come on. Let's get out of here."

"Are you sure?"

"I've never been more sure of anything."

Belinda gave her a watery smile and got up from her chair. Fleur bumped the edge of the table with her hip, and a little of Belinda's drink sloshed over the rim. Only then did she notice how full the glass was. She stared at it for a moment. Belinda didn't seem to have taken so much as a sip.

At the end of their first week in Iowa, Jake finally had a day off. He slept late, went for a run, then took a shower. He was just stepping out of the tub when he heard a knock. He tucked a towel around his hips and opened the door. Belinda stood on the other side.

She wore a simple blue and lavender wrap dress, and she dangled a white paper sack from her fingertips. "Want some breakfast?"

A feeling of inevitability came over him. Why the hell not? "Do you have coffee in there?"

"Strong and black."

He gestured her in. She pulled the DO NOT DISTURB sign off the knob, hung it outside, then closed the door and withdrew two Styrofoam cups. As she handed his over, he smelled her perfume. She was one of the most fascinating women he'd ever met.

"Do you consider yourself a rebel, Jake?"

He peeled off the lid and dropped it in the wastebasket. "I guess I've never thought about it."

"I think you are." She sat in the room's only chair and crossed her legs so that her skirt fell open over her knees. "You're a rebel without a cause. A man who follows his own drummer. That's one of the things that excites me about you."

"There's more?" He smiled, only to realize that she was perfectly serious.

"Oh yes. Do you remember when you were on the run in *Devil Slaughter*? I loved that. I love it when it's just you against them. That's the kind of picture Jimmy would have made if he hadn't died."

"Jimmy?" He tossed the pillows against the headboard and settled into them.

"James Dean. You've always reminded me of him." She rose and came toward the bed. In the dim light of the room, her blue eyes bathed him in admiration. "I've been so lonely," she whispered. "Would you like me to get undressed for you?"

He'd gotten sick of playing games, and her directness was refreshing. "That's the best offer I've had in months."

"I want to please you." She sat on the side of the bed and leaned forward to kiss him. As their lips met, her hands clasped his shoulders and began stroking his arms. He kissed her more deeply and touched her breast through the silky fabric of the dress. She immediately pulled away and began unfastening her blouse.

"Hey, slow down," he said gently.

She looked up at him, her eyes clouded with confusion. "Don't you want to see me?"

"We've got all day."

"I only want to please you."

"That works two ways." He pushed her beneath him and slipped his hand under her skirt.

When Belinda felt Jake's hand on her thigh, she saw the scene in *Devil Slaughter* where Bird Dog tangled with the beautiful Englishwoman. She remembered how he'd pulled her off her horse into his arms, how he'd run his hands over her body searching for the knife he knew she carried. As Jake's hand circled her thigh, she pretended he was searching her.

Her mouth fell open to his kisses . . . wonderful, deep kisses. She'd meant to undress for him, but he took off her clothes, one item at a time. It didn't feel right seeing his face so close, so she shut her eyes again and visualized the way he looked on the screen.

Better. So much better. . .

She parted her legs to offer herself. His beard scraped her skin, deliciously hurting her. And then he stopped.

★

As Jake gazed at Belinda's closed eyes, he knew he'd made a big mistake. She was completely passive, like some kind of vestal virgin offering herself up to the gods. The adoration she'd showered him with since they day they'd met now felt faintly creepy. He could do whatever he wanted, but this was like making love to a blow-up doll.

Her eyes flickered open. He had the urge to wave his hands in front of her to see if she was still there. "Is something wrong?" she asked.

He told himself to do it and get it over with, but the image of Flower's face popped into his head, and what had only seemed creepy now felt sordid. "Second thoughts," he said, pulling away from her. "Sorry."

She reached up and touched his shoulder. He waited for the cross-examination to begin—tried to figure out what to say—but to his shock, it didn't happen. "All right," she said.

Moments later, she was gone.

Three days passed, but as Jake sat on the back of a tractor, his bare chest oiled with phony sweat, the incident continued to bother him. He spotted Belinda perched by the wardrobe trailer reading a magazine. He'd been doing his best to avoid her. Unnecessary, as it turned out, because she treated him exactly as she had before. She didn't seem to expect anything from him, and that alone was unsettling.

"Here's your shirt."

He hadn't seen Lynn approach. "Since when are you working wardrobe?" he said, as he took the denim shirt from her.

"I wanted to talk to you without anybody listening in." Lynn folded her arms over the phony pregnancy padding beneath her maternity top. Something in her determined expression made him wary. "I saw Belinda go into your room the other morning."

Shit. "So what?" He came down off the tractor and patted her stomach to distract her. "How's the baby doing?"

"You're making a big mistake."

"I need to find Johnny Guy." He started moving away, but she stepped in front of him.

"She's nothing but a well-dressed celebrity fucker."

Lynn was right, but Belinda's sophistication had kept him from seeing the truth. "Nice talk," he said. "I saw her running lines with you yesterday. What is it with you women?"

"Did you even once think about Fleur?"

He wasn't letting her drag Flower into this, and he slipped on the shirt. "This doesn't have anything to do with you or with her."

"Don't be stupid. You have to know the way she feels about you."

His hands stalled on the shirt buttons. "What are you talking about?"

"Apparently you and Belinda are the only ones who haven't figured out that she's fallen for you."

"You're crazy. She's a kid."

"Since when? I'll bet anything you've dated women her age. Probably slept with a few of them, too. I don't get your big brother act."

"That's the way I feel about her."

"It's not the way she feels about you."

"You're wrong." But even as he said it, he knew he was kidding himself, and the coffee he'd drunk turned sour in his stomach. Fleur had given him subtle signs, all of which he'd chosen to ignore. From the day he'd met her, he'd sensed a fragility about her that made her off-limits to someone like him, so he'd deliberately taken on the big brother role to keep her safe.

"She's my friend, Jake, and despite the fact that she doesn't slobber all over you, she really cares about you." Lynn rubbed her fake belly. "Fleur also loves her mother, and you're setting her up for something nasty if she figures out what you and Belinda have been up to. I don't want to see her hurt."

Neither did he, and once again he cussed himself out for letting things with Belinda go as far as they had. "Nothing happened with Belinda and me." Not exactly true. "And even if you're right about Fleur, you know she'll forget all about me as soon as the picture is over."

"Are you sure? She's a beautiful, intelligent young woman who's attracted to you, and I don't think she gives her heart away easily."

"You're making too much of it." He poked her padded stomach. "This pregnancy has whacked your hormones."

"You could do a lot worse than Fleur Savagar."

"What are you saying? I'm supposed to keep my hands off Belinda, who damned well knows what she's doing, but stick it to the kid with the big eyes. I don't get you, Lynn."

"A problem you seem to have with most women."

★

They finished their location work in Iowa and returned to L.A. As August unfolded and they entered the final weeks of shooting, Fleur grew increasingly miserable. Jake had been acting strangely ever since they'd gotten back. He'd stopped ordering her around, and he never teased her anymore. Instead he treated her with professional courtesy. He'd even stopped calling her "Flower." She hated it. She also felt a growing resentment toward Belinda, who acted as though their confrontation in Iowa had never happened and continued making plans for their future while she waved off any doubts Fleur expressed. Fleur was trapped.

She and Jake had just finished shooting a scene when Johnny Guy pulled them aside. "I want to talk about the love scene. We start shooting it on Friday morning, and you both need to be thinking about it."

Fleur didn't want to think about it.

"I'm not going to over-rehearse the scene," Johnny Guy said. "I don't want any damned choreographed ballet dance. I want sex, dirty and raw." He curled his hand over Fleur's shoulder. "I'll clear the set to keep you as comfortable as I can, honey. Just me, the AD, boom, and camera. That's about as stripped down as we can get."

"Maybe you could put Jenny on boom instead of Frank,"

Jake said. "And, Fleur, if you want somebody from SAG standing by, we can do that, too."

"I don't know what you mean," she said. "Check my contract. I don't need a closed set. We're using a body double, remember?"

"Shit." Jake shoved his hand through his hair.

Johnny Guy shook his head. "Your agent talked about a body double, but we wouldn't sign you under those conditions. Not with the way we're filming the scene. Your people knew that."

Alarm shot through her. "There's a mistake. I'm calling my agent."

"You do that, honey." The kindness in Johnny Guy's eyes added to her anxiety. "Go into Dick's office where you can have some privacy."

Fleur rushed to the producer's office and phoned Parker Dayton, her film agent. By the time she hung up, she was nauseous. She dashed out of the studio and rushed for her car.

She found Belinda at one of Beverly Hills's most fashionable watering holes, lunching with the wife of a television producer she wanted to impress. Belinda took one look at her face and stood up. "Darling, whatever are you doing—"

"I need to talk to you." The Porsche keys cut into Fleur's palm.

Belinda took Fleur's arm and smiled down at her luncheon partner. "Excuse us for a moment, will you?" She pulled Fleur into the restroom and locked the door. "What's this all about?" she said coldly.

Fleur gripped the keys tighter. The pain of their sharp edges digging into her skin almost felt good, maybe because she knew she could make it stop. "I just talked to Parker Dayton. He said there was nothing about a body double in my contract. He said you told him I'd changed my mind."

Belinda shrugged. "They wouldn't agree to it, baby.

Parker pushed them, but they said it was nonnegotiable. They wouldn't film the scene with a double."

"So you lied to me? Even though you know how I feel about working nude?"

Belinda pulled a pack of cigarettes from her purse. "You wouldn't have signed if you'd known you couldn't use a double. I had to protect you. Surely you can see that now."

"I'm not doing it."

"Of course you are." Belinda looked faintly alarmed. "My God, a breach-of-contract suit would finish you in Hollywood. You're not ruining your career because of some silly bourgeois prudery."

The keys cut deeper, and Fleur asked the question she'd held back for so long. "Is it my career, Belinda, or is it yours?"

"What a wicked, ungrateful thing to say!" Belinda pitched the cigarette she'd just lit to the floor and stubbed it out with the toe of her shoe. "You listen to me, Fleur, and pay attention to exactly what I'm telling you. If you do anything to jeopardize this film, things will never be the same between us."

Fleur stared at her mother. A chill slithered through her. "You don't mean that."

"I've never meant anything more."

As Fleur gazed into Belinda's face, she saw only determination. Her lungs compressed, and she ran from the restroom. Belinda called out for her, but Fleur didn't stop. She wove through the tables and out onto the street. The thin soles of her sandals slapped the pavement as she began to run, up one street, down another, trying to outrace her misery. She had no destination in mind, but she couldn't stop. Then she saw the phone booth.

Her hands shook as she placed the call, and her dress stuck to her skin.

"It's . . . me," she said when he answered.

"I can barely hear you. Is something wrong, *enfant*?"

"Yes, something's really wrong. She—she lied to me." Struggling to breathe, she told him what had happened.

"You signed a contract without reading it first?" he said when she finished.

"Belinda always takes care of that."

"I am very much afraid, *enfant*," he said quietly, "that you have learned a most difficult lesson about your mother. She is not to be trusted. Ever."

Ironically, Alexi's attack on Belinda made Fleur feel an automatic need to defend her. She didn't.

She waited until she knew Belinda would be at her hair appointment before she went home. As soon as she got there, she changed into a swimsuit and threw herself into the pool. Jake found her as she was climbing out.

He wore a pair of ratty navy shorts and a T-shirt so faded that only the outlines of Beethoven's face were still visible on the front. One of his sweat socks had fallen into accordion folds around his ankle. He was rumpled and mussed, a hard-fisted cowboy misplaced in Beverly Hills. She was absurdly, insanely glad to see him. "Go away, Koranda. Nobody invited you."

"Get your shoes on. We're going for a run."

"I don't feel like it."

"Don't piss me off. You've got a minute and a half to change your clothes."

"Or what?"

"I call in Bird Dog."

"I'm scared." She grabbed a towel and took her time drying off. "I'll run with you, but only because I was planning to go out anyway."

"Understood."

She went into the house and changed. If what she felt for Jake was puppy love, she prayed the real thing never came along. It was too painful. Every night as she fell asleep, she imagined they were making love in a sun-drenched room filled with flowers and soft music. She saw them lying on a bed with pastel sheets that billowed over their bodies in the breeze from the open window. He pulled a flower from a vase by the bed and brushed the petals over her nipples and her stomach. She opened her legs, and he touched her there, too. They were in love, and they were alone. No camera. No crew. Just the two of them.

She snared her hair in a ponytail and tightened it with a hard yank. He was waiting for her in the driveway. They began to run, but they'd barely made it a half mile before she had to stop. "I can't today. You go on."

Normally he would have teased her, but today he didn't. Instead he slowed. "We'll walk back. Let's take my car to the park and shoot some baskets instead. If we're lucky, it'll be deserted, and we won't have to sign any autographs."

She knew they had to talk about what had happened, and it would be easier if she didn't have to look him in the eye. "All right."

He'd driven over in his truck, a '66 Chevy pickup with a Corvette racing engine. If he'd been any other actor, she might have been able to pull off the nude scene. As much as she would have hated it, she could have detached from what was happening and gotten through it. But not with Jake. Not while she dreamed about a room filled with flowers and music.

"I don't want to do the scene," she said.

"I know." He stopped the truck next to the park and pulled a basketball from behind the seat. They walked across the grass to the deserted basketball court. He began to dribble. "The scene isn't sleazy, Flower. It's necessary." He made a quick dunk and then passed the ball to her.

She dribbled toward the basket, shot, and hit the rim. "I don't work nude."

"Your people don't seem to understand that."

"They understand it."

"Then why did this happen?"

Because she'd trusted her mother. "Because I didn't read the contract before I signed it, that's how."

He made a quick jump from the side and sank a clean shot. "We're not after the raincoat crowd. It'll be handled tastefully."

"Tastefully! What does that mean?" She batted the ball at his chest. "Let me tell you what it means. It means it won't be your noodle everybody is seeing!" She stomped off the court.

"Flower." She spun around and caught him smiling. He wiped it off and tucked the ball under his arm. "Sorry. It was just your manner of expression." He walked over to her and brushed his index finger under her chin. "It won't be your noodle, either, kiddo. The most the audience will see is your backside. Mine, too, for that matter. They may not even see your breasts. It depends on how it's edited."

"You'll see them."

"Actually, Flower . . . it won't be a new experience. Not that I've seen yours in particular, but there are only so many variations. If you think about it, I should be the one complaining. How many noodles have you seen?"

"Enough," she lied. "And that's not the point." Her ponytail tugged at her scalp, and she pulled out the rubber band. "You think this is funny, don't you?"

"Only the 'noodle' part, not the fact that you were misled. I'd kick some major ass if I were you. But, bottom line, that scene is necessary to the film, and you're going to have to come through."

He cupped the side of her neck and gazed straight into her eyes. She had the horrible feeling she'd seen him do this in one of his films, where he had to convince some stupid female to do exactly what he wanted. But what if the tenderness was real? She desperately wanted to believe that.

"Flower, this is important," he said softly. "Will you do it? Will you do it for me?"

Right then, she knew it wasn't real at all. He was manipulating her. She jerked away. "Stop pretending I have a choice. I signed a contract. You know I have to do it."

She ran back toward the bike path. He didn't care anything about her. All he cared about was his movie.

6*

Jake watched her running away from him, and something tightened inside his chest. She was so damned beautiful with her hair streaming behind her like spilled gold paint. As she covered the ground with long, clean strides, he realized she was the only woman he'd ever been able to run with. From the very beginning, those knockout chorus girl legs had been a perfect match for his own.

A lot of things about her matched him. That smart-aleck mouth and quirky sense of humor. Her boundless energy. But not her innocence. That wasn't a match at all. Not her innocence, and not her fragile little-girl's heart.

Chapter 12

Johnny Guy cleared the set of all but the necessary few, then called everyone together while Fleur was in makeup. "The first person who cracks a joke or does anything to make Fleur uncomfortable today is out on his butt, and the union can go screw itself."

Dick Spano winced.

Johnny Guy cornered Jake. "You watch those wisecracks today."

"You worry about yourself," Jake retorted.

They were glaring at each other as Fleur came on the set. She wore a yellow cotton dress and white sandals. A baby-blue eyelet ribbon held her hair back from her face. She'd worn this yellow dress most of the week as they shot the dialogue that led up to the love scene, but today was the day it came off, and she was miserable.

"Let's run through what we're going to do, honey lamb." Johnny Guy led her into the old farmhouse room with its faded wallpaper and iron bed. "You're going to stand on that mark and look over at Matt. Keep looking at him while you unbutton your dress and step out of it. After we get that, I'll shoot you from behind while you take off your bra and panties. Real easy stuff. Don't try to rush it. And, Jako, when she's taking off her underwear, I'll start coming in on you. Questions?"

"I'm clear," Jake said.

Fleur yawned and looked at her wrist. "Yeah. Me, too." The set was unnaturally quiet. No one called out insults, and none of the normal chatter flew back and forth. The tomblike silence made her even more queasy.

"You okay, Flower?" Jake said.

"Peachy." She pretended to adjust the shoulder strap on her sundress.

Jake gave her a crooked smile. "It's not the end of the world."

"Easy for you to say. Your underpants don't have teddy bears on them."

"You're kidding."

"They thought it would add to Lizzie's character."

Jake's smile turned into a glower. "That's the stupidest thing I ever heard."

"Exactly what I told them."

Jake strode past her. "Johnny Guy, some idiot put Flower in panties with teddy bears on them."

"I'm the idiot, Jako. You got a problem?"

"Damned right. Lizzie should be in the sexiest underwear they make. Innocence on the outside and corruption underneath. You're screwing with my metaphor."

"Fuck your metaphor."

The two men began to argue. Finally something felt normal. She hoped they kept at it all day. Unfortunately they remembered she was there and apologized.

Johnny Guy sent her back to wardrobe to change underwear. The red lace replacement set didn't hide anything, and she yearned for the teddy bears. Johnny Guy called for action. Slowly she began unbuttoning the top of the dress.

"Cut! You need to look at Matt, honey."

She ordered herself to think only of Lizzie. Lizzie had undressed for a dozen men. She'd been scheming for this moment ever since Matt had returned. But as the cameras started to roll, she couldn't make herself believe the man watching her was anyone other than Jake.

It took four more takes, but the yellow dress finally slid to the floor. She stood in front of Jake wearing nothing more than a few scraps of red lace. She told herself this was no more revealing than a lingerie ad, but it didn't feel like that.

She slipped into a terry-cloth robe while the crew moved the camera. They were shooting her from the back as she took off the bra and panties. She was supposed to be slightly out of focus as the camera concentrated on Matt's reaction. But she wouldn't be out of focus to Jake.

She made them wait while she went to the bathroom, but she could only stall so long. The cameras rolled. During the next take, she fumbled with the clasp of the bra. After that Johnny Guy had to remind her to hold her head up. The set felt like a morgue, and the absence of chatter added to her agitation.

As they got ready for the fifth take, she gazed desperately at Jake. He'd spent all morning not looking at her unless he had to, but now, instead of helping her, he let his eyes sweep down over her. He shrugged. "Your body is nice and everything, kiddo, but I'd appreciate it if we could get out of here before the tip-off. The Sixers are playing the Nets tonight."

The cameraman laughed. Johnny Guy gave Jake a murderous glare, but Fleur felt a little better. Some of the tension on the set eased, and the skeletal crew began talking in normal tones.

With the next take, she got her bra off. She tried to pretend it was Matt looking at her breasts. She leaned forward just as Johnny Guy wanted her to and slipped her thumbs into the sides of her panties. Her stomach pitched. She gave a little tug and pulled them down.

Jake's eyes followed the panties, then returned to look at what they'd been covering up. This wasn't the way she wanted Jake to see her, not with everyone else looking, not with cameras rolling and anyone who could afford a movie ticket able to see this moment that should have been private.

She hated herself for selling out. This might be right for other actresses, but she was a fake actress and it wasn't right for her. She wanted to give herself to Jake with love—not performing a piece of business she was getting paid for.

The camera couldn't see her facial expression, but Jake could. "Cut," he said. "Just cut it. Shit."

*

It didn't take long for Belinda's contacts to call and tell her what was happening. They been working on a closed set today, but Belinda should have gone anyway. If she'd been there, she could have helped.

She smoked and paced the living room. Nothing was going right. She'd never imagined Fleur would stay angry with her for so long, but her daughter had barely spoken to her since Tuesday when she'd found out she couldn't use a body double. And now this.

Belinda lit another cigarette and waited.

Fleur came home early and walked past Belinda without saying a word. Belinda followed her upstairs. "Baby, don't be like this."

"I don't want to talk about it," Fleur said with a quiet dignity that further unsettled Belinda.

"How much longer are you going to punish me?"

"I'm not punishing you." Fleur went into her room and dropped her purse on the bed.

"I'd call three days of silence punishment," Belinda retorted.

Fleur rounded on her. "What you did to me was wrong."

Fleur's intensity frightened Belinda. "I'm not perfect, baby. Sometimes my ambition for you gets the better of me."

"No kidding."

Fleur's sarcasm was a relief. Belinda made her way to

her daughter's side. "You're special, baby, and I won't ever let you forget that, no matter how much you try to. The rules for celebrities aren't the same as the rules for ordinary people."

"I don't believe that."

Belinda stroked her cheek. "I love you with all my heart, do you believe that?"

Fleur softened enough to nod.

Belinda's eyes filled with tears. "I only want the best for you. Your destiny was carved out the instant you were conceived. Fame is in your blood." She held out her arms. "Forgive me, baby. Please say you forgive me."

Fleur let Belinda hug her. Gradually her stiff muscles relaxed. "I forgive you," she whispered. "But please . . . Promise you won't ever lie to me again."

Belinda's heart filled with love for her beautiful, naïve daughter. She stroked her hair. "I promise. I'll never lie to you again."

★

Just before dark, Belinda grabbed the keys to her Mercedes. If she didn't do something quickly, everything she'd worked for would slip away. She parked in Fleur's space at the studio and nodded to the guard as she went inside. None of the three men sitting in the dark projection room noticed her. They were too absorbed in the images on the screen.

"The entire fucking sympathy of the movie shifts to her." Johnny Guy twisted the cap on what looked like a bottle of Maalox. "It's as if we're watching Snow White get raped. I swear to God, Jako, if you say 'I told you so,' I'll kick your ass."

"The film's imploding on us," Jake said tonelessly.

Belinda felt a chill.

"Let's not jump the gun," Dick Spano said. "Fleur had a bad day, that's all."

Johnny Guy popped an antacid. "You weren't there, Dicky. She doesn't have it in her to pull off that scene."

Jake raked his fingers through his hair. "I'll drive up to my place, turn off the phones for the weekend, and do some rewrites. We'll have to cut some of her footage."

Belinda dug her fingernails into her palms. Cut Fleur's footage? She wouldn't allow it.

"Do what you have to," Johnny Guy said. "I'll make some notes for you. I'm sorry about this, Jako. Really."

Spano jabbed the air with his cigar. "I don't get why she froze up like that. We all know some of the guys she's dated. Big-time players. It's not like she's never taken her clothes off for a man."

"But she hasn't taken them off for Jake," Johnny Guy said.

Spano cigar's tip glowed. "What does that mean?"

Jake sighed. "Leave it alone, Johnny Guy."

The director glanced over at Spano. "Fleur's fallen hard for our boy."

Belinda went absolutely still.

Johnny Guy popped another antacid. "I guess he can't help being irresistible."

"Go to hell," Jake said without any rancor.

Johnny Guy rubbed the back of his head. "Do what you can over the weekend with the rewrites. It's not the end of the world, but this is going to hurt."

Belinda's mind raced as she slipped out of the room. Fleur had fallen in love with Jake? Why hadn't she noticed?

Because she'd been too caught up in her own fascination with him. She thought she knew her daughter so well, but she hadn't seen what should have been perfectly obvious. Of course Fleur had fallen for him. What woman wouldn't? If she looked back, she could see the signs. But watching her dreams come true had made her oblivious. A thrill shot through her. She located Jake's pickup in the parking lot and waited for him. She wouldn't let them cut Fleur's scenes.

He approached a little before midnight. She stepped out into the pool of light behind his truck. Ever since Iowa, he'd been avoiding her, and he didn't look happy to see her now. She accepted his rejection with the same fatalistic resignation she'd accepted Flynn's abandonment. She wasn't important enough to hold him. But when he'd kissed her that day, she'd felt as though she'd gotten a little piece of Jimmie back, and she could be satisfied with that.

"Don't do the rewrites," she said as he reached her. "It's a waste of your time. Fleur can do those scenes."

"Somebody's been eavesdropping."

She shrugged. "I saw the rushes, and I heard all of you talking. But there's no need to change anything."

He pulled a set of keys from his jeans pocket. "If you saw the rushes, you know we can't use anything we shot today. Believe me, I don't want to do this, but unless a miracle happens, we don't have any choice."

"Make the miracle, Jake," she said softly. "You can do it."

He locked eyes with her. "What are you talking about?"

She stepped closer to him, her mouth dry. "We both know why Fleur can't let herself go in that scene. She's afraid you'll see the way she feels about you. But you can fix that."

"I don't know what you mean."

How could a man who wrote so brilliantly about human complexity be so obtuse? She smiled at him. "Break down that wall. Take her away with you this weekend and break down the wall she's put up."

He seemed to freeze, and then his voice grew cold. "Maybe you'd better explain exactly what you mean by that."

She gave a small, nervous laugh. "Fleur will be twenty next month. She's well past the age of consent."

His lips barely moved. "I still don't understand what you're getting at. Spell it out, Belinda. Spell it out so I'm sure I've got it right."

She wouldn't retreat, and she lifted her chin. "I think you should make love to her."

"Jesus."

"Don't look so shocked. It's the obvious solution."

"Only in your twisted mind." His voice whipped her, and his eyes raked her with contempt. "Making love is what people do for pleasure. It's not a business deal. You're pimping your own daughter."

"Jake . . ."

"What you're talking about is fucking. Fuck my daughter, Koranda, so she won't blow her movie career. Fuck her so she won't blow *my* career."

"It's not like that!" she cried. "You make it sound so ugly."

"Then make it pretty for me."

"You have to be attracted to her. She's one of the most beautiful women in the world. And she's in love with you." Of course, she was, Belinda thought. Fleur had always been a creature of grand passions. She had to love Jake.

His contempt turned to disgust. "Have you forgotten that morning in Iowa?"

"Nothing happened. It doesn't count."

"It counts in my mind."

"Fleur wants you, Jake. And her feelings for you are all that stand in the way of finishing this film exactly the way you want it to be. Only you can break through her reserve." Belinda had waited her whole life for this, and she wouldn't let his squeamishness dissuade her. "What's the harm?" She ignored her uneasiness and looked him straight in the eye. "It's not like she's never been with a man."

Jake flinched.

Belinda hurried on. "She hasn't been promiscuous, don't think that. I sheltered her as much as I could. But a mother can only do so much. And this way her feelings for you will be able to run their natural course. She'll be better for it. The movie will be better. Everybody wins."

"You don't win, Belinda." He gazed down at her with eyes so cold they chilled her to the bone. "You're the biggest loser I've ever met."

He climbed in his truck, and the engine growled to life.

The tires screamed as he whipped out of his parking place. She watched until the taillights disappeared.

When she got home, she slipped inside Fleur's dark bedroom. Her daughter was asleep. Tenderly she brushed away a long lock of blond hair that curled over her cheek.

Fleur stirred. "Belinda?"

"It's all right, darling. Go back to sleep."

"Smelled your perfume," Fleur murmured, and then she was quiet.

Belinda sat awake for the rest of the night. She'd never been more right about anything than she was about this. Fleur and Jake could become one of Hollywood's great couples, like Gable and Lombard, or Liz Taylor and Mike Todd. Jake needed a woman who was larger than life, just like him.

The more she thought about it, the more she understood how right this was. Of course Fleur had frozen up during the filming today. She'd been mortified to have everyone watching what should have been their first private moment—the first time she shared herself with him. Once Fleur had worked through that, she'd do the scene brilliantly. But Fleur needed to be intimate with Jake before she could set herself free.

As Belinda smoked one cigarette after another, she wrote a script in her head. The scenario was so simple it was almost transparent. Still, that's what made it appealing. Wasn't this Hollywood, where disbelief was suspended every day?

She practiced on a pad of unlined stationery, using handwritten notes Jake had made on Fleur's script as her guide. The end product wouldn't bear close scrutiny, but it was good enough. She'd put the rest in place tomorrow.

Fleur spent most of Saturday on horseback, but it didn't make her forget what had happened. People were depending on her, and she'd failed them. Monday would be even worse. What would she do after the undressing part was over and she had to make love to Jake?

When she got home, she found Belinda sunbathing by the pool. Her mother had to know by now what had happened on Friday, and she braced herself for a cross-examination, but Belinda merely smiled. "I have the most fabulous idea. Cool off with a swim, then let's both get dressed up and go out to dinner. Just the two of us. Someplace fabulously expensive."

Fleur had no appetite, but she didn't want to spend Saturday night wallowing, either. Besides, she and Belinda needed to do something together that didn't involve work. "I'd like that."

She changed into her suit, swam for a while, and took a shower. When she came out, Belinda was sitting on the side of her bed waiting for her. Her mother's blond hair gleamed against her coral knit suit. "I went shopping today," she said. "Look what I found for you."

A very short crocheted dress made of oatmeal-colored string lay on the bed along with a flesh-colored slip and a pair of lace panties. No chance of going unnoticed in that. She'd be all legs, and the flesh slip under that wide-open knit would make her look naked. But she couldn't refuse Belinda's peace offering. "Thanks. It's great."

"And look at these." Belinda opened a shoebox and pulled out a pair of candy-striped wedged sandals with ribbon ties at the ankles. "This is going to be such fun."

Fleur got dressed, and, just as she suspected, she was all flesh and legs. Belinda piled her hair on top of her head, fastened big gold hoops in her ears, and added a dab of perfume. Her eyes filled with tears as she gazed at Fleur's reflection in the mirror. "I love you so much."

"I love you, too."

They went downstairs. Belinda retrieved her purse from the table in the hallway. "Oh . . . I forgot." She picked up an envelope. "This is so odd. I found it in the mailbox. It's addressed to you, but there's no stamp on it. Someone must have personally delivered it."

Fleur took the envelope. Only her name was printed on front. She tore it open and pulled out two sheets of white stationery. Untidy handwriting covered the top sheet.

Dear Flower,

It's after midnight and I can't see any lights, so I'll leave this in your mailbox and hope you find it first thing Saturday morning. I have to see you now. Please, Flower, if you care about me, drive up to my place in Morro Bay as soon as you get this. It'll take you about three hours. Here's a map. Don't disappoint me, kiddo. I need you.

Love,

Jake

P.S. Don't tell anyone about this. Not even Belinda.

Fleur stared at the note. She was supposed to have found this hours ago. What if something horrible had happened? Her heart pounded. He needed her.

"What is it?" Belinda asked.

Fleur stared at the last line. "This is . . . from Lynn. Something's wrong. I have to go to her right away."

"Go where? It's late."

"I'll call you." She grabbed her purse. As she shot through the house to the garage, she wished he'd left his number so she could call him and tell him she was coming.

All the way to Morro Bay, she tried to figure out what had happened. She wanted to believe he'd finally realized he cared about her, and with each mile, her hopes grew. Maybe Friday's events had forced him to stop looking at her as a kid sister.

It was after eleven by the time she passed through Morro Bay and found the turnoff marked on the map. The road was deserted, and she drove for almost ten minutes before she saw the mailbox that was her next marker. The steep uphill gravel road was treacherously narrow, with pine and chaparral stretching on both sides. Finally she saw lights.

The cantilevered wedge of concrete and glass seemed to grow from the barren hillside. A dimly lit drive curved up to the house. She parked and stepped out of the car. The wind tossed her hair, and the air smelled of salt and rain.

He must have heard the car because the front door opened just as she reached for the bell, and the light behind him outlined his tall, lean body.

"Flower?"

"Hello, Jake."

Chapter 13

Fleur waited for Jake to invite her in, but he just stood there scowling at her. He wore jeans and an inside-out black sweatshirt with the sleeves chopped off. He looked exhausted. The bones of his face were sharper than ever and he hadn't shaved. But she saw something on his face besides exhaustion, something that reminded her of that first day on the set when she'd watched him beat up Lynn. He looked hard-bitten and mean.

"Can I use the bathroom?" she asked nervously.

For a moment she didn't think he was going to let her in. Finally he gave a tired shrug and stepped aside. "I never argue with fate."

"What?"

"Help yourself."

The interior of the house was like nothing she'd ever seen. Great concrete angles delineated the areas, and ramps took the place of stairs. The glass walls and soaring spaces blurred the boundaries between inside and out. Even its colors were those of the outdoors: the pewter of the ocean, the whites and grays of rock and stone.

"It's beautiful, Jake."

"The bathroom's down that ramp."

She looked at him nervously. Something was very wrong. As she walked in the direction he'd indicated, she spotted a study with a wall of books and an old library table holding a typewriter. Crumpled balls of paper littered the floor. A few had found their way to the bookshelves.

She shut the door and gazed at the biggest bathroom she'd ever seen, a cavern of black and bronze tile with a glass wall and a vast sunken tub that hung over the edge of the cliff. Everything in the room was oversized: the tub, the shower stall sculpted into the wall, even the twin sinks.

She caught sight of herself in the mirror and hated what she saw. The flesh-colored slip made it seem as if she was naked underneath the string knit dress. But then, as she thought about how forbidding Jake looked, she decided the dress wasn't that bad. She definitely didn't look like anybody's kid sister tonight. The Glitter Baby had come to call on Bird Dog Caliber.

When she came out, Jake was sitting in the living room, a glass in his hand filled with something that looked like straight whiskey.

"I thought you only drank beer," she said.

"That's right. Anything else turns me into a bad-tempered drunk."

"Then why—?"

"What are you doing here?"

She stared at him. He didn't know. At that moment, it became horrifyingly clear. He hadn't written the note. Her cheeks burned with embarrassment. How could she have been stupid enough to believe he needed her? She'd seen only what she wanted to. She couldn't think of anything else to do but reach into her purse and hand him the note.

The seconds ticked by as he scanned the pages. Her mind raced. Was this supposed to be some kind of joke? But who would have done such a thing? She immediately thought of Lynn. Her costar was the only person who suspected how Fleur felt about Jake, and Lynn loved to play matchmaker. She'd done this, and Fleur was going to kill her. After she killed herself.

"Frigging door-to-door delivery." Jake crumpled the note and hurled it toward the empty fireplace. "You were set up. That's not my handwriting."

"I've just figured that out." She ran her fingers along the strap of her purse. "It must have been somebody's idea of a joke. Not a good one."

Abruptly he drained his glass. His eyes flicked over the little string dress, lingered on her breasts, then took in her legs. He'd never looked at her like this, as if he'd finally figured out she was a woman. She felt a subtle shift in the balance between them, and her embarrassment began to fade.

"What went wrong on Friday?" he said. "I've met actresses who don't like taking off their clothes, but I've never seen anything like what happened to you."

"Not exactly professional, was I?"

"Let's just say that you blew your chance at a career as a stripper." He headed for a bar made from wood and stone and refilled his whiskey glass. "Tell me about it."

She sat on a couch that jutted from the wall and tucked her foot under her hip. The little string dress rode up on her thighs. He noticed. She watched as he took a deep swig from his glass. "There's nothing much to tell," she said. "I hate it, that's all."

"Taking off your clothes, or life in general?"

"I don't like this business." She took a deep breath. "I don't like acting, and I don't like making films."

"Then why are you doing it?" He propped his arm on the bar. If he'd had a dusty trail hat on his head and a polished brass rail to prop his boot heel on, he would have brought Bird Dog to life. "Never mind. That was a stupid question. Belinda uses you."

She automatically went on the defensive. "Belinda only wants what's best for me, but lives get tangled up together. She can't comprehend that people might be looking for different things from life."

"Do you believe that? Do you really believe she's only thinking about your welfare?"

"Yes, that's what I believe." She wouldn't let anyone but herself criticize her mother. "I know how important the scene with Matt and Lizzie is. I'm really going to try on Monday. If I really try—"

"You weren't trying on Friday? Come off it, kiddo. This is Uncle Jake you're talking to."

She shot up off the couch. "Don't do that! I hate it when you do that. I'm not a child, and you're not my uncle."

Suddenly his eyes narrowed and his jaw set in a hard line. "We needed a woman to play Lizzie. Instead we hired a kid."

His words should have wiped her out. They should have broken her into a million pieces and sent her flying from the house in tears, but they were too outrageous. She stared into that tough face and felt a primitive surge of excitement. He wasn't looking at her as if she was a kid. Beneath those shielded blue eyes, she glimpsed something she'd never seen before, something she could easily identify because she'd been feeling it so long herself. Despite his hostility, Jake wanted her.

Her skin broke out in gooseflesh. In that moment, she understood everything Lizzie understood, and she knew exactly what gave Lizzie her power.

"The only kid in the room," she said softly, "is you."

He didn't like that. "Don't play games with me. I've played them with the best, and believe me, you're still minor league."

He was deliberately trying to hurt her, and she could think of only one reason. So she'd run. She settled back on the couch and slipped her fingers into her hair. "Is that so?"

"Careful, Flower. Don't do anything you're going to regret, especially when you're wearing that dress."

She smiled. "What's wrong with my dress?"

"Don't mess around, okay?"

"How could I mess around?" she said with fake innocence. "I'm minor league, remember?"

His brow furrowed. "I'd better drive you into Morro Bay. There's a nice inn where you can stay."

Sunday Morning Eclipse would finish shooting in two weeks, and she might never see him again. If she needed to prove to him that she was a woman, now was her chance, while she wore this silly string dress with its illusion of flesh and its short hem that showcased the legs he couldn't stop looking at. She saw the desire in his eyes. A man's desire for a woman. She stood and walked over to the window. Her hair swished across her shoulders, the gold hoops skipped at her ears, and the little string dress played peekaboo with her hips. She tugged on one of the hoops and turned to face him, her heart pounding. "You seem jittery. Is there any reason?"

His voice snagged on a rough edge in his throat. "Maybe it's because you're not looking as ugly as usual to me tonight, Flower. I think you'd better go."

She summoned all her cover-girl tricks. She leaned against the glass, angled her hips, and extended her legs. "If you want me to go . . ." She bent one knee just until it opened enough to expose the inner curve of her thigh. " . . . you'll have to make me."

Something inside him seemed to snap. He slapped his glass down on the bar just as he'd done in a dozen films. "You want to play games? Okay, baby. Let's play."

He started coming toward her, and she belatedly remembered this wasn't a movie but her real life. She told herself to get out of his way, but he caught her before she could take a step. Her hips bumped into the window. He curled his hands around her arms. "Come on, kid," he whispered. "Show me what you've got."

His head swooped down, and he closed his mouth over hers. His teeth ground into her bottom lip as he forced her mouth open. She tasted whiskey on his tongue and tried to tell herself this was Jake. His hands slipped under her dress to her panties. He slid them down just far enough to cup her bare buttocks. When he pulled her hard against him, her newfound sense of power evaporated.

He pushed her dress higher, and the fly of his jeans scraped the bare flesh of her stomach. His tongue probed her mouth. He was too fierce. She wanted soft music and beautiful flowers. She wanted sinuous bodies blurred beneath a soft-focus lens, not this raw carnal attack. She pushed against his chest. "Stop."

The harsh sound of his breathing rasped in her ear. "This is what you want, isn't it? You want me to treat you like a woman."

"Like a woman, not a whore." The lover of her daydreams had vanished. She pulled away from him and stumbled toward the front door, desperate to get outside before she burst into tears. But she needed her purse. Her car keys. She turned back to get them in time to see him pick up the telephone.

Her lust-crazed attacker had vanished. He looked tired and sad. She studied him more closely, trying to see him with her head instead of her bruised heart. Suddenly he became as transparent as one of the glass walls in this cantilevered house.

He spoke into the receiver, all business now. "Do you have a suite available for tonight?"

She walked toward him, her keys and purse forgotten.

He fixed his eye on the fireplace so he didn't have to look at her. "Yes. Yes, that'll be fine. No, just one night—"

She took the phone from him and set it back on its cradle.

He wasn't a man who could be easily taken by surprise. He pulled on his hostility like an ill-fitting costume. "Haven't you had enough for tonight?"

She stared him straight in the eye. "No," she said softly. "I want more."

A pulse ticked in his throat. "You don't know what you're doing."

"Nobody's ever accused you of being the world's greatest actor, but even for you, that was a lousy performance." She softly mocked him. "Big bad Bird Dog Caliber trying to scare off the good girl."

He raked his hands through his hair. "Leave it alone. Just leave it alone."

"You're a chicken. No guts."

"I'll drive you to the inn."

"You want me," she said. "I know you do."

His jaw clenched, but he kept his voice even. "After you get a good night's sleep—"

"I want to sleep here."

"I'll pick you up at the inn tomorrow morning and take you to breakfast. How about that?"

She shaped her lips into a model's pout. "Golly, Uncle Jake, it sounds super. Will you buy me a lollipop, too?"

His face darkened. "How much am I supposed to take? What the hell do you want from me?"

"I want you to stop trying to protect me."

"You're a kid, damn it! You need protecting."

"That kid crap is getting old, Jake. Really old."

"Go away, Fleur. Please. For your own good."

She couldn't take one more person telling her what was best for her, especially not Jake. "I'll decide that." She tried not to show her heart in her eyes. "I want you to make love with me."

"Not interested."

"You're a liar."

She saw the exact moment when she won. His head came up, and his lips thinned. "All right then. Let's see what you're made of. " He caught her arm and steered her across the room toward a ramp, not exactly dragging her, but coming close. They went up the slope, through an arch, up another ramp. She wanted to slow down. "Jake . . ."

"Shut up, okay?"

"I want to—"

"I don't."

He led her into the master bedroom, which had the biggest bed she'd ever seen. It rested on a platform directly beneath an enormous skylight. He scooped her in his arms, just like in her daydreams, climbed the two steps, and dropped her in an unceremonious heap on the gray and black satin spread.

"Last chance, Flower," he growled, his expression forbidding. "Before we hit the point of no return."

She refused to move.

"Okay, kiddo." He crossed his arms over his chest and pulled off his sweatshirt. "It's time to play with the big boys."

Her grip tightened on the coverlet. "Jake?"

"Yeah."

"You're making me nervous."

He opened the snap of his jeans. "Tough."

He was still trying to scare her away, and he whipped off his jeans. Seconds later, he stood at the bottom of the bed, clad only in a pair of black briefs. She wished he were wearing friendly white cotton, or something baggy and faded like his swim trunks. She'd seen his chest a dozen times, but never so much of his stomach. It was flat and solid, taut, sculpted muscle. Her gaze dropped to the forbidding vertical shaft the briefs were too small and too tight to conceal.

"You're overdressed."

He wanted her to back off, but she wouldn't. He needed to understand exactly how tough she was.

His hand shackled one of her ankles, and her toughness began to dissolve. He untied her sandal and pulled it off, then did the same with its mate. His eyes lingered on her exposed skin. She pushed herself into the pillows. He was so grim. "I don't want it to be like this," she said.

His eyes touched her breasts, her hips, swept down her legs. "Too bad." He leaned forward and tugged open the tie at the top of her dress.

"I'd rather not—"

He caught her by the shoulders and drew her up into a kneeling position.

She gulped. "I think we should—"

He whipped the little string dress over her head. "I'm sick of playing the good guy around you. From the day we met . . ." He reached for the hem of her slip.

She pushed his hand away. "Not like this. This isn't how I want it to be."

"We're playing by grown-up rules now." He tugged on her slip and pulled it free of her hair. She was kneeling on the bed in nothing but panties and her swaying gold hoops.

"Now I can see all those parts of you I had to pretend not to look at on Friday."

"I know what you're trying to do, and I won't let you. I won't let you make this *bad* for me."

His voice was tight and hard. "I don't know what you're talking about."

She curled her hands at her sides. "You're trying to ruin this. You want to keep this from being *important*."

"It's isn't important." The mattress sagged under his weight. He covered her body with his own, and reached beneath them to tug off her panties. "It's fun. That's all." His fingers found her, their touch almost clinical. "Do you like the way this feels?"

"Stop it."

"How do you want it? Fast? Slow? Tell me how you want it, babe."

"I want flowers," she whispered. "I wanted you to touch my body with flowers."

A shudder passed through him. He rolled away from her with a muffled curse and lay on his back staring up at the night through the skylight. She didn't understand him at all.

"Why do you want to hurt me?" she asked.

He reached out and touched her hand. "If I were a better man . . . But I'm not." He turned toward her and gently traced the curve of her shoulder with his fingers. "All right, baby," he whispered. "No more games. Let's do it right."

His mouth found hers in a soft, tender kiss that melted the great chill inside her. It wasn't anything like their kisses on camera. Their noses bumped. He opened his mouth and closed it over hers, the sound sweet and sloppy. His tongue slipped past the barrier of her teeth, where she touched it with her own. It was wet and rough and perfect. She wrapped her arms around his shoulders and pulled him so close she could feel his heartbeat with her breast.

Finally he drew back. His fingers played in her hair, and his eyes gazed gently down at her. "I don't have any flowers," he whispered, "so I'll have to touch you with something else." He dipped his head and caught her nipple in his mouth. It swelled beneath his tongue, and she moaned as waves of pleasure washed through her.

Like a lazy cowboy with all the time in the world, he roamed her body with his hands. His kisses trailed over her stomach while he stroked her thighs, setting fires in all the empty spaces inside her. Then he drew up her knees and gently pushed them apart.

Moonlight washing through the skylight painted silvery shadows on his back. His fingers played at the tight web of curls. Gently he opened her. "Flower petals," he whispered. "I found them." And then he covered her with his soft, sulky mouth.

The feeling was like nothing she'd ever imagined. She called his name, but whether out loud or only in her mind, she didn't know. Spirals of pleasure whirled inside her, throwing off sparkling pinwheels that glowed brighter and hotter, ready to explode. "No . . ."

Her strangled cry made him look up, but she couldn't think how to tell him that she didn't want to go on this flight by herself. He smiled and slid his body beside hers. "Give up?" he murmured, his voice sexy, teasing, and absolutely irresistible.

She felt the strong outline of him against her thigh and slipped her hand beneath the waistband of his briefs. He was smooth and hard as a shaft of marble, and he let out a soft gasp as her fingers closed around him.

"What's the matter, cowboy?" she whispered. "Can't you take it?"

His breathing came in soft, sudden gasps. "Doesn't . . . affect me . . . one way or the other."

She laughed and eased herself up to see him better. Her hair brushed his chest. She peeled his briefs off and experimented with the power of her touch. Here . . . there . . . here again. She stroked with the end of her finger, the pad of her thumb, a lock of her hair. Finally she touched him with the tip of her tongue.

His cry was hoarse and deep.

She licked him like a cat as a deep, fierce joy at the power she possessed swelled inside her. His hands settled around her shoulders, and he pulled her to his chest.

"I give up," he said hoarsely, nibbling at her bottom lip.

"Quitter," she murmured.

His fingers went to her breast and squeezed her nipple. "Looks like I'm going to have to remind you who's the boss."

"Good luck with that." She touched his crooked tooth with the tip of her tongue.

"The lady's a slow learner." He covered her with the lean length of his body. "Open up, baby. You're about to meet your master."

She opened for him gladly, burning to receive him. To love him. She laughed up into smoky-blue eyes that were bright with desire.

Jake heard the sweet, soft woman's sound coming from deep in her throat, and it seared the edges of his soul. Gazing into her eyes, he wordlessly begged her to hold something back, but she smiled all her love up at him, and the softness in her face sliced him in two. He pushed himself deep within her. He hadn't expected her to be so tight. He hadn't expected . . .

She let out a small cry. "Finally . . ." she whispered.

It could have meant anything, but he felt the bottom drop out of his stomach. "Flower . . . My God . . ." He began to pull away, but she dug her fingers into his buttocks.

"No," she cried. "If you do, I'll never forgive you."

He wanted to throw back his head and howl over his stupidity. Despite Belinda's lies and Fleur's own false boasts, he should have known she was a virgin. He should have scared her away as he'd intended to, but corruption of the innocent was his specialty, and he'd been too damned selfish.

He felt her chorus-girl legs wind around his own, felt her pulling him more deeply inside, even though it had to hurt her. He couldn't find the strength to hurt her more by drawing away. Summoning all his will, he held himself still, giving her time to grow accustomed to his size. "I'm sorry, Flower. I didn't know."

She moved her hips, trying to draw him tighter.

He stroked her hair, played at her lips. "Give it a minute," he whispered.

"I'm okay."

He wondered how he could stay so hard inside her. Jake Koranda, king of the shit heads. Still hard as a pike. Sticking it to the kid with the big eyes.

He buried his head in her neck and tangled his fingers in her hair and began moving gently inside her. She shuddered. Her fingers dug into his shoulders.

He stopped at once. "Hurt?"

"No," she gasped. "Please—"

He drew back so he could see her face. Her eyes were squeezed shut, her lips parted, not with pain, but with passion. He lifted his hips and stroked, deep and long inside her. Once . . . twice . . . He watched her shatter beneath him.

He calmed her through the aftershocks. Finally her eyes drifted open, unfocused, and then gradually clearing. She murmured something he couldn't make out, then she smiled up at him. "Wonderful," she whispered.

He couldn't hold back his smile. "Glad you were pleased."

"I didn't imagine it would be quite so—so—"

"Boring?"

She laughed.

"Tedious?" he suggested.

"Not exactly the words I'm looking for."

"How about—"

"Stupendous," she offered. "Colossal."

"Flower?"

"Yes?"

"I don't know if you've noticed, but we're not exactly done yet."

"We're not—" Her eyes suddenly widened. "Oh."

He watched as her comprehension changed to embarrassment. "I—I'm sorry," she said with a stutter. "I didn't mean to be a pig or anything. I didn't know—I mean . . ." Her voice trailed miserably away.

He tugged on her earlobe with his lips. "You can doze off now if you want to," he whispered. "Read a book or something. I'll try not to bother you." Once again he began to move inside her. He felt her body relax and then gradually grow tense again. Her fingers dug into his sides. She was so soft and good, so sweet . . .

"Oh," she whispered. "It's going to happen again, isn't it?"

"You can bet on it."

Moments later, they fell off the end of the world together.

Chapter 14

“You’re not talking me out of being pissed.”

“Stuff it, Bird Dog.” Fleur had awakened a little after two in the morning to discover she was alone in bed. She’d slipped on her panties and Jake’s black sweatshirt with the sawed-off sleeves, then headed for the kitchen, where she found him devouring a serving bowl piled with ice cream. He started to go at her the minute he saw her, and they’d been arguing ever since.

“You should have told me before we did it.” He dropped his dish in the sink and pulled on the faucet.

“Did it? You’ve got a real gift for self-expression. You should be a writer when you grow up. That would be, what? When you’re fifty?”

“Don’t be such a wise-ass. It wasn’t right, Flower, not telling me you were a . . . newcomer.”

She smiled sweetly. “Afraid I wouldn’t respect you in the morning?” She was getting good at matching him wisecrack for wisecrack, but she wished he’d stop arguing and kiss her. She began opening drawers at random, looking for a rubber band.

“Damn, it, Flower! I wouldn’t have been so rough.”

“That was rough? You’ve got to be kidding. I could

take you with my eyes closed." She found a rubber band and pulled her hair into a ponytail high on her head. Then she walked into the living room and scooped up a batch of chunky candles she'd seen on the table.

He followed her in as if she were a kid who needed watching. "What are you doing?"

"Getting ready to take a bath."

"It's almost three in the morning."

"So what? I'm stinky."

For the first time since she'd walked into the kitchen, he relaxed. "Yeah? Why is that?" He almost managed the cocky grin that made her want to slap him and kiss him at the same time.

"You're the expert. You tell me." His sweatshirt didn't completely cover her panties, and she twitched her rear as she walked away from him.

She set the candles around the edge of the sunken tub, lit them, and poured in a generous amount of bubble bath from a bottle sitting on the side. Somehow she didn't think it was Jake's. She hated every single woman he'd ever dated.

While the tub filled, she twisted her ponytail into a loose knot and secured it with a clip she found in the makeup pouch she kept in her purse. No matter what Jake said, she didn't regret what had happened between them. So much of her life had been forced upon her. This choice had been hers alone. And when he'd been inside her, she'd felt as if her heart would burst with the enormity of her love for him.

She slipped into the water. The candles flickered in the wall of glass suspended over the side of the cliff, and she felt like she was floating in space. She remembered that sweet moment when he'd entered her and his tenderness afterward.

"Is this a private party, or can anybody join?"

He was already unzipping his jeans, so the question was rhetorical. "Depends on whether you're done with your lecture."

"Lecture's over." He muttered something as he stepped into the tub and eased down beside her.

"What did you say?"

"Nothing."

"Tell me."

"All right. I said I was sorry."

She pushed herself up on her elbows. "Sorry for what? Exactly what are you sorry for?"

He must have heard the unsteadiness in her voice because he pulled her into his arms. "Nothing, babe. I'm not sorry for a damned thing except being so rough on you."

And then he was kissing her and she was kissing him back, and her hair came undone and neither of them noticed. They wrapped their legs and arms together, fell back in the bubbles, and Fleur twisted her hair around them both. Jake pulled the plug so they could breathe, then began loving her in that delicious way that made her cry out again and again until he stilled her with his kisses.

Afterward he wrapped her in a towel. "Now that you've worn me out," he said, "how about feeding me? I'm a lousy cook, and I haven't had anything but ice cream and potato chips since I got here."

"Don't look at me. I'm a rich kid, remember."

He fastened a matching towel around his hips. "Are you telling me you don't know how to cook?"

"I might remember how to hard-boil an egg."

"Even I can do better than that."

For the next hour, they made a mess of the kitchen. They grilled steaks that didn't have the decency to thaw in the middle, incinerated a loaf of French bread under the broiler, and fixed a salad from a head of browning lettuce and some limp carrots. It was the best meal Fleur had ever eaten.

*

They planned to go for a run on Sunday morning but went back to bed instead and made love all over again. In the afternoon they played cards and told terrible jokes and took another erotic bath. Jake woke her just before dawn on Monday morning for the trip back to Los Angeles. Since they both had cars, they had to drive separately. He kissed her after she got in the Porsche. "Don't straighten out any curves, okay?"

"You, either."

She'd called Belinda the day before and guiltily repeated her lie about Lynn needing her. Now she drove straight to the studio.

When she came out from hair and makeup, Jake and Johnny Guy were already arguing, this time about the revision Jake hadn't finished that weekend. Jake gave her an impersonal nod. She hated the idea of everyone gossiping about them, and she told herself she appreciated his discretion. Still, she felt just a little disappointed.

Johnny Guy came over. "Now, honey, I know Friday was a little hard on you, but we'll try to make things easier today. I've made some changes—"

"I don't need any changes," Fleur heard herself say. "Let's do it right."

He looked at her doubtfully. She gave him a cocky thumbs-up, as if she were a fighter pilot about to take off on a dawn patrol. She could do this. And this time she wouldn't let Jake forget that he was looking at a woman, not a kid.

Jake reappeared in costume. As Johnny Guy began outlining the scene, Jake interrupted. "I thought we decided to cut most of this. We already know she can't handle it. Let's not waste any more time."

Johnny Guy didn't let her respond. "The little lady says she wants to give it a try." He turned toward the crew. "Showtime, boys and girls. Let's get to work."

The cameras rolled. Jake glowered at her from across the tiny bedroom. She grinned at him, her hands going to her buttons. He was too cocky, and she was going to show him. She stepped out of the dress without taking her eyes from his. They had secrets now, the two of them. He was funny and maddening and dear, and she loved him with all her heart. He had to feel the same—at least a little bit—or he could never have made such sweet love to her.

Please love me. Just a little.

She unfastened her bra. Jake scowled and stepped off his mark. "Cut it!"

"Goddamn it, Jako, I'm the one who calls 'cut'! She was doing great. What's wrong with you?" Johnny Guy slapped his leg. "Nobody calls 'cut' except me! Nobody!" The tirade went on, and Jake grew more sullen. Finally he complained that a chair had been moved out of position. Johnny Guy nearly hit him.

"It's okay," she said to the director, feeling very much like a woman in control. "I'm ready to go again."

The cameras rolled. Jake's face was a thundercloud. The bra came off. She unfastened it slowly, tantalizing him, torturing him with her delicious, newfound power. Bending over, she pulled off her panties and walked over to him.

His body was rigid as she unbuttoned his shirt and slipped her hands inside. She touched the spot she'd kissed just that morning. She pushed her hips against his, and then did something that hadn't been rehearsed. She leaned forward and flicked her tongue over one of his nipples.

"Cut and print!" Johnny Guy yelled, jumping around like a jubilant jack-in-the-box. "Beautiful, honey lamb! Just beautiful!"

Jake scowled, grabbed the white terry-cloth robe from the wardrobe girl, and shoved Fleur into it.

During a break, she sought out Lynn. Since she didn't want her to know she'd gone to Jake's house, she couldn't come out and ask her directly if she'd sent the note, so she had to poke around. But Lynn refused to take the bait. Sooner or later, Fleur vowed, she'd weasel the truth out of her.

Things went well for the rest of the morning, and by late afternoon they'd reshot all the material from Friday and begun shooting the two of them in bed. Johnny Guy captured everything—Matt's tension, his guilt, the anguish simmering just beneath the surface . . . and Lizzie's relentless seduction. Jake barely talked to her unless the cameras were rolling, but it was an intense scene, and they both needed to stay focused.

As soon as they wrapped for the day, he disappeared. Neither of them had gotten much sleep for the past two nights, and she told herself he was tired. But as the next few days passed and he continued to keep his distance, she ran out of comforting excuses. He was avoiding her.

The weekend came and went, and her hopes that he'd call her turned to misery. Monday morning arrived, and she thought about forcing a confrontation, but she was too afraid she'd end up begging him to love her, and she couldn't bear that. Jake was telling her loud and clear not to place any significance on what had happened between them in Morro Bay.

Instead of days, she began counting the hours until she was done. Thursday was her last day on the set. She moved mechanically through her scene with Lynn, did some close-ups, and went home in despair.

"Did Jake say anything to you about Johnny Guy's party this weekend?" Belinda asked over dinner that evening. "Surely he's planning to attend."

"I don't know. We didn't talk about it." Fleur would never talk to Belinda about her feelings for Jake, and she excused herself from the table.

Johnny Guy's wife, Marcella, was one of Hollywood's favorite hostesses, and she'd invited everyone who was anyone to the party she was throwing to celebrate the completion of *Sunday Morning Eclipse.* Fleur was a slow learner. Right up until the last minute, she'd entertained the frail hope that Jake would ask her to go with him. Instead she ended up going with Belinda.

Marcella had filled the Kellys' Brentwood home with flowers, candles, and music. Fleur knew the only way she could get through the night with any kind of dignity was by playing the Glitter Baby, and she wore an ecru silk gown with shimmering horizontal stripes of mocha, beige, and terra-cotta. The tubular dress had a subtle Egyptian feeling that she'd emphasized with matching gold cuff bracelets and flat sandals that had a jeweled clasp at the instep. She'd braided her hair wet and brushed it out after it had dried so it fell down her back in a cascade of tiny waves. Marcella Kelly told her she looked like a blond Cleopatra.

Marcella was as sophisticated as Johnny Guy was homespun. While he walked around with a can of Orange Crush and a Cuban cigar, she encouraged her guest to try the hors d'oeuvres—salmon cured in tequila, canapés decorated with edible cactus leaves, and tiny beignets stuffed with hydroponically grown vegetables.

Fleur studied the crowd over the top of Dick Spano's head, but Jake was nowhere to be seen. Belinda had wedged Kirk Douglas into a corner. The actor, who had a slightly bemused expression, was undoubtedly being bombarded with the history of every film he'd made, some of which he'd probably just as soon forget. Fleur sipped her drink and pretended to listen to the male rising star who'd popped up at her side. Outside, she heard a clap of thunder. Then the crowd shifted, and she spotted Jake.

He'd arrived with Lynn and the documentary filmmaker who was Lynn's latest lover. Fleur's heart constricted. Marcella Kelly swooped down on him and began leading him through her guests, a prize catch put on display. Fleur couldn't endure it. She excused herself from the rising star and locked herself in the bathroom, where she leaned back against the door and told herself—no matter what—she'd hold on to her pride tonight. He was going to remember her dressed like Cleopatra with a Hollywood heartthrob dancing attendance at her side.

Finally she made herself leave the bathroom and slip

back into the crowd. Rain had begun tapping on the mullioned windows. She looked around and saw that Jake had disappeared. Moments later, she realized Belinda was nowhere to be seen, either.

It could have been coincidence, but she knew her mother too well, and she immediately felt uneasy. *I only do what's best for you, baby.* What if Belinda had figured out how Fleur felt and decided to interfere? Just the thought of it made Fleur shudder.

She began to search for her, weaving through the guests as she moved from room to room while an invisible conversation played out in her head. *Just give her a chance, Jake, and I know you'll fall in love with her the same way she's fallen for you. The two of you are a perfect match.*

Fleur would never forgive her.

When her downstairs search came up empty, she slipped upstairs, and though she managed an embarrassing intrusion on Lynn and her lover, she couldn't find her mother. Just as she was getting ready to return downstairs, however, she heard noises coming from Marcella Kelly's bedroom. She peeked in.

"There's nothing more to talk about. Let's go back to the party."

It was Jake's voice. With her heart in her throat, Fleur slipped into the bedroom.

"Two more minutes for old time's sake," Belinda said. "Remember how much fun we had together in that awful motel in Iowa? I'll never forget that morning."

The intimate note in Belinda's voice caught Fleur by surprise. As she took another step into the room, their reflections jumped out at her from a floor-length antique mirror, Belinda in shrimp-pink Karl Lagerfeld and Jake wearing a jacket that looked almost respectable. They stood in some kind of dressing alcove. He crossed his arms over his chest. Belinda reached out and touched him. The soft, terrible expression on her face made Fleur's mouth go dry.

"It must be your mission in life to break the hearts of the Savagar women," she said. "I understand a rebel spirit, and I knew from the beginning that I wasn't special enough for you. But Fleur is. Don't you see that? The two of you belong together, and you're breaking her heart."

Fleur dug her fingernails into her palms.

Jake pulled away from her. "Don't do this."

"I sent her to you!" she exclaimed. "I sent her to you, and now you're violating my trust."

"Trust! You sent her to me to save five minutes of film that you didn't want to end up on the cutting room floor. Five minutes of your precious Glitter Baby's career. Fuck my daughter, Koranda, so Baby can save her career. That's what you told me."

Fleur's stomach pitched.

"Don't be so sanctimonious," Belinda hissed. "I saved your picture."

"The picture wasn't in that much danger."

"That's not how it looked to me. I did what I had to."

"Yeah, right. You dropped your daughter on my doorstep for Mommy's magic bedroom cure. Tell me something, Belinda. Is this going to be the pattern with you? Trying out your daughter's lovers first? Auditioning them to make sure they meet your standards before you let them into Baby's bed?"

The room reeled around her.

Jake's contempt scorched the air. "What the hell kind of woman are you?"

"I'm a woman who loves her daughter."

"Bullshit. You don't even know your daughter. The only person you love is yourself." He spun around and came face-to-face with Fleur's reflection in the mirror.

Fleur couldn't move. The pain in her chest twisted like some terrible beast, stealing her breath and turning the world black and ugly.

Jake was beside her in an instant. "Flower . . ."

Belinda let out a soft sharp gasp. "Oh my God. My

baby." She ran to Fleur and grabbed her arms. "It's all right, baby."

Tears rolled down Fleur's cheeks. She pushed them away and stepped backward—jerky and awkward, trying to escape the awful beast clawing at her. "Don't touch me. Don't either of you touch me!"

Belinda's face twisted. "Baby . . . Let me explain. I had to help you. I had to . . . Don't you see? You could have ruined it for us—your career, all our plans, our dreams. You're a celebrity now. The rules are different for you. Don't you see that?"

"Shut up!" Fleur cried. "You're filthy. Both of you."

"Please, baby . . ."

Fleur drew back her hand and slapped her mother as hard as she could. Belinda cried out and stumbled backward.

"Fleur!" Jake rushed toward her.

She clenched her teeth and let out the snarl of a feral animal. "Stay away!"

"Listen to me, Fleur." He reached for her, and she went wild, swinging at him, screaming at him, kicking him, killing him . . . Oh God, kill him. He tried to catch her arms, but she broke away and ran from the room, down the stairs. Dozens of startled faces stared at her as she raced through the foyer and out the door.

A driving downpour lashed at her. She wished it were ice, hard slivers of ice that would cut her up and slice her into tiny pieces of flesh and bone small enough to be washed away. She pulled up her wet skirt and raced down the curved driveway. The straps of the sandals bit into her feet and the soles slid on the wet blacktop, but she didn't slow down. She cut across the grass and ran for the gates.

She heard him behind her, calling her name over the rain, and she ran faster. Her hair stuck to her cheeks. He cursed, and the sound of pounding feet grew louder. He caught her by the shoulder and threw her off balance. She tripped on the wet silk, and they fell together, just as they had that very first time in front of the farmhouse.

"Stop it, Flower. Please, stop." He pulled her to him and held her tight there on the rain-soaked ground. His fingers tangled in her wet hair, and his breathing was rough and uneven. "You can't go off like this. Let me take you home. Let me explain."

She'd believed he'd wanted her that night. The little oatmeal string dress and the flesh-colored slip and the shining gold hoops that had swung from her ears . . . All of it had been chosen by Belinda. Her mother had sent her to him in costume. "Get your hands off me!"

He tightened his grip and turned her so she was facing him. His jacket was soaked and mud-streaked. Rivulets of rainwater ran down the slopes of his face. "Listen to me. What you heard wasn't the whole story."

She barred her teeth. "Were you my mother's lover?"

"No . . ." He dragged his thumbs over her cheeks. "She came to my room, but I stopped. I didn't—"

"*She* wrote that note! She sent me to you so you could make love to me!"

"Yes. But what happened that night was only between you and me."

"*You shit!*" She swung at him with her fist. "Don't try to tell me you took me to bed because you fell in love with me!"

He caught her wrists. "Flower, there are different kinds of love. I care about you. I—"

"Shut up!" She tried to punch him again. "*I loved you!* I loved you with every part of me, and I don't want to hear any of your shit. Let me go!"

Slowly his grip eased, and he released her. She stumbled to her feet. Her wet hair hung over her face, and her words came out in little gusts. "If you really want to help me . . . get Lynn. And then . . . keep Belinda away from me. For an hour. Keep her away . . . for an hour."

"Flower . . ."

"Do it, you bastard. I deserve that much."

They stood in the rain, their chests heaving, rain dripping from their hair. He nodded and turned back to the house.

Lynn drove Fleur home without asking questions. She didn't want to leave her alone, but Fleur insisted she was going right to bed. As soon as Lynn drove off, however, Fleur threw some clothes into her largest suitcase, tore off her ruined dress, and stuffed her legs into jeans. Jake and Belinda had plotted over her, used her . . . And she'd made it so easy. She wondered if they'd talked about her when they were in bed together. Jake had said it hadn't gone all the way, but it had gone far enough, and her stomach roiled.

She closed the suitcase, called the airline, and booked herself on the next flight to Paris. Only one more thing to do before she left . . .

By the time Jake let Belinda go, she was frantic. Her panic swelled when she reached the house and saw that the Porsche was gone. She ran to Fleur's room and found the bed littered with discarded clothing. The wet Egyptian dress lay on the floor. She picked it up and pressed it to her cheek. Of course Fleur was upset, but she'd be back. She needed a little time to calm down, that was all. Belinda and Fleur were inseparable; everybody knew that. More than mother and daughter. They were best friends.

Belinda noticed the light in the bathroom. With the ruined dress still in her hands, she went over to turn it off.

She spotted the scissors first, gleaming against the white basin, and then she let out a soft, anguished cry. A great mound of wet blond hair littered the floor.

Jake drove aimlessly, trying not to think, but the icy lump wouldn't dissolve in his chest. The day they'd passed out strength of character, he'd been at the goddamned end of the line. When Fleur had shown up at his door, he should have scared her away like he wanted to. But he hadn't been able to resist her.

He left the suburbs behind, and soon he was driving through the wet, deserted streets that made up the heart of L.A. He shrugged out of his ruined jacket and drove in his shirtsleeves. She'd been beautiful. Sensuous, exciting . . . He'd hurt her that first time, but she'd still held on to him, still kept right on trusting him.

The playground was at the end of a street littered with trash and broken dreams. The jungle gym had lost its horizontal bars, and the swing set had no swings. A single floodlight shone over a backboard holding a rusted rim and the fragments of what once had been a net. He parked his car and reached in the back for his basketball. Only a kid would be dumb enough to trust as she did. A kid who hadn't been knocked around enough by life to smarten up.

But she sure as hell had been knocked around now. He stepped through a muddy pothole on his way across the street to the empty playground. She'd been so knocked around, she'd never be dumb again.

He reached the cracked asphalt and began to dribble the ball. It hit the asphalt, slapped his hand, felt good, like something he understood. He didn't want to remember her lying in his bathtub encircled by candles. Beautiful, wet, dreamy-eyed. He didn't want to think about what he'd done to her.

He drove for the basket and slammed the ball home. The rim quivered and his hand stung, but the crowd began to roar. He had to pull out all the stops—show the crowd his stuff—make them scream so loud he couldn't hear anything else, especially not the taunting voices inside him.

He spun past an opponent and took the ball to center court. He faked to the right, to the left, then came off the dribble for a quick jump shot. The crowd went wild, screaming out for him. *Doc! Doc! Doc!*

He grabbed the ball and spotted Kareem just ahead waiting for him, a cold killing machine. Kareem, superhuman, the face of his nightmares. Fake him. He started to swing left, but Kareem was a machine who read minds. Quick, before he sees it in your eyes, before he feels it through his pores, before he knows all your darkest secrets. Now.

He wheeled to the right lightning fast, jumped, flew through the air . . . Man can't fly, but I can. . . . Past Kareem . . . into the stratosphere . . . SLAM!

Doc! They were on their feet. *Doc!* They screamed.

Kareem looked at him, and they silently acknowledged each other with the perfect respect that passed between legends. Then the moment was gone and they were enemies again.

The ball was alive beneath his fingertips. He thought only of the ball. It was a perfect world. A world where a man could walk like a giant and never feel shame. A world with referees who clearly signaled right and wrong. A world without tender babies and broken hearts.

Jake Koranda. Actor. Playwright. Winner of the Pulitzer Prize. He wanted to give it all up and live his fantasy. He wanted to be Julius Erving running down the court on feet with wings, leaping into the clouds, flying higher, farther, freer than any man. Slamming the ball to glory. *Yes.*

The screams of the crowd faded, and he stood alone in a pool of rusty light exactly at the end of nowhere.

Baby on the Run

Chapter 15

Fleur tried to sleep on the plane to Paris, but every time she shut her eyes, she heard Jake and Belinda. *Fuck my daughter, Koranda, so she can save her career.*

"Mademoiselle Savagar?" A liveried chauffeur approached her as she stood by the baggage carousel at Orly. "Your father is waiting for you."

She followed the chauffeur through the crowded terminal to a limousine parked at the curb. He held the door open for her, and she slipped inside, into Alexi's arms. "*Papa.*"

He pulled her close. "So, *chérie*, you have finally decided to come home to me."

She buried her face in the expensive fabric of his suit coat and began to cry. "It's been so awful. I've been so stupid."

"There, there, *enfant*. Rest now. Everything will be fine."

He began to stroke her, and it felt so comforting that she closed her eyes.

When they reached the house, Alexi helped her to her room. She asked him to sit by her side until she fell asleep, and he did.

It was late when she awakened the next morning. A maid served her coffee in the dining room along with two croissants, which she pushed away. She couldn't imagine ever putting food into her mouth again.

Alexi came in, leaned over, and kissed her cheek. He frowned as he noticed the jeans and pullover she'd slipped into after her shower. "Did you bring no other clothes with you, *chérie*? We will have to get you some today."

"I have other things. I just didn't have the energy to put them on." She could see that he was displeased, and she wished she'd made an effort to look better.

He surveyed her critically. "How could you do such a thing to your hair? You look like a boy."

"It was a good-bye present for my mother."

"I see. Then we will have it taken care of today."

He gestured for the maid to pour him coffee, then pulled a cigarette from the silver case he carried in the breast pocket of his suit coat. "Tell me what happened."

"Has Belinda called you?"

"Several times. She's quite frantic. I told her you were on your way to the Greek islands, but you wouldn't tell me which one. I also told her to leave you alone."

"Which means she's on her way to Greece."

"*Naturellement*."

They were silent for a moment and then Alexi asked, "Does all this have anything to do with a certain actor?"

"How did you know?"

"I make it my business to know everything that affects those who belong to me."

She looked down into her coffee, trying to hide the fact that her eyes were once again filling with tears. She was tired of crying, tired of the wrenching pain inside her. "I fell in love with him," she said. "We went to bed together."

"Inevitable."

She couldn't contain her bitterness. "My mother had been there first."

Two narrow ribbons of smoke curled from Alexi's nostrils. "Also inevitable, I'm afraid. Your mother is a woman of little willpower where movie stars are concerned."

"They struck a deal."

"Suppose you tell me."

Alexi listened as Fleur repeated the conversation she'd overheard between Jake and Belinda. When she was done, he said, "Your mother's motivations seem clear, but what about your lover's?"

She flinched at his choice of words. "His motivations were crystal-clear. This movie meant everything to him. The love scene had to work. When I froze, he saw the whole project bombing."

"Unfortunate, *chérie*, that you didn't make a better choice for your first lover."

"Obviously I'm not the world's best judge of character."

He leaned back in his chair and crossed his legs. On another man the gesture would have looked effeminate, but Alexi made it elegantly masculine. "You are planning to stay with me for some time, I hope. I think it would be best for you."

"For a while anyway. Until I can get my bearings. That is, if you'll have me."

"I've waited for this longer than you can imagine, *chérie*. It would be my pleasure." He stood. "There's something I want to show you. I've been feeling a bit like a child waiting for Christmas."

"What is it?"

"You'll see." She followed him through the house and across the gardens toward the museum. He put the key in the lock and turned it. "Close your eyes."

She did as he asked. He led her through the doorway into the cool, faintly musty interior of the museum. She remembered the last time she'd been here, the day she'd met her brother. She didn't know whether her father had ever found Michel. She should have asked, but she hadn't.

"This has been a fortunate time for me," Alexi said. "I'm seeing all my dreams fulfilled." She heard him flick a switch. "Open your eyes."

The museum was dark except for a pair of spotlights in

the center. They shone down on the platform that had been empty the last time she was there. Now it held the most magnificent automobile she'd ever seen. It was gleaming black, exquisitely balanced, with an endlessly long hood that looked like a cartoon of a millionaire's car. She would have recognized it anywhere, and she let out a soft exclamation. "It's the Royale. You found it!"

"I had not seen it since 1940." He repeated the story he'd told her so many times. "There were three of us, *chérie*. We drove it deep into the sewers of Paris and wrapped it in canvas and straw. All through the war, I didn't go near it for fear I'd be followed. Then, when I went back after the Liberation, the car was gone. The other two men who knew about it were killed in North Africa. I think now that the Germans found it. It has taken me more than thirty years to locate it."

"But how? What happened?"

"Decades of inquiries, money applied in proper and improper places." He flicked a handkerchief from his breast pocket and wiped an invisible fleck of dust from the fender. "All that matters is that I now own the most important collection of *pur sang* Bugattis in the world, and the Royale is the crown jewel."

Much later, after he'd shown her every feature on the Bugatti, she went to her room where a hairdresser was waiting. The man asked no questions but cut Fleur's hair close to her head and told her he could do no more until it grew. She looked horrible, like a prisoner—big eyes smudged with dark circles, oversized head, no hair. Still, her ugly reflection gave her a perverse sense of pleasure. Now her exterior matched the way she felt inside.

Alexi frowned when he saw her and sent her back to her room to put on makeup, but it didn't help much. They went for a walk around the grounds and talked about what they would do when she felt better. She took a nap in the afternoon. At dinner, she picked at breast of veal then went to Alexi's study to listen to Sibelius. He held her hand, and as the music washed over her, some of the painful knots inside her began to loosen. She'd been stupid to let Belinda keep her apart from her father these past few years, but she'd always let her mother manipulate her. She'd been afraid to rebel in even the smallest way for fear she'd lose Belinda's love. A love she knew now that she'd never really had.

She leaned her head against Alexi's shoulder and shut her eyes. She could no longer work up any real anger against him. In her pain, she'd finally found forgiveness. He was the only person in her life with nothing to gain by loving her.

That night she couldn't sleep. She found an old bottle of Belinda's sleeping pills, swallowed two capsules, and slumped down on the edge of her bed. The worst part was losing her self-respect. She'd let Belinda lead her around by the nose. She'd panted like a puppy dog as she followed her mother's every wish. *Love me, Mommy. Don't leave me, Mommy.* And then there was Jake. She'd built stupid fantasies around him and tried to make herself believe he loved her back. She concentrated on her pain, picking at it like a scab.

"Are you ill, *chérie*?"

Alexi stood knotting the sash of his robe in the doorway. She'd never seen him mussed. His thin steel-gray hair was as neat as if he'd just come from his barber. "No, not ill."

"You look like a young boy with your awful mangled hair. *Pauvre enfant*. Get in bed, now."

He tucked her in as if she were a child. "*Je t'aime, Papa*," she said softly, squeezing his hand where it lay on top of the covers.

He brushed his lips over hers. They were dry and unexpectedly rough. "Turn over. I will rub your back and help you fall asleep."

She did as she was told. It felt good. His hands slid under her shirt, and as he massaged her skin, her tension eased.

The sleeping pill did its work, and she drifted into a dream of Jake. Jake making love to her. Jake kissing her neck and touching her through the silky fabric of her underpants.

After the first few days in Paris, Fleur's life began to settle into a semblance of routine. She got up late, then listened to music or thumbed through a magazine. In the afternoon she napped until one of the maids awakened her in time to shower and dress before Alexi came home. Sometimes they walked the grounds together, but walking made her tired, and they didn't go far. It was hard for her to sleep at night, so Alexi rubbed her back.

She knew she had to stop moping, and she tried to make plans, but she couldn't go back to the States right away. Looking the way she did, it was doubtful anyone would recognize her, but if that happened, she'd have to face reporters, which was impossible.

August turned into September. Belinda kept calling, and Alexi kept putting her off. He told her Fleur must have changed her mind about Greece and said the detectives he'd hired thought she might be in the Bahamas. He lectured Belinda on her failure as a mother and made her cry.

Fleur started thinking of Greece. She'd always loved the islands. She could buy a house there, and a horse, too. The islands would heal her heartbreak. She told Alexi she wanted to tap into some of the money he'd been handling for her, but he said it was tied up in long-term investments. She told him to untie it. He said she should understand it wasn't so simple and that she shouldn't worry about money. He'd buy her anything she wanted. She told him she wanted a house on the Aegean and a horse. He said they'd talk about it when she felt better.

The conversation made her uneasy. It had been so simple to let Alexi take care of everything. The bills were always paid, and she and Belinda had as much money as they needed.

She tried to force herself to exercise. One day, she made it through the gates and out onto the Rue de la Bienfaisance. A runner with a bright orange headband whipped by. She couldn't remember what it felt like to have so much energy, and she returned to the house.

That night, she woke up with her nightgown soaked with perspiration. She'd dreamed about Jake again. She was back at the gates of the Couvent de l'Annonciation watching him drive away. She went into her bathroom to get a sleeping pill, but the container was empty. She'd taken the last one two nights ago. She headed for Belinda's room to see if she could find more. On her way, she saw a dim light at the end of the corridor. It came from the steps leading to the attic. Curious, she climbed to the top and entered the strangest room she'd ever seen.

The ceiling had been painted blue with fluffy white clouds racing across it. A bedraggled parachute, collapsed on one side, hung over the narrow iron bed. Alexi sat in a straight-backed wooden chair, his shoulders slumped, staring into an empty glass. Belinda had told her Michel used to stay in the attic. This had been his room.

"Alexi?"

"Leave me alone. Get out of here."

She'd been so wrapped up in her own pain that she hadn't thought about her father's. She knelt beside his chair. She'd never known him to drink too much, but now he smelled of liquor. "You miss him, don't you?" she asked softly.

"You know nothing about it."

"I know about missing people. I know what it's like to miss someone you love."

He lifted his head, and his cold, empty eyes frightened her. "Your sentiment is touching, but unnecessary. Michel is a weakling, and I have cut him out of my life."

Like me, she thought. *Like you once cut me out.* "Then what are you doing in his room?"

"I've had too much to drink, and I'm indulging myself. You of all people should understand that."

She was hurt. "You think I indulge myself?"

"Of course you do. The way you put Belinda on a pedestal. The way you've made me over in your mind into the father you always wanted."

She felt a chill. She stood and rubbed her arms. "I haven't had to make you over. These last few years, you've been wonderful to me."

"I've been exactly what I knew you wanted me to be."

She suddenly yearned to be back to her room. "I'm . . . going to bed now."

"Wait." He set the empty glass on the table. "Pay no attention. I am having my own fantasy, so I shouldn't mock yours. I've been daydreaming about what would have happened if Michel had been a son worthy of me instead of a perverted weakling who should never have been born."

"That's medieval," she said. "Millions of men are homosexuals. It's not that big a deal."

He came out of the chair so suddenly she thought he was going to hit her. "You know nothing about it! Nothing! Michel is a Savagar." He stalked across the room, his frenetic movements scaring her. "Such obscenity is unthinkable for a Savagar. It is your mother's blood. I should never have married her. She was the one mistake of my life, and I have never been able to recover from it. Her neglect perverted Michel. If you had not been born, she would have been a proper mother to him."

The liquor was talking. This wasn't her father. She had to get away before she heard anything more. She turned to the door, but he was already beside her.

"You do not know me well at all." He ran his hand up her arm. "I think we must talk now. I've attempted to be patient, but it's been long enough."

She tried to step away, but he didn't let her go. "Tomorrow," she said. "When you're sober."

"I am not drunk. Merely melancholy." He put his hands on her neck and ran his thumb gently over her ear. "You should have seen your mother when she was even younger than you are now. So full of optimism . . . So passionate.

And as self-centered as a child. I have plans for you, *chérie*. Plans that I made when you were sixteen, the day I first saw you."

"What kind of plans?"

"You're frightened. Lie on Michel's bed and let me rub your back so we can talk."

She didn't want to lie on Michel's bed. She wanted to go to her room and lock the door and pull the covers over her head.

"Come, *chérie*. I've upset you. Let me make it better." He smiled so warmly her tension eased. He missed Michel tonight, that was all. And she was jealous, as usual, still trying to forget her brother existed. He steered her toward the bed.

She lay down on the bare mattress and folded her hands under her cheek. The bed sagged as he sat beside her and began rubbing her back through the thin material of her robe. "I've waited patiently for you, *chérie*. I've given you two years. I've let you fall in love. I've let you and your mother smear the Savagar name with your vulgar career."

She stiffened. "What do you—"

"Shhh. I'm talking now, *chérie*, and you must listen. The night I saw you lean over the coffin to kiss your grandmother's lips, I knew a great injustice had been done. You were everything my son should have been, but you were too attached to your mother. Even last month, you would tolerate no criticism of her. I had to give you time to see for yourself who she truly is so your false sentimentality wouldn't stand between us. It's been a painful lesson, but a necessary one. Now you know how she really feels about you. And now you're finally ready to take your place beside me."

She turned over onto her back and looked up at him. "I don't know what you mean. Take my place beside you?"

He curled his hands around her shoulders and massaged them. His eyelids were half closed, almost sleepy. She wanted to leave before something terrible happened.

She looked up at the parachute. It hung limp and yellowed above her.

"You belong with me, *chérie.* At my side. You belong with me in a way your mother never did." He slipped his fingers just inside the open collar of her robe. "I am going to shape you into a magnificent woman. I have such wonderful plans for you." His hands dipped lower, pushing open the neck of the robe . . . moved lower again.

"Alexi!" She reached up and caught his wrists.

He smiled so gently she was embarrassed at what she'd thought he was going to do.

"It is right, *chérie*, for us to be together. Do you not see it every time you look at yourself? Can't you see your mother's unfaithfulness whenever you look in the mirror?"

Unfaithfulness? For a moment she couldn't think what the word meant.

"It's time for you to know the truth. Give up the fantasy, *enfant.* Give it up. The truth will be much better."

"No . . ."

"You're not my daughter, *chérie.* Surely you've felt that. Your mother was pregnant when I married her."

The beast had come back. The great, ugly beast who wanted to chew her into pieces. "I don't believe you. You're lying to me."

"You are the bastard of Errol Flynn, my oldest enemy."

It was a joke. She even tried to smile to show him she was a good sport. But the smile died, and the painted clouds on the ceiling blurred as she remembered Johnny Guy talking about Belinda and Errol Flynn and the Garden of Allah.

Alexi leaned over and pressed his cheek to hers. "Do not cry, *enfant.* It's better this way. Don't you see?"

The clouds swam before her, and the beast nibbled at her flesh, taking tiny bites that weren't big enough to do the job right. He touched her lightly through her robe.

"So beautiful. Small and delicate, not plump like your mother's."

"*No! Damn you!*" She shoved his hands away and tried to get up, but the beast had devoured her strength.

"I am sorry, *chérie*. I've been foolish, and I'm quite embarrassed." He let her go. "I must give you time to adjust, to see things as I do, to see that there is no harm in our being together. We share no blood. You are not *pur sang*."

"You're my father," she whispered.

"Never!" he said harshly. "I've never thought of myself as your father. These past few years have been a courtship. Even your mother understood that."

She pushed herself up. The mattress buttons dug into her knees.

"Don't dwell on this now," he said. "I've been unforgivably clumsy. We'll go on as we have until you're ready."

"Ready?" Her voice was thick, as if she were drowning. "Ready for what?"

"We'll talk of it later."

"Now! Tell me now!"

"You're clearly distraught."

"I want to hear everything."

"It will seem strange to you. You've had no time to adjust."

"What do you want from me, Alexi?"

He sighed. "I want you to stay with me, to let me spoil you. I want you to grow your hair so you'll be beautiful again."

There was more. She knew it. "Tell me."

"You've not had enough time."

"*Tell me!*" Her fingers dug into the mattress, and she offered up a silent prayer. *Don't say what I know you're going to say. Don't say you want me to be your lover.*

He didn't.

He said he wanted her to have his child.

*

Alexi explained his plan as Fleur stood at the dirty attic window and looked out on the roof. Something pink lay on the tiles, the featherless body of a baby bird that had fallen from a nest in one of the chimneys. Alexi walked around the attic room, his hands in the pockets of his robe, and neatly laid it out for her. As soon as she got pregnant, he would take her away somewhere for the duration, and then, when it was over, announce that he had adopted a child. The baby would have his blood, her blood, and Flynn's blood.

She stared out at the little featherless body. It never had a chance at life, never even had a chance to grow its feathers.

He assured her that his motives weren't those of a lecherous old man—*You said it, Daddy, not me*—and after it was over, they could go back to their old relationship, and he'd be her loving father, just as she wanted.

"I'm hiring a lawyer," she said, but her voice was so tight that the words came out as a broken whisper, and she had to repeat herself. "I'm hiring a lawyer. I want my money."

He laughed. "Hire an army of them, if you wish. You signed the papers yourself. I even explained it to you. It's all quite legal."

"I want my money."

"Don't worry about the money, *chérie*. Tomorrow I'll buy you anything you want. Diamonds for your fingers. Emeralds to match your eyes."

"No."

"Your mother was alone once," he said. "She was penniless, with no prospects for the future. And pregnant, although of course I didn't know that at the time. You need me now just as much as your mother needed me then."

She had to ask him. Before she walked out of this room, she had to ask, except she was crying again, and she could barely force out the strangled words. "What do you know about me?"

Her question puzzled him.

She was choking. "What do you know about me that makes you think I would do something so horrible? What weakness do you see? You're not stupid. You wouldn't make this obscene proposal if you didn't think there was a chance I'd accept it. What's *wrong* with me?"

He shrugged. It was an elegant gesture, and also a little pitying. "It's not your fault, *chérie.* The circumstances forced it on you, but you must understand that, by yourself, you are nothing more than a pretty decoration. You don't have any real value. You don't know how to *do* anything."

She wiped her nose with the back of her hand. "I'm the most famous model in the world."

"The Glitter Baby is Belinda's creation, *chérie.* You would fail without her. And if you were to succeed . . . Well, it wouldn't be your own success, would it? I'm offering you a function and the promise that I will never turn my back on you. We both know that's what's most important to you."

He believed she was going to do it. She could see it in his perfect arrogance. He'd looked inside her, seen what was there, and decided that she was weak enough to do this obscene thing.

With a choked sob, she ran from the attic room and down the stairs to her own room, where she locked the door and pressed her back against it.

Before long, she heard his footsteps in the hallway. He paused outside her door. She squeezed her eyes shut, barely able to breathe. He moved away. She slid down along the door and sat on the floor, where she curled her body over her bent knees. She stayed like that, listening to the pounding of her own heart until the deepest hours of the night.

*

The key turned soundlessly in the lock as she let herself into the museum. She set down her shoulder bag and flicked on the panel of lights. Her palms were sweating, and she rubbed them on her jeans while she walked toward the small tool room at the back.

Everything was scrupulously neat, just as he was. She

remembered the feel of his hands when they'd touched her breasts, and she crossed her arms over her chest. She forced herself to concentrate on the rows of tools. Finally she found what she wanted. She lifted it off the narrow shelf and tested its weight in her hands. Belinda was wrong. The rules were the same for everyone. If people didn't follow the rules, they lost their humanity.

She closed the door and walked across the museum to the Royale. The ceiling lights shone like tiny stars in the gleaming black finish. The car had been cherished. Alexi had wrapped it in canvas and straw so no harm would come to it.

She lifted the crowbar high above her head and brought it down on the shiny black hood. The jaws of the beast snapped shut.

Chapter 16

Fleur cashed a check at American Express using her Gold Card as ID. When she arrived at the Gare de Lyon, she pushed through the crowd to the schedule board and studied the blur of numbers and cities. The next train was leaving for Nîmes, which was four hundred miles from Paris. Four hundred miles from Alexi Savagar's retribution.

She'd destroyed the Royale, systematically smashing the hood and the windshield, grille and lights, beating in the fenders and the sides. Then she'd attacked the heart of the car, Ettore Bugatti's peerless engine. The thick stone walls of the museum had held in the noise, and no one tried to stop her as she put an end to Alexi's dream.

The old couple already occupying the compartment regarded her suspiciously. She should have cleaned herself up first so she wasn't so conspicuous. She turned to stare out the window. There was blood on her face, and the cut on her cheek from the flying glass stung. It was only a small cut, but she should clean it so it didn't get infected and leave a scar.

She envisioned her face with a little scar on her cheek. And then she imagined the scar beginning at her hairline, cutting a diagonal across her forehead, and thickening to bisect one eyebrow. It would pucker her eyelid and cut down over her cheek to her jaw. That would just about do it, she thought. A scar like that would keep her safe for the rest of her life.

Just before the train pulled out of the station, two young women came into the compartment carrying a supply of American magazines. Fleur watched their reflections in the window as they settled into their seats and began studying the other occupants in typical tourist fashion. It seemed as if weeks had passed since she'd slept, and she was so tired she felt light-headed. She closed her eyes and concentrated on the rhythm of the train. As she drifted into an uneasy sleep, she heard the echo of smashing metal and the crunch of broken glass.

The American girls were talking about her when she woke up. "It has to be her," one of them whispered. "Ignore her hair. Look at those eyebrows."

Where was the scar? Where was that pretty white scar cutting her eyebrow in half?

"Don't be silly." the other girl whispered. "What would Fleur Savagar be doing traveling by herself? Besides, I read that she's in California making a movie."

Panic beat inside her like the pounding of a crowbar. She'd been recognized a hundred times before and this was no different, but being connected with the Glitter Baby made her feel sick. Slowly she opened her eyes.

The girls were looking at a magazine. Fleur could just make out the page in the window's reflection, a sportswear ad she'd done for Armani. Her hair flew in every direction from beneath the brim of a big, floppy hat.

The girl directly across from her finally picked up the magazine and leaned forward. "Excuse me," she said. "Has anybody ever said that you look exactly like Fleur Savagar, the model?"

She stared back at them.

"She doesn't speak English," the girl finally said.

Her companion flipped the magazine closed. "I told you it wasn't her."

They reached Nîmes, and Fleur found a room in an inexpensive hotel near the railroad station. As she lay in bed that night, the numbness inside her finally broke apart. She began to cry, racking sobs of loneliness and betrayal and awful, boundless despair. She had nothing left. Belinda's love had been a lie, and Alexi had soiled her forever. Then there was Jake . . . The three of them together had raped her soul.

People survive by their ability to make judgments, yet every judgment she'd made was wrong. *You are nothing*, Alexi had said. As the night settled around her, she understood the meaning of hell. Hell was being lost in the world, even from yourself.

★

"I am sorry, mademoiselle, but this account has been closed." Fleur's Gold Card disappeared, tucked like a magician's trick into the palm of the clerk's hand.

Panic gripped her. She needed money. With money, she could hide someplace where she'd be safe from Alexi and where no one would recognize her, someplace where Fleur Savagar could cease to exist. But that wasn't possible now. As she hurried through the streets of Nîmes, she tried to shake off the feeling that Alexi was watching her. She saw him in the doorways, in the reflections of store windows, in the faces passing her in the street. She fled back to the train station. *Run*. She had to run.

★

When Alexi saw the wreckage of the Royale, he felt his own mortality for the first time. It took the form of a slight paralysis in his right side that lasted nearly two days. He closed himself in his room and saw no one.

All day, he lay in bed, holding a handkerchief in his left hand. Sometimes he stared at his reflection in the mirror.

The right side of his face sagged.

It was almost imperceptible, except for the mouth. No matter how hard he tried, he couldn't control the trickle of saliva that seeped from the corner. Each time he lifted his handkerchief to wipe it away, he knew that the mouth was what he would never forgive.

The paralysis gradually faded, and when he could control his mouth, he called in the doctors. They said it was a small stroke. A warning. They ordered him to cut back on his schedule, stop smoking, watch his diet. They mentioned hypertension. Alexi listened patiently and then dismissed them.

He put his collection of automobiles up for sale at the beginning of December. The auction attracted buyers from all over the world. He was advised to stay away, but he wanted to watch. As each car went on the block, he studied the faces of the buyers, printed their expressions in his mind so he would always remember.

After the auction was over, he had the museum dismantled, stone by stone.

Fleur sat at a battered table in the back of a student café in Grenoble and stuffed every cloying bite of her second pastry into her mouth until nothing was left. For nearly a year and a half, food had provided her only sense of security. As her jeans had grown tighter and she'd been able to pinch that first definitive fold of fat at the base of her ribs, the thick fog of numbness had lifted long enough for her to feel a brief sense of accomplishment. The Glitter Baby had disappeared.

She imagined Belinda's expression if she could see her precious daughter now. Twenty-one years old, overweight, with cropped hair, and cheap, ugly clothes. And Alexi . . . She could hear his contempt tucked away inside some honeyed endearment like a piece of candy with a tainted center.

She counted out her money carefully and left the café, pulling the collar of her man's parka tighter around her neck. It was February, and the dark, icy sidewalk still held remnants of that morning's snow. She tugged her wool hat further down over her head, more to protect herself from the cold than from fear that anyone would recognize her. That hadn't happened in nearly a year.

A line had already begun to form at the cinema, and as she took her place at the end, a group of American exchange students fell in behind her. The flat sounds of their accents grated on her ears. She couldn't remember the last time she'd spoken English. She didn't care if she ever spoke it again.

Despite the cold, the palms of her hands were sweating, and she shoved them more deeply into the pockets of her parka. At first she'd told herself she wouldn't even read the reviews of *Sunday Morning Eclipse*, but she hadn't been able to stop herself. The critics had been kinder to her than she'd expected. One called her performance "a surprisingly promising debut." Another commented on the "sizzling chemistry between Koranda and Savagar." Only she knew how one-sided that chemistry had been.

Now she simply existed, taking whatever job she could find and sneaking into university lecture halls when she wasn't working. Two months ago, she'd gone to bed with a sweet-natured German student who'd sat next to her in an economics lecture at the Université d'Avignon. She hadn't wanted Jake to be the only man she'd made love with. Not long afterward, she'd imagined Alexi's presence breathing down her neck, and she'd left Avignon for Grenoble.

A French girl standing in line ahead of her began to tease her date. "Aren't you afraid I won't be interested in you tonight after I've spent two hours watching Jake Koranda?"

He glanced over at the movie poster. "You're the one who should be worried. I'll be watching Fleur Savagar. Jean-Paul saw the film last week, and he's still talking about her body."

Fleur huddled more deeply into the collar of her parka. She had to see for herself.

She found a seat in the last row of the theater. The opening credits rolled, and the camera panned a long stretch of flat Iowa farmland. Dusty boots walked down a gravel road. Suddenly Jake's face flooded the screen. She'd once loved him, but the white-hot fire of betrayal had burned up that love, leaving only cold ash behind.

The first few scenes flicked by, and then Jake stood in front of the Iowa farmhouse. A young girl jumped up from a porch swing. The pastries Fleur had stuffed down clumped in her stomach as she watched herself run into his arms. She remembered the solidness of his chest, the touch of his lips. She remembered his laughter, his jokes, the way he'd held her so tight she'd thought he'd never let her go.

Her chest constricted. She couldn't stay in Grenoble any longer. She had to leave. Tomorrow. Tonight. Now.

The last thing she heard as she rushed from the theater was Jake's voice. "When did you get so pretty, Lizzie?"

Run. She had to run until she disappeared, even from herself.

Alexi sat in the leather chair behind the desk in his study and lit a cigarette, the last of the five he permitted himself to smoke each day. The reports were delivered to him at exactly three o'clock every Friday afternoon, but he always waited until nighttime when he was alone to study them. The photographs before him looked much like the others that had been sent to him over the past few years. Ugly barbershop hair, threadbare jeans, scuffed leather boots. All that fat. For someone who should be at the apex of her beauty, she looked obscene.

He'd been so certain she would go back to New York and resume her career, but she'd surprised him by staying in France. Lyon, Aix-en-Provence, Avignon, Grenoble, Bordeaux, Montpelier—all towns with universities. She foolishly believed she could hide from him in anonymous throngs of students. As if such a thing were possible.

After six months she'd begun to take classes at some of the universities. At first he'd been mystified by her choice of courses: lectures in calculus, contract law, anatomy, sociology. Eventually he'd discerned the pattern and realized she chose only classes held in large lecture halls where there was little chance of anyone discovering she wasn't a registered student. Officially enrolling was out of the question, since she had no money. He'd seen to that.

His eyes slid down the list of ridiculously menial jobs she'd held to support herself for the past two years: washing dishes, cleaning stables, waiting tables. Sometimes she worked for photographers, not as a model—such an idea was ludicrous now—but setting up lights and handling equipment. She'd unwittingly discovered the only possible defense she could use against him. What could he take from a person who had nothing?

He heard footsteps and quickly slipped the photographs back into the leather folder. When they were tucked away, he walked over to the door and unlocked it.

Belinda's hair was sleep-tousled and her mascara smudged. "I dreamed about Fleur again," she whispered. "Why do I keep dreaming about her? Why doesn't it get better?"

"Because you keep holding on," he said. "You will not let her go."

Belinda closed her hand over his arm, imploring him. "You know where she is. Tell me, please."

"I am protecting you, *chérie*." His cold fingers trailed down her cheek. "I do not wish to expose you to your daughter's hatred."

Belinda finally left him alone. He returned to his desk, where he studied the report again, then locked it in his wall safe. For now, Fleur had nothing of value that he could destroy, but the time would come when she did. He was a patient man, and he would wait, even if it took years.

*

The bell over the front door of the Strasbourg photo shop jangled just as Fleur set the last box of film on the shelf. Unexpected noises still startled her, even though two and half years had passed since she'd fled from Paris. She told herself that if Alexi wanted her, he would have found her by now. She glanced at the wall clock. Her employer had been running a special on baby photographs that had kept them busy all week, but she'd hoped the rush was over for the afternoon so she could get to her economics lecture. Dusting her hands on her jeans, she pushed aside the curtain that separated the small reception area from the studio.

Gretchen Casimir stood on the other side. "Good God!" she exclaimed.

Fleur felt as if someone had clamped a vise around her chest.

"Good God!" she repeated.

Fleur told herself it was inevitable that someone would find her—she should be grateful it had taken this long—but she didn't feel grateful. She felt trapped and panicky. She shouldn't have stayed in Strasbourg so long. Four months was too long.

Gretchen pulled off her sunglasses. Her gaze swept over Fleur's figure. "You look like a blimp. I can't possibly use you like this."

Her hair was longer than Fleur remembered, and the auburn color was brighter. Her pumps looked like Mario of Florence, the beige linen suit was definitely Perry Ellis, and the scarf de rigueur Hermès. Fleur had nearly forgotten what such clothes looked like. She could live for six months on what Gretchen was wearing.

"You must have gained forty pounds. And that hair! I couldn't sell you to *Field and Stream*."

Fleur tried to pull the old screw-you grin out of mothballs, but it wouldn't fit on her face. "Nobody's asking you to," she said tightly.

"This escapade has cost you a fortune," Gretchen said. "The broken contracts. The lawsuits."

Fleur tried to slip a hand into her jeans pocket, but the fabric was stretched so tight she could only manage a thumb. She didn't care. If she weighed her former one hundred and thirty pounds, she'd lose even her fleeting feelings of safety. "Send the bill to Alexi," she said. "He has two million dollars of mine that should cover it. But I imagine you've already found that out." Alexi knew where she was. He was the one who'd sent Gretchen here. The room closed in on her.

"I'm taking you back to New York," Gretchen said, "and getting you into a fat farm. It'll be months before you'll be in shape to work. That awful hair is going to hurt you, so don't think I can get your old price, and don't think that Parker can get you another film right away."

"I'm not going back," Fleur said. It felt odd to speak English.

"Of course you are. Look at this place. I can't believe you actually work here. My God, after *Sunday Morning Eclipse* came out, some of the top directors in Hollywood wanted you." She stabbed the stem of her sunglasses into the pocket of her suit jacket so the lenses hung out. "This silly quarrel between you and Belinda has gone on long enough. Mothers and daughters have problems all the time. There's no reason to make such a *thing* out of it."

"That's none of your business."

"Grow up, Fleur. This is the twentieth century, and no man is worth splitting up two women who care about each other."

So that was what everyone believed, that she and Belinda had quarreled over Jake. She barely thought about him anymore. Occasionally she saw a picture of him in a magazine, usually scowling at the photographer who'd invaded his privacy. Sometimes he was with a beautiful woman, and her stomach always did an unpleasant flip. It was like stumbling unexpectedly across a dead cat or bird. The corpse was harmless, but it still made you jump.

Jake's acting career was stronger than ever, but even though *Sunday Morning Eclipse* had earned him a screenwriting Oscar, he'd stopped writing. No one seemed to know why, and Fleur didn't care.

Gretchen made no effort to conceal her scorn. "Look at yourself. You're twenty-two years old, hiding away in the middle of nowhere, living like a pauper. Your face is all you have, and you're doing your best to ruin that. If you don't listen to me you're going to wake up one morning, old and alone, satisfied with whatever crumbs you can pick up. Is that what you want? Are you that self-destructive?"

Was she? The worst of the pain was gone. She could even look at a newspaper picture of Belinda and Alexi with a certain detachment. Of course her mother had gone back to him. Alexi was one of the most important men in France, and Belinda needed the limelight the way other people needed oxygen. Sometimes Fleur thought about returning to New York, but she could never model again, and what would she do there? The fat kept her safe, and it was easier to drift through the present than to rush into an uncertain future. Easier to forget about the girl who'd been so determined to make everybody love her. She didn't need other people's love anymore. She didn't need anyone but herself.

"Leave me alone," she said to Gretchen. "I'm not going back."

"I have no intention of leaving until—"

"Go away."

"You can't keep on like—"

"Get out!"

Gretchen let her eyes slide over the ugly man's shirt, over the bulging jeans. She assessed her, judged her, and Fleur felt the exact moment when Gretchen Casimir decided she was no longer worth the effort.

"You're a loser," she said. "You're sad and pitiful, living a dead-end life. Without Belinda, you're nothing."

The venom behind Gretchen's words didn't make them

any less true. Fleur had no ambition, no plans, no pride of accomplishment—nothing but a mute kind of survival reflex. Without Belinda, she was nothing.

An hour later, she fled the photo shop and boarded the next train out of Strasbourg.

Fleur's twenty-third birthday came and went. A week before Christmas, she threw some things into a duffel bag, picked up her Eurail pass, and left Lille to board a train to Vienna. France was the only place in Europe where she could work legally, but she had to get away for a few days or she'd suffocate. She could no longer remember how it felt to be slim and strong, or what it was like not to worry about paying the rent on a shabby room with a rust-stained sink and damp patches on the ceiling.

She chose Vienna on a whim after she read *The World According to Garp.* A place with bears on unicycles and a man who could only walk on his hands seemed just about right. She found a cheap room in an old Viennese pension with a gilded birdcage elevator the concierge told her had been broken by the Germans during the war. After lugging her duffel bag up six flights of stairs, she opened the door to a minuscule room with scarred furniture and wondered which war he meant. She peeled off her clothes, pulled the coverlet over her, and, as the wind rattled the windows and the elevator creaked, she went to sleep.

The next morning she walked through the Schönbrunn Palace and then had an inexpensive lunch at the Leupold near Rooseveltplatz. A waiter set a plate of tiny Austrian dumplings called *Nockerln* in front of her. They were delicious, but she had a hard time getting them down. There were no bears on unicycles in Vienna, no men who walked on their hands, only the same old problems that no amount of running away could solve. She'd never been the bravest, the fastest, or the strongest. It had all been an illusion.

A Burberry trench coat and Louis Vuitton briefcase brushed by her table, then backtracked. "Fleur? Fleur Savagar?"

It took her a moment to recognize the man standing in front of her as Parker Dayton, her former agent. He was in his mid-forties with one of those faces that looked as if it had been perfectly formed by a Divine Sculptor and then, just before the clay was dry, given a push inward. Even the neatly trimmed ginger-colored beard he'd grown since she'd last seen him couldn't quite hide the less-than-impressive chin or balance out the squished-in nose.

She'd never liked Parker. Belinda had selected him to handle Fleur's movie career on the strength of Gretchen's recommendation, but it turned out he was Gretchen's lover at the time and not a member of the upper echelon of agents. Still, from the evidence offered by the Vuitton briefcase and the Gucci shoes, business seemed to have picked up.

"You look like shit." Without waiting for an invitation, he took a seat across from her and settled his briefcase on the floor. He stared at her. She stared back. He shook his head. "It cost Gretchen a bundle to settle on the modeling contracts you broke." His hand tapped the table, and she had the feeling he was itching to pull out his calculator so he could punch in the numbers for her.

"It didn't cost Gretchen a penny," she said. "I'm sure Alexi paid the bills with my money, and *I* could afford it."

He shrugged. "You're one reason I pretty much stick to music now." He lit a cigarette. "I'm managing Neon Lynx. You have to have heard of them. They're America's hottest rock group. That's why I'm in Vienna." He fumbled in his pockets and finally pulled out a ticket. "Come to the concert tonight as my guest. We've been sold out for weeks."

She'd seen the posters plastered all over the city. Tonight was the opening concert in their first European tour. She took the ticket and mentally calculated what she could get for scalping it. "I can't see you as a rock manager."

"If a rock band hits, it's like you've got a license to print money. Lynx was playing a third-rate club on the Jersey shore when I found them. I knew they had something, but they weren't packaging it right. They didn't have any style, you know what I mean? I could have turned them over to a manager, but business wasn't too great at the time, so I decided, what the hell, I'd give it a shot myself. I made some changes and put 'em on the map. I'll tell you the truth. I expected them to hit, but not this big. We had riots in two cities on our last tour. You wouldn't believe—"

He waved to someone behind her, and a second man joined them. He was maybe in his early thirties with bushy hair and a Fu Manchu mustache.

"Fleur, this is Stu Kaplan, road manager for Neon Lynx."

To Fleur's relief he didn't seem to recognize her. The men ordered coffee, then Parker turned to Stu. "Did you take care of it?"

Stu tugged on his Fu Manchu. "I spent half an hour on the phone with that goddamned employment agency before I found anybody who spoke English. Then they told me they might have a girl for me in a week. Christ, we'll be in freakin' Germany next week."

Parker frowned. "I'm not getting involved, Stu. You're the one who's going to have to work without a road secretary."

They talked for a few minutes. Parker excused himself to go to the men's room, and Stu turned to Fleur. "He a friend of yours?"

"More an old acquaintance."

"He's a freakin' dictator. 'I'm not getting involved, Stu.' Hell, it's not my fault she got knocked up."

"Your road secretary?"

He nodded mournfully into his coffee, his Fu Manchu

drooping. "I told her we'd pay for the abortion and everything, but she said she was going back to the States to have it done right." Stu looked up and stared at Fleur accusingly. "For chrissake, this is Vienna. Freud's from here, isn't he? They gotta have good doctors in Vienna."

She thought of several things to say and discarded them all. He groaned, "I mean it wouldn't be so bad if this had happened in Pittsburgh or somewhere, but freakin' Vienna . . ."

"What exactly does a road secretary do?" The words came out of her unintended. She was drifting, just as always.

Stu Kaplan looked at her with his first real spark of interest. "It's a cushy job—answering phones, double-checking arrangements, helping out with the band a little. Nothing hard." He took a sip of coffee. "You—uh—speak any German?"

She sipped, too. "A little." Also Italian and Spanish.

Stu leaned back in his chair. "The job pays two hundred a week, room and board provided. You interested?"

She had a job waiting tables in Lille. She had her classes and a cheap room, and she no longer did anything impulsively. But this felt safe. Different. She could handle it for a month or so. She didn't have anything better to do. "I'll take it."

Stu whipped out a business card. "Pack your suitcase and meet me at the Intercontinental in an hour and a half." He scrawled something on the card and rose. "Here's the suite number. Tell Parker I'll see him there."

Parker came back to the table, and Fleur told him what had happened. He laughed. "You can't have that job."

"Why not?"

"You couldn't stick it. I don't know what Stu told you, but being road secretary to any band is a hard job, and with a band like Neon Lynx it's even tougher."

There it was, the open acknowledgment that she wasn't

worth anything without Belinda. She should leave and forget all about this, but what had been nothing more than an impulse had suddenly become important. "I've had tough jobs."

He patted her hand patronizingly. "Let me explain something. One of the reasons Neon Lynx has stayed on top is because they're spoiled, arrogant bastards. It's their image, and, frankly, I encourage it. Their arrogance is a big part of what makes them so great when they perform. But it also makes them impossible to work for. And road secretary isn't what you'd call a high-prestige job. Let's face it. You're used to giving orders, not taking them."

A lot Parker Dayton knew. She dug in with a stubbornness she'd forgotten she possessed. "I can handle it."

The man who didn't have a sense of humor laughed again. "You wouldn't last an hour. I don't know what happened with you three years ago, but you screwed yourself pretty good. Here's some free advice. Take a pass on the bread and cookies, then call Gretchen and get yourself back in front of the cameras."

She stood up. "Stu Kaplan can hire his own road secretary, right?"

"Under normal circumstances, but . . ."

"Okay, then. He offered me the job, and I'm taking it."

She was out of the restaurant before he could say anything more, but halfway down the street she had to lean against the side of a building to catch her breath. What was she doing? She told herself this was safe, nothing more than a secretary's job, but her heart rate refused to slow down.

When she walked into the suite at the Intercontinental an hour later, she felt as if she'd walked into Bedlam. A group of reporters was talking to Parker and two extravagantly dressed young men she assumed were band members. Waiters wheeled in trays of food, and three phones rang at the same time. The insanity of what she'd done hit her full force. She had to get out of here, but Stu had already picked up two of the phones and was gesturing for her to pick up the third.

She answered with an unsteady voice. It was the manager of the Munich hotel where the group was staying the next night. He told her he'd heard rumors about the destruction of two hotel suites in London and regretted to inform her that Neon Lynx was no longer welcome at his establishment. She put her hand over the receiver and told Stu what had happened.

Within seconds, she realized that the pleasant Stu Kaplan of the coffee shop was not the same man standing in front of her. "Tell him it was Rod Stewart, for chrissake! Use your freakin' head, and don't bother me with the little shit." He tossed a clipboard at her, smacking her in the knuckles. "Double-check the arrangements while you got him on the phone. Double-check everything, and then check it again."

Her stomach clenched. She couldn't do this. She couldn't work at a job with someone screaming at her and expecting her to know things that had never been explained. Parker Dayton gave her a smug smile with I-told-you-so written all over it. As she turned away from him, she caught sight of her reflection across the room. The mirror that hung above the sofa was the same size as those blown-up photographs Belinda had hung on the apartment walls in New York. Those oversized, beautiful faces had never seemed to belong to her. But neither did the pasty, tense reflection staring back at her.

She tightened her damp palms around the receiver. "I'm sorry to keep you waiting, but you can't blame Neon Lynx for damage they didn't do." Her voice sounded thin from lack of air. She took a quick breath, then began a systematic assassination of Rod Stewart's character. When she was done, she launched into a determined review of the room assignments from the instructions on the clipboard, then went on to detail arrangements for luggage carts and food. As the manager relayed the instructions back to her, and she realized she'd convinced him to change his mind, she felt a rush of satisfaction far out of proportion to what she'd done.

She hung up the phone, and it rang again. One of the roadies had been busted for drugs. This time she was prepared for Stu's yelling.

"For chrissake, don't you know how to handle anything?" He grabbed his jacket. "Take care of things here while I get the son of a bitch out of jail. And I'm telling you right now . . . Those motherfucking Austrian police had better speak English." He pitched another clipboard at her. "Here's the schedule and the assignments. Get those stage passes stamped for the VIPs and call Munich to make sure they've taken care of transportation from the airport. We were short on limos the last time. And check on the charter from Rome. Make them give us a backup." He was still hurling instructions as he walked out the door.

She fielded eight more phone calls and spent a half hour with the airlines before she noticed that she hadn't taken off her coat. Parker Dayton asked if she'd had enough yet. She gritted her teeth and told him she was having a terrific time, but as soon as he left the suite, she sagged into her chair. Parker was leaving the tour in three days to go back to New York. That's how long she had to last. Three days.

She took a few minutes between phone calls to study the promotional kit, and when the lead guitarist for Neon Lynx walked in, she recognized him as Peter Zabel. He was in his early twenties, with a small, compact body and curly, shoulder-length black hair. Two earrings decorated his right lobe, one an enormous diamond and the other a long white feather. He asked her to put a call through to his broker in New York. He was worried about his Anaconda Copper.

After he got off the phone, he slouched down on the couch and propped his boots up on the coffee table. They had three-inch Lucite heels with embedded goldfish. "I'm the only one in the band who looks to the future," he said suddenly. "The other guys think this is going to last forever, but I know it doesn't happen that way, so I'm building a portfolio."

"Probably a good idea." She reached for the backstage passes and began to stamp them.

"Damned straight it's a good idea. What's your name anyway?"

She hesitated. "Fleur."

"You look familiar. You a dyke?"

"Not at the moment." She slammed the stamp down on the VIP pass. Whom did she think she was kidding? Three days was forever.

Peter got up and headed for the door. Suddenly he stopped and turned back. "I know where I saw you. You used to be a model or something. My kid brother had your poster up in his room, and you were in that movie I saw. Fleur . . . what's it?"

"Savagar," she made herself say. "Fleur Savagar."

"Yeah. That's right." He didn't seem impressed. He tugged on the white feather earring. "Listen, I hope you don't mind my saying so, but if you'd had a portfolio, you would of had something to fall back on after you was washed up."

"I'll remember that for the future." The door shut behind him, and she realized that she was smiling for the first time in weeks. Around this crew anyway, the Glitter Baby was yesterday's news. She felt as if she had more air to breathe.

The tour was opening that night at a sports arena north of Vienna, and once Stu came back with the errant roadie, she didn't have a minute to think. First there was a ticket mix-up, and then the one-hour warning calls to the band. She had to be in the lobby early to double-check transportation and take care of tips. Then she had to make a second set of phone calls to the band members telling them the limos were ready. Stu yelled at her about everything, but he seemed to yell at everybody except the band, so she tried to ignore it. As far as she could tell, there were only two cardinal rules: keep the band happy, and double-check everything.

As the members of Neon Lynx wandered into the lobby, she identified each one. Peter Zabel she'd met. Kyle Light, the bass player, wasn't hard to spot. He had thin blond hair, dead eyes, and a wasted look. Frank LaPorte, the drummer, was a belligerent redhead with a Budweiser can in his hand. Simon Kale, the keyboard player, was the fiercest-looking black man she'd ever seen, with a shaved and oiled head, silver chains draping an overdeveloped chest, and something that looked suspiciously like a machete hanging from his belt.

"Where's that freakin' Barry?" Stu called out. "Fleur, go up and get that son of a bitch down here. And don't do anything to upset him, for chrissake."

Fleur reluctantly headed for the elevator and the penthouse suite of lead singer Barry Noy. The promotional kit billed him as the new Mick Jagger. He was twenty-four, and his photographs showed him with long, sandy-colored hair and fleshy lips permanently set in a sneer. From bits and pieces of conversations, she'd gathered that Barry was "difficult," but she didn't let herself think too hard about what that might mean.

She knocked at the door of his suite, and when there was no answer, she tried the knob. It was unlocked. "Barry?"

He was stretched out on the couch, his forearm thrown across his eyes and his sandy hair dangling over the couch pillows toward the carpet. He wore the same satin trousers as the other members of the band, except his were Day-Glo orange with a red sequined star strategically placed over the crotch.

"Barry? Stu sent me up to get you. The limos are here, and we're ready to go."

"I can't play tonight."

"Uh . . . Why's that?"

"I'm depressed." He gave a protracted sigh. "I swear I have never been so depressed in my entire fucking life. I can't sing when I'm depressed."

Fleur glanced at her watch, a man's gold Rolex Stu had loaned her that afternoon. She had five minutes. Five minutes and two and a half days. "What are you depressed about?"

For the first time he looked at her. "Who are you?"

"Fleur. The new road secretary."

"Oh yeah, Peter told me about you. You used to be a big movie star or something." He threw his arm back over his eyes. "I'm telling you, life is really shit. I mean I am *really* hot now. I can have any woman I want, but that bitch Kissy has me wrapped around her finger. I bet I called New York a hundred times today, but either I couldn't get through or she never answered the phone."

"Maybe she was out."

"Yeah. She was out all right. Out with some stud."

She had four minutes. "Would any woman in her right mind go out with another man when she could have you?" she said, even as she was thinking that any woman in her right mind would go out with a penguin before she'd go out with him. "I'll bet your timing was bad. The time zones are confusing. Why don't you try her after the concert? It'll be early morning in New York. You're sure to get her then."

He seemed interested. "You think so?"

"I'm sure of it." Three and a half minutes. If they had to wait for the elevator, she'd be in trouble. "I'll even put through the call for you."

"You'll come here after the concert and help me get the call through?"

"Sure."

He grinned. "Hey, that's great. Hey, I think I'm going to like you."

"Good. I'm sure I'm going to like you." *In a pig's eye, you degenerate.* Three minutes. "Let's go downstairs."

Barry propositioned her in the elevator between the ninth and tenth floors. When she refused him, he turned sullen, so she told him she thought she might have a venereal disease. That seemed to make him happy, and she delivered him to the lobby with thirty seconds to spare.

Chapter 17

They arrived at the ice hockey arena. The stage had been erected at one end of the rink, and hundreds of fans pushed against the wooden barricades. Ignoring the opening band, they called out for Barry and the group. Stu threw a clipboard at Fleur and told her to double-check everything. By the time she went backstage to watch the show, the crowd's screams had grown deafening. Just as she put in the pink rubber earplugs the stage manager handed her, the rink went dark. A voice bellowed over the loudspeaker, introducing the band in German. The screams turned into a solid wall of sound, and four spotlights hit the stage like atomic blasts. The beams of light collided and Neon Lynx ran forward.

The crowd exploded. Barry leaped into the air, his hair flying. He thrust his hips so the red sequined star on his crotch caught fire. Frank LaPorte twirled his drumsticks, and Simon Kale slammed the keyboard. Fleur watched as a young girl, not more than twelve or thirteen, fainted over the barricade. The crowd pressed against her, and no one paid attention.

The music was raucous and visceral, blatantly sexual, and Barry Noy played the crowd for all he was worth. As the song ended, the crowd surged the barricades, and she could see that the guards were getting nervous. The spotlights flashed blue and red in crisscrossing swords of light, and the band went into its next number.

She was afraid somebody would get killed. One of the roadies came up to stand beside her. "Is it always like this?" she asked.

"Naw. Guess it's because we're used to the States. Freakin' crowd's dead tonight."

After the show she stood with Stu in the underground garage that had been roped off by the Viennese police and counted limos. The band came out, all five of them soaked with sweat. Barry grabbed her by the arm. "Got to talk to you."

As he pulled her toward the lead limo, she started to protest. Stu glared at her, and she remembered rule number one. Keep the band happy. Translated that meant keep Barry Noy happy.

She piled into the limousine, and he pulled her down on the seat beside him. She heard the clink of chains, and Simon Kale climbed in with them. She remembered how he'd twirled that dangerous machete on stage, and she regarded him warily. He lit a cigarillo and turned to stare out the window.

The limousine drove from the garage into a crowd of screaming fans. Suddenly a young girl broke through the police barricade and rushed toward the car, pulling up her shirt as she ran to expose bare pubescent breasts. A policeman caught her. Barry paid no attention.

"So how did you think I was tonight?" He took a slug from a can of Bud.

"You were great, Barry," she replied, with all the sincerity she could muster. "Just great."

"You didn't think I was off tonight? Friggin' crowd was dead."

"Oh no. You weren't off at all. You were terrific."

"Yeah, you're right." He drained the beer and crumpled

the can in his fist. "I wish Kissy could have been here. She wouldn't come to Europe with me. What does that tell you about the kind of ditzy broad she is?"

"It tells me a lot, Barry."

A snort came from the other side of the limo.

"What does Kissy do?" she asked.

"She says she's an actress, but I've never seen her on television or anything. Shit, I'm getting depressed again."

If there was anything she didn't need, it was a depressed Barry Noy. "That's probably it, then. Actresses trying to get work can't afford to leave town whenever they want. They might miss their big break."

"Yeah, maybe you're right. Hey, I'm sorry about your VD and everything."

Simon Kale looked over at her, and she thought she saw a flicker of interest in his eyes.

"Thanks," she said sadly. "I'm doing my best to cope."

★

She should have been prepared for the pandemonium of the hotel lobby, but she wasn't. The hotel had orders not to give out any information, but there were women everywhere. As the members of the band made their way toward the heavily guarded elevators, she saw Peter Zabel reach out and grab the arm of a buxom redhead. Frank LaPorte inspected a freckled blonde, then gestured toward both her and her bubble-gum-chewing companion. Only Simon Kale ignored the crowd of women.

"I can't believe this," she muttered.

Stu heard her. "We're all hoping they don't speak English. That way we won't have to talk to them, too."

"That's disgusting!"

"It's rock and roll, kid. Rockers are kings as long as they can stay on top." Stu put his arm around a frizzy-haired blonde and headed toward the elevators. Before he got in, he called back to her. "Stick close to Barry. He told me he likes you. And check the IDs on those girls who went with Frank. They looked young to me, and I don't want any more trouble with the police. Then get hold of that freakin' Kissy and make sure she meets us in Munich tomorrow. Tell her we'll pay her two fifty a week."

"Hey, that's fifty more than I'm getting!"

"You're expendable, kid." The elevator doors slid shut.

She slumped against a pillar. The world of rock and roll.

It was one o'clock in the morning, and she was exhausted. She was going to forget about Frank and his groupies. They probably deserved each other. She was going to forget about Barry and his stupid Kissy, and she was going to bed. In the morning she'd tell Parker he'd been right about her. She couldn't handle the job.

But when the doors closed on the elevator, she found herself punching in the floor of Frank LaPorte's suite.

The two girls with him checked out, so she said a polite good-night and left them. She took the elevator up another floor to Barry's suite. As she dragged her body down the hallway, she thought of the beautiful hotel room waiting for her. Hot water, clean sheets, and heat.

The guard let her in, and she was relieved to see that everybody still had clothes on. The three girls, none of whom looked particularly happy, were playing cards. Barry was stretched out on the couch watching television. His face lit up when he saw her. "Hey, Fleur, I was just getting ready to call your room. I thought you forgot." He grabbed his wallet from the coffee table and riffled through it for a scrap of paper he shoved toward her. "Here's Kissy's number. How 'bout calling her from your room. I gotta get some sleep. And take two of those bimbos with you when you leave."

She clenched her teeth. "Any two in particular?"

"I don't know. Whichever ones speak English, I guess."

Fifteen minutes later, Fleur let herself into her own hotel room. She undressed and stared wistfully at her bed, then picked up the telephone. As she waited for the call to go through, she glanced at the scrap of paper in her hand. Kissy Sue Christie. Lord.

A voice answered on the fifth ring. It was distinctly Southern and very angry. "Barry, I swear to God . . ."

"It's not Barry," Fleur said quickly. "Miss Christie?"

"Yes."

"This is Fleur, the new road secretary for Neon Lynx."

"Did Barry get you to call me?"

"Actually . . ."

"Never mind. Just deliver a message." In a soft, breathy voice that oozed generations of ladylike Southern breeding, Kissy Sue Christie reeled off a list of instructions, the majority of which concerned Barry Noy and his anatomy. The contrast between her voice and the obscene instructions was too much for Fleur, and she laughed. The sound echoed in her ears, rusty and unfamiliar, like a nearly forgotten song.

"Am I amusin' you?" the voice asked with a Southern chill.

"I'm sorry. It's just that it's really late, and I'm so tired I can hardly keep my eyes open. And . . . you're saying everything I've been thinking all day. The man is—"

"— toad spit," Kissy Sue concluded.

Fleur laughed again, then got hold of herself. "I apologize for calling so late. I was under orders."

"It's okay. What's Stu offering now to get me to come over? Last time it was two hundred a week."

"It's up to two fifty now."

"No kidding. Shoot, I'd love to go to Europe, too. I even have some vacation time coming up. The only places I've seen outside South Carolina are New York and Atlantic City, but to tell you the truth, Fleur, I'd swear off men completely before I ever went to bed with Barry Noy again."

Fleur settled back on the bed and thought it over. "You know, Kissy, there just might be a way . . ."

Fleur's wake-up call came at six-thirty the next morning. She waited for the familiar heaviness to settle over her, but it didn't come. She'd barely had four hours of sleep, but it had been deep and restful. No pitching and tossing. No sudden heart pounding. No dreams about the people she used to love. She felt . . .

Competent.

She settled back into the pillows and tried the idea on for size. She had a terrible job. The people were awful—spoiled, rude, and blatantly immoral—but she'd survived her first day and done a good job. Better than good. She'd done a *great* job. They hadn't thrown anything at her she hadn't been able to handle, including Barry Noy. She was going to show Parker Dayton . . .

She stopped herself. She didn't care about Parker Dayton. She didn't care about Alexi, or Belinda, or anybody. The only person's opinion she cared about was her own.

The band's arrival in Munich was hectic beyond belief, and Stu coped by yelling at her. This time she yelled back, which made him pout and say he didn't know what she was getting so mad about. The next two nights' concerts were a repeat of the concert in Vienna, with girls fainting over the barricades and a crowd of groupies waiting in the hotel lobby.

Right before the last concert, Fleur sent a limousine to the airport to pick up the long-awaited Miss Christie, but to her dismay, it came back empty. She told Barry the plane had been delayed and then spent the next two hours while the band performed trying fruitlessly to track Kissy down. Finally she had to tell Stu, who yelled at her and said that she could personally explain the screw-up to Barry. After the concert.

Barry took it just about as she expected.

She calmed him down with some half-baked promises she probably couldn't keep and dragged herself to her hotel room. On the way, she passed Simon Kale in the hallway.

He wore gray slacks and an open-collared black silk shirt with a single gold chain at the neck. It was the most conservative outfit she'd seen on anyone other than Parker since she'd joined the Neon Lynx circus, but she suspected he had a switchblade tucked in one of his pockets.

She fell asleep within seconds of hitting the pillow, only to be awakened an hour later by a phone call from the hotel manager telling her the guests were complaining about the noise coming from the fifteenth floor. "I have not been able to reach Herr Stu Kaplan, madam, so you must put a stop to it."

She had a fairly good idea of what was in store for her when she stepped into the elevator and found Herr Stu Kaplan passed out with an empty V.O. bottle and half his Fu Manchu shaved off.

It took thirty minutes of begging and cajoling for her to get the party crowd in the suite thinned down to twenty-five, which was, she decided, the best she could do. She stepped over Frank LaPorte as she carried the telephone into a closet to call the lobby and tell them to put guards back on the elevators. When she came out, she saw that Barry had left with some of the women, and she decided it was safe to return to her room. But she was wide-awake now, tomorrow was a layover day, and she deserved a little fun—or at least a drink before she turned in.

After a short struggle with a cork, she poured several inches of champagne into a glass. Peter called her over to talk about OPEC, much to the disgust of the girls who were clamoring for his attention. Just as she began her second glass of champagne, she heard a furious pounding on the door. Groaning, she set down her glass and walked across the suite. "Party's over," she called through the door crack.

"Let me in!" The voice was female and vaguely desperate.

"I can't," Fleur told the crack. "Fire regulations."

"Fleur, is that you?"

"How did you—" Fleur suddenly realized the voice had

a strong Southern accent. She released the lock and pulled open the door.

Kissy Sue Christie tumbled into the room.

She looked like a rumpled sugarplum. She had short licorice curls, a candy apple mouth, and big gumdrop eyes. She wore black leather pants and an electric pink camisole with a broken strap. Except for a generous spill of breasts, everything about her was tiny. It was also vaguely lopsided, since she was missing one high-heeled shoe, but even lopsided, Kissy Sue Christie looked exactly the way Fleur had always wanted to look.

Kissy threw the bolt on the door and began her own inspection. "Fleur Savagar," she said. "I had the strangest feeling over the telephone it was you, even though you didn't tell me your last name. I'm mildly psychic." She checked the lock. "There's this Lufthansa pilot I'm trying desperately to avoid. I would have been here earlier, but I was unexpectedly delayed." She gazed around the suite. "Tell me I'm a lucky girl and Barry's not here."

"You're a lucky girl."

"I suppose it's too much to hope that he was electrocuted tonight or otherwise stricken?"

"Neither of us could be that lucky." Fleur suddenly remembered her duties. "Where's your luggage? I'll phone down and have somebody take you to your room."

"Actually," Kissy said, "my room is already occupied." She tugged on the broken pink camisole strap. "Is there someplace we could talk? And I wouldn't look unfavorably on the offer of a drink."

Fleur scooped up her champagne bottle, two glasses, and Kissy. She had an urge to tuck Kissy in her pocket.

The only unoccupied space was the bathroom, so she locked them both in and took a seat on the floor. While she poured the champagne, Kissy kicked off her remaining shoe. "To tell you God's honest truth, I think I made a mistake letting him escort me to my room."

Fleur took a wild stab. "The Lufthansa pilot?"

Kissy nodded. "It started as a mild flirtation, but I guess it got a little out of hand." She sipped delicately at her champagne, then licked her top lip with the tip of her pink tongue. "I know this is going to sound strange to you, but like I said, I'm mildly psychic, and I have this strong feeling we're going to be friends. I might as well tell you from the start—I have a little bitty problem with promiscuity."

This had all the earmarks of an interesting conversation, and Fleur settled herself more comfortably against the side of the tub. "How little bitty?"

"Depends on your viewpoint." Kissy tucked her feet beneath her and leaned against the door. "Do you like hunks?"

Fleur refilled her cup and thought about it. "I guess I'm sort of off men right now. Kind of neutral, you know what I mean?"

Kissy's gumdrop eyes widened. "Gosh, no. I'm sorry."

Fleur giggled. Whether it was from the champagne or Kissy or the lateness of the hour, she didn't know, but she was fed up with self-hatred. It felt good to laugh again.

"Sometimes I think hunks have just about ruined my life," Kissy said mournfully. "I tell myself I'm going to reform, but the next thing I know, I look up and there's this piece of gorgeous male flesh standin' right in my path with big, broad shoulders and those little bitty hips, and I can't find it in my heart to pass him by."

"Like Lufthansa?"

Kissy almost smacked her lips. "He had this dimple—right here." She pointed to a spot on her chin. "That dimple, it did something to me, even though the rest of him wasn't much. See, that's my problem, Fleur—I can always find something. It's cost me a lot."

"What do you mean?"

"The pageant, for one thing."

"Pageant?"

"Uhmm. Miss America. My mommy and daddy raised me from the cradle to go to Atlantic City."

"And you didn't make it?"

"Oh, I made it all right. I won Miss South Carolina without any trouble. But the night before the Miss America pageant, I committed an indiscretion."

"Hunks?" Fleur suggested.

"Two of them. Both judges. Not at the same time, of course. Well, not exactly. One was a United States senator and the other was a tight end for the Dallas Cowboys." Her eyelids drifted shut at the memory. "And oh my, Fleur, did he ever have one."

"You were caught?"

"In the act. I tell you, to this very day it annoys me. I got kicked out, but they both stayed on. Now does that seem proper to you? Men like that being judges in the greatest beauty pageant in the world?"

It seemed grossly unfair to Fleur, and she said so.

"I suppose it all worked out, though. I was on my way back to Charleston when I met this truck driver who looked like John Travolta. He helped me get to New York and find a place to stay where I wouldn't have to worry about being mutilated on my doorstep. I got a job working at an art gallery while I waited for my big break, but I have to tell you, it's been slow in coming."

"The competition's tough." Fleur refilled Kissy's glass.

"It's not the competition," Kissy said indignantly. "I'm exceptionally talented. Among other things, I was born to do Tennessee Williams. Sometimes I think he wrote those crazy women just for me."

"Then what's the problem?"

"Trying to get the auditions in the first place. Directors take one look at me and won't even let me try out. They say I'm not the right physical type, which is another way of saying that I'm too short and my boobies are too big and I look altogether frivolous. That's the one that really annoys me. I'd have been Phi Beta Kappa if I'd stayed in college for my senior year. I'm tellin' you, Fleur, beautiful women like you with legs and cheekbones and all the other blessings of God can't imagine what it's like."

Fleur hadn't been beautiful in a long time, and she nearly choked. "You're the most gorgeous thing I've ever seen. All my life I've wanted to be little and pretty like you."

This struck them both as being terrifically funny, and they dissolved in giggles. Fleur noticed their bottle was empty so she went on a scouting mission. When she returned with a fresh bottle, the bathroom was empty.

"Kissy?"

"Is he gone?" A loud whisper came from behind the shower curtain.

"Who?"

Kissy pushed back the curtain and climbed out. "Somebody had to use the facility. I think it was Frank, who is a base pig, in my opinion."

They resettled in their old spots. Kissy tucked several wayward licorice curls behind her ear and looked at Fleur thoughtfully. "You ready to talk yet?"

"What do you mean?"

"I'm not exactly blind to the fact that I'm sharin' this bathroom with a woman who used to be one of the most famous models in the world, as well as a promising new actress. A woman who disappeared off the face of God's earth after some interesting rumors about her association with one of our great country's truly outstanding hunks. I'm not obtuse."

"I didn't think you were." Fleur picked at the edge of the bathmat with her fingernail.

"Well? Are we friends or not? I've told you some of the very best parts of my life story, and you haven't told me one thing about yours."

"We've just met." As soon as she said it, Fleur knew that it was wrong and hurtful, even though she wasn't exactly sure why.

Kissy's eyes filled with tears, which made them look melty and soft, like blue gumdrops left too long in the sun. "Do you think that makes a difference? This is a lifelong friendship being formed right now. There's got to be trust." She brushed her tears away, picked up the champagne, and took a swig directly from the bottle. Then she looked Fleur straight in the eye and held the bottle out to her.

Fleur thought about all the secrets locked inside her for so long. She saw her loneliness, her fear, and the self-respect she'd lost along the way. All she had to show for the past three years—nearly three and a half—was an eclectic university education. Kissy was offering her a way out. But honesty was dangerous, and Fleur hadn't let herself take a risk for a very long time.

Slowly she reached for the bottle and took a long swallow. "It's sort of a complicated story," she said finally. "I guess it started before I was born . . ."

It took Fleur nearly two hours to tell it all. Sometime between her trip to Greece with Belinda and her first modeling assignment, she and Kissy escaped the pounding on the bathroom door by moving to Fleur's hotel room. Kissy curled up on one of the double beds while Fleur propped herself against the headboard of the other. She kept the champagne bottle that was helping her through the story balanced on her chest. Kissy occasionally interrupted with pithy, one-word character assassinations of the people involved, but Fleur remained almost detached. Champagne definitely helped, she decided, when you were spilling your sordid secrets.

"That's heartbreaking!" Kissy exclaimed, when Fleur finally finished. "I don't know how you can tell that story without falling apart."

"I'm cried out, Kissy. If you live with it long enough, even high tragedy gets to be mundane."

"Like *Oedipus Rex*." Kissy dabbed at her eyes. "I was in the chorus when I was in college. We must have performed that play for every high school in the state." She flipped onto her back. "There's a master's thesis in here somewhere."

"How do you figure?"

"Do you remember the characteristics of a tragic hero? He's a person of high stature brought down by a tragic flaw, like hubris, the sin of pride. He loses everything. Then he achieves a catharsis, a cleansing through his suffering. Or *her* suffering," she said pointedly.

"Me?"

"Why not? You had high stature, and you sure have been brought down."

"What's my tragic flaw?" Fleur asked.

Kissy thought for a moment. "Shitty parents."

Late the next morning, after showers, aspirin, and room-service coffee, they heard a knock at the door. Kissy opened it and emitted a loud squeal. Fleur looked up just in time to see the Belle of the Confederacy hurl herself into Simon Kale's forbidding arms.

The three of them had breakfast in the revolving dining room on top of Munich's Olympia Tower, where they could gaze out over the Alps, sixty-five miles away. As they ate, Fleur heard the story of Kissy and Simon's long-standing friendship. They'd been introduced not long after Kissy's arrival in New York by one of Simon's classmates at Juilliard. Simon Kale, Fleur discovered, was a classically trained musician and as menacing as Santa Claus.

He laughed as he wiped one corner of his mouth with his napkin. "You should have seen Fleur taming King Barry with her story about having a venereal disease. She was magnificent."

"And you didn't try to help her out, did you?" Kissy gave him a none-too-gentle punch in the arm. "Instead you gave her that I-eat-white-girls-for-breakfast look, just to amuse yourself."

Simon acted wounded. "I haven't eaten a white girl in years, Kissy, and I'm hurt that you would suggest such a perversion."

"Simon's discreetly gay," Kissy informed Fleur. And

then, in a loud whisper, "I don't know about you, Fleurinda, but I regard homosexuality as a personal insult."

By the time breakfast was over, Fleur decided she liked Simon Kale. Beneath his threatening facade lay a kind and gentle man. As she watched his delicate gestures and finicky mannerisms, she'd have bet every penny of her meager income that he would have been more comfortable in the body of a ninety-pound weakling. Maybe that was why she liked him. They both lived in bodies that didn't feel like home.

When they got back to the hotel, Simon excused himself, and Kissy and Fleur set out for Barry's suite. It had been cleaned up since last night's party, and Barry was once again in residence, nervously pacing the carpet as they entered. He was so glad to see Kissy that he barely listened to her breathlessly convoluted lie about why she was late, and several minutes elapsed before he even noticed Fleur. He made it obvious with a less than subtle glance toward the door that her presence was no longer required. Fleur pretended not to notice.

Kissy leaned forward and whispered something in his ear. As Barry listened, his expression grew increasingly horrified. When Kissy finished, she gazed down at the floor like a naughty child.

Barry looked at Fleur. He looked at Kissy. Then he looked at Fleur again. "What is this?" he cried. "A friggin' epidemic?"

★

Kissy's two weeks of vacation from the gallery ended, and she and Fleur said a tearful good-bye at Heathrow, with Fleur promising to telephone that evening at Parker Dayton's expense. When she returned to the hotel, she was depressed for the first time since she'd started her job. She already missed Kissy's quirky sense of humor and even quirkier view of life.

A few days later Parker called with a job offer. He

wanted her to work for him in New York at nearly double her current salary. Panic-stricken, she hung up the telephone and called Kissy at the gallery.

"I don't know why you're so surprised, Fleurinda," Kissy said. "You're on the phone with him two or three times a day, and he's as impressed with your work as everybody else. He may be slime mold, but he's not stupid."

"I—I'm not ready to go back to New York. It's too soon."

The distinct sound of a snort traveled through three thousand miles of ocean cable. "You're not going to start whining again, are you? Self-pity kills your sex drive."

"My sex drive is nonexistent."

"See. What did I tell you?"

Fleur twisted the phone cord. "It's not that simple, Kissy."

"Do you want to be back where you were a month ago? Ostrich time is over, Fleurinda. It's time to return to the real world."

Kissy made it sound so easy, but how long could Fleur stay in New York before the press discovered her? And she still didn't like Parker. What if her job with him didn't work out? What would she do then?

Her stomach rumbled, and she realized she hadn't had anything to eat since the night before. Another change this job had made in her life. Her jeans were already too loose, and her hair had grown down over her ears. Everything was changing.

She hung up the telephone and walked over to the hotel window where she pushed back the drapery to gaze down on the wet Glasgow street. A jogger dodged a taxi in the rain. She remembered when she'd been a dedicated runner like that, going out regardless of weather. The bravest, the fastest, the strongest . . . Now she doubted she could run a city block without stopping to catch her breath.

"Hey, Fleur, you seen Kyle?" It was Frank, a can of Budweiser already opened at nine o'clock in the morning. Fleur grabbed her parka and brushed past him. She rushed out into the hallway, into the elevator, through the well-dressed crowd of businessmen in the lobby.

The rain was an icy January drizzle, and by the time she reached the corner, it had trickled off the stubby ends of her hair and under the neck of her parka. As she crossed the street, her feet squished in her cheap wet sneakers. They had no cushioning, no thick padding to support her arches and protect the balls of her feet.

She pulled her hands out of her pockets and gazed up at the steel-gray sky. One long block stretched before her. Just one block. Could she make it that far?

She began to run.

Chapter 18

Kissy's apartment sat above an Italian restaurant in the Village. The interior decorating looked just like her: lollipop colors, a collection of stuffed teddy bears, and a poster of Tom Selleck taped to the bathroom door. As Kissy was showing Fleur how the makeshift shower worked, a bright pink lip print on the poster caught Fleur's eye. "Kissy Sue Christie, is that your lipstick on Tom Selleck?"

"So what if it is?"

"You could at least have aimed for his mouth."

"Where's the fun in that?"

Fleur laughed. Kissy had taken the fact that Fleur would be her roommate for granted, and Fleur was more than grateful. Despite her success with Neon Lynx, her self-confidence was shaky at best, and she was plagued with doubts about her decision to return to New York.

Parker begrudgingly gave her a week to get settled before she had to report to work, and she forced herself to leave the safe haven of the apartment and get reacquainted with the city she'd once loved. It was early February, and New York was at its worst, but she found it beautiful. Best of all, no one recognized her.

She ran every morning that week, only a few blocks before she had to walk to catch her breath, but each day she felt stronger. Sometimes she passed a place she and Belinda had visited together, and she felt a sharp, bittersweet pang. But there was no room in her new life for misplaced sentimentality. She was carving out her own future, and she wouldn't take any dirty laundry from the past with her. She tested herself by sitting through an Errol Flynn retrospective, but she didn't feel anything for the dashing swashbuckler on the screen.

The day before Fleur had to start work, Kissy threw out all her clothes. "You're not going to wear those vile rags, Fleur Savagar. You look like a bag lady."

"I like looking like a bag lady! Give me my clothes back."

"Too late."

Fleur ended up trading in her old jeans for ones that fit her slimmer shape and bought a supply of funky tops to go with them—a Mexican peasant shirt, an old varsity letter sweater, and some turtlenecks. Kissy frowned and left a copy of *Dress for Success* conspicuously displayed on the coffee table.

"You're wasting your time, Magnolia Blossom," Fleur said. "I'm working for Parker Dayton, not Xerox. The entertainment world has a more casual dress code."

"There's casual and there's dowdy."

Fleur could peel away only so many layers at a time. "Go kiss Tom Selleck."

It didn't take her long to discover Parker wanted his pound of flesh for the generous salary she'd forced him to pay. Her days blended into nights and spilled over into the weekends. She visited Barry Noy's purple-painted Tudor in the Hamptons to console him on his loss of Kissy. She wrote press releases, studied contracts, and fielded calls from promoters. The business, finance, and law classes she'd sat in on immediately began to pay off. She discovered she had a talent for negotiation.

She'd known she couldn't remain anonymous forever, but by dressing inconspicuously and staying away from anyplace connected with the fashion world, she avoided attracting attention for almost six weeks. In March, however, her luck ran out. The *Daily News* announced that former Glitter Baby Fleur Savagar was back in New York working at the Parker Dayton Agency.

The phone calls started coming in, and a few reporters showed up at the office. But all of them wanted the Glitter Baby back, signing perfume contracts, going to marvelous parties, and talking about her rumored affair with Jake Koranda. "I have a new life now," she said politely, "and I won't be making any further comments."

Try as they might, she refused to elaborate.

A photographer appeared to capture the Glitter Baby's whirling cloud of streaky blond hair and couture fashion. They got baggy blue jeans and a Yankees cap. After two weeks, the story died of boredom. The fabulous Glitter Baby was yesterday's news.

Over the next three months, Fleur learned who the record producers were and managed to keep track of the television executives as they played musical chairs at the networks. She was smart, dependable; she honored her commitments, and people began to ask for her. By midsummer she'd fallen in love with the entire business of making stars.

"It's great to pull other people's strings instead of having my own pulled," she told Kissy one hot Sunday afternoon in August as they sat on a bench in Washington Square eating dripping ice cream cones. The park held its usual colorful complement of characters: tourists, leftover hippies, skinny kids with ghetto blasters hoisted on their shoulders.

After six months in New York, Fleur's hair swung in a jaw-length blunt cut that shimmered in the summer sun. She was tan and too slim for the shorts that sat on her hipbones. Kissy frowned over the top of her ice cream cone.

"We are getting you some clothes that aren't made out of denim."

"Don't start. We're talking about my job, not fashion."

"Wearing something decent won't turn you back into the Glitter Baby."

"You're imagining things."

"You think looking good will somehow ruin everything you're building for yourself." She adjusted her red plastic barrettes, which were shaped like lips. "You hardly ever look in a mirror. A few seconds to slick on lipstick, another couple of seconds to run a comb through your hair. You are a world-class champion at avoiding your reflection."

"You look at yours enough for both of us."

But Kissy was on a roll, and Fleur couldn't distract her. "You're fighting a losing battle, Fleurinda. The old Fleur Savagar can't hold a candle to the new one. You're going to be twenty-four next month, and your face has something it didn't have when you were nineteen. Even those disgusting clothes can't hide the fact that you have a better body now than when you were modeling. I hate to be the bearer of tragic news, but you've turned from boringly gorgeous into a classic beauty."

"You Southerners do love your drama."

"Okay, no more nagging." Kissy circled the double-decker mound of raspberry ripple with her tongue. "I'm glad you love your job. You even seem to love the ugly parts, like having Parker for a boss and dealing with Barry Noy."

Fleur caught a dab of mint chocolate chip before it dropped on her shorts. "It almost scares me how much. I love the wheeling and dealing and the fact that something is always happening. Every time I head off another crisis, I feel like one of the nuns just pasted a gold star next to my name."

"You're turning into one of those awful overachievers."

"It feels good." She gazed across the square. "When I was a kid, I thought my father would let me go home if

I could be the best at everything. After it all fell apart, I lost faith in myself." She hesitated. "I think . . . maybe I'm starting to get that back." Her self-confidence was too frail to hold up for examination, even from her best friend, and she wished she hadn't been so open. Fortunately Kissy's thoughts took a different path.

"I don't understand how you can't miss acting."

"You saw *Eclipse*. I was never going to win any Academy Awards." Unlike Jake and his screenplay.

"You were great in that part," Kissy insisted.

Fleur made a face. "I had a couple of good scenes. The rest were barely adequate. I never felt comfortable." In deference to Kissy's feelings, she didn't mention that she also found the whole process of filmmaking, with all the standing around, boring beyond belief.

"You put your heart into modeling, Fleurinda."

"I put my determination into it, not my heart."

"Either way, you were the best."

"Thanks to a lucky combination of chromosomes. Modeling never had anything to do with who I was." She drew in her legs to save them from amputation by a skateboard. One of the drug dealers stopped talking to stare. She gazed off into space. "The night Alexi and I played out our smutty little scene, he said I was nothing more than a pretty, oversized decoration. He said I couldn't really *do* anything."

"Alexi Savagar is a whacko prick."

Fleur smiled at hearing Kissy dismiss Alexi so inelegantly. "But he was also right. I didn't know who I was. I guess I still don't, not entirely, but at least I'm on the right path. I spent three and a half years running from myself. Granted, I acquired a world-class university education along the way, but I'm not running anymore." And she wasn't. Something had changed inside her. Something that finally made her want to fight for herself.

Kissy pitched the end of her cone into the trash. "I wish I had your drive."

"What are you talking about? You're always juggling your schedule at the gallery so you can get your hours in and still hit the auditions. You go to class in the evenings. The parts will come, Magnolia. I've talked to a lot of people about you."

"I know you have, and I appreciate it, but I think it's time I face the fact that it's not going to happen." Kissy wiped her fingers on her very short pink shorts. "Directors won't let me read for anything other than comic sexpots, and I'm terrible in that kind of part. I'm a serious actress, Fleur."

"I know you are, honey." Fleur put all the conviction she could muster behind her words, but it wasn't easy. Kissy—with her pouty mouth, pillowy breasts, and smudge of raspberry ripple on her chin—was a perfect comic sexpot.

"I got a raise at the gallery." She made it sound as thought she'd gotten a terminal disease. "Maybe if I had a more disagreeable job, I'd push myself harder. I should never have gotten my minor in art history. It's turned into my security blanket." Her eyes automatically slid over a good-looking college student walking past, but her heart wasn't in it. "I can only take so much rejection, and I've just about had my fill. I do a good job at the gallery, and I get recognized for it. Maybe that should be enough."

Fleur squeezed her hand. "Hey, what happened to Miss Positive Thinking?"

"I think I'm thunked out."

Fleur hated the idea of Kissy giving up, but with her own history, she wasn't in a position to criticize. She rose from the bench. "Let's go. If we play our cards right, we can catch the beginning of *Butch Cassidy and the Sundance Kid* on television before we have to get dressed for our dates." She dropped the remainder of her cone and napkin in the trash.

"Good idea. How many times will this make?"

"Five or six. I lost count."

"You haven't told anybody about this, have you?"

"Are you nuts? Do you think I want the whole world to know we're perverts?"

They left the park walking side by side, a dozen pairs of male eyes following them.

Fleur's daily runs had firmed her muscles, and as the extra pounds melted away, her sexuality emerged from its long hibernation. The flow of water over her body in the shower, the slide of a soft sweater on her skin—everyday acts became sensual experiences. She wanted to be held by someone who shaved, someone with biceps and a hairy chest, someone who cussed and drank beer. Her body was starved for male contact, and as part of her self-improvement campaign, she began dating a personable young actor named Max Shaw, who was appearing off-off-Broadway in a Tom Stoppard play. He was Hollywood handsome, a rangy blond whose only drawback was a tendency to use phrases like "practicing my craft." They had fun together, and she wanted him.

She donned jeans and the black tank top she'd bought on the clearance table at Ohrbach's for their date the night of her twenty-fourth birthday. They'd planned to go to a party, but she said she'd had a tough week and suggested they skip it. Max wasn't stupid, and half an hour later, they found themselves in his apartment.

He poured her a glass of wine and settled next to her on the foam slab that served as both couch and bed in his studio apartment. The smell of his cologne bothered her. Men should smell of soap and a clean shirt. Like Jake.

But her memories of her treacherous first lover were shackles made of dusty cobwebs, easy to break free of, and they drifted away as she kissed Max. Before long, they were naked.

He pushed all the right buttons, and she had the release she'd been craving, but she felt empty afterward. She told him she had an early meeting and couldn't stay. After she left his apartment, she began to tremble. Instead of feeling energized like Kissy after one of her casual encounters, Fleur felt as though she'd given up something important.

She saw Max a few more times, but each encounter left her more depressed, and she eventually ended it. Someday she'd meet a man she could give herself to with all her heart. Until then, she'd keep things casual and direct her energy into her job.

Christmas arrived, then New Year's. The longer she worked for Parker, the more she disagreed with the way he ran his business. Olivia Creighton, for example, had spent most of the fifties as the queen of the B movies, specializing in torn dresses and being rescued by Rory Calhoun. With those days gone, Parker, along with Olivia's personal manager, a man named Bud Sharpe, had decided to capitalize on what was left of her name with commercial endorsements. But Olivia still wanted to act.

"What do you have for me now?" The actress sighed into the telephone when she heard Fleur's voice. "Laxative commercials?"

"Florida condominiums. The company wants a more glamorous image, and they know you'll give it to them." Fleur tried, but she couldn't manufacture any more enthusiasm than Olivia.

"Did anything happen with that new Mike Nichols play?" Olivia asked after a moment's silence.

Fleur toyed with a pencil on her desk. "It wasn't a lead, and Bud wouldn't consider it for you. Not enough money. I'm sorry."

Fleur had argued with Bud and Parker over Olivia, but she couldn't convince either of them to let Olivia have a shot at the Nichols play.

After she hung up, she slipped into the loafers she'd kicked off under her desk and went to see Parker. She'd worked for him for a year and had gradually assumed so much responsibility that he'd begun to rely on her for everything, but he still didn't like it when she questioned his judgment. The new Lynx album was bombing, Barry got lazier all the time, and Simon had started talking about setting up his own group, but Parker behaved as if Lynx would go on forever, and he used Fleur to pacify his other clients. Although she was gaining valuable experience because of his neglect, she didn't believe this was the way to run an agency.

"I've got an idea I want to talk over with you." She sat on the plush burgundy couch across from his desk. His squished-in face looked even more unpleasant than usual.

"Why don't you send me another of your memos?"

"I believe in the personal touch."

His voice dripped cynicism. "But I look forward to all those bright college-girl suggestions. They make great toilet paper."

It was going to be one of those days. He'd probably had a fight with his wife.

"What is it this time?" he said. "More nonsense about computerization? A new filing system? A frigging newsletter for our clients?"

She ignored his testiness. "Something more fundamental." Acting under the flies/honey/vinegar theory, she adopted her most chipper manner. "I've been thinking about what happens when we negotiate a contract for our bigger clients. First, we have to clear everything with the client's personal manager. Then, after our legal looks it over, the personal manager studies it, passes it on to a business manager, who passes it on to another lawyer. Once the deal has gone through, there's a publicist, and then—"

"Get to the point. I'm dying of old age here."

She carved a column in the air with her hand. "Here's the client. Here we are. We get ten percent for finding the client a job. The personal manager gets fifteen percent for directing the client's career, the business manager five percent for handling money, the attorney another five percent for studying the small print, and the press agent gets two or three thousand a month for publicizing. Everybody takes a cut."

Parker's high-back chair squeaked as he shifted his weight. "Any client who's big enough to have a team like that is in the top tax bracket, so all those commissions get deducted."

"They still have to be paid. Compare that to the way you operate with Lynx. You're their agent and personal manager. We do their tour publicity, and the pie isn't split so many ways. With some smart expansion, we could make that kind of service available to your best clients. We could charge twenty percent commission, which is ten percent more than we're getting now, but fifteen percent less than the client is paying out to all those different people. We make more, the client pays less, and everybody's happy."

He waved her off. "Lynx is a different situation. I knew from the beginning that I had a gold mine, and I wasn't letting it get away from me. But an operation on the scale you're talking about would be too expensive to run. Besides, most clients wouldn't want their business centralized like that, even if it cost less. It would leave them too open to mismanagement, not to mention embezzlement."

"Regular audits get built into the package. But the current system leaves them open to mismanagement, too. Three-quarters of these managers care more about their own cut than their client's interests. Olivia Creighton is a perfect example. She hates doing commercials, but Bud Sharpe won't let her accept any of the parts she's been offered because they don't pay as much as condominium commercials. Olivia has some good years left, and that's shortsighted management."

Parker had started glancing at his watch, and she knew she was beat, but still, she plunged on. "We can make money with this kind of organization, and it would be more efficient for clients. If we're discriminating, being represented by Parker Dayton would become a real status symbol. We'd be a 'caviar agency' with great clients beating down our door."

"Fleur, I'm going to try this one more time, and you'd better watch my lips. I don't want to be William Morris. I don't want to be ICM. I'm happy with things just the way they are."

She shouldn't have wasted her breath. But as she headed back to her office, she couldn't stop thinking about her idea. If someone honest and reliable had taken care of her interests when she was nineteen, she wouldn't be out two million dollars.

She thought about her "caviar agency" all that day and into the next week. Putting together the kind of operation she imagined would be much more expensive than a standard agency. The nature of the project required a prestigious address and a diversified, well-paid staff. It would take a fortune just to get started. Still, the more she thought about it, the more certain she became that the right person could make it work. Unfortunately the right person had only five thousand dollars in her savings account and an under-abundance of courage.

That evening she met Simon Kale for tandoori at the Indian Pavilion. "What would you do if you weren't already filthy rich and you needed big money?" she found herself asking.

He plucked some fennel seeds from the bowl in front of him. "I'd clean apartments. Really, Fleur, it's impossible to find good help. I'd pay a fortune for someone reliable."

"I'm serious. How would you go about it if you only had five thousand dollars in the bank and you needed a lot more? Like six figures more."

"Are we eliminating drug dealing?"

She lifted an eyebrow at him.

"Well, then . . ." He selected another fennel seed. "I'd say the fastest way would be to pick up our telephone and call that bitch Gretchen Casimir."

"That's not an option." Modeling was the one thing she wouldn't consider. If she did this—not that she would, but if she did—it would have to be all hers.

"Have we considered prostitution?"

"Fishnet stockings are so unflattering."

He brushed a stray seed from the sleeve of his silky gray shirt. "Since we're being so picky, the best way would probably be to demand a loan from a filthy rich friend."

She smiled at him. "You'd do it, too, wouldn't you? I'd only have to ask."

He pursed his lips. "Which, of course, you won't."

She leaned across the table and planted a kiss on his cheek. "Any other ideas?"

"Mmm . . . Peter, I suppose. He's your best bet, considering all these silly restrictions you've set up."

"Our Peter Zabel? Lead guitarist for Neon Lynx? How could he help me?"

"Tell me you're kidding, pet. You used to place all those phone calls to his brokers for him. Peter knows more about making money than anyone I've met. He's made a fortune for me in precious metals and new stock issues. I can't believe he never gave you any tips."

Fleur nearly knocked over her water glass. "Do you mean I was supposed to take him seriously?"

"Fleur . . . Fleur . . . Fleur . . ."

"But he's such an idiot!"

"His banker would most definitely disagree."

Another week passed before Fleur got up the courage to call Peter and lay out the situation in the vaguest terms. "What do you think? Speaking hypothetically. Could a person do anything with only five thousand dollars to start?"

"Depends on whether you're willing to lose it or not," Peter said. "High return means high risk. You're talking commodities trading—currency, fuel oil, wheat. If sugar goes down a penny a pound, you lose your nest egg. Very risky. You could end up worse off than you are now."

"I supposed . . . Yes." And then she was horrified to hear herself go on. "I don't care. Tell me what I have to do."

Peter explained the basics, and she began spending every spare minute with her head buried in the books and articles he recommended on commodities trading. She read the *Journal of Commerce* on the subway, and she fell asleep with *Barron's* propped on her pillow. All her classes in business and economics helped her grasp the basics, but did she really have the guts to do this? No. But she was going to do it anyway.

Following Peter's advice, she invested two thousand in soybeans, bought a contract for liquefied propane, and, after studying weather forecasts, spent the rest on orange juice. Florida had a killer freeze, the soybeans rotted from too much rain, but liquefied propane went through the roof. She ended up with seven thousand. This time she divided it between copper, durum wheat, and more soybeans. Copper and wheat tanked, but soybeans pulled through to the tune of nine thousand dollars.

She reinvested every penny.

On April Fool's Day, Kissy landed the plum role of Maggie in a workshop production of *Cat on a Hot Tin Roof.* She danced around their apartment as she broke the news to Fleur. "I'd given up! Then this girl who was in a couple of my acting classes called. She remembered this scene I'd done . . . I can't believe it! We start rehearsals next week. There's no money, and it's not a big enough production to attract anybody important, but at least I'll be acting again."

Once rehearsals began, Fleur didn't see Kissy for days at a time, and when she did, Kissy was distracted. Not a single hunk passed through their apartment, and Fleur finally accused her of celibacy.

"I'm storing up my sexual energy," Kissy replied.

The day of the production, Fleur was so nervous she couldn't eat. She didn't want to see Kissy humiliated, and there was no way her little fluff ball of a roommate could take command of a heavyweight part like Maggie. Kissy belonged in sitcoms, exactly where she didn't want to be.

A freight elevator took Fleur up to a chilly Soho loft with clanging pipes and peeling paint. The small stage at one end held nothing except a big brass bed. Fleur tried to convince herself the bed was a good omen where Kissy was concerned.

The audience was made up of other unemployed actors and starving artists, without a casting agent in sight. A bearded guy who smelled like linseed oil leaned forward from the row of chairs behind her. "So, are you a friend of the bride or the groom?"

"Uh—the bride," she replied.

"Yeah, I thought so. Hey, I dig your hair."

"Thanks." Her hair brushed her shoulders now and attracted more attention than she liked, but cutting it felt like a weakness.

"You want to go out sometime?"

"No, thanks."

"That's cool."

Fortunately the play started right then. Fleur took a deep breath and mentally crossed her fingers. The audience heard the sound of a shower running offstage, and Kissy made her entrance in an antique lace dress. Her accent was as thick as summer jasmine. She stripped off the dress and stretched. Her fingers formed tiny claws in the air. The man sitting next to Fleur shifted in his seat.

For two hours the audience sat spellbound as Kissy prowled and hissed and scratched her way across the stage. With dark, desperate eroticism and a voice like dime-store talcum powder, she radiated Maggie the Cat's sexual frustration. It was one of the most riveting performances Fleur had ever seen, and it came straight from the soul of Kissy Sue Christie.

By the time the play was over, Fleur was drained. Now she understood Kissy's problem in a way she couldn't have before. If Fleur, Kissy's best friend, hadn't believed she could be a serious dramatic actress, how could Kissy hope to convince a director?

Fleur pushed her way through the crowd. "You were incredible!" she exclaimed, when she reached Kissy's side. "I've never seen anything like it!"

"I know," Kissy replied with a giggle. "Come tell me how wonderful I was while I change out of costume."

Fleur followed her to the makeshift dressing room where Kissy introduced her to the other female cast members. She chatted with all of them, then perched on a chair next to Kissy's dressing table and told her another dozen times how wonderful she'd been.

"Everybody decent?" a masculine voice inquired from the other side of the door. "I need to pick up the costumes."

"I'm the only one left, Michael," Kissy called out. "Come on in. I have somebody I want you to meet."

The door opened. Fleur turned.

"Fleurinda, you've heard me talk about our brilliant costume designer and the future dressmaker to the Beautiful People. Fleur Savagar meet Michael Anton."

Everything stopped like a damaged frame of film frozen in a movie projector. He wore an antique purple satin bowling shirt and a pair of loosely cut wool trousers held up by suspenders. At twenty-three, he wasn't much taller than he'd been the last time she'd seen him, maybe five feet, seven inches. He had shiny blond hair that fell in long waves level with his chin, a set of narrow shoulders, a small chest, and delicately carved features.

Gradually Kissy realized that something was wrong. "Do you two know each other?"

Michael Anton nodded. Fleur reached deep inside her. "This is one of your better moments, Kissy," she said, as lightly as she could manage. "Michael is my brother Michel."

"Oh boy." Kissy's gaze flicked from one to the other. "Should I play some organ music or something?"

Michel shoved one hand into the pocket of his trousers and leaned against the door. "How about a few notes on the kazoo?"

He carried himself with the languid grace of old money and the assurance of someone born with an aristocratic bloodline. Just like Alexi. But as he gazed at her, she saw eyes as blue as spring hyacinths.

She curled stiff fingers around her purse. "Did you know I was in New York?"

"I knew."

She couldn't stand there with him any longer. "I have to go." She gave Kissy a quick peck on the cheek and left the dressing room without so much as a nod in his direction.

Kissy caught up with her on the street. "Fleur! Wait! I had no idea."

She faked a smile. "Don't worry about it. It was just a shock, that's all."

"Michael is . . . He's really a terrific guy."

"That's . . . great." She spotted a cab and stepped out from the curb to hail it. "Go to your cast party, Magnolia, and make them all bow when you come in the room."

"I think I'd better go home with you."

"Not on your life. This is your big night, and you're going to enjoy every minute." She climbed into the cab, waved, and shut the door. As the taxi pulled away, she sagged back into the seat and let the old bitterness swamp her.

★

In the weeks that followed, Fleur tried to forget about Michel, but one evening she found herself walking along West Fifty-fifth Street studying the numbers painted above the shop doors, now closed for the night. She found the address she was looking for. The location was good, but the unimposing storefront had badly lit windows . . . and the most beautiful garments she'd ever seen.

Michel had bucked the tide of current fashion trends

where women were dressing up in evening tuxedos and neckties so they could look like men. The small window held a quartet of outrageously feminine dresses that conjured up lavish Renaissance paintings. As she gazed at the silks, jerseys, and gracefully draped crepe de chine, she couldn't remember how long it had been since she'd spent money on decent clothes. These exquisite garments rebuked her.

★

Spring drifted into summer and then into fall. Kissy's theater company folded, so she joined another group that performed almost exclusively in New Jersey. Fleur celebrated her twenty-fifth birthday by making Parker give her another raise. She bought cocoa beans with it.

She lost more often than she won, but when the wins came, they came big. She studied hard to learn from her mistakes, and her initial five thousand quadrupled, then quadrupled again. The more money she made, the harder it became for her to sink it back into risky speculations, but she forced herself to keep writing out the checks. Forty thousand dollars was as useless to her as five thousand had been.

Winter settled in. She developed an enchantment with copper and made almost thirty thousand dollars in six weeks, but the stress was giving her stomach pains. Beef went up, pork fell. She kept going—investing, reinvesting, and biting her fingernails to the quick.

By the first day of June, a year and a half after she'd jumped on her financial roller-coaster, she stared at her balance sheets, hardly able to believe what she saw. She'd done it. With nothing more than sheer nerve, she'd accumulated enough to start her business. The next day, she put everything into nice, safe, thirty-day certificates of deposit at Chase Manhattan.

A few evenings later as she was letting herself into the apartment, she heard the phone ring. She stepped over a pair of Kissy's heels, crossed the room, and picked up the receiver.

"Hello, *enfant.*"

It had been more than five years since she'd heard that familiar endearment. She tightened her grip on the telephone and made herself take a slow, steadying breath. "What do you want, Alexi?"

"No social amenities?"

"You have exactly one minute, and then I'm hanging up."

He sighed, as if she'd wounded him. "Very well, *chérie.* I called to congratulate you on your recent financial gains. Rather foolhardy, but then one doesn't argue with success. I understand you started looking for office space today."

She felt a chill. "How do you know that?"

"I've told you, *chérie.* I make it my business to know everything that affects those I care about."

"You don't care about me," she said, her throat tight. "Stop playing games."

"On the contrary, I care very much about you. I've waited a long time for this, *chérie.* I hope you don't disappoint me."

"A long time for what? What are you talking about?"

"Guard your dream, *chérie.* Guard it better than I guarded mine."

Chapter 19

Fleur rested her elbows on the deck rail and watched the tawny dune grass bend against the breeze in the last of the evening light. The Long Island beach house, an angular structure of glass and weathered clapboard, blended with the sand and water. She was glad she'd been invited here for the Fourth of July weekend. She needed to get away from the city for a while, and she also needed a distraction from that mental tape recorder that wouldn't stop replaying Alexi's words. *Guard your dream.* Alexi hadn't forgotten what she'd done to the Royale—not that she'd expected him to—and he still wanted his revenge. But other than keeping her eyes open, she didn't know what she could do about it.

She pushed aside her worries and thought about the four-story Upper East Side townhouse she'd leased for her new offices. The renovations were under way, and she hoped to be able to move in by mid-August, but before then she had to hire a staff. If a few breaks came her way and she had no big emergencies, she had enough money to keep the agency afloat until spring. Unfortunately a business like hers needed at least a year to get established, so she was at risk from the start, but that just meant she'd have to work harder, something she'd discovered she was good at.

She'd hoped to keep her salary from Parker coming in a little longer, but when he found out what she was up to, he'd fired her. They'd had an acrimonious parting. Lynx had broken up, and Parker had delegated too much of his business to Fleur. Now he was blaming her for the desperate game of catch-up he had to play with resentful clients.

Fleur had made the decision to expand the clients of her "caviar agency" beyond musicians and actors to include a select group of writers, maybe even artists—whoever she thought had the potential to rise to the top. She'd already signed Rough Harbor, the rock group Simon Kale was founding, and she'd stolen Olivia Creighton out from under Bud Sharpe's greedy fingers. Then there was Kissy. All three offered the earnings potential she was looking for, but three clients weren't enough to keep her aloft after her start-up money ran out.

She slipped her sunglasses on top of her head and thought about Kissy. Other than a hypnotically restrained performance as Irena in a workshop production of *The Cherry Orchard* and a one-liner Fleur had gotten her on a CBS soap opera, nothing much had happened for her since *Cat on a Hot Tin Roof*, and Kissy had stopped going to auditions again. Recently too many men had been passing through her bedroom door, each one a little more muscle-bound and a little stupider than the last. Kissy needed a showcase, and Fleur hadn't figured out how to find one for her, which wasn't the best omen for someone who only had until spring to prove herself.

Through the glass doors, she spotted Charlie Kincannon, their host for the weekend. Charlie had backed Kissy's workshop production of *The Cherry Orchard*, which was how Fleur had met him. It was painfully obvious that he'd fallen for Kissy, but since he was smart, sensitive, and successful, Kissy was ignoring him. She preferred beefcake losers.

The patio doors slid open behind her, and Kissy stepped out onto the deck. She'd dressed for the party in a one-piece pink and blue candy-striped romper, big silver heart-shaped earrings, and flat-soled pink sandals with beaded straps across her toes. She looked like a seven-year-old with breasts. "It's getting late, Fleurinda, and what's-his-name's guests are starting to show up. Aren't you going to change your clothes?" She took a sip of her piña colada from a lipstick-tipped straw.

"In a minute." The white shorts Fleur had pulled over her black tank suit had a mustard stain on the front, and her hair was stiff from salt water. Since Charlie Kincannon had backed several off-Broadway plays, she hoped to make some contacts at tonight's party, and she needed to look decent. First, though, she reached for Kissy's piña colada and took a sip. "I wish you'd stop calling him what's-his-name. Charlie Kincannon is a very nice man, not to mention rich."

Kissy wrinkled her nose. "Then you date him."

"I just might. I like him, Kissy. I really do. He's the first man you've hung around with who doesn't eat bananas and gaze longingly at the Empire State Building."

"Cute. I give him to you with my blessings." Kissy reclaimed her piña colada. "He reminds me of a Baptist minister I used to know. He wanted to save me, but he was afraid I wouldn't put out if he did."

"You're not 'putting out' for Charlie Kincannon. If you have such an overpowering need to play the sexpot, do it onstage, where you can make us both some money."

"Spoken like a true bloodsucker. You're going to make a great agent. By the way, did you notice those guys on the beach this afternoon tripping over themselves trying to catch your attention?"

"The one with the sippy cup or the kid with the *Star Wars* light saber?" If she listened to Kissy, she'd believe every man in the world wanted her. She brushed the sand from her legs and headed inside. "I'd better get in the shower."

"Put something decent on. Never mind. I'm wasting my breath."

"I'm a business tycoon now. I have to look serious."

"That stupid black dress you brought makes you look dead, not serious."

Fleur ignored her and headed inside. The house had angular ceilings, slate floors, and minimalist Japanese furniture. She spotted the owner sitting on a sand-colored couch, staring mournfully into what looked like a double shot of bourbon. "Could I talk to you for a minute, Fleur?" he asked.

"Sure."

He pushed aside his copy of *Rabbit Redux* so she could sit next to him. Charlie Kincannon reminded her of a character Dustin Hoffman might play—the kind of man who, despite all his money, manages to look a little out of step with the rest of the world. He had short dark hair and pleasant, slightly irregular features, with a set of serious brown eyes framed by horn-rimmed glasses.

"Is something wrong?" she asked.

He swirled the liquor in his glass. "It embarrasses me to sound like an adolescent, but how do you assess my chances with Kissy?"

She hedged. "It's sort of hard to tell."

"In other words, no chance at all."

He looked so sad and sweet that her heart went out to him. "It isn't your fault. Kissy's a little self-destructive right now, and that means she's doing an even worse job than normal of seeing men as people."

He thought it over, his brown eyes growing even more serious. "Our situation is an interesting role reversal for me. I'm used to women being the aggressors. I know I'm not a sex object, but they usually overlook that because I'm rich."

Fleur smiled and liked him even more. Still, she had a

friend to protect. "Exactly what do you want from her?"

"I don't know what you mean?"

"Do you want a real relationship or is this just about sex?"

"Of course I want a real relationship. I can get sex anywhere."

He looked so offended she was satisfied. She thought it over. "I don't know if it will work or not, but except for Simon, you're the only man who's figured out how intelligent Kissy is. Maybe you'd catch her attention if you ignored her body and concentrated on her brain."

He gave her a reproachful look. "I don't mean to sound like a chauvinist, but it's difficult to ignore Kissy's body, especially for someone like myself who has such a strong sex drive."

She smiled sympathetically. "That's my best shot."

A few guests had begun to arrive, and a man's voice, lightly accented, drifted toward her. "The house is amazing. Look at that view."

She stiffened and turned her head in time to see Michel step into the living room. He was part of Kissy's workshop group, so she should have realized he'd be invited. Her pleasure in the weekend vanished.

They'd run into each other twice in the year since they'd met, and both times they'd exchanged the barest minimum of conversation. Michel's companion was a muscular young man with dark hair that fell over his eyes. A dancer, she decided, as his feet automatically came to rest in first position.

The glass doors were her closest escape. She gave him a brief nod, excused herself from Charlie, and slipped back outside.

The moon had come out, Kissy had disappeared, and the beach was deserted. Fleur needed a few minutes to put her armor on before she went back inside to get cleaned up. She walked down to the water, then wandered along the cool, wet sand away from the house. She had to stop letting herself get thrown off stride so easily, but every time she saw Michel, she felt as if she'd been thrust back into her childhood.

She stubbed her toe on a rock she hadn't seen sticking out of the sand. She'd walked farther than she'd intended, and she turned to go back, but just then, a man stepped out from the dunes fifty yards ahead of her. Something about his stillness, combined with being alone on a deserted beach, made her instantly alert. He stood darkly silhouetted against the night, a tall man, bigger than anyone she wanted to tangle with, and he wasn't trying to disguise his interest in her. She automatically glanced toward the distant lights of the beach house, but it was too far away for anyone to hear if she yelled for help.

Living in New York had made her paranoid. He was probably one of Charlie's guests who'd drifted away from the party just as she had. In the moonlight, she dimly made out a shaggy head of Charles Manson hair and an even shaggier mustache. The words to "Helter Skelter" skimmed through her brain. She picked up her stride and edged closer to the water.

Abruptly he tossed down his beer can and began coming toward her. He covered the sand in long, swift strides, and every cell in her body went on full alert. Paranoid or not, she had no intention of waiting around to see what he wanted. She dug in her feet and began to run.

At first, she could only hear the sound of her own breathing, but she soon grew aware of the soft pounding of feet on the sand behind her. Her heart thudded. He was coming after her, and she had to outrun him. She told herself she could do it. She ran all the time now. Her muscles were strong. All she had to do was pick up the pace.

She stayed in the hard-packed sand near the water. She extended her legs, pumped her arms. As she ran, she kept her eyes on the beach house, but it was still agonizingly far ahead. If she headed for the dunes, she'd sink into deeper sand, but so would he. She grabbed more air. He couldn't keep up with her forever. She could do this, and she pushed herself harder.

He stayed with her.

Her lungs burned, and she lost her rhythm. She sucked in ragged gasps of air. The word "rape" rattled around in her head. *Why didn't he fall back?*

"Leave me alone," she screamed. The words were garbled, barely comprehensible, and she'd lost more precious air.

He shouted something. Near. Almost in her ear. Her chest was on fire. He touched her shoulder, and she screamed. The next thing she knew, the ground rushed up, and he was falling with her. As they hit the sand, he shouted the word again, and this time she heard.

"*Flower!*"

He fell on top of her. She gasped for air beneath his weight and tasted grit. With the last of her strength, she clenched her hand into a fist and swung hard. She heard a sharp exclamation. His weight eased, and the ends of his hair brushed her cheek as he raised himself on his arms above her. His breath fanned her face, and she hit him again.

He pulled back, and she went after him. Scrambling to her knees, she hit him again and again with her fists. She didn't bother aiming, but caught whatever she could reach—an arm, his neck, his chest, every blow punctuated with a sob.

Finally he made a vise of his arms and squeezed. "Stop it, Flower! It's me. It's Jake."

"I know it's you, you bastard! Let me go!"

"Not till you've calmed down."

She gasped for air against the soft fabric of his T-shirt. "I'm calm."

"No you're not."

"Yes I am!" She slowed her breathing, quieted her voice. "I'm calm. Really."

"Are you sure?"

"I'm sure."

Gradually he released her. "All right, then. I was—"

She slugged him in the head. "*You son of a bitch!*"

"Ouch!" He threw up his arm.

She caught him in the shoulder with her next blow. "You arrogant, hateful—"

"Stop it!" He snagged her wrist. "If you hit me again, I swear, I'll deck you."

She seriously doubted he'd follow through, but her adrenaline rush was beginning to fade, her hands hurt, and she was so wobbly she was afraid she'd throw up if she took another swing.

He crouched in the sand before her. His tangled, unkempt hair fell nearly to his shoulders, and his mustache obscured all of his mouth except for that impossible, sulky bottom lip. With a Nike T-shirt that didn't make it to his waist, faded maroon shorts, and his long, outlaw's hair, he looked like he should be carrying a cardboard sign that read, WILL KILL FOR FOOD.

"Why didn't you tell me it was you?" she managed on a thin stream of air.

"I thought you recognized me."

"How could I recognize you? It's dark, and you look like a wanted poster."

He released her wrist, and she struggled to her feet. It shouldn't have happened this way, with her wearing mustard-stained white shorts and a ponytail slipping out of its rubber band. She'd imagined herself dripping in diamonds when she met him again. She wanted to be standing on the steps of the casino at Monte Carlo with a European prince on one arm and Lee Iacocca on the other.

"I'm making a new Caliber picture," he said. "Bird Dog goes blind, so I have to learn to use the Colts by sound." He rubbed his shoulder as he stood. "Since when did you turn into such a chickenshit?"

"Since I saw a man who looks like a serial killer coming out from behind a sand dune."

"If I have a black eye . . ."

"Here's hoping."

"Damn it, Fleur . . ."

None of this was playing out as she'd imagined. She'd wanted to be cool and aloof, to act as if she barely remembered him. "So you're making a new Caliber movie. How many women do you slap around in this one?"

"Bird Dog's getting more sensitive."

"That's gotta be a real stretch for you."

"Don't be a bitch, okay?"

Fireworks went off in her head, and she was once again standing in the rain on the front lawn of Johnny Guy Kelly's house finishing a conversation that had barely gotten started. She spit out her words through a rigid jaw. "You used me to get your picture finished. I was a stupid, naïve kid who didn't want to take her clothes off, but Mr. Big Shot's love machine made short work of that. You made me happy to take everything off. Did you think about me when they handed you your Oscar?"

She wanted to see guilt. Instead he launched a counterattack. "You were your mother's victim, not mine—at least not much. Take it up with her. And while you're doing that, remember you weren't the only one who got screwed. I've lost more than you can imagine."

Her fury ignited. "You! Are you seriously trying to paint yourself as the injured party?" Her hand flew back of its own volition. She hadn't planned to hit him again, but her arm had a will of its own.

He caught it before she made contact. "Don't you dare."

"I think you'd better take your hands off her." A familiar voice drifted toward them from the dunes. Both of them turned to see Michel standing there. He looked like a boy who'd accidentally wandered into the company of giants.

Jake loosened his grip on her arm but didn't let her go.

"This is a private party, pal, so how about minding your own business?"

Michel came closer. He was dressed in a madras blazer and yellow net-T-shirt, with wisps of blond hair blowing across his delicately carved cheek. "Let's go back to the house, Fleur."

She stared at her brother and realized he'd somehow appointed himself her protector. It was laughable. He stood half a head shorter than she did, and yet here he was challenging Jake Koranda, a man with quicksilver reflexes and an outlaw's squint.

Jake's lip curled. "This is between her and me, so unless you want your ass kicked, leave us alone."

It sounded like a line from a Caliber movie, and she almost stopped the confrontation right then. She could have stopped it . . . but she didn't. Michel, her protector. Would he really stay here and defend her?

"I'll be happy to leave," Michel said softly. "But Fleur goes with me."

"Don't count on it," Jake retorted.

Michel slipped his hands in the pockets of his shorts and held his ground. He knew he couldn't physically remove her from Jake, so he'd decided to wait him out.

Bird Dog wasn't used to confronting a soft-spoken opponent with wispy blond hair and a delicate physique. His eyes dropped to half mast as he turned to her. "A friend of yours?"

"He's . . ." She swallowed hard. "This is my brother, Michael An—"

"I'm Michel Savagar."

Jake studied them both, then stepped back, the corner of his mouth twisting. "You should have told me that right away. I make it a rule never to be in the same place with more than one Savagar at a time. See you around, Fleur." He strode off down the beach.

Fleur studied the sand, then lifted her head and gazed at her brother. "He could have broken you in two."

Michel shrugged.

"Why did you do it?" she asked softly.

He looked past her to study the ocean. "You're my sister," he said. "It's my responsibility as a man." He headed toward the house.

"Wait." She moved automatically. The sand tugged at her feet like old hurts, but she pulled herself free. Images of the beautiful gowns she'd seen in his shop window flashed through her head. Who was he?

He waited for her to reach his side, but when she got there, she didn't know what to say. She cleared her throat. "Do you . . . want to go someplace and talk?"

Several seconds ticked by. "All right."

They didn't speak as he drove his ancient MG to a roadhouse in Hampton Bays where Willie Nelson sang on the jukebox and the waitress brought them clams, french fries, and a pitcher of beer. Fleur began, haltingly, to tell him about growing up at the *couvent.*

He told her about his schooling and his love for his grandmother. She learned that Solange had left him the money that was supporting his business. An hour slipped by and then another. She explained how it felt to be an outcast, and he talked about his terror when he'd realized he was gay. As the neon sign outside the roadhouse window flashed blue across his hair, she leaned against the back of the scarred wooden booth and told him about Flynn and Belinda.

His eyes grew dark and bitter. "It explains so much."

They spoke of Alexi and understood each other perfectly. The roadhouse began to close up for the night. "I was so jealous of you," she finally said. "I thought you had everything I'd been denied."

"And I wanted to be you," he said. "Away from them both."

Dishes clattered in the kitchen, and the waitress glared at them. Fleur saw that Michel had something more he wanted to say, but he was having trouble forming the words.

"Tell me."

He gazed down at the battered tabletop. "I want to design for you," he said. "I always have."

★

The next morning she pulled on a tangerine bikini, fastened her hair into a loose top knot, and slipped into a short white cover-up. The living room was deserted, but through the windows she saw Charlie and Michel lounging on the deck with the Sunday papers. She smiled as she took in Michel's outfit for the day, a pair of Bermuda shorts and an emerald-green shirt with "One Day Dry Cleaning" emblazoned across the back. After so many years of misdirected hatred, she'd been given the unexpected gift of a brother. She could hardly take it in.

She went into the kitchen and poured herself a cup of coffee. "How about making that two cups?"

She spun around and saw Jake standing in the doorway. His long hair was damp from his shower. He wore a gray T-shirt and a pair of faded swim trunks that looked like the same ones he'd worn six years ago when Belinda had invited him for a backyard barbecue. She'd already figured out that last night's encounter hadn't been accidental. He was one of Charlie's party guests, he'd known she was here, and he'd gone out looking for her.

She turned away. "Get your own damned coffee."

"I didn't mean to scare you last night." His arm brushed hers as he reached for the coffeepot. She smelled Dial soap and mint toothpaste. "I wasn't completely sober. I'm sorry, Flower."

She crossed her arms over her chest. "I'm sorry, too. That I didn't split your head open."

He leaned back against the counter and took a sip of his coffee. "You did okay in *Eclipse*. Better than I expected."

"Gee, thanks."

"Go for a walk on the beach with me?"

She started to refuse, only to hear one of Charlie's

houseguests coming downstairs. This was as good an opportunity as any to say what she needed to. "After you."

They slipped out the side door, avoiding the group on the deck. Fleur pulled off her espadrilles and tossed them aside. The wind tugged at Jake's Wild West hair. Neither of them spoke until they got near the water. "I talked to your brother for a while this morning," he said. "Michael's a nice guy."

Did he really think he could melt away the years so easily? "A nice guy for a dress designer, you mean."

"You're not provoking me, no matter how hard you try."

She'd see about that.

He flopped down on the sand. "Okay, Flower, let's have it out."

The acid words churned inside her, all the rage and bitterness ready to spill out. But as she watched a father and son fly a Chinese kite with a blue and yellow tail, she realized she couldn't say any of it, not if she wanted to hold on to even a shred of her pride. "No lasting scars," she said. "You weren't that important." She made herself settle next to him in the sand. "And you're the one who's had to live with what you did."

He squinted against the sun. "If it wasn't that important, why did you give up a career that was earning you a fortune? And why haven't I been able to write anything since *Sunday Morning Eclipse*?"

"You're not writing at all?" She felt a stab of satisfaction.

"You haven't seen any new plays running around with my name on them, have you? I've got a frigging case of concrete writer's block."

"Too bad."

He threw a shell toward the water. "Funniest thing. I was writing just dandy before you and Mama came along."

"Hold on. You're blaming me?"

"No." He sighed. "I'm just being a prick."

"Finally something you're good at."

He looked her square in the eyes. "What happened between us that weekend didn't have anything to do with *Eclipse*."

"Come off it." Despite her determination, the words spilled out. "That picture meant everything to you, and I was ruining your big opportunity. A nineteen-year-old kid with an absurdly misdirected case of puppy love. You were a grown man, and you knew better."

"I was twenty-eight. And, believe me, you didn't look like a kid that night."

"My mother was your lover!"

"If it's any consolation, we never did the dirty deed."

"I don't want to hear."

"All I can say in my defense is that I was a lousy judge of character."

Fleur knew her mother well enough to believe Belinda had made it easy for him, but she didn't care. "So if you were Mr. Innocent, why haven't you been able to write since then? I can't pretend to see into the murky depths of your psyche, but there must be some connection between your writing block and what you did to that stupid nineteen-year-old kid."

He came to his feet, spraying her with sand. "Since when did I get nominated for sainthood? Nineteen and looking the way you did wasn't a *kid*." He pulled off his T-shirt and ran down to the water, where he dived under a wave, then swam out. His form was as lousy as ever. Big he-man movie star. Bastard. She wanted to retaliate, and when he finally emerged, she unfastened her beach robe and let it drop. Underneath was the tiny tangerine bikini Kissy had bought her, and she made sure he got a front-row view as she performed a perfect runway walk to the water, planting one foot directly in front of the other so that her hips swayed. At the edge, she lifted her arms to fasten a tendril of hair that had come loose from the pins, casually stretching as she did it to make her legs look even longer.

She stole a glance out of the corner of her eye to see if

he was watching. He was. Good. Let him eat his shriveled little heart out.

She plunged into the water and swam for a while, then came out and walked back to where he was sitting. He held her beach robe on his lap, and as she leaned down to pick it up, he moved it just out of her reach. "Give a guy a break. I've been working with horses for three months, and this is a nice change of scenery."

She straightened, then walked away. Jake Koranda was as dead to her as the grandmother she'd never known.

Jake watched Fleur until she disappeared into the beach house. The beautiful nineteen-year-old who'd sent him into a tailspin couldn't hold a candle to this woman. She'd become every man's fantasy. Was it his imagination, or did that pert little butt sit higher than ever on those knockout legs? He should have given her back the robe so he didn't have to torture himself watching her body in that ridiculous tangerine bikini tied together with those little bits of string. He could eat that bikini off her in three good bites.

He headed for the water to cool off. The guy flying the kite with his kid had spotted Flower as soon as she came over the dunes, and now he was backing into the water to get a better view. It had always been that way—men stumbling over themselves while she sailed past, oblivious to the stir she'd created. She was the ugly duckling who wouldn't look into a mirror long enough to see that she'd changed into a swan.

He swam for a while, then went back to the beach. Fleur's cover-up lay in the sand. As he picked it up, he caught the same light floral scent he'd smelled the night before when she was struggling in his arms. He'd been a real prick, and she'd stood up to him. She always had, in one way or another.

He dug his heels into the sand. The music started playing in his head. Otis Redding. Creedence Clearwater. She'd brought back all the sounds of Vietnam. He'd never forget kneeling on Johnny Guy's lawn with her wet and sobbing in his arms. She'd ripped a hole through the wall he'd built inside him—a wall he'd thought was secure—and he hadn't been able to write a word since then for fear he'd bring the whole damned thing crashing down. Writing was the only way he'd ever been able to express himself, and without it, he felt as though he was living half a life.

As he gazed toward the beach house, he wondered if the woman she'd become could hold the key to unlocking this prison he'd fallen into.

Chapter 20

Dark, erotic dreams invaded Fleur's sleep after she got back to the city. She wondered if their wrestling match on the beach had recharged some kind of internal sexual battery. Wouldn't that be ironic? She was hungry for the touch of a man, but she was too tightly strung right now to think about looking for a lover.

Two weeks after the beach party, she sat on a straight-backed chair in Michel's boutique while he locked up for the evening. At first they'd invented excuses to talk to each other. He called to see if she'd gotten stuck in traffic on her way back from Long Island. She called to ask his advice about an outfit she wanted to buy Kissy for her birthday. Finally they abandoned subterfuge and openly enjoyed each other's company.

"I went over your books last night." She'd brushed some sawdust from her jeans. "Bottom line . . . Your finances are a mess."

He flipped off the store's front lights. "I'm an artist, not a businessman. That's why I hired you."

"My newest client." She smiled. "It never occurred to me to represent a designer, but I'm excited about it. Your gowns and dresses are the most innovative work this city has seen in years. All I have to do is make people want them." She waved her hands over an imaginary crystal ball. "I see fame, fortune, and brilliant management in your future." As an afterthought, she added, "I also see a new lover."

He stepped behind her and pulled the rubber band from her ponytail. She'd spent all day with the carpenters at the townhouse, and she was a mess. "Stick with fame and fortune and leave my lovers alone," he said. "I know you didn't like Damon, but—"

"He's a whiny twit." Damon was the dark-haired dancer who had been with Michel the night of Charlie's beach party. "Your choice of men is worse than Kissy's. Her hunks are only dumb. Yours is snide, too."

"Only because you intimidated him. Hand me your hairbrush. You look like bad Bette Davis. And those jeans are making me bilious. Really, Fleur, I don't think I can stand these clothes of yours much longer. I've shown you the designs—"

She snatched the brush from her purse. "Hurry up and finish my hair. I have to meet Kissy, and I only stopped by to tell you that you're a financial screw-up. You also know zip about merchandising. Still, I forgive you. Come to dinner with Kissy and me tomorrow night at the townhouse."

"Aren't you missing a few necessities for throwing a dinner party? Like walls and furniture?"

"It's informal." She hopped up, gave him a kiss, and left. As she stepped out onto West Fifty-fifth Street, she wondered if he'd sensed how nervous she was about the announcement she intended to make at her improvised dinner party.

✶

She'd leased the red brick townhouse on the Upper West Side with an option to buy. Because the house's four stories had been awkwardly divided—horizontally instead of vertically—she'd gotten a good price, and she'd been able to adapt the unusual arrangement to her advantage. She intended to live in the smaller rear section of the house and use the larger front section for office space. If all went well, she'd be able to move in by mid-August, a month from now.

"No one's going to confuse this with La Grenouille," Michel said as he gingerly lowered himself into a folding chair she'd set in front of the table fashioned from two sawhorses and some sheets of plywood in what would soon be her office.

Kissy looked pointedly at Michel's white clam diggers and Greek peasant shirt. "They wouldn't let you in La Grenouille, so stop complaining."

"I heard you were there, though," he said. "With a certain Mr. Kincannon."

"And a group of his nerdy friends." Kissy wrinkled her nose. Even though she saw Charlie Kincannon frequently, she barely mentioned him, which didn't bode well for his plan to win her heart.

Fleur began ladling out lemon chicken and spicy Szechuan shrimp from carryout cartons. "I wish you'd move in with me, Kissy. The attic is finished, so you'd have plenty of privacy, not to mention twice as much room as our apartment. There's a kitchen up there, the plumbing works, and you'll even have a separate entrance off the front hallway so I won't be able to cluck my tongue over your playmates."

"I like my place. And I've told you—moving makes me crazy. I never do it if I don't have to."

Fleur gave up. Kissy was so down on herself right now that she didn't feel as though she deserved anything more than what she had, and no amount of persuasion could convince her otherwise.

Kissy dabbed her mouth with a paper napkin. "Why the mystery? You said you wanted Michel and me here so you could make an announcement. What's up?"

Fleur gestured toward the wine. "Pour, Michel. We're going to drink a toast."

"Beaujolais with Chinese? Really, Fleur."

"Don't criticize, just do your job." He filled their glasses, and Fleur lifted hers, determined to project a confidence she didn't feel. "Tonight we drink to my two favorite clients, as well as the genius who's going to put you both on top. Namely me." She clicked their glasses and took a sip. "Michel, why haven't you ever had a showing of your designs?"

He shrugged. "I had one my first year, but it cost me a fortune and nobody came. My stuff isn't like anything else on Seventh Avenue, and I don't have a name."

"Right." She looked at Kissy. "And no one will let you audition for the kind of parts you want because of the way you look."

Kissy pushed a shrimp around and gave a glum nod.

"What both of you need for your careers to take off is a showcase, and I've figured out how we're going to get one." Fleur set down her glass. "Of the three of us, which one stands the best shot at getting media attention?"

"Rub it in," Kissy grumbled.

Michel stated the obvious. "You do. We all know that."

"I beg to disagree," Fleur said. "Except for the week or so after the story broke, I've been in New York over two years without getting any publicity. Even Adelaide Abrams didn't care I was back. The newspapers don't want Fleur Savagar, who's a total bore. They want the Glitter Baby." She handed them the evening paper, which she'd folded open to Adelaide's gossip column.

Kissy read it aloud.

> Superstar Jake Koranda was seen wandering the beaches of Quogue Fourth of July weekend with none other than Glitter Baby Fleur Savagar. Koranda, taking a break from the Arizona filming of his newest Caliber picture, was a guest at the vacation home of millionaire pharmaceutical heir Charles Kincannon. According to friends, the GB and Koranda only had eyes for each other. So far, no comment from either Koranda's West

Coast office or the elusive Glitter Baby, who's been quietly making a name for herself in New York these past few years as a talent agent.

Kissy looked up from the article, her face stricken. "I'm sorry, Fleurinda. I know how you hate having the past dredged up. And once Abrams gets hold of a story, she won't let it go. I don't know who talked to her, but—"

"I'm the one who planted the story," Fleur said.

They stared at her.

"Would you care to let us in on the reason?" her brother asked.

Fleur took a deep breath and lifted her glass. "Drag out those designs you've been saving up for me, Michel. The Glitter Baby's coming back, and she's taking the two of you with her."

Pain was harder to bear sober, Belinda had discovered, since she'd forced herself to stop drinking. She slipped a cassette into the tape deck and pressed the button with the tip of her finger. As the room filled with the sounds of Barbra Streisand singing "The Way We Were," she lay back against the satin bed pillows and let the tears trickle down her cheeks.

All the rebels were dead. First it had been Jimmy on the road to Salinas, and then Sal Mineo in that brutal murder. Finally Natalie Wood. The three leading actors from *Rebel Without a Cause* had all died before their time, and Belinda was afraid she would be next.

She and Natalie were almost exactly the same age, and Natalie had loved Jimmy, too. He teased her when they were shooting *Rebel* because she was just a kid to him. Bad Boy Jimmy Dean playing with Natalie's feelings.

Death terrified Belinda, and yet she kept a secret supply of pills stashed in the bottom of an old jewelry box near the spinning gold charm Errol Flynn had given her. She couldn't stand living her life like this much longer, but a strain of optimism still ran deep inside her that said things might get better. Alexi might die.

Belinda missed her baby so much. Alexi said he'd put Belinda in a sanitarium if she tried to contact Fleur. A sanitarium for chronic alcoholics, even though she hadn't let herself touch a drop of liquor for almost two years. Although Alexi never left the house anymore, she hardly ever saw him. He conducted his business from a suite of rooms on the first floor, working through a series of assistants who wore dark suits and somber expressions and passed her in the hallways without speaking. Almost no one spoke to her. Her days and nights blended together, stretching behind and before her in an unending line, each one exactly like the last until she couldn't find a reason to go on living except the hope that Alexi would die.

In the old days, when she walked into a ball or a restaurant on Alexi's arm, she became the most important woman in the room. People sought her out to curry favor. They told her how beautiful she was, how amusing. Without Alexi, the invitations had stopped.

She remembered how it had been in California when she was the Glitter Baby's mother. She'd been charged with energy until she was luminescent. Everything she touched became special. That was the best time of all.

The song came to an end. She got out of bed and pushed the rewind button to play it again. The music kept her from hearing the door open, and she didn't know that Alexi had entered until she turned around.

It had been nearly a month since he'd visited her rooms, and she wished that her hair was combed and that her eyes weren't red from crying. She nervously toyed with the front of her robe. "I—I'm a wreck."

"But always beautiful," he replied. "Fix yourself for me, *chérie*. I'll wait."

This was what made him so dangerous. Not his terrible cruelties, but his awful tenderness. Both were intentional, and each, in its own way, entirely sincere.

While he took a seat in the room's most comfortable chair, she gathered up what she needed and slipped into the bathroom. When she came out, he lay on the bed, all the lamps turned off except one on the opposite side of the room. The dim light hid his unhealthy pallor, as well as the network of fine lines at the corners of her own eyes.

She wore a simple white nightgown. Her toenails were bare of polish and her scrubbed face clean of makeup. She'd threaded a ribbon through her hair.

She lay back on the bed without speaking. He pushed her nightgown to her waist. She kept her legs tightly closed while he caressed her and slowly removed her underpants. When he pushed at her knees, she whimpered as if she were afraid, and he rewarded her for the whimper with one of the deep caresses she liked so much. She tried to push her legs closed again to please him, but he'd begun to kiss the insides of her thighs, and her eyelids drifted shut. This was their unspoken pact. Now that his teenage mistresses were gone, she played the child bride for him, and he let her keep her eyes shut so she could remember Flynn and dream about James Dean.

Usually he left as soon as it was over, but this time he lay still, a sheen of sweat visible on the flaccid skin of his chest. "Are you all right?" she asked.

"Would you hand me my robe, *chérie*? There are some pills in the pocket."

She got the robe for him and turned away as he pulled out the vial of pills. Instead of making him weaker, his illness had strengthened his power. Now, with his first-floor fortress and the army of watchful assistants carrying out his orders, he'd made himself invulnerable.

She went into the bathroom to shower. When she came out, he was still there, sitting in a chair and sipping a drink.

"I ordered whiskey for you." He pointed with his glass toward a tumbler on a silver tray.

How typically cruel of him. The cruelty coming after the tenderness in a tightly woven pattern of contradictions that had directed the course of her life for more than twenty-five years. "You know I don't drink anymore."

"Really, *chérie*, you shouldn't lie to me. Do you think I don't know about the empty bottles your maid finds hidden in the bottom of the wastebasket?"

There were no empty bottles. This was his way of threatening her to make certain she did his bidding. She remembered the pictures of the sanitarium he'd shown her, a collection of ugly gray buildings in the most remote part of the Swiss Alps. "What do you want from me, Alexi?"

"You are a stupid woman. A stupid, helpless woman. I cannot imagine why I ever loved you." A small muscle ticked near his temple. "I'm sending you away," he said abruptly.

A chill shot through her. The ugly gray buildings sat like great cold stones in the snow. She thought of the pills hidden away in the bottom of her old jewelry box.

All the rebels were dead now.

He crossed his legs and took a sip from his drink. "The sight of you depresses me. I do not wish to have you near me any longer."

Death from the pills would be painless. It wouldn't be like the suffocating salt water that had closed over Natalie's head or the terrible pain Jimmy had felt when he died. She'd simply go to bed and drift into endless sleep.

The hard Russian eyes of Alexi Savagar sliced through the layers of her skin like a razor. "I am sending you to New York," he said. "What you do once you are there no longer concerns me."

Baby Resurrected

Chapter 21

The bronze satin gown hugged her body with its high neck, bare arms, and slashed skirt. She wanted to part her hair in the middle and wear it in a low Spanish knot like a flamenco dancer, but Michel wouldn't let her. "That big streaky mane is the Glitter Baby's trademark. For tonight, you have to wear it down."

Fleur had just moved into her living quarters at the townhouse, but Michel ordered her to dress at the apartment where Kissy could supervise. Her former roommate stuck her head in the bedroom. "The limo's outside."

"Wish me luck," Fleur said.

"Not so fast." Kissy turned Fleur toward the mirror. "Look at yourself."

"Come on, Kissy, I don't have time—"

"Stop squirming and look in the mirror."

Fleur glanced at her reflection. The gown was exquisite. Instead of deemphasizing her height, Michel's lean design accentuated it. The diagonal slash of skirt started at mid-thigh and crossed over her body, offering tantalizing glimpses of long legs through the filmy black *point d'esprit* flounce that filled the space.

Slowly she lifted her eyes. In a few weeks, she'd be

twenty-six, and her face had a new maturity. She catalogued her separate parts—the wide-spaced green eyes, the marking-pen brows, the mouth that spread all over—and then, for an instant, it all came together, and her face finally seemed to belong to her.

The moment passed, the impression faded, and she turned away. "Just shows what a fabulous dress and good makeup will do."

Kissy looked disappointed. "You never see yourself."

"Don't be silly." She picked up her purse and dashed downstairs to the limousine. Just before she got in, she looked up at the window and saw Michel and Kissy standing there watching her. She gave them her very cockiest grin. The Glitter Baby was back.

What she hadn't counted on was Belinda.

Adelaide Abrams slowly dropped her hand from Fleur's arm and nodded toward the doorway of the Orlani Gallery where Belinda stood wrapped in golden sable, as fragile and beautiful as a butterfly. Fleur fought to control the whirlwind of emotions spinning inside her. She took one deep breath and then another as Belinda approached. Fleur hadn't seen her mother for six years, and she felt as if she were shattering into a thousand ice-cold pieces.

Belinda extended one hand and pressed the other to the bodice of her dress as if she were touching something hidden there. "People are watching, darling. For appearances, at least."

"I don't play to the crowd anymore." Fleur turned her back and walked away from the scent of Shalimar, from the sight of delicately etched lines, like the veins of an autumn leaf, crinkling the corners of her mother's blue eyes.

As she made her way across the gallery, she smiled automatically and exchanged a few words here and there with people she recognized. She even managed a short interview with the reporter from *Harper's*. But all the time she wondered why it had to happen tonight. How had Belinda known the Glitter Baby would be reappearing?

Kissy and Michel were scheduled to arrive soon. Their appearance was the point of all this, and Belinda's presence had thrown it all off balance.

"Fleur Savagar?" A young man dressed in black stopped in front of her and held out a long florist's box. "A delivery for you."

Adelaide Abrams appeared at her side like magic. "An admirer?"

"I don't know." Fleur flipped open the box and pushed aside the nest of tissue paper. Lying beneath were a dozen long-stemmed white roses . . . She lifted her head and looked across the gallery. She locked eyes with Belinda and slowly pulled one of the roses from the box.

Belinda's forehead creased and her shoulders drooped. She stared at the white rose, then turned toward the door and fled from the gallery.

Adelaide poked in the box. "There's no card."

"I know who they're from." Fleur took in the empty doorway.

"His initials wouldn't happen to be J.K., would they?" Adelaide asked.

Fleur fixed a bright smile on her face. "Secret admirers are meant to be secret. Especially ones who've made a career out of protecting their privacy."

Adelaide gave her a sly wink. "You're a good girl, Fleur, despite your occasional lapses."

As Adelaide disappeared, Fleur shoved the rose back into the box. The cloying smell stuck in her nostrils and clung to her throat. Fleur had been expecting something like this ever since Alexi's phone call. He was letting her know he hadn't forgotten anything.

She pushed the lid back on and set the box on a bench. She wanted to stuff it in the nearest trash can, but she couldn't afford to with Adelaide Abrams looking on. Let her think they came from Jake. He was a big boy, and he could take care of himself. She also needed the publicity, and she didn't have a single qualm about using him as he'd once used her.

She saw Michel and Kissy standing in the doorway. Michel wore a white tuxedo with a black nylon T-shirt. He'd dressed Kissy in a tiny pink and silver version of a prom dress, perfectly proportioned for her size. She clung to his arm, feminine, helpless, lips slightly pursed as if she were ready to expel a breathless boop-boopy-doop.

Fleur took the long way through the crowd, giving everyone time to watch where she was going. When she reached the doorway, she brushed cheeks with them both and whispered in Michel's ear that Belinda had just left. He gazed at her searchingly. She had no idea what to tell him.

Kissy and Michel's entrance coupled with Fleur's greeting had attracted attention, just as she'd planned. *Women's Wear Daily* got to them first, and Fleur made the introductions. Both Michel and Kissy performed like champs, bored sophistication on his part, a frothy cloud of pink and silver exuberance on hers. When they had finished with *WWD*, *Harper's*, and Adelaide Abrams, the three of them circulated through the gallery, stopping to chat with everyone they met. She introduced her brother as Michel Savagar instead of Michael Anton. Not long after they'd been reunited, he'd decided to stop hiding under an assumed name. Michel remained aloof and mysterious while Kissy chattered like a magpie, and Fleur directed the conversation exactly where she wanted it.

"Isn't my brother the most magnificent designer . . . ? My brother designed my gown. I'm glad you like it . . . My brother is obscenely talented. I'm trying to get him to share his gift, but he's so stubborn . . ."

She responded to questions about Kissy's identity with a smile. "Isn't she outrageous? So adorable. One of the Charleston Christies. Michel designed her dress, too."

When they asked what Kissy did for a living, Fleur waved

an airy hand. "A little acting, but that's more a hobby than anything else."

The women's envious gazes flickered between Fleur's incredible bronze satin and Kissy's reimagined prom dress. "My brother has so many women begging him to design for them," she confided, "but right now he's only designing for Kissy and me. Confidentially I'm hoping to change that."

Several people commented on Belinda's appearance. Fleur answered as briefly as possible and then changed the subject. She told everyone about her new agency—Fleur Savagar and Associates, Celebrity Management—and issued early invitations to the big open house she planned to throw in a few weeks. A good-looking celebrity heart surgeon invited her to dinner the next evening. She accepted. He was charming, and she needed a chance to show off Michel's iris and blue silk sheath.

By the time they got into the limousine after the party, Fleur was fighting off a headache, and Michel picked up her hand. "You're exhausted. You don't have to put yourself through this, you know."

"Yes, I do. We couldn't buy this kind of publicity. Besides, it's long past time I figure out how to live with who I am, and that includes the Glitter Baby."

She thought of the roses she'd abandoned at the gallery, and suddenly she understood their message as clearly as if Alexi had sent her a letter. He'd kept Belinda out of her life for all these years. Now he'd sent her back.

A week later, the phone calls began. They usually came around two in the morning. When Fleur answered, she heard music turned low in the background—Barbra Streisand, Neil Diamond, Simon and Garfunkel—but the caller never spoke. Fleur had no hard evidence that the calls were coming from Belinda. No scent of Shalimar magically wafted through the telephone lines. But she was certain all the same.

She hung up without saying a word, but the calls began

to wear on her, and whenever she turned a corner, she found herself waiting for Belinda to appear.

*

Fleur made Michel shut down his store and bring in the people who'd done the Kamali boutique to refashion the space with better display areas, a more elegant storefront, and the name Michel Savagar embossed over the doorway in bold red script on a deep purple background.

She and Kissy immediately made themselves an integral part of New York's social scene. Wherever they went, they wore Michel's wonderful designs. They lunched at Orsini's then popped into David Webb to pick up an eighteen-karat bauble, which one of them later returned because "It wasn't quite right." They stopped at Helene Arpels for a new pair of evening pumps, then danced at Club A or Regine's. As they lunched, shopped, and danced, they modeled silk dresses that floated like sea foam around their hips, a slim skimp of blue jersey with a gathered side seam, an evening gown that shimmered with tomato-red sequined panels. Within a week, every fashion-forward social butterfly in New York began asking about Michel Savagar's dresses. Just as Fleur had hoped, they wanted them even more when they discovered the garments weren't available.

Fleur and Kissy publicly gossiped about Michel. "My grandmother ruined him with all the money she left him," Fleur confided to Adelaide Abrams from a banquette at Chez Pascal where she also showed off a silk wrap dress printed with gossamer water lilies. "People who don't have to work for a living get lazy."

The next day she confided in the gossipy wife of a department store heir. "Michel's afraid commercialism will stifle his creativity. But he *is* working on something, and I do have some plans . . . Oh, never mind."

Kissy was less subtle. "I'm almost positive he's secretly putting together a collection," she told everyone. And then her candy apple mouth formed a little pout, and she patted the skirt of whatever sugarplum confection she was showing off that day. "I don't think it's right that he won't confide in me. Except for his sister, I'm his very dearest friend, and I can keep a secret as well as anyone."

While Fleur and Kissy spread the word about Michel's idealism and indifference to commercial success, Michel was working eighteen-hour days overseeing every detail of a collection he was financing with the last of Solange Savagar's money.

Fleur was surviving on four hours of sleep. Every minute she didn't spent playing the social butterfly she was in her office interviewing for staff, planning her open house, and dodging the last of the workmen. Several actors approached her about representation, but none of them had the special qualities she was looking for.

Fleur loved the way the townhouse renovations had turned out, despite the challenges the structure had presented. Her offices occupied the larger front section of the house and her living quarters the smaller rear portion. She'd decorated the office spaces in black and white with shots of gray and indigo. Her private office and the reception area occupied the front of the main floor, while the other offices were set off a balcony above. She'd added tubular ocean liner railing and black art deco columns with chrome collars to border the balcony, along with an open curved staircase that looked as if Fred Astaire and Ginger Rogers would be dancing the Continental down it at any moment.

Her first two hires were Will O'Keefe, a cheerful redhead from North Dakota, who was an experienced publicist and talent agent, and David Bennis, gray-haired and professorial, who'd take charge of business and financial management, as well as give her agency an air of stability. She also hired a single mother named Riata Lawrence as office manager. For now, she didn't have enough clients to keep them all busy, but they were part of the facade of success she had to create, right along with her beautifully decorated office and couture wardrobe.

A week before the open house, Will stepped over the last of the drop cloths outside her office. Since they weren't officially open for business until after the open house, she wore jeans and an orange Mickey Mouse sweatshirt instead of the executive wardrobe Michel had designed for her.

"You've made Abrams's column again," Will said. "Unfortunately this isn't one of our plants."

Fleur took the paper and read.

> Belinda Savagar spent yesterday afternoon in Yves Saint Laurent's men's boutique helping thirty-year-old heartthrob Shawn Howell pick out a new set of YSL silk sheets. Wonder what French industrialist hubby Alexi Savagar has to say about all that laundry?

Fleur hadn't seen Belinda since the Orlani Gallery two weeks ago, but she was still getting the middle-of-the-night phone calls.

The next day, Will handed over Adelaide's newest column:

> Shawn Howell nuzzled with Belinda Savagar in the Elm Room at Tavern on the Green. Who says May/December romances don't work? Shawn and Belinda seem to be getting it just right. No comment from Glitter Baby Fleur Savagar, even though she and Shawn used to be an item.

Some item. Fleur had detested Shawn Howell from their first arranged date.

Adelaide went on to write:

Old feuds die hard. Maybe Mom and the Glitter Baby will patch it up for Christmas. Peace on earth, girls.

Fleur pitched the column into the wastebasket.

*

She'd just gotten off the phone with another actor she didn't want to represent when Will O'Keefe stuck his head into her office, his lightly freckled face pale. "We have a big problem. Yesterday Olivia Creighton called to chew me out because she hadn't received her open house invitation. I sent her another one and didn't think anything more about it until an hour ago when Adelaide Abrams called with the same complaint. Fleur, I've checked around. No one's received their invitation."

"That's impossible. We mailed them ages ago."

"That's what I thought." His expression grew graver. "I just spoke with Riata. She had them sitting in an open box on her desk. The day she planned to mail them, she came back from lunch and they were gone. She assumed I'd mailed them. Unfortunately she didn't bother to check."

Fleur sank into her new desk chair and tried to think.

"Do you want me to call everyone?" he asked. "Explain what happened and issue the invitation over the phone? Or should we change the date? We only have four days."

Fleur made up her mind. "No phone calls and no explanations. Have new invitations hand-delivered this afternoon with flowers from Ronaldo Maia." It would cost a fortune, but trying to explain would only make her look incompetent. "Put my mind at ease and double-check the rest of the arrangements. Let's make sure there haven't been any other slip-ups."

He was back ten minutes later, and even before he spoke, she could see he had bad news. "Someone canceled the caterer last week. They've booked another party for our date."

"Great," Fleur muttered. "This is just great." She rubbed

her eyes and spent the rest of the afternoon shopping for a new caterer.

For the next four days she worked until she was exhausted and waited for another disaster. Nothing out of the ordinary happened, but she couldn't make herself relax, and by the afternoon of the open house, she felt as if her nerves had been scraped raw. She ran out for a quick meeting with a new casting agent. When she came back, a soot-streaked Will met her at the entrance.

"We've had a fire."

Her stomach pitched. "Is anybody hurt? How bad was it?"

"It could have been worse. David and I were in the hallway, and we smelled smoke coming from the basement. We grabbed a fire extinguisher and put the flames out before they could do much damage."

"Are you all right? Where's David?"

"We're both fine. He's cleaning up."

"Thank God. How did it start? What happened?"

He wiped the back of his hand over his smudged cheek. "You'd better see for yourself."

As she followed him to the basement, she shuddered to think what would have happened if the fire had broken out tonight when the house was full of people. He pointed toward the broken window directly above some charred lumber the contractor hadn't gotten around to clearing out. Fleur walked closer and pushed at the glass shards on the floor with the toe of her sneaker. "It was broken from the outside."

"I was down here this morning," Will said, "and there was nothing combustible over here. No paint cans, turpentine, nothing like that. A couple of punks out for kicks must have broken the window and tossed something inside."

Except it was five in the afternoon, not the time most punks were on the prowl. "Air things out," she said. "I'll take care of the upstairs."

Within an hour, they'd removed the charred lumber and

sprayed the office with Opium to camouflage what was left of the acrid smell. As Will left to get dressed for the party, she stopped him. "I appreciate what you and David did. I'm only glad no one was hurt."

"All in a day's work." He fastened the last button and turned to leave. "Oh, I forgot . . . Flowers arrived while you were out. Riata put them in water. She said there was no card."

Fleur went into her office. The flowers sat in a tall chrome vase on her desk.

One dozen white roses.

Chapter 22

Fleur came to a stop halfway up the circular staircase and smiled down at her guests. Assorted executives from the entertainment and publishing industries had shown up, along with enough famous faces to keep the reporters and photographers Will had invited happy. Michel had outdone himself with the long-sleeved ecru silk sheath he'd designed for her. The bodice shimmered with poppies picked out in tiny brown and tan beads. On Michel's orders, she'd secured her hair in a low chignon at the back of her neck and speared it with a jeweled chopstick. The Glitter Baby was living up to her name.

The jazz quartet playing on the balcony came to the end of their number. The crowd gradually quieted and gazed up at her. She drew on her old acting lessons and pretended she did this sort of thing all the time.

"Welcome, everyone, to the official opening of Fleur Savagar and Associates, Celebrity Management." Her guests applauded politely, but she spotted skepticism on more than a few faces. She introduced Will and David, then spoke enthusiastically of Simon's band and Olivia Creighton's new part on *Dragon's Bay.* Finally she gestured for Michel to join her on the staircase.

"I'm very sad to announce that my talented brother, Michel Savagar, will be sharing his incredible designs with the world in November when he shows his first collection." She'd caught the attention of the women in the crowd, and this time the applause was more vigorous. She pretended to frown at him. "Unfortunately that means I'll no longer be his most important client."

"You will always be most important to me," he said, his accent heavier than normal, which would have made her laugh if she weren't the one who'd suggested he emphasize his French roots.

The reporters furiously scribbled away in their notebooks as she announced the details of the showing. She thanked her guests for attending, the jazz quartet began playing again, and well-wishers surrounded Michel. She reached for a champagne flute as Kissy approached. "Good job, Fleurinda. You introduced all your clients except me."

"I have other plans for you, my pet. As you very well know."

Kissy pulled her gaze from a hunky music producer. "All Olivia Creighton wants to talk about is her new part on *Dragon's Bay.* It's only six episodes, and it's not even a lead."

"I'll bet it will be when Olivia's done with it." Fleur took a sip of champagne. "The nighttime soaps are hot, and she's perfect for television. I think she could be as big as Joan Collins."

It had taken Fleur almost a month to convince the *Dragon's Bay* producers to let Olivia audition, and then it took another few days to convince Olivia that being forced to audition was less demeaning than doing more condominium commercials. But as soon as the producers heard her read, they offered her the job. The money was unimpressive, but Fleur would fix that the next time around. Olivia's mature, sexy beauty and confident bearing held a strong appeal to middle-aged women, and Fleur was betting all that would translate into higher ratings for the show.

The hunky music executive disappeared, and Kissy finally gave Fleur her full attention. "You look incredible tonight. A little intimidating."

"Really? How?"

"Sort of like the 'other woman' in the movies. The sophisticated blond bitch-goddess who tries to steal the hero from the rosy-cheeked heroine."

"Excellent." A blond bitch-goddess didn't have to worry about the little things in life. Or the big things—like Alexi Savagar trying to destroy her.

She'd told Kissy and Michel about the fire, but hadn't yet mentioned Alexi's involvement. From the moment Belinda had walked into the Orlani Gallery, Alexi had been playing a cat-and-mouse game. The missing invitations were bad enough, but this afternoon he'd gotten serious.

Kissy nudged her. "Have you been watching Michel and Simon?"

"Disappointing." With his massive size and shaved head, Simon was the most noticeable man in the crowd to everyone but Michel.

"They both have such bad taste in men," Kissy said. "I guess we shouldn't be surprised that they haven't paid any attention to each other."

"That little twit Damon won't leave Michel's side."

Kissy frowned. "Michel and Simon are terrific people. The temptation to do some matchmaking is almost irresistible."

Fleur watched Michel laugh at something Damon said. "It's none of our business."

"I know you're right."

"Michel doesn't butt into my personal life, and I owe him the same courtesy."

"You're a good sister."

"So how about a small dinner party in a few weeks?"

"Exactly what I was thinking."

With that piece of business out of the way, Kissy surveyed the crowd. "Didn't you tell me you invited Charlie

Kincannon?" The inquiry seemed casual, but Fleur wasn't fooled.

"Uh-huh."

"Did you get the impression that he was coming?"

"I'm not sure. Haven't you talked to him?"

"Not for a couple of weeks."

"Problems?"

Kissy shrugged. "I guess he's gay or something."

"Just because a fabulous man ignores you doesn't mean he's gay."

"He's hardly fabulous."

"Christie Brinkley seems to think so. I heard they were dating." Lying to her best friend was a rotten thing to do, but Kissy refused to take Charlie seriously, and Fleur decided the end justified the means.

"Christie Brinkley! She has to be a foot taller than he is."

"Charlie's very self-confident behind his geeky and fabulously rich facade. I don't think he worries too much about externals."

"I really don't care." Kissy sniffed. "Besides, I've never found Christie all that attractive."

"Yeah. What's so great about perfect features and a magnificent body?"

"You think I deserve this, don't you?"

"Oh yes."

"I haven't fallen for him, so get that smug look off your face. Charlie's not interested in me that way. We're friends."

Will drew Fleur away to talk to a reporter before she could suggest that Kissy cut the crap. As she finished posing for photographers, she bumped into Shawn Howell, who definitely hadn't been on her guest list. Shawn's teen idol face wasn't nearly as cute at thirty as it had been at twenty-two when Fleur had to endure the dates Belinda had arranged. Since then, his career had tanked, and he reportedly owed the IRS a quarter of a million dollars.

"Hello, gorgeous." He bypassed her cheek for a direct

shot at her mouth. His tongue flicked her bottom lip. "You don't mind a couple of gate crashers at your party, do you?"

A strobe flashed next to them. "Apparently not."

"Hey, it's business, right?" He grinned and rubbed his hand down her spine like a high school boy checking for a bra. "I hear you're in the market for clients, and I'm looking for a new agent, so maybe I'll give you a try."

"I don't think we're a good fit." She started to slip past him, then stopped as a sense of dread swept through her. "What did you mean by 'a couple of gate crashers'?"

"Belinda's waiting in your office. She asked me to tell you."

For a moment Fleur was tempted to leave her own party, but she didn't run anymore, and this was something she couldn't put off.

★

Belinda stood with her back to the door looking at a Louise Nevelson lithograph Fleur had bought with the profits from a delivery of palladium. As Fleur stared at the small, straight line of her mother's spine, she felt a stab of yearning. She remembered how she used to throw herself into Belinda's arms when her mother appeared at the front door of the *couvent*, how she'd bury her face in the crook of her neck. Belinda had been her only champion. She'd defended her against the nuns and told her she was the most wonderful girl in all the world.

"I'm sorry, baby," Belinda said, still staring at the Nevelson. "I know you don't want me here."

Fleur went over to sit behind her desk, using its authority to protect herself from the flood of painful emotion that made her want to rush across the room and hold tight to the person she used to care about more than anyone. "Why did you come?"

Belinda turned. She wore a frilly ice-blue dress and satin French heels with pale blue ribbons that tied around her ankles. The outfit was too youthful for a forty-five-year-old woman, but it looked perfect on her. "I tried to stay away. Ever since I saw the white roses that night at the Orlani . . . But I couldn't manage it any longer."

"What did the roses mean to you?"

Belinda fumbled with the jeweled clasp on her evening bag and reached inside for a cigarette. "You should never have destroyed the Royale." She pulled out a gold lighter and flicked it with unsteady fingers. "Alexi hates you."

"I don't care." Fleur hated the catch in her voice. "Alexi means nothing to me."

"I wanted to tell you," Belinda said softly. "You'll never know how many times I wanted to tell you about your real father." With a faraway look in her eyes, she gazed across the office. "We lived together for three months at the Garden of Allah. Errol Flynn was a great star, Fleur. An immortal. You look so much like him."

Fleur brought her hand down on the desk. "How could you lie to me? All those years! Why couldn't you have told me the truth instead of letting me wonder why my father sent me away?"

"Because I didn't want to hurt you, baby."

"Your lies hurt more than the truth ever could. All that time I thought it was my fault that Alexi banished me from the family."

"But, baby, if I'd told you the truth, you would have hated me."

Her mother looked fragile and helpless, and Fleur couldn't stand to hear any more. She fought for control. "Why did Alexi send you to me? I know he did."

Belinda gave a soft, nervous laugh. "Because he thinks I'm no good for you. Isn't that silly, baby? When I saw the roses that night at the gallery, I understood he wanted me to go to you. That's why I've been staying away."

"Until tonight."

"I couldn't manage it any longer. I had to see if we could start over. I miss you so much, baby."

Fleur held herself stiffly and stared at Belinda. Gradually her mother wilted. "I'll go now. Watch out for Alexi." She walked to the door. "And remember. I never meant to cause you hurt. I love you too much."

Even after all this time, Belinda still didn't understand that what she'd done was wrong. Fleur gripped the edge of her desk. "You pimped me."

Belinda looked confused. "The man was Jake Koranda, baby. I would never have given you to anyone else." She hesitated for a moment and then slipped out the door.

Fleur was exhausted by the time the last of her guests left, but the open house had been a huge success, worth every tired muscle. She slipped into the front hallway and passed through the door that led to her private living quarters in the back of the house. She smelled the eucalyptus she'd piled in wicker baskets, the only decorating touch her bank account permitted for now. Walking into the living room, she flicked on the lights, then collapsed on her secondhand couch. A fringed paisley shawl only marginally disguised its shabbiness, but the peaceful room began to soothe the jagged edges of her tension.

The two-story expanse of metal-paned windows in front of her had come from an old New England textile mill. Through them she saw her small, sunken garden with its lacework of tree branches. Pyracantha bearing bright orange berries climbed the high brick walls. Someday this nearly empty room would be a true haven. She imagined a warm combination of rich walnut furniture, cozy rugs, and antique tables topped with flowers.

The second-floor living room was an open loft fronted by a railing. Fleur wandered over to the railing in her stocking feet. She gazed down the expanse of industrial windows to the kitchen and dining area below. The weathered brick floor held the antique cherry harvest table Michel had given her as a housewarming gift. Now it was surrounded with mismatched chairs, but someday she'd own beautiful old ladder-backs and nubby hand-woven rugs.

She flicked off the living room lights and made her way to her bedroom. On the way, she unzipped her dress and stepped out of it. Wearing her bra and a pair of tap pants, she walked across her bare bedroom floor to her closet. The most beautiful couture wardrobe in New York was stashed away in a bedroom with only a secondhand chest of drawers, a creaky chair, and a double bed missing a headboard. She switched on the closet light and hung up her dress. While she gazed at the array of beautiful clothes Michel had made for her, she took the pins from her hair. As she shook it out, something in the periphery of her vision caught her eye. She gasped and spun around.

Jake lay asleep on her bed.

He lifted his arm and covered his eyes. "Do you have to make so much noise?"

The jeweled hair ornaments fell from her fingers. She stalked over to the bed, her hair flying. "What are you doing here? Get out! How did you get in? I swear—"

"Your secretary let me in." He yawned. "She thinks I'm a better actor than Bobby De Niro."

"You're not. All you know how to do is snarl and squint." She pushed her hair out of her face. "And you had no right to turn your cheap charm loose on my secretary." First the basement fire, then Belinda, and now this. She kicked the mattress. "Out of here! This is my house."

He flipped on the bedside light, and her body—the same body that refused to wake up for any of the men she dated—stirred to life. Although he'd shaved his mustache and cut his hair since the beach party, Jake didn't look any more civilized. He looked rough and male and infinitely desirable.

He rested his weight on his elbow and performed his own inspection, which reminded her she was standing before him in a vanilla demi-bra and matching satin tap pants. He rubbed the corner of his mouth. "Does all your underwear look like that?"

"Except for my Strawberry Shortcake panties. Now haul your ass out of my bed."

"Could you maybe put on a robe? Something flannel that smells like bacon grease."

"No."

He sat up and dropped his rangy legs over the side of the bed. "I understand you're pissed I didn't make your party, but parties aren't my scene. Still, it was nice of you to invite me."

"I didn't invite you." Will must have. She snatched up her robe from a chair next to the bed and shoved her arms into the sleeves.

Jake's eyes slid over her. "Is it too late to change my mind about the bacon grease?"

She remembered what Kissy had said about the cool, blond bitch-goddess. She crossed her arms over her breasts and tried to look the part. "What do you want?"

"I've got a business deal for you, but you don't seem to be in the mood to talk." He rose and stretched. "We can discuss it in the morning while you fix me breakfast."

"What kind of business deal?"

"In the morning. Where do you want me to sleep?"

"On a park bench."

He sat back on her bed. "Thanks, this'll be just fine. Nice, firm mattress."

She gave him her coldest stare and tried to figure out how to handle this. As much as she wanted to, she couldn't ignore his comment about a business deal, and he obviously wasn't saying any more tonight. "Take the room at the end of the hall," she snapped. "The bed's too short for you and the mattress is lumpy, but if you bang on the wall, the rats will hardly bother you."

"Are you sure you're not going to be lonesome in here by yourself?"

"Oh no. I'm looking forward to sleeping alone for a change."

His eyes narrowed. "Sorry to spoil your track record."

She smiled. "It's okay. A girl needs a little beauty rest now and then."

That shut him up, and he left her alone.

She stomped into the bathroom and turned on the water to wash her face. What kind of business deal did he have in mind? Was it possible he wanted her to represent him? The idea made her queasy. Jake Koranda's name on her client roster would give her instant credibility. Just like that, all her worries about the future of her agency would disappear.

She brought herself back to reality. An established superstar would hardly turn himself over to new management just because that new management happened to be an old lover. Unless he felt guilty and wanted to make it up to her.

Highly unlikely. She rinsed her face and reached for a hand towel. Still . . . if she could land Jake, she'd have taken a giant step toward making Fleur Savagar and Associates the gold standard for celebrity management.

The bravest, the fastest, the strongest . . .

★

She awakened late the next morning to the smell of freshly brewed coffee drifting up from the kitchen. She pulled on her oldest pair of athletic gray warm-ups and fastened her hair into a ponytail. When she reached the kitchen, she found Jake sitting at the harvest table, his legs stretched in front of him as he drank a cup of coffee. She went to the refrigerator and poured herself a glass of orange juice. She had to play this just right. "I'll make the toast if you make the eggs," she said.

"Are you sure you can handle the responsibility? As I remember, cooking isn't your strong point."

"Which is why you're making the eggs." She pulled out a carton and set it on the counter for him along with a stainless steel bowl. Then she grabbed a grapefruit, dropped it on the cutting board, and severed it with one sharp thwack.

"Careful there."

"I'm practicing for bigger and better things." She gestured toward a bottom drawer. "If Bird Dog needs an apron, he can find one in there. Ignore the pink ruffle."

"You're all heart."

Neither of them spoke again until they were settled across from each other at the harvest table. She could barely swallow her toast. In the clear light of a new day, the notion that he might sign with her seemed even more far-fetched, but she had to know for sure. She took a sip of coffee. "Don't you have an incredibly expensive house somewhere in the Village?"

"Yeah, but too many people bother me there, so I sometimes disappear. That's one of the things I wanted to talk to you about. Can we work something out with your attic?"

"My attic?"

"Your office manager showed it to me last night when she was giving me the tour. It's a great space—private, self-contained. I need a place where I can hide out for a while and work. A place no one will think to look for me."

She couldn't believe it. Jake didn't want her as an agent. He wanted a landlady! Disappointment choked her. She threw down her napkin. "Are you so used to people kissing your butt that you think I'll do it, too?" She rose from her chair and pointed toward the door. "You're not living in my house. Ever. Now get out. I'm sick of looking at you."

He swiped at his plate with a triangle of toast. "I'm going to take that as a definite maybe."

"Don't even try to be cute. You've—"

"Let me finish. I told you last night that I had a business deal. Sit down and eat those excellent scrambled eggs while we talk about it."

She sat down, but she didn't touch her eggs.

He pushed his plate back and wiped his mouth with his napkin. "I can't keep going on like this. The Caliber picture's done, and I'm taking six months off so I can start writing again. If I don't work this thing through now, I never will. I want you to represent me."

She couldn't believe she'd heard him right. He wanted her to be his agent? Her spirits soared. Their past relationship would make this the most difficult challenge she could possibly face, but she was tough enough to handle it. She struggled to pull herself together. "I'd be glad to represent you. I know I can make your life easier. As you might have heard, I'm offering total celebrity management to an elite group of clients. I can handle all your business and legal affairs, negotiate film deals, take care of publicity—"

He waved her off. "I have good people doing all that."

She went absolutely still. "Then exactly what are you offering me?"

"I want you to handle everything I write."

She stared at him. "Big deal."

"If you want my name on your client roster, this is the way to get it."

"You haven't written anything since *Eclipse*!" She wanted to scream. "Your name as a writer on my client roster won't get me anything but snickers." She snatched up her plate and took it to the sink.

"You're the one who blocked me, kiddo. Now all you have to do is unblock me."

The plate broke as she set it down too hard. "Why do you keep saying that?"

"The problem started when you came along."

"That's no answer."

His chair scraped the floor. "It's all the answer you're going to get."

She didn't even try to hide her animosity. "And how am I supposed to unblock you? On my back?"

"If that's what works for you."

Before she could take a swing at him, he detoured toward the coffeepot. "I need some help working through the block. Whatever went wrong happened when we were making *Eclipse*."

She threw the broken plate into the trash. "You don't *have* to write. You sure don't need the money."

"Writing is what I do, Flower. Acting is satisfying, and it's made me rich, but it's writing that lets me breathe." He turned away, as if confessing even that small amount compromised him. "I won't be living in your pocket. All I want is privacy. And I don't need to tell you that if I start writing again, your agency will pick up a fat piece of change."

"That's a big 'if.' And why do you have to write in my house?"

He shrugged off her question. "I just do."

The same old Jake. He dangled little pieces of himself in front of her, then snatched them back before she could get a good look. But even as a dozen venomous thoughts raced through her mind, she knew he'd boxed her in. She had to take the chance, despite the risks she could see all too clearly. If only she hadn't planted the stories about the two of them . . . She imagined people's smirks if word got out that she'd committed herself to representing a writer who didn't write anymore. Everyone would say that Jake was only letting her use his name because they were sleeping together. They'd point out that he didn't trust her to handle his film deals, just a writing career that had gone sour years ago. She'd look like a woman trying to build a business from her bedroom.

But what if she could get him to start writing again? What if she could break through that block and get him to produce another Koranda play? She wouldn't have to worry about gossip then, or about her money running out. It was a gamble she couldn't pass up. At the same time, she had to make sure she wouldn't be paying a personal price for once again getting involved with the man who'd hurt her so badly.

★

The gossip began two days later, but not about Jake. On Monday afternoon as Fleur was about to leave the office to have lunch with a talented new singer she hoped to woo, she received a phone call from a network vice-president she'd gotten to known.

"There's some gossip floating around I think you should hear about," he said. "Somebody's going out of their way to remind people of those broken modeling contracts you left behind when you fled the country."

She rubbed her eyes and tried to sound unconcerned. "That's old news. Isn't there anything better to gossip about?"

"It's lousy PR for a woman trying to start a business based on client trust."

He didn't need to spell it out for her. The implication was clear. If she'd broken contracts before, she'd do it again. She could think of only one reason for those stories to resurface now. Alexi had made his next move.

The young singer didn't show up for lunch, a message Fleur had no trouble interpreting. She got back to the office in time to take a call from Olivia Creighton.

"I've been hearing some terrible stories about you, Fleur. I'm sure none of them are true, and you know how I adore you, but after what happened with poor Doris Day and all her money, a woman can't be too careful. I'm not comfortable with instability."

"Of course not." Fleur thought of the six antique Baccarat goblets and case of Pouilly Fuissé Olivia had sent her just the week before to celebrate her contract for *Dragon's Bay*. Now the celebration was over. She made a lunch date for Olivia to meet David Bennis With his leather elbow patches and his smelly pipe, he radiated stability better than anyone, and Fleur hoped he could reassure Olivia, but as she headed for David's office, she didn't like the feeling that she was once again using someone else to solve her problems.

★

Later that day, she found Michel in the second floor of a converted factory in Astoria, where weary seamstresses were working on the garments for his collection. He had less than seven weeks left, and he was exhausted from the strain of trying to get everything together so quickly. She wished she didn't have to add to his worries, but she couldn't postpone telling him what was happening any longer. By now, Alexi understood exactly how important the success of Michel's collection was to her, and she didn't need a crystal ball to figure out where he'd try to strike next.

Michel straightened the scarf she'd tied at the neck of her white cashmere sheath. He had to reach up to do it because she was wearing the stiletto heels that were a standard part of her business wardrobe ever since she'd realized her height sometimes worked to her advantage. She told him about the missing invitations and the fire. Michel listened in silence. When she got to the end, she squeezed his arm. "As of tonight, I'm putting this workroom under twenty-four-hour guard."

He looked physically ill. "Do you really think he'll go after the samples?"

"I'm sure of it. Destroying the samples before you can show them is the way he can do the most damage."

He gazed around the workroom. "If we make it through this, there'll be something else."

"I know." She rubbed her cheek. "Let's hope he gets bored. There's not much else we can do."

*

Jake settled into the attic a few days after the party, but he didn't spend much time there the first week, opting instead to stay in his townhouse in the Village and attend rehearsals of a revival of one of his older plays. Once Fleur heard his footsteps late at night as she fell asleep. Two days later, she heard the sound of water running, but she never heard a typewriter.

To her consternation, word immediately got out that

she'd be representing Jake's so far nonexistent future literary endeavors. The last thing anyone in his West Coast office wanted was for her to succeed at what they hadn't been able to accomplish, and she suspected they were responsible for the leak. That, coupled with continued stories about her broken modeling contracts, was chipping away at the small amount of credibility she'd been able to build up. A well-established actor and rising young writer she'd been close to signing both backed off, and Olivia was getting increasingly skittish.

As the second week of October arrived, Jake began spending more nights in the attic apartment, but Fleur never saw him and never once heard the sound of a typewriter. Acting on the theory that exercise improves creativity and would, at the least, get him out of bed in the morning, she started pushing notes under his door inviting him to join her on her daily run. One crisp fall morning, three weeks after they'd sealed their deal, she came outside to find him sitting on the front step waiting for her.

He wore a gray UCLA sweatshirt, navy sweatpants, and beat-up Adidas. As he spotted her, his pouty bottom lip curled in a smile, and her heart gave an alarming hiccup. When she was a kid, just the sight of him had made her melt, but all he meant to her now was a business deal, and she'd never let him get to her like that again. She took the three front steps in one leap and ran past him.

"You never heard of warming up?" he called out from behind her.

"Don't need it. I'm already hot." She looked back over her shoulder. "Think you can keep up with me, cowboy?"

"Ain't met a woman yet who could outrun me," he replied, all full of sagebrush and buffalo chips.

"I don't know about that. Seems to me you've been living a pretty indolent life."

He drew up next to her. "Playing basketball three afternoons a week with a bunch of inner city teenagers who call me 'mister' isn't exactly taking it easy."

She sidestepped a muddy puddle and headed west, toward Central Park. "I'm surprised you can keep up at your advanced age."

"I can't. My knees are shot, and I can't jump anymore, so I usually get pulled from the game before the third quarter is over. They only put up with me because I bought the uniforms."

As they slipped around a delivery truck blocking the sidewalk, Fleur thought about how much she liked Jake's self-deprecating sense of humor. Next to his body, it was the best thing about him. His body and his no-nonsense masculinity. And his face. She loved his face. What she didn't love was his manipulative behavior and two-bit morality. He'd taken her to the mountaintop, then shoved her off. But she couldn't keep rehashing the past. She had a job to do, and she'd left him alone long enough. "I haven't noticed a typewriter banging away over my head since you moved in."

"Don't push me, okay?" His face closed up.

She thought for a moment and decided to take a risk. "I'm having a dinner party on Saturday night. Why don't you come?" She'd was just getting around to throwing the party she and Kissy had discussed at the open house, the one that would allow Michel and Simon to get to know each other. Being among congenial people might be a good first step toward loosening Jake up. And the others would entertain him so she wouldn't have to.

"Sorry, Flower, but formal dinner parties aren't my thing."

"It's not exactly formal. The guests cook. It'll just be Michel, Simon Kale, and Kissy. I invited Charlie Kincannon, but he's going to be out of town."

"Do you really know somebody named Kissy?"

"I guess you didn't meet her at Charlie's beach party. She's my best friend. Although . . ." She hesitated. "It might be best not to walk into any dark rooms with her."

"An interesting comment to make about a friend. Care to explain?"

"You'll find out soon enough." They shot past a woman walking a pair of Chihuahuas. "Pick up the pace. One of us has to work today."

They ran for a while without talking. Finally Jake looked over at her. "My publicist sent me some press clippings I just got around to reading. You and I were a pretty hot item in the New York gossip columns at the end of the summer."

"Really?" Those columns had appeared more than two months ago. She'd wondered when he'd get around to mentioning them.

"You're not a good enough actress to pull off the innocent act."

"Sure I am."

He reached out and caught her arm, pulling her to a stop. "You planted those stories."

"I needed the publicity."

His chest rose and fell under his T-shirt as he steadied his breathing. "You know how I feel about my privacy."

"Technically I didn't violate your privacy since none of the stories were true."

He didn't crack a smile. "I don't like cheap tricks."

"That's funny. I thought you invented them."

His mouth tightened in an unfriendly line. "Keep my name out of the newspapers, Fleur. Consider this your only warning." He turned away and took off across the street.

"I'm not your publicist, remember?" she called out after him. "All I represent is your pathetic literary career."

He picked up his pace and didn't look back.

Chapter 23

* * * * * * *

To Fleur's surprise, Jake was the first to arrive for her Saturday night dinner party, knocking on the door at precisely eight o'clock. Although she'd taken the precaution of tucking a few bottles of Mexican beer in the refrigerator, she hadn't really expected him to show up. He wore semi-respectable dark gray slacks and a lighter gray long-sleeved dress shirt that made his eyes seem bluer. He thrust a gift-wrapped package into her hands as he took in her ivory wool trousers and copper silk blouse. "Don't you ever look bad?"

She frowned at the package. "Should I call the bomb squad?"

"Stop being a wise-ass and open it."

She pulled off the gift wrap to reveal a fresh new copy of *The Joy of Cooking*. "Just what I've always not wanted."

"I knew you'd love it."

He followed her into the kitchen, and she put the cookbook on the counter. Considering her limited personal resources, she loved how welcoming everything looked. She'd waxed the old harvest table until the dark wood shone. At a secondhand store, she'd found a chipped bean pot that she'd filled with chrysanthemums to use as a centerpiece. The store had also yielded up a charming set of faded tan and olive checked tea towels for placemats. She smelled Jake's clean shirt and toothpaste as he came up behind her. She started as his hands lifted the back of her hair and touched her neck just beneath the collar of her blouse.

"Jeez, you're jumpy." Something small and cool settled between her breasts. She looked down and saw a trumpet-shaped blue and green enamel flower hanging on a thin gold chain. Tiny diamonds sparkled on the blossoms like dew. As she turned to him, she glimpsed something soft and unguarded in his expression. The present slipped away, and for a moment it seemed as if they'd returned to the time when things were easy between them. "It's beautiful," she said. "You didn't have to—"

"No big deal. It's a morning glory. I've noticed that's not your best time of day." He turned away, ending the moment.

The morning glory charm slipped from her fingers. Just for a moment, she'd let down her guard. She wouldn't let it happen again.

"How's come I don't smell food?" he said. "Should I be worried?"

"The cook hasn't arrived yet," she replied lightly.

Right on cue, the front buzzer rang, and she hurried to open it.

"I've brought my own knives," Michel said. Tonight he wore khakis and a long-sleeved blue T-shirt with a narrow piece of what had once been a man's striped necktie sewn diagonally across the chest. He headed for the kitchen. "I found these wonderful grapes at this little hole-in-the-wall off Canal Street. Did you go to the fish market I told you about for the halibut?"

"Aye, aye, sir." As he set the grocery bag on the counter, she saw how tired he looked, and she was glad she'd planned this evening for him. He spotted Jake.

"Michel, you remember Jake Koranda. I disarmed him at the door, so feel free to insult him as much as you want."

Jake smiled and shook hands with Michel.

Simon arrived five minutes later. As luck would have it, he'd seen every Caliber picture and barely noticed Michel in his eagerness to talk with Jake. Michel, in the meantime, was getting ready to cook and treating Fleur to a long list of mishaps he was absolutely convinced would ruin his collection. In terms of matchmaking, the evening wasn't getting off to a promising start.

Kissy appeared and headed for the kitchen. "Sorry I'm late, but Charlie called me from Chicago just as I was leaving."

"Things must be improving," Fleur said. "At least you're talking again."

Kissy looked glum. "I think I've lost my touch. No matter what I do, he—" She broke off as she saw Jake leaning against the counter. "Ohmygod."

Fleur rescued a spoon Michel had dropped. "Kissy, meet Jake Koranda. Jake, Kissy Sue Christie."

Kissy was all gumdrop eyes and candy apple mouth as she stared up at Jake. An oil slick of a grin spread over his face. Kissy looked like a kindergarten snack. "My pleasure." She smiled her dippy what's-your-name-sailor-boy smile, and Jake puffed up like a rooster.

Fleur should have been amused. Instead she felt as if she were thirteen again, taller than the other girls, gawky and awkward with bruised elbows, bandaged knees, and a face too big for her body. Kissy, on the other hand, looked like a teenage boy's wet dream, and, before long, she and Jake were making the salad together while Simon acted as bartender. Fleur fought her jealousy as she helped Michel fix one of his signature dishes, fish with grapes in a vermouth butter sauce.

When Jake and Simon started talking about horses, Kissy slipped to Fleur's side. "He's even hotter in person than he is on the screen. That man belongs in the Hunk Hall of Fame."

"His tooth is crooked," Fleur retorted.

"I'll bet nothing else is."

★

Everyone except Fleur had a wonderful time. Michel and Simon finally began to talk over Michel's spectacular halibut dish, and as the breadbasket made its second pass, they were listing their favorite restaurants. Before long, they'd begun a casual discussion about checking out a trendy place in the East Village. Kissy tried to catch Fleur's eye for a congratulatory salute, but Fleur pretended not to notice.

Kissy and Jake were trading jokes as if they'd known each other for years. Then they began comparing notes about a new singer they both liked. Why didn't they just go to bed and get it over with?

When it was time for dessert, Fleur brought out a French almond cake she'd bought that afternoon at her favorite bakery. Everyone loved it, but she could barely eat a bite. She suggested they take their Irish coffee into the living room. Kissy sat on the couch. Normally Fleur would have sat next to her, but now she grabbed one of the big floor pillows instead, leaving the rest of the couch free for Jake, who immediately claimed it.

Everyone except Fleur started arguing about the all-time best rock groups. Her unhappiness settled into a lump in the pit of her stomach that she didn't want to examine too closely. Kissy sent her a sympathetic smile. Fleur looked away.

Kissy cleared her throat. "Fleurinda, you promised I could borrow your amber earrings. Show me where they are before I walk off without them."

Fleur hadn't promised Kissy any such thing, and she started to say so, only to find herself on the receiving end of one of Kissy's steel magnolia glares. She wouldn't put it past her former friend to stage a scene, so she rose reluctantly and followed Kissy to the bedroom.

When they got there, Kissy crossed her arms over her pillowy breasts. "You'd better get that whipped puppy look off your face right now, or I swear to God, I'm going back in that living room and French him right in front of you."

"I don't know what you're talking about."

Kissy looked at her with disgust. "I'm about ready to give up on you. You're twenty-six. That's too old not to know yourself better."

"I know myself just fine."

Instead of responding, Kissy started tapping the toe of one bright red ballet flat. Fleur felt herself wilt. "Sorry," she mumbled.

"You should be. You're acting crazy."

"You're right. And I don't even know why."

"Because you're green-eyed jealous, that's why."

"I'm not jealous! Not the way you mean anyway."

Kissy wasn't having it. "Since when have you ever known me not to flirt with a good-looking guy, let alone a man like that? Yummy. And what did you do? Not one thing, that's what. You just slinked off into the corner. I'm ashamed of you."

Fleur was ashamed of herself, too. "It wasn't about Jake. I'm not that stupid. It was about feeling like an overgrown teenager again."

"I'm not buying it," Magnolia Blossom said. "Don't you think it's time you stop kidding yourself and take a hard look at your feelings for that gorgeous man sitting in your living room?"

"My feelings for him are made up of dollar signs. Really, Kissy. I've practically lost Olivia, and the only clients who want me to represent them are ones I don't want to represent, like that cretin Shawn Howell. Jake's not even pretending to write, and—" She stopped. "That's no excuse. I'm sorry, Kissy. You're right. I've been acting infantile. Forgive me."

Kiss finally softened. "All right. But only because I feel the same way every time I see you and Charlie together."

"Charlie and me? Why?"

Kissy sighed and refused to meet Fleur's eyes. "He likes you so much, and I know I can't compete with you when it comes to looks. Every time I see the two of you talking, I feel like the Pillsbury Doughboy."

Fleur didn't know whether to laugh or cry. "It seems like I'm not the only one who doesn't know herself very well." She gave Kissy a bear hug, then glanced at her watch. "*Butch Cassidy* is on television tonight. If I'm calculating right, we should be able to take a peek, then get back to the party before we're missed. Do you want to indulge?"

"You bet." Kissy flipped on the small television perched on a secondhand table in the corner of the bedroom. "Do you think we're getting too old for this?"

"Probably. We should give it up for Lent."

"Or not."

The Hole-in-the-Wall Gang had just robbed the Overland Flyer, and Paul Newman's Butch, along with Robert Redford's mustachioed Sundance Kid, were drinking on the balcony of the whorehouse. Kissy and Fleur settled on the edge of the bed as the schoolteacher Etta Place climbed the steps to her small frame house, lit the lamp inside, and unfastened the top buttons of her shirtwaist. When she reached her bedroom, she pulled off the garment and hung it in the closet. Then she turned and screamed as she saw the chiseled features of the Sundance Kid staring menacingly at her from across the room.

"Keep going, Teacher Lady," he said.

She stared at him with wide, frightened eyes. Slowly he picked up his gun and leveled it at her. "That's okay. Don't mind me. Keep on going."

She hesitantly unfastened the long undergarment and then stepped out of it. Clasping it modestly in front of her, she tried to hide her eyelet-trimmed camisole from the outlaw's eyes.

"Let down your hair," he ordered.

She dropped the undergarment and pulled out the hairpins.

"Shake your head."

No sensible woman was going to argue with the Sundance Kid when he had a pistol trained on her belly, and the schoolteacher did as she was told. All she had left was the camisole, and Sundance didn't have to talk. He raised his pistol and cocked the hammer.

Etta slowly opened the low row of buttons until the camisole parted in a V. Sundance's hands moved to his waist. He unfastened his gun belt and pushed it aside, then stood and approached her. He slipped his hands inside the open garment.

"Do you know what I wish?" Etta asked.

"What?"

"*That once you'd get here on time!*"

As Etta threw her arms around Redford's neck, Fleur sighed and got up to turn off the set. "It's hard to believe that scene was written by a man, isn't it?"

Kissy gazed at the blank screen. "William Goldman's a great screenwriter, but I'll bet anything his wife wrote that scene while he was in the shower. What I wouldn't give . . ."

"Uhmm. It's the ultimate female sexual fantasy."

"All that male sexual menace coming from a lover you know will never hurt you." Kissy licked her lips.

Fleur touched her morning glory necklace. "Too bad they don't make men like that anymore."

Jake stood in the hallway outside the partially opened door and listened to the two women. He hadn't intended to eavesdrop, but Fleur had looked funny all evening, and they were gone so long he'd decided to check up on her. Now he was sorry. This was exactly the kind of conversation a man should never hear. What did women want? In public the rhetoric was all about male sensitivity and equality, but in private, here they were, two intelligent women having orgasms over caveman macho.

Maybe he was a little jealous. He was one of the biggest box office draws of the decade, and he was living right above Fleur Savagar's head, but all she wanted to do was take verbal potshots at him. He wondered if Redford had to put up with this kind of crap. If there was any justice in the world, Redford was sitting in front of his television someplace in Sundance, Utah, watching his wife go melty-eyed over one of Bird Dog Caliber's rough-'em-up love scenes. The thought gave him a small moment of satisfaction, but, as he slipped away, the emotion faded. No matter how you looked at it, this wasn't the easiest time to be a man.

*

The next morning Jake showed up to run with her, but as they made their way around the Central Park Reservoir, he barely spoke. She had to find some way to motivate him to at least attempt to write. When they returned to the house, she impulsively invited him in for Sunday morning breakfast. Maybe he'd be more communicative with a full stomach. But he declined.

"That's right," she replied coolly. "Your schedule's been a real killer lately with all that time you're spending pounding away at your typewriter."

He tugged open the zipper of his sweatshirt. "You don't know anything."

"Are you even trying to write?"

"For your information, I've already filled up a legal pad."

Jake composed at the typewriter, and she didn't believe him. "Show me."

He scowled and brushed past her into the house.

She showered, then slipped into jeans and her favorite cable-knit sweater. She'd been so preoccupied with Michel's collection, Olivia's skittishness, and trying to anticipate Alexi's next move that she hadn't focused on the problem over her head. Jake Koranda had made a deal with her to start writing again, and he wasn't following through.

At ten o'clock, she went out into the front hallway and unlocked the door that led to the attic apartment. He didn't answer when she knocked at the top of the stairs. She slipped her key in the lock.

The attic was a large, open space lit by both a skylight and smaller, rectangular windows on two sides. Fleur hadn't been up here since Jake had moved in, and she saw that he'd furnished it sparsely with a few comfortable chairs, a bed, a long couch, and an L-shaped arrangement of desk and table that held a typewriter and a ream of paper still in its wrapper.

He had his feet propped on the desk, and he was tossing a basketball from one hand to the other. "I don't remember inviting you in," he said. "I don't like interruptions when I'm working."

"I wouldn't dream of interrupting your creative process. Just pretend I'm not here." She went into the small kitchen that sat behind a curve of counter and opened the cupboards until she found a can of coffee.

"Go away, Fleur. I don't want you here."

"I'll leave as soon as we have a business meeting."

"I'm not in the mood for a meeting." The basketball passed back and forth, right palm to left.

She plugged in the coffeepot and walked over to perch on the desk. "The thing is," she said, "you're dead wood, and I can't afford to have anything pulling me under right now. Everyone in town thinks you signed with me because we're sleeping together. Only one thing's going to stop the gossip. Another Koranda play."

"Tear up our contract."

She swatted the basketball from his hand. "Stop being such a crybaby."

Easygoing, wisecracking Jake Koranda disappeared, leaving her face-to-face with Bird Dog. "Get out. This isn't any of your goddamned business."

She didn't move. "Make up your mind. First you say I'm the one who blocked you, and now you tell me it's none of my business. You can't have it both ways."

His feet dropped to the ground. "Out." He grasped her arm and steered her toward the door.

She was suddenly angry, not because he was manhandling her and not even because he was threatening the future of her business, but because he was wasting his talent. "Big hotshot playwright." She jerked away. "That typewriter has an inch of dust on it."

"I'm not ready yet!" He stalked across the room and grabbed his jacket from a chair.

"I don't see what's so hard about it." She made her way to his desk and ripped the wrapper off a ream of paper. "Anybody can put a piece of paper in a typewriter. See how I'm doing it. Nothing could be easier."

He shoved his arms into the sleeves.

She dropped into the desk chair and flicked on the switch. The machine hummed to life. "Watch this. Act One, Scene One." She picked out the letters on the keyboard. "Where are we, Jake? What does the stage set look like?"

"Don't be a bitch."

"Don't . . . be . . . a . . . bitch." She typed out the words. "Typical Koranda dialogue—tough and anti-female. What comes next?"

"Stop it, Fleur!"

"Stop . . . it . . . Fleur. Bad name choice. Too close to this amazing woman you already know."

"*Stop it!*" He shot across the room. His hand came down on top of hers, jamming the keys. "This is all a big joke to you, isn't it?"

Bird Dog had slipped away, and she saw the pain beneath his anger. "It's not a joke," she said softly. "It's something you have to do."

He didn't move. And then he lifted his hand and brushed her hair. She closed her eyes. He pulled away and headed into the kitchen. She heard him pour a cup of coffee. Her fingers shook as she tugged the paper from the typewriter. Jake came toward her, mug in hand. She slipped in a fresh sheet of paper.

"What are you doing?" He sounded tired, a little hoarse.

She took an unsteady breath. "You're going to write today. I'm not letting you put it off any longer. This is it."

"Our deal's off." He sounded defeated. "I'm moving out of the attic."

She hardened herself against his sadness. "I don't care where you move. But we have an agreement, and we're sticking to it."

"Is that all you care about? Your two-bit agency."

His anger was phony, and she wouldn't let him bait her. "You're writing today."

He stepped behind her, set down his coffee mug, and settled his hands lightly on her shoulders. "I don't think so."

He lifted her hair and pressed his mouth into the softness just beneath her ear. His breath felt warm on her skin, and the soft touch of his lips made all her senses come alive. For a moment, she let herself give in to the sensations he was arousing. Just for a moment . . .

His hands slipped under her sweater and slid up over her bare skin to the lacy cups of her bra. He toyed with her nipples through the silk. His touch felt so good. Ripples of pleasure scuttled through her body. He unfastened the center clasp of her bra and pushed aside the cups. As he slipped up her sweater and bared her breasts, the ripples turned into waves of heat rushing through her veins. He pushed her shoulders back against the chair so her breasts tilted upward and began teasing the nipples with his thumbs. His lips caught her earlobe, then trailed along her neck. He was a master seducer playing with her body, going from one erogenous point to another as if he were following a chart in a sex manual.

Right then, she knew she was being bought.

She shoved his hands away from their carefully calculated seduction and jerked down her sweater. "You're a real bastard." She rose from the chair. "This was the easiest way to close me out, wasn't it?"

He stared at a point just past her head. Doors slammed shut, shades pulled down, shutters locked tight. "Don't push me."

She was furious with herself for giving in so easily, furious with him, and unbearably sad. "The circle's complete now," she said. "You've played Bird Dog for so long that he's finally taken over. He's eating up what was left of your decency."

He stalked across the room and pulled the door open.

She gripped the edge of the desk. "Making those crappy movies is easier than doing your real work."

"Get out."

"Mr. Tough Guy has a yellow streak a mile wide." She dropped back down in the chair. Her hands were shaking so badly she could barely push the typewriter keys. "Act One, Scene One, damn you . . ."

"You're crazy."

"Act One, Scene One. What's the first line?"

"You're out of your frigging mind!"

"Come on, you know exactly what this play's about."

"*It's not a play!*" He stalked over to her, his expression so tormented that she winced. One of his hands knotted into a fist. "It's a book! I have to write a book. A book about 'Nam."

She took a deep breath. "A war book? That's right up Bird Dog's alley."

His voice grew quiet. "You don't know anything."

"Then explain it to me."

"You weren't there. You wouldn't understand."

"You're one of the best writers in the country. Make me understand."

He turned his back to her. Silence fell between them. She heard the distant sound of a police siren, the rattle of a truck passing below. "You couldn't tell them apart," he finally said. "You had to regard everybody as the enemy."

His voice was controlled, but it seemed to be coming from far away. He turned and looked at her as if he wanted to make certain she understood. She nodded, even though she didn't. If what had happened in Vietnam was blocking his writing, why did he blame her?

"You'd be walking next to a rice paddy and spot a couple of little kids—four or five years old. Next thing you knew, one of them was throwing a grenade at you. Shit. What kind of war is that?"

She slipped her fingers back on the keys and began to type, trying to get it all down, hoping she was doing the right thing but not sure at all.

He didn't seem to notice the sound of the typewriter. "The village was a VC stronghold. The guerrillas had cost us a lot of men. Some of them had been tortured, mutilated. They were our buddies . . . guys we'd gotten to know as well as our own family. We were supposed to go in and waste the village. The civilians knew the rules. If you weren't guilty, don't run! *Don't for chrissake run!* Half the company was stoned or doped up—it was the only way you could make it." He took a ragged breath. "We were airlifted to a landing strip near the village, and as soon as the strip was secure, the artillery opened up. When everything was clear, we went in. We herded them all together in the middle of the village. They didn't run—they knew the rules—but some of them were shot anyway." His face had grown ashen. "A little girl . . . she had on a ragged shirt that didn't cover her belly, and the shirt had these little yellow ducks on it. And when it was over, and the village was burning, and somebody turned Armed Forces Vietnam on the radio and Otis Redding started singing 'Sittin' on the Dock of the Bay' . . . The little girl had flies all over her belly."

He stabbed his hand toward the typewriter. "Did you get that part about the music? The music is important. Everybody who's been in 'Nam remembers the music."

"I—I don't know. You're going so fast."

"Let me in." He pushed her aside, ripped out the sheet that was in the typewriter, and inserted a new one. He shook his head once as if to clear it, and then he began to type.

She went over to the couch and waited. He didn't take his eyes off the pages that began sliding like magic through his typewriter. The room was cool, but his forehead beaded with sweat as he punched the keys. The images he'd drawn were already etched in her brain. The village, the people, the shirt with the little yellow ducks. Something terrible had happened that day.

He didn't notice as she slipped out of the room.

★

She went to dinner with Kissy that evening. When she returned, she could still hear his typewriter. She made a sandwich for him and cut a slab of the French almond cake left over from the dinner party. This time she didn't bother to knock before she used her key.

He sat hunched over the typewriter, his face lined with fatigue. Coffee mugs and paper littered the desk. He grunted as she set the tray down and collected the cups to wash. She cleaned out the coffeepot and refilled it so it was ready to go again.

Dread had been building inside her ever since this morning. She kept thinking about *Sunday Morning Eclipse* and the massacre Matt had witnessed in Vietnam. Now she couldn't stop asking a terrible question. Had Jake been a helpless witness to a massacre like the character he'd created, or had he been an active participant?

She wrapped her arms around herself and left the attic.

★

She received her first phone call from Dick Spano later that week. "I've got to find Jake."

"He never calls me," she said, which was literally true.

"If he does, tell him I'm looking for him."

"I really don't think he will."

That evening, she went up to the attic to tell Jake about the call. His eyes were red-rimmed, his jaw covered with stubble, and he looked as if he hadn't slept. "I don't want to talk to anybody," he said. "Keep them away from me, will you?"

She did her best. She put off his business manager, his lawyer, and all of their secretaries, but someone as famous as Jake couldn't simply disappear, and after five more days passed, and the callers grew more alarmed, she knew she had to do something, so she called Dick Spano. "I've heard from Jake," she said. "He's started to write again, and he wants to hide out for a while."

"I have to talk to him. I've got a deal that won't wait. Tell me where he is."

She tapped a pen on her desk. "I think he's in Mexico. He wouldn't say exactly where."

Dick swore, then bombarded her with a long list of things she was to tell him if he called her again. She wrote them all down and tucked the note in her pocket.

October turned into November, and as the date for Michel's fashion show drew near, the gossip about her broken contracts refused to die. As if that wasn't bad enough, the phony stories she'd planted at the end of the summer about her relationship with Jake were continuing to damage her. The gossips said Fleur Savagar was nothing more than a washed-up fashion model trying to start a business on her back. None of the clients she'd been pursuing had signed with her, and each night she fell asleep only to jolt awake a few hours later and listen to the sound of Jake's typewriter. In the morning, she used her key to check on him, and after a while, it became difficult to tell which of them was the more haggard.

She spent the day before Michel's show at the hotel, scurrying between technicians and the carpenters setting up the runway. She drove everyone crazy with her insistence on security passes and guards at the door. Even Kissy lost patience with her, but everything rested on Michel's collection, and Alexi had less than twenty-four hours to do his worst. Fleur called Michel at the Astoria factory to make sure the guards were doing their job.

"Every time I look out, they're where they're supposed to be," he said.

As he hung up, she had to remind herself to breathe. She'd hired the best security company in the state. Now she had to trust them to do their job.

Willie Bonaday burped and reached into his uniform pocket for a roll of Tums. Sometimes he chewed them one after another to help pass the time until the daytime shift took over. He'd been working this job for a month now, and tonight was the last night. Willie thought it was a lot of trouble to go to for a bunch of dresses, but as long as he got his paycheck, he minded his own business.

Four of them worked each shift, and they had the place sealed up tighter than a drum. Willie sat just inside the front door of the old Astoria factory, while his partner, Andy, was at the back and two of the younger men were outside the workshop doors on the second floor where the dresses were locked up. In the morning, the boys on the day shift would accompany the big dress racks on the drive to the hotel. By evening, the job would be over.

A couple of years back, Willie had guarded Reggie Jackson. That was the kind of job he liked. When him and his brother-in-law were sitting around watching the Giants, he wanted to shoot the bull about guarding Reggie Jackson, not a bunch of dresses. Willie picked up the *Daily News.* As he turned to the sports section, a battered orange van with BULLDOG ELECTRONICS painted on the side drove past the front entrance. Willie didn't notice.

The man driving the van turned into an alley across the street without even glancing at the factory. He didn't have to. He'd driven by every night for the past week, each time in a different vehicle, and he knew exactly what he'd see. He knew about Willie, although he didn't know his name, and he knew about the guard at the back entrance and the locked room on the second floor with the guards stationed outside. He knew about the day shift that would arrive in a few hours, and the dim interior lights kept on in the factory at night. Only the lights were important to him.

The warehouse across the street from the factory had been abandoned for years, and the rusty padlock at the back gave easily beneath the jaws of the bolt cutters. He pulled an equipment case from the van. It was heavy, but the weight didn't bother him. When he was safely inside the warehouse, he switched on his flashlight and shone it at the floor as he walked toward the front of the building. The flashlight annoyed him. Its beam of light spread out in a smear—no clear boundaries, no precision. It was sloppy light.

Light was his specialty. Pure beams of pencil-slim light. Coherent light that didn't spread out in undisciplined pools like a flashlight beam.

He spent nearly an hour setting up. Normally it didn't take so long, but he'd been forced to modify his equipment with a high-powered telescope, and the mounting was difficult. He didn't mind, though, because he liked challenges, especially ones that paid so well.

When he'd finished setting up, he cleaned his hands on the rag he carried with him and then wiped a circle in the dirty glass of the warehouse window. He took his time sighting and focusing the telescope, making certain everything was exactly the way he wanted it. He could pick out each of the tiny lead plug centers without any difficulty. They were clearer to him than if he'd been standing in the middle of that second-story room.

When he was ready, he gently pulled the switch on the laser, directing the pure beam of ruby-red light right at the lead plug that was farthest away. The plug needed only a hundred and sixty-five degrees of heat to melt, and within seconds he could see that the hot ruby light of the laser had done its work. He picked out the next plug, and it, too, dissolved under the force of the pencil-thin beam of light. In a matter of minutes, all the lead plugs had melted, and the heads of the automatic fire sprinkler system were spraying water over the racks of dresses.

Satisfied, the man packed up his equipment and left the warehouse.

Fleur

Chapter 24

The phone call from the security company woke Fleur at four in the morning. She listened to the lengthy explanation from the man on the other end of the line. "Don't wake my brother," she said just before she hung up. And then she pulled the covers over her head and went back to sleep.

The doorbell woke her. She squinted at her clock and wondered if florists delivered white roses at six in the morning but decided she wasn't getting up to find out. She stuck her head under the pillow and dozed off. Out of nowhere, someone jerked the pillow away. She screamed and bolted upright in bed.

Jake towered above her in jeans and a zippered sweatshirt that he'd thrown on over his bare chest. His hair was shaggy, his jaw unshaven, and his eyes had an empty, haunted look. "What's wrong with you? Why didn't you answer the door?"

Fleur grabbed the pillow out of his hands and hit him in the stomach. "It's six-thirty in the morning!"

"You run at six o'clock! Where were you?"

"*In bed!*"

He shoved his hands into his pockets and looked sulky.

"How was I supposed to know you were sleeping? When I didn't see you from my window, I thought something was wrong."

She couldn't postpone this day any longer, and she kicked away the covers. He didn't even pretend not to notice that her gown was bunched around her thighs. She stretched out to switch on the bedside light and deliberately rearranged her legs like a girl in a mattress ad, with her toes pointed and her arches delicately curved. Considering all the problems lying ahead of her today, it wasn't the greatest reflection on her character that she needed to make sure Jake Koranda got a great view of her legs.

"I'll make breakfast," he said abruptly.

She took a quick shower, then slipped into jeans and an old ski sweater. Jake glanced up at her from the eggs he was cracking into a skillet. Standing over her stove, he looked taller than ever, with his shoulders straining the seams of his sweatshirt in a way that was aggressively and indisputably male. It took a moment for her head to semi-clear. "How did you get in? I double-checked the doors before I went to bed last night."

"You want your eggs scrambled or fried?"

"Jake . . ."

"I can't chitchat and make breakfast at the same time. You could help, you know, instead of standing there like the Queen of England. Although you're a lot better-looking."

A typically male evasive action, but she let him get away with it because she was hungry. She pitched in with toast and orange juice, then poured the coffee. Once they settled at the table, however, she attacked. "You got to my office manager again. Riata made you a duplicate of her key."

He loaded up his fork.

"Admit it," she said. "There's no other way you could have gotten in."

"How come you put more butter on your toast than mine?"

"Riata has a key. I have a key. Michel has a key. That's it. If I fire her, it'll be on your conscience."

"You're not firing her." He traded his toast for hers. "Your brother gave me a duplicate key a few nights after the dinner party. He told me what your father's been up to. Michel is worried about you, and I can't say I'm exactly happy knowing that bastard has you in his crosshairs. When you didn't go out to run this morning, I was afraid he'd gotten to you."

She was touched, so she glared at him. "Alexi won't hurt me physically. Michel should know that. He wants me alive and suffering. Don't you have enough of your own problems right now?"

"I don't like what he's doing."

She retrieved her toast. "I'm not exactly crazy about it myself."

They ate in silence for a while. Jake took a sip of coffee. "You don't usually wear jeans and sneakers to work. What's up?"

"I'm riding with the dress racks over to the hotel. The men aren't due here for an hour, and it's going to be a long day." She regarded him pointedly. "That's why I wanted to sleep in this morning. Besides, I couldn't leave while all this was in the house." She made a vague gesture toward her living room.

Jake had already spotted the rows of metal racks bearing garments draped in black plastic. "Do you want to tell me about it or should I guess?"

"You know Michel's showing his collection today."

"And those are the pieces?"

She nodded and told him about the factory in Astoria and the phone call she'd received at four that morning. "The security people aren't exactly sure how the sprinkler system was set off, but all the dresses hanging on the racks in the workroom were waterlogged."

He lifted an inquisitive eyebrow.

"Everything in the workroom was thrift shop stuff," she said. "Kissy, Simon, Charlie, and I made the switch last night after Michel and all the seamstresses went home." She tried to feel some sense of satisfaction for having outwitted Alexi, but she'd only have to start worrying again as soon as this was over. She rose and walked toward the phone. "I have to call Michel so he doesn't have a heart attack if he stops at the factory this morning."

He came up out of his chair. "Wait a minute. Are you telling me Michel doesn't know you moved his dresses over here?"

"It's not his problem. I'm the one who chopped up the Bugatti, and I'm the one Alexi's after. Michel has enough to worry about."

Jake shot out from behind the table. "Suppose Alexi sent one of his thugs here? What would you have done then?"

"The factory was crawling with guards. Alexi had no reason to suspect the samples were here."

"You know what your problem is? You don't think!" As he came toward her, the pocket of his sweatshirt hit the edge of the counter, and she heard a loud thunk. For the first time she noticed that one side of the garment hung down farther than the other. He immediately shoved his hand in the pocket.

She set the receiver back on its hook. "What do you have?"

"What do you mean?"

Something prickled at the base of her spine. "In your pocket. What is it?"

"Pocket? My keys."

"What else?"

He shrugged. "A twenty-two automatic."

She looked at him blankly. "A what?"

"A gun."

"Are you crazy?" She charged toward him. "You brought a gun in here! In my house? Do you think this is one of your movies?"

His gaze was steady and unrepentant. "No apologies. I didn't know what I'd find when I walked in."

Out of nowhere, she found herself thinking about a little girl with yellow ducks on her shirt and a massacre. A creeping fear she absolutely did not want to let in pummeled at the door of her consciousness.

"Stay here while I throw on some clothes," he said as he left the kitchen.

Every instinct she possessed told her that Jake could never have taken part in an atrocity, not even in the middle of a war. But her brain wasn't as easily persuaded. She wished she'd never let him back into her life. Even with everything she knew about him, she was once again letting him burrow under her defenses.

By the time he reappeared, the white roses had arrived.

His face set in grim lines. "That son of a bitch."

"The good news is that he doesn't seem to have figured out his plans went awry."

"Let's keep it that way." He picked up the phone and dialed a number from memory. "Michel, it's Jake. I'm heading for the hotel with Wonder Woman and your collection. I'll tell you the whole story when I see you."

"You don't have to do that," she said when he hung up. "I can handle this."

"Humor me."

The men arrived, and Jake did everything but frisk them before he let them in the house. He kept guard as they loaded up the racks, then rode in the back of the truck with her to the hotel. When they got there, he stood off to the side, but he never let her out of his sight, and once she saw his hand creep into the pocket of his parka. Although he tried to look inconspicuous, it wasn't long before one of the hotel workers recognized him, and he was soon surrounded by autograph seekers shoving everything from packing slips to parking tickets in front of him to sign. She knew how much he hated this kind of public attention, but he stayed where he was until all the racks were set up.

After that, she didn't see him for a while, but each time she decided he'd finally gone home, she'd catch a glimpse of him lounging in the shadows by a stairwell or a service entrance, a ball cap pulled low on his head. His presence comforted her, and she didn't like that. Once this was over, she needed to have a long, hard talk with herself.

In the midst of all the backstage chaos, she made herself exude a confidence she didn't feel. So much depended on what happened during the next few hours. There had been an overwhelming demand for invitations, so they were showing the collection twice, both early and midafternoon. Each model had a separate dress rack with all her pieces arranged in order, along with the proper accessories. Customarily the racks were set up the day before, but since Fleur wouldn't let the dresses out of her safekeeping until that morning, everything had to be organized in very little time. There were last-minute hunts for missing accessories and a nearly disastrous mix-up with shoes, all of it accompanied by dark glances in her direction. In the meantime, a camera crew set up to videotape the collection for boutiques and department stores.

An hour before the first show, Fleur changed into the dress she'd brought along. It was one of the first pieces Michel had designed for her—a lacquer-red sheath with a center slit that ran from her neck to breasts, and another that descended from above the knee to the mid-calf hem. Beaded jet butterflies perched on one shoulder, and miniature versions sat on the toes of her red satin heels.

Kissy appeared at her side backstage, looking pale and tense. "This was the worst idea you ever had. It'll never work. I think I'm running a temperature. I bet I've got the flu. I know I do."

"You have butterflies. Take a deep breath. You'll be fine."

"Butterflies! These are not butterflies, Fleur Savagar. These are giant turkey buzzards."

Fleur hugged her, then went out to mingle with the

crowd filling the ballroom. By the time she'd finished talking to fashion editors and posing for photographers, the ends of her fingers had gone numb from nerves. She took the small gilt chair that had been reserved for her near the front of the runway and squeezed Charlie Kincannon's hand.

He leaned over and whispered, "I've been eavesdropping, and I'm getting worried. People think Michel's designs will be froufrou, whatever that means."

"It means he makes women look like women, and the fashion press doesn't know how to deal with that, but they'll come around." She wished she felt as confident as she sounded, but the truth was that any new designer who thumbed his nose at current fashion trends was in danger of being slaughtered by the powerful fashion arbiters. Michel was the new kid on the block in a tough, territorial neighborhood. The *Women's Wear Daily* reporter looked hostile, and Fleur understood exactly what Kissy meant about turkey buzzards.

The house lights dimmed, and sad, bluesy music began to play. Fleur dug her fingernails into her palms. Complicated theatrics at couture showings had gone out of style right along with ruffles and lace. The trend was simplicity —the runway, the models, and the clothes. Once again, they were bucking the tide, and it was all because of her. She was the one who'd talked Michel into this stupid idea.

The chatter in the ballroom began to die. The music grew louder, and the lights on the stage behind the runway came up on a moody *tableau vivant* set behind a filmy gauze curtain that made the scene dreamlike. Silhouettes of scenery—a wrought-iron railing, a lamppost, the shadow of palm fronds and broken shutters—suggested a shabby New Orleans courtyard on a steamy summer night.

Gradually the figures of the models became visible. They draped the set in their filmy dresses—their breasts, elbows, and knees jutting out in exaggerated angles like the figures in a Thomas Hart Benton painting. Some held palmetto fans frozen in midair. One bent forward, her hair trailing toward the floor like the branches of a willow, a hairbrush poised in her hand. Fleur heard whispers coming from the audience, sidelong glances to gauge the reaction of others, but no one seemed anxious to commit until they knew which way the tide was turning.

Suddenly one figure moved away from the others, growing visibly upset as she stepped into a pool of blue light. She looked at the audience for a moment, then blinked her eyes as if she were trying to make up her mind whether or not to confide in them. Finally she began to talk. She told them about Belle Reve, the plantation she'd lost, and about Stanley Kowalski, the subhuman her dear sister Stella had married. Her voice was agitated, her face weary and tortured. Finally she fell silent and lifted her hand toward them, wordlessly begging for understanding. The bluesy music began again. Defeated, she faded back into the shadows.

There was a moment of stunned silence and then the audience began to applaud, slowly at first, but gradually growing stronger. Kissy's extraordinary monologue as Blanche DuBois in *A Streetcar Named Desire* had stunned them. Fleur felt Charlie sag with relief. "They love her, don't they?"

She nodded, then held her breath, hoping they loved Michel's designs as much. No matter how inspiring Kissy's performance had been, the afternoon was ultimately about fashion.

The tempo of the music picked up and one by one the models broke their poses and moved out from behind the gauze curtain to walk down the runway. They wore filmy summer dresses that called up memories of scented flowers, hot Southern nights, and a streetcar named Desire. The lines were soft and feminine without being fussy, delicately fashioned for women who were tired of looking like men. New York hadn't seen anything like it in years.

Fleur listened to the murmurs around her and heard the

scratch of pens on notepads. The applause was polite for the first few dresses, but as one followed another and the members of the audience slowly began to absorb the beauty of Michel's designs, the applause built until the sound engulfed the great ballroom.

As the final dress cleared the runway, Charlie let out his breath in a long, tortured exhalation. "I feel like I've lived a lifetime in the last fifteen minutes."

Her fingers cramped, and she realized she'd been digging them into his knee. "Only one?"

Two more tableaux followed, each greeted more enthusiastically than the last. A steamy *Night of the Iguana* rain forest showcased Kissy in a second monologue and also served as a background for informal wear in wildly colorful jungle blossom prints. Finally Kissy performed her dazzling Maggie the Cat against the shadowy outline of a huge brass bed as an introduction to an exotic collection of evening gowns that evoked images of delicious decadence and brought the house to its feet.

When the show was over, Fleur watched Michel and Kissy take their bows. Life would never be the same for either one of them. She couldn't have found a better way to thank Kissy for her unwavering friendship and Michel for all those years of misplaced hatred than by making sure they each received the public recognition they deserved. As she hugged Charlie, she realized the success of her two clients would impact her own career, too. This afternoon had given her a giant shot of credibility.

The audience began to swarm around her, and she caught sight of Jake at the very back of the ballroom. Just before he slipped away, he gave her a silent thumbs-up.

★

The next week passed in a whirlwind of telephone calls and interviews. *Women's Wear Daily* did a cover story on Michel's collection, calling it the "New Femininity," and fashion editors lined up for news about his future plans. Michel sailed through the press conference Fleur scheduled for him and afterward took her to dinner. They grinned at each other over their menus.

"The Savagar brats haven't done too badly for themselves, have they, Big Sis?"

"Not badly at all, Little Bro." She touched the poplin sleeve of the safari jacket he wore over a burgundy silk shirt, French commando sweater, and Swiss Army necktie. "I love you, Michel. Big heaps. I should tell you more often."

"Me, too. Even bigger heaps." He was quiet for a moment, then he cocked his head so that his hair brushed his shoulder. "Does it bother you that I'm gay?"

She propped her hand on her chin. "I'd rather see you live happily ever after with someone who'd give me a tribe of nieces and nephews, but since I'm not going to have that, I want to see you in a stable relationship with a man who's worthy of you."

"Someone like Simon Kale?"

"Now that you mention it . . ."

He set down his menu and looked at her with sad eyes. "It's not going to work, Fleur. I know you've been counting on it, but it's not going to happen."

She was embarrassed. "I've stepped over the line, haven't I?"

"Yes." He smiled. "And do you know how much it means to me that somebody cares whether I'm happy?"

"I'm going to take that as a free license to interfere in your life."

"Don't." He took a sip from his wineglass. "Simon is a special person, and we've developed a solid friendship, but that's all it'll ever be. Simon is strong and self-sufficient. He doesn't really need anybody."

"That's important to you, isn't it? Being needed?"

He nodded. "I know you don't like Damon. And you're right. He can be selfish, and he's not the most intellectual person I've met. But he loves me, Fleur, and he needs me."

Fleur swallowed her disappointment. "I never said Damon didn't have good taste."

She thought about Jake. His erotic pull on her grew stronger every time she saw him. She didn't trust him, but she wanted him. And why couldn't she have him? She turned the idea over in her mind. No emotional commitment. Just good, dirty sex. That's all her attraction to him had ever been about. And wasn't that the essence of real liberation? Women didn't have to play games. They shouldn't play games. She should look Jake straight in the eye and tell him she wanted to—

To what? "Go to bed" was too wishy-washy, "make love" had implications, "screw" was tacky, and "fuck" was just plain awful.

Was she going to buckle under just because of a language barrier? How would a man do it? How would Jake do it?

Why wouldn't Jake do it?

Right then she knew she could never be the sexual aggressor, no matter how much she wanted him. Whether her reluctance was rooted in cultural conditioning or biological instinct made no difference because women's liberation got all tangled up when it hit the bedroom door.

★

Fleur tried to tune out the typewriter. Instead she concentrated on sending Kissy from one audition to the next and attempted to figure out what Alexi's next move would be. All the people who'd been dodging her phone calls now wanted to talk to her, and by the first week of December, a month after Michel's showing, Kissy was signed to appear in a limited run of *The Fifth of July.* Afterward, she'd fly to London for a supporting role in a big-budget action-adventure film.

She and Kissy hadn't talked about anything but business for weeks, and she was more than happy one evening to open her front door and see her friend standing there with a pizza and a big bottle of Tab. Before long, they were settled in the living room around Fleur's new coffee table.

"Just like old times, huh, Fleurinda?" Kissy said as "Tequila Sunrise" played in the background. "Except now that we're rich and famous, maybe we should switch to beluga, although I can't imagine trading in an all-American pepperoni pizza for Commie fish food."

Fleur took a sip from one of the Baccarat goblets Olivia Creighton had given her. "Do you think we're hypocrites because we drink diet soda with pizza? It seems like we should commit ourselves one way or the other."

"You worry about ethics while I eat. I haven't had anything since breakfast, and I'm starved." She bit into the piece she'd just pulled from the box. "I don't think I've ever been so happy in my life."

"You really do love pizza."

"It's not the pizza." Kissy sank her teeth into another bite, but this time she swallowed before she spoke. "It's the play, the movie, everything. Bob Fosse said hello to me yesterday. Not 'Hi, kid' but 'Hello, Kissy.' Bob Fosse!"

Fleur felt a bubble of pleasure growing inside her. She'd made this happen.

The image of Belinda's happy face flashed through her mind, and her pleasure vanished. Was this how her mother had felt manipulating Fleur's career?

Kissy was nervous about the film she'd be making in London, and she pumped Fleur about *Eclipse*. Eventually she switched to the subject of Jake. "You haven't said much about him lately."

Fleur set aside her pizza. "He's barely looked up from his typewriter in weeks. When I go upstairs to check on him, he doesn't even see me." But they still ran together sometimes in the morning, although they never spoke about anything important, and Jake had shown up in her kitchen for breakfast a couple of times.

"Translated that means that you're not sleeping together."

The topic of Jake was too complicated, so she settled on the simplest response. "He was my mother's lover."

"Not technically," Kissy replied. "And I've been thinking about that. Everything I've heard about her indicates Belinda's a very seductive woman. Jake was a young guy. She came on to him. You and Jake weren't lovers at the time, and whatever happened between them didn't have anything to do with you."

"She had to know how I felt about him," Fleur said bitterly, "but she jumped into bed with him anyway."

"That speaks volumes about her, but not about him." Kissy tucked her legs under her. "You don't really still believe that old garbage about Jake seducing you for the sake of his movie, do you? I've only met him a few times, but that's obviously not his style. I'm sure he has his faults, but blind ambition doesn't seem to be one of them."

"He has his faults, all right. He's the most emotionally dishonest person I've ever met. You should see the way he puts up a barrier against anyone who gets too close. He'll give me little glimpses of who he is, then he slams the door. That's fine in a casual friendship, but not for someone who loves him."

Kissy set down the pizza crust and stared at her. Fleur's cheeks grew hot. "I'm not in love with him! God, Kissy, I was talking generally. Yes, there are things about him I love—mainly his looks and his body. But . . ." She let her hand fall into her lap. "I can't afford him. I've had too many dishonest, manipulative people in my life, and I don't need another one."

Kissy mercifully changed the subject. They chatted about Olivia Creighton's latest neurosis, and what clothes Kissy should take to London. Eventually, however, Kissy seemed to run out of things to say, and that's when Fleur realized the name "Charlie Kincannon" hadn't crossed her lips all evening. But Kissy's eyes were sparkling, and she could barely sit still to eat. Maybe her excitement wasn't all about work. "Something's going on with you and Charlie."

"Charlie?"

"It is! Spit it out."

"Really, Fleur, such a vulgar expression."

She pulled the pizza crust from Kissy's fingers. "No more food until you tell me what's happening."

Kissy hesitated and then pulled her knees up. "Don't laugh, okay? I know you'll think this is silly . . ." She twisted a curl around her finger. "Actually . . ." Her throat worked as she swallowed. "I think I might be in love."

"Why would I think that's silly?"

"Because Charlie isn't exactly the most likely companion for me, considering my history."

Fleur smiled. "I've always thought you and Charlie were the most likely of companions. You were the one who didn't agree."

Now that Kissy's news was out, she wanted to tell everything before she lost her nerve. "I feel so stupid. He's the most wonderful man I ever met, but I didn't know how to relate to a guy who wanted me for something other than sex. Every time I tried to seduce him, he started talking about Kierkegaard, or dadaism, or the Knicks, for God's sake. And . . . listen to this . . . No matter what we were talking about, he never once tried to dominate the conversation. He didn't talk *at* me like other men do. He was genuinely interested in my opinions. He *challenged* me. And the more we talked, the more I remembered how smart I really am." Kissy's eyes suddenly filled with tears. "Fleur, it felt so good."

Fleur's own eyes stung. "Charlie's a special person, and so are you."

"The funny thing was that at first all I could think about was getting him into bed, which, let's face it, is where I'm most comfortable. I'd brush up against him or tell him my muscles were sore and I needed a back rub. Or when he'd come to pick me up, I wouldn't quite have all my clothes on. But no matter how brazen I acted, he didn't seem to notice. After a while, I started to forget about seducing him and just started enjoying his company. That's when I realized he wasn't quite as unaffected by me as he pretended. But it still took forever for him to get serious."

At Kissy's dreamy expression, Fleur smiled. "Looks like it was worth the wait."

Kissy grinned. "I didn't let him touch me."

"You're kidding?"

"It was so nice being *courted*. Then, two weeks ago, he came over to the apartment one night after rehearsal. He started kissing me, and I was really enjoying it, but I started to feel afraid. You know. Afraid that after everything that had gone on, I'd disappoint him. I could tell by his expression that he knew how I felt because he just smiled that sweet, understanding smile of his. And then he said we ought to play Scrabble."

"Scrabble?" There was such a thing as carrying restraint too far, and Fleur was disappointed in Charlie.

"Well . . . not regular Scrabble. Sort of—strip Scrabble."

Good for you, Charlie. Fleur arched an eyebrow. "Might one ask how this particular perversion is played?"

"It's really pretty simple. For every twenty points your opponent scores, you have to take off one item of clothing. And you know, Fleur, as much as I wanted to go to bed with him, I really did like being courted, and I happen to be a truly exceptional Scrabble player." She swept a dramatic arc through the air. "I started out strong with 'klepht' and 'pewit.' "

"I'm impressed."

"Then I hit him right between the eyes with 'whey' and 'jargon' on a double word score."

"That must have taken his breath away."

"It did. But he came back with 'jaw' off my 'jargon' and 'wax' off 'pewit.' Still, it was obvious that we weren't in the same league—I *never* do three-letter words unless I'm desperate. By the time I made 'viscacha,' he was down to his briefs and one sock. I still had my slip and everything under it." Her forehead puckered in a frown. "That's when it happened."

"I'm breathless with anticipation."

"He hit me with 'qaid.' "

"There's no such word."

"Oh yes there is. A Northern African tribal leader, although generally only world-class Scrabble players and crossword addicts know it."

"And?"

"Don't you see? The son of a bitch was hustling me!"

"Dear God."

"To make a long story short, he laid 'zebu' in on a horizontal and then capped it with 'zloty' on the vertical. My 'quail' looked pretty pitiful after that, but worse was to come."

"I don't know if I can bear the tension."

" 'Phlox' on a triple word score."

"That devil."

Chapter 25

By Christmas, Fleur had picked up three great new clients—two actors and a singer. Alexi hadn't made any new moves against her, and the old stories about her broken contracts seem to be fading. The gossip about her relationship with Jake continued, but word had started to leak that he was writing again, and the gossip no longer held as much sting. Rough Harbor's first album was performing above expectations, and the unqualified success of Michel's collection was still bringing an avalanche of good publicity. When Kissy got rave reviews after her play premiered on January 3, Fleur felt as if all her own dreams were coming true. So why wasn't she happier? She avoided probing her inner psyche too deeply by working even harder.

Jake stopped showing up for their morning run, and when she went upstairs to check on him, he barely spoke. He'd been working on his book for nearly three months, and he'd grown increasingly gaunt. His hair hung long over his collar, and he forgot to shave for days at a time.

One cold Friday night in the second week of January, something awakened her. Total silence. What had happened to the typewriter? She stirred.

"It's okay, Flower," a rough voice whispered. "It's just me."

The dim lights sifting in from her winter garden illuminated the room just enough so she could see Jake hunched in a chair not far from her bed, his rangy legs stretched in front of him.

"What are you doing?" she muttered.

"Watching you sleep." His voice was as soft and dark as the night room. "The light's a paintbrush in your hair. Do you remember how we wrapped your hair around us when we made love?"

The blood rushed through her sleep-heavy body. "I remember."

"I never wanted to hurt you," he said raggedly. "You got caught in the crossfire."

She didn't want to think about the past. "That was a long time ago. I'm not so naïve now."

"I don't know about that." His voice developed an edge. "For somebody who wants me to believe she's made a career out of sleeping around, you don't seem to have a lot of men coming through here."

She wanted him to stay soft and sweet. She wanted him talking about paintbrushes and the light in her hair. "Not with you living over my head, that's for sure. We go to their places."

"Is that so?" Slowly he uncurled from the chair and began unbuttoning his shirt. "If you're passing it out for free, I guess it's time I took my turn."

She bolted up in bed. "I'm not passing it out for free!"

He stripped off his shirt. "This could have happened between us months ago. All you had to do was ask."

"Me! What about you?"

He didn't say anything. Instead his hand went to the snap on his jeans.

"Stop right there."

"Let's not." His zipper fell open in a V, revealing a bare, flat stomach. "The book's done."

"It is?"

"And I can't quit thinking about you."

Her emotions tangled into a knot. She wanted him so much. But something was terribly wrong. If his book was finished, he should be relieved. Instead he seemed haunted, and she needed to find out why. "Zip your pants, cowboy," she said quietly. "We need to talk first."

"The hell we do." He kicked off his shoes, whipped away the blankets covering her, and gazed down at the ice-blue nightgown twisted high on her thighs. "Nice." He peeled off his jeans.

"No."

"Just be quiet, will you?" He reached for the hem of her gown.

"We're going to talk." She started to pull away, but he snared the skirt of her nightgown, holding her in place.

"Later."

She clamped her fingers around his wrist. "I'm not into recreational sex, not with you."

He let her go abruptly and slapped the wall above her head with the flat of his hand. "How about mercy fucking then? Are you into mercy fucking, because if you are, you've got yourself one hell of an opportunity here."

She saw the pain he couldn't hide, and her heart ached. "Oh, Jake."

The shutters banged shut. "Forget it!" He grabbed his jeans and shoved his legs into them. "Forget I was ever here." He snatched up his shirt and headed into the hallway.

"Wait!" She pushed herself out of bed, only to get tangled in the cast-off blankets. By the time she freed herself, her front door had slammed. She heard the thud of his feet on the steps leading to the attic. She remembered the deep shadows under his eyes, the feeling of desperation rolling off him. Without thinking it through, she went into the hallway and up the stairs to the attic.

The door was locked against her. "Open up."

Nothing but silence came from the other side.

"I mean it, Jake. Open this door right now."

"Go away."

She swore under her breath and went back downstairs to get her key. By the time she got his door unlocked, she was shaking.

He sat on the unmade bed, leaning against the headboard with a bottle of beer propped on his bare chest and his jeans still unzipped. His hostility crackled like dry ice. "You ever heard of tenant's rights?"

"You don't have a lease." She stepped over his shirt, which lay crumpled on the floor, and walked toward him. When she reached the bed, she studied him, trying to read his mind, but all she saw were the harsh lines of exhaustion around his mouth and the desperation that had etched itself into the shadows under his eyes. "If anybody needs mercy," she said quietly, "it's me. It's been a long time."

His expression tightened, and she realized right away that he wasn't going to make this easy for himself. He'd revealed too much need, and now he had to throw up some camouflage. He took a swig of beer and looked at her as if she were a cockroach who'd just crawled across his floor. "Maybe some poor slob would take you to bed if you weren't such a ballbuster."

She'd love to take a swing at him, but he was only capable of self-destruction tonight, and she suspected that's what he wanted. "It's not like I haven't had plenty of offers."

"I'll just bet you have." He sneered. "Pretty boys with Cuisinarts and BMWs."

"Among others."

"How many?"

Why couldn't he just admit he needed her instead of putting them both through this? She had to stay in charge of this dangerous game he wanted to play. "Dozens," she replied. "Hundreds."

"I'll bet."

"I'm legendary."

"In your own mind." He took another slug of beer, then swiped his mouth with the back of his hand. "And now you want me to take the edge off your sexual frustrations. Play stud for you."

The man was shameless. "If you don't have anything better to do."

He shrugged and kicked the blankets away. "I guess not. Take off your nightgown."

"No way, cowboy. You want it off—you take it off. And while you're at it, get rid of those jeans so I can see what you've got."

"What *I've* got?"

"Consider this an audition."

He couldn't even manage a smile, and she knew he'd reached his breaking point. "On second thought," she said, "why don't you just lie there? I'm feeling aggressive." She peeled her nightgown over her head, but her hair got tangled in the strap. She was standing naked and vulnerable in front of him. Her fingers trembled as she tried to free her hair, but she only made the snare worse.

"Lean over," he said softly.

He pulled her down to the side of the bed. She sat with her back to him and her bare hip brushing his denim-covered thigh.

The nightgown slipped free. "There."

He made no move to touch her. She gazed across the room, her spine stiff, her hands crossed in her lap, and she knew she couldn't go any further. She heard him sliding off his jeans. Why did he have to make this so difficult? Maybe he wouldn't even kiss her. Maybe he'd just pull her back on the bed and have sex with her without even kissing her. Wham, bam—nice knowing you, kiddo, but I'll be moving on now. And wouldn't that be just like him? He was such a son of a bitch. Playing on her sympathies. Refusing to talk except to insult her. Getting ready to run out on her again!

"Flower?" His hand touched her shoulder.

She spun on him. "I won't do it if you don't kiss me. I mean it! If you don't kiss me, you can go to hell."

He blinked.

"And don't you think for one minute—"

He caught her by the back of her neck and dragged her down over his bare chest. "I need you, Flower," he whispered. "I need you real bad."

His mouth closed over hers in a deep, sweet tongue kiss. She floated through the kiss, bathed in it, drank it and ate it, and didn't want it ever to stop. He rolled her onto her back and pressed her into the mattress with his weight.

The kiss lost its sweetness, becoming dark and desperate. His breathing grew more ragged, and she arched her back to press her hips closer. Sweat broke out on his body, mingling with her own, and suddenly his hands were all over her. Rough, clumsy hands—at her breasts and waist, on her hips and buttocks, pushing inside her.

There was something so desperate about his touch. She was frightened for him, frightened for herself. All the frustration, the years of denial, formed a fiery ball in her chest. She wrapped her arms around his shoulders and met his fierceness with her own. "Love me, Jake," she whispered. "Please love me."

His fingers dug into the soft skin of her thighs, spreading them far apart, and his weight settled between them. Without warning, he thrust deep and hard within her. She cried out. He grabbed her head between his hands and covered her mouth with his own. He kissed her desperately as he drove inside her. She came at once, breaking apart in a joyless orgasm. He didn't stop. He stayed with her, tongue in her mouth, hands in her hair, pushing harder . . . faster . . . letting out a harsh, anguished cry as he spilled himself deep within her.

He pulled away as soon as it was over. She lay staring at the ceiling. His desperation . . . his dark silence . . . the bleakness of their lovemaking . . . His book was done, and he'd just said good-bye.

Love me, Jake. Please love me. The words she'd spoken in the throes of lovemaking came back to her, and she felt sick inside.

They lay on the bed, not even their hands touching. Nothing.

"Flower?"

In her mind she saw a long stretch of sun-scorched sand spreading bleak and empty before her. She had so much—her job, her friends—but all she could see was the barren sand.

"Flower, I want to talk to you."

She turned her back to him and burrowed her face into the pillow. Now he wanted to talk. Now that it was all over. Her head ached and her mouth felt dry and acrid. The mattress creaked as he left the bed. "I know you're not asleep."

"What do you want?" she finally said.

He switched on the gooseneck lamp that sat on his desk. She rolled over to face him. He stood next to the desk, unself-conscious in his nakedness. "Do you have anything going this weekend that you can't cancel?" he said. "Anything important?"

He wanted to play out the final scene, the great goodbye. "Let me reach under the pillow and check my appointment calendar," she said wearily.

"Damn it! Go throw some things in a suitcase. I'll get you in half an hour."

★

Two hours later they were in a chartered jet flying to God-knew-where, and Jake was asleep in the seat next to her. Was there some basic flaw in her makeup that made her keep falling in love with this man who couldn't love her back? She didn't try to slide around it anymore. She loved Jake Koranda.

She'd fallen in love with him when she was nineteen years old, and now she'd done it all over again. He was the only man she'd ever known who seemed to belong to her.

Jake, who went out of his way to close himself off, was part of her. Maybe she had a death wish. Again and again, he left her emotionally stranded at the gates of the *couvent*. He didn't *give* anything back. He wouldn't talk about anything important—the war, his first marriage, what had happened when they were making *Eclipse*. Instead he deflected her with wisecracks. And if she wanted to be honest, she knew she did the same to him. But it was different with her. She did it because she had to protect herself. What did he have to protect?

It was seven in the morning when they landed in Santa Barbara. Jake turned up the collar on his leather jacket against the early chill, or maybe the prying eyes of a lurking fan. He carried an attaché case in one hand and guided her by the elbow toward the parking lot with the other. They stopped next to a dark maroon Jaguar sedan. He unlocked the door and slung his case, along with her overnight bag, into the back.

"It'll be a while before we get there," he said with an unexpected gentleness. "Try to get some sleep."

The cantilevered glass and concrete house looked almost the same as she remembered it. What a perfect spot for the farewell they still had to play out. "A return to the scene of the crime?" she said as he pulled up in front.

He turned off the ignition. "I don't know that I'd exactly call it a crime, but we have some ghosts to put to rest, and this seems like the right place to do it."

She was tired and upset, and she couldn't help sniping at him. "Too bad you couldn't find a root beer stand. As long as we're dealing with the business of lost innocence . . ."

He ignored her.

While he took a shower, she changed into a swimsuit. After she'd wrapped herself in a warm robe, she went out to test the water in the pool. It wasn't heated nearly enough to combat the late morning January chill, but she shed her robe anyway and dived in. She gasped from the chill and began to swim laps, but the tension coiled inside her refused to unravel. She got out, pulled an oversized bath towel around her, and lay down on one of the chaises in the sun, where she instantly fell asleep.

Hours later, a small Mexican woman with shiny black hair awakened her and announced that dinner would be ready soon if she'd like to change first. Fleur deliberately avoided the big bathroom with the sunken tub where they'd made love all those years ago, choosing a smaller guest bathroom instead. By the time she'd finished her shower and swept her hair back from her face with a set of combs, her grogginess had disappeared. She pulled on light gray slacks and an open-necked sage-green blouse. Just before she stepped out into the living room, she slipped on the necklace Jake had given her, but then she fastened the button between her breasts so he wouldn't see she was wearing it.

He was clean-shaven and dressed almost respectably in jeans and a light blue sweater, but the lines of exhaustion around his mouth hadn't eased. Neither of them had much appetite, and their meal was tense and silent. She couldn't get past the feeling that everything that had passed between them was about to be resolved, and there wouldn't be a happy ending. Loving Jake had always been a one-way street.

Eventually the housekeeper appeared with coffee. She set the pot down harder than necessary to protest the injustice that had been done to her meal. Jake dismissed her for the night and sat without moving until he heard the back door close. He pushed himself away from the table and disappeared. When he came back, he was carrying a fat manila envelope. She stared at it, and then she stared at him. "You really did finish your book."

He shoved his hand through his hair. "I'm going out for a while. You can—if you want, you can read this."

She took the envelope gingerly. "Are you sure? I know I pushed you into this. Maybe—"

"Don't sell the serial rights while I'm out." He tried to

smile, but he couldn't make it. "This one's just for you, Flower. Nobody else."

"What do you mean?"

"Exactly what I said. I wrote it for you. Only you."

She didn't understand. How could he have spent the last three months destroying himself over a manuscript that only she would read? A manuscript he never intended to see published? Once again, she thought of the little girl wearing a shirt with yellow ducks. There could be only one explanation. The contents were too incriminating. She felt nauseous.

He turned away. She heard his footsteps pass through the kitchen. He went out the same back door the housekeeper had used such a short time ago. Fleur took her coffee over to the window and stared out into the lavender evening. He'd written about massacres twice, first a fictionalized version in *Sunday Morning Eclipse* and now the true story in the pages sealed inside the manila envelope. She thought about the two faces of Jake Koranda. The brutal face of Bird Dog Caliber and the sensitive face of the playwright who explored the human condition with so much insight. She'd always believed Bird Dog was the fake, but now she wondered if she'd gotten it all wrong just as she'd gotten so many other things wrong about him.

It was a long time before she could make herself pick up the manila envelope and pull out the manuscript. She settled into a chair near the windows, turned on the light, and began to read.

★

Jake dribbled toward the basketball hoop on the side of the garage and went in for a quick dunk, but the leather soles of his boots slipped on the concrete, and the ball hit the rim. For a moment he thought about going back inside for his sneakers, but he couldn't bear to see her reading.

He tucked the basketball under his arm and wandered to the stone wall that kept the hillside in place. He wished he had a six-pack of Mexican beer, but he wasn't going back into the house to get it. He wasn't going anywhere close to her. He couldn't stand watching her disillusionment for a second time.

He leaned against the rough stones. He should have come up with another way of ending things between them, a way that would have distanced him from her disgust. The pain was too sharp to bear, so he imagined the sounds of the crowd in his head. He envisioned himself in center court at the Philadelphia Spectrum, wearing a Seventy-sixers uniform with the number six on his chest. *Doc.*

Doc . . . Doc . . . He tried to make his mind form the image, but it wouldn't take shape.

He stood up and carried the ball back around the garage to the hoop. He began to dribble. He was Julius Erving, a little slower than he used to be, but still a giant, still flying . . . *Doc.*

Instead of the roar of the crowd, he heard a different sort of music playing in his head.

Inside the house, the hours slipped by and the pile of discarded manuscript pages grew at Fleur's feet. Her hair slipped from its combs, and her back got a crick from sitting in the same place for so long. As she reached the final page, she could no longer hold back her tears.

> When I think of 'Nam, I think of the music that was always playing. Otis . . . the Stones . . . Wilson Pickett. Most of all, I think of Creedence Clearwater and their bad moon rising over that badass land. Creedence was playing when they loaded me on the plane in Saigon to go home, and as I filled my lungs with that last breath of monsoon-heavy, dope-steady air, I knew the bad moon had blown me away. Now, fifteen years later, it's still got me.

Chapter 26

Fleur found Jake by the garage, sitting on the ground just beyond the reach of the floodlights. He was leaning against a stone wall, a basketball propped in his lap, and he looked as though he'd walked through the fires of hell, which wasn't far from the truth. She knelt beside him. He stared up at her, the shutters drawn and tightly locked, daring her to pity him.

"You'll never know how much you scared me," she said. "I forgot about you and your damned metaphors. All that talk about massacres, and the little girl in the shirt with the yellow ducks . . . I saw you wiping out a village full of innocent civilians. You scared me so bad . . . It was like I couldn't trust my own instincts about you. I thought you'd been part of some obscene massacre."

"I was. The whole frigging war was a massacre."

"Metaphorically speaking, maybe, but I'm a little more literal-minded."

"Then you must have been relieved to learn the truth," he said bitterly. "John Wayne ended his military career in a psychiatric ward pumped full of Thorazine because he couldn't take the heat."

There it was. The secret that haunted him. The reason

he'd erected such indomitable walls around himself. He was afraid the world would find out he'd broken apart.

"You weren't John Wayne. You were a twenty-one-year-old kid from Cleveland who hadn't gotten many breaks in life and was seeing too much."

"I freaked out, Flower. Don't you understand that? I was screaming at ceilings."

"It doesn't matter. You can't have it both ways. You can't write beautiful, sensitive plays that look into people's hearts and not expect to be torn apart when you see human suffering."

"A lot of guys saw the same things, but they didn't freak."

"A lot of guys weren't you."

She reached out for him, but before she could touch him, he stood up and turned his back toward her. "I managed to arouse all your protective instincts, didn't I?" The words whipped her with their scorn. "I made you feel sorry for me. Believe me, that wasn't what I wanted to do."

She stood, too, but this time she didn't try to touch him. "When you gave me the manuscript, you should have told me I wasn't supposed to react to it. Did you expect me to respond as though I'd just seen one of your stupid Caliber pictures? I can't do that. I don't like watching you drill people full of bullet holes. I liked you a lot better curled up on that cot in the hospital, screaming your heart out because you weren't able to stop what happened in the village. Your pain made me suffer with you, and if you can't handle that, then you shouldn't have given me the book."

Instead of settling him, her words seemed to make him angrier. "You didn't understand a damned thing."

He stalked away, and she didn't go after him. This was about him, not her. She made her way to the pool and stripped down to her bra and panties. Shivering with cold, she looked into the dark, forbidding water. Then she dived in. The frigid water stole her breath. She swam to the deep end and turned over to float on her back. Cold . . . suspended . . . waiting.

She felt a deep, wrenching pity for the boy he'd been, raised without any softness by a mother who was too tired and too angry over the unfairness of her life to give her child the love he'd needed. He'd looked for a father in the men who frequented the neighborhood bars. Sometimes he found one; sometimes he didn't. She considered the irony of the college scholarship he'd received—not for his fine, sensitive mind, but for a ruthless slam dunk.

As she floated in the icy water, she thought about his marriage to Liz. He'd continued to love her long after their relationship was over. How typical of him. Jake didn't give his love easily, but once he gave it, he didn't withdraw it easily, either. He'd been numb with pain when he'd enlisted, and he'd futilely tried to distract himself with war, death, and drugs. He hadn't cared if he survived, and it frightened her to think about how reckless he'd been. When he hadn't been able to stop what happened in the village, he'd broken. And despite all those long months in the VA hospital, he'd never really recovered.

As she looked into the night sky, she thought she understood why that was.

"The water's cold. You'd better get out." He stood at the side of the pool, his posture neither friendly nor unfriendly. He held a beer in one hand. An orange beach towel dangled from the other.

"I'm not ready."

He hesitated, then carried the towel and the beer over to a lounge chair.

She studied the racing clouds overhead. "Why did you blame me for the block?"

"The problem started when I met you. Before you came along, everything was fine."

"Got any ideas about that?"

"A few."

"Care to toss them out?"

"Not particularly."

She pulled her legs under her and began to tread water.

"I'll tell you why you couldn't write. I was storming the fort. Breaching those walls. You'd built them thick and strong, but this funny nineteen-year-old kid who ate you up with her eyes was tearing them down as fast as you could build them. You were scared to death that once those walls took their first shot, you'd never be able to build them up again."

"You're making it more complicated than it was. I couldn't write after you left because I felt guilty, that's all, and we both know that wasn't your fault."

"No!" She cut through the water until her feet touched bottom. "You didn't feel guilty. That's a cop-out." Her throat was tight. "You didn't feel guilty because you didn't have anything to feel guilty about. You made love to me because you wanted me, because you even loved me a little." A painful lump made it hard to breathe. "You had to have loved me, Jake. I couldn't have generated all that feeling by myself."

"You don't know anything about what I felt."

She stood shivering in the water, the wet bra clinging to her breasts, the flower necklace stuck to her skin. Suddenly she saw it all so clearly that she wondered why she hadn't understood it before. "This is about macho. That's all this is. With *Sunday Morning Eclipse*, your writing had become too self-revealing, and then I came along at the same time and all your warning flashers went off. You didn't stop writing because of me. You stopped because you were afraid to peel off any more layers. You didn't want everybody to know that the tough guy on the screen—the tough guy you'd had to be while you were growing up—wasn't anyplace close to the real man."

"You sound like a shrink."

Her teeth had begun to chatter, making her words come out in short, broken bursts. "Even when you joke about your screen image, you're subtly winking your eye. Like you're saying—'Hey, everybody, sure it's just acting, but we all know I'm still one hell of a man.' "

"That's bull."

"You started playing the tough guy when you were a kid. If you hadn't, you'd have gotten swallowed up by those Cleveland streets. But after a while, you started believing that's who you really were, this man who could handle anything. A man like Bird Dog." She climbed up the steps, shivering as the air hit her. "Bird Dog's exactly who you want to be—someone who's emotionally dead. Who never feels pain. A man who's *safe*."

"You're full of crap!" The beer bottle slammed down on the table.

Instead of accepting that he wasn't invulnerable, he was lashing out against the closest target. Her. She gripped the railing, her shoulders hunched against the cold, her chest tight with anguish. "Bird Dog's not half the man you are. Can't you see that? Your breakdown is a sign of your humanity, not your weakness."

"Bullshit!"

Her teeth were chattering so hard she could barely speak. "If you want to heal yourself, go inside and read your own damned book!"

"Fucking unbelievable, you're so wrong."

"Read your book and try to feel a little compassion for that poor, brave kid who'd had his nerves burned raw—"

He jumped up from his chair, his face white with fury. "You missed the whole point! You don't get it! You didn't see what's right in front of you. This isn't about pity!"

"Read your book!" she cried into the cold night. "Read about the kid who didn't have a single person in the world who gave a damn about him!"

"Why can't you understand?" he shouted. "This isn't about pity! This is about *disgust*!" He kicked away a chair that stood in his path and sent it crashing into the pool. "I want you to feel disgust so you *get out of my fucking life!*"

He stormed toward the house, and the gates of the *couvent* slammed shut on her for the thousandth time. He walked away like they all did, leaving her stranded, cold, and alone. She sank down on the concrete, shivering and numb. The old cedars around the house groaned. She grabbed for the orange beach towel and wrapped herself in it. Then she rested her head on her pillow of ruined clothes and drew up into a ball. Finally she let herself cry until she had no tears left.

*

Jake stood next to the window in the dark living room and looked down on her crumpled at the side of the pool. She was a beautiful, shining creature of light and goodness, and he'd dragged her into hell. Something swift and sharp tore at the backs of his eyelids. He wanted to take on her pain as his own. But he didn't go to her—wouldn't let himself go. He'd given her the book. He'd written it just for her so she'd understand why he couldn't offer her everything he wanted to, everything that exquisite creature deserved, everything he was too weak—too unworthy—to give.

He remembered the night he'd walked in on her when she and Kissy were watching *Butch Cassidy.* Redford wouldn't have ended up lying on a cot curled up like a fetus. The Doc wouldn't have cracked up. And neither would Bird Dog. How could she love a man who'd ended up as he had?

He turned away from the window. He shouldn't have brought her here, shouldn't have let her back into his life, shouldn't love her so goddamned much. If he'd learned anything by now, he'd learned that he wasn't cut out for love. Love tore down the defenses he needed to get through the day. Because she was so strong herself, she didn't want to accept that he was weak. The other guys hadn't cracked up, but he had.

She'd scattered the manuscript pages around the chair where she'd been reading, and in his mind he could see her sitting there, those long legs tucked up under her, that big, beautiful face creased in concentration. He walked over to the chair and knelt down to stack the pages. He was going to build a fire and burn them before he went to bed. They were like live grenades lying around, and he couldn't sleep until he'd destroyed them, because if anyone but Flower ever found out what was in them, he might as well put a pistol to his head and blow out his brains.

He walked back over to the window. She was quiet now. Maybe she'd fallen asleep. He hoped so.

He returned to the chair where she'd been sitting, and his eyes fell on the top page. He picked it up and studied the layout, the quality of the type, the fact that he'd run the right margin too close to the edge. He took in all those separate, unimportant facts, and then he began to read.

> CHAPTER ONE
>
> Everything in 'Nam was booby-trapped. A pack of cigarettes, a lighter, a candy bar wrapper—all those things could blow up in your face. But we didn't expect anything other than another small, dead body when we saw the baby lying at the side of the road outside Quang Tri. Who could have imagined that anyone would booby-trap the body of a baby? It was the ultimate rape of innocence . . .

Sometime during the night Jake carried her inside. He bumped her head trying to get her through the guest room door and cursed, but when he laid her down and whispered good night, she heard a horrible tenderness that made her pretend she'd fallen back to sleep.

Emotionally dishonest. That's what she'd told Kissy about him, and she'd been right. She'd had enough pain in her life, and she was bailing out. Loving a man who batted around her heart like one of his basketballs had grown too awful to bear.

Early the next morning, she found him asleep on one of the couches, his mouth slightly open, his arm dipping into the puddle of manuscript pages scattered on the floor beneath him. She located the key to his Jag and threw everything into her overnight case as quietly as she could. His truck was parked in the garage, so she wasn't leaving him stranded.

The car started right away. As she slipped it into reverse and backed around in the drive, the morning sun struck her in the eyes. They were still swollen from the night before. She reached into her purse for sunglasses. The driveway was steep and rutted. Jake and his insecurities. He'd made the approach to the house nearly impassable, all so he could guard his precious, stupid privacy.

She started to crawl down the drive. A movement in the rearview mirror caught her attention. It was Jake running toward the car. His shirttail had come undone, his hair stood up on one side of his head, and he looked as if he wanted to murder someone. She couldn't hear what he was yelling. Probably just as well.

She hit the accelerator, took the next curve too fast, and felt the car bottom out on one of the ruts. She overcompensated by jerking the steering wheel to the right. The Jag swerved. Before she could straighten, the front wheel was hanging over a ditch.

She turned off the ignition and rested her arms on top of the steering wheel, waiting for Jake and his anger, or Jake and his wisecracks, or Jake and whatever other facade he'd decide to throw up between them. Why couldn't he let her go? Why couldn't they finally take the easy way out?

The driver's door swung open, but she didn't move. His breathing sounded as ragged as hers had on that Fourth of July night six months ago. She pushed the sunglasses higher on her nose.

"You didn't take your necklace." His voice was higher-pitched than normal. He cleared his throat. "I want you to have your necklace, Flower."

The morning glory pendant slipped into her lap. She felt the warmth of the metal from where he'd clutched it in his hand. She stared straight ahead through the windshield. "Thank you."

"I—I had it made especially for you." He cleared his throat again. "This guy I know. I did a pencil drawing for him."

"It's beautiful." She spoke politely, as if she'd just received it. Still she wouldn't look at him.

His feet shifted in the gravel. "I don't want you to go, Flower. All that stuff last night . . ." His voice sounded hoarse, as if he were getting a cold. "I'm sorry."

She wouldn't cry, but the effort cost her, and her words sounded as broken as her heart. "I can't—I can't take any more. Let me go."

He drew a ragged breath. "I did what you said. I read the book. You . . . You were right. I—I've been locked up inside myself too long. Afraid. But when I went to get you by the pool last night . . . All of a sudden I knew I was a hell of a lot more afraid of losing you than I was of anything that happened fifteen years ago."

She finally turned to look at him, but he wouldn't meet her eyes. She pulled off her sunglasses and heard him clear his throat again and suddenly realized he was crying.

"Jake?"

"Don't look at me."

She turned away, but then his hands were on her arms, and he was pulling her from the car. He squeezed her to his chest so tightly she could barely breathe. "Don't leave me." He choked out the words. "I've been alone for so long . . . all my life. Don't leave me. Jesus, I love you so much. Please, Flower."

She felt him crumbling. All the protective layers he'd built around himself were breaking away. She finally had what she wanted—Jake Koranda with his emotions stripped raw. Jake letting her see what he'd never shown to anyone else. And it broke her heart.

She covered his tears with her mouth, swallowed them, made them disappear. She tried to heal him with her touch. She wanted to make him whole again, as whole as she was. "It's all right, cowboy," she whispered. "It's all right. I love you. Just don't shut me out anymore. I can take anything but that."

He gazed down at her, his eyes red-rimmed, all the cockiness stripped away. "What about you? How long are you going to keep shutting me out? When are you going to let me in?"

"I don't know what you—" She stopped herself and rested her cheek against his jaw. His smokescreens were no different from her own. All her life, she'd tried to find her personal value in the opinions of others—the nuns at the *couvent*, Belinda, Alexi. And now it was her business. Yes, she wanted her agency to succeed, but if it failed, she wouldn't be any less a person. There was nothing wrong with her. She'd been just as much a victim of her misconceptions as Jake.

Try to feel some compassion for the kid you were, she'd told him. Maybe it was time she took her own advice and felt a little compassion for the frightened child she'd been.

"Jake?"

He muttered something into her neck.

"You'll have to help me," she said.

He slipped his fingers in her hair, and they kissed long enough to lose track of time. When they finally moved apart, he said, "I love you, Flower. Let's get this car out of here and drive down to the water. I want to look at the ocean and hold you close and tell you everything I've wanted to say for a long time. And I think you have some things to tell me, too."

She thought of everything she needed to tell him. About the *couvent* and Alexi, about Belinda and Errol Flynn, about her lost years and her ambitions. She nodded.

They got the car back on the road. Jake drove, and as they began their slow crawl down the drive, he picked up her hand and kissed her fingertips. She smiled, and then she gently pulled away. Her purse held a compact with a pocket mirror. She flipped it open and began to study her face.

What she saw was unsettling and disturbing, but she

didn't turn away as she'd been doing for so many years. Instead she stared at her reflection and tried to take in her features with her heart instead of her brain.

Her face was part of her. It might be too big to fit her personal definition of beauty, but she saw intelligence in her reflection, sensitivity in her eyes, humor in her wide mouth. It was a good face. Well-balanced. It belonged to her, and that made it good. "Jake?"

"Hmmm?"

"I really am pretty, aren't I?"

He looked at her and grinned, a wisecrack ready to slip from his mouth. But then he saw her expression, and his grin disappeared. "I think you're the prettiest woman I've ever seen," he said simply.

She sighed and settled back into her seat, a satisfied smile on her face.

The motorcycle rider waited until the Jag disappeared around the bend before he came out from behind the scrub. He lifted his helmet, took in the road. Then he headed up the rutted drive to the cantilevered house.

Chapter 27

They returned an hour later, shivering with cold from their rambling, kiss-filled walk along the ocean. Jake lit a fire and laid a comforter in front of it. They undressed each other and made love—slow and tender. He mounted her. She, him. Her hair drifted around them both.

Afterward, they ceremoniously burned his manuscript, and as one page after another went up in flames, Jake seemed to grow younger. "I think I can forget it now."

She rested her head against his bare shoulder. "Don't forget. Your past will always be part of you, and you have nothing to be ashamed of."

He picked up the poker and pushed a loose page back into the flames, but he didn't say anything, and she didn't push him. He needed time. It was enough for now that he could talk to her about what had happened.

She called the office and told David she needed a few days off. "It's about time you took a vacation," he said.

She and Jake shut out the world. Their happiness felt iridescent, and their tender, passionate lovemaking filled them both with a sense of wonder.

On their third morning, she was lying in bed wearing only a T-shirt when he came out of the bathroom wrapped in a towel. She inched up against the suede headboard. "Let's go horseback riding."

"There's no good place to ride around here."

"What do you mean? There's a stable not three miles away. We passed it yesterday when we out for a drive. I haven't been on a horse in months."

He picked up a pair of jeans and seemed to be inspecting it for wrinkles, something she'd never known him to care one thing about. "Why don't you go by yourself? I need to catch up on some work. Besides, I have to ride all the time. It'd be a busman's holiday."

"It won't be fun without you."

"You're the one who pointed out that we have to get used to separations." He stumbled over her sneakers.

She looked at him more closely. He was fidgety, and an outrageous suspicion struck her. "How many Westerns have you made?"

"I don't know."

"Take a guess."

"Five . . . six. I don't know." He seemed to have developed a sudden reluctance to drop his towel in front of her. Snatching up his jeans, he carried them back into the bathroom.

"How about . . . seven?" she called out brightly.

"Yeah, maybe. Yeah, I guess that's about right." She heard him turn on the faucet and then the sounds of a noisy toothbrushing. He finally reappeared—bare chest, jeans still unzipped, a dab of toothpaste at the corner of his mouth.

She offered her most polite smile. "Seven Westerns, did you say?"

He fumbled with his zipper. "Uh-huh."

"A lot of time in the saddle."

"Damned zipper's stuck."

She nodded her head thoughtfully. "A *lot* of saddle time."

"I think it's broken."

"So tell me? Have you always been afraid of horses, or is it something recent?"

His head shot up. "Yeah, sure. Yeah, right."

She didn't say a word. She merely smiled.

"Me? Afraid of horses?"

Not a word.

Another jerk on the zipper. "A lot you know."

He was determined to gut it out. He even managed an appropriately belligerent sneer. Her smile passed from sweet to saccharine. Finally he dropped his head. "I wouldn't exactly say I was afraid," he muttered.

"What exactly would you say?" she cooed.

"We just don't get along, that's all."

She let out a whoop of laughter and fell back on the bed. "You're afraid of horses! Bird Dog's afraid of horses! You'll have to be my slave forever. I can blackmail you with this for the rest of your life. Backrubs, home-cooked meals, kinky sex—"

He looked hurt. "I like dogs."

"Do you now?"

"Big ones, too."

"Really?"

"Rotweillers. Shepherds. Bull mastiffs. The bigger the dog, the more I like it."

"I'm impressed."

"Damned right you are."

"Very impressed. I was starting to think you were more of a Chihuahua guy."

"Are you crazy? Those suckers bite."

She laughed and threw herself into his arms.

On their last day together, she lay with her head in his lap and thought about how much she didn't want to fly home alone tomorrow, but Jake needed to stay in California for a few weeks to take care of all the business he'd neglected while he'd been writing his book.

He made a paintbrush out of a lock of her hair. "I've been thinking . . ." He trailed the curl over her lips. "What about—what do you think would happen . . ." He painted her cheekbone. "What if we . . . got married?"

A rush of joy shot through her. She lifted her head. "Really?"

"Why not?"

Her joy bubble slipped aside just enough to reveal a tiny yellow caution light. "I think—I think it's too fast."

"We've known each other for seven years. That's not exactly fast."

"But we haven't been together for seven years. Neither of us can stand to fail at this. We bruise too easily. And we have to be absolutely sure."

"I couldn't be surer."

Neither could she. At the same time . . . "Let's give ourselves a chance to see how we handle the separation of having two careers—how we deal with the rough spots that are going to come along."

"I thought women were supposed to be romantics. What happened to impulse and passion?"

"They're opening in Vegas for Wayne Newton."

"You've got a smart mouth." He lowered himself over her and began nibbling at her bottom lip. "Let's do something about that."

His mouth moved to her breast, and she told herself she was right not to leap to marry him. They'd both received important insights about themselves this weekend, and they needed time to adjust.

But there was another reason. Some small part of her still didn't entirely trust Jake, and she couldn't handle another abandonment.

His kisses dipped lower, her senses ignited, and the world faded away around them.

⁂

Success bred success, and now that it didn't matter so much, everything she touched seemed to turn to gold. She renegotiated Olivia Creighton's *Dragon's Bay* contract, then signed one of the most promising of Hollywood's new wave of actors. Kissy's movie was going fabulously well in London, Rough Harbor's album was getting the kind of airplay that signaled a big hit, and orders were rolling in for Michel's designs. As icing on the cake, she came back from a business lunch one afternoon to find a Mailgram on her desk, the crux of which read:

ELOPING AT HIGH NOON TOMORROW STOP WILL PHONE AFTER HONEYMOON STOP CHARLIE JUST TOLD ME HOW RICH HE REALLY IS STOP AINT LOVE GRAND

Fleur laughed and leaned back in her chair. Ain't love grand, indeed.

Jake flew out from L.A. for a long weekend of sex, conversation, and laughter, but he had go back to do some overdubbing. She talked to him two or three times a day, sometimes more. He called as soon as he woke up in the morning, and she called before she went to bed at night. "This is good," she said. "Since we can't touch each other, we're learning to relate on a more cerebral level."

His reply was typical Koranda. "Cut the crap and tell me what color panties you're wearing."

One Friday evening toward the end of February, she returned from the housewarming Michel and Damon had thrown to celebrate moving into their new co-op. Just as she let herself in, the phone rang. She smiled and picked it up. "I said I'd call you, lover boy."

"Fleur? Oh God, baby, you've got to help me! Please, baby—"

Her fingers tightened around the receiver. "Belinda?"

"Don't let him do this! I know you hate me, but please, don't let him get away with this."

"Where are you?"

"In Paris. I—I thought I was rid of him. I should have known—" Her words grew muffled, and she began to sob.

Fleur squeezed her eyes shut. "Tell me what's happened."

"He sent two of his henchmen to New York after me. They were waiting in my apartment when I came home yesterday, and they forced me to go with them. They're going to take me to Switzerland. He's going to lock me up, baby. Because I stayed away from you in New York. He's threatened me for years, and now he's going to—"

There was a sudden click, and the line went dead.

Fleur slumped on the edge of her bed, the receiver still clasped in her hand. She didn't owe her mother anything. Belinda was the one who'd chosen to stay married to Alexi. She'd been too attached to the limelight his world cast over her to get a divorce, and whatever was happening to her now was her own fault.

Except—Belinda was her mother.

She set the receiver back on the cradle and forced herself to examine the relationship she'd avoided looking at for so long. The memories of their times together slipped before her like the pages of Jake's manuscript, and she saw with new eyes what she hadn't been able to see before. She saw her mother for who she was—a weak, frivolous woman who wanted the best from life but didn't have either the ability or the strength of character to get it on her own. And then she saw her mother's love—selfish, self-serving, laced with conditions and manipulations—but love nonetheless. Love so heartfelt that Belinda had never been able to understand how Fleur could ever doubt it.

She booked herself on a morning flight to Paris. It was too early to call Jake, so she left a note on Riata's desk telling her to let him know she had some emergency business out of town and not to worry if she didn't call him for a few days. She didn't want either Jake or Michel to discover where she was going. The last thing she needed was for Jake to show up in Paris with a pair of Colt revolvers and a bullwhip. And Michel had suffered enough from Belinda's indifference.

As she left the house, she played out various scenarios in her head, each one uglier than the last. Belinda might think this was only about her, but Fleur knew better. Alexi was using Belinda as human bait to bring his daughter back to him.

The house on the Rue de la Bienfaisance stood gray and silent in the Parisian winter twilight. It looked as unfriendly as Fleur remembered, and as she gazed out the window of the limousine she'd taken from her hotel, she thought about the first time she'd seen the house. She'd been so frightened that day—afraid to meet her father, aching to see her mother, worried that she'd dressed wrong. At least this time, she didn't have to be concerned about her clothes.

Beneath her satin and velvet evening wrap, she wore the last gown Michel had designed for her, a wine velvet sheath with tight-fitting sleeves and a deeply slashed bodice embroidered at the edge with a web of tiny burgundy beads. The dress had the uneven hem that was becoming Michel's trademark, knee-high on one side, dipping to mid-calf on the other, with beadwork emphasizing the diagonal. She'd put her hair up for the evening, arranging it more elaborately than usual, and added garnet earrings that winked through the tendrils fanning her ears. At sixteen she might have thought it wise to appear at Alexi's door in casual dress, but at twenty-six she knew differently.

A young man in a three-piece suit answered the door. One of the henchmen Belinda had referred to? He looked like a mortician who just happened to have a degree from Harvard Business School. "Your father has been expecting you."

I'll just bet he has. She handed over her evening cape. "I'd like to see my mother."

"This way please."

She followed him into the front salon. The room stood cold and empty, its only ornamentation a display of white roses that fanned the mantelpiece like a funeral spray. She shivered.

"Dinner will be ready momentarily," the mortician said. "Would you like a drink first? Some champagne perhaps?"

"I'd like to see my mother."

He turned as if she hadn't spoken and disappeared down the hallway. She hugged herself against the cryptlike chill of the room. The wall sconces cast grotesque shadows on the gruesome ceiling frescoes.

Enough of this. Just because the mortician had closed the door to seal her in didn't mean she had to stay here. The heels of her pumps clicked against the marble as she slipped out into the hallway. Head held high against invisible eyes, she walked past the priceless Gobelin tapestries on her way toward the grand staircase. When she reached the top, another mortician with neat hair and a dark suit stepped out to block her from going farther. "You have lost your way, mademoiselle."

It was a statement, not a question, and she knew she'd made her first mistake. He wasn't going to let her pass, and she couldn't afford an early defeat when she needed to conserve all her strength for her battle with Alexi. She cut her losses. "It's been so long since I was here that I'd forgotten how large the house is." She retreated to the salon, where the first mortician waited to lead her to the dining room.

Another spray of white roses and a single china place setting adorned the long mahogany banquet table. Alexi had launched a war of nerves, carefully orchestrating everything to make her feel powerless. She glanced at the diamond watch Jake had sent her and pretended to stifle a yawn. "I hope the food is decent tonight. I'm hungry."

Surprise flickered across his face before he nodded and excused himself. Who were these men with their dark suits and officious manner? And where was Belinda? For that matter, where was Alexi?

A liveried servant appeared to attend her. She sat alone

in her wine velvet gown at the end of the vast, gleaming table, her garnets and beads winking in the candlelight, and concentrated on eating her dinner with every appearance of relish. She even asked for a small second helping of chestnut soufflé. At the end, she ordered a cup of tea and a brandy. Alexi could dictate how he played his portion of their game. She would determine how she played hers.

The mortician appeared again while she toyed with the brandy. "If Mademoiselle would please come with me . . ."

She took another sip, then dipped into her purse for compact and lipstick. The mortician made his impatience known. "Your father is waiting."

"I came here to see my mother." She snapped the compact open. "I have no business with Monsieur Savagar until after I've spoken with her. If he won't permit that, I'll leave immediately."

The mortician hadn't anticipated this. He hesitated and then nodded. "Very well, I'll take you to her."

"I'll find my own way." She returned the compact to her purse, swept past him into the hallway, and headed back up the grand staircase. The man she'd encountered earlier appeared at the top, but this time he made no effort to stop her, and she walked past him as if he were invisible.

Almost seven years had gone by since she'd last been in the house on the Rue de la Bienfaisance, but nothing had changed. The Persian carpets still muffled her footsteps, and the fifteenth-century Madonnas continued to roll their eyes heavenward from their gilded frames. In this house, time was measured in centuries, while decades slipped by unnoticed.

As she walked the opulent, silent hallways, she thought of the house she wanted to share with Jake—a big, rambling home, with doors that banged and floorboards that squeaked and banisters children could slide down. A house that measured time in noisy decades. Jake as the father of her children . . . their children. Unlike Alexi, Jake would yell at them when he got mad. He'd also hug them and kiss them and fight the whole world if necessary to keep them safe.

Why was she hesitating? Marrying him was what she wanted more than anything. If it meant she had to accept both sides of him—well, she was wise to his tricks by now, and he wouldn't find it so easy to shut her out when something bothered him. He also wasn't exactly getting a bargain. She wouldn't give up her career, and nothing would ever make her work up any real interest in housekeeping. Besides, he wasn't the only one who'd gotten good at shutting people out.

In the cryptlike chill of the house, her doubts fell away. There was no other man on earth she'd trust to be the father of her children, and she was going to call him that night and tell him so.

She'd reached Belinda's room, so she pulled her thoughts away from the future to deal with the present. A few moments passed after she knocked before she heard movement. The door eased open, and Belinda's face peered through the crack. "Baby?" Her voice quivered as if she hadn't used it for some time. "Is it really you? I—I'm a mess, baby. I didn't think—" Her fingers fluttered like a captive bird as her hand went to her cheek.

"You didn't think I'd come."

Belinda pushed aside a rumpled lock of hair that had tumbled over her eye. "I—I didn't want to count on it. I know I shouldn't have asked you."

"Are you going to let me in?"

"Oh . . . Yes. Yes." She moved out of the way. As the door shut behind her, Fleur noticed that her mother smelled like stale cigarettes instead of Shalimar. She remembered the bright bird of paradise who used to arrive at the *couvent* carrying a fragrance so sweet it instantly dispelled the musty scent of worn habits and lost prayers.

Belinda's makeup had faded, leaving only an oily trace of blue shadow in her eyelid creases. Her face was too pale to hold its own against the saffron silk of her rumpled Chinese robe. Fleur noticed a stain on the bodice, and the saggy front pocket looked as if it had been forced to hold one too many cigarette lighters. Belinda's hand once again went to her cheek. "Let me go wash my face. I always liked to be pretty for you. You always thought I was so pretty."

Fleur caught her mother's hand. It felt as small as a child's. "Sit down and tell me what's happened."

Belinda did as she was ordered, an obedient child bowing to a stronger force. She lit a cigarette, and in her breathless, young woman's voice, she told Fleur about Alexi's threats to put her in a sanitarium. "I haven't been drinking, baby. He knows that, but he uses the past like a sword over my head to threaten me whenever I upset him." She blew a puff of smoke. "He didn't like what happened when I went to New York. He thought I'd try harder to be with you. He expected me to embarrass you, but all I did was embarrass him."

"You had an affair with Shawn Howell."

She flicked her ash into a porcelain ashtray. "He left me for an older woman, did you know that? Funny, isn't it? Alexi closed off my accounts, and the other woman was rich."

"Shawn Howell is a cretin."

"He's a star, baby. It's just a matter of time before he makes a comeback." She looked at Fleur with her old reproach. "You could have helped him, you know. Now that you're a big agent, you could have helped an old friend."

Fleur saw the displeasure in her mother's eyes and waited for the old guilt to wash over her, but it didn't come. Instead she experienced the exasperation of a mother confronting an unreasonable child. "I'm sure I could have helped him, but I didn't want to. He doesn't have any talent, and I don't like him."

Belinda set her cigarette in the ashtray, and her lips formed a pout. "I don't understand you at all." She scanned Fleur's dress. "Michel designed that, didn't he? I never dreamed he was so talented. Everyone in New York was talking about him." Her eyes narrowed vindictively, and Fleur understood she was about to be punished for refusing to help Shawn. "I went to see Michel. Such a beautiful boy. He looks just like me. Everybody says so."

Did Belinda really think she could make her jealous? Fleur felt a flash of pity for her brother. Michel hadn't told her about the visit, but she could imagine how painful it had been.

"We had a wonderful time," Belinda said defiantly. "He told me he'd introduce me to all his famous friends and design my wardrobe." Fleur could hear the echo of a child's voice in her mother's words. *And we won't let you play with us.*

"Michel's a special person."

Belinda couldn't hold it together any longer, and her face crumpled. She bent forward in her chair and shoved her fingers through her hair. "He looked at me like Alexi does. Like I'm some sort of insect. You're the only one who's ever understood me. Why does everybody make things so hard for me?"

Fleur didn't waste her breath pointing out that Belinda's own choices were what had made her life so hard. "It would probably be best if you stayed away from Michel."

"He hates me even more than Alexi does. Why does Alexi want to lock me up?"

Fleur stubbed out her mother's smoldering cigarette. "What's happening with Alexi right now doesn't have very much to do with you. He's using you to bring me here. He wants to settle old scores."

Belinda's head shot up, and her petulance fell away. "Of course! I should have thought of that." She stood abruptly. "You have to leave right away. He's dangerous. I should have realized . . . I can't let him hurt you. Let me think."

Belinda began pacing the carpet, one hand pushing her hair back from her face, the other reaching for her cigarettes as she tried to figure out how to protect her child.

Fleur was annoyed and touched. For the first time, she understood how blurred the roles between mothers and daughters could become as they grew older.

It's my turn to be the mommy. No, you be the baby. No, I wanna be the mommy.

As Belinda paced the floor, trying to figure out how to shelter her daughter, Fleur knew her time of being Belinda's baby was gone forever. Belinda could no longer control the way Fleur viewed either the world or herself.

"I'm staying at the Ritz," she said. "I'll come back in the morning, and we'll settle his." She needed to take Belinda with her, but the mortician and his cohorts would make that impossible. She had to find another way.

Belinda gave her a swift, desperate hug. "Don't come back, baby. I should have realized it was you he wanted all along. It'll be all right. Please, don't come back."

Fleur looked into her mother's eyes and saw that she was as sincere as she knew how to be. "I'll be fine."

She made her way back through the maze of hallways to the staircase. The mortician waited for her at the bottom. She regarded him evenly. "I'll see Monsieur Savagar now."

"I'm sorry, mademoiselle, but you'll have to wait. Your father is not yet ready to see you." He indicated the rococo chair that sat outside the library doors.

So the warfare dragged on. She waited until the mortician disappeared, then made her way to the front salon, where she plucked one full-blown white rose from the mantelpiece and pushed it into the deep V of the velvet bodice. It gleamed against her skin. She carried its heavy fragrance with her as she returned to the hallway and the library doors.

Even through the heavy paneling, she could feel Alexi's presence on the other side—grasping for her, clinging to her as tenaciously as the scent of the rose. Alexi, malicious and confident, marking off the minutes in his war of nerves. Slowly she turned the knob.

Only one dim lamp burned in the ornate room, throwing the periphery in shadow. Even so, she could see that the vigorous man she remembered had shrunk. He sat behind his desk, his right hand resting on top, his left hand hidden in his lap. He was dressed as immaculately as ever—a dark suit and a starched shirt with a platinum collar pin at the neck—but everything seemed too big. She saw a small gap at the neck of the shirt, took in a looseness at the shoulders, but she didn't let herself believe for a moment that these were signs of frailty. Even in the room's shadows, she saw that his narrow Russian eyes missed nothing. They slid over her, taking in her face and hair, sweeping along her dress, and finally coming to rest on the white rose between her breasts.

"You should have been mine," he said.

Chapter 28

"I wanted to be yours," Fleur replied, "but you wouldn't permit it.'

"You are a *bâtarde.* Not *pur sang.*"

"That's right. How could I forget?" She wished she could see his features more clearly, and she stepped closer to the desk. "All my Irish Flynn blood is too uncivilized for you, isn't it?" She had the satisfaction of seeing him stiffen. "I understand one of his ancestors was hung for stealing sheep. Definitely bad blood. Then there was all that drinking and whoring." She paused deliberately. "His young girls . . ."

The hand resting on the desktop curled in upon itself. "You are foolish to play games with me that you have no hope of winning."

"Then let's end the game. Stop terrorizing Belinda."

"I intend to institutionalize your mother. Lock her up in a sanitarium for incurable alcoholics."

"That might be difficult considering that she no longer drinks."

Alexi chuckled. "You're still naïve. Nothing is difficult when one has money and power."

The day had been long, and she could feel her own weariness catching up with her. She wanted to go back to the hotel, call Jake, and feel that life was sane again. "Do you really think I'd sit by and let you do that? I'd scream so long and so loud that the whole world would hear."

"Of course you would. I don't know why Belinda hasn't realized that. I'd have to silence you first, and that would be quite impossible without resorting to barbaric measures."

Fleur thought of Jake with his blazing Colts and ready fists. Jake, who was so much more civilized than the old man sitting in front of her. She took a chair across from him and wished he'd turn on the desk lamp so she could see his expression more clearly. "You've never had any intention of locking her up."

"From the beginning, you've been a worthy opponent. I expected you to discover the fire in the basement, but substituting the dresses was quite clever."

"When you've been around a snake long enough, you learn how to crawl in the dirt. Tell me what you want."

"How very American you've grown. Blunt and vulgar. No patience for *nuance*. It must be the influence of those crude friends with whom you keep company."

A chill crept through her. Was he talking about Kissy? Michel? Or was it Jake . . . ? Alarms shrieked inside her. She had to keep her relationship with Jake tucked safely away, well hidden from Alexi's ruthless calculations. He surely knew Jake had lived in her attic. Maybe he even knew about her trip to his house. But he had no way of knowing she'd fallen back in love with him.

She crossed her legs and launched her counterattack. "I'm happy with my friends. Especially my brother. You made a disastrous mistake, you know. Michel is an extraordinary talent, and he has a brilliant career ahead of him. Admittedly he's bad at business, but I'm very good at business, and I've made sure his money is tucked safely away."

"A dress designer," Alexi said contemptuously. "How can he hold up his head?"

She laughed. "Believe me, with the entire city courting him, he doesn't have any trouble. It's funny. He's so much like you. The way he carries himself, his walk, his mannerisms—they all come from you. He even has your habit of looking at someone he doesn't like with his eyes narrowed and his brow lifted. You can practically see the person shrink. It's very intimidating. Of course, he also has the humanity that you lack, which makes him a far more powerful person."

"Michel is a *tapette*!"

"And your mind is too small to see beyond that." She heard his sharp intake of breath and concentrated on keeping her gaze even with his. "Poor Alexi. Maybe sometime I'll be able to pity you."

He slammed his hand down on the desk. "Do you feel any remorse for what you did? Any shame for destroying an object of such remarkable beauty?"

"The Bugatti was a work of art, and it's sad that it no longer exists. But that's not really what you're asking, is it? You want to know if I'm sorry." She pressed her fingers into the beadwork on her skirt. Alexi leaned slightly forward, and she heard the soft creak of leather as he shifted his weight. "Not ever," she said. "Not for one moment have I ever been sorry." The beads bit into her fingers. "You declared yourself the emperor of your own private kingdom, a man who's above the law, just like Belinda's movie stars. But nobody is above the laws of decency, and people who try to crush others should be punished. What you did to me was horrible, and I punished you. It's as simple as that. You can threaten Belinda and keep on trying to ruin my business, but you'll *never* make me regret what I did."

"I'll destroy you."

"I think I've grown too strong for that, but if I've miscalculated—if you somehow manage to destroy my business—then so be it. I still won't regret what I did. You don't have any more power over me."

The chair screeched as Alexi settled back into its depths. "I said I would destroy your dream, *chérie*, and that is what

I intend to do. The score will finally be even between us."

"You're bluffing. There's nothing you can do to hurt me."

"I never bluff." He slid a small envelope across the desktop. She looked at it for a moment. A chill passed through her. She reached out to take it. "A keepsake," he said.

She slit open the envelope, and a battered piece of metal fell into her lap. The letters embossed upon it were still visible: BUGATTI. It was the red metal oval from the front of the Royale.

He pushed something else across the desk. In the dim light, it took a moment before she saw what it was. Her blood froze.

"A dream for a dream, *chérie*."

It was a tabloid newspaper—an American paper with that day's date—and the headline leaped out at her:

NEW KORANDA BIO REVEALS CRACK-UP

"No." She shook her head, willing the ugly words to disappear, even as her eyes skimmed the sentences.

> Actor/playwright Jake Koranda, best known for playing the renegade cowboy Bird Dog Caliber, suffered a nervous breakdown while serving in the United States Army in Vietnam . . . Fleur Savagar, the actor's literary agent and recent companion, revealed in a press release today that Koranda was hospitalized for post-traumatic stress syndrome. . .
>
> According to Savagar, details of the breakdown will be revealed in the actor's new autobiography . . . "Jake has been honest about his emotional and psychological problems," Savagar said, "and I'm certain the public will respect him for that honesty and look upon his terrible experience with compassion and pity."

Fleur could read no further. There were photographs—one of Jake as Bird Dog, another of the two of them running in the park, a third of her alone, with a sidebar bearing the headline, GLITTER BABY SCORES BIG AS AGENT FOR THE STARS. She put the tabloid on the desk and slowly stood up. The battered Bugatti oval fell to the carpet.

"I have been patient for seven years," Alexi whispered from across the desk. "Now the score is settled. Now you, too, have lost what you care about most. It wasn't your business that was the real dream, was it, *chérie*?"

Her heart contracted into a small mass of frozen tissue that would never again pulse with life. All this time she'd thought it was the agency he was after, but Alexi had known better. He'd known from the beginning that Jake was as elemental to her as food and water. Jake was the dream.

But something inside her refused to give Alexi his victory. "Jake will never believe this," she said, her voice little more than a whisper, but calm, as calm as the center of a storm.

"He's a man accustomed to the betrayal of women," Alexi replied. "He'll believe it."

"How did you do this? Jake and I destroyed the book together."

"I'm told there was a man with a special camera watching the house. Such things have been possible for years."

"You're lying. The manuscript was never out of Jake's—" She stopped. It had been. The morning Jake had come running after her . . . They'd gone for a walk on the beach. "Jake knows I'd never do anything like this."

"Does he? He's been betrayed before. And he knows how important your business is to you. You used his name before to gain publicity. He has no reason to believe you wouldn't do it again."

Every word he spoke was true, but she couldn't let him see that. "You've lost," she said. "You've underestimated Jake, and you've underestimated me." She reached out quickly—so quickly that he couldn't have anticipated it—and snapped on the desk lamp.

With a harsh exclamation, he jerked up his arm and sent the lamp smashing to the floor, where it rocked crazily from side to side, casting cruel, moving blades of light over him. He covered the side of his face, but he was too late. By then she'd already seen what he wanted to hide.

The slackness on the left side of his face was so subtle that someone who didn't know him well might not have noticed. There was an extra fold of skin beneath his eye, a looseness in his cheek, the slightest dip at the corner of his mouth. Another person with the same malady might have given it little thought, but for a proud man obsessed with perfection, even so slight an imperfection was intolerable. She understood—she even felt a flash of pity—but she pushed it aside. "Now your face is as ugly as your soul."

"*Bitch! Sale garce!*" He tried to kick at the lamp, but his left side wasn't as responsive as his right, and he only succeeded in knocking away the shade so the rocking light flashed more brutally across his face.

"You've made a fatal mistake," she said. "Jake and I love each other in a way you can never comprehend because you don't have a heart. All you feel is the need to control. If you understood about love and trust, you'd know that all your schemes and all your plots aren't worth anything. Jake trusts me with his life, and he'll never believe this."

"No!" he cried. "I've beaten you!" The weak side of his face began to quiver, as she saw the first flicker of doubt.

"You've lost," she replied. And then she turned her back on him and left the library. She walked down the icy hallway to the front door and stepped out into the cold, clear February night.

Her limousine was gone—Alexi had planned to keep her here—but she wouldn't reenter the house. She walked down the drive toward the gates that led to the street. Every word she'd spoken to Alexi was a lie. He'd calculated correctly. She could try to explain it to Jake. She would try. He might even believe Alexi was responsible. But he'd still blame her. Exposure was Jake's deepest fear, and this was something he'd never forgive.

A dream for a dream. Alexi had finally beaten her.

He stood at the library window, the fingers of his right hand clutching the edge of the drapery, and watched her tall, straight figure grow smaller as she disappeared down the drive. It was a cold night, and she wasn't wearing a coat, but she didn't huddle into the chill, or hug her arms, or in any way acknowledge the temperature. She was magnificent.

The leafless branches of the old chestnuts formed a skeletal cathedral over her head. He remembered how the trees looked when they were in blossom and how—years before—another woman had disappeared down that same drive into those blossoms. Neither woman had been worthy of him. Both had betrayed him. Yet, even so, he had loved them.

A great sense of desolation filled him. For seven years, he'd been obsessed with Fleur, and now it was over. He no longer knew how he would fill his days. His assistants were well trained to handle his business affairs, and his hideous facial deformity kept him from ever again appearing in public.

A dull ache throbbed in his left shoulder, and he kneaded it with his hand. Her walk was so straight and proud, and tiny fires glittered on her dress as the beads caught the lamplights. The Glitter Baby. She lifted her arm, and something fell to the ground. He was too far away to see what it was, but, even so, he knew. As clearly as if she'd been standing next to him, he knew exactly what she'd thrown away. A white rose.

It was then that the pain hit him.

Belinda found him on the library floor next to the window, his body curled into a comma. "Alexi?" She knelt beside him, speaking his name softly because his henchmen weren't far away, and she wasn't supposed to be in here.

"B-Belinda?" His voice was thick and slurred. She picked up his head to cradle it in the lap of her saffron robe and gave a startled cry as she saw that the side of his face was grotesquely twisted.

"Oh, Alexi . . ." She pulled him to her. "My poor, poor Alexi. What's happened to you?"

"Help me. Help—" His agonized whisper horrified her. She wanted to tell him to *stop talking like that this very minute.* She felt a damp spot on her thigh and saw that saliva had leaked from the side of his mouth through her robe. It was too much. She wanted to run away. Instead she thought of Fleur.

His mouth worked to form the words. "G-get help. I—I need help."

"Hush . . . Save your strength. Don't try to talk."

"Please . . ."

"Rest, my darling." His suit coat gaped and one of the lapels was turned under. They'd been married for twenty-seven years, and she'd never seen his suit coat untidy. She straightened the lapel.

"H-help me."

She gazed down at him. "Don't try to talk, my darling. Just rest. I won't leave you. I'll hold you until you don't need me any longer."

She could see the fear in his eyes then, at first the merest spark. Gradually it grew more intense until she knew he finally understood. She stroked his thin hair with the tips of her trembling fingers. "My poor darling," she said. "My poor, poor darling. I loved you, you know. You're the only one who ever really understood me. If only you hadn't taken my baby away."

"Do not—do this. I beg you—" The muscles in his right side tensed, but he was too weak to lift his arm. His lips had a blue tinge, and his breathing grew more labored. She didn't want him to suffer, and she tried to think how to comfort him. Finally she opened her robe and cradled him to her bare breast.

Eventually he grew still. As she gazed down at the face of the man who had shaped her life, a pair of tears perfectly balanced themselves on the bottom lashes of her incomparable hyacinth-blue eyes. "Good-bye, my darling."

Jake felt as if all the air had been knocked out of him. A basketball whizzed past his arm and bounced into the empty bleachers, but he couldn't move. Even the noises of the game going on behind him faded away. Cold seeped through the sweat-drenched jersey into his bones, and he struggled for breath.

"Jake, I'm sorry." His secretary stood with him at the side of the court, her face pale, her forehead knitted with concern. "I—I knew you'd want to see it right away. The phones are ringing off the wall. We'll have to issue a statement—"

He crushed the newspaper in his fist and pushed past her. He headed for the scarred wooden door. The sound of his breathing echoed off the chipped plaster walls of the L.A. gym as he fled down the steps to the empty locker room. He shoved his legs into his jeans over his shorts, grabbed a shirt, and raced from the old brick building where he'd played basketball on and off for ten years. As the door slammed behind him, he knew he'd never be back.

The Jag's tires squealed as he peeled out of the parking lot into the street. He'd buy up all the newspapers. Every copy. He'd send planes all over the country to every store, every newsstand in the universe. He'd buy them and burn them and—

A fire engine shrieked in the distance. He remembered the day he'd come home and found Liz. Then he'd been able to fight. He'd smashed his fist into that bastard's face until his knuckles bled. He remembered the way Liz's arms had felt as she fell to her knees and clutched his legs, wrapping her arms around them like a movie poster from *A Hatful of Rain.* She'd cried and begged him to forgive her while that poor bastard lay on the linoleum floor with his pants around his ankles and his nose pushed to the side of his face. When Liz had betrayed him, he'd had a target for his rage.

Sweat dripped into his eyes. He blinked it away. He'd written the book for Fleur, spilled out his guts. . .

He clutched the steering wheel and tasted gunmetal in the back of his mouth. The taste of fear. Cold metal fear.

Chapter 29

Belinda gazed at the suitcase that lay open on Fleur's bed as if she'd never before seen one. "You can't leave me now, baby. I need you."

Fleur struggled to hold herself together. Only a few more hours, and she'd be away from this house forever. Only a few more hours, and she could lick her wounds in private. "The funeral was a week ago," she said, "and you're doing just fine."

Belinda lit another cigarette.

The burden of dealing with Alexi's death had fallen entirely on Fleur's shoulders. A massive stroke, the doctor had said. One of Alexi's assistants had found him lying on the library floor next to the front window. He'd apparently collapsed not long after she'd left him, and Fleur couldn't help but wonder if he'd been standing there watching her when it happened. His death left her feeling neither triumph nor grief, only the knowledge that a powerful force had disappeared from her life.

Michel wouldn't fly over for the funeral. "I can't do it," he'd told her during one of their daily phone calls. "I know it's not fair to you, but I can't pretend to mourn him, and

I can't handle Belinda looking at me with those calf eyes now that people know my name."

Fleur decided it was for the best. She needed all her energy to deal with the arrangements, and the added tension of Michel and Belinda's strained relationship would only make things more difficult.

Belinda blew a thin ribbon of smoke. "You know all this legal nonsense makes my head spin. I can't cope."

"You won't have to. I told you that. David Bennis is going to work with Alexi's staff. He'll be able to handle everything from New York."

Making Alexi's assistants understand they were now taking orders from her had been one more challenge she'd faced and won. But she still had to deal with Belinda's neediness and the way her own stomach lurched every time she received a phone call.

"I want you to handle my business affairs, not some stranger." Fleur didn't respond, and Belinda's mouth formed the same pout she'd launched in her daughter's direction a dozen times over the past week when she didn't get her way. "I hate this house. I can't spend the night here."

"Then move to a hotel."

"You're cold, Fleur. You've gotten very cold with me. And I don't like the way you've shut me out. All these stories about Jake in Vietnam . . . I had to read about it in the newspaper. I'm sure you've talked to him, but you won't tell me a thing."

Fleur hadn't talked to him. Jake refused to take her calls. A fresh stab of pain pierced her heart as she remembered the efficient voice of his secretary on the other end of the line. "I'm sorry, Miss Savagar, but I don't know where he is . . . No, he hasn't left any messages for you."

Fleur had tried both his house in California and his place in New York to no avail. She'd contacted his secretary again, and this time she'd met open hostility. "Haven't you done enough harm? He's being hounded by reporters.

Why don't you get the message? He doesn't want to talk to you."

That had been five days ago, and Fleur hadn't tried to call him since.

She latched her suitcase. "If you don't want to live here, Belinda, you should move. You're a rich woman, and you can live wherever you want. I offered to go apartment shopping with you, but you put me off."

"I've changed my mind. Let's go tomorrow."

"Too late. My plane takes off at three o'clock." But not for New York, as Belinda thought.

"Baby!" Belinda said with a wail, "I'm not used to being alone."

Knowing her mother, Fleur doubted she'd be on her own for very long. "You're stronger than you think." *Both of us are*, she thought.

Tears filled Belinda's eyes. "I can't believe you're deserting me. After everything I've done for you."

Fleur planted a swift kiss on her mother's cheek. "You'll be fine."

On the way to the airport, the limousine stalled in traffic. Fleur studied the shop windows until a Cityrama bus blocked her view. The limousine crawled forward another thirty feet, swung in front of the bus, and she found herself gazing into Jake's face on a billboard advertising *Disturbance at Blood River.* The flat brim of his hat shaded his eyes, his cheeks were grizzled, and he had a cheroot clamped in the corner of his mouth. Bird Dog Caliber—a man without weakness, a man who didn't need anybody. What had made her think that she could finally civilize him?

She closed her eyes. She had a business to run, and she couldn't afford to be away any longer, but she needed a few days—just a few days alone—before she went back. She needed to be in a place where no one could find her, a place where she could stop spending her days waiting for a phone call that would never come. She'd healed from heartbreak before. She could do it again.

She'd do it on Mykonos.

*

The white stucco cottage sat in an olive grove not far from a deserted beach. She toasted herself in the sun, took long, barefoot walks along the ocean, and told herself time would heal her wounds. But she felt numb and color-blind. On Mykonos—where the whites were so white they hurt the eyes, and the turquoise of the Aegean so bright it redefined the hue—everything had faded to gray. She didn't feel hunger when she forgot to eat, or pain when she stepped on a sharp rock. She walked along the ocean—saw that her hair was blowing—but she couldn't feel the breeze touch her skin, and she wondered if the terrible numbness would ever go away.

At night, tortured memories of making love with Jake awakened her. His lips on her breasts . . . the feel of him stretching her, pulsing . . . If he'd loved her as she loved him, he'd have known she could never betray him. This was what she'd been afraid of all along. This was the reason she'd put him off when he'd suggested marriage. She hadn't trusted him to love her enough, and she'd been right. He hadn't loved her enough to stand strong.

By the third day, she knew Mykonos held no magical healing powers. She'd neglected her business too long, and she had to return to New York. Still, she lingered another two days before she made herself call David and tell him when she was returning.

She was numb and grief-stricken, but she wasn't broken.

*

By the time she got off the plane at Kennedy, it had begun to snow. Her wool slacks itched her thighs where they were peeling from the sun, and her stomach was queasy from two hours of turbulence over the Atlantic. The snow made getting a cab more arduous than usual, and the one she finally found had a broken heater. It was well after midnight before she slipped the bolt on her door and let herself into her living room.

The house was damp and nearly as cold as the cab. Dropping her suitcase, she pushed up the thermostat and then kicked off her shoes. With her coat still on, she walked down to the kitchen, filled a glass with water, and tossed in two Alka-Seltzers. As the tablets fizzed, the cold from the brick floor seeped through her stockings. She was getting into bed, turning up her electric blanket, and not moving until morning. First, though, she'd take the hottest shower she could stand.

She waited until she was in the bathroom before she pulled off her coat and her clothes. After she pinned her hair on top of her head, she slid open the shower doors and let the hot water wash over her. In six hours she would force herself to get up and run in the park, no matter how bad she felt. This time she wouldn't crumble. She'd go through the motions one day at a time until, finally, the pain would be bearable.

When she'd dried off, she pulled a beige satin nightgown from a hook next to the shower. She'd forgotten to turn on her electric blanket, so she slipped into the matching robe. The temperature change from Mykonos was too drastic. Even though she'd just gotten out of the shower, she was already cold. The sheets were going to feel like ice.

She pushed open the bathroom door and fumbled to tie the sash of her robe. Odd. She thought she'd flipped the light on before she'd come into the bedroom. God, it was freezing. The windows were rattling from the blizzard kicking up outside. Why hadn't the furnace turned—

She screamed.

"Stay right where you are, lady, and don't move."

A whimper caught in her throat.

He sat on the far side of the room with only his face visible in the patch of light from the open bathroom door. His mouth barely moved. "You do what I say and nobody gets hurt."

She stumbled backward toward the bathroom. He lifted his arm, and she found herself looking down the long, silver barrel of a gun. "That's far enough," he said.

Her heart jumped into her throat. "Please . . ."

"Let go."

At first she didn't understand what he meant. Then she realized he was talking about her robe sash. Quickly she dropped it.

"Now the robe."

She didn't move.

He lifted the gun so that it was aimed at her chest.

"You're crazy," she gasped. "You're—"

The hammer clicked. "Take it off."

Her hands flew to the front of the robe. She opened it and slipped her arms out. The fabric made a soft, hissing sound as it dropped to the floor.

He lifted the barrel ever so slightly. "Let your hair down."

"Sweet Jesus . . ." Her hands fumbled with the pins, and as her hair came down, drops of water splattered on her bare shoulders.

"That's nice. Real pretty. Now the gown."

"Don't . . ." she pleaded.

"Pull down the straps slow. One at a time."

She slipped down the first strap and then stopped.

"Go on." He made a sharp gesture with the gun. "Do what I tell you."

"No."

He sat up straighter. "What did you say?"

"You heard me."

"Don't push me, Teacher Lady."

Fleur clamped her arms over her chest.

Shit, Jake thought. Now what was he supposed to do?

⋆

"Just hold me for a minute, okay?" she said.

He set the pearl-handled Colt on the table next to the bed and walked over to where she was standing. Her skin was like ice. He opened his parka and put it around her, then cuddled her against his flannel shirt. "You're no fun."

She gave a choked sob.

"Hey, are you crying?" She nodded against his jaw. "I'm sorry, sweetheart. I didn't mean to make you cry. I guess my timing wasn't too good."

She shook her head, too dazed to figure out how he knew about *Butch Cassidy* and her fantasy.

"It seemed like a good idea," he said, "especially when I couldn't decide what to say when I saw you."

She spoke against his flannel shirt. "Bird Dog can't resolve this for us. We have to settle it ourselves."

He tilted up her chin. "You've got to learn to separate fantasy from reality. Bird Dog's a movie character. I like playing him—he gives me a chance to get rid of my aggressions—but he's not me. I'm the one who's afraid of horses, remember?"

She stared up at him.

"Come on, you're freezing." He led her over to the bed and pulled back the covers. In a daze, she settled between the cold sheets. He quickly divested himself of his parka and boots. Still wearing his shirt and jeans, he slid in next to her. "The pilot must be out on your furnace," he said. "It's colder than hell in here."

She reached over to flick on the light. "Why wouldn't you take my calls? I went crazy. I thought . . ."

"I know what you thought." He settled his weight on his forearm and looked down at her. His face twisted. "I'm sorry, Flower. The press was everywhere, and all the old stuff came back to grab me." He shook his head. "I couldn't think straight. I let you down."

"When did you figure out it was Alexi?"

"I'd give anything to say I knew it right away." He gazed blindly across the room. "But I'm an old pro at trying to blame you for things I can't handle. It was a week before my head cleared enough to figure that out."

"A week?" Just about the time she left for Mykonos.

He brushed his thumb over the corner of her mouth and whispered, "I'll make it up to you. I promise."

He looked so tortured, she couldn't stand it, so she glared at him. "Darned right you will. Starting with diamonds."

His voice caught. "As many as you want."

She bit his thumb.

He wrapped a lock of her hair around his finger. "I still can't figure out how he managed to do it. That manuscript was never out of my sight."

Now she was the one who looked away. "Yes, it was. The night I read it. You went outside, remember? I was alone with that manuscript for hours."

"Don't be a brat." He caught her chin and turned it toward him. Then he kissed her again. Her heart swelled. Even though he didn't understand how it could be otherwise, he knew she hadn't betrayed him. He was taking her loyalty on faith.

She cupped that tough, stubborn jaw. "Someone got into the house and photographed the manuscript while we were walking along the ocean that first day. I found the negatives after he died."

"You found them?" His head came up. "What did you do with them?"

"Burned them, of course."

"Damn." He looked annoyed.

She couldn't believe it. She came up on her elbows. "Damn?"

"I wish you'd talked to me first," he muttered. "That's all."

She couldn't help it. She pulled the comforter over her head and screamed.

For a moment there was silence. Finally he tugged at the comforter. When he got as far as her nose, he peered down at her. "It's going to mean a lot of rewriting, that's all." His bottom lip looked as sulky as ever.

She nodded toward the Colt. "Is that thing loaded?"

"Of course not."

"Too bad."

The windowpanes rattled. He moved the gun out of reach. "Your various friends started calling me after the tabloid article appeared. When they realized how screwed up I was, all hell broke loose. Kissy flew back from her honeymoon. God, that woman can cuss. Simon threatened to go to the newspapers and tell everyone I was gay. Michel hit me." Fleur looked at him sharply, and he threw up his hands. "I didn't hit him back. Honest to God." He sank back under the covers with her. "Even some cretin named Barry Noy got hold of me."

"You're kidding."

"God is my witness." He stroked her hair. "Do you have any idea how many people love you?"

Her eyes filled with tears. He kept talking and stroking her hair. "I was pretty ragged by the time Belinda found me three days ago. She has a way about her, that mother of yours. She looked at me with those blue eyes and told me I was the most exciting star in Hollywood and that I was throwing away the only woman in the world who was good enough for me." He shook his head. "But listen to this, Flower. Not one—not *one* of those interfering sons of bitches had any idea where I could find you!" He shuddered. "Until David Bennis called me yesterday, I thought this time I'd lost you for good. Mykonos! Who the hell goes to Mykonos? If you *ever* run away from me like that again—"

"Me!"

He crushed her to his chest so hard she thought her ribs would crack. "I'm so sorry, babe. I love you so much. You mean everything to me. When that story broke, everybody was trying to get to me. Peel off my skin. Pick at my bones." He kissed away a tear that had escaped from the corner of her eyes. "Then the letters started to arrive. They came from all over the country. Guys who'd been in 'Nam and couldn't get it out of their souls. Teachers, bankers, garbagemen, a lot of guys who couldn't hold on to a job. Some of them are still having nightmares. Others said 'Nam was the best time of their lives, and they'd do it all over again. Guys told me about broken marriages and good marriages, about their kids. A few of the letters said I was 'perpetuating the myth of the crazed Vietnam vet.' But we weren't crazed. We were just a bunch of kids who'd seen too much. As I read those letters, I finally understood I'd written something the whole country needs to see. I'm going to publish my book, Flower, and I'm going to include those letters."

"Are you sure?"

"I'm not living in the shadows anymore. I want to walk in the sun. But I can't do that without you."

She put her arms around his shoulders and buried her face in his neck. "Do you have any idea how much I love you?"

"Enough to start talking about station wagons and a two-career marriage?"

"And kids," she said without hesitation. "I want babies. Lots and lots of babies."

He grinned the crooked-tooth grin that drove her crazy and slid his hand up under her nightgown. "Want to start now?" He didn't wait for an answer but settled his mouth over hers. After a few moments, he drew back. "Flower?"

"Uh-huh?"

"I'm not enjoying this kiss."

"S-sorry." She tried to force her teeth to stop chattering, but it was no use. "I'm just s-so *cold.* I can see my breath in the air!"

He groaned and pulled back the covers. "Come on. You'll have to hold the flashlight for me."

With his parka draped over her satin gown and her feet encased in wool sweat socks, she followed him to the basement. While he knelt on the concrete to light the pilot, she stuck her free hand under his shirt. "Jake?"

"Yeah?"

"After the house heats up—"

"Hold that flashlight steady, will you? I almost have it."

"After the house heats up, what would you think about—I mean, would you think it was silly if—"

"There, that's got it." He shook out the match and straightened up. "What were you saying?"

"What?"

"You were saying something. Would I mind if—"

She swallowed. "Nothing. I forget."

"Liar." He slipped his hands inside the parka and around her waist so he could draw her against him. "Don't you know there's nothing I'd rather do?" His lips caught her earlobe, then traveled across her cheek until he could whisper against her mouth. "You'll have to put your hair back up again with those pins. That was my favorite part."

As it turned out, Jake found other parts he liked even better . . .

When it was over, the room was warm, and they were sated. They kicked away all the covers and dozed. Fleur finally stirred from the cozy comfort of his chest. "Next time I get to hold the gun," she said as she eased back into her pillow.

He nipped her bare shoulder. "Nobody holds a gun on Bird Dog."

"Is that so?" She cocked her finger and pointed it as his chest.

"Wow. That's a fast draw you have there."

"Fastest draw in the Big Apple." She blew on her finger. "Seems like Bird Dog's going to have to adjust his thinking."

Jake rubbed his thumb against the corner of her mouth. "Seems like Bird Dog already has."

He smiled, and she smiled back. Snow tapped at the windowpane. The furnace hissed. They gazed at each other with perfect trust.

Epilogue

The young man's body formed a perfect arc as he dived into the turquoise water of the pool behind Belinda's Bel Air home. His name was Darian Boothe—the final "e" had been her idea—and when he came to the surface, she blew him a kiss. "Wonderful, darling. I love watching you."

He gave her a smile that she suspected might not be totally sincere. As he pulled himself out of the water, his biceps knotted, and his tiny red nylon Speedo rode up into the crack of his rear. She hoped the network would buy his pilot. If they didn't, he'd be miserable, and she'd have to expend too much energy trying to cheer him up. On the other hand, if they did buy it, he'd move out and forget about her, but it wouldn't be difficult to find another handsome young actor who needed her help.

She moved her legs farther apart so the sun could reach the insides of her oiled thighs, and pulled her sunglasses back over her eyes. She was tired. It hadn't been easy to fall back asleep after Jake's phone call last night telling her the twins had been born.

She'd known Fleur was having twins ever since the sonogram, so it wasn't a surprise, but Belinda couldn't imagine getting used to being a grandmother of three. Fleur and Jake had been married for three years. Three years and three children. It was embarrassing. And they didn't plan to stop there. Her beautiful daughter had turned into a brood-mare.

Only to herself did Belinda admit that Fleur had turned into something of a disappointment. Her daughter sent thoughtful gifts and called several times a week, but she didn't really *listen* to Belinda anymore. Belinda tried to be fair. With the opening of Fleur's West Coast office last year, not even the most dedicated skeptic could say that she hadn't turned her agency into a huge success. And she *had* been photographed for *Vogue* wearing Michel's gorgeous new line of maternity clothes. But it was clear to Belinda, if no one else, that Fleur wasn't living up to her potential. All that beauty gone to waste . . . God knew, she didn't need it to sit behind a desk. Then, on weekends, she and Jake buried themselves at that godforsaken farmhouse in Connecticut instead of staying in Manhattan where they could be the brightest, most sought-after couple in town.

Belinda remembered her last visit to the farmhouse two months ago. It had been early July, just after the Fourth. She'd stepped out of her car directly into a pile of dog refuse from one of those dirty animals Fleur insisted upon keeping. Her new Maud Frizon pumps were ruined. She rang the front doorbell. No one answered, so she had to let herself into the house.

The interior was cool and fragrant with kitchen smells, but it wasn't Belinda's idea of what the inside of a house belonging to two such famous people should look like. Wide-pegged floors instead of marble. Two braided rugs—"*rag* rugs" they'd called them in Indiana—instead of Persian carpets. A basketball was shoved into one corner of the foyer. A galvanized watering can held some very ordinary garden flowers. And, on the console, she spotted something that looked suspiciously like the Peretti evening bag she'd given Fleur two Christmases earlier, except now Big Bird's fuzzy yellow head stuck out the top.

Belinda had removed her soiled pumps and padded through the silent downstairs into the dining room. A manuscript sat on the sideboard, but Belinda wasn't tempted to look at it, although she knew dozens of people would give anything to get an early peek at a new Koranda play. Despite all his awards and honors, Jake's writing didn't interest her. And the book about Vietnam that had won him his second Pulitzer was the most depressing thing she'd ever read.

She liked his movies so much better than his writing and wished he made more of them, but there'd been only one Bird Dog picture in the last three years, and Fleur had thrown a fit about that. She and Jake had argued for days, but Jake wouldn't budge. He told her he liked playing Bird Dog, and she could just suffer through it every few years. She ended up going on location with him whenever she could get away from work and spending her time wrangling the horses.

Just then, Belinda heard Fleur's laughter drifting through the open window. She pushed back the lace curtain.

There her pregnant daughter lay, her head in her husband's lap, both of them sprawled underneath a gnarled cherry tree that should have been removed years ago. Fleur wore faded navy maternity shorts and one of Jake's shirts with the bottom buttons unfastened to make room for her stomach. Belinda wanted to cry. Her daughter's beautiful blond hair was pulled back with a rubber band, a long scratch ran along the calf of one sunburned leg, and a mosquito bite marred her ankle. Worst of all, Jake was popping cherries into her mouth with one hand while he stroked her stomach with the other.

Fleur tilted her head, and Belinda saw the sheen of cherry juice on her chin. Jake kissed her, then slid his hand under her shirt to cup her breast. Embarrassed, Belinda started to turn away, only to hear a car door slam followed by a high-pitched, happy shriek. Belinda's pulses quickened, and she leaned forward to catch her first glimpse of Meg in weeks.

Meg . . .

Fleur and Jake looked up as the child came running around the side of the house. She dashed past a green plastic wading pool and launched her chubby body at them. Jake caught her before she could reach Fleur and pulled her into the crook of his arm. "Whoa, Cookie Bird. You're gonna make Mommy's tummy pop."

"Great start to her sex education, cowboy." Fleur tugged down the elastic leg on Meg's cotton sunsuit. "I see ice cream around that mouth? Did you pull a fast one on Nanny again?"

Meg plopped her index finger into her mouth and took a contemplative suck, then turned to her father and gave him her biggest grin. He laughed, pulled her close, and buried his head in her neck.

"Con artist." Fleur leaned forward and closed her mouth over a chubby thigh, almost as if she were tasting her daughter's skin.

The diving board banged, and Darian Boothe somersaulted into the pool, bringing Belinda back to her own house in Bel Air and the reminder that her daughter now had two more babies. As she lay in the sun with the scent of chlorine filling her nostrils, she thought of how contemptuously Alexi would have regarded Fleur's childbearing. Poor Alexi.

But she didn't like thinking about him, so she thought about Darian Boothe instead and whether the network would buy the pilot. Then she thought of Fleur, who was still so beautiful she made Belinda's heart ache. And Meg . . .

It wasn't much of a name—far too plain for a beautiful little girl with her father's mouth, her mother's eyes, and Errol Flynn's gleaming chestnut hair. Still, any name with

Koranda after it was going to look fabulous on a marquee, and blood would tell.

More than thirty years had passed since the night James Dean had died on the road to Salinas. Belinda stretched in the California sun. All in all, she hadn't done too badly for herself.

Author's Note

So many people have helped directly and indirectly with this book, both in its original form and this newly revised edition. My special thanks to those in fashion and film who answered my questions so graciously: David Price, Calvin Klein Ltd.; Ford Models, Inc.; and the production staff and cast of *Flanagan*. A wonderful group of writers offered both wise counsel and practical information: Dionne Brennan Polk, Mary Shukis, Rosanne Kohake, Ann Rinaldi, Barbara Bretton, and Joi Nobisso. Friends and former neighbors shared their specialized knowledge with me: Simone Baldeon, Thelma Canty, Don Cucurello, Dr. Robert Pallay, Joe Phillips, and the staff of the Hillsborough (New Jersey) Public Library. My original editor, Maggie Crawford, loved this project from the beginning. Since then, my current editor, Carrie Feron, has wisely and enthusiastically steered it through its rebirth, along with my terrific agent, Steven Axelrod. How do I thank all the fabulous people at HarperCollins, William Morrow, and Avon Books, who continue to watch over me so well? Every writer should be so blessed. And to Bill and Dr. J.—thanks for the inspiration.

Susan Elizabeth Phillips
www.susanelizabethphillips.com

Turn the page for a sneak peek at

Susan Elizabeth Phillips's

exciting new novel

What I Did for Love

How did this happen? Georgie York, once the co-star of America's favorite television sitcom, has been publicly abandoned by her famous husband, her film career has tanked, her father is driving her crazy, and her public image as a spunky heroine is taking a serious beating.

What should a down-on-her-luck actress do? NOT go to Vegas . . . NOT run into her detestable former co-star—dreamboat-from-hell Bramwell Shepard . . . and NOT get caught up in an ugly incident that leads to a calamitous elopement. Before she knows it, Georgie has a fake marriage, a fake husband, and maybe (or not) a fake sex life.

Two enemies find themselves working without a script in a town where the spotlight shines bright . . . and where the strongest emotions can wear startling disguises.

Available February 2009 in hardcover

From William Morrow

An Imprint of HarperCollins Publishers

The jackals swarmed her as she stepped out into the late April afternoon. When Georgie had ducked into the perfume shop on Beverly Boulevard, only three of them had been stalking her, but now there were fifteen—twenty—maybe more—a howling, feral pack loose in L.A., cameras unsheathed, ready to rip the last bit of flesh from her bones.

Their strobes blinded her, but she told herself she could handle whatever they threw at her. Hadn't she been doing exactly that for the past year? They began to shout their rude questions—too many questions, too fast, too loud, words running together until nothing made sense. One of them shoved something in her hands—a tabloid—and screamed into her ear. "This just hit the stands, Georgie. What do you have to say?"

Georgie automatically glanced down, and there on the front page of *Flash* was a sonogram of a baby. Lance and Jade's baby. The baby that should have been hers.

All the blood rushed from her head. The strobes fired, the cameras snapped, and the back of her hand flew to her mouth. After so many months of holding it together, she lost her way, and her eyes flooded with tears.

The cameras caught everything—the hand at her mouth, the tears in her eyes. She'd finally given the jackals what they'd spent the past year preying to capture—photographs of funny, thirty-one-year-old Georgie York with her life shattered around her.

She dropped the tabloid and turned to flee, but they'd trapped her. She tried to back up, but they were behind her, in front of her, surrounding her with their hot strobes and heartless shouts. Their smell clogged her nostrils—sweat, cigarettes, acrid cologne. Someone stepped on her foot. An elbow caught her in the side. They pressed closer, stealing her air, suffocating her . . .

Bramwell Shepard watched the nasty scene unfold from the restaurant steps next door. He'd just emerged from lunch when the commotion broke out, and he paused at the top of the steps to take it in. He hadn't seen Georgie York in a couple of years, and then it had only been a glimpse. Now, as he watched the paparazzi attack, the old, bitter feelings returned.

His higher position on the steps gave him a vantage point to observe the chaos. Some of the paps held their cameras over their heads; others shoved their lenses in her face. She'd been dealing with the press since she was a kid, but nothing had prepared her for the pandemonium of this past year. Too bad there were no heroes waiting around to rescue her.

Bram had spent eight miserable years rescuing Georgie from thorny situations, but his days of playing gallant Skip Scofield to Georgie's spunky Scooter Brown were long behind him. This time Scooter Brown could save her own ass—or, more likely, wait around for Daddy to do it.

The paparazzi hadn't spotted him. He wasn't on their radar screens these days, not that he wouldn't have been if they could ever catch him in the same frame with Georgie. *Skip and Scooter* had been one of the most successful sitcoms in television history. Eight years on the air, eight years off, but the public hadn't forgotten, especially when it came to America's favorite good girl, Scooter Brown, as played by real life by Georgie York.

A better man might have felt sorry for her current predicament, but he'd only worn the hero badge on screen. His mouth twisted as he looked down at her. *How's your spunky, can-do attitude working for you these days, Scooter?*

Things suddenly took an uglier turn. Two of the paps got into a shoving match, and one of them bumped her hard. She lost her balance and started to fall, and as she fell her head came up, and that's when she spotted him. Through the madness, the wild jockeying and crazy shoving, through the clamor and chaos, she somehow spotted him standing there barely thirty feet away. Her face registered a jolt of shock, not from the fall—she'd somehow caught herself before both knees hit—but from the sight of him. Their eyes locked, the cameras pressed closer, and the plea for help written on her face made her look like a kid again. He stared at her—not moving—simply taking in those gumdrop green eyes, still hopeful that one more present might be lurking beneath the Christmas tree. Then her eyes clouded, and he saw the exact moment when she realized he wasn't going to help her—that he was the same selfish bastard he'd always been.

What the hell did she expect? When had she ever been able to count on him for anything? Her funny girl's face twisted with contempt, and she turned her attention back to fighting off the cameras.

He belatedly realized he was missing a golden opportunity, and he started down the steps. But he'd waited too long. She'd already thrown the first punch. It wasn't a good punch, but it did the job, and a couple of the paps stepped in to form a wedge so she could get to her car. She flung herself inside and, moments later, peeled away from the curb. As she plunged erratically into the Friday afternoon L.A. traffic, the paparazzi raced to their illegally parked black SUVs and took off after her.

If the restaurant's valet service hadn't chosen that moment to deliver his Audi, Bram would probably have dismissed the incident, but as he slid behind the wheel, his curiosity got the best of him. Where did a tabloid princess go to lick her wounds when she had no place left to hide?

The lunch he'd just sat through had been a bust, and he had nothing better to do with his time, so he decided to fall in behind the paparazzi cavalcade. Although he couldn't see her Prius, he could tell by the way the paps wove through the traffic that Georgie was driving erratically. She cut over toward Sunset. He flipped on the radio, flipped it back off, pondered his current situation. His mind began to toy with an intriguing scenario.

Eventually, the cavalcade hit the PCH heading north, and that's when it struck him. Her likely destination. He rubbed his thumb over the top of the steering wheel.

And wasn't life full of interesting coincidences? . . .

More Praise for **The Martian**

"Gripping . . . Grade: A."

—AVClub.com

"Weir delivers with *The Martian*."

—Associated Press

"Smart, funny, and white-knuckle intense . . . the best book I've read in ages."

—Hugh Howey, author of *Wool*

"A book I just couldn't put down!"

—Astronaut Chris Hadfield

"An impressively geeky debut."

—*Entertainment Weekly*

"Harkens back to masters such as Robert Heinlein, Isaac Asimov, and Arthur C. Clarke."

—*San Jose Mercury News*

"One of the best thrillers I've read in a long time."

—Douglas Preston, author of *Impact*

"*The Martian* kicked my ass! Relentlessly entertaining and inventive."

—Ernest Cline, author of *Ready Player One*

"Brilliant . . . a celebration of human ingenuity [and] the purest example of real-science sci-fi for many years . . . Utterly compelling."

—*Wall Street Journal*

"A hugely entertaining novel [that] reads like a rocket ship afire . . . Weir has fashioned in Mark Watney one of the most appealing, funny, and resourceful characters in recent fiction."

—*Chicago Tribune*

"As gripping as they come . . . you'll be rooting for Watney the whole way, groaning at every setback and laughing at his pitch-black humor. Utterly nail-biting and memorable."

—*Financial Times*

"Terrific stuff, a crackling good read."

—*USA Today*

"A perfect novel in almost every way."

—*Crimespree* magazine

"Almost literally an un-put-downable book. I recommend it to anyone who loves the manned space program, or who loves science, or who loves a brilliantly written novel of unrelenting suspense and intelligence."

—Dan Simmons, *New York Times* bestselling author of *Drood* and *Hyperion*

"*Robinson Crusoe* on Mars, twenty-first-century style. Set aside a chunk of free time when you start this one. You're going to need it because you won't want to put it down."

—Steve Berry, *New York Times* bestselling author of *The King's Deception*

"An exciting, insightful science-based tale [that] kept me turning the pages to see what ingenious solution our hero would concoct to survive yet another impossible dilemma."

—Terry Brooks, *New York Times* bestselling author of *The Sword of Shannara*

"A great read with inspiring attention to technical detail and surprising emotional depth. Loved it!"

—Daniel H. Wilson, *New York Times* bestselling author of *Robopocalypse*

"An excellent first novel . . . Weir laces the technical details with enough keen wit to satisfy hard science fiction fan and general reader alike [and] keeps the story escalating to a riveting conclusion."

—*Publishers Weekly* (starred review)

"Gripping . . . shapes up like Defoe's *Robinson Crusoe* as written by someone brighter."

—Larry Niven, Hugo and Nebula Award–winning author of the Ringworld series and *Lucifer's Hammer*

"Weir combines the heart-stopping with the humorous in this brilliant debut novel. . . . The perfect mix of action and space adventure."

—*Library Journal* (starred review)

"The tension simply never lets up, from the first page to the last, and at no point does the believability falter for even a second. You can't shake the feeling that this could all really happen."

—Patrick Lee, *New York Times* bestselling author of *The Runner*

"Riveting . . . a tightly constructed and completely believable story of a man's ingenuity and strength in the face of seemingly insurmountable odds."

—*Booklist*

"A page-turning thriller . . . this survival tale with a high-tech twist will pull you right in."

—*Suspense* magazine

"Sharp, funny, and thrilling, with just the right amount of geekery . . . Weir displays a virtuosic ability to write about highly technical situations without leaving readers far behind. The result is a story that is as plausible as it is compelling."

—*Kirkus Reviews*

THE MARTIAN

THE MARTIAN

A NOVEL

ANDY WEIR

B\D\W\Y
Broadway Books
New York

This is a work of fiction. Names, characters, places, and incidents either are the product of the author's imagination or are used fictitiously. Any resemblance to actual persons, living or dead, events, or locales is entirely coincidental.

Published in the United States by Broadway Books, an imprint of the Crown Publishing Group, a division of Penguin Random House LLC, New York.
www.crownpublishing.com

Originally self-published as an ebook in 2011 and subsequently published in hardcover in slightly different form in the United States by Crown Publishers, an imprint of the Crown Publishing Group, a division of Penguin Random House LLC, New York, in 2014, and as a trade paperback by Broadway Books, an imprint of the Crown Publishing Group, a division of Penguin Random House LLC, New York, in 2014.

Library of Congress Cataloging-in-Publication data is available upon request.

ISBN 978-1-101-90500-5
eBook ISBN 978-0-8041-3903-8

Printed in the United States of America

Book design by Elizabeth Rendfleisch
Map by Fred Haynes
Photograph by Antonio M. Rosario/Stockbyte/Getty Images

10 9 8 7 6 5 4 3 2 1

First Movie Tie-in Mass Market Edition

For Mom,
who calls me "Pickle,"
and Dad,
who calls me "Dude."

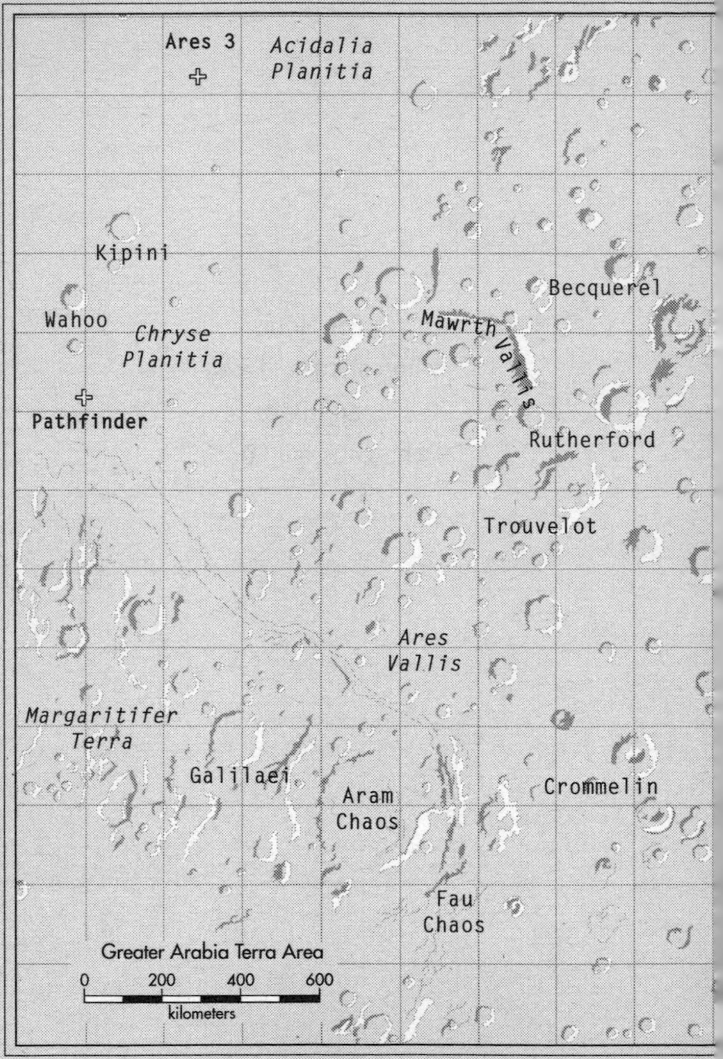

Ares 3

Acidalia Planitia

Kipini

Becquerel

Wahoo

Chryse Planitia

Mawrth Vallis

Pathfinder

Rutherford

Trouvelot

Ares Vallis

Margaritifer Terra

Galilaei

Aram Chaos

Crommelin

Fau Chaos

Greater Arabia Terra Area

0 200 400 600

kilometers

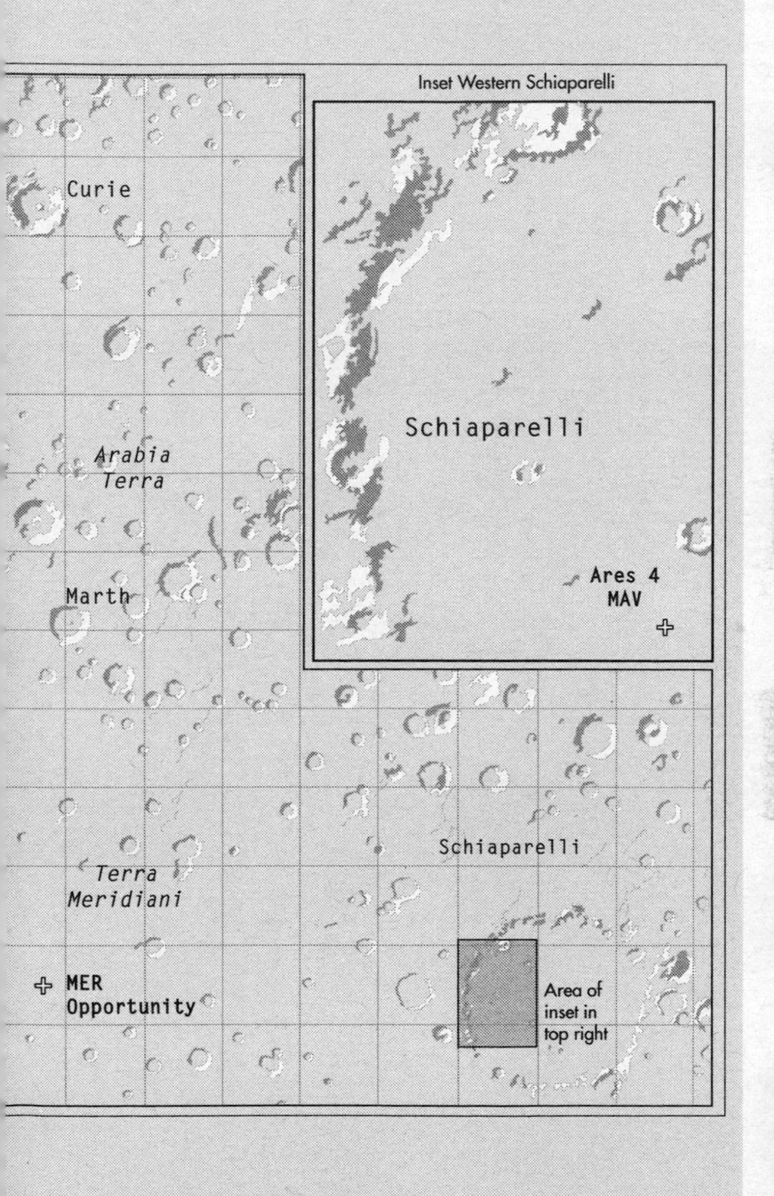
Inset Western Schiaparelli
Schiaparelli
Ares 4
MAV
Curie
Arabia
Terra
Marth
Schiaparelli
Terra
Meridiani
MER
Opportunity
Area of
inset in
top right

CHAPTER 1

LOG ENTRY: SOL 6

I'm pretty much fucked.

That's my considered opinion.

Fucked.

Six days into what should be the greatest month of my life, and it's turned into a nightmare.

I don't even know who'll read this. I guess someone will find it eventually. Maybe a hundred years from now.

For the record . . . I didn't die on Sol 6. Certainly the rest of the crew thought I did, and I can't blame them. Maybe there'll be a day of national mourning for me, and my Wikipedia page will say, "Mark Watney is the only human being to have died on Mars."

And it'll be right, probably. 'Cause I'll surely die here. Just not on Sol 6 when everyone thinks I did.

Let's see . . . where do I begin?

The Ares Program. Mankind reaching out to Mars to send people to another planet for the very first time and expand the horizons of humanity blah, blah, blah. The Ares 1 crew did their thing and came back heroes. They got the parades and fame and love of the world.

Ares 2 did the same thing, in a different location on Mars. They got a firm handshake and a hot cup of coffee when they got home.

Ares 3. Well, that was my mission. Okay, not *mine* per se. Commander Lewis was in charge. I was just one of her crew. Actually, I was the very lowest ranked member of the crew. I would only be "in command" of the mission if I were the only remaining person.

What do you know? I'm in command.

I wonder if this log will be recovered before the rest of the crew die of old age. I presume they got back to Earth all right. Guys, if you're reading this: It wasn't your fault. You did what you had to do. In your position I would have done the same thing. I don't blame you, and I'm glad you survived.

I guess I should explain how Mars missions work, for any layman who may be reading this. We got to Earth orbit the normal way, through an ordinary ship to *Hermes*. All the Ares missions use *Hermes* to get to and from Mars. It's really big and cost a lot so NASA built only one.

Once we got to *Hermes*, four additional unmanned missions brought us fuel and supplies while we prepared for our trip. Once everything was a go, we set out for Mars. But not very fast.

Gone are the days of heavy chemical fuel burns and trans-Mars injection orbits.

Hermes is powered by ion engines. They throw argon out the back of the ship really fast to get a tiny amount of acceleration. The thing is, it doesn't take much reactant mass, so a little argon (and a nuclear reactor to power things) let us accelerate constantly the whole way there. You'd be amazed at how fast you can get going with a tiny acceleration over a long time.

I could regale you with tales of how we had great fun on the trip, but I won't. I don't feel like reliving it right now. Suffice it to say we got to Mars 124 days later without strangling each other.

From there, we took the MDV (Mars descent vehicle) to the surface. The MDV is basically a big can with some light thrusters and parachutes attached. Its sole purpose is to get six humans from Mars orbit to the surface without killing any of them.

And now we come to the real trick of Mars exploration: having all of our shit there in advance.

A total of fourteen unmanned missions deposited everything we would need for surface operations. They tried their best to land all the supply vessels in the same general area, and did a reasonably good job. Supplies aren't nearly so fragile as humans and can hit the ground really hard. But they tend to bounce around a lot.

Naturally, they didn't send us to Mars until they'd confirmed that all the supplies had made it to the surface and their containers weren't breached. Start to finish, including supply missions, a Mars mission takes about three years. In fact, there were Ares 3 supplies en route to Mars while the Ares 2 crew were on their way home.

The most important piece of the advance supplies, of course, was the MAV. The Mars ascent vehicle. That was how we would get back to *Hermes* after surface operations were complete. The MAV was soft-landed (as opposed to the balloon bounce-fest the other supplies had). Of course, it was in constant communication with Houston, and if there had been any problems with it, we would have passed by Mars and gone home without ever landing.

The MAV is pretty cool. Turns out, through a neat set of chemical reactions with the Martian atmosphere, for every kilogram of hydrogen you bring to Mars, you can make thirteen kilograms of fuel. It's a slow process, though. It takes twenty-four months to fill the tank. That's why they sent it long before we got here.

You can imagine how disappointed I was when I discovered the MAV was gone.

It was a ridiculous sequence of events that led to me almost dying, and an even more ridiculous sequence that led to me surviving.

The mission is designed to handle sandstorm gusts up to 150 kph. So Houston got understandably nervous when we got whacked with 175 kph winds. We all got in our flight space suits and huddled in the middle of the Hab, just in case it lost pressure. But the Hab wasn't the problem.

The MAV is a spaceship. It has a lot of delicate parts. It can put up with storms to a certain extent, but it can't just get sandblasted forever. After an hour and a half of sustained wind, NASA gave the order to abort. Nobody wanted to stop a month-long mission after only six days, but if the MAV took any more punishment, we'd all have gotten stranded down there.

We had to go out in the storm to get from the Hab to the MAV. That was going to be risky, but what choice did we have?

Everyone made it but me.

Our main communications dish, which relayed signals from the Hab to *Hermes*, acted like a parachute, getting torn from its foundation and carried with the torrent. Along the way, it crashed through the reception antenna array. Then one of those long thin antennae slammed into me end-first. It tore through my suit like a bullet through butter, and I felt the worst pain of my life as it ripped open my side. I vaguely remember having the wind knocked out of me (pulled out of me, really) and my ears popping painfully as the pressure of my suit escaped.

The last thing I remember was seeing Johanssen hopelessly reaching out toward me.

I awoke to the oxygen alarm in my suit. A steady, obnoxious beeping that eventually roused me from a deep and profound desire to just fucking die.

The storm had abated; I was facedown, almost totally buried in sand. As I groggily came to, I wondered why I wasn't more dead.

The antenna had enough force to punch through the suit and my side, but it had been stopped by my pelvis. So there was only one hole in the suit (and a hole in me, of course).

I had been knocked back quite a ways and rolled down a steep hill. Somehow I landed facedown, which forced the antenna to a strongly oblique angle that put a lot of torque on the hole in the suit. It made a weak seal.

Then, the copious blood from my wound trickled down toward the hole. As the blood reached the site of the breach, the water in it quickly evaporated from the airflow and low pressure, leaving a gunky residue behind. More blood came in behind it and was also reduced to gunk. Eventually, it sealed the gaps around the hole and reduced the leak to something the suit could counteract.

The suit did its job admirably. Sensing the drop in pressure, it constantly flooded itself with air from my nitrogen tank to equalize. Once the leak became manageable, it only had to trickle new air in slowly to relieve the air lost.

After a while, the CO_2 (carbon dioxide) absorbers in the suit were expended. That's really the limiting factor to life support. Not the amount of oxygen you bring with you, but the amount of CO_2 you can remove. In the Hab, I have the oxygenator, a large piece of equipment that breaks apart CO_2 to give the oxygen back. But the space suits have to be portable, so they use a simple chemical absorption process with expendable filters. I'd been asleep long enough that my filters were useless.

The suit saw this problem and moved into an emergency mode the engineers call "bloodletting." Having no way to separate out the CO_2, the suit deliberately vented air to the Martian atmosphere, then backfilled with nitrogen. Between the breach and the bloodletting, it quickly ran out of nitrogen. All it had left was my oxygen tank.

So it did the only thing it could to keep me alive. It started backfilling with pure oxygen. I now risked dying from oxygen toxicity, as the excessively high amount of oxygen threatened to burn up my nervous system, lungs, and eyes. An ironic death for someone with a leaky space suit: too much oxygen.

Every step of the way would have had beeping alarms, alerts, and warnings. But it was the high-oxygen warning that woke me.

The sheer volume of training for a space mission is astounding. I'd spent a week back on Earth practicing emergency space suit drills. I knew what to do.

Carefully reaching to the side of my helmet, I got the breach kit. It's nothing more than a funnel with a valve at the small end and an unbelievably sticky resin on the wide end. The idea is you have the valve open and stick the wide end over a hole. The air can escape through the valve, so it doesn't interfere with the resin making a good seal. Then you close the valve, and you've sealed the breach.

The tricky part was getting the antenna out of the way. I pulled it out as fast as I could, wincing as the sudden pressure drop dizzied me and made the wound in my side scream in agony.

I got the breach kit over the hole and sealed it. It held. The suit backfilled the missing air with yet more oxygen. Checking my arm readouts, I saw the suit was now at 85 percent oxygen. For reference, Earth's atmosphere is about 21 percent. I'd be okay, so long as I didn't spend too much time like that.

I stumbled up the hill back toward the Hab. As I crested the rise, I saw something that made me very happy and something that made me very sad: The Hab was intact (yay!) and the MAV was gone (boo!).

Right that moment I knew I was screwed. But I

didn't want to just die out on the surface. I limped back to the Hab and fumbled my way into an airlock. As soon as it equalized, I threw off my helmet.

Once inside the Hab, I doffed the suit and got my first good look at the injury. It would need stitches. Fortunately, all of us had been trained in basic medical procedures, and the Hab had excellent medical supplies. A quick shot of local anesthetic, irrigate the wound, nine stitches, and I was done. I'd be taking antibiotics for a couple of weeks, but other than that I'd be fine.

I knew it was hopeless, but I tried firing up the communications array. No signal, of course. The primary satellite dish had broken off, remember? And it took the reception antennae with it. The Hab had secondary and tertiary communications systems, but they were both just for talking to the MAV, which would use its much more powerful systems to relay to *Hermes*. Thing is, that only works if the MAV is still around.

I had no way to talk to *Hermes*. In time, I could locate the dish out on the surface, but it would take weeks for me to rig up any repairs, and that would be too late. In an abort, *Hermes* would leave orbit within twenty-four hours. The orbital dynamics made the trip safer and shorter the earlier you left, so why wait?

Checking out my suit, I saw the antenna had plowed through my bio-monitor computer. When on an EVA, all the crew's suits are networked so we can see each other's status. The rest of the crew would have seen the pressure in my suit drop to nearly zero, followed immediately by my bio-signs going flat. Add to that watching me tumble down a hill with a spear through me in the middle of a sandstorm . . . yeah. They thought I was dead. How could they not?

They may have even had a brief discussion about recovering my body, but regulations are clear. In the event a crewman dies on Mars, he stays on Mars. Leaving his body behind reduces weight for the MAV on the trip back. That means more disposable fuel and a larger margin of error for the return thrust. No point in giving that up for sentimentality.

So that's the situation. I'm stranded on Mars. I have no way to communicate with *Hermes* or Earth. Everyone thinks I'm dead. I'm in a Hab designed to last thirty-one days.

If the oxygenator breaks down, I'll suffocate. If the water reclaimer breaks down, I'll die of thirst. If the Hab breaches, I'll just kind of explode. If none of those things happen, I'll eventually run out of food and starve to death.

So yeah. I'm fucked.

CHAPTER 2

LOG ENTRY: SOL 7

Okay, I've had a good night's sleep, and things don't seem as hopeless as they did yesterday.

Today I took stock of supplies and did a quick EVA to check up on the external equipment. Here's my situation:

The surface mission was supposed to be thirty-one days. For redundancy, the supply probes had enough food to last the whole crew fifty-six days. That way if one or two probes had problems, we'd still have enough food to complete the mission.

We were six days in when all hell broke loose, so that leaves enough food to feed six people for fifty days. I'm just one guy, so it'll last me three hundred days. And that's if I don't ration it. So I've got a fair bit of time.

I'm pretty flush on EVA suits, too. Each crew member had two space suits: a flight spacesuit to wear during descent and ascent, and the much bulkier and more robust EVA suit to wear when doing surface operations. My flight spacesuit has a hole in it, and of course the crew was wearing the other five when they returned to *Hermes*. But all six EVA suits are still here and in perfect condition.

The Hab stood up to the storm without any problems. Outside, things aren't so rosy. I can't find the satellite dish. It probably got blown kilometers away.

The MAV is gone, of course. My crewmates took it up to *Hermes*. Though the bottom half (the landing stage) is still here. No reason to take that back up when weight is the enemy. It includes the landing gear, the fuel plant, and anything else NASA figured it wouldn't need for the trip back up to orbit.

The MDV is on its side and there's a breach in the hull. Looks like the storm ripped the cowling off the reserve chute (which we didn't have to use on landing). Once the chute was exposed, it dragged the MDV all over the place, smashing it against every rock in the area. Not that the MDV would be much use to me. Its thrusters can't even lift its own weight. But it might have been valuable for parts. Might still be.

Both rovers are half-buried in sand, but they're in good shape otherwise. Their pressure seals are intact. Makes sense. Operating procedure when a storm hits is to stop motion and wait for the storm to pass. They're made to stand up to punishment. I'll be able to dig them out with a day or so of work.

I've lost communication with the weather stations, placed a kilometer away from the Hab in four directions. They might be in perfect working order for all I know. The Hab's communications are so weak right now it probably can't even reach a kilometer.

The solar cell array was covered in sand, rendering it useless (hint: solar cells need sunlight to make electricity). But once I swept the cells off, they returned to full efficiency. Whatever I end up doing, I'll have plenty of power for it. Two hundred square meters of solar cells, with hydrogen fuel cells to store plenty of reserve. All I need to do is sweep them off every few days.

Things indoors are great, thanks to the Hab's sturdy design.

I ran a full diagnostic on the oxygenator. Twice. It's perfect. If anything goes wrong with it, there's a short-term spare I can use. But it's solely for emergency use while repairing the main one. The spare doesn't actually pull CO_2 apart and recapture the oxygen. It just absorbs the CO_2 the same way the space suits do. It's intended to last five days before it saturates the filters, which means thirty days for me (just one person breathing, instead of six). So there's some insurance there.

The water reclaimer is working fine, too. The bad news is there's no backup. If it stops working, I'll be drinking reserve water while I rig up a primitive distillery to boil piss. Also, I'll lose half a liter of water per day to breathing until the humidity in the Hab reaches its maximum and water starts condensing on every surface. Then I'll be licking the walls. Yay. Anyway, for now, no problems with the water reclaimer.

So yeah. Food, water, shelter all taken care of. I'm going to start rationing food right now. Meals are pretty minimal already, but I think I can eat a three-fourths portion per meal and still be all right. That should turn my three hundred days of food into four hundred. Foraging around the medical area, I found the main bottle of vitamins. There's enough multivitamins there to last years. So I won't have any nutritional problems (though I'll still starve to death when I'm out of food, no matter how many vitamins I take).

The medical area has morphine for emergencies. And there's enough there for a lethal dose. I'm not going to slowly starve to death, I'll tell you that. If I get to that point, I'll take an easier way out.

Everyone on the mission had two specialties. I'm a botanist and mechanical engineer; basically, the mission's fix-it man who played with plants. The mechanical engineering might save my life if something breaks.

I've been thinking about how to survive this. It's not completely hopeless. There'll be humans back on Mars in about four years when Ares 4 arrives (assuming they didn't cancel the program in the wake of my "death").

Ares 4 will be landing at the Schiaparelli crater, which is about 3200 kilometers away from my location here in Acidalia Planitia. No way for me to get there on my own. But if I could communicate, I might be able to get a rescue. Not sure how they'd manage that with the resources on hand, but NASA has a lot of smart people.

So that's my mission now. Find a way to communicate with Earth. If I can't manage that, find a way to communicate with *Hermes* when it returns in four years with the Ares 4 crew.

Of course, I don't have any plan for surviving four years on one year of food. But one thing at a time here. For now, I'm well fed and have a purpose: Fix the damn radio.

LOG ENTRY: SOL 10

Well, I've done three EVAs and haven't found any hint of the communications dish.

I dug out one of the rovers and had a good drive around, but after days of wandering, I think it's time to give up. The storm probably blew the dish far away and then erased any drag-marks or scuffs that might have led to a trail. Probably buried it, too.

I spent most of today out at what's left of the communications array. It's really a sorry sight. I may as well yell toward Earth for all the good that damned thing will do me.

I could throw together a rudimentary dish out of metal I find around the base, but this isn't some walkie-talkie I'm working with here. Communicating from Mars to Earth is a pretty big deal, and requires extremely specialized equipment. I won't be able to whip something up with tinfoil and gum.

I need to ration my EVAs as well as food. The CO_2 filters are not cleanable. Once they're saturated, they're done. The mission accounted for a four-hour EVA per crew member per day. Fortunately, CO_2 filters are light and small, so NASA had the luxury of sending more than we needed. All told, I have about 1500 hours' worth of CO_2 filters. After that, any EVAs I do will have to be managed with bloodletting the air.

Fifteen hundred hours may sound like a lot, but I'm faced with spending at least four years here if I'm going to have any hope of rescue, with a minimum of several hours per week dedicated to sweeping off the solar array. Anyway. No needless EVAs.

In other news, I'm starting to come up with an idea for food. My botany background may come in useful after all.

Why bring a botanist to Mars? After all, it's famous for not having anything growing there. Well, the idea was to figure out how well things grow in Martian gravity, and see what, if anything, we can do with Martian soil. The short answer is: quite a lot . . . almost. Martian soil has the basic building blocks needed for plant growth, but there's a lot of stuff going on in Earth soil that Mars soil doesn't have, even when it's placed in an Earth atmosphere and given plenty of water. Bacterial activity, certain nutrients provided by animal life, etc. None of that is happening on Mars. One of my tasks for the mission was to see how plants grow here, in various combinations of Earth and Mars soil and atmosphere.

That's why I have a small amount of Earth soil and a bunch of plant seeds with me.

I can't get too excited, however. It's about the amount of soil you'd put in a window box, and the only seeds I have are a few species of grass and ferns. They're the most rugged and easily grown plants on Earth, so NASA picked them as the test subjects.

So I have two problems: not enough dirt, and nothing edible to plant in it.

But I'm a botanist, damn it. I should be able to find a way to make this happen. If I don't, I'll be a really hungry botanist in about a year.

LOG ENTRY: SOL 11

I wonder how the Cubs are doing.

LOG ENTRY: SOL 14

I got my undergrad degree at the University of Chicago. Half the people who studied botany were hippies who thought they could return to some natural world system. Somehow feeding seven billion people through pure gathering. They spent most of their time working out better ways to grow pot. I didn't like them. I've always been in it for the science, not for any New World Order bullshit.

When they made compost heaps and tried to conserve every little ounce of living matter, I laughed at them. "Look at the silly hippies! Look at their pathetic attempts to simulate a complex global ecosystem in their backyard."

Of course, now I'm doing exactly that. I'm saving every scrap of biomatter I can find. Every time I finish a meal, the leftovers go to the compost bucket. As for other biological material . . .

The Hab has sophisticated toilets. Shit is usually vaccum-dried, then accumulated in sealed bags to be discarded on the surface.

Not anymore!

In fact, I even did an EVA to recover the previous bags of shit from before the crew left. Being completely desiccated, this particular shit didn't have bacteria in it anymore, but it still had complex proteins and would serve as useful manure. Adding it to water and active bacteria would quickly get it inundated, replacing any population killed by the Toilet of Doom.

I found a big container and put a bit of water in it, then added the dried shit. Since then, I've added my own shit to it as well. The worse it smells, the better things are going. That's the bacteria at work!

Once I get some Martian soil in here, I can mix in the shit and spread it out. Then I can sprinkle the Earth soil on top. You might not think that would be an important step, but it is. There are dozens of species of bacteria living in Earth soil, and they're critical to plant growth. They'll spread out and breed like . . . well, like a bacterial infection.

People have been using human waste as fertilizer for centuries. It's even got a pleasant name: "night soil." Normally, it's not an ideal way to grow crops, because it spreads disease: Human waste has pathogens in it that, you guessed it, infect humans. But it's not a problem for me. The only pathogens in this waste are the ones I already have.

Within a week, the Martian soil will be ready for plants to germinate in. But I won't plant yet. I'll bring in more lifeless soil from outside and spread some of the live soil over it. It'll "infect" the new soil and I'll have double what I started with. After another week, I'll double it again. And so on. Of course, all the while, I'll be adding all new manure to the effort.

My asshole is doing as much to keep me alive as my brain.

This isn't a new concept I just came up with. People have speculated on how to make crop soil out of Martian dirt for decades. I'll just be putting it to the test for the first time.

I searched through the food supplies and found all sorts of things that I can plant. Peas, for instance. Plenty of beans, too. I also found several potatoes. If *any* of them can still germinate after their ordeal, that'll be great. With a nearly infinite supply of vitamins, all I need are calories of any kind to survive.

The total floor space of the Hab is about 92 square meters. I plan to dedicate all of it to this endeavor. I don't mind walking on dirt. It'll be a lot of work, but I'm going to need to cover the entire floor to a depth of 10 centimeters. That means I'll have to transport 9.2 cubic meters of Martian soil into the Hab. I can get maybe one-tenth of a cubic meter in through the airlock at a time, and it'll be backbreaking work to collect it. But in the end, if everything goes to plan, I'll have 92 square meters of crop-able soil.

Hell yeah I'm a botanist! Fear my botany powers!

LOG ENTRY: SOL 15

Ugh! This is backbreaking work!

I spent twelve hours today on EVAs to bring dirt into the Hab. I only managed to cover a small corner of the base, maybe five square meters. At this rate it'll take me weeks to get all the soil in. But hey, time is one thing I've got.

The first few EVAs were pretty inefficient; me filling small containers and bringing them in through the airlock. Then I got wise and just put one big container in the airlock itself and filled that with small containers till it was full. That sped things up a lot because the airlock takes about ten minutes to get through.

I ache all over. And the shovels I have are made for taking samples, not heavy digging. My back is killing me. I foraged in the medical supplies and found some Vicodin. I took it about ten minutes ago. Should be kicking in soon.

Anyway, it's nice to see progress. Time to start getting the bacteria to work on these minerals. After lunch. No three-fourths ration today. I've earned a full meal.

LOG ENTRY: SOL 16

One complication I hadn't thought of: water.

Turns out being on the surface of Mars for a few million years eliminates all the water in the soil. My master's degree in botany makes me pretty sure plants need wet dirt to grow in. Not to mention the bacteria that has to live in the dirt first.

Fortunately, I have water. But not as much as I want. To be viable, soil needs 40 liters of water per cubic meter. My overall plan calls for 9.2 cubic meters of soil. So I'll eventually need 368 liters of water to feed it.

The Hab has an excellent water reclaimer. Best technology available on Earth. So NASA figured, "Why send a lot of water up there? Just send enough for an emergency." Humans need three liters of water per day to be comfortable. They gave us 50 liters each, making 300 liters total in the Hab.

I'm willing to dedicate all but an emergency 50 liters to the cause. That means I can feed 62.5

square meters at a depth of 10 centimeters. About two-thirds of the Hab's floor. It'll have to do. That's the long-term plan. For today, my goal was five square meters.

I wadded up blankets and uniforms from my departed crewmates to serve as one edge of a planter box with the curved walls of the Hab being the rest of the perimeter. It was as close to five square meters as I could manage. I filled it with sand to a depth of 10 centimeters. Then I sacrificed 20 liters of precious water to the dirt gods.

Then things got disgusting. I dumped my big container o' shit onto the soil and nearly puked from the smell. I mixed this soil and shit together with a shovel, and spread it out evenly again. Then I sprinkled the Earth soil on top. Get to work, bacteria. I'm counting on you. That smell's going to stick around for a while, too. It's not like I can open a window. Still, you get used to it.

In other news, today is Thanksgiving. My family will be gathering in Chicago for the usual feast at my parents' house. My guess is it won't be much fun, what with me having died ten days ago. Hell, they probably just got done with my funeral.

I wonder if they'll ever find out what really happened. I've been so busy staying alive I never thought of what this must be like for my parents. Right now, they're suffering the worst pain anyone can endure. I'd give anything just to let them know I'm still alive.

I'll just have to survive to make up for it.

LOG ENTRY: SOL 22

Wow. Things really came along.

I got all the sand in and ready to go. Two-thirds of the base is now dirt. And today I executed my first dirt-doubling. It's been a week, and the former Martian soil is rich and lovely. Two more doublings and I'll have covered the whole field.

All that work was great for my morale. It gave me something to do. But after things settled down a bit, and I had dinner while listening to Johanssen's Beatles music collection, I got depressed again.

Doing the math, this won't keep me from starving.

My best bet for making calories is potatoes. They grow prolifically and have a reasonable caloric content (770 calories per kilogram). I'm pretty sure the ones I have will germinate. Problem is I can't grow enough of them. In 62 square meters, I could grow maybe 150 kilograms of potatoes in 400 days (the time I have before running out of food). That's a grand total of 115,500 calories, a sustainable average of 288 calories per day. With my height and weight, if I'm willing to starve a little, I need 1500 calories per day.

Not even close.

So I can't just live off the land forever. But I can extend my life. The potatoes will last me 76 days.

Potatoes grow continually, so in those 76 days, I can grow another 22,000 calories of potatoes, which will tide me over for another 15 days. After that, it's kind of pointless to continue the trend. All told it buys me about 90 days.

So now I'll start starving to death on Sol 490

instead of Sol 400. It's progress, but any hope of survival rests on me surviving until Sol 1412, when Ares 4 will land.

There's about a thousand days of food I don't have. And I don't have a plan for how to get it.

Shit.

CHAPTER 3

LOG ENTRY: SOL 25

Remember those old math questions you had in algebra class? Where water is entering a container at a certain rate and leaving at a different rate and you need to figure out when it'll be empty? Well, that concept is critical to the "Mark Watney doesn't die" project I'm working on.

I need to create calories. And I need enough to last the 1387 sols until Ares 4 arrives. If I don't get rescued by Ares 4, I'm dead anyway. A sol is 39 minutes longer than a day, so it works out to be 1425 days. That's my target: 1425 days of food.

I have plenty of multivitamins; over double what I need. And there's five times the minimum protein in each food pack, so careful rationing of portions takes care of my protein needs for at least four years. My general nutrition is taken care of. I just need calories.

I need 1500 calories every day. I have 400 days

of food to start off with. So how many calories do I need to generate per day along the entire time period to stay alive for around 1425 days?

I'll spare you the math. The answer is about 1100. I need to create 1100 calories per day with my farming efforts to survive until Ares 4 gets here. Actually, a little more than that, because it's Sol 25 right now and I haven't actually planted anything yet.

With my 62 square meters of farmland, I'll be able to create about 288 calories per day. So I need almost four times my current plan's production to survive.

That means I need more surface area for farming, and more water to hydrate the soil. So let's take the problems one at a time.

How much farmland can I really make?

There are 92 square meters in the Hab. Let's say I could make use of all of it.

Also, there are five unused bunks. Let's say I put soil in on them, too. They're 2 square meters each, giving me 10 more square meters. So we're up to 102.

The Hab has three lab tables, each about 2 square meters. I want to keep one for my own use, leaving two for the cause. That's another 4 square meters, bringing the total to 106.

I have two Martian rovers. They have pressure seals, allowing the occupants to drive without space suits during long periods traversing the surface. They're too cramped to plant crops in, and I want to be able to drive them around anyway. But both rovers have an emergency pop-tent.

There are a lot of problems with using pop-tents as farmland, but they have 10 square meters of floor space each. Presuming I can overcome the problems, they net me another 20 square meters, bringing my farmland up to 126.

One hundred and twenty-six square meters of farmable land. That's something to work with. I still don't have the water to moisten all that soil, but like I said, one thing at a time.

The next thing to consider is how efficient I can be in growing potatoes. I based my crop yield estimates on the potato industry back on Earth. But potato farmers aren't in a desperate race for survival like I am. Can I get a better yield?

For starters, I can give attention to each individual plant. I can trim them and keep them healthy and not interfering with each other. Also, as their flowering bodies breach the surface, I can replant them deeper, then plant younger plants above them. For normal potato farmers, it's not worth doing because they're working with literally millions of potato plants.

Also, this sort of farming annihilates the soil. Any farmer doing it would turn their land into a dust bowl within twelve years. It's not sustainable. But who cares? I just need to survive for four years.

I estimate I can get 50 percent higher yield by using these tactics. And with the 126 square meters of farmland (just over double the 62 square meters I now have) it works out to be over 850 calories per day.

That's real progress. I'd still be in danger of starvation, but it gets me in the range of survival. I might be able to make it by nearly starving but not quite dying. I could reduce my caloric use by minimizing manual labor. I could set the temperature of the Hab higher than normal, meaning my body would expend less energy keeping its temperature. I could cut off an arm and eat it, gaining me valuable calories and reducing my overall caloric need.

No, not really.

So let's say I could clear up that much farmland. Seems reasonable. Where do I get the water? To go from 62 to 126 square meters of farmland at 10 centimeters deep, I'll need 6.4 more cubic meters of soil (more shoveling, whee!) and that'll need over 250 liters of water.

The 50 liters I have is for me to drink if the water reclaimer breaks. So I'm 250 liters short of my 250-liter goal.

Bleh. I'm going to bed.

LOG ENTRY: SOL 26

It was a backbreaking yet productive day.

I was sick of thinking, so instead of trying to figure out where I'll get 250 liters of water, I did some manual labor. I need to get a whole assload more soil into the Hab, even if it is dry and useless right now.

I got a cubic meter in before getting exhausted.

Then, a minor dust storm dropped by for an hour and covered the solar collectors with crap. So I had to suit up *again* and do *another* EVA. I was in a pissy mood the whole time. Sweeping off a huge field of solar cells is boring and physically demanding. But once the job was done, I came back to my Little Hab on the Prairie.

It was about time for another dirt-doubling, so I figured I might as well get it over with. It took an hour. One more doubling and the usable soil will all be good to go.

Also, I figured it was time to start up a seed crop. I'd doubled the soil enough that I could afford to leave a little corner of it alone. I had twelve potatoes to work with.

I am one lucky son of a bitch they aren't freeze-dried or mulched. Why did NASA send twelve whole potatoes, refrigerated but not frozen? And why send them along with us as in-pressure cargo rather than in a crate with the rest of the Hab supplies? Because Thanksgiving was going to happen while we were doing surface operations, and NASA's shrinks thought it would be good for us to make a meal together. Not just to eat it, but to actually prepare it. There's probably some logic to that, but who cares?

I cut each potato into four pieces, making sure each piece had at least two eyes. The eyes are where they sprout from. I let them sit for a few hours to harden a bit, then planted them, well spaced apart, in the corner. Godspeed, little taters. My life depends on you.

Normally, it takes at least 90 days to yield full-sized potatoes. But I can't wait that long. I'll need to cut up all the potatoes from this crop to seed the rest of the field.

By setting the Hab temperature to a balmy 25.5°C, I can make the plants grow faster. Also, the internal lights will provide plenty of "sunlight," and I'll make sure they get lots of water (once I figure out where to get water). There will be no foul weather, or any parasites to hassle them, or any weeds to compete with for soil or nutrients. With all this going for them, they should yield healthy, sproutable tubers within forty days.

I figured that was enough being Farmer Mark for one day.

A full meal for dinner. I'd earned it. Plus, I'd burned a ton of calories, and I wanted them back.

I rifled through Commander Lewis's stuff until I found her personal data-stick. Everyone got to bring whatever digital entertainment they wanted, and I was tired of listening to Johanssen's Beatles albums for now. Time to see what Lewis had.

Crappy TV shows. That's what she had. Countless entire runs of TV shows from forever ago.

Well. Beggars can't be choosers. *Three's Company* it is.

LOG ENTRY: SOL 29

Over the last few days, I got in all the dirt that I'll need. I prepped the tables and bunks for holding the weight of soil, and even put the dirt in place. There's still no water to make it viable, but I have some ideas. Really bad ideas, but they're ideas.

Today's big accomplishment was setting up the pop-tents.

The problem with the rovers' pop-tents is they weren't designed for frequent use.

The idea was you'd throw out a pop-tent, get in, and wait for rescue. The airlock is nothing more than valves and two doors. Equalize the airlock with your side of it, get in, equalize with the other side, get out. This means you lose a lot of air with each use. And I'll need to get in there at least once a day. The total volume of each pop-tent is pretty low, so I can't afford to lose air from it.

I spent *hours* trying to figure out how to attach a pop-tent airlock to a Hab airlock. I have three airlocks in the Hab. I'd be willing to dedicate two to pop-tents. That would have been awesome.

The frustrating part is pop-tent airlocks *can* attach to other airlocks! You might have injured people in there, or not enough space suits. You need to be able to get people out without exposing them to the Martian atmosphere.

But the pop-tents were designed for your crew-mates to come rescue you in a rover. The airlocks on the Hab are much larger and completely different from the airlocks on the rovers. When you think about it, there's really no reason to attach a pop-tent to the Hab.

Unless you're stranded on Mars, everyone thinks you're dead, and you're in a desperate fight against time and the elements to stay alive. But, you know, other than that edge case, there's no reason.

So I finally decided I'd just take the hit. I'll be losing some air every time I enter or exit a pop-tent. The good news is each pop-tent has an air feed valve on the outside. Remember, these are emergency shelters. The occupants might need air, and you can provide it from a rover by hooking up an air line. It's nothing more than a tube that equalizes the rover's air with the pop-tent's.

The Hab and the rovers use the same valve and tubing standards, so I was able to attach the pop-tents directly to the Hab. That'll automatically replenish the air I lose with my entries and exits (what we NASA folk call ingress and egress).

NASA was not screwing around with these emergency tents. The moment I pushed the panic button in the rover, there was an ear-popping whoosh as the pop-tent fired out, attached to the rover airlock. It took about two seconds.

I closed the airlock from the rover side and ended up with a nice, isolated pop-tent. Setting up the equalizer hose was trivial (for once I'm using equipment the way it was designed to be used). Then, after a few trips through the airlock (with the air-loss automatically equalized by the Hab) I got the dirt in.

I repeated the process for the other tent. Everything went really easily.

Sigh . . . water.

In high school, I played a lot of Dungeons and Dragons. (You may not have guessed this botanist/mechanical engineer was a bit of a nerd in high school, but indeed I was.) In the game I played a cleric. One of the magic spells I could cast was "Create Water." I always thought it was a really stupid spell, and I never used it. Boy, what I wouldn't give to be able to do that in real life right now.

Anyway. That's a problem for tomorrow.

For tonight, I have to get back to *Three's Company*. I stopped last night in the middle of the episode where Mr. Roper saw something and took it out of context.

LOG ENTRY: SOL 30

I have an idiotically dangerous plan for getting the water I need. And boy, do I mean *dangerous*. But I don't have much choice. I'm out of ideas and I'm due for another dirt-doubling in a few days. When I do the final doubling, I'll be doubling on to all that new soil I've brought in. If I don't wet it first, it'll just die.

There isn't a lot of water here on Mars. There's ice at the poles, but they're too far away. If I want water, I'll have to make it from scratch. Fortunately, I know the recipe: Take hydrogen. Add oxygen. Burn.

Let's take them one at a time. I'll start with oxygen.

I have a fair bit of O_2 reserves, but not enough to make 250 liters of water. Two high-pressure tanks at one end of the Hab are my entire supply (plus the air in the Hab of course). They each contain 25 liters of liquid O_2. The Hab would use them only in an emergency; it has the oxygenator to balance the atmosphere. The reason the O_2 tanks are here is to feed the space suits and rovers.

Anyway, the reserve oxygen would only be enough to make 100 liters of water (50 liters of O_2 makes 100 liters of molecules that only have one O each). That would mean no EVAs for me, and no emergency reserves. And it would make less than half the water I need. Out of the question.

But oxygen's easier to find on Mars than you might think. The atmosphere is 95 percent CO_2. And I happen to have a machine whose sole purpose is liberating oxygen from CO_2. Yay, oxygenator!

One problem: The atmosphere is very thin—less than 1 percent of the pressure on Earth. So it's hard to collect. Getting air from outside to inside is nearly impossible. The whole purpose of the Hab is to keep that sort of thing from happening. The tiny amount of Martian atmosphere that enters when I use an airlock is laughable.

That's where the MAV fuel plant comes in.

My crewmates took away the MAV weeks ago. But the bottom half of it stayed behind. NASA isn't in the habit of putting unnecessary mass into orbit. The landing gear, ingress ramp, and fuel plant are still here. Remember how the MAV made its own fuel with help from the Martian atmosphere? Step one of that is to collect CO_2 and store it in a high-pressure vessel. Once I get the fuel plant hooked up to the Hab's power, it'll give me half a liter of liquid CO_2 per hour, indefinitely. After ten sols it'll have made 125 liters of CO_2, which will make 125 liters of O_2 after I feed it through the oxygenator.

That's enough to make 250 liters of water. So I have a plan for oxygen.

The hydrogen will be a little trickier.

I considered raiding the hydrogen fuel cells, but I need those batteries to maintain power at night. If I don't have that, it'll get too cold. I could bundle up, but the cold would kill my crops. And each fuel cell has only a small amount of H_2 anyway. It's just not worth sacrificing so much usefulness for so little gain. The one thing I have going for me is that energy is not a problem. I don't want to give that up.

So I'll have to go a different route.

I often talk about the MAV. But now I want to talk about the MDV.

During the most terrifying twenty-three minutes of my life, four of my crewmates and I tried not to shit ourselves while Martinez piloted the MDV down to the surface. It was kind of like being in a tumble-dryer.

First, we descended from *Hermes*, and decelerated our orbital velocity so we could start falling properly. Everything was smooth until we hit the atmosphere. If you think turbulence is rough in a jetliner going 720 kph, just imagine what it's like at 28,000 kph.

Several staged sets of chutes deployed automatically to slow our descent, then Martinez manually piloted us to the ground, using the thrusters to slow descent and control our lateral motion. He'd trained for this for years, and he did his job extraordinarily well. He exceeded all plausible expectations of landings, putting us just nine meters from the target. The guy just plain owned that landing.

Thanks, Martinez! You may have saved my life!

Not because of the perfect landing, but because he left so much fuel behind. Hundreds of liters of unused hydrazine. Each molecule of hydrazine has four hydrogen atoms in it. So each liter of hydrazine has enough hydrogen for *two* liters of water.

I did a little EVA today to check. The MDV has 292 liters of juice left in the tanks. Enough to make almost 600 liters of water! Way more than I need!

There's just one catch: Liberating hydrogen from hydrazine is . . . well . . . it's how rockets work. It's really, really hot. And dangerous. If I do it in an oxygen atmosphere, the hot and newly liberated hydrogen will explode. There'll be a lot of H_2O at the end, but I'll be too dead to appreciate it.

At its root, hydrazine is pretty simple. The Germans used it as far back as World War II for rocket-assisted fighter fuel (and occasionally blew themselves up with it).

All you have to do is run it over a catalyst (which I can extract from the MDV engine) and it will turn into nitrogen and hydrogen. I'll spare you the chemistry, but the end result is that five molecules of hydrazine becomes five molecules of harmless N_2 and ten molecules of lovely H_2. During this process, it goes through an intermediate step of being ammonia. Chemistry, being the sloppy bitch it is, ensures there'll be some ammonia that doesn't react with the hydrazine, so it'll just stay ammonia. You like the smell of ammonia? Well, it'll be prevalent in my increasingly hellish existence.

The chemistry is on my side. The question now is how do I actually make this reaction happen slowly, and how do I collect the hydrogen? The answer is: I don't know.

I suppose I'll think of something. Or die.

Anyway, much more important: I simply can't abide the replacement of Chrissy with Cindy. *Three's Company* may never be the same after this fiasco. Time will tell.

CHAPTER 4

LOG ENTRY: SOL 32

So I ran into a bunch of problems with my water plan.

My idea is to make 600 liters of water (limited by the hydrogen I can get from the hydrazine). That means I'll need 300 liters of liquid O_2.

I can create the O_2 easily enough. It takes twenty hours for the MAV fuel plant to fill its 10-liter tank with CO_2. The oxygenator can turn it into O_2, then the atmospheric regulator will see the O_2 content in the Hab is high, and pull it out of the air, storing it in the main O_2 tanks. They'll fill up, so I'll have to transfer O_2 over to the rovers' tanks and even the space suit tanks as necessary.

But I can't create it very quickly. At half a liter of CO_2 per hour, it will take twenty-five days to make the oxygen I need. That's longer than I'd like.

Also, there's the problem of storing the hydrogen.

The air tanks of the Hab, the rovers, and all the space suits add up to exactly 374 liters of storage. To hold all the materials for water, I would need a whopping 900 liters of storage.

I considered using one of the rovers as a "tank." It would certainly be big enough, but it just isn't designed to hold in that much pressure. It's made to hold (you guessed it) one atmosphere. I need vessels that can hold fifty times that much. I'm sure a rover would burst.

The best way to store the ingredients of water is to make them be water. So what's what I'll have to do.

The concept is simple, but the execution will be incredibly dangerous.

Every twenty hours, I'll have 10 liters of CO_2 thanks to the MAV fuel plant. I'll vent it into the Hab via the highly scientific method of detaching the tank from the MAV landing struts, bringing it into the Hab, then opening the valve until it's empty.

The oxygenator will turn it into oxygen in its own time.

Then, I'll release hydrazine, *very slowly*, over the iridium catalyst, to turn it into N_2 and H_2. I'll direct the hydrogen to a small area and burn it.

As you can see, this plan provides many opportunities for me to die in a fiery explosion.

Firstly, hydrazine is some serious death. If I make any mistakes, there'll be nothing left but the "Mark Watney Memorial Crater" where the Hab once stood.

Presuming I don't fuck up with the hydrazine,

there's still the matter of burning hydrogen. I'm going to be setting a fire. In the Hab. On purpose.

If you asked every engineer at NASA what the worst scenario for the Hab was, they'd all answer "fire." If you asked them what the result would be, they'd answer "death by fire."

But if I can pull it off, I'll be making water continuously, with no need to store hydrogen or oxygen. It'll be mixed into the atmosphere as humidity, but the water reclaimer will pull it out.

I don't even have to perfectly match the hydrazine end of it with the fuel plant CO_2 part. There's plenty of oxygen in the Hab, and plenty more in reserve. I just need to make sure not to make so much water I run myself out of O_2.

I hooked up the MAV fuel plant to the Hab's power supply. Fortunately they both use the same voltage. It's chugging away, collecting CO_2 for me.

Half-ration for dinner. All I accomplished today was thinking up a plan that'll kill me, and that doesn't take much energy.

I'm going to finish off the last of *Three's Company* tonight. Frankly, I like Mr. Furley more than the Ropers.

LOG ENTRY: SOL 33

This may be my last entry.

I've known since Sol 6 there was a good chance I'd die here. But I figured it would be when I ran out of food. I didn't think it would be this early.

I'm about to fire up the hydrazine.

Our mission was designed knowing that anything might need maintenance, so I have plenty of tools. Even in a space suit, I was able to pry the access panels off the MDV and get at the six hydrazine tanks. I set them in the shadow of a rover to keep them from heating up too much. There's more shade and a cooler temperature near the Hab, but fuck that. If they're going to blow up, they can blow up a rover, not my house.

Then I pried out the reaction chamber. It took some work and I cracked the damn thing in half, but I got it out. Lucky for me I don't need a proper fuel reaction. In fact, I really, super-duper don't want a proper fuel reaction.

I brought the reaction chamber in. I briefly considered only bringing one tank of hydrazine in at a time to reduce risk. But some back-of-the-napkin math told me even one tank was enough to blow the whole Hab up. So I brought them all in. Why not?

The tanks have manual vent valves. I'm not 100 percent sure what they're for. Certainly we were never expected to use them. I think they're there to release pressure during the many quality checks done during construction and before fueling. Whatever the reason, I have valves to work with. All it takes is a wrench.

I liberated a spare water hose from the water reclaimer. With some thread torn out of a uniform (sorry, Johanssen), I attached it to the valve output. Hydrazine is a liquid, so all I have to do is lead it to the reaction chamber (more of a "reaction bowl" now).

Meanwhile, the MAV fuel plant is still working. I've already brought in one tank of CO_2, vented it, and returned it for refilling.

So there are no more excuses. It's time to start making water.

If you find the charred remains of the Hab, it

means I did something wrong. I'm copying this log over to both rovers, so it's more likely it'll survive.

Here goes nothin'.

LOG ENTRY: SOL 33 (2)

Well, I didn't die.

First thing I did was put on the inner lining of my EVA suit. Not the bulky suit itself, just the inner clothing I wear under it, including the gloves and booties. Then I got an oxygen mask from the medical supplies and some lab goggles from Vogel's chem kit. Almost all of my body was protected and I was breathing canned air.

Why? Because hydrazine is *very* toxic. If I breathe too much of it, I'll get major lung problems. If I get it on my skin, I'll have chemical burns for the rest of my life. I wasn't taking any chances.

I turned the valve until a trickle of hydrazine came out. I let one drop fall into the iridium bowl.

It undramatically sizzled and disappeared.

But hey, that's what I wanted. I just freed up hydrogen and nitrogen. Yay!

One thing I have in abundance here are bags. They're not much different from kitchen trash bags, though I'm sure they cost $50,000 because of NASA.

In addition to being our commander, Lewis was also the geologist. She was going to collect rock and soil samples from all over the operational area (10-kilometer radius). Weight limits restricted how much she could actually bring back to Earth, so she was going to collect first, then sort out the most interesting 50 kilograms to take home. The bags were to store and tag the samples. Some are smaller than a Ziploc, while others are as big as a Hefty lawn and leaf bag.

Also, I have duct tape. Ordinary duct tape, like you buy at a hardware store. Turns out even NASA can't improve on duct tape.

I cut up a few Hefty-sized bags and taped them together to make a sort of tent. Really it was more of a supersized bag. I was able to cover the whole table where my hydrazine mad scientist setup was. I put a few knickknacks on the table to keep the plastic out of the iridium bowl. Thankfully, the bags are clear, so I can still see what's going on.

Next, I sacrificed a space suit to the cause. I needed an air hose. I have a surplus of space suits, after all. A total of six; one for each crew member. So I don't mind murdering one of them.

I cut a hole in the top of the plastic and duct-taped the hose in place. Nice seal, I think.

With some more string from Johannsen's clothing, I hung the other end of the hose from the top of the Hab's dome by two angled threads (to keep them well clear of the hose opening). Now I had a little chimney. The hose was about one centimeter wide. Hopefully a good aperture.

The hydrogen will be hot after the reaction, and it'll want to go up. So I'll let it go up the chimney, then burn it as it comes out.

Then I had to invent fire.

NASA put a lot of effort into making sure nothing here can burn. Everything is made of metal or flame-retardant plastic and the uniforms are synthetic. I needed something that could hold a flame, some kind of pilot light. I don't have the skills to keep enough H_2 flowing to feed a flame without killing myself. Too narrow a margin there.

After a search of everyone's personal items (hey, if they wanted privacy, they shouldn't have abandoned me on Mars with their stuff) I found my answer.

Martinez is a devout Catholic. I knew that. What I didn't know was he brought along a small wooden cross. I'm sure NASA gave him shit about it, but I also know Martinez is one stubborn son of a bitch.

I chipped his sacred religious item into long splinters using a pair of pliers and a screwdriver. I figure if there's a God, He won't mind, considering the situation I'm in.

If ruining the only religious icon I have leaves me vulnerable to Martian vampires, I'll have to risk it.

There were plenty of wires and batteries around to make a spark. But you can't just ignite wood with a small electric spark. So I collected ribbons of bark from local palm trees, then got a couple of sticks and rubbed them together to create enough friction to . . .

No not really. I vented pure oxygen at the stick and gave it a spark. It lit up like a match.

With my mini-torch in hand, I started a slow hydrazine flow. It sizzled on the iridium and disappeared. Soon I had short bursts of flame sputtering from the chimney.

The main thing I had to watch was the temperature. Hydrazine breaking down is extremely exothermic. So I did it a bit at a time, constantly watching the readout of a thermocouple I'd attached to the iridium chamber.

Point is, the process worked!

Each hydrazine tank holds a little over 50 liters, which would be enough to make 100 liters of water. I'm limited by my oxygen production, but I'm all excited now, so I'm willing to use half my reserves. Long story short, I'll stop when the tank is half-empty, and I'll have 50 liters of water at the end!

LOG ENTRY: SOL 34

Well, that took a really long time. I've been at it all night with the hydrazine. But I got the job done.

I could have finished faster, but I figured caution's best when setting fire to rocket fuel in an enclosed space.

Boy is this place a tropical jungle now, I'll tell ya.

It's almost 30°C in here, and humid as all hell. I just dumped a ton of heat and 50 liters of water into the air.

During this process, the poor Hab had to be the mother of a messy toddler. It's been replacing the oxygen I've used, and the water reclaimer is trying to get the humidity down to sane levels. Nothing to be done about the heat. There's actually no air-conditioning in the Hab. Mars is cold. Getting rid of excess heat isn't something we expected to deal with.

I've now grown accustomed to hearing the alarms blare at all times. The fire alarm has finally stopped, now that there's no more fire. The low oxygen alarm should stop soon. The high humidity alarm will take a little longer. The water reclaimer has its work cut out for it today.

For a moment, there was yet another alarm. The water reclaimer's main tank was full. Booyah! That's the kind of problem I want to have!

Remember the space suit I vandalized yesterday? I hung it on its rack and carried buckets of water to it from the reclaimer. It can hold an atmosphere of air in. It should be able to handle a few buckets of water.

Man I'm tired. Been up all night, and it's time to sleep. But I'll drift off to dreamland in the best mood I've been in since Sol 6.

Things are finally going my way. In fact, they're going great! I have a chance to live after all!

LOG ENTRY: SOL 37

I am fucked, and I'm gonna die!

Okay, calm down. I'm sure I can get around this.

I'm writing this log to you, dear future Mars archaeologist, from Rover 2. You may wonder why I'm not in the Hab right now. Because I fled in terror, that's why! And I'm not sure what the hell to do next.

I guess I should explain what happened. If this is my last entry, you'll at least know why.

Over the past few days, I've been happily making water. It's been going swimmingly. (See what I did there? "Swimmingly"?)

I even beefed up the MAV fuel plant compressor. It was very technical (I increased the voltage to the pump). So I'm making water even faster now.

After my initial burst of 50 liters, I decided to settle down and just make it at the rate I get O_2. I'm not willing to go below a 25-liter reserve. So when I dip too low, I stop dicking with hydrazine until I get the O_2 back up to well above 25 liters.

Important note: When I say I made 50 liters of water, that's an assumption. I didn't *reclaim* 50 liters of water. The additional soil I'd filled the Hab with was extremely dry and greedily sucked up a lot of the humidity. That's where I want the water to go anyway, so I'm not worried, and I wasn't surprised when the reclaimer didn't get anywhere near 50 liters.

I get 10 liters of CO_2 every fifteen hours now that I souped up the pump. I've done this process four times. My math tells me that, including my initial 50-liter burst, I should have added 130 liters of water to the system.

Well my math was a damn liar!

I'd gained 70 liters in the water reclaimer and the space-suit-turned-water-tank. There's plenty of condensation on the walls and domed roof, and the soil is certainly absorbing its fair share. But that doesn't account for 60 liters of missing water. Something was wrong.

That's when I noticed the other O_2 tank.

The Hab has two reserve O_2 tanks. One on each side of the structure, for safety reasons. The Hab can decide which one to use whenever it wants. Turns out it's been topping off the atmosphere from Tank 1. But when I add O_2 to the system (via the oxygenator), the Hab evenly distributes the gain between the two tanks. Tank 2 has been slowly gaining oxygen.

That's not a problem. The Hab is just doing its job. But it does mean I've been gaining O_2 over time. Which means I'm not consuming it as fast as I thought.

At first, I thought "Yay! More oxygen! Now I can make water faster!" But then a more disturbing thought occurred to me.

Follow my logic: I'm gaining O_2. But the amount I'm bringing in from outside is constant. So the only way to "gain" it is to be using less than I thought. But I've been doing the hydrazine reaction with the assumption that I was using all of it.

The only possible explanation is that I haven't been burning all the released hydrogen.

It's obvious now, in retrospect. But it never occurred to me that some of the hydrogen just wouldn't burn. It got past the flame, and went on its merry way. Damn it, Jim, I'm a botanist, not a chemist!

Chemistry is messy, so there's unburned hydrogen in the air. All around me. Mixed in with the oxygen. Just . . . hanging out. Waiting for a spark so it can *blow the Hab up!*

Once I figured this out and composed myself, I got a Ziploc-sized sample bag and waved it around a bit, then sealed it.

Then, a quick EVA to a rover, where we keep the atmospheric analyzers. Nitrogen: 22 percent. Oxygen: 9 percent. Hydrogen: 64 percent.

I've been hiding here in the rover ever since.

It's Hydrogenville in the Hab.

I'm very lucky it hasn't blown. Even a small static discharge would have led to my own private *Hindenburg.*

So, I'm here in Rover 2. I can stay for a day or two, tops, before the CO_2 filters from the rover and my space suit fill up. I have that long to figure out how to deal with this.

The Hab is now a bomb.

CHAPTER 5

LOG ENTRY: SOL 38

I'm still cowering in the rover, but I've had time to think. And I know how to deal with the hydrogen.

I thought about the atmospheric regulator. It pays attention to what's in the air and balances it. That's how the excess O_2 I've been importing ends up in the tanks. Problem is, it's just not built to pull hydrogen out of the air.

The regulator uses freeze-separation to sort out the gasses. When it decides there's too much oxygen, it starts collecting air in a tank and cooling it to 90 kelvin. That makes the oxygen turn to liquid, but leaves the nitrogen (condensation point: 77K) still gaseous. Then it stores the O_2.

But I can't get it to do that for hydrogen, because hydrogen needs to be below 21K to turn liquid. And the regulator just can't get temperatures that low. Dead end.

Here's the solution:

Hydrogen is dangerous because it can blow up. But it can only blow up if there's oxygen around. Hydrogen without oxygen is harmless. And the regulator is all about pulling oxygen out of the air.

There are four different safety interlocks that prevent the regulator from letting the Hab's oxygen content get too low. But they're designed to work against technical faults, not deliberate sabotage (bwa ha ha!).

Long story short, I can trick the regulator into pulling all the oxygen out of the Hab. Then I can wear a space suit (so I can breathe) and do whatever I want without fear of blowing up.

I'll use an O_2 tank to spray short bursts of oxygen at the hydrogen, and make a spark with a couple of wires and a battery. It'll set the hydrogen on fire, but only until the small bit of oxygen is used up.

I'll just do that over and over, in controlled bursts, until I've burned off all the hydrogen.

One tiny flaw with that plan: It'll kill my dirt.

The dirt is only viable soil because of the bacteria growing in it. If I get rid of all the oxygen, the bacteria will die. I don't have 100 billion little space suits handy.

It's half a solution anyway.

Time to take a break from thinking.

Commander Lewis was the last one to use this rover. She was scheduled to use it again on Sol 7, but she went home instead. Her personal travel kit's still in the back. Rifling through it, I found a protein bar and a personal USB, probably full of music to listen to on the drive.

Time to chow down and see what the good commander brought along for music.

LOG ENTRY SOL 38 (2)

Disco. God damn it, Lewis.

LOG ENTRY: SOL 39

I think I've got it.

Soil bacteria are used to winters. They get less active, and require less oxygen to survive. I can lower the Hab temperature to 1°C, and they'll nearly hibernate. This sort of thing happens on Earth all the time. They can survive a couple of days this way. If you're wondering how bacteria on Earth survive longer periods of cold, the answer is they don't. Bacteria from further underground where it is warmer breed upward to replace the dead ones.

They'll still need some oxygen, but not much. I think a 1 percent content will do the trick. That leaves a little in the air for the bacteria to breathe, but not enough to maintain a fire. So the hydrogen won't blow up.

But that leads to yet another problem. The potato plants won't like the plan.

They don't mind the lack of oxygen, but the cold will kill them. So I'll have to pot them (bag them, actually) and move them to a rover. They haven't even sprouted yet, so it's not like they need light.

It was surprisingly annoying to find a way to make the heat stay on when the rover's unoccupied. But I figured it out. After all, I've got nothing but time in here.

* * *

So that's the plan. First, bag the potato plants and bring them to the rover (make sure it keeps the damn heater on). Then drop the Hab temperature to 1°C. Then reduce the O_2 content to 1 percent. Then burn off the hydrogen with a battery, some wires, and a tank of O_2.

Yeah. This all sounds like a great idea with no chance of catastrophic failure.

That was sarcasm, by the way.

Well, off I go.

LOG ENTRY: SOL 40

Things weren't 100 percent successful.

They say no plan survives first contact with implementation. I'd have to agree. Here's what happened:

I summoned up the courage to return to the Hab. Once I got there, I felt a little more confident. Everything was how I'd left it. (What did I expect? Martians looting my stuff?)

It would take a while to let the Hab cool, so I started that right away by turning the temperature down to 1°C.

I bagged the potato plants, and got a chance to check up on them while I was at it. They're rooting nicely and about to sprout. One thing I hadn't accounted for was how to bring them from the Hab to the rovers.

The answer was pretty easy. I put all of them in Martinez's space suit. Then I dragged it out with me to the rover I'd set up as a temporary nursery.

Making sure to jimmy the heater to stay on, I headed back to the Hab.

By the time I got back, it was already chilly.

Down to 5°C already. Shivering and watching my breath condense in front of me, I threw on extra layers of clothes. Fortunately I'm not a very big man. Martinez's clothes fit over mine, and Vogel's fit over Martinez's. These shitty clothes were designed to be worn in a temperature-controlled environment. Even with three layers, I was still cold. I climbed into my bunk and under the covers for more warmth.

Once the temperature got to 1°C, I waited another hour, just to make sure the bacteria in the dirt got the memo that it was time to take it slow.

The next problem I ran into was the regulator. Despite my swaggering confidence, I wasn't able to outwit it. It *really* does not want to pull too much O_2 out of the air. The lowest I could get it to was 15 percent. After that, it flatly refused to go lower, and nothing I did mattered. I had all these plans about getting in and reprogramming it. But the safety protocols turned out to be in ROMs.

I can't blame it. Its whole purpose is to *prevent* the atmosphere from becoming lethal. Nobody at NASA thought, "Hey, let's allow a fatal lack of oxygen that will make everyone drop dead!"

So I had to use a more primitive plan.

The regulator uses a different set of vents for air sampling than it does for main air separation. The air that gets freeze-separated comes in through a single large vent on the main unit. But it samples the air from nine small vents that pipe back to the main unit. That way it gets a good average of the Hab, and one localized imbalance won't throw it off.

I taped up eight of the intakes, leaving only one of them active. Then I taped the mouth of a Hefty-sized bag over the neck-hole of a spacesuit

(Johanssen's this time). In the back of the bag, I poked a small hole and taped it over the remaining intake.

Then I inflated the bag with pure O_2 from the suit's tanks. "Holy shit!" the regulator thought, "I better pull O_2 out right away!"

Worked great!

I decided not to wear a space suit after all. The atmospheric pressure was going to be fine. All I needed was oxygen. So I grabbed an O_2 canister and breather mask from the medical bay. That way, I had a hell of a lot more freedom of motion. It even had a rubber band to keep it on my face!

Though I did need a space suit to monitor the actual Hab oxygen level, now that the Hab's main computer was convinced it was 100 percent O_2. Let's see . . . Martinez's space suit was in the rover. Johanssen's was outwitting the regulator. Lewis's was serving as a water tank. I didn't want to mess with mine (hey, it's custom-fitted!). That left me two space suits to work with.

I grabbed Vogel's suit and activated the internal air sensors while leaving the helmet off. Once the oxygen dropped to 12 percent, I put the breather mask on. I watched it fall further and further. When it reached 1 percent, I cut power to the regulator.

I may not be able to reprogram the regulator, but I can turn the bastard off completely.

The Hab has emergency flashlights in many locations in case of critical power failure. I tore the LED bulbs out of one and left the two frayed power wires very close together. Now, when I turned it on, I got a small spark.

Taking a canister of O_2 from Vogel's suit, I attached a strap to both ends and slung it over my shoulder. Then I attached an air line to the tank and crimped it with my thumb. I turned on a very slow trickle of O_2; small enough that it couldn't overpower the crimp.

Standing on the table with a sparker in one hand and my oxygen line in the other, I reached up and gave it a try.

And holy hell, it worked! Blowing the O_2 over the sparker, I flicked the switch on the flashlight and a wonderful jet of flame fired out of the tube. The fire alarm went off, of course. But I'd heard it so much lately, I barely noticed it anymore.

Then I did it again. And again. Short bursts. Nothing flashy. I was happy to take my time.

I was elated! This was the best plan ever! Not only was I clearing out the hydrogen, I was making more water!

Everything went great right up to the explosion.

One minute I was happily burning hydrogen; the next I was on the other side of the Hab, and a lot of stuff was knocked over. I stumbled to my feet and saw the Hab in disarray.

My first thought was: "My ears hurt like hell!"

Then I thought, "I'm dizzy," and fell to my knees. Then I fell prone. I was *that* dizzy. I groped my head with both hands, looking for a head wound I desperately hoped would not be there. Nothing seemed to be amiss.

But feeling all over my head and face revealed the true problem. My oxygen mask had been ripped off in the blast. I was breathing nearly pure nitrogen.

The floor was covered in junk from all over the Hab. No hope of finding the medical O_2 tank.

No hope of finding anything in this mess before I passed out.

Then I saw Lewis's suit hanging right where it belonged. It hadn't moved in the blast. It was heavy to start with and had 70 liters of water in it.

I rushed over, quickly cranked on the O_2, and stuck my head into the neck hole (I'd removed the helmet long ago, for easy access to the water). I breathed a bit until the dizziness faded, then took a deep breath and held it.

Still holding my breath, I glanced over to the space suit and Hefty bag I'd used to outsmart the regulator. The bad news is I'd never removed them. The good news is the explosion removed them. Eight of the nine intakes for the regulator were still bagged, but this one would at least tell the truth.

Stumbling over to the regulator, I turned it back on.

After a two-second boot process (it was made to start up fast for obvious reasons), it immediately identified the problem.

The shrill low-oxygen alarm blared throughout the Hab as the regulator dumped pure oxygen into the atmosphere as fast as it safely could. *Separating* oxygen from the atmosphere is difficult and time-consuming, but *adding* it is as simple as opening a valve.

I clambered over debris back to Lewis's space suit and put my head back in for more good air. Within three minutes, the regulator had brought the Hab oxygen back up to par.

I noticed for the first time how burned my clothing was. It was a good time to be wearing three layers of clothes. Mostly the damage was on my sleeves. The outer layer was gone. The middle layer was singed and burned clean through in places. The inner layer, my own uniform, was in reasonably good shape. Looks like I lucked out again.

Also, glancing at the Hab's main computer, I saw the temperature had gone up to 15°C. Something very hot and very explodey had happened, and I wasn't sure what. Or how.

And that's where I am now. Wondering what the hell happened.

After all that work and getting blown up, I'm exhausted. Tomorrow I'll have to do a million equipment checks and try to figure out what exploded, but for now I just want to sleep.

I'm in the rover again tonight. Even with the hydrogen gone, I'm reluctant to hang out in a Hab that has a history of exploding for no reason. Plus, I can't be sure there isn't a leak.

This time, I brought a proper meal, and something to listen to that isn't disco.

LOG ENTRY: SOL 41

I spent the day running full diagnostics on every system in the Hab. It was incredibly boring, but my survival depends on these machines, so it had to be done. I can't just assume an explosion did no long-term damage.

I did the most critical tests first. Number one was the integrity of the Hab canvas. I felt pretty confident it was in good shape, because I'd spent a few hours asleep in the rover before returning to the Hab, and the pressure was still good. The computer reported no change in pressure over that time, other than a minor fluctuation based on temperature.

Then I checked the oxygenator. If that stops working and I can't fix it, I'm a dead man. No problems.

Then the atmospheric regulator. Again, no problem.

Heating unit, primary battery array, O_2 and N_2 storage tanks, water reclaimer, all three airlocks, lighting systems, main computer . . . on and on I went, feeling better and better as each system proved to be in perfect working order.

Got to hand it to NASA. They don't screw around when making this stuff.

Then came the critical part . . . checking the dirt. I took a few samples from all over the Hab (remember, it's all dirt flooring now) and made slides.

With shaking hands, I put a slide into the microscope and brought the image up on-screen. There they were! Healthy, active bacteria doing their thing! Looks like I won't be starving to death on Sol 400 after all. I plopped down in a chair and let my breathing return to normal.

Then I set about cleaning up the mess. And I had a lot of time to think about what had happened.

So what happened? Well, I have a theory.

According to the main computer, during the blast, the internal pressure spiked to 1.4 atmospheres, and the temperature rose to 15°C in under a second. But the pressure quickly subsided back to 1 atm. This would make sense if the atmospheric regulator were on, but I'd cut power to it.

The temperature remained at 15°C for some time afterward, so any heat expansion should still have been present. But the pressure dropped down again, so where did that extra pressure go? Raising the temperature and keeping the same number of atoms inside should permanently raise the pressure. But it didn't.

I quickly realized the answer. The hydrogen (the only available thing to burn) combined with oxygen (hence combustion) and became water. Water is a thousand times as dense as a gas. So the heat added to the pressure, and the transformation of hydrogen and oxygen into water brought it back down again.

The million dollar question is, where the hell did the oxygen come from? The whole plan was to limit oxygen and keep an explosion from happening. And it was working for quite a while before blowing up.

I think I have my answer. And it comes down to me brain-farting. Remember when I decided not to wear a space suit? That decision almost killed me.

The medical O_2 tank mixes pure oxygen with surrounding air, then feeds it to you through a mask. The mask stays on your face with a little rubber band that goes around the back of your neck. Not an airtight seal.

I know what you're thinking. The mask leaked oxygen. But no. I was breathing the oxygen. When I was inhaling, I made a nearly airtight seal with the mask by sucking it to my face.

The problem was *exhaling*. Do you know how much oxygen you absorb out of the air when you take a normal breath? I don't know either, but it's not 100 percent. Every time I exhaled, I added more oxygen to the system.

It just didn't occur to me. But it should have. If your lungs grabbed up all the oxygen, mouth-to-mouth resuscitation wouldn't work. I'm such a dumb-ass for not thinking of it! And my dumbassery almost got me killed!

I'm really going to have to be more careful.

It's a good thing I burned off most of the hydrogen before the explosion. Otherwise that would have been the end. As it is, the explosion wasn't strong enough to pop the Hab. Though it was strong enough to almost blast my eardrums in.

This all started with me noticing a 60-liter shortfall in water production. Between deliberate burn-off and a bit of unexpected explosion, I'm back on track. The water reclaimer did its job last night and pulled 50 liters of the newly created water out of the air. It's storing it in Lewis's spacesuit, which I'll call "The Cistern" from now on, because it sounds cooler. The other 10 liters of water was directly absorbed by the dry soil.

Lots of physical labor today. I've earned a full meal. And to celebrate my first night back in the Hab, I'll kick back and watch some shitty twentieth-century TV courtesy of Commander Lewis.

The Dukes of Hazzard, eh? Let's give it a whirl.

LOG ENTRY: SOL 42

I slept in late today. I deserved it. After four nights of awful sleep in the rover, my bunk felt like the softest, most profoundly beautiful feather bed ever made.

Eventually, I dragged my ass out of bed and finished some post-explosion cleanup.

I moved the potato plants back in today. And just in time, too. They're sprouting. They look healthy and happy. This isn't chemistry, medicine, bacteriology, nutrition analysis, explosion dynamics, or any other shit I've been doing lately. This is *botany*. I'm sure I can at least grow some plants without screwing up.

Right?

You know what really sucks? I've only made 130 liters of water. I have another 470 liters to go. You'd think after almost killing myself *twice*, I'd be able to stop screwing around with hydrazine. But nope. I'll be reducing hydrazine and burning hydrogen in the Hab, every ten hours, for another ten days. I'll do a better job of it from now on. Instead of counting on a clean reaction, I'll do frequent "hydrogen cleanings" with a small flame. It'll burn off gradually instead of building up to kill-Mark levels.

I'll have a lot of dead time. Ten hours for each tank of CO_2 to finish filling. It only takes twenty minutes to reduce the hydrazine and burn the hydrogen. I'll spend the rest of the time watching TV.

And seriously . . . It's clear that General Lee can outrun a police cruiser. Why doesn't Rosco just go to the Duke farm and arrest them when they're *not* in the car?

CHAPTER 6

VENKAT KAPOOR returned to his office, dropped his briefcase on the floor, and collapsed into his leather chair. He took a moment to look out the windows. His office in Building 1 afforded him a commanding view of the large park in the center of the Johnson Space Center complex. Beyond that, dozens of scattered buildings dominated the view all the way to Mud Lake in the distance.

Glancing at his computer screen, he noted forty-seven unread e-mails urgently demanding his attention. They could wait. Today had been a sad day. Today was the memorial service for Mark Watney.

The President had given a speech, praising Watney's bravery and sacrifice, and the quick actions of Commander Lewis in getting everyone else to safety. Commander Lewis and the surviving crew, via long-range communication from *Hermes*, gave eulogies for their departed comrade from deep space. They had another ten months of travel yet to endure.

The administrator had given a speech as well, reminding everyone that space flight is incredibly dangerous, and that we will not back down in the face of adversity.

They'd asked Venkat if he was willing to make a speech. He'd declined. What was the point? Watney was dead. Nice words from the director of Mars operations wouldn't bring him back.

"You okay, Venk?" came a familiar voice from the doorway.

Venkat swiveled around. "Guess so," he said.

Teddy Sanders swept a rogue thread off his otherwise immaculate blazer. "You could have given a speech."

"I didn't want to. You know that."

"Yeah, I know. I didn't want to, either. But I'm the administrator of NASA. It's kind of expected. You sure you're okay?"

"Yeah, I'll be fine."

"Good," Teddy said, adjusting his cuff links. "Let's get back to work, then."

"Sure." Venkat shrugged. "Let's start with you authorizing my satellite time."

Teddy leaned against the wall with a sigh. "This again."

"Yes," Venkat said. "This again. What is the problem?"

"Okay, run me through it. What, exactly, are you after?"

Venkat leaned forward. "Ares 3 was a failure, but we can salvage something from it. We're funded for five Ares missions. I think we can get Congress to fund a sixth."

"I don't know, Venk . . ."

"It's simple, Teddy." Venkat pressed on. "They evac'd after six sols. There's almost an entire mission's worth of supplies up there. It would only cost a fraction of a normal mission. It normally takes fourteen presupply probes to prep a site. We might be able to send what's missing in three. Maybe two."

"Venk, the site got hit by a 175 kph sandstorm. It'll be in really bad shape."

"That's why I want imagery," Venkat said. "I just need a couple of shots of the site. We could learn a lot."

"Like what? You think we'd send people to Mars without being sure everything was in perfect working order?"

"Everything doesn't have to be perfect," Venkat said quickly. "Whatever's broken, we'd send replacements for."

"How will we know from imagery what's broken?"

"It's just a first step. They evac'd because the wind was a threat to the MAV, but the Hab can withstand a lot more punishment. It might still be in one piece.

"And it'll be really obvious. If it popped, it'd completely blow out and collapse. If it's still standing, then everything inside will be fine. And the rovers are solid. They can take any sandstorm Mars has to offer. Just let me take a look, Teddy, that's all I want."

Teddy paced to the windows and stared out at the vast expanse of buildings. "You're not the only guy who wants satellite time, you know. We have Ares 4 supply missions coming up. We need to concentrate on Schiaparelli crater."

"I don't get it, Teddy. What's the problem

here?" Venkat asked. "I'm talking about securing us another mission. We have twelve satellites in orbit around Mars; I'm sure you can spare one or two for a couple of hours. I can give you the windows for each one when they'll be at the right angle for Ares 3 shots—"

"It's not about satellite time, Venk," Teddy interrupted.

Venkat froze. "Then . . . but . . . what . . ."

Teddy turned to face him. "We're a public domain organization. There's no such thing as secret or secure information here."

"So?"

"Any imagery we take goes directly to the public."

"Again, so?"

"Mark Watney's body will be within twenty meters of the Hab. Maybe partially buried in sand, but still very visible, and with a comm antenna sticking out of his chest. Any images we take will show that."

Venkat stared. Then glared. "*This* is why you denied my imagery requests for two months?"

"Venk, come on—"

"Really, Teddy?" he said. "You're afraid of a PR problem?"

"The media's obsession with Watney's death is finally starting to taper off," Teddy said evenly. "It's been bad press after bad press for two months. Today's memorial gives people closure, and the media can move on to some other story. The last thing we want is to dredge everything back up."

"So what do we do, then? He's not going to decompose. He'll be there forever."

"Not forever," Teddy said. "Within a year, he'll be covered in sand from normal weather activity."

"A year?" Venkat said, rising to his feet. "That's ludicrous. We can't wait a year for this."

"Why not? Ares 4 won't even launch for another five years. Plenty of time."

Venkat took a deep breath and thought for a moment.

"Okay, consider this: Sympathy for Watney's family is really high. Ares 6 could bring the body back. We don't say that's the *purpose* of the mission, but we make it clear that would be part of it. If we framed it that way, we'd get more support in Congress. But not if we wait a year. In a year, people won't care anymore."

Teddy rubbed his chin. "Hmm . . ."

■■■

MINDY PARK stared at the ceiling. She had little else to do. The three a.m. shift was pretty dull. Only a constant stream of coffee kept her awake.

Monitoring the status of satellites around Mars had sounded like an exciting proposition when she took the transfer. But the satellites tended to take care of themselves. Her job turned out to be sending e-mails as imagery became available.

"Master's degree in mechanical engineering," she muttered. "And I'm working in an all-night photo booth."

She sipped her coffee.

A flicker on her screen announced that another set of images was ready for dispatch. She checked the name on the work order. Venkat Kapoor.

She posted the data directly to internal servers and composed an e-mail to Dr. Kapoor. As she entered the latitude and longitude of the image, she recognized the numbers.

"31.2°N, 28.5°W . . . Acidalia Planitia . . . Ares 3?"

Out of curiosity, she brought up the first of the seventeen images.

As she'd suspected, it was the Ares 3 site. She'd heard they were going to image it. Slightly ashamed of herself, she scoured the image for any sign of Mark Watney's dead body. After a minute of fruitless searching, she was simultaneously relieved and disappointed.

She moved on to perusing the rest of the image. The Hab was intact; Dr. Kapoor would be happy to see that.

She brought the coffee mug to her lips, then froze.

"Um . . . ," she mumbled to herself. "Uhhh . . ."

She brought up the NASA intranet and navigated through the site to the specifics of the Ares missions. After some quick research, she picked up her phone.

"Hey, this is Mindy Park at SatCon. I need the mission logs for Ares 3, where can I get 'em? . . . Uh huh . . . uh-huh . . . Okay . . . Thanks."

After some more time on the intranet, she leaned back in her seat. She no longer needed the coffee to keep awake.

Picking up the phone again, she said, "Hello, Security? This is Mindy Park in SatCon. I need the emergency contact number for Dr. Venkat Kapoor. . . . Yes it's an emergency."

■ ■ ■

MINDY FIDGETED in her seat as Venkat trudged in. To have the director of Mars operations visiting SatCon was unusual. Seeing him in jeans and a T-shirt was even more unusual.

"You Mindy Park?" he asked with the scowl of a man operating on two hours of sleep.

"Yes," she quavered. "Sorry to drag you in."

"I'm assuming you had a good reason. So?"

"Um," she said, looking down. "Um, it's. Well. The imagery you ordered. Um. Come here and look."

He pulled another chair to her station and seated himself. "Is this about Watney's body? Is that why you're shook up?"

"Um, no," she said. "Um. Well . . . uh." She winced at her own awkwardness and pointed to the screen.

Venkat inspected the image. "Looks like the Hab's in one piece. That's good news. Solar array looks good. The rovers are okay, too. Main dish isn't around. No surprise there. What's the big emergency?"

"Um," she said, touching her finger to the screen. "That."

Venkat leaned in and looked closer. Just below the Hab, beside the rovers, two white circles sat in the sand. "Hmm. Looks like Hab canvas. Maybe the Hab didn't do well after all? I guess pieces got torn off and—"

"Um," she interrupted. "They look like rover pop-tents."

Venkat looked again. "Hmm. Probably right."

"How'd they get set up?" Mindy asked.

Venkat shrugged. "Commander Lewis probably ordered them deployed during the evac. Not a bad idea. Have the emergency shelters ready in case the MAV didn't work and the Hab breached."

"Yeah, um," Mindy said, opening a document on her computer, "this is the entire mission log for Sols 1 through 6. From MDV touchdown to MAV emergency liftoff."

"Okay, and?"

"I read through it. Several times. They never threw out the pop-tents." Her voice cracked at the last word.

"Well, uh . . . ," Venkat said, furrowing his brow. "They obviously did, but it didn't make it into the log."

"They activated two emergency pop-tents and never told anyone?"

"Hmm. That doesn't make a lot of sense, no. Maybe the storm messed with the rovers and the tents autodeployed."

"So after autodeploying, they detached themselves from the rovers and lined up next to each other twenty meters away?"

Venkat looked back to the image. "Well obviously they activated somehow."

"Why are the solar cells clean?" Mindy said, fighting back tears. "There was a huge sandstorm. Why isn't there sand all over them?"

"A good wind could have done it?" Venkat said, unsure.

"Did I mention I never found Watney's body?" she said, sniffling.

Venkat's eyes widened as he stared at the picture. "Oh . . . ," he said quietly. "Oh God . . ."

Mindy put her hands over her face and sobbed quietly.

■ ■ ■

"FUCK!" Annie Montrose said. "You have got to be fucking kidding me!"

Teddy glared across his immaculate mahogany desk at his director of media relations. "Not helping, Annie."

He turned to his director of Mars operations. "How sure are we of this?"

"Nearly a hundred percent," Venkat said.

"Fuck!" Annie said.

Teddy moved a folder on his desk slightly to the right so it would line up with his mouse pad. "It is what it is. We have to deal with it."

"Do you have any idea the *magnitude* of shit storm this is gonna be?" she retorted. "You don't have to face those damn reporters every day. I do!"

"One thing at a time," Teddy said. "Venk, what makes you sure he's alive?"

"For starters, no body," Venkat explained. "Also, the pop-tents are set up. And the solar cells are clean. You can thank Mindy Park in SatCon for noticing all that, by the way.

"But," Venkat continued, "his body could have been buried in the Sol 6 storm. The pop-tents might have autodeployed and wind could have blown them around. A 30 kph windstorm some time later would have been strong enough to clean the solar cells but not strong enough to carry sand. It's not likely, but it's possible.

"So I spent the last few hours checking everything I could. Commander Lewis had two outings in Rover 2. The second was on Sol 5. According to the logs, after returning, she plugged it into the Hab for recharging. It wasn't used again, and thirteen hours later they evac'd."

He slid a picture across the desk to Teddy.

"That's one of the images from last night. As you can see, Rover 2 is facing *away* from the Hab. The charging port is in the nose, and the cable isn't long enough to reach."

Teddy absently rotated the picture to be parallel with the edges of his desk. "She must have parked it facing the Hab or she wouldn't have been able to plug it in," he said. "It's been moved since Sol 5."

"Yeah," Venkat said, sliding another picture to Teddy. "But here's the real evidence. In the lower right of the image you can see the MDV. It's been taken apart. I'm pretty sure they wouldn't have done that without telling us.

"And the clincher is on the right of the image," Venkat pointed. "The landing struts of the MAV. Looks like the fuel plant has been completely removed, with considerable damage to the struts in the process. There's just no way that could have happened before liftoff. It would have endangered the MAV way too much for Lewis to allow it."

"Hey," Annie said. "Why not talk to Lewis? Let's go to CAPCOM and ask her directly."

Rather than answer, Venkat looked to Teddy knowingly.

"Because," Teddy said, "if Watney really is alive, we don't want the Ares 3 crew to know."

"What!?" Annie said. "How can you not tell them?"

"They have another ten months on their trip home," Teddy explained. "Space travel is dangerous. They need to be alert and undistracted. They're sad that they lost a crewmate, but they'd be devastated if they found out they'd abandoned him alive."

Annie looked to Venkat. "You're on board with this?"

"It's a no-brainer," Venkat said. "Let 'em deal with that emotional trauma when they're not flying a spaceship around."

"This'll be the most talked-about event since Apollo 11," Annie said. "How will you keep it from them?"

Teddy shrugged. "Easy. We control all communication with them."

"Fuck," Annie said, opening her laptop. "When do you want to go public?"

"What's your take?" he asked.

"Mmm," Annie said. "We can hold the pics for twenty-four hours before we're required to release them. We'll need to send out a statement along with them. We don't want people working it out on their own. We'd look like assholes."

"Okay," Teddy agreed, "put together a statement."

"That'll be fun," she grumbled.

"Where do we go from here?" Teddy asked Venkat.

"Step one is communication," Venkat said. "From the pics, it's clear the comm array is ruined. We need another way to talk. Once we can talk, we can assess and make plans."

"All right," Teddy said. "Get on it. Take anyone you want from any department. Use as much overtime as you want. Find a way to talk to him. That's your only job right now."

"Got it."

"Annie, make sure nobody gets wind of this till we announce."

"Right," Annie said. "Who else knows?"

"Just the three of us and Mindy Park in SatCon," Venkat said.

"I'll have a word with her," Annie said.

Teddy stood and opened his cell phone. "I'm going to Chicago. I'll be back tomorrow."

"Why?" Annie asked.

"That's where Watney's parents live," Teddy said. "I owe them a personal explanation before it breaks on the news."

"They'll be happy to hear their son's alive," Annie said.

"Yes, he's alive," Teddy said. "But if my math is right, he's doomed to starve to death before we can possibly help him. I'm not looking forward to the conversation."

"Fuck," Annie said, thoughtfully.

■ ■ ■

"NOTHING? Nothing at all?" Venkat groaned. "Are you kidding me? You had twenty experts working for twelve hours on this. We have a multibillion-dollar communications network. You can't figure out *any* way to talk to him?"

The two men in Venkat's office fidgeted in their chairs.

"He's got no radio," said Chuck.

"Actually," said Morris, "he's got a radio, but he doesn't have a dish."

"Thing is," Chuck continued, "without the dish, a signal would have to be really strong—"

"Like, melting-the-pigeons strong," Morris supplied.

"—for him to get it," Chuck finished.

"We considered Martian satellites," Morris said. "They're way closer. But the math doesn't work out. Even SuperSurveyor 3, which has the strongest transmitter, would need to be fourteen times more powerful—"

"Seventeen times," Chuck said.

"Fourteen times," Morris asserted.

"No, it's seventeen. You forgot the amperage minimum for the heaters to keep the—"

"Guys," Venkat interrupted, "I get the idea."

"Sorry."

"Sorry."

"Sorry if I'm grumpy," Venkat said. "I got like two hours sleep last night."

"No problem," Morris said.

"Totally understandable," Chuck said.

"Okay," Venkat said. "Explain to me how a single windstorm removed our ability to talk to Ares 3."

"Failure of imagination," Chuck said.

"Totally didn't see it coming," Morris agreed.

"How many backup communications systems does an Ares mission have?" Venkat asked.

"Four," Chuck said.

"Three," Morris said.

"No, it's four," Chuck corrected.

"He said *backup* systems," Morris insisted. "That means not including the primary system."

"Oh right. Three."

"So four systems total, then," Venkat said. "Explain how we lost all four."

"Well," Chuck said, "The primary ran through the big satellite dish. It blew away in the storm. The rest of the backups were in the MAV."

"Yup," Morris agreed. "The MAV is, like, a communicating *machine*. It can talk to Earth, *Hermes*, even satellites around Mars if it has to. And it has three independent systems to make sure nothing short of a meteor strike can stop communication."

"Problem is," Chuck said, "Commander Lewis and the rest of them took the MAV when they left."

"So four independent communications systems became one. And that one broke," Morris finished.

Venkat pinched the bridge of his nose. "How could we overlook this?"

Chuck shrugged. "Never occurred to us. We never thought someone would be on Mars *without* an MAV."

"I mean, come on!" Morris said. "What are the odds?"

Chuck turned to him. "One in three, based on empirical data. That's pretty bad if you think about it."

■ ■ ■

THIS WAS going to be rough and Annie knew it. Not only did she have to deliver the biggest mea culpa in NASA's history, every second of it would be remembered forever. Every movement of her arms, intonation of her voice, and expression on her face would be seen by millions of people over and over again. Not just in the immediate press cycle, but for decades to come. Every documentary made about Watney's situation would have this clip.

She was confident that none of that concern showed on her face as she took to the podium.

"Thank you all for coming on such short notice," she said to the assembled reporters. "We have an important announcement to make. If you could all take your seats."

"What this about, Annie?" Bryan Hess from NBC asked. "Something happen with *Hermes*?"

"Please take your seats," Annie repeated.

The reporters milled about and argued over seats for a brief time, then finally settled down.

"This is a short but very important announcement," Annie said. "I won't be taking any questions at this time, but we will have a full press conference with Q&A in about an hour. We have recently reviewed satellite imagery from Mars and have confirmed that astronaut Mark Watney is, currently, still alive."

After one full second of utter silence, the room exploded with noise.

...

A WEEK after the stunning announcement, it was still the top story on every news network in the world.

"I'm getting sick of daily press conferences," Venkat whispered to Annie.

"I'm getting sick of hourly press conferences," Annie whispered back.

The two stood with countless other NASA managers and executives bunched up on the small stage in the press room. They faced a pit of hungry reporters, all desperate for any scrap of new information.

"Sorry I'm late," Teddy said, entering from the side door. He pulled some flash cards from his pocket, squared them in his hands, then cleared his throat.

"In the nine days since announcing Mark

Watney's survival, we've received a massive show of support from all sectors. We're using this shamelessly every way we can."

A small chuckle cascaded through the room.

"Yesterday, at our request, the entire SETI network focused on Mars. Just in case Watney was sending a weak radio signal. Turns out he wasn't, but it shows the level of commitment everyone has toward helping us.

"The public is engaged, and we will do our best to keep everyone informed. I've recently learned CNN will be dedicating a half-hour segment every weekday to reporting on just this issue. We will assign several members of our media relations team to that program, so the public can get the latest information as fast as possible.

"We have adjusted the orbits of three satellites to get more view time on the Ares 3 site and hope to catch an image of Mark outside soon. If we can see him outside, we will be able to draw conclusions on his physical health based on stance and activities.

"The questions are many: How long can he last? How much food does he have? Can Ares 4 rescue him? How will we talk to him? The answers to these questions are not what we want to hear.

"I can't promise we'll succeed in rescuing him, but I can promise this: The entire focus of NASA will be to bring Mark Watney home. This will be our overriding and singular obsession until he is either back on Earth or confirmed dead on Mars."

■ ■ ■

"NICE SPEECH," Venkat said as he entered Teddy's office.

"Meant every word of it," Teddy said.

"Oh, I know."

"What can I do for you, Venk?"

"I've got an idea. Well, JPL has an idea. I'm the messenger."

"I like ideas," Teddy said, gesturing to a seat.

Venkat sat down.

"We can rescue him with Ares 4. It's very risky. We ran the idea by the Ares 4 crew. Not only are they willing to do it, but now they're really pushing hard for it."

"Naturally," Teddy said. "Astronauts are inherently insane. And really noble. What's the idea?"

"Well," Venkat began, "it's in the rough stages, but JPL thinks the MDV can be misused to save him."

"Ares 4 hasn't even launched yet. Why misuse an MDV? Why not make something better?"

"We don't have time to make a custom craft. Actually, he can't even survive till Ares 4 gets there, but that's a different problem."

"So tell me about the MDV."

"JPL strips it down, loses some weight, and adds some fuel tanks. Ares 4's crew lands at the Ares 3 site, very efficiently. Then, with a full burn, and I mean a *full* burn, they can lift off again. It can't get back to orbit, but it can go to the Ares 4 site on a lateral trajectory that's, well, really scary. Then they have an MAV."

"How are they losing weight?" Teddy asked. "Don't they already have it as light as it can be?"

"By removing safety and emergency equipment."

"Wonderful," Teddy said. "So we'd be risking the lives of six more people."

"Yup," Venkat said. "It would be safer to leave the Ares 4 crew in *Hermes* and only send the pilot down with the MDV. But that would mean giving up the mission, and they'd rather risk death."

"They're astronauts," Teddy said.

"They're astronauts," Venkat confirmed.

"Well. That's a ludicrous idea and I'll never okay it."

"We'll work on it some more," Venkat said. "Try to make it safer."

"Do that. Any idea how to keep him alive for four years?"

"Nope."

"Work on that, too."

"Will do," Venkat said.

Teddy swiveled his chair and looked out the window to the sky beyond. Night was edging in. "What must it be like?" he pondered. "He's stuck out there. He thinks he's totally alone and that we all gave up on him. What kind of effect does that have on a man's psychology?"

He turned back to Venkat. "I wonder what he's thinking right now."

LOG ENTRY: SOL 61

How come Aquaman can control whales? They're mammals! Makes no sense.

CHAPTER 7

LOG ENTRY: SOL 63

I finished making water some time ago. I'm no longer in danger of blowing myself up. The potatoes are growing nicely. Nothing has conspired to kill me in weeks. And seventies TV keeps me disturbingly more entertained than it should. Things are stable here on Mars.

It's time to start thinking long-term.

Even if I find a way to tell NASA I'm alive, there's no guarantee they'll be able to save me. I need to be proactive. I need to figure out how to get to Ares 4.

Won't be easy.

Ares 4 will be landing at the Schiaparelli crater, 3200 kilometers away. In fact, their MAV is already there. I know because I watched Martinez land it.

It takes eighteen months for the MAV to make its fuel, so it's the first thing NASA sends along. Sending it forty-eight months early gives it plenty of extra time in case fuel reactions go slower than expected. But much more importantly, it means a precision soft landing can be done remotely by a pilot in orbit. Direct remote operation from Houston isn't an option; they're anywhere from four to twenty light-minutes away.

Ares 4's MAV spent eleven months getting to Mars. It left before us and got here around the same time we did. As expected, Martinez landed it beautifully. It was one of the last things we did before piling into our MDV and heading to the surface. Ahh, the good old days, when I had a crew with me.

I'm lucky. Thirty-two hundred km isn't that bad. It could have been up to 10,000 km away. And because I'm on the flattest part of Mars, the first 650 kilometers is nice, smooth terrain (Yay Acidalia Planitia!) but the rest of it is nasty, rugged, crater-pocked hell.

Obviously, I'll have to use a rover. And guess what? They weren't designed for massive overland journeys.

This is going to be a research effort, with a bunch of experimentation. I'll have to become my own little NASA, figuring out how to explore far from the Hab. The good news is I have lots of time to figure it out. Almost four years.

Some stuff is obvious. I'll need to use a rover. It'll take a long time, so I'll need to bring supplies. I'll need to recharge en route, and rovers don't have solar cells, so I'll need to steal some from the Hab's solar farm. During the trip I'll need to breathe, eat, and drink.

Lucky for me, the tech specs for everything are right here in the computer.

I'll need to trick out a rover. Basically it'll have to be a mobile Hab. I'll pick Rover 2 as my target. We have a certain bond, after I spent two days in it during the Great Hydrogen Scare of Sol 37.

There's too much shit to think about all at once. So for now, I'll just think about power.

Our mission had a 10-kilometer operational radius. Knowing we wouldn't take straight-line paths, NASA designed the rovers to go 35 kilometers on a full charge. That presumes flat, reasonable terrain. Each rover has a 9000-watt-hour battery.

Step one is to loot Rover 1's battery and install it in Rover 2. Ta-daa! I just doubled my full-charge range.

There's just one complication. Heating.

Part of the battery power goes to heating the rover. Mars is really cold. Normally, we were expected to do all EVAs in under five hours. But I'll be living in it twenty-four and a half hours a day. According to the specs, the heating equipment soaks up 400 watts. Keeping it on would eat up 9800 watt hours per day. Over half my power supply, every day!

But I do have a free source of heat: me. A couple million years of evolution gave me "warm-blooded" technology. I can just turn off the heater and wear layers. The rover has good insulation, too. It'll have to be enough; I need every bit of power.

According to my boring math, moving the rover eats 200 watt hours of juice to go 1 kilometer, so using the full 18,000 watt hours for motion (minus a negligible amount for computer, life support, etc.) gets me 90 kilometers of travel. Now we're talkin'.

I'll never *actually* get 90 kilometers on a single charge. I'll have hills to deal with, and rough terrain, sand, etc. But it's a good ballpark. It tells me that it would take *at least* 35 days of travel to get to Ares 4. It'll probably be more like 50. But that's plausible, at least.

At the rover's blazing 25 kph top speed, it'll take me three and a half hours before I run the battery down. I can drive in twilight, and save the sunny part of the day for charging. This time of year I get about thirteen hours of light. How many solar cells will I have to pilfer from the Hab's farm?

Thanks to the fine taxpayers of America, I have over 100 square meters of the most expensive solar paneling ever made. It has an astounding 10.2 percent efficiency, which is good because Mars doesn't get as much sunlight as Earth. Only 500 to 700 watts per square meter (compared to the 1400 Earth gets).

Long story short: I need to bring twenty-eight square meters of solar cell. That's fourteen panels.

I can put two stacks of seven on the roof. They'll stick out over the edges, but as long as they're secure, I'm happy. Every day, after driving, I'll spread them out then . . . wait all day. Man it'll be dull.

Well it's a start. Tomorrow's mission: transfer Rover 1's battery to Rover 2.

LOG ENTRY: SOL 64

Sometimes things are easy, and sometimes they're not. Getting the battery out of Rover 1 was easy. I removed two clamps on the undercarriage and it dropped right out. The cabling was easy to detach, too, just a couple of complicated plugs.

Attaching it to Rover 2, however, is another story. There's nowhere to put it!

The thing is *huge*. I was barely able to drag it. And that's in Mars gravity.

It's just too big. There's no room in the undercarriage for a second one. There's no room on the roof, either. That's where the solar cells will go. There's no room inside the cabin, and it wouldn't fit through the airlock anyway.

But fear not, I found a solution.

For emergencies completely unrelated to this one, NASA provided six square meters of extra Hab canvas and some really impressive resin. The same kind of resin, in fact, that saved my life on Sol 6 (the patch kit I used on the hole in my suit).

In the event of a Hab breach, everyone would run to the airlocks. Procedure was to let the Hab pop rather than die trying to prevent it. Then, we'd suit up and assess the damage. Once we found the breach, we'd seal it with the spare canvas and resin. Then reinflate and we're good as new.

The six square meters of spare canvas was a convenient one by six meters. I cut 10-centimeter-wide strips, then used them to make a sort of harness.

I used the resin and straps to make two 10-meter circumference loops. Then I put a big patch of canvas on each end. I now had poor man's saddlebags for my rover.

This is getting more and more *Wagon Train* every day.

The resin sets almost instantly. But it gets stronger if you wait an hour. So I did. Then I suited up and headed out to the rover.

I dragged the battery to the side of the rover and looped one end of the harness around it. Then I threw the other end over the roof. On the other side, I filled it with rocks. When the two weights were roughly equal, I was able to pull the rocks down and bring the battery up.

Yay!

I unplugged Rover 2's battery and plugged in Rover 1's. Then I went through the airlock to the rover and checked all systems. Everything was a-okay.

I drove the rover around a bit to make sure the harness was secure. I found a few largish rocks to drive over, just to shake things up. The harness held. Hell yeah.

For a short time, I wondered how to splice the second battery's leads into the main power supply. My conclusion was "Fuck it."

There's no need to have a continuous power supply. When Battery 1 runs out, I can get out, unplug Battery 1, and plug in Battery 2. Why not? It's a ten-minute EVA, once per day. I'd have to swap batteries again when I'm recharging them, but again, so what?

I spent the rest of the day sweeping off the solar cell farm. Soon, I shall be looting it.

LOG ENTRY: SOL 65

The solar cells were a lot easier to manage than the battery.

They're thin, light, and just lying around on the ground. And I had one additional bonus: I was the one who set them up in the first place.

Well, okay. It wasn't just me. Vogel and I worked together on it. And boy did we drill on it. We spent almost an entire *week* drilling on the solar array alone. Then we drilled more whenever they figured we had spare time. The array was mission-critical. If we broke the cells or rendered them useless, the Hab wouldn't be able to make power, and the mission would end.

You might wonder what the rest of the crew was doing while we assembled the array. They were setting up the Hab. Remember, everything in my glorious kingdom came here in boxes. We had to set it up on Sols 1 and 2.

Each solar cell is on a lightweight lattice that holds it at a 14-degree angle. I'll admit I don't know why it's a 14-degree angle. Something about maximizing solar energy. Anyway, removing the cells was simple, and the Hab can spare them. With the reduced load of only supporting one human instead of six, a 14 percent energy production loss is irrelevant.

Then it was time to stack them on the rover.

I considered removing the rock sample container. It's nothing more than a large canvas bag attached to the roof. Way too small to hold the solar cells. But after some thought I left it there, figuring it would provide a good cushion.

The cells stacked well (they were made to, for

transport to Mars), and the two stacks sat nicely on the roof. They hung over the left and right edges, but I won't be going through any tunnels, so I don't care.

With some more abuse of the emergency Hab material, I made straps and tied the cells down. The rover has external handles near the front and back. They're there to help us load rocks on the roof. They made perfect anchor points for the straps.

I stood back and admired my work. Hey, I earned it. It wasn't even noon and I was done.

I came back to the Hab, had some lunch, and worked on my crops for the rest of the sol. It's been thirty-nine sols since I planted the potatoes (which is about forty Earth days), and it was time to reap and resow.

They grew even better than I had expected. Mars has no insects, parasites, or blights to deal with, and the Hab maintains perfect growing temperature and moisture at all times.

They were small compared to the taters you'd usually eat, but that's fine. All I wanted was enough to support growing new plants.

I dug them up, being careful to leave their plants alive. Then I cut them up into small pieces with one eye each and reseeded them into new dirt. If they keep growing this well, I'll be able to last a good long time here.

After all that physical labor, I deserved a break. I rifled through Johanssen's computer today and found an endless supply of digital books. Looks like she's a big fan of Agatha Christie. The Beatles, Christie . . . I guess she's an Anglophile or something.

I remember liking Hercule Poirot TV specials

back when I was a kid. I'll start with *The Mysterious Affair at Styles*. Looks like that's the first one.

LOG ENTRY: SOL 66

The time has come (ominous musical crescendo) for some missions!

NASA gets to name their missions after gods and stuff, so why can't I? Henceforth, rover experimental missions will be "Sirius" missions. Get it? Dogs? Well if you don't, fuck you.

Sirius 1 will be tomorrow.

The mission: Start with fully charged batteries and solar cells on the roof, drive until I run out of power, and see how far I get.

I won't be an idiot. I'm not driving directly away from the Hab. I'll drive a half-kilometer stretch, back and forth. I'll be within a short walk of home at all times.

Tonight, I'll charge up both batteries so I can be ready for a little test drive tomorrow. I estimate three and a half hours of driving, so I'll need to bring fresh CO_2 filters. And, with the heater off, I'll wear three layers of clothes.

LOG ENTRY: SOL 67

Sirius 1 is complete!

More accurately, Sirius 1 was aborted after one hour. I guess you could call it a "failure," but I prefer the term "learning experience."

Things started out fine. I drove to a nice flat spot a kilometer from the Hab, then started going back and forth over a 500-meter stretch.

I quickly realized this would be a crappy test. After a few laps, I had compressed the soil enough to have a solid path. Nice, hard ground, which makes for abnormally high energy efficiency. Nothing like it would be on a long trip.

So I shook it up a bit. I drove around randomly, making sure to stay within a kilometer of the Hab. A much more realistic test.

After an hour, things started to get cold. And I mean *really cold*.

The rover's always cold when you first get in it. When you haven't disabled the heater, it warms up right away. I expected it to be cold, but Jesus Christ!

I was fine for a while. My own body heat plus three layers of clothing kept me warm, and the rover's insulation is top-notch. The heat that escaped my body just warmed up the interior. But there's no such thing as perfect insulation, and eventually the heat left to the great outdoors, while I got colder and colder.

Within an hour, I was chattering and numb. Enough was enough. There's no way I could do a long trip like this.

Turning the heater on, I drove straight back to the Hab.

Once I got home, I sulked for a while. All my brilliant plans foiled by thermodynamics. Damn you, Entropy!

I'm in a bind. The damn heater will eat half my battery power every day. I could turn it down, I guess. Be a little cold but not freezing to death. Even then I'd still lose at least a quarter.

This will require some thought. I have to ask myself . . . What would Hercule Poirot do? I'll have to put my "little gray cells" to work on the problem.

LOG ENTRY: SOL 68

Well, shit.

I came up with a solution, but . . . remember when I burned rocket fuel in the Hab? This'll be more dangerous.

I'm going to use the RTG.

The RTG (radioisotope thermoelectric generator) is a big box of plutonium. But not the kind used in nuclear bombs. No, no. This plutonium is *way* more dangerous!

Plutonium-238 is an incredibly unstable isotope. It's so radioactive that it will get red hot all by itself. As you can imagine, a material that can *literally fry an egg* with radiation is kind of dangerous.

The RTG houses the plutonium, catches the radiation in the form of heat, and turns it into electricity. It's not a reactor. The radiation can't be increased or decreased. It's a purely natural process happening at the atomic level.

As long ago as the 1960s, NASA began using RTGs to power unmanned probes. They have lots of advantages over solar power. They're not affected by storms; they work day or night; they're entirely internal, so you don't need delicate solar cells all over your probe.

But they never used large RTGs on manned missions until the Ares Program.

Why not? It should be pretty damned obvious why not! They didn't want to put astronauts next to a glowing hot ball of radioactive death!

I'm exaggerating a little. The plutonium is inside

a bunch of pellets, each one sealed and insulated to prevent radiation leakage, even if the outer container is breached. So for the Ares Program, they took the risk.

An Ares mission is all about the MAV. It's the single most important component. It's one of the few systems that can't be replaced or worked around. It's the *only* component that causes a complete mission scrub if it's not working.

Solar cells are great in the short term, and they're good for the long term if you have humans around to clean them. But the MAV sits alone for years quietly making fuel, then just kind of hangs out until its crew arrives. Even doing nothing, it needs power, so NASA can monitor it remotely and run self-checks.

The prospect of scrubbing a mission because a solar cell got dirty was unacceptable. They needed a more reliable source of power. So the MAV comes equipped with an RTG. It has 2.6 kilograms of plutonium-238, which makes almost 1500 watts of heat. It can turn that into 100 watts of electricity. The MAV runs on that until the crew arrive.

One hundred watts isn't enough to keep the heater going, but I don't care about the electrical output. I want the heat. A 1500-watt heater is so warm I'll have to tear insulation out of the rover to keep it from getting too hot.

As soon as the rovers were unstowed and activated, Commander Lewis had the joy of disposing of the RTG. She detached it from the MAV, drove four kilometers away, and buried it. However safe it may be, it's still a radioactive core and NASA didn't want it too close to their astronauts.

The mission parameters don't give a specific location to dump the RTG. Just "at least four kilometers away." So I'll have to find it.

I have two things working for me. First, I was assembling solar panels with Vogel when Commander Lewis drove off, and I saw she headed due south. Also, she planted a three-meter pole with a bright green flag over where she buried it. Green shows up extremely well against the Martian terrain. It's made to ward us off, in case we get lost on a rover EVA later on.

So my plan is: Head south four kilometers, then search around till I see the green flag.

Having rendered Rover 1 unusable, I'll have to use my mutant rover for the trip. I can make a useful test mission of it. I'll see how well the battery harness holds up to a real journey, and how well the solar cells do strapped to the roof.

I'll call it Sirius 2.

LOG ENTRY: SOL 69

I'm no stranger to Mars. I've been here a long time. But I've never been out of sight of the Hab before today. You wouldn't think that would make a difference, but it does.

As I made my way toward the RTG's burial site, it hit me: Mars is a barren wasteland and I am *completely* alone here. I already knew that, of course. But there's a difference between knowing it and really experiencing it. All around me there was nothing but dust, rocks, and endless empty desert in all directions. The planet's famous red color is from iron oxide coating everything. So it's not just a desert. It's a desert so old it's literally rusting.

The Hab is my only hint of civilization, and seeing it disappear made me way more uncomfortable than I like to admit.

I put those thoughts behind me by concentrating on what was in front of me. I found the RTG right where it was supposed to be, four kilometers due south of the Hab.

It wasn't hard to find. Commander Lewis had buried it atop a small hill. She probably wanted to make sure everyone could see the flag, and it worked great! Except instead of avoiding it, I beelined to it and dug it up. Not exactly what she was going for.

It was a large cylinder with heat-sinks all around it. I could feel the warmth it gave off even through my suit's gloves. That's really disconcerting. Especially when you know the root cause of the heat is radiation.

No point in putting it on the roof; my plan was to have it in the cabin anyway. So I brought it in with me, turned off the heater, then drove back to the Hab.

In the ten minutes it took to get home, even with the heater off, the interior of the rover became an uncomfortably hot 37°C. The RTG would definitely be able to keep me warm.

The trip also proved that my rigging worked. The solar cells and extra battery stayed beautifully in place while traversing eight kilometers of random terrain.

I declare Sirius 2 to be a successful mission!

I spent the rest of the day vandalizing the interior of the rover. The pressure compartment is made of carbon composite. Just inside that is insulation, which is covered by hard plastic. I used a sophisticated method to remove sections of plastic (hammer), then carefully removed the solid foam insulation (hammer again).

After tearing out some insulation, I suited up and took the RTG outside. Soon, the rover cooled down again, and I brought it back in. I watched as the temperature rose slowly. Nowhere near as fast as it had on my trip back from the burial site.

I cautiously removed more insulation (hammer) and checked again. After a few more cycles of this, I had enough insulation torn out that the RTG could barely keep up with it. In fact, it was a losing battle. Over time, heat will slowly leach out. That's fine. I can turn on the heater for short bursts when necessary.

I brought the insulation pieces with me back into the Hab. Using advanced construction techniques (duct tape), I reassembled some of them into a square. I figure if things ever get really cold, I can tape that to a bare patch in the rover, and the RTG will be winning the "heat fight."

Tomorrow, Sirius 3 (which is just Sirius 1 again, but without freezing).

LOG ENTRY: SOL 70

Today, I write to you from the rover. I'm halfway through Sirius 3 and things are going well.

I set out at first light and drove laps around the Hab, trying to stay on untouched ground. The first battery lasted just under two hours. After a quick EVA to switch the cables, I got back to driving. When all was said and done, I had driven 81 kilometers in 3 hours and 27 minutes.

That's *very* good! Mind you, the land around the Hab is really flat, as is all of Acidalia Planitia.

I have no idea what my efficiency would be on the nastier land en route to Ares 4.

The second battery still had a little juice left, but I can't just run it down all the way before I stop; remember, I need life support while recharging. The CO_2 gets absorbed through a chemical process, but if the fan that pushes it isn't working, I'll choke. The oxygen pump is also kind of important.

After my drive, I set up the solar cells. It was hard work; last time I had Vogel's help. They aren't heavy, but they're awkward. After setting up half of them, I figured out I could drag them rather than carry them, and that sped things up.

Now I'm just waiting for the batteries to recharge. I'm bored, so I'm updating the log. I have all the Poirot books in my computer. That'll help. It's going to take twelve hours to recharge, after all.

What's that, you say? Twelve hours is wrong? I said thirteen hours earlier? Well, my friend, let me set you straight.

The RTG is a *generator*. It's a paltry amount of power, compared to what the rover consumes, but it's not nothing. It's one hundred watts. It'll cut an hour off my total recharge time. Why not use it?

I wonder what NASA would think about me fucking with the RTG like this. They'd probably hide under their desks and cuddle with their slide rules for comfort.

LOG ENTRY: SOL 71

As predicted, it took twelve hours to charge the batteries to full. I came straight home as soon as they were done.

Time to make plans for Sirius 4. And I think it'll be a multiday field trip.

Looks like power and battery recharging are solved. Food's not a problem; there's plenty of space to store things. Water's even easier than food. I need two liters per day to be comfortable.

When I do my trip to Ares 4 for real, I'll need to bring the oxygenator. But it's big and I don't want to screw with it right now. So I'll rely on O_2 and CO_2 filters for Sirius 4.

CO_2 isn't a problem. I started this grand adventure with 1500 hours of CO_2 filters, plus another 720 for emergency use. All systems use standard filters (Apollo 13 taught us important lessons). Since then, I've used 131 hours of filter on various EVAs. I have 2089 left. Eighty-seven days' worth. Plenty.

Oxygen's a little trickier. The rover was designed to support three people for two days, plus some reserve for safety. So its O_2 tanks can hold enough to last me seven days. Not enough.

Mars has almost no atmospheric pressure. The inside of the rover has one atmosphere. So the oxygen tanks are on the inside (less pressure differential to deal with). Why does that matter? It means I can bring along other oxygen tanks, and equalize them with the rover's tanks without having to do an EVA.

So today, I detached one of the Hab's two 25-liter liquid oxygen tanks and brought it into the rover. According to NASA, a human needs 588 liters of oxygen per day to live. Compressed liquid

O_2 is about 1000 times as dense as gaseous O_2 in a comfortable atmosphere. Long story short: With the Hab tank, I have enough O_2 to last 49 days. That'll be plenty.

Sirius 4 will be a twenty-day trip.

That may seem a bit long, but I have a specific goal in mind. Besides, my trip to Ares 4 will be at least forty days. This is a good scale model.

While I'm away, the Hab can take care of itself, but the potatoes are an issue. I'll saturate the ground with most of the water I have. Then, I'll deactivate the atmospheric regulator, so it doesn't pull water out of the air. It'll be humid as hell, and water will condense on every surface. That'll keep the potatoes well watered while I'm away.

A bigger problem is CO_2. The potatoes need to breathe. I know what you're thinking. "Mark, old chap! *You* produce carbon dioxide! It's all part of the majestic circle of nature!"

The problem is: Where will I put it? Sure, I exhale CO_2 with every breath, but I don't have any way to store it. I could turn off the oxygenator and atmospheric regulator and just fill the Hab with my breath over time. But CO_2 is deadly to me. I need to release a bunch at once and run away.

Remember the MAV fuel plant? It collects CO_2 from the Martian atmosphere. A 10-liter tank of compressed liquid CO_2, vented into the Hab, will be enough CO_2 to do the trick. That'll take less than a day to create.

So that's everything. Once I vent the CO_2 into the Hab, I'll turn off the atmospheric regulator and oxygenator, dump a ton of water on the crops, and head out.

Sirius 4. A huge step forward in my rover research. And I can start tomorrow.

CHAPTER 8

"HELLO, AND thank you for joining us," Cathy Warner said to the camera. "Today on CNN's *Mark Watney Report*: Several EVAs over the past few days . . . what do they mean? What progress has NASA made on a rescue option? And how will this affect the Ares 4 preparations?

"Joining us today is Dr. Venkat Kapoor, director of Mars operations for NASA. Dr. Kapoor, thank you for coming."

"A pleasure to be here, Cathy," Venkat said.

"Dr. Kapoor," Cathy said, "Mark Watney is the most-watched man in the solar system, wouldn't you say?"

Venkat nodded. "Certainly the most watched by NASA. We have all twelve of our Martian satellites taking pictures whenever his site's in view. The European Space Agency has both of theirs doing the same."

"All told, how often do you get these images?"

"Every few minutes. Sometimes there's a gap, based on the satellite orbits. But it's enough that we can track all his EVA activities."

"Tell us about these latest EVAs."

"Well," Venkat said, "it looks like he's preparing Rover 2 for a long trip. On Sol 64, he took the battery from the other rover and attached it with a homemade sling. The next day, he detached fourteen solar cells and stacked them on the rover's roof."

"And then he took a little drive, didn't he?" Cathy prompted.

"Yes he did. Sort of aimlessly for an hour, then back to the Hab. He was probably testing it. Next time we saw him was two days later, when he drove four kilometers away, then back. Another incremental test, we think. Then, over the past couple of days, he's been stocking it up with supplies."

"Hmm," Cathy said, "most analysts think Mark's only hope of rescue is to get to the Ares 4 site. Do you think he's come to the same conclusion?"

"Probably," Venkat said. "He doesn't know we're watching. From his point of view, Ares 4 is his only hope."

"Do you think he's planning to go soon? He seems to be getting ready for a trip."

"I hope not," Venkat said. "There's nothing at the site other than the MAV. None of the other presupplies. It would be a very long, very dangerous trip, and he'd be leaving the safety of the Hab behind."

"Why would he risk it?"

"Communication," Venkat said. "Once he reaches the MAV, he could contact us."

"So that would be a good thing, wouldn't it?"

"Communication would be a *great* thing. But traversing thirty-two hundred kilometers to Ares 4 is incredibly dangerous. We'd rather he stayed put. If we could talk to him, we'd certainly tell him that."

"He can't stay put forever, right? Eventually he'll need to get to the MAV."

"Not necessarily," Venkat said. "JPL is experimenting with modifications to the MDV so it can make a brief overland flight after landing."

"I'd heard that idea was rejected as being too dangerous," Cathy said.

"Their first proposal was, yes. Since then, they've been working on safer ways to do it."

"With only three and a half years before Ares 4's scheduled launch, is there enough time to make and test modifications to the MDV?"

"I can't answer that for sure. But remember, we made a lunar lander from scratch in seven years."

"Excellent point." Cathy smiled. "So what are his odds right now?"

"No idea," Venkat said. "But we're going to do everything we can to bring him home alive."

■ ■ ■

MINDY GLANCED nervously around the conference room. She'd never felt so thoroughly outranked in her life. Dr. Venkat Kapoor, who was four levels of management above her, sat to her left.

Next to him was Bruce Ng, the director of JPL. He'd flown all the way to Houston from Pasadena just for this meeting. Never one to let precious time go to waste, he typed furiously on his laptop.

The dark bags under his eyes made Mindy wonder just how overworked he truly was.

Mitch Henderson, the flight director for Ares 3, swiveled back and forth in his chair, a wireless earpiece in his ear. It fed him a real-time stream of all the comm chatter from Mission Control. He wasn't on shift, but he was kept apprised at all times.

Annie Montrose entered the conference room, texting as she walked. Never taking her eyes off her phone, she deftly navigated around the edge of the room, avoiding people and chairs, and sat in her usual spot. Mindy felt a pang of envy as she watched the director of media relations. She was everything Mindy wanted to be. Confident, high-ranking, beautiful, and universally respected within NASA.

"How'd I do today?" Venkat asked.

"Eeeh," Annie said, putting her phone away. "You shouldn't say things like 'bring him home alive.' It reminds people he might die."

"Think they're going to forget that?"

"You asked my opinion. Don't like it? Go fuck yourself."

"You're such a delicate flower, Annie. How'd you end up NASA's director of media relations?"

"Beats the fuck out of me," Annie said.

"Guys," Bruce said, "I need to catch a flight back to LA in three hours. Is Teddy coming or what?"

"Quit bitching, Bruce," Annie said. "None of us want to be here."

Mitch turned the volume down on his earpiece and faced Mindy. "Who are you, again?"

"Um," Mindy said, "I'm Mindy Park. I work in SatCon."

"You a director or something?"

"No, I just work in SatCon. I'm a nobody."

Venkat looked to Mitch. "I put her in charge of tracking Watney. She gets us the imagery."

"Huh," said Mitch. "Not the director of SatCon?"

"Bob's got more to deal with than just Mars. Mindy's handling all the Martian satellites, and keeps them pointed at Mark."

"Why Mindy?" Mitch asked.

"She noticed he was alive in the first place."

"She gets a promotion 'cause she was in the hot seat when the imagery came through?"

"No." Venkat frowned, "she gets a promotion 'cause she figured out he was alive. Stop being a jerk, Mitch. You're making her feel bad."

Mitch raised his eyebrows. "Didn't think of that. Sorry, Mindy."

Mindy looked at the table and managed to say, "'kay."

Teddy entered the room. "Sorry I'm late." He took his seat and pulled several folders from his briefcase. Stacking them neatly, he opened the top one and squared the pages within. "Let's get started. Venkat, what's Watney's status?"

"Alive and well," Venkat said. "No change from my e-mail earlier today."

"What about the RTG? Does the public know about that yet?" Teddy asked.

Annie leaned forward. "So far, so good," she said. "The images are public, but we have no obligation to tell them our analysis. Nobody has figured it out yet."

"Why did he dig it up?"

"Heat, I think," Venkat said. "He wants to make the rover do long trips. It uses a lot of energy keeping warm. The RTG can heat up the interior without soaking battery power. It's a good idea, really."

"How dangerous is it?" Teddy asked.

"As long as the container's intact, no danger at all. Even if it cracks open, he'll be okay if the pellets inside don't break. But if the pellets break, too, he's a dead man."

"Let's hope that doesn't happen," Teddy said. "JPL, how are the MDV plans coming along?"

"We came up with a plan a long time ago," Bruce said. "You rejected it."

"Bruce," Teddy cautioned.

Bruce sighed. "The MDV wasn't made for lift-off and lateral flight. Packing more fuel in doesn't help. We'd need a bigger engine and don't have time to invent one. So we need to lighten the MDV. We have an idea for that.

"The MDV can be its normal weight on primary descent. If we made the heat shield and outer hull detachable, they could ditch a lot of weight after landing at Ares 3, and have a lighter ship for the traverse to Ares 4. We're running the numbers now."

"Keep me posted," Teddy said. He turned to Mindy. "Miss Park, welcome to the big leagues."

"Sir," Mindy said. She tried to ignore the lump in her throat.

"What's the biggest gap in coverage we have on Watney right now?"

"Um," Mindy said. "Once every forty-one hours, we'll have a seventeen-minute gap. The orbits work out that way."

"You had an immediate answer," Teddy said. "Good. I like it when people are organized."

"Thank you, sir."

"I want that gap down to four minutes," Teddy said. "I'm giving you total authority over satellite trajectories and orbital adjustments. Make it happen."

"Yes, sir," Mindy said, with no idea how to do it.

Teddy looked to Mitch. "Mitch, your e-mail said you had something urgent?"

"Yeah," Mitch said. "How long are we gonna keep this from the Ares 3 crew? They all think Watney's dead. It's a huge drain on morale."

Teddy looked to Venkat.

"Mitch," Venkat said. "We discussed this—"

"No, *you* discussed it," Mitch interrupted. "They think they lost a crewmate. They're devastated."

"And when they find out they *abandoned* a crewmate?" Venkat asked. "Will they feel better then?"

Mitch poked the table with his finger. "They deserve to know. You think Commander Lewis can't handle the truth?"

"It's a matter of morale," Venkat said. "They can concentrate on getting home—"

"I make that call," Mitch said. "I'm the one who decides what's best for the crew. And I say we bring them up to speed."

After a few moments of silence, all eyes turned to Teddy.

He thought for a moment. "Sorry, Mitch, I'm with Venkat on this one," he said. "But as soon as we come up with a plan for rescue, we can tell *Hermes*. There needs to be some hope, or there's no point in telling them."

"Bullshit," Mitch grumbled, crossing his arms. "Total bullshit."

"I know you're upset," Teddy said calmly.

"We'll make it right. Just as soon as we have some idea how to save Watney."

Teddy let a few seconds of quiet pass before moving on.

"Okay, JPL's on the rescue option," he said with a nod toward Bruce. "But it would be part of Ares 4. How does he stay alive till then? Venkat?"

Venkat opened a folder and glanced at the paperwork inside. "I had every team check and double-check the longevity of their systems. We're pretty sure the Hab can keep working for four years. Especially with a human occupant fixing problems as they arise. But there's no way around the food issue. He'll start starving in a year. We *have* to send him supplies. Simple as that."

"What about an Ares 4 presupply?" said Teddy. "Land it at Ares 3 instead."

"That's what we're thinking, yeah," Venkat confirmed. "Problem is, the original plan was to launch presupplies a year from now. They're not ready yet.

"It takes eight months to get a probe to Mars in the best of times. The positions of Earth and Mars right now . . . it's not the best of times. We figure we can get there in nine months. Presuming he's rationing his food, he's got enough to last three hundred and fifty more days. That means we need to build a presupply in *three months*. JPL hasn't even started yet."

"That'll be tight," Bruce said. "Making a presupply is a six-month process. We're set up to pipeline a bunch of them at once, not to make one in a hurry."

"Sorry, Bruce," Teddy said. "I know we're asking a lot, but you have to find a way."

"We'll find a way," Bruce said. "But the OT alone will be a nightmare."

"Get started. I'll find you the money."

"There's also the booster," Venkat said. "The only way to get a probe to Mars with the planets in their current positions is to spend a buttload of fuel. We only have one booster capable of doing that. The Delta IX that's on the pad right now for the EagleEye 3 Saturn probe. We'll have to steal that. I talked to ULA, and they just can't make another booster in time."

"The EagleEye 3 team will be pissed, but okay," said Teddy. "We can delay their mission if JPL gets the payload done in time."

Bruce rubbed his eyes. "We'll do our best."

"He'll starve to death if you don't," Teddy said.

▪▪▪

VENKAT SIPPED his coffee and frowned at his computer. A month ago it would have been unthinkable to drink coffee at nine p.m. Now it was necessary fuel. Shift schedules, fund allocations, project juggling, out-and-out looting of other projects . . . he'd never pulled so many stunts in his life.

"NASA's a large organization," he typed. *"It doesn't deal with sudden change well. The only reason we're getting away with it is the desperate circumstances. Everyone's pulling together to save Mark Watney, with no interdepartmental squabbling. I can't tell you how rare that is. Even then, this is going to cost tens of millions, maybe hundreds of millions of dollars. The MDV modifications alone*

are an entire project that's being staffed up. Hopefully, the public interest will make your job easier. We appreciate your continued support, Congressman, and hope you can sway the committee toward granting us the emergency funding we need."

He was interrupted by a knock at his door. Looking up, he saw Mindy. She wore sweats and a T-shirt, her hair in a sloppy ponytail. Fashion tended to suffer when work hours ran long.

"Sorry to bother you," Mindy said.

"No bother," Venkat said. "I could use a break. What's up?"

"He's on the move," she said.

Venkat slouched in his chair. "Any chance it's a test drive?"

She shook her head. "He drove straightaway from the Hab for almost two hours, did a short EVA, then drove for another two. We think the EVA was to change batteries."

Venkat sighed heavily. "Maybe it's just a longer test? An overnight trip kind of thing?"

"He's seventy-six kilometers from the Hab," Mindy said. "For an overnight test, wouldn't he stay within walking distance?"

"Yes, he would," Venkat said. "Damn it. We've had teams run every conceivable scenario. There's just no way he can make it to Ares 4 with that setup. We never saw him load up the oxygenator or water reclaimer. He can't possibly have enough basics to live long enough."

"I don't think he's going to Ares 4," Mindy said. "If he is, he's taking a weird path."

"Oh?" said Venkat.

"He went south-southwest. Schiaparelli crater is southeast."

"Okay, maybe there's hope," Venkat said. "What's he doing right now?"

"Recharging. He's got all the solar cells set up," Mindy said. "Last time he did that, it took twelve hours. I was going to sneak home for some sleep if that's okay."

"Sure, sounds good. We'll see what he does tomorrow. Maybe he'll go back to the Hab."

"Maybe," Mindy said, unconvinced.

■ ■ ■

"WELCOME BACK," Cathy said to the camera. "We're chatting with Marcus Washington, from the US Postal Service. So, Mr. Washington, I understand the Ares 3 mission caused a postal service first. Can you explain that to our viewers?"

"Uh yeah," said Marcus. "Everyone thought Mark Watney was dead for over two months. In that time, the postal service issued a run of commemorative stamps honoring his memory. Twenty thousand were printed and sent to post offices around the country."

"And then it turned out he was alive," Cathy said.

"Yeah," said Marcus. "We don't print stamps of living people. So we stopped the run immediately and recalled the stamps, but thousands were already sold."

"Has this ever happened before?" Cathy asked.

"No. Not once in the history of the postal service."

"I bet they're worth a pretty penny now."

Marcus chuckled. "Maybe. But like I said,

thousands were sold. They'll be rare, but not super-rare."

Cathy chuckled then addressed the camera. "We've been speaking with Marcus Washington of the United States Postal Service. If you've got a Mark Watney commemorative stamp, you might want to hold on to it. Thanks for dropping by, Mr. Washington."

"Thanks for having me," Marcus said.

"Our next guest is Dr. Irene Shields, flight psychologist for the Ares missions. Dr. Shields, welcome to the program."

"Thank you," Irene said, adjusting her microphone clip.

"Do you know Mark Watney personally?"

"Of course," Irene said. "I did monthly psych evaluations on each member of the crew."

"What can you tell us about him? His personality, his mind-set?"

"Well," Irene said, "he's very intelligent. All of them are, of course. But he's particularly resourceful and a good problem-solver."

"That may save his life," Cathy interjected.

"It may indeed," Irene agreed. "Also, he's a good-natured man. Usually cheerful, with a great sense of humor. He's quick with a joke. In the months leading up to launch, the crew was put through a grueling training schedule. They all showed signs of stress and moodiness. Mark was no exception, but the *way* he showed it was to crack more jokes and get everyone laughing."

"He sounds like a great guy," Cathy said.

"He really is," Irene said. "He was chosen for the mission in part because of his personality. An Ares crew has to spend thirteen months together. Social compatibility is key. Mark not only fits well in any social group, he's a catalyst to make the group work better. It was a *terrible* blow to the crew when he 'died.'"

"And they still think he's dead, right? The Ares 3 crew?"

"Yes, they do, unfortunately," Irene confirmed. "The higher-ups decided to keep it from them, at least for now. I'm sure it wasn't an easy decision."

Cathy paused for a moment, then said, "All right. You know I have to ask: What's going through his head right now? How does a man like Mark Watney respond to a situation like this? Stranded, alone, no idea we're trying to help?"

"There's no way to be sure," Irene said. "The biggest threat is giving up hope. If he decides there's no chance to survive, he'll stop trying."

"Then we're okay for now, right?" Cathy said. "He seems to be working hard. He's prepping the rover for a long trip and testing it. He plans to be there when Ares 4 lands."

"That's one interpretation, yes," Irene said.

"Is there another?"

Irene carefully formed her answer before speaking. "When facing death, people want to be heard. They don't want to die alone. He might just want the MAV radio so he can talk to another soul before he dies.

"If he's lost hope, he won't care about survival. His only concern will be making it to the radio. After that, he'll probably take an easier way out than starvation. The medical supplies of an Ares mission have enough morphine to be lethal."

After several seconds of complete silence in the studio, Cathy turned to the camera. "We'll be right back."

■ ■ ■

"HEYA, VENK." Bruce's voice came from the speakerphone on Venkat's desk.

"Bruce, hi," said Venkat, typing on his computer. "Thanks for clearing up some time. I wanted to talk about the presupply."

"Sure thing. What's on your mind?"

"Let's say we soft-land it perfectly. How will Mark know it happened? And how will he know where to look?"

"We've been thinking about that," said Bruce. "We've got some ideas."

"I'm all ears," Venkat said, saving his document and closing his laptop.

"We'll be sending him a comm system anyway, right? We could have it turn on after landing. It'll broadcast on the rover and EVA suit frequencies. It'll have to be a strong signal, too.

"The rovers were only designed to communicate with the Hab and each other; the signal origin was presumed to be within twenty kilometers. The receivers just aren't very sensitive. The EVA suits are even worse. But as long as we have a strong signal we should be good. Once we land the presupply, we'll get its exact location from satellites, then broadcast that to Mark so he can go get it."

"But he's probably not listening," said Venkat. "Why would he be?"

"We have a plan for that. We're going to make a bunch of bright green ribbons. Light enough to flutter around when dropped, even in Mars's atmosphere. Each ribbon will have 'MARK: TURN ON YOUR COMM' printed on it. We're working on a release mechanism now. During the landing sequence, of course. Ideally, about a thousand meters above the surface."

"I like it," Venkat said. "All he needs to do is notice one. And he's sure to check out a bright green ribbon if he sees one outside."

"Venk," said Bruce. "If he takes the 'Watney-mobile' to Ares 4, this'll all be for nothing. I mean, we can land it at Ares 4 if that happens, but . . ."

"But he'll be without a Hab. Yeah," Venkat said. "One thing at a time. Let me know when you come up with a release mechanism for those ribbons."

"Will do."

After terminating the call, Venkat opened his laptop to get back to work. There was an e-mail from Mindy Park waiting for him. "*Watney's on the move again.*"

■ ■ ■

"STILL GOING in a straight line," Mindy said, pointing to her monitor.

"I see," Venkat said. "He's sure as hell not going to Ares 4. Unless he's going around some natural obstacle."

"There's nothing for him to go around," Mindy said. "It's Acidalia Planitia."

"Are those the solar cells?" Venkat asked, pointing to the screen.

"Yeah," Mindy said. "He did the usual two-hour drive, EVA, two-hour drive. He's one hundred and fifty-six kilometers from the Hab now."

They both peered at the screen.

"Wait . . . ," Venkat said. "Wait, no way . . ."

"What?" Mindy asked.

Venkat grabbed a pad of Post-its and a pen. "Give me his location, and the location of the Hab."

Mindy checked her screen. "He's currently at . . . 28.9 degrees north, 29.6 degrees west." With a few keystrokes, she brought up another file. "The Hab's at 31.2 degrees north, 28.5 degrees west. What do you see?"

Venkat finished taking down the numbers. "Come with me," he said, quickly walking out.

"Um," Mindy stammered, following after. "Where are we going?"

"SatCon break room," Venkat said. "You guys still have that map of Mars on the wall?"

"Sure," Mindy said. "But it's just a poster from the gift shop. I've got high-quality digital maps on my computer—"

"Nope. I can't draw on those," he said. Then, rounding the corner to the break room, he pointed to the Mars map on the wall. "I can draw on that."

The break room was empty save for a computer technician sipping a cup of coffee. He looked up in alarm as Venkat and Mindy stormed in.

"Good, it has latitude and longitude lines," Venkat said. Looking at his Post-it, then sliding his finger along the map, he drew an X. "That's the Hab," he said.

"Hey," the technician said. "Are you drawing on our poster?"

"I'll buy you a new one," Venkat said without looking back. Then, he drew another X. "That's his current location. Get me a ruler."

Mindy looked left and right. Seeing no ruler, she grabbed the technician's notebook.

"Hey!" the technician protested.

Using the notebook as a straight-edge, Venkat

drew a line from the Hab to Mark's location and beyond. Then took a step back.

"Yup! That's where he's going!" Venkat said excitedly.

"Oh!" Mindy said.

The line passed through the exact center of a bright yellow dot printed on the map.

"*Pathfinder!*" Mindy said. "He's going to *Pathfinder*!"

"Yup!" Venkat said. "Now we're getting somewhere. It's like eight hundred kilometers from him. He can get there and back with supplies on hand."

"And bring *Pathfinder* and Sojourner rover back with him," Mindy added.

Venkat pulled out his cell phone. "We lost contact with *Pathfinder* in 1997. If he can get it online again, we can communicate. It might just need the solar cells cleaned. Even if it's got a bigger problem, he's an engineer!" Dialing, he added, "Fixing things is his job!"

Smiling for what felt like the first time in weeks, he held the phone to his ear and awaited a response. "Bruce? It's Venkat. Everything just changed. Watney's headed for *Pathfinder*. Yeah! I know, right!? Dig up everyone who was on that project and get them to JPL now. I'll catch the next flight."

Hanging up, he grinned at the map. "Mark, you sneaky, clever, son of a bitch!"

CHAPTER 9

LOG ENTRY: SOL 79

It's the evening of my eighth day on the road. Sirius 4 has been a success so far.

I've fallen into a routine. Every morning I wake up at dawn. First thing I do is check oxygen and CO_2 levels. Then I eat a breakfast pack and drink a cup of water. After that, I brush my teeth, using as little water as possible, and shave with an electric razor.

The rover has no toilet. We were expected to use our suits' reclamation systems for that. But they aren't designed to hold twenty days' worth of output.

My morning piss goes in a resealable plastic box. When I open it, the rover reeks like a truck-stop men's room. I could take it outside and let it boil off. But I worked hard to make that water, and the last thing I'm going to do is waste it. I'll feed it to the water reclaimer when I get back.

Even more precious is my manure. It's critical to the potato farm, and I'm the only source on Mars. Fortunately, when you spend a lot of time in space, you learn how to shit in a bag. And if you think things are bad after opening the piss box, imagine the smell after I drop anchor.

After I'm done with that lovely routine, I go outside and collect the solar cells. Why didn't I do it the previous night? Because trying to dismantle and stack solar cells in *total darkness* isn't fun. I learned that the hard way.

After securing the cells, I come back in, turn on some shitty seventies music, and start driving. I putter along at 25 kph, the rover's top speed. It's comfortable inside. I wear hastily made cutoffs and a thin shirt while the RTG bakes the interior. When it gets too hot I detach the insulation duct-taped to the hull. When it gets too cold, I tape it back up.

I can go almost two hours before the first battery runs out. I do a quick EVA to swap cables, then I'm back at the wheel for the second half of the day's drive.

The terrain is very flat. The undercarriage of the rover is taller than any of the rocks around here, and the hills are gently sloping affairs, smoothed by eons of sandstorms.

When the other battery runs out, it's time for another EVA. I pull the solar cells off the roof and lay them on the ground. For the first few sols, I lined them up in a row. Now I plop them wherever, trying to keep them close to the rover out of sheer laziness.

Then comes the incredibly dull part of my day. I sit around for twelve hours with nothing to do. And I'm getting sick of this rover. The inside's the size of a van. That may seem like plenty of room, but try being trapped in a van for eight days. I look forward to tending my potato farm in the wide open space of the Hab.

I'm nostalgic for the Hab. How fucked up is that?

I have shitty seventies TV to watch, and a bunch of Poirot novels to read. But mostly I spend my time thinking about getting to Ares 4. I'll have to do it someday. How the hell am I going to survive a 3200-kilometer trip in this thing? It'll probably take fifty days. I'll need the water reclaimer and the oxygenator, maybe some of the Hab's main batteries, then a bunch more solar cells to charge everything. . . . Where will I put it all? These thoughts pester me throughout the long, boring days.

Eventually, it gets dark and I get tired. I lie among the food packs, water tanks, extra O_2 tank, piles of CO_2 filters, box of pee, bags of shit, and personal items. I have a bunch of crew jumpsuits to serve as bedding, along with my blanket and pillow. Basically, I sleep in a pile of junk every night.

Speaking of sleep . . . G'night.

LOG ENTRY: SOL 80

By my reckoning, I'm about 100 kilometers from *Pathfinder*. Technically it's "Carl Sagan Memorial Station." But with all due respect to Carl, I can call it whatever the hell I want. I'm the King of Mars.

As I mentioned, it's been a long, boring drive. And I'm still on the outward leg. But hey, I'm an astronaut. Long-ass trips are my business.

Navigation is tricky.

The Hab's nav beacon only reaches 40 kilometers, so it's useless to me out here. I knew that'd be an issue when I was planning this little road trip, so I came up with a brilliant plan that didn't work.

The computer has detailed maps, so I figured I could navigate by landmarks. I was wrong. Turns out you can't navigate by landmarks if you can't find any god damned landmarks.

Our landing site is at the delta of a long-gone river. NASA chose it because if there are any microscopic fossils to be had, it's a good place to look. Also, the water would have dragged rock and soil samples from thousands of kilometers away. With some digging, we could get a broad geological history.

That's great for science, but it means the Hab's in a *featureless wasteland*.

I considered making a compass. The rover has plenty of electricity, and the med kit has a needle. Only one problem: Mars doesn't have a magnetic field.

So I navigate by Phobos. It whips around Mars so fast it actually rises and sets twice a day, running west to east. It isn't the most accurate system, but it works.

Things got easier on Sol 75. I reached a valley with a rise to the west. It had flat ground for easy driving, and I just needed to follow the edge of the hills. I named it "Lewis Valley" after our fearless leader. She'd love it there, geology nerd that she is.

Three sols later, Lewis Valley opened into a wide plain. So, again, I was left without references and relied on Phobos to guide me. There's probably symbolism there. Phobos is the god of fear, and I'm letting it be my guide. Not a good sign.

But today, my luck finally changed. After two sols wandering the desert, I found something to navigate by. It was a five-kilometer crater, so small it didn't even have a listed name. But it was on the maps, so to me it was the Lighthouse of Alexandria. Once I had it in sight, I knew exactly where I was.

I'm camped near it now, as a matter of fact.

I'm finally through the blank areas of the map. Tomorrow, I'll have the Lighthouse to navigate by, and Hamelin crater later on. I'm in good shape.

Now on to my next task: sitting around with nothing to do for twelve hours.

I better get started!

LOG ENTRY: SOL 81

Almost made it to *Pathfinder* today, but I ran out of juice. Just another 22 kilometers to go!

An unremarkable drive. Navigation wasn't a problem. As Lighthouse receded into the distance, the rim of Hamelin crater came into view.

I left Acidalia Planitia behind a long time ago. I'm well into Ares Vallis now. The desert plains are giving way to bumpier terrain, strewn with ejecta that never got buried by sand. It makes driving a chore; I have to pay more attention.

Up till now, I've been driving right over the rock-strewn landscape. But as I travel farther south, the rocks are getting bigger and more plentiful. I have to go around some of them or risk damage to my suspension. The good news is I don't have to do it for long. Once I get to *Pathfinder,* I can turn around and go the other way.

The weather's been very good. No discernible

wind, no storms. I think I got lucky there. There's a good chance my rover tracks from the past few sols are intact. I should be able to get back to Lewis Valley just by following them.

After setting up the solar panels today, I went for a little walk. I never left sight of the rover; the last thing I want to do is get lost on foot. But I couldn't stomach crawling back into that cramped, smelly rat's nest. Not right away.

It's a strange feeling. Everywhere I go, I'm the first. Step outside the rover? First guy ever to be there! Climb a hill? First guy to climb that hill! Kick a rock? That rock hadn't moved in a million years!

I'm the first guy to drive long-distance on Mars. The first guy to spend more than thirty-one sols on Mars. The first guy to grow crops on Mars. First, first, first!

I wasn't expecting to be first at anything. I was the fifth crewman out of the MDV when we landed, making me the seventeenth person to set foot on Mars. The egress order had been determined years earlier. A month before launch, we all got tattoos of our "Mars numbers." Johanssen almost refused to get her "15" because she was afraid it would hurt. Here's a woman who had survived the centrifuge, the vomit comet, hard-landing drills and 10k runs. A woman who fixed a simulated MDV computer failure while being spun around upside-down. But she was afraid of a tattoo needle.

Man, I miss those guys.

Jesus Christ, I'd give anything for a five-minute conversation with anyone. Anyone, anywhere. About anything.

I'm the first person to be alone on an entire planet.

Okay, enough moping. I *am* having a conversation with someone: whoever reads this log. It's a bit one-sided but it'll have to do. I might die, but damn it, someone will know what I had to say.

And the whole point of this trip is to get a radio. I could be reconnected with mankind before I even die.

So here's another first: Tomorrow I'll be the first person to recover a Mars probe.

LOG ENTRY: SOL 82

Victory! I found it!

I knew I was in the right area when I spotted Twin Peaks in the distance. The two small hills are under a kilometer from the landing site. Even better, they were on the far side of the site. All I had to do was aim for them until I found the lander.

And there it was! Right where it was supposed to be! I excitedly stumbled out and rushed to the site.

Pathfinder's final stage of descent was a balloon-covered tetrahedron. The balloons absorbed the impact of landing. Once it came to rest, they deflated, and the tetrahedron unfolded to reveal the probe.

It's actually two separate components. The lander itself, and the Sojourner rover. The lander was immobile, while Sojourner wandered around and got a good look at the local rocks. I'm taking both back with me, but the important part is the lander. That's the part that can communicate with Earth.

I can't explain how happy I was to find it. It was a *lot* of work to get here, and I'd succeeded.

The lander was half-buried. With some quick and careful digging, I exposed the bulk of it, though the large tetrahedron and the deflated balloons still lurked below the surface.

After a quick search, I found Sojourner. The little fella was only two meters from the lander. I vaguely remember it was farther away when they last saw it. It probably entered a contingency mode and started circling the lander, trying to communicate.

I quickly deposited Sojourner in my rover. It's small, light, and easily fit in the airlock. The lander was a different story.

I had no hope of getting the whole thing back to the Hab. It was just too big, but I only needed the probe itself. It was time for me to put on my mechanical engineer hat.

The probe was on the central panel of the unfolded tetrahedron. The other three sides were each attached to the central panel with a metal hinge. As anyone at JPL will tell you, probes are delicate things. Weight is a serious concern, so they're not made to stand up to much punishment.

When I took a crowbar to the hinges, they popped right off!

Then things got difficult. When I tried to lift the central panel assembly, it didn't budge.

Just like the other three panels, the central panel had deflated balloons underneath it.

Over the decades, the balloons had ripped and filled with sand.

I could cut off the balloons, but I'd have to dig to get to them. It wouldn't be hard, it's just sand. But the other three panels were in the damn way.

I quickly realized I didn't give a crap about the condition of the other panels. I went back to my rover, cut some strips of Hab material, then braided them into a primitive but strong rope. I can't take credit for it being strong. Thank NASA for that. I just made it rope-shaped.

I tied one end to a panel and the other to the rover. The rover was made for traversing extremely rugged terrain, often at steep angles. It may not be fast, but it has great torque. I towed the panel away like a redneck removing a tree stump.

Now I had a place to dig. As I exposed each balloon, I cut it off. The whole task took an hour.

Then I hoisted the central panel assembly up and carried it confidently to the rover!

At least, that's what I wanted to do. The damn thing is still heavy as hell. I'm guessing it's 200 kilograms. Even in Mars's gravity that's a bit much. I could carry it around the Hab easily enough, but lifting it while wearing an awkward EVA suit? Out of the question.

So I dragged it to the rover.

Now for my next feat: getting it on the roof.

The roof was empty at the moment. Even with mostly full batteries, I had set up the solar cells when I stopped. Why not? Free energy.

I'd worked it out in advance. On the way here, two stacks of solar panels occupied the whole roof. On the way back, I'll use a single stack to make room for the probe. It's a little more dangerous; the stack might fall over. Also, the cells will be a pain in the ass to stack that high. But I'll get it done.

I can't just throw a rope over the rover and hoist *Pathfinder* up the side. I don't want to break it. I mean, it's already broken; they lost contact in 1997. But I don't want to break it *more*.

I came up with a solution, but I'd done enough physical labor for one day, and I was almost out of daylight.

Now I'm in the rover, looking at Sojourner. It seems all right. No physical damage on the outside. Doesn't look like anything got too baked by the sunlight. The dense layer of Mars crap all over it protected it from long-term solar damage.

You may think Sojourner isn't much use to me. It can't communicate with Earth. Why do I care about it?

Because it has a lot of moving parts.

If I establish a link with NASA, I can talk to them by holding a page of text up to the lander's camera. But how would they talk to me? The only moving parts on the lander are the high-gain antenna (which would have to stay pointed at Earth) and the camera boom. We'd have to come up with a system where NASA could talk by rotating the camera head. It would be painfully slow.

But Sojourner has six independent wheels that rotate reasonably fast. It'll be much easier to communicate with those. I could draw letters on the wheels. NASA could rotate them to spell things at me.

That all assumes I can get the lander's radio working at all.

Time to turn in. I've got a lot of backbreaking physical labor to do tomorrow. I'll need my rest.

LOG ENTRY: SOL 83

Oh God, I'm sore.

But it's the only way I could think of to get the lander safely onto the roof.

I built a ramp out of rocks and sand. Just like the ancient Egyptians did.

And if there's one thing Ares Vallis has, it's rocks!

First, I experimented to find out how steep the grade could be. I piled some rocks near the lander and dragged it up the pile and back down again. Then I made the pile steeper and made sure I could drag the lander up and down. I repeated this over and over until I found the best grade for my ramp: 30 degrees. Anything more was too risky. I might lose my grip and send the lander tumbling down the ramp.

The roof of the rover is over two meters from the ground. So I'd need a ramp almost four meters long. I got to work.

The first few rocks were easy. Then they started feeling heavier and heavier. Hard physical labor in a space suit is murder. Everything's more effort because you're lugging 20 kilograms of suit around with you, and your movement is limited. I was panting within twenty minutes.

So I cheated. I upped my O_2 mixture. It really helped a lot. Probably shouldn't make that a habit. Also, I didn't get hot. The suit leaks heat faster than my body could ever generate it. The heating system is what keeps the temperature bearable. My physical labor just meant the suit didn't have to heat itself as much.

After hours of grueling labor, I finally got the ramp made. Nothing more than a pile of rocks against the rover, but it reached the roof.

I stomped up and down the ramp first, to make sure it was stable, then I dragged the lander up. It worked like a charm!

I was all smiles as I lashed the lander in place. I

made sure it was firmly secured, and even stacked the solar cells in a big single stack (why waste the ramp?).

But then it hit me. The ramp would collapse as I drove away, and the rocks might damage the wheels or undercarriage. I'd have to take the ramp apart to keep that from happening.

Ugh.

Tearing the ramp down was easier than putting it up. I didn't need to carefully put each rock in a stable place. I just dropped them wherever. It only took me an hour.

And now I'm done!

I'll start heading home tomorrow, with my new 200-kilogram broken radio.

CHAPTER 10

LOG ENTRY: SOL 90

Seven days since *Pathfinder*, and seven days closer to home.

As I'd hoped, my inbound tracks gave me a path back to Lewis Valley. Then it was four sols of easy driving. The hills to my left made it impossible to get lost, and the terrain was smooth.

But all good things come to an end. I'm back in Acidalia Planitia now. My outgoing tracks are long gone. It's been sixteen days since I was last here. Even timid weather would clear them out in that time.

On my way out, I should have made a pile of rocks every time I camped. The land is so flat they'd be visible for kilometers.

On second thought, thinking back to making that damn ramp . . . ugh.

So once again I am the desert wanderer, using

Phobos to navigate and hoping I don't stray too far. All I need to do is get within 40 kilometers of the Hab and I'll pick up the beacon.

I'm feeling optimistic. For the first time, I think I might get off this planet alive. With that in mind, I'm taking soil and rock samples every time I do an EVA.

At first, I figured it was my duty. If I survive, geologists will love me for it. But then it started to get fun. Now, as I drive, I look forward to that simple act of bagging rocks.

It just feels nice to be an astronaut again. That's all it is. Not a reluctant farmer, not an electrical engineer, not a long-haul trucker. An astronaut. I'm doing what astronauts do. I missed it.

LOG ENTRY: SOL 92

I got two seconds of signal from the Hab beacon today, then lost it. But it's a good sign. I've been traveling vaguely north-northwest for two days. I must be a good hundred kilometers from the Hab; it's a miracle I got any signal at all. Must have been a moment of perfect weather conditions.

During the boring-ass days, I'm working my way through *The Six Million Dollar Man* from Commander Lewis's inexhaustible collection of seventies tripe.

I just watched an episode where Steve Austin fights a Russian Venus probe that landed on Earth by mistake. As an expert in interplanetary travel, I can tell you there are *no* scientific inaccuracies in the story. It's quite common for probes to land on the wrong planet. Also, the probe's large, flat-panel hull is ideal for the high-pressure Venusian atmosphere. And, as we all know, probes often refuse to obey directives, choosing instead to attack humans on sight.

So far, *Pathfinder* hasn't tried to kill me. But I'm keeping an eye on it.

LOG ENTRY: SOL 93

I found the Hab signal today. No more chance to get lost. According to the computer, I'm 24,718 meters away.

I'll be home tomorrow. Even if the rover has a catastrophic failure, I'll be fine. I can *walk* to the Hab from here.

I don't know if I've mentioned this before, but I am really fucking sick of being in this rover. I've spent so much time seated or lying down, my back is all screwed up. Of all my crewmates, the one I miss most right now is Beck. He'd fix my aching back.

Though he'd probably give me a bunch of shit about it. "Why didn't you do stretching exercises? Your body is important! Eat more fiber," or whatever.

At this point, I'd welcome a health lecture.

During training, we had to practice the dreaded "Missed Orbit" scenario. In the event of a second-stage failure during MAV ascent, we'd be in orbit, but too low to reach *Hermes*. We'd be skimming the upper atmosphere, so our orbit would rapidly decay. NASA would remotely operate *Hermes* and bring it in to pick us up. Then we'd get the hell out of there before *Hermes* caught too much drag.

To drill this, they made us stay in the MAV simulator for three miserable days. Six people in an ascent vehicle originally designed for a twenty-three-minute flight. It got a little cramped. And by "a little cramped" I mean "we wanted to kill each other."

I'd give anything to be in that cramped capsule with those guys again.

Man, I hope I get *Pathfinder* working again.

LOG ENTRY: SOL 94

Home sweet home!

Today I write from my gigantic, cavernous Hab!

The first thing I did when I got in was wave my arms wildly while running in circles. Felt great! I was in that damn rover for twenty-two sols and couldn't even walk without suiting up.

I'll need to endure twice that to get to Ares 4, but that's a problem for later.

After a few celebratory laps around the Hab, it was time to get to work.

First, I fired up the oxygenator and atmospheric regulator. Checking the air levels, everything looked good. There was still CO_2, so the plants hadn't suffocated without me exhaling for them.

Naturally I did an exhaustive check on my crops, and they're all healthy.

I added my bags of shit to the manure pile. Lovely smell, I can tell you. But once I mixed some soil in, it died down to tolerable levels. I dumped my box o' pee into the water reclaimer.

I'd been gone over three weeks and had left the Hab very humid for the sake of the crops. That much water in the air can cause any amount of electrical problems, so I spent the next few hours doing full systems checks on everything.

Then I kind of lounged around for a while. I wanted to spend the rest of the day relaxing, but I had more to do.

After suiting up, I went out to the rover and dragged the solar cells off the roof. Over the next few hours, I put them back where they belonged, wiring them into the Hab's power grid.

Getting the lander off the roof was a hell of a lot easier than getting it up there. I detached a strut from the MAV platform and dragged it over to the rover. By leaning it against the hull and digging the other end into the ground for stability, I had a ramp.

I should have brought that strut with me to the *Pathfinder* site. Live and learn.

There's no way to get the lander in the airlock. It's just too big. I could probably dismantle it and bring it in a piece at a time, but there's a pretty compelling reason not to.

With no magnetic field, Mars has no defense against harsh solar radiation. If I were exposed to it, I'd get so much cancer, the cancer would have cancer. So the Hab canvas shields from electromagnetic waves. This means the Hab itself would block any transmissions if the lander were inside.

Speaking of cancer, it was time to get rid of the RTG.

It *pained* me to climb back into the rover, but it had to be done. If the RTG ever broke open, it would kill me to death.

NASA decided four kilometers was the safe distance, and I wasn't about to second-guess them. I drove back to where Commander Lewis had originally dumped it, ditched it in the same hole, and drove back to the Hab.

I'll start work on the lander tomorrow.

Now to enjoy a good, long sleep in an actual cot. With the comforting knowledge that when I wake, my morning piss will go into a toilet.

LOG ENTRY: SOL 95

Today was all about repairs!

The *Pathfinder* mission ended because the lander had an unknown critical failure. Once JPL lost contact with the lander, they had no idea what became of Sojourner. It might be in better shape. Maybe it just needs power. Power it couldn't get with its solar panels hopelessly caked with dust.

I set the little rover on my workbench and pried open a panel to peek inside. The battery was a lithium thionyl chloride nonrechargeable. I figured that out from some subtle clues: the shape of the connection points, the thickness of the insulation, and the fact that it had "LiSOCl2 NON-RCHRG" written on it.

I cleaned the solar panels thoroughly, then aimed a small, flexible lamp directly at them. The battery's long dead. But the panels might be okay, and Sojourner can operate directly off them. We'll see if anything happens.

Then it was time to take a look at Sojourner's daddy. I suited up and headed out.

On most landers, the weak point is the battery. It's the most delicate component, and when it dies, there's no way to recover.

Landers can't just shut down and wait when they have low batteries. Their electronics won't work unless they're at a minimum temperature. So they have heaters to keep the electronics warm.

It's a problem that rarely comes up on Earth, but hey. Mars.

Over time, the solar panels get covered with dust. Then winter brings colder temperatures and less daylight. This all combines into a big "fuck you" from Mars to your lander. Eventually it's using more power to keep warm than it's getting from the meager daylight that makes it through the dust.

Once the battery runs down, the electronics get too cold to operate, and the whole system dies. The solar panels will recharge the battery somewhat, but there's nothing to tell the system to reboot. Anything that could make that decision would be electronics, which would not be working. Eventually, the now-unused battery will lose its ability to retain charge.

That's the usual cause of death. And I sure hope it's what killed *Pathfinder*.

I piled some leftover parts of the MDV into a makeshift table and ramp. Then I dragged the lander up to my new outdoor workbench. Working in an EVA suit is annoying enough. Bending over the whole time would have been torture.

I got my tool kit and started poking around. Opening the outer panel wasn't too hard and I identified the battery easily enough. JPL labels everything. It's a 40 amp-hour Ag-Zn battery with an optimal voltage of 1.5. Wow. They really made those things run on nothin' back then.

I detached the battery and headed back inside. I checked it with my electronics kit, and sure enough it's dead, dead, dead. I could shuffle across a carpet and hold more charge.

But I knew what the lander needed: 1.5 volts.

Compared to the makeshift crap I've been gluing together since Sol 6, this was a breeze. I have voltage controllers in my kit! It only took me fifteen minutes to put a controller on a reserve power line, then another hour to go outside and run the line to where the battery used to be.

Then there's the issue of heat. It's a good idea to keep electronics above −40°C. The temperature today is a brisk −63°C.

The battery was big and easy to identify, but I had no clue where the heaters were. Even if I knew, it'd be too risky to hook them directly to power. I could easily fry the whole system.

So instead, I went to good old "Spare Parts" Rover 1 and stole its environment heater. I've gutted that poor rover so much, it looks like I parked it in a bad part of town.

I lugged the heater to my outdoor "workbench," and hooked it to Hab power. Then I rested it in the lander where the battery used to be.

Now I wait. And hope.

LOG ENTRY: SOL 96

I was really hoping I'd wake up to a functional lander, but no such luck. Its high-gain antenna is right where I last saw it. Why does that matter? Well, I'll tell ya . . .

If the lander comes back to life (and that's a big if), it'll try to establish contact with Earth. Problem is nobody's listening. It's not like the *Pathfinder* team is hanging around JPL just in case their long-dead probe is repaired by a wayward astronaut.

The Deep Space Network and SETI are my best

bets for picking up the signal. If either of them caught a blip from *Pathfinder*, they'd tell JPL.

JPL would quickly figure out what was going on, especially when they triangulated the signal to my landing site.

They'd tell the lander where Earth is, and it would angle the high-gain antenna appropriately. That there, the angling of the antenna, is how I'll know if it linked up.

So far, no action.

There's still hope. Any number of reasons could be delaying things. The rover heater is designed to heat air at one atmosphere, and the thin Martian air severely hampers its ability to work. So the electronics might need more time to warm up.

Also, Earth is only visible during the day. I (hopefully) fixed the lander yesterday evening. It's morning now, so most of the intervening time has been night. No Earth.

Sojourner's showing no signs of life, either. It's been in the nice, warm environment of the Hab all night, with plenty of light on its sparkling clean solar cells. Maybe it's running an extended self-check, or staying still until it hears from the lander or something.

I'll just have to put it out of my mind for now.

Pathfinder LOG: SOL 0

BOOT SEQUENCE INITIATED

TIME 00:00:00

LOSS OF POWER DETECTED, TIME/DATE UNRELIABLE

LOADING OS . . .

VXWARE OPERATING SYSTEM (C) WIND RIVER SYSTEMS

PERFORMING HARDWARE CHECK:

INT. TEMPERATURE: -34°C

EXT. TEMPERATURE: NONFUNCTIONAL
BATTERY: FULL
HIGAIN: OK
LOGAIN: OK
WIND SENSOR: NONFUNCTIONAL
METEOROLOGY: NONFUNCTIONAL
ASI: NONFUNCTIONAL
IMAGER: OK
ROVER RAMP: NONFUNCTIONAL
SOLAR A: NONFUNCTIONAL
SOLAR B: NONFUNCTIONAL
SOLAR C: NONFUNCTIONAL
HARDWARE CHECK COMPLETE

BROADCASTING STATUS
LISTENING FOR TELEMETRY SIGNAL . . .
LISTENING FOR TELEMETRY SIGNAL . . .
LISTENING FOR TELEMETRY SIGNAL
SIGNAL ACQUIRED . . .

CHAPTER 11

"SOMETHING'S COMING IN . . . yes . . . yes! It's *Pathfinder*!"

The crowded room burst into applause and cheers. Venkat slapped an unknown technician on the back while Bruce pumped his fist in the air.

The ad-hoc *Pathfinder* control center was an accomplishment in itself. Over the last twenty days, a team of JPL engineers had worked around the clock to piece together antiquated computers, repair broken components, network everything, and install hastily made software that allowed the old systems to interact with the modern Deep Space Network.

The room itself was formerly a conference room; JPL had no space ready for the sudden need. Already jam-packed with computers and equipment, the cramped space had turned positively claustrophobic with the many spectators now squeezing into it.

One Associated Press camera team pressed

against the back wall, trying—and failing—to stay out of everyone's way while recording the auspicious moment. The rest of the media would have to satisfy themselves with the live AP feed, and await a press conference.

Venkat turned to Bruce. "God damn, Bruce. You really pulled a rabbit out of your hat this time! Good work!"

"I'm just the director," Bruce said modestly. "Thank the guys who got all this stuff working."

"Oh I will!" Venkat beamed. "But first I have to talk to my new best friend!"

Turning to the headsetted man at the communications console, Venkat asked, "What's your name, new best friend?"

"Tim," he said, not taking his eyes off the screen.

"What now?" Venkat asked.

"We sent the return telemetry automatically. It'll get there in just over eleven minutes. Once it does, *Pathfinder* will start high-gain transmissions. So it'll be twenty-two minutes till we hear from it again."

"Venkat's got a doctorate in physics, Tim," Bruce said. "You don't need to explain transmission time to him."

Tim shrugged. "You can never tell with managers."

"What was in the transmission we got?" Venkat asked.

"Just the bare bones. A hardware self-check. It's got a lot of 'nonfunctional' systems, 'cause they were on the panels Watney removed."

"What about the camera?"

"It says the imager's working. We'll have it take a panorama as soon as we can."

LOG ENTRY: SOL 97

It worked!

Holy shit, it worked!

I just suited up and checked the lander. The high-gain antenna is angled *directly* at Earth! *Pathfinder* has no way of knowing where it is, so it has no way of knowing where Earth is. The *only* way for it to find out is getting a signal.

They know I'm alive!

I don't even know what to say. This was an insane plan and somehow it worked! I'm going to be talking to someone again. I spent three months as the loneliest man in history and it's finally over.

Sure, I might not get rescued. But I won't be alone.

The whole time I was recovering *Pathfinder,* I imagined what this moment would be like. I figured I'd jump up and down a bit, cheer, maybe flip off the ground (because this whole damn planet is my enemy), but that's not what happened. When I got back to the Hab and took off the EVA suit, I sat down in the dirt and cried. Bawled like a little kid for several minutes. I finally settled down to mild sniffling and then felt a deep calm.

It was a good calm.

It occurs to me: Now that I might live, I have to be more careful about logging embarrassing moments. How do I delete log entries? There's no obvious way. . . . I'll get to it later. I've got more important things to do.

I've got people to talk to!

■ ■ ■

VENKAT GRINNED as he took the podium in the JPL press room.

"We received the high-gain response just over half an hour ago," he said to the assembled press. "We immediately directed *Pathfinder* to take a panoramic image. Hopefully, Watney has some kind of message for us. Questions?"

The sea of reporters raised their hands.

"Cathy, let's start with you," Venkat said, pointing to the CNN reporter.

"Thanks," she said. "Have you had any contact with the Sojourner rover?"

"Unfortunately, no," he replied. "The lander hasn't been able to connect to Sojourner, and we have no way to contact it directly."

"What might be wrong with Sojourner?"

"I can't even speculate," Venkat said. "After spending that long on Mars, *anything* could be wrong with it."

"Best guess?"

"Our best guess is he took it into the Hab. The lander's signal wouldn't be able to reach Sojourner through Hab canvas." Pointing to another reporter, he said, "You, there."

"Marty West, NBC News," Marty said. "How will you communicate with Watney once everything's up and running?"

"That'll be up to Watney," said Venkat. "All we have to work with is the camera. He can write notes and hold them up. But how we talk back is trickier."

"How so?" Marty asked.

"Because all we have is the camera platform. That's the only moving part. There are plenty of ways to get information across with just the platform's rotation, but no way to tell Watney about them. He'll have to come up with something and tell us. We'll follow his lead."

Pointing to the next reporter, he said, "Go ahead."

"Jill Holbrook, BBC. With a twenty-two-minute round-trip and nothing but a single rotating platform to talk with, it'll be a dreadfully slow conversation, won't it?"

"Yes it will," Venkat confirmed. "It's early morning in Acidalia Planitia right now, and just past three a.m. here in Pasadena. We'll be here all night, and that's just for a start. No more questions for now. The panorama is due back in a few minutes. We'll keep you posted."

Before anyone could ask a follow-up, Venkat strode out the side door and hurried down the hall to the makeshift *Pathfinder* control center. He pressed through the throng to the communications console.

"Anything, Tim?"

"Totally," he replied. "But we're staring at this black screen because it's way more interesting than pictures from Mars."

"You're a smart-ass, Tim," Venkat said.

"Noted."

Bruce pushed his way forward. "Still another few seconds on the clock," he said.

The time passed in silence.

"Getting something," Tim said. "Yup. It's the panoramic."

Sighs of relief and muted conversation replaced tense silence as the image began coming through. It filled out from left to right at a snail's pace due to the bandwidth limitations of the antique probe sending it.

"Martian surface . . . ," Venkat said as the lines slowly filled in. "More surface . . ."

"Edge of the Hab!" Bruce said, pointing to the screen.

"Hab." Venkat smiled. "More Hab now . . . more Hab . . . Is that a message? That's a message!"

As the image grew, it revealed a handwritten note, suspended at the camera's height by a thin metal rod.

"We got a note from Mark!" Venkat announced to the room.

Applause filled the room, then quickly died down. "What's it say?" someone asked.

Venkat leaned closer to the screen. "It says . . . 'I'll write questions here—Are you receiving?' "

"Okay . . . ?" said Bruce.

"That's what it says." Venkat shrugged.

"Another note," said Tim, pointing to the screen as more of the image came through.

Venkat leaned in again. "This one says 'Point here for yes.' "

He folded his arms. "All right. We have communication with Mark. Tim, point the camera at 'Yes.' Then, start taking pictures at ten-minute intervals until he puts another question up."

LOG ENTRY: SOL 97 (2)

"Yes!" They said, "Yes!"

I haven't been this excited about a "yes" since prom night!

Okay, calm down.

I have limited paper to work with. These cards were intended to label batches of samples. I have about fifty cards. I can use both sides, and if it comes down to it, I can re-use them by scratching out the old question.

The Sharpie I'm using will last much longer than the cards, so ink isn't a problem. But I have to do all my writing in the Hab. I don't know what kind of hallucinogenic crap that ink is made of, but I'm pretty sure it would boil off in Mars's atmosphere.

I'm using old parts of the antenna array to hold the cards up. There's a certain irony in that.

We'll need to talk faster than yes/no questions every half hour. The camera can rotate 360 degrees, and I have plenty of antenna parts. Time to make an alphabet. But I can't just use the letters A through Z. Twenty-six letters plus my question card would be twenty-seven cards around the lander. Each one would only get 13 degrees of arc. Even if JPL points the camera perfectly, there's a good chance I won't know which letter they meant.

So I'll have to use ASCII. That's how computers manage characters. Each character has a numerical code between 0 and 255. Values between 0 and 255 can be expressed as 2 hexadecimal digits. By giving me pairs of hex digits, they can send any character they like, including numbers, punctuation, etc.

How do I know which values go with which characters? Because Johanssen's laptop is a wealth of information. I knew she'd have an ASCII table in there somewhere. All computer geeks do.

So I'll make cards for 0 through 9, and A through F. That makes 16 cards to place around the camera, plus the question card. Seventeen cards means over 21 degrees each. Much easier to deal with.

Time to get to work!

Spell with ASCII. 0–F at 21-degree increments. Will watch camera starting 11:00 my time. When message done, return to this position. Wait 20 minutes after completion to take picture (so I can write and post reply). Repeat process at top of every hour.

S . . . T . . . A . . . T . . . U . . . S

No physical problems. All Hab components functional. Eating 3/4 rations. Successfully growing crops in Hab with cultivated soil. Note: Situation not Ares 3 crew's fault. Bad luck.

H . . . O . . . W . . . A . . . L . . . I . . . V . . . E

Impaled by antenna fragment. Knocked out by decompression. Landed facedown, blood sealed hole. Woke up after crew left. Bio-monitor computer destroyed by puncture. Crew had reason to think me dead. Not their fault.

C . . . R . . . O . . . P . . . S . . . ?

Long story. Extreme botany. Have 126 m2 farmland growing potatoes. Will extend food supply, but not enough to last until Ares 4 landing. Modified rover for long-distance travel, plan to drive to Ares 4.

W . . . E . . . S . . . A . . . W . . . — . . . S . . . A . . . T . . . L . . . I . . . T . . . E

Government watching me with satellites? Need tinfoil hat! Also need faster way to communicate. Speak&Spell taking all damn day. Any ideas?

B . . . R . . . I . . . N . . . G . . . S . . . J . . . R . . . N . . . R . . . O . . . U . . . T

Sojourner rover brought out, placed 1 meter due north of lander. If you can contact it, I can draw hex numbers on the wheels and you can send me six bytes at a time.

S . . . J . . . R . . . N . . . R . . . N . . . O . . . T . . . R . . . S . . . P . . . N . . . D

Damn. Any other ideas? Need faster communication.

W . . . O . . . R . . . K . . . I . . . N . . . G . . . O . . . N . . . I . . . T

Earth is about to set. Resume 08:00 my time tomorrow morning. Tell family I'm fine. Give crew my best. Tell Commander Lewis disco sucks.

■ ■ ■

VENKAT BLINKED his bleary eyes several times as he tried to organize the papers on his desk. His temporary desk at JPL was nothing more than a folding table set up in the back of a break room. People were in and out picking up snacks all day, but on the plus side the coffeepot was nearby.

"Excuse me," said a man approaching the table.

"Yes, they're out of Diet Coke," Venkat said without looking up. "I don't know when Site Services refills the fridge."

"I'm actually here to talk to you, Dr. Kapoor."

"Huh?" said Venkat, looking up. He shook his head. "Sorry, I was up all night." He gulped his coffee. "Who are you again?"

"Jack Trevor," said the thin, pale man before Venkat. "I work in software engineering."

"What can I do for you?"

"We have an idea for communication."

"I'm all ears."

"We've been looking through the old *Pathfinder* software. We got duplicate computers up and running for testing. Same computers they used to find a problem that almost killed the original mission. Real interesting story, actually; turns out there was a priority inversion in Sojourner's thread management and—"

"Focus, Jack," interrupted Venkat.

"Right. Well, the thing is, *Pathfinder* has an OS update process. So we can change the software to anything we want."

"How does this help us?"

"*Pathfinder* has two communications systems. One to talk to us, the other to talk to Sojourner. We can change the second system to broadcast on the Ares 3 rover frequency. And we can have it pretend to be the beacon signal from the Hab."

"You can get *Pathfinder* talking to Mark's rover?"

"It's the only option. The Hab's radio is dead, but the rover has communications equipment made for talking to the Hab and the other rover. Problem is, to implement a new comm system, both ends of it need to have the right software running. We can remotely update *Pathfinder,* but not the rover."

"So," Venkat said, "you can get *Pathfinder* to talk to the rover, but you can't get the rover to listen or talk back."

"Right. Ideally, we want our text to show up on the rover screen, and whatever Watney types to be sent back to us. That requires a change to the rover's software."

Venkat sighed. "What's the point of this discussion if we can't update the rover's software?"

Jack grinned as he continued. "*We* can't do the patch, but Watney can! We can just send the data, and have him enter the update into the rover himself."

"How much data are we talking about?"

"I have guys working on the rover software

right now. The patch file will be twenty meg, minimum. We can send one byte to Watney every four seconds or so with the 'Speak&Spell.' It'd take three years of constant broadcasting to get that patch across. Obviously, that's no good."

"But you're talking to me, so you have a solution, right?" Venkat probed, resisting the urge to scream.

"Of course!" Jack beamed. "Software engineers are sneaky bastards when it comes to data management."

"Enlighten me," said Venkat.

"Here's the clever part," Jack said, conspiratorially. "The rover currently parses the signal into bytes, then identifies the specific sequence the Hab sends. That way, natural radio waves won't throw off the homing. If the bytes aren't right, the rover ignores them."

"Okay, so what?"

"It means there's a spot in the code base where it's got the parsed bytes. We can insert a tiny bit of code, just twenty instructions, to write the parsed bytes to a log file before checking their validity."

"This sounds promising . . . ," Venkat said.

"It is!" Jack said excitedly. "First, we update *Pathfinder* so it knows how to talk to the rover. Then, we tell Watney exactly how to hack the rover software to add those twenty instructions. Then we have *Pathfinder* broadcast new software to the rover. The rover logs the bytes to a file. Finally, Watney launches the file as an executable and the rover patches itself!"

Venkat furrowed his brow, taking in far more information than his sleep-deprived mind wanted to accept.

"Um," Jack said. "You're not cheering or dancing."

"So we just need to send Watney those twenty instructions?" Venkat asked.

"That, and how to edit the files. And where to insert the instructions in the files."

"Just like that?"

"Just like that!"

Venkat was silent for a moment. "Jack, I'm going to buy your whole team autographed *Star Trek* memorabilia."

"I prefer *Star Wars*," he said, turning to leave. "The original trilogy only, of course."

"Of course," Venkat said.

As Jack walked away, a woman approached Venkat's table.

"Yes?" Venkat said.

"I can't find any Diet Coke, are we out?"

"Yes," Venkat said. "I don't know when Site Services refills the fridge."

"Thanks," she said.

Just as he was about to get back to work, his mobile rang. He groaned loudly at the ceiling as he snatched the phone from his desk.

"Hello?" he said as cheerfully as he could.

"I need a picture of Watney."

"Hi, Annie. Nice to hear from you, too. How are things back in Houston?"

"Cut the shit, Venkat. I need a picture."

"It's not that simple," Venkat explained.

"You're talking to him with a fucking camera. How hard can it be?"

"We spell out our message, wait twenty minutes, and *then* take a picture. Watney's back in the Hab by then."

"So tell him to be around when you take the next picture," Annie demanded.

"We can only send one message per hour, and only when Acidalia Planitia is facing Earth," Venkat said. "We're not going to waste a message just to tell him to pose for a photo. Besides, he'll be in his EVA suit. You won't even be able to see his face."

"I need something, Venkat," Annie said. "You've been in contact for twenty-four hours and the media is going ape shit. They want an image for the story. It'll be on every news site in the world."

"You have the pictures of his notes. Make do with that."

"Not enough," Annie said. "The press is crawling down my throat for this. And up my ass. Both directions, Venkat! They're gonna meet in the middle!"

"It'll have to wait a few days. We're going to try and link *Pathfinder* to the rover computer—"

"A few days!?" Annie gasped. "This is all anyone cares about right now. In the world. This is the biggest story since Apollo 13. Give me a fucking picture!"

Venkat sighed. "I'll try to get it tomorrow."

"Great!" she said. "Looking forward to it."

LOG ENTRY: SOL 98

I have to be watching the camera when it spells things out. It's half a byte at a time. So I watch a pair of numbers, then look them up on an ASCII cheat sheet I made. That's one letter.

I don't want to forget any letters, so I scrape

them into the dirt with a rod. The process of looking up a letter and scraping it in the dirt takes a couple of seconds. Sometimes when I look back at the camera, I've missed a number. I can usually guess it from context, but other times I just miss out.

Today, I got up hours earlier than I needed to. It was like Christmas morning! I could hardly wait for 08:00 to roll around. I had breakfast, did some unnecessary checks on Hab equipment, and read some Poirot. Finally the time came!

CNHAKRVR2TLK2PTHFDRPRP4LONGMSG

Yeah. Took me a minute. "Can hack rover to talk to *Pathfinder*. Prepare for long message."

That took some mental gymnastics to work out. But it was great news! If we could get that set up, we'd only be limited by transmission time! I set up a note that said, *Roger*.

Not sure what they meant by "long message," but I figured I better be ready. I went out fifteen minutes before the top of the hour and smoothed out a big area of dirt. I found the longest antenna rod I had, so I could reach into the smooth area without having to step on it.

Then I stood by. Waiting.

At exactly the top of the hour, the message came.

LNCHhexiditONRVRCMP,OPENFILE-/usr/lib/habcomm.so-SCROLLTILIDXONLFTIS:2AAE5,OVRWRT141BYTSWTHDATAWE'LLSNDNXTMSG,STANDINVIEW4NXTPIC20MINFTERTHSDONE

Jesus. Okay . . .

They want me to launch "hexedit" on the rover's computer, then open the file /usr/lib/habcomm.so, scroll until the index reading on the left of the screen is 2AAE5, then replace the bytes there with a 141-byte sequence NASA will send in the next message. Fair enough.

Also, for some reason, they want me to hang around for the next pic. Not sure why. You can't see any part of me when I'm in the suit. Even the faceplate would reflect too much light. Still, it's what they want.

I went back in and copied down the message for future reference. Then I wrote a short note and came back out. Usually I'd pin up the note and go back in. But this time I had to hang around for a photo op.

I gave the camera a thumbs-up to go along with my note, which said, *Ayyyyyy!*

Blame the seventies TV.

■ ■ ■

"I ASK for a picture, and I get the Fonz?" Annie asked, admonishing Venkat.

"You got your picture, quit bitching," he said, cradling the phone on his shoulder. He paid more attention to the schematics in front of him than the conversation.

"Ayyyyyy!" Annie mocked. "Why would he do that?"

"Have you *met* Mark Watney?"

"Fine, fine," Annie said. "But I want a pic of his face ASAP."

"Can't do that."

"Why not?"

"Because if he takes off his helmet, he'll die.

Annie, I have to go, one of the JPL programmers is here and it's urgent. Bye!"

"But—" Annie said as he hung up.

Jack, in the doorway, said, "It's not urgent."

"Yeah, I know," Venkat said. "What can I do for you?"

"We were thinking," Jack began. "This rover hack might get kind of detailed. We may have to do a bunch of back-and-forth communication with Watney."

"That's fine," Venkat said. "Take your time, do it right."

"We could get things done faster with a shorter transmission time," Jack said.

Venkat gave him a puzzled look. "Do you have a plan for moving Earth and Mars closer together?"

"Earth doesn't have to be involved," Jack said. "*Hermes* is seventy-three million kilometers from Mars right now. Only four light-minutes away. Beth Johanssen is a great programmer. She could talk Mark through it."

"Out of the question," Venkat said.

"She's the mission sysop." Jack pressed on. "This is her exact area of expertise."

"Can't do it, Jack. The crew still doesn't know."

"What is with you? Why won't you just tell them?"

"Watney's not my only responsibility," Venkat said. "I've got five other astronauts in deep space who have to concentrate on their return trip. Nobody thinks about it, but statistically they're in more danger than Watney right now. He's on a planet. They're in space."

Jack shrugged. "Fine, we'll do it the slow way."

LOG ENTRY: SOL 98 (2)

Ever transcribed 141 random bytes, one-half of a byte at a time?

It's boring. And it's tricky when you don't have a pen.

Earlier, I had just written letters in the sand. But this time, I needed a way to get the numbers onto something portable. My first plan was: Use a laptop!

Each crewman had their own laptop. So I have six at my disposal. Rather, I *had* six. I now have five. I thought a laptop would be fine outside. It's just electronics, right? It'll keep warm enough to operate in the short term, and it doesn't need air for anything.

It died instantly. The screen went black before I was out of the airlock. Turns out the "L" in "LCD" stands for "Liquid." I guess it either froze or boiled off. Maybe I'll post a consumer review. "Brought product to surface of Mars. It stopped working. 0/10."

So I used a camera. I've got lots of them, specially made for working on Mars. I wrote the bytes in the sand as they came in, took a picture, then transcribed them in the Hab.

It's night now, so no more messages. Tomorrow, I'll enter this into the rover and the geeks at JPL can take it from there.

▪▪▪

A NOTABLE smell hung in the air of the makeshift *Pathfinder* control room. The ventilation system was not designed for so many people, and everyone had been working every waking moment without much time for personal hygiene.

"Come on up here, Jack," said Venkat. "You get to be the most Timward today."

"Thanks," said Jack, taking Venkat's place next to Tim. "Heya, Tim!"

"Jack," said Tim.

"How long will the patch take?" Venkat asked.

"Should be pretty much instant," Jack answered. "Watney entered the hack earlier today, and we confirmed it worked. We updated *Pathfinder*'s OS without any problems. We sent the rover patch, which *Pathfinder* rebroadcast. Once Watney executes the patch and reboots the rover, we should get a connection."

"Jesus, what a complicated process," Venkat said.

"Try updating a Linux server sometime," Jack said.

After a moment of silence, Tim said, "You know he was telling a joke, right? That was supposed to be funny."

"Oh," said Venkat. "I'm a physics guy, not a computer guy."

"He's not funny to computer guys, either."

"You're a very unpleasant man, Tim," Jack said.

"System's online," said Tim.

"What?"

"It's online. FYI."

"Holy crap!" Jack said.

"It worked!" Venkat announced to the room.

■■■

[11:18] JPL: Mark, this is Venkat Kapoor. We've been watching you since Sol 49. The whole world's been rooting for you. Amazing job, getting Pathfinder. We're working on rescue plans. JPL is adjusting Ares 4's MDV to do a short overland flight. They'll pick you up, then take you with them to Schiaparelli. We're putting together a supply mission to keep you fed till Ares 4 arrives.

[11:29] WATNEY: Glad to hear it. Really looking forward to not dying. I want to make it clear it wasn't the crew's fault. Side question: What did they say when they found out I was alive? Also, "Hi, Mom!"

[11:41] JPL: Tell us about your "crops." We estimated your food packs would last until Sol 400 at 3/4 ration per meal. Will your crops affect that number? As to your question: We haven't told the crew you're alive yet. We wanted them to concentrate on their own mission.

[11:52] WATNEY: The crops are potatoes, grown from the ones we were supposed to prepare on Thanksgiving. They're doing great, but the available farmland isn't enough for sustainability. I'll run out of food around Sol 900. Also: Tell the crew I'm alive! What the fuck is wrong with you?

[12:04] JPL: We'll get botanists in to ask detailed questions and double-check your work. Your life is at stake, so we want to be sure. Sol 900 is great news. It'll give us a lot more time to get the supply mission together. Also, please watch your language. Everything you type is being broadcast live all over the world.

[12:15] WATNEY: Look! A pair of boobs! -> (.Y.)

■ ■ ■

"THANK YOU, Mr. President," Teddy said into the phone. "I appreciate the call, and I'll pass your congratulations on to the whole organization."

He terminated the call and put his phone on the corner of his desk, flush with the desktop's edges.

Mitch knocked on the open door to the office.

"This a good time?" Mitch asked.

"Come in, Mitch," Teddy said. "Have a seat."

"Thanks," Mitch said, sitting in a fine leather couch. He reached up to his earpiece and lowered the volume.

"How's Mission Control?" Teddy asked.

"Fantastic," Mitch said. "All's well with *Hermes*. And everyone's in great spirits thanks to what's going on at JPL. Today was a damn good day for a change!"

"Yes, it was," Teddy agreed. "Another step closer to getting Watney back alive."

"Yeah, about that," said Mitch. "You probably know why I'm here."

"I can take a guess," said Teddy. "You want to tell the crew Watney's alive."

"Yes," Mitch said.

"And you're bringing this up with me while Venkat is in Pasadena, so he can't argue the other side."

"I shouldn't have to clear this with you or Venkat or anyone else. I'm the flight director. It should have been my call from the beginning, but you two stepped in and overrode me. Ignoring all that, we agreed we'd tell them when there was hope. And now there's hope. We've got communication, we have a plan for rescue in the works, and his farm buys us enough time to get him supplies."

"Okay, tell them," Teddy said.

Mitch paused. "Just like that?"

"I knew you'd be here sooner or later, so I already thought it through and decided. Go ahead and tell them."

Mitch stood up. "All right. Thanks," he said as he left the office.

Teddy swiveled in his chair and looked out his windows to the night sky. He pondered the faint, red dot among the stars. "Hang in there, Watney," he said. "We're coming."

CHAPTER 12

WATNEY SLEPT peacefully in his bunk. He shifted slightly as some pleasant dream put a smile on his face. He'd done three EVAs the previous day, all filled with labor-intensive Hab maintenance. So he slept deeper and better than he had in a long time.

"Good morning, crew!" Lewis called out. "It's a brand-new day! Sol 6! Up and at 'em!"

Watney added his voice to a chorus of groans.

"Come on," Lewis prodded, "no bitching. You got forty minutes more sleep than you would've on Earth."

Martinez was first out of his bunk. An air force man, he could match Lewis's navy schedule with ease. "Morning, Commander," he said crisply.

Johanssen sat up, but made no further move toward the harsh world outside her blankets. A career software engineer, mornings were never her forte.

Vogel slowly lumbered from his bunk, checking his watch. He wordlessly pulled on his jumpsuit, smoothing out what wrinkles he could. He sighed inwardly at the grimy feeling of another day without a shower.

Watney turned away, hugging a pillow to his head. "Noisy people, go away," he mumbled.

"Beck!" Martinez called out, shaking the mission's doctor. "Rise and shine, bud!"

"Yeah, okay," Beck said blearily.

Johanssen fell out of her bunk, then remained on the floor.

Pulling the pillow from Watney's hands, Lewis said, "Let's move, Watney! Uncle Sam paid a hundred thousand dollars for every second we'll be here."

"Bad woman take pillow," Watney groaned, unwilling to open his eyes.

"Back on Earth, I've tipped two-hundred-pound men out of their bunks. Want to see what I can do in 0.4 g?"

"No, not really," Watney said, sitting up.

Having rousted the troops, Lewis sat at the comm station to check overnight messages from Houston.

Watney shuffled to the ration cupboard and grabbed a breakfast at random.

"Hand me an 'eggs,' will ya," Martinez said.

"You can tell the difference?" Watney said, passing Martinez a pack.

"Not really," Martinez said.

"Beck, what'll you have?" Watney continued.

"Don't care," Beck said. "Give me whatever."

Watney tossed a pack to him.

"Vogel, your usual sausages?"

"*Ja*, please," Vogel responded.

"You know you're a stereotype, right?"

"I am comfortable with that," Vogel replied, taking the proffered breakfast.

"Hey Sunshine," Watney called to Johanssen. "Eating breakfast today?"

"Mnrrn," Johanssen grunted.

"Pretty sure that's a no," Watney guessed.

The crew ate in silence. Johanssen eventually trudged to the ration cupboard and got a coffee packet. She clumsily added hot water, then sipped until wakefulness crept in.

"Mission updates from Houston," Lewis said. "Satellites show a storm coming, but we can do surface ops before it gets here. Vogel, Martinez, you'll be with me outside. Johanssen, you're stuck tracking weather reports. Watney, your soil experiments are bumped up to today. Beck, run the samples from yesterday's EVA through the spectrometer."

"Should you really go out with a storm on the way?" Beck asked.

"Houston authorized it," Lewis said.

"Seems needlessly dangerous."

"Coming to Mars was needlessly dangerous," Lewis said. "What's your point?"

Beck shrugged. "Just be careful."

■■■

THREE FIGURES looked eastward. Their bulky EVA suits rendered them nearly identical. Only the European Union flag on Vogel's shoulder distinguished him from Lewis and Martinez, who wore the Stars and Stripes.

The darkness to the east undulated and flickered in the rays of the rising sun.

"The storm," Vogel said in his accented English, "it is closer than Houston reported."

"We've got time," Lewis said. "Focus on the task at hand. This EVA's all about chemical analysis. Vogel, you're the chemist, so you're in charge of what we dig up."

"Ja," Vogel said. "Please dig thirty centimeters and get soil samples. At least one hundred grams each. Very important is thirty centimeters down."

"Will do," Lewis said. "Stay within a hundred meters of the Hab," she added.

"Mm," Vogel said.

"Yes, ma'am," said Martinez.

They split up. Greatly improved since the days of Apollo, Ares EVA suits allowed much more freedom of motion. Digging, bending over, and bagging samples were trivial tasks.

After a time, Lewis asked, "How many samples do you need?"

"Seven each, perhaps?"

"That's fine," Lewis confirmed. "I've got four so far."

"Five here," Martinez said. "Of course, we can't expect the navy to keep up with the air force, now can we?"

"So that's how you want to play it?" Lewis said.

"Just call 'em as I see 'em, Commander."

"Johanssen here." The sysop's voice came over the radio. "Houston's upgraded the storm to 'severe.' It's going to be here in fifteen minutes."

"Back to base," Lewis said.

▪▪▪

THE HAB shook in the roaring wind as the astronauts huddled in the center. All six of them now wore their flight space suits, in case they had to scramble for an emergency takeoff in the MAV. Johanssen watched her laptop while the rest watched her.

"Sustained winds over one hundred kph now," she said. "Gusting to one twenty-five."

"Jesus, we're gonna end up in Oz," Watney said. "What's the abort wind speed?"

"Technically one fifty kph," Martinez said. "Any more than that and the MAV's in danger of tipping."

"Any predictions on the storm track?" Lewis asked.

"This is the edge of it," Johanssen said, staring at her screen. "It's gonna get worse before it gets better."

The Hab canvas rippled under the brutal assault as the internal supports bent and shivered with each gust. The cacophony grew louder by the minute.

"All right," Lewis said. "Prep for abort. We'll go to the MAV and hope for the best. If the wind gets too high, we'll launch."

Leaving the Hab in pairs, they grouped up outside Airlock 1. The driving wind and sand battered them, but they were able to stay on their feet.

"Visibility is almost zero," Lewis said. "If you get lost, home in on my suit's telemetry. The wind's gonna be rougher away from the Hab, so be ready."

Pressing through the gale, they stumbled toward the MAV, with Lewis and Beck in the lead and Watney and Johanssen bringing up the rear.

"Hey," Watney panted. "Maybe we could shore up the MAV. Make tipping less likely."

"How?" Lewis huffed.

"We could use cables from the solar farm as guylines." He wheezed for a few moments, then continued. "The rovers could be anchors. The trick would be getting the line around the—"

Flying wreckage slammed Watney, carrying him off into the wind.

"Watney!" Johanssen exclaimed.

"What happened?" Lewis said.

"Something hit him!" Johanssen reported.

"Watney, report," Lewis said.

No reply.

"Watney, report," Lewis repeated.

Again, she was met with silence.

"He's offline," Johanssen reported. "I don't know where he is!"

"Commander," Beck said, "before we lost telemetry, his decompression alarm went off!"

"Shit!" Lewis exclaimed. "Johanssen, where did you last see him?"

"He was right in front of me and then he was gone," she said. "He flew off due west."

"Okay," Lewis said. "Martinez, get to the MAV and prep for launch. Everyone else, home in on Johanssen."

"Dr. Beck," Vogel said as he stumbled through the storm, "how long can a person survive decompression?"

"Less than a minute," Beck said, emotion choking his voice.

"I can't see anything," Johanssen said as the crew crowded around her.

"Line up and walk west," Lewis commanded.

"Small steps. He's probably prone; we don't want to step over him."

Staying in sight of one another, they trudged through the chaos.

Martinez fell into the MAV airlock and forced it closed against the wind. Once it pressurized, he quickly doffed his suit. Having climbed the ladder to the crew compartment, he slid into the pilot's couch and booted the system.

Grabbing the emergency launch checklist with one hand, he flicked switches rapidly with the other. One by one, the systems reported flight-ready status. As they came online, he noted one in particular.

"Commander," he radioed. "The MAV's got a seven-degree tilt. It'll tip at 12.3."

"Copy that," Lewis said.

"Johanssen," Beck said, looking at his arm computer, "Watney's bio-monitor sent something before going offline. My computer just says 'Bad Packet.' "

"I have it, too," Johanssen said. "It didn't finish transmitting. Some data's missing, and there's no checksum. Gimme a sec."

"Commander," Martinez said. "Message from Houston. We're officially scrubbed. The storm's definitely gonna be too rough."

"Copy," Lewis said.

"They sent that four and a half minutes ago," Martinez continued, "while looking at satellite data from nine minutes ago."

"Understood," Lewis said. "Continue prepping for launch."

"Copy," Martinez said.

"Beck," Johanssen said. "I have the raw packet.

It's plaintext: BP 0, PR 0, TP 36.2. That's as far as it got."

"Copy," Beck said morosely. "Blood pressure zero, pulse rate zero, temperature normal."

The channel fell silent for some time. They continued pressing forward, shuffling through the sandstorm, hoping for a miracle.

"Temperature normal?" Lewis said, a hint of hope in her voice.

"It takes a while for the—" Beck stammered. "It takes a while to cool."

"Commander," Martinez said. "Tilting at 10.5 degrees now, with gusts pushing it to eleven."

"Copy," Lewis said. "Are you at pilot-release?"

"Affirmative," Martinez replied. "I can launch anytime."

"If it tips, can you launch before it falls completely over?"

"Uh," Martinez said, not expecting the question. "Yes, ma'am. I'd take manual control and go full throttle. Then I'd nose up and return to preprogrammed ascent."

"Copy that," Lewis said. "Everyone home in on Martinez's suit. That'll get you to the MAV airlock. Get in and prep for launch."

"What about you, Commander?" Beck asked.

"I'm searching a little more. Get moving. And Martinez, if you start to tip, launch."

"You really think I'll leave you behind?" Martinez said.

"I just ordered you to," Lewis replied. "You three, get to the ship."

They reluctantly obeyed Lewis's order and made their way toward the MAV. The punishing wind fought them every step of the way.

Unable to see the ground, Lewis shuffled forward. Remembering something, she reached to her back and got a pair of rock-drill bits. She had added the one-meter bits to her equipment that morning, anticipating geological sampling later in the day. Holding one in each hand, she dragged them along the ground as she walked.

After twenty meters, she turned around and walked the opposite direction. Walking a straight line proved to be impossible. Not only did she lack visual references, the endless wind pushed her off course. The sheer volume of attacking sand buried her feet with each step. Grunting, she pressed on.

Beck, Johanssen, and Vogel squeezed into the MAV airlock. Designed for two, it could be used by three in emergencies. As it equalized, Lewis's voice came over the radio.

"Johanssen," she said, "would the rover IR camera do any good?"

"Negative," Johanssen replied. "IR can't get through sand any better than visible light."

"What's she thinking?" Beck asked after removing his helmet. "She's a geologist. She knows IR can't get through a sandstorm."

"She is grasping," Vogel said, opening the inner door. "We must get to the couches. Please hurry."

"I don't feel good about this," Beck said.

"Neither do I, Doctor," said Vogel, climbing the ladder, "but the commander has given us orders. Insubordination will not help."

"Commander," Martinez radioed, "we're tilting 11.6 degrees. One good gust and we're tipping."

"What about the proximity radar?" Lewis said. "Could it detect Watney's suit?"

"No way," Martinez said. "It's made to see *Hermes* in orbit, not the metal in a single space suit."

"Give it a try," Lewis said.

"Commander," said Beck, putting on a headset as he slid into his acceleration couch, "I know you don't want to hear this, but Watn— . . . Mark's dead."

"Copy," Lewis said. "Martinez, try the radar."

"Roger," Martinez radioed.

He brought the radar online and waited for it to complete a self-check. Glaring at Beck, he said, "What's the matter with you?"

"My friend just died," Beck answered. "And I don't want my commander to die, too."

Martinez gave him a stern look. Turning his attention back to the radar, he radioed, "Negative contact on proximity radar."

"Nothing?" Lewis asked.

"It can barely see the Hab," he replied. "The sandstorm's fucking things up. Even if it wasn't, there's not enough metal in— Shit!"

"Strap in!" he yelled to the crew. "We're tipping!"

The MAV creaked as it tilted faster and faster.

"Thirteen degrees," Johanssen called out from her couch.

Buckling his restraints, Vogel said, "We are far past balance. We will not rock back."

"We can't leave her!" Beck yelled. "Let it tip, we'll fix it!"

"Thirty-two metric tons including fuel," Martinez said, his hands flying over the controls. "If it hits the ground, it'll do structural damage to the tanks, frame, and probably the second-stage engine. We'd never be able to fix it."

"You can't abandon her!" Beck said. "You can't."

"I've got one trick. If that doesn't work, I'm following her orders."

Bringing the orbital maneuvering system online, he fired a sustained burn from the nose cone array. The small thrusters fought against the lumbering mass of the slowly tilting spacecraft.

"You are firing the OMS?" Vogel asked.

"I don't know if it'll work. We're not tipping very fast," Martinez said. "I think it's slowing down . . ."

"The aerodynamic caps will have automatically ejected," Vogel said. "It will be a bumpy ascent with three holes in the side of the ship."

"Thanks for the tip," Martinez said, maintaining the burn and watching the tilt readout. "C'mon . . . "

"Still thirteen degrees," Johanssen reported.

"What's going on up there?" Lewis radioed. "You went quiet. Respond."

"Stand by," Martinez replied.

"Twelve point nine degrees," Johanssen said.

"It is working," Vogel said.

"For now," Martinez said. "I don't know if maneuvering fuel will last."

"Twelve point eight now," Johanssen supplied.

"OMS fuel at sixty percent," Beck said. "How much do you need to dock with *Hermes*?"

"Ten percent if I don't fuck anything up," Martinez said, adjusting the thrust angle.

"Twelve point six," Johanssen said. "We're tipping back."

"Or the wind died down a little," Beck postulated. "Fuel at forty-five percent."

"There is danger of damage to the vents," Vogel cautioned. "The OMS was not made for prolonged thrusts."

"I know," Martinez said. "I can dock without nose vents if I have to."

"Almost there . . . ," Johanssen said. "Okay we're under 12.3."

"OMS cutoff," Martinez announced, terminating the burn.

"Still tipping back," Johanssen said. "11.6 . . . 11.5 . . . holding at 11.5."

"OMS Fuel at twenty-two percent," Beck said.

"Yeah, I see that," Martinez replied. "It'll be enough."

"Commander," Beck radioed, "you need to get to the ship now."

"Agreed," Martinez radioed. "He's gone, ma'am. Watney's gone."

The four crewmates awaited their commander's response.

"Copy," she finally replied. "On my way."

They lay in silence, strapped to their couches and ready for launch. Beck looked at Watney's empty couch and saw Vogel doing the same. Martinez ran a self-check on the nose cone OMS thrusters. They were no longer safe for use. He noted the malfunction in his log.

The airlock cycled. After removing her suit, Lewis made her way to the flight cabin. She wordlessly strapped into her couch, her face a frozen mask. Only Martinez dared speak.

"Still at pilot-release," he said quietly. "Ready for launch."

Lewis closed her eyes and nodded.

"I'm sorry, Commander," Martinez said. "You need to verbally—"

"Launch," she said.

"Yes, ma'am," he replied, activating the sequence.

The retaining clamps ejected from the launch gantry, falling to the ground. Seconds later, preignition pyros fired, igniting the main engines, and the MAV lurched upward.

The ship slowly gained speed. As it did, wind shear blew it laterally off course. Sensing the problem, the ascent software angled the ship into the wind to counteract it.

As fuel was consumed, the ship got lighter, and the acceleration more pronounced. Rising at this exponential rate, the craft quickly reached maximum acceleration, a limit defined not by the ship's power, but by the delicate human bodies inside.

As the ship soared, the open OMS ports took their toll. The crew rocked in their couches as the craft shook violently. Martinez and the ascent software kept it trim, though it was a constant battle. The turbulence tapered off and eventually fell to nothing as the atmosphere became thinner and thinner.

Suddenly, all force stopped. The first stage had been completed. The crew experienced weightlessness for several seconds, then were pressed back into their couches as the next stage began. Outside, the now-empty first stage fell away, eventually to crash on some unknown area of the planet below.

The second stage pushed the ship ever higher, and into low orbit. Lasting less time than the massive first stage, and thrusting much more smoothly, it seemed almost like an afterthought.

Abruptly, the engine stopped, and an oppressive calm replaced the previous cacophony.

"Main engine shutdown," Martinez said. "Ascent time: eight minutes, fourteen seconds. On course for *Hermes* intercept."

Normally, an incident-free launch would be cause for celebration. This one earned only silence broken by Johanssen's gentle sobbing.

■ ■ ■

Four months later . . .

Beck tried not to think about the painful reason he was doing zero-g plant growth experiments. He noted the size and shape of the fern leaves, took photos, and made notes.

Having completed his science schedule for the day, he checked his watch. Perfect timing. The data dump would be completing soon. He floated past the reactor to the Semicone-A ladder.

Traveling feet-first along the ladder, he soon had to grip it in earnest as the centripetal force of the rotating ship took hold. By the time he reached Semicone-A he was at 0.4 g.

No mere luxury, the centripetal gravity of *Hermes* kept them fit. Without it, they would have spent their first week on Mars barely able to walk. Zero-g exercise regimens could keep the heart and bones healthy, but none had been devised that would give them full function from Sol 1.

Because the ship was already designed for it, they used the system on the return trip as well.

Johanssen sat at her station. Lewis sat in the adjacent seat while Vogel and Martinez hovered nearby. The data dump carried e-mails and videos from home. It was the high point of the day.

"Is it here yet?" Beck asked as he entered the bridge.

"Almost," Johanssen said. "Ninety-eight percent."

"You're looking cheerful, Martinez," Beck said.

"My son turned three yesterday." He beamed. "Should be some pics of the party. How about you?"

"Nothing special," Beck said. "Peer reviews of a paper I wrote a few years back."

"Complete," Johanssen said. "All the personal e-mails are dispatched to your laptops. Also there's a telemetry update for Vogel and a system update for me. Huh . . . there's a voice message addressed to the whole crew."

She looked over her shoulder to Lewis.

Lewis shrugged. "Play it."

Johanssen opened the message, then sat back.

"*Hermes*, this is Mitch Henderson," the message began.

"Henderson?" Martinez said, puzzled. "Talking directly to us without CAPCOM?"

Lewis held her hand up to signal for silence.

"I have some news," Mitch's voice continued. "There's no subtle way to put this: Mark Watney's still alive."

Johanssen gasped.

"Wha—" Beck stammered.

Vogel stood with his mouth agape as a shocked expression swept across his face.

Martinez looked to Lewis. She leaned forward and pinched her chin.

"I know that's a surprise," Mitch continued. "And I know you'll have a lot of questions. We're going to answer those questions. But for now I'll just give you the basics.

"He's alive and healthy. We found out two months ago and decided not to tell you; we even censored personal messages. I was *strongly* against all that. We're telling you now because we finally have communication with him and a viable rescue plan. It boils down to Ares 4 picking him up with a modified MDV.

"We'll get you a full write-up of what happened, but it's definitely not your fault. Mark stresses that every time it comes up. It was just bad luck.

"Take some time to absorb this. Your science schedules are cleared for tomorrow. Send all the questions you want and we'll answer them. Henderson out."

The message's end brought stunned silence to the bridge.

"He . . . He's alive?" Martinez said, then smiled.

Vogel nodded excitedly. "He lives."

Johanssen stared at her screen in wide-eyed disbelief.

"Holy shit," Beck laughed. "Holy shit! Commander! He's alive!"

"I left him behind," Lewis said quietly.

The celebrations ceased immediately as the crew saw their commander's expression.

"But," Beck began, "we all left togeth—"

"You followed orders," Lewis interrupted. "I left him behind. In a barren, unreachable, godforsaken wasteland."

Beck looked to Martinez pleadingly. Martinez opened his mouth, but could find no words to say.

Lewis trudged off the bridge.

CHAPTER 13

The employees of Deyo Plastics worked double shifts to finish the Hab canvas for Ares 3. There was talk of triple shifts, if NASA increased the order again. No one minded. The overtime pay was spectacular, and the funding was limitless.

Woven carbon thread ran slowly through the press, which sandwiched it between polymer sheets. The completed material was folded four times and glued together. The resulting thick sheet was then coated with soft resin and taken to the hot-room to set.

LOG ENTRY: SOL 114

Now that NASA can talk to me, they won't shut the hell up.

They want constant updates on every Hab system, and they've got a room full of people trying to micromanage my crops. It's *awesome* to have a bunch of dipshits on Earth telling me, a botanist, how to grow plants.

I mostly ignore them. I don't want to come off as arrogant here, but I'm the best botanist on the planet.

One big bonus: e-mail! Just like the days back on *Hermes,* I get data dumps. Of course, they relay e-mail from friends and family, but NASA also sends along choice messages from the public. I've gotten e-mail from rock stars, athletes, actors and actresses, and even the President.

One of them was from my alma mater, the University of Chicago. They say once you grow crops somewhere, you have officially "colonized" it. So technically, I colonized Mars.

In your *face,* Neil Armstrong!

But my favorite e-mail was the one from my mother. It's exactly what you'd expect. Thank God you're alive, stay strong, don't die, your father says hello, etc.

I read it fifty times in a row. Hey, don't get me wrong, I'm not a mama's boy or anything. I'm a full-grown man who only occasionally wears diapers (you have to in an EVA suit). It's totally manly and normal for me to cling to a letter from my mom. It's not like I'm some homesick kid at camp, right?

Admittedly, I have to schlep to the rover five times a day to check e-mail. They can get a message from Earth to Mars, but they can't get it another ten meters to the Hab. But hey, I can't bitch. My odds of living through this are way higher now.

Last I heard, they'd solved the weight problem on Ares 4's MDV. Once it lands here, they'll ditch the heat shield, all the life support stuff, and a bunch of empty fuel tanks. Then they can take the seven of us (Ares 4's crew plus me) all the way to Schiaparelli. They're already working on my duties for the surface ops. How cool is that?

In other news, I'm learning Morse code. Why? Because it's our backup communications system. NASA figured a decades-old probe isn't ideal as a sole means of communication.

If *Pathfinder* craps out, I'll spell messages with rocks, which NASA will see with satellites. They can't reply, but at least we'd have one-way communication. Why Morse code? Because making dots and dashes with rocks is a lot easier than making letters.

It's a shitty way to communicate. Hopefully it won't come up.

All chemical reactions complete, the sheet was sterilized and moved to a clean room. There, a worker cut a strip off the edge, divided it into squares, and put each through a series of rigorous tests.

Having passed inspection, the sheet was then cut to shape. The edges were folded over, sewn, and resealed with resin. A man with a clipboard made final inspections, independently verifying the measurements, then approved it for use.

LOG ENTRY: SOL 115

The meddling botanists have grudgingly admitted I did a good job. They agree I'll have enough food to last till Sol 900. Bearing that in mind, NASA has fleshed out the mission details of the supply probe.

At first, they were working on a desperate plan to get a probe here before Sol 400. But I bought another five hundred sols of life with my potato farm, so they have more time to work on it.

They'll launch next year during the Hohmann Transfer Window, and it'll take almost nine months to get here. It should arrive around Sol 856. It'll have plenty of food, a spare oxygenator, water reclaimer, and comm system. Three comm systems, actually. I guess they aren't taking any chances, what with my habit of being nearby when radios break.

Got my first e-mail from *Hermes* today. NASA's been limiting direct contact. I guess they're afraid I'll say something like "You abandoned me on Mars, you assholes!" I know the crew was surprised to hear from the Ghost of Mars Missions Past, but c'mon! I wish NASA was less of a nanny sometimes. Anyway, they finally let one e-mail through from the Commander:

> Watney, obviously we're very happy to hear you survived. As the person responsible for your situation, I wish there was more I could do to directly help. But it looks like NASA has a good rescue plan. I'm sure you'll continue to show your incredible resourcefulness and get through this. Looking forward to buying you a beer back on Earth.
>
> —Lewis

My reply:

> Commander, pure bad luck is responsible for my situation, not you. You made the right call and saved everyone else. I know it must have

been a tough decision, but any analysis of that day will show it was the right one. Get everyone else home and I'll be happy.

I will take you up on that beer, though.

—Watney

The employees carefully folded the sheet and placed it in an argon-filled airtight shipping container. The man with the clipboard placed a sticker on the package. "Project Ares 3; Hab Canvas; Sheet AL102."

The package was placed on a charter plane and flown to Edwards Air Force Base in California. It flew abnormally high, at great cost of fuel, to ensure a smoother flight.

Upon arrival, the package was carefully transported by special convoy to Pasadena. Once there, it was moved to the JPL Spacecraft Assembly Facility. Over the next five weeks, engineers in white bodysuits assembled Presupply 309. It contained AL102 as well as twelve other Hab Canvas packages.

LOG ENTRY: SOL 116

It's almost time for the second harvest.

Ayup.

I wish I had a straw hat and some suspenders.

My reseed of the potatoes went well. I'm beginning to see that crops on Mars are extremely prolific, thanks to the billions of dollars' worth of life support equipment around me. I now have four hundred healthy potato plants, each one making lots of calorie-filled taters for my dining enjoyment. In just ten days they'll be ripe!

And this time, I'm not replanting them as seed.

This is my food supply. All natural, organic, Martian-grown potatoes. Don't hear that every day, do you?

You may be wondering how I'll store them. I can't just pile them up; most of them would go bad before I got around to eating them. So instead, I'll do something that wouldn't work at all on Earth: throw them outside.

Most of the water will be sucked out by the near-vacuum; what's left will freeze solid. Any bacteria planning to rot my taters will die screaming.

In other news, I got an e-mail from Venkat Kapoor:

> Mark, some answers to your earlier questions:
>
> No, we will not tell our Botany Team to "Go fuck themselves." I understand you've been on your own for a long time, but we're in the loop now, and it's best if you listen to what we have to say.
>
> The Cubs finished the season at the bottom of the NL Central.
>
> The data transfer rate just isn't good enough for the size of music files, even in compressed formats. So your request for "Anything, oh God, ANYTHING but Disco" is denied. Enjoy your boogie fever.
>
> Also, an uncomfortable side note . . . NASA is putting together a committee. They want to see if there were any avoidable mistakes that led you to being stranded. Just a heads-up. They may have questions for you later on.
>
> Keep us posted on your activities.
>
> —Kapoor

My reply:

Venkat, tell the investigation committee they'll have to do their witch hunt without me. And when they inevitably blame Commander Lewis, be advised I'll publicly refute it. I'm sure the rest of the crew will do the same.

Also, please tell them that each and every one of their mothers is a prostitute.

—Watney

PS: Their sisters, too.

The presupply probes for Ares 3 launched on fourteen consecutive days during the Hohmann Transfer Window. Presupply 309 was launched third. The 251-day trip to Mars was uneventful, needing only two minor course adjustments.

After several aerobraking maneuvers to slow down, it made its final descent toward Acidalia Planitia. First, it endured reentry via a heat shield. Later, it released a parachute and detached the now-expended shield.

Once its onboard radar detected it was thirty meters from the ground, it cut loose the parachute and inflated balloons all around its hull. It fell unceremoniously to the surface, bouncing and rolling, until it finally came to rest.

Deflating its balloons, the onboard computer reported the successful landing back to Earth.

Then it waited twenty-three months.

LOG ENTRY: SOL 117

The water reclaimer is acting up.

Six people will go through 18 liters of water per

day. So it's made to process 20. But lately, it hasn't been keeping up. It's doing 10, tops.

Do I generate 10 liters of water per day? No, I'm not the urinating champion of all time. It's the crops. The humidity inside the Hab is a lot higher than it was designed for, so the water reclaimer is constantly filtering it out of the air.

I'm not worried about it. If need be, I can piss directly onto the plants. The plants will take their share of water and the rest will condense on the walls. I could make something to collect the condensation, I'm sure. Thing is, the water can't go anywhere. It's a closed system.

Okay, *technically* I'm lying. The plants aren't entirely water-neutral. They strip the hydrogen from some of it (releasing the oxygen) and use it to make the complex hydrocarbons that are the plant itself. But it's a very small loss and I made like 600 liters of water from MDV fuel. I could take *baths* and still have plenty left over.

NASA, however, is absolutely shitting itself. They see the water reclaimer as a critical survival element. There's no backup, and they think I'll die instantly without it. To them, equipment failure is terrifying. To me, it's "Tuesday."

So instead of preparing for my harvest, I have to make extra trips to and from the rover to answer their questions. Each new message instructs me to try some new solution and report the results back.

So far as we've worked out it's not the electronics, refrigeration system, instrumentation, or temperature. I'm sure it'll turn out to be a little hole somewhere, then NASA will have four hours of meetings before telling me to cover it with duct tape.

* * *

Lewis and Beck opened Presupply 309. Working as best they could in their bulky EVA suits, they removed the various portions of Hab canvas and laid them on the ground. Three entire presupply probes were dedicated to the Hab.

Following a procedure they had practiced hundreds of times, they efficiently assembled the pieces. Special seal-strips between the patches ensured airtight mating.

After erecting the main structure of the Hab, they assembled the three airlocks. Sheet AL102 had a hole perfectly sized for Airlock 1. Beck stretched the sheet tight to the seal-strips on the airlock's exterior.

Once all airlocks were in place, Lewis flooded the Hab with air and AL102 felt pressure for the first time. Lewis and Beck waited an hour. No pressure was lost; the setup had been perfect.

LOG ENTRY: SOL 118

My conversation with NASA about the water reclaimer was boring and riddled with technical details. So I'll paraphrase it for you:

Me: "This is obviously a clog. How about I take it apart and check the internal tubing?"

NASA: (after five hours of deliberation) "No. You'll fuck it up and die."

So I took it apart.

Yeah, I know. NASA has a lot of ultra-smart people and I should really do what they say. And I'm being too adversarial, considering they spend all day working on how to save my life.

I just get sick of being told how to wipe my ass. Independence was one of the qualities they looked for when choosing Ares astronauts. It's a thirteen-month mission, most of it spent many light-minutes away from Earth. They wanted people who would act on their own initiative.

If Commander Lewis were here, I'd do whatever she said, no problem. But a committee of faceless bureaucrats back on Earth? Sorry, I'm just having a tough time with it.

I was really careful. I labeled every piece as I dismantled it, and laid everything out on a table. I have the schematics in the computer, so nothing was a surprise.

And just as I'd suspected, there was a clogged tube. The water reclaimer was designed to purify urine and strain humidity out of the air (you exhale almost as much water as you piss). I've mixed my water with soil, making it mineral water. The minerals built up in the water reclaimer.

I cleaned out the tubing and put it all back together. It completely solved the problem. I'll have to do it again someday, but not for a hundred sols or so. No big deal.

I told NASA what I did. Our (paraphrased) conversation was:

Me: "I took it apart, found the problem, and fixed it."

NASA: "Dick."

AL102 shuddered in the brutal storm. Withstanding forces far greater than it was designed for, it rippled violently against the airlock seal-strip. Other sections of canvas undulated along their seal-strips together, acting as a single sheet, but AL102 had no such luxury. The airlock barely moved, leaving AL102 to take the full force of the tempest.

The layers of plastic, constantly bending, heated the resin from pure friction. The new, more yielding environment allowed the carbon fibers to separate.

AL102 stretched.

Not much. Only four millimeters. But the carbon fibers, usually 500 microns apart, now had a gap eight times that width in their midst.

After the storm abated, the lone remaining astronaut performed a full inspection of the Hab. But he didn't notice anything amiss. The weak part of canvas was concealed by a seal-strip.

Designed for a mission of thirty-one sols, AL102 continued well past its planned expiration. Sol after sol went by, with the lone astronaut traveling in and out of the Hab almost daily. Airlock 1 was closest to the rover charging station, so the astronaut preferred it to the other two.

When pressurized, the airlock expanded slightly; when depressurized, it shrunk. Every time the astronaut used the airlock, the strain on AL102 relaxed, then tightened anew.

Pulling, stressing, weakening, stretching . . .

LOG ENTRY: SOL 119

I woke up last night to the Hab shaking.

The medium-grade sandstorm ended as suddenly as it began. It was only a category three storm with 50 kph winds. Nothing to worry about. Still, it's a bit disconcerting to hear howling winds when you're used to utter silence.

I'm worried about *Pathfinder*. If the sandstorm damaged it, I'll have lost my connection to NASA.

Logically, I shouldn't worry. The thing's been on the surface for decades. A little gale won't do any harm.

When I head outside, I'll confirm *Pathfinder*'s still functional before moving on to the sweaty, annoying work of the day.

Yes, with each sandstorm comes the inevitable Cleaning of the Solar Cells, a time-honored tradition among hearty Martians such as myself. It reminds me of growing up in Chicago and having to shovel snow. I'll give my dad credit; he never claimed it was to build character or teach me the value of hard work.

"Snowblowers are expensive," he used to say. "You're free."

Once, I tried to appeal to my mom. "Don't be such a wuss," she suggested.

In other news, it's seven sols till the harvest, and I still haven't prepared. For starters, I need to make a hoe. Also, I need to make an outdoor shed for the potatoes. I can't just pile them up outside. The next major storm would cause the Great Martian Potato Migration.

Anyway, all that will have to wait. I've got a full day today. After cleaning the solar cells, I have to check the whole solar array to make sure the storm didn't hurt it. Then I'll need to do the same for the rover.

I better get started.

■ ■ ■

AIRLOCK 1 SLOWLY depressurized to 0.006 atmospheres. Watney, wearing an EVA suit, stood inside it waiting for the cycle to complete. He had done it literally hundreds of times. Any apprehension he may have had on Sol 1 was long gone. Now it was merely a boring chore before exiting to the surface.

As the depressurization continued, the Hab's atmosphere compressed the airlock, and AL102 stretched for the last time.

On Sol 119, the Hab breached.

The initial tear was less than one millimeter. The perpendicular carbon fibers should have prevented the rip from growing. But countless abuses had stretched the vertical fibers apart and weakened the horizontal ones beyond use.

The full force of the Hab's atmosphere rushed through the breach. Within a tenth of a second, the rip was a meter long, running parallel to the seal-strip. It propagated all the way around until it met its starting point. The airlock was no longer attached to the Hab.

The unopposed pressure launched the airlock like a cannonball as the Hab's atmosphere explosively escaped through the breach. Inside, the surprised Watney slammed against the airlock's back door with the force of the expulsion.

The airlock flew forty meters before hitting the ground. Watney, barely recovered from the earlier shock, now endured another as he hit the front door, face-first.

His faceplate took the brunt of the blow, the safety glass shattering into hundreds of small cubes. His head slammed against the inside of the helmet, knocking him senseless.

The airlock tumbled across the surface for a further fifteen meters. The heavy padding of Watney's suit saved him from many broken bones. He tried to make sense of the situation, but he was barely conscious.

Finally done tumbling, the airlock rested on its side amid a cloud of dust.

Watney, on his back, stared blankly upward through the hole in his shattered faceplate. A gash in his forehead trickled blood down his face.

Regaining some of his wits, he got his bearings. Turning his head to the side, he looked through the back door's window. The collapsed Hab rippled in the distance, a junkyard of debris strewn across the landscape in front of it.

Then, a hissing sound reached his ears. Listening carefully, he realized it was not coming from his suit. Somewhere in the phone booth–sized airlock, a small breach was letting air escape.

He listened intently to the hiss, then he touched his broken faceplate. Then he looked out the window again.

"You fucking kidding me?" he said.

CHAPTER 14

AUDIO LOG TRANSCRIPT: SOL 119

You know what!? Fuck this! Fuck this airlock, fuck that Hab, and fuck this whole planet!

Seriously, this is it! I've had it! I've got a few minutes before I run out of air and I'll be damned if I spend them playing Mars's little game. I'm so god damned sick of it I could puke!

All I have to do is sit here. The air will leak out and I'll die.

I'll be done. No more getting my hopes up, no more self-delusion, and no more problem-solving. I've fucking *had it!*

AUDIO LOG TRANSCRIPT: SOL 119 (2)

Sigh . . . okay. I've had my tantrum and now I have to figure out how to stay alive. Again. Okay, let's see what I can do here . . . .

I'm in the airlock. I can see the Hab out the window; it's a good 50 meters away. Normally, the airlock is *attached* to the Hab. So that's a problem.

The airlock's on its side, and I can hear a steady hiss. So either it's leaking or there are snakes in here. Either way, I'm in trouble.

Also, during the . . . whatever the fuck happened . . . I got bounced around like a pinball and smashed my faceplate. Air is notoriously uncooperative when it comes to giant, gaping holes in your EVA suit.

Looks like the Hab is completely deflated and collapsed. So even if I had a functional EVA suit to leave the airlock with, I wouldn't have anywhere to go. So that sucks.

I gotta think for a minute. And I have to get out of this EVA suit. It's bulky, and the airlock is cramped. Besides, it's not like it's doing me any good.

AUDIO LOG TRANSCRIPT: SOL 119 (3)

Things aren't as bad as they seem.

I'm still fucked, mind you. Just not as deeply.

Not sure what happened to the Hab, but the rover's probably fine. It's not ideal, but at least it's not a leaky phone booth.

I have a patch kit on my EVA suit, of course. The same kind that saved my life back on Sol 6. But don't get excited. It won't do the suit any good. The patch kit is a cone-shaped valve with super-sticky resin on the wide end. It's just too small to deal with a hole larger than eight centimeters. And really, if you have a nine-centimeter hole, you're going to be dead way before you could whip out the kit.

Still, it's an asset, and maybe I can use it to stop the airlock leak. And that's my top priority right now.

It's a small leak. With the faceplate gone, the EVA suit is effectively managing the whole airlock. It's been adding air to make up for the missing pressure. But it'll run out eventually.

I need to find the leak. I think it's near my feet, judging by the sound. Now that I'm out of the suit, I can turn around and get a look. . . .

I don't see anything. . . . I can hear it, but . . . it's down here somewhere, but I don't know where.

I can only think of one way to find it: Start a fire!

Yeah, I know. A lot of my ideas involve setting something on fire. And yes, deliberately starting a fire in a tiny, enclosed space is usually a terrible idea. But I need the smoke. Just a little wisp of it.

As usual, I'm working with stuff that was deliberately designed not to burn. But no amount of careful design by NASA can get around a determined arsonist with a tank of pure oxygen.

Unfortunately, the EVA suit is made entirely of nonflammable materials. So is the airlock. My clothes are fireproof as well, even the thread.

I was originally planning to check the solar array, doing repairs as needed after last night's storm. So I have my toolbox with me. But looking through it, I see it's all metal or nonflammable plastic.

I just realized I do have something flammable: my own hair. It'll have to do. There's a sharp knife in the tool kit. I'll shave some arm hairs off into a little pile.

Next step: oxygen. I don't have anything so refined as pure oxygen flow. All I can do is muck with the EVA suit controls to increase oxygen percentage in the whole airlock. I figure bumping it to 40 percent will do.

All I need now is a spark.

The EVA suit has electronics, but it runs on very low voltage. I don't think I could get an arc with it. Besides, I don't want to mess with the suit. I need it working to get from the airlock to the rover.

The airlock itself has electronics, but it ran on Hab power. I guess NASA never considered what would happen if it was launched fifty meters. Lazy bums.

Plastic might not burn, but anyone who's played with a balloon knows it's great at building up static charge. Once I do that, I should be able to make a spark just by touching a metal tool.

Fun fact: This is exactly how the Apollo 1 crew died. Wish me luck!

AUDIO LOG TRANSCRIPT: SOL 119 (4)

I'm in a box full of burning-hair smell. It's not a good smell.

On my first try, the fire lit, but the smoke just drifted randomly around. My own breathing was screwing it up. So I held my breath and tried again.

My second try, the EVA suit threw everything off. There's a gentle flow of air coming out of the faceplate as the suit constantly replaces the missing air. So I shut the suit down, held my breath, and tried again. I had to be quick; the pressure was dropping.

My third try, the quick arm movements I used to set the fire messed everything up. Just moving around makes enough turbulence to send the smoke everywhere.

The fourth time I kept the suit turned off, held my breath, and when the time came to light the fire, I did it very slowly. Then I watched as the little wisp of smoke drifted toward the floor of the airlock, disappearing through a hairline fracture.

I have you now, little leak!

I gasped for air and turned the EVA suit back on. The pressure had dropped to 0.9 atmospheres during my little experiment. But there was plenty of oxygen in the air for me and my hair-fire to breathe. The suit quickly got things back to normal.

Looking at the fracture, I see that it's pretty tiny. It would be a cinch to seal it with the suit's patch kit, but now that I think about it, that's a bad idea.

I'll need to do some kind of repair to the faceplate. I don't know how just yet, but the patch kit and its pressure-resistant resin are probably really important. And I can't do it bit by bit, either. Once I break the seal on the patch kit, the binary components of the resin mix and I have sixty seconds before it hardens. I can't just take a little to fix the airlock.

Given time, I might be able to come up with a plan for the faceplate. Then, I could take a few seconds during that plan to scrape resin over the airlock fracture. But I don't have time.

I'm down to 40 percent of my N_2 tank. I need to seal that fracture now, and I need to do it without using the patch kit.

First idea: Little Dutch Boy. I'm licking my palm and placing it over the crack.

Okay . . . I can't quite make a perfect seal, so there's airflow . . . getting colder now . . . getting pretty uncomfortable . . . Okay, fuck this.

On to idea number two. Tape!

I have duct tape in my toolbox. Let's slap some on and see if it slows the flow. I wonder how long it will last before the pressure rips it. Putting it on now.

There we go . . . still holding . . .

Lemme check the suit . . . . Readouts say the pressure is stable. Looks like the duct tape made a good seal.

Let's see if it holds. . . .

AUDIO LOG TRANSCRIPT: SOL 119 (5)

It's been fifteen minutes, and the tape is still holding. Looks like that problem is solved.

Sort of anticlimactic, really. I was already working out how to cover the breach with ice. I have two liters of water in the EVA suit's "hamster-feeder." I could have shut off the suit's heating systems and let the airlock cool to freezing. Then I'd . . . Well, whatever.

Coulda done it with ice. I'm just sayin'.

All right. On to my next problem: How do I fix the EVA suit? Duct tape might seal a hairline crack, but it can't hold an atmosphere of pressure against the size of my broken faceplate.

The patch kit is too small, but still useful. I can spread the resin around the edge of where the face-plate was, then stick something on to cover the hole. Problem is, what do I use to cover the hole? Something that can stand up to a lot of pressure.

Looking around, the only thing I see that can hold an atmosphere is the EVA suit itself. There's plenty of material to work with, and I can even cut it. Remember when I was cutting Hab canvas into strips? Those same shears are right here in my tool kit.

Cutting a chunk out of my EVA suit leaves it with another hole. But a hole I can control the shape and location of.

Yeah . . . I think I see a solution here. I'm going to cut off my arm!

Well, no. Not *my* arm. The EVA suit's arm. I'll cut right below the left elbow. Then I can cut along its length, turning it into a rectangle. It'll be big enough to seal the faceplate, and it'll be held in place by the resin.

Material designed to withstand atmospheric pressure? Check.

Resin designed to seal a breach against that pressure? Check.

And what about the gaping hole on the stumpy arm? Unlike my faceplate, the suit's material is flexible. I'll press it together and seal it with resin. I'll have to press my left arm against my side while I'm in the suit, but there'll be room.

I'll be spreading the resin pretty thin, but it's literally the strongest adhesive known to man. And it doesn't have to be a perfect seal. It just has to last long enough for me to get to safety.

And where will that "safety" be? Not a damn clue.

Anyway, one problem at a time. Right now I'm fixing the EVA suit.

Cutting the arm off the suit was easy; so was cutting along its length to make a rectangle. Those shears are strong as hell.

Cleaning the glass off the faceplate took longer than I'd expected. It's unlikely it would puncture EVA suit material, but I'm not taking any chances. Besides, I don't want glass in my face when I'm wearing it.

Then came the tricky part. Once I broke the seal on the patch kit, I had sixty seconds before the resin set. I scooped it off the patch kit with my fingers and quickly spread it around the rim of the faceplate. Then I took what was left and sealed the arm hole.

I pressed the rectangle of suit material onto the helmet with both hands while using my knee to keep pressure on the arm's seam.

I held on until I'd counted 120 seconds. Just to be sure.

It seemed to work well. The seal looked strong and the resin was rock-hard. I did, however, glue my hand to the helmet.

Stop laughing.

In retrospect, using my fingers to spread the resin wasn't the best plan. Fortunately, my left hand was still free. After some grunting and a lot of profanities, I was able to reach the toolbox. Once I got a screwdriver, I chiseled myself free (feeling really stupid the whole time). It was a delicate process because I didn't want to flay the skin off my fingers. I had to get the screwdriver between the helmet and the resin. I freed my hand and didn't draw blood, so I call that a win. Though I'll have hardened resin on my fingers for days, just like a kid who played with Krazy Glue.

Using the arm computer, I had the suit over-pressurize to 1.2 atmospheres. The faceplate patch bowed outward but otherwise held firm. The arm filled in, threatening to tear the new seam, but stayed in one piece.

Then I watched the readouts to see how airtight things were.

Answer: Not very.

It absolutely *pissed* the air out. In five minutes it leaked so much it pressurized the whole airlock to 1.2 atmospheres.

The suit is designed for eight hours of use. That works out to 250 milliliters of liquid oxygen. Just to be safe, the suit has a full liter of O_2 capacity. But that's only half the story. The rest of the air is nitrogen. It's just there to add pressure. When the suit leaks, that's what it backfills with. The suit has two liters of liquid N_2 storage.

Let's call the volume of the airlock two cubic meters. The inflated EVA suit probably takes up half of it. So it took five minutes to add 0.2 atmospheres to 1 cubic meter. That's 285 grams of air (trust me on the math). The air in the tanks is around 1 gram per cubic centimeter, meaning I just lost 285 milliliters.

The three tanks combined had 3000 milliliters to start with. A lot of that was used to maintain pressure while the airlock was leaking. Also, my breathing turned some oxygen into carbon dioxide, which was captured by the suit's CO_2 filters.

Checking the readouts, I see that I have 410 milliliters of oxygen, 738 milliliters of nitrogen. Together, they make almost 1150 milliliters to work with. That, divided by 285 milliliters lost per minute . . .

Once I'm out of the airlock, this EVA suit will only last four minutes.

Fuck.

AUDIO LOG TRANSCRIPT: SOL 119 (7)

Okay, I've been thinking some more.

What good is going to the rover? I'd just be trapped there instead. The extra room would be nice, but I'd still die eventually. No water reclaimer, no oxygenator, no food. Take your pick; all of those problems are fatal.

I need to fix the Hab. I know what to do; we practiced it in training. But it'll take a long time. I'll have to scrounge around in the now-collapsed canvas to get the spare material for patching. Then I have to find the breach and seal-strip a patch in place.

But it'll take hours to repair, and my EVA suit is useless.

I'll need another suit. Martinez's used to be in the rover. I hauled it all the way to the *Pathfinder* site and back, just in case I needed a spare. But when I returned, I put it back in the Hab.

Damn it!

All right, so I'll need to get another suit before going to the rover. Which one? Johanssen's is too small for me (tiny little gal, our Johanssen). Lewis's is full of water. Actually, by now it's full of slowly sublimating ice. The mangled, glued-together suit I have with me is my original one. That leaves just Martinez, Vogel, and Beck's.

I left Martinez's near my bunk, in case I needed

a suit in a hurry. Of course, after that sudden decompression, it could be anywhere. Still, it's a place to start.

Next problem: I'm like 50 meters from the Hab. Running in 0.4 g while wearing a bulky EVA suit isn't easy. At best, I can trundle 2 meters per second. That's a precious 25 seconds; almost an eighth of my four minutes. I've got to bring that down.

But how?

AUDIO LOG TRANSCRIPT: SOL 119 (8)

I'll roll the damn airlock.

It's basically a phone booth on its side. I did some experiments.

I figured if I want it to roll, I'll need to hit the wall as hard as possible. And I have to be in the air at the time. I can't press against some other part of the airlock. The forces would cancel each other out and it wouldn't move at all.

First I tried launching myself off one wall and slamming into the other. The airlock slid a little, but that's it.

Next, I tried doing a super-push-up to get airborne (0.4 g yay!) then kicking the wall with both feet. Again, it just slid.

The third time, I got it right. The trick was to plant both my feet on the ground, near the wall, then launch myself to the top of the opposite wall and hit with my back. When I tried that just now, it gave me enough force and leverage to tip the airlock and roll it one face toward the Hab.

The airlock is a meter wide, so . . . sigh . . . I have to do it like fifty more times.

I'm gonna have a hell of a backache after this.

AUDIO LOG TRANSCRIPT: SOL 120

I have a hell of a backache.

The subtle and refined "hurl my body at the wall" technique had some flaws. It worked only one out of every ten tries, and it hurt a lot. I had to take breaks, stretch out, and generally convince myself to body-slam the wall again and again.

It took all damn night, but I made it.

I'm ten meters from the Hab now. I can't get any closer, 'cause the debris from the decompression is all over the place. This isn't an "all-terrain" airlock. I can't roll over that shit.

It was morning when the Hab popped. Now it's morning again. I've been in this damn box for an entire day. But I'm leaving soon.

I'm in the EVA suit now, and ready to roll.

All right . . . Okay . . . Once more through the plan: Use the manual valves to equalize the airlock. Get out and hurry to the Hab. Wander around under the collapsed canvas. Find Martinez's suit (or Vogel's if I run into it first). Get to the rover. Then I'm safe.

If I run out of time before finding a suit, I'll just run to the rover. I'll be in trouble, but I'll have time to think and materials to work with.

Deep breath . . . here we go!

LOG ENTRY: SOL 120

I'm alive! And I'm in the rover!

Things didn't go exactly as planned, but I'm not dead, so it's a win.

Equalizing the airlock went fine. I was out on

the surface within thirty seconds. Skipping toward the Hab (the fastest way to move in this gravity), I passed through the field of debris. The rupture had really sent things flying, myself included.

It was hard to see; my faceplate was covered by the makeshift patch. Fortunately, my arm had a camera. NASA discovered that turning your whole EVA-suited body to look at something was a strenuous waste of time. So they mounted a small camera on the right arm. The feed is projected on the inner faceplate. This allows us to look at things just by pointing at them.

The faceplate patch wasn't exactly smooth or reflective, so I had to look at a rippled, messed-up version of the camera feed. Still, it was enough to see what was going on.

I beelined for where the airlock used to be. I knew there had to be a pretty big hole there, so I'd be able to get in. I found it easily. And boy is it a nasty rip! It's going to be a pain in the ass to fix it.

That's when the flaws in my plan started to reveal themselves. I only had one arm to work with. My left arm was pinned against my body, while the stumpy arm of the suit bounced freely. So as I moved around under the canvas, I had to use my one good arm to hold the canvas up. It slowed me down.

From what I could see, the interior of the Hab is chaos. Everything's moved. Entire tables and bunks are meters away from where they started. Lighter objects are wildly jumbled, many of them out on the surface. Everything's covered in soil and mangled potato plants.

Trudging onward, I got to where I'd left Martinez's suit. To my shock, it was still there!

"Yay!" I naively thought. "Problem solved."

Unfortunately, the suit was pinned under a table, which was held down by the collapsed canvas. If I'd had both arms, I could have pulled it free, but with only one, I just couldn't do it.

Running low on time, I detached the helmet. Setting it aside, I reached past the table to get Martinez's patch kit. I found it with the help of the arm-camera. I dropped it in the helmet and hauled ass out of there.

I barely made it to the rover in time. My ears were popping from pressure loss just as the rover's airlock filled with wonderful 1-atmosphere air.

Crawling in, I collapsed and panted for a moment.

So I'm back in the rover. Just like I was back on the Great *Pathfinder* Recovery Expedition. Ugh. At least this time it smells a little better.

NASA's probably pretty worried about me by now. They probably saw the airlock move back to the Hab, so they know I'm alive, but they'll want status. And as it happens, it's the rover that communicates with *Pathfinder*.

I tried to send a message, but *Pathfinder* isn't responding. That's not a big surprise. It's powered directly from the Hab, and the Hab is offline. During my brief, panicked scramble outside, I saw that *Pathfinder* was right where I left it, and the debris didn't reach that far out. It should be fine, once I get it some power.

As for my current situation, the big gain is the helmet. They're interchangeable, so I can replace my broken-ass one with Martinez's. The stumpy arm is still an issue, but the faceplate was the main source of leaks. And with the fresh patch kit, I can seal the arm with more resin.

But that can wait. I've been awake for over

twenty-four hours. I'm not in any immediate danger, so I'm going to sleep.

LOG ENTRY: SOL 121

Got a good night's sleep and made real progress today.

First thing I did was reseal the arm. Last time, I had to spread the resin pretty thin; I'd used most of it for the faceplate patch. But this time I had a whole patch kit just for the arm. I got a perfect seal.

I still only had a one-armed suit, but at least it didn't leak.

I'd lost most of my air yesterday, but I had a half hour of oxygen left. Like I said earlier, a human body doesn't need much oxygen. Maintaining pressure was the problem.

With that much time, I was able to take advantage of the rover's EVA tank-refill. Something I couldn't do with the leaky suit.

The tank-refill is an emergency measure. The expected use of the rover is to start with full EVA suits and come back with air to spare. It wasn't designed for long trips, or even overnighters. But, just in case of emergency, it has refill hoses mounted on the exterior. Inside space was limited already, and NASA concluded that most air-related emergencies would be outdoors.

But refilling is slow, slower than my suit was leaking. So it wasn't any use to me until I swapped helmets. Now, with a solid suit capable of holding pressure, refilling the tanks was a breeze.

After refilling, and making sure the suit was still not leaking, I had a few immediate tasks to take care of. Much as I trust my handiwork, I wanted a two-armed suit.

I ventured back into the Hab. This time, not being rushed, I was able to use a pole to leverage the table off Martinez's suit. Pulling it loose, I dragged it back to the rover.

After a thorough diagnostic to be sure, I finally had a fully functional EVA suit! It took me two trips to get it, but I got it.

Tomorrow, I'll fix the Hab.

LOG ENTRY: SOL 122

The first thing I did today was line up rocks near the rover to spell "A-okay." That should make NASA happy.

I went into the Hab again to assess damage. My priority will be to get the structure intact and holding pressure. From there, I can work on fixing stuff that broke.

The Hab is normally a dome, with flexible support poles maintaining the arch and rigid, folding floor material to keep its base flat. The internal pressure was a vital part of its support. Without it, the whole thing collapsed. I inspected the poles, and none of them had broken. They're just lying flat is all. I'll have to re-couple a few of them, but that'll be easy.

The hole where Airlock 1 used to be is huge, but surmountable. I have seal-strips and spare canvas. It'll be a lot of work, but I can get the Hab together again. Once I do, I'll reestablish power and get *Pathfinder* back online. From there, NASA can tell me how to fix anything I can't figure out on my own.

I'm not worried about any of that. I have a much bigger problem.

The farm is dead.

With a complete loss of pressure, most of the water boiled off. Also, the temperature is well below freezing. Not even the bacteria in the soil can survive a catastrophe like that. Some of the crops were in pop-tents off the Hab. But they're dead, too. I had them connected directly to the Hab via hoses to maintain air supply and temperature. When the Hab blew, the pop-tents depressurized as well. Even if they hadn't, the freezing cold would have killed the crops.

Potatoes are now extinct on Mars.

So is the soil bacteria. I'll never grow another plant so long as I'm here.

We had it all planned out. My farm would give me food till Sol 900. A supply probe would get here on Sol 856; way before I ran out. With the farm dead, that plan is history.

The ration packs won't have been affected by the explosion. And the potatoes I've already grown may be dead, but they're still food. I was just about to harvest, so it was a good time for this to happen, I guess.

The rations will last me till Sol 400. I can't say for sure how long the potatoes will last, until I see how many I got. But I can estimate. I had 400 plants, probably averaging 5 potatoes each: 2000 taters. At 150 calories each, I'll need to eat 10 per sol to survive. That means they'll last me 200 sols. Grand total: I have enough food to last till Sol 600.

By Sol 856 I'll be long dead.

CHAPTER 15

[08:12] WATNEY: Test.

[08:25] JPL: Received! You gave us quite a scare there. Thanks for the "A-okay" message. Our analysis of satellite imagery shows a complete detachment of Airlock 1. Is that correct? What's your status?

[08:39] WATNEY: If by "detachment" you mean "shot me out like a cannon" then yeah. Minor cut on my forehead. Had some issues with my EVA suit (I'll explain later). I patched up the Hab and repressurized it (main air tanks were intact). I just got power back online. The farm is dead. I've recovered as many potatoes as I could and stored them outside. I count 1841. That will last me 184 days. Including the remaining mission rations, I'll start starving on Sol 584.

[08:52] JPL: Yeah, we figured. We're working on solutions to the food issue. What's the status of the Hab systems?

[09:05] WATNEY: Primary air and water tanks were unharmed. The rover, solar array, and Pathfinder were out of the blast range. I'll run diagnostics on the Hab's systems while I wait for your next reply. By the way, who am I talking to?

[09:18] JPL: Venkat Kapoor in Houston. Pasadena relays my messages. I'm going to handle all direct communication with you from now on. Check the oxygenator and water reclaimer first. They're the most important.

[09:31] WATNEY: Duh. Oxygenator functioning perfectly. Water reclaimer is completely offline. Best guess is water froze up inside and burst some tubing. I'm sure I can fix it. The Hab's main computer is also functioning without any problems. Any idea what caused the Hab to blow up?

[09:44] JPL: Best guess is fatigue on the canvas near Airlock 1. The pressurization cycle stressed it until it failed. From now on, alternate Airlock 2 and 3 for all EVAs. Also, we'll be getting you a checklist and procedures for a full canvas exam.

[09:57] WATNEY: Yay, I get to stare at a wall for several hours! Let me know if you come up with a way for me to not starve.

[10:11] JPL: Will do.

■ ■ ■

"It's Sol 122," Bruce said. "We have until Sol 584 to get a probe to Mars. That's four hundred and sixty-two sols, which is four hundred and seventy-five days."

The assembled department heads of JPL furrowed their brows and rubbed their eyes.

He stood from his chair. "The positions of Earth and Mars aren't ideal. The trip will take four hundred and fourteen days. Mounting the probe to the booster and dealing with inspections will take thirteen days. That leaves us with just forty-eight days to make this probe."

Sounds of whispered exasperation filled the room. "Jesus," someone said.

"It's a whole new ball game," Bruce continued. "Our focus is food. Anything else is a luxury. We don't have time to make a powered-descent lander. It'll have to be a tumbler. So we can't put anything delicate inside. Say good-bye to all the other crap we'd planned to send."

"Where's the booster coming from?" asked Norm Toshi, who was in charge of the reentry process.

"The EagleEye 3 Saturn probe," Bruce said. "It was scheduled to launch next month. NASA put it on hold so we can have the booster."

"I bet the EagleEye team was pissed about that," Norm said.

"I'm sure they were," Bruce said. "But it's the only booster we have that's big enough. Which brings me to my next point: We only get one shot at this. If we fail, Mark Watney dies."

He looked around the room and let that sink in.

"We do have some things going for us," he finally said. "We have some of the parts built for the Ares 4 presupply missions. We can steal from them, and that'll save us some time. Also, we're sending food, which is pretty robust. Even if there's a reentry problem and the probe impacts at high velocity, food is still food.

"And we don't need a precision landing. Watney can travel hundreds of kilometers if necessary. We just need to land close enough for him to reach it. This ends up being a standard tumble-land pre-supply. All we have to do is make it quickly. So let's get to it."

■ ■ ■

[08:02] JPL: We've spun up a project to get you food. It's been in progress for a week or so. We can get it to you before you starve, but it'll be tight. It'll just be food and a radio. We can't send an oxygenator, water reclaimer, or any of that other stuff without powered descent.

[08:16] WATNEY: No complaints here! You get me the food, I'll be a happy camper. I've got all Hab systems up and running again. The water reclaimer is working fine now that I replaced the burst hoses. As for water supply, I have 620 liters remaining. I started with 900 liters (300 to start with, 600 more from reducing hydrazine). So I lost almost 300 liters to sublimation. Still, with the water reclaimer operational again, it's plenty.

[08:31] JPL: Good, keep us posted on any mechanical or electronic problems. By the way, the name of the probe we're sending is Iris. Named after the Greek goddess who traveled the heavens with the speed of wind. She's also the goddess of rainbows.

[08:47] WATNEY: Gay probe coming to save me. Got it.

■ ■ ■

RICH PURNELL sipped coffee in the silent building. He ran a final test on the software he'd written. It passed. With a relieved sigh, he sank back in his chair. Checking the clock on his computer, he shook his head. 3:42 a.m.

As an astrodynamicist, Rich rarely had to work late. His job was to find the exact orbits and course corrections needed for any given mission. Usually, it was one of the first parts of a project, all the other steps being based on the orbit.

But this time, things were reversed. Iris needed an orbital path, and nobody knew when it would launch.

Planets move as time goes by. A course calculated for a specific launch date will work only for that date. Even a single day's difference would result in missing Mars entirely.

So Rich had to calculate *many* courses. He had a range of twenty-five days during which Iris might launch. He calculated one course for each.

He began an e-mail to his boss.

Mike, he typed, *Attached are the courses for Iris, in 1-day increments. We should start peer review and vetting so they can be officially accepted. And you were right, I was here almost all night.*

It wasn't that bad. Nowhere near the pain of calculating orbits for Hermes. I know you get bored when I go into the math, so I'll summarize: The small, constant thrust of Hermes's ion drives is much harder to deal with than the large point-thrusts of presupply probes.

All 25 of the courses take 414 days, and vary only slightly in thrust duration and angle. The fuel requirement is nearly identical for the orbits and is well within the capacity of EagleEye's booster.

It's too bad. Earth and Mars are really badly positioned. Heck, it's almost easier to—

He stopped typing.

Furrowing his brow, he stared into the distance.

"Hmm," he said.

He grabbed his coffee cup and went to the break room for a refill.

▪ ▪ ▪

TEDDY SCANNED the crowded conference room. It was rare to see such an assembly of NASA's most important people all in one place. He squared a small stack of notes he'd prepared and placed them neatly in front of him.

"I know you're all busy," Teddy said. "Thank you for making time for this meeting. I need status on Project Iris from all departments. Venkat, let's start with you."

"The mission team's ready," Venkat said, looking at spreadsheets on his laptop. "There was a minor turf war between the Ares 3 and Ares 4 presupply control teams. The Ares 3 guys said they should run it, because while Watney's on Mars, Ares 3 is still in progress. The Ares 4 team points out it's their coopted probe in the first place. I ended up going with Ares 3."

"Did that upset Ares 4?" Teddy asked.

"Yes, but they'll get over it. They have thirteen other presupply missions coming up. They won't have time to be pissy."

"Mitch," Teddy said to the flight controller, "what about the launch?"

Mitch pulled the earpiece from his ear. "We've got a control room ready," he said. "I'll oversee the launch, then hand cruise and landing over to Venkat's guys."

"Media?" Teddy said, turning to Annie.

"I'm giving daily updates to the press," she said, leaning back in her chair. "Everyone knows Watney's fucked if this doesn't work. The public hasn't been this engaged in ship construction since Apollo 11. CNN's *The Watney Report* has been the number one show in its time slot for the past two weeks."

"The attention is good," Teddy said. "It'll help get us emergency funding from Congress." He looked up to a man standing near the entrance. "Maurice, thanks for flying out on short notice."

Maurice nodded.

Teddy gestured to him and addressed the room. "For those who don't know him, this is Maurice Stein from Cape Canaveral. He was the scheduled pad leader for EagleEye 3, so he inherited the role for Iris. Sorry for the bait and switch, Maurice."

"No problem," said Maurice. "Glad I can help out."

Teddy flipped the top page of his notes face-down beside the stack. "How's the booster?"

"It's all right for now," said Maurice. "But it's not ideal. EagleEye 3 was set to launch. Boosters aren't designed to stand upright and bear the stress of gravity for long periods. We're adding external supports that we'll remove before launch.

It's easier than disassembly. Also the fuel is corrosive to the internal tanks, so we had to drain it. In the meantime, we're performing inspections on all systems every three days."

"Good, thank you," Teddy said. He turned his attention to Bruce Ng, who stared back at him with heavy bloodshot eyes.

"Bruce, thank you for flying out, too. How's the weather in California these days?"

"I wouldn't know," Bruce said. "I rarely see the outdoors."

Subdued laughter filled the room for a few seconds.

Teddy flipped another page. "Time for the big question, Bruce. How's Iris coming along?"

"We're behind," Bruce said with a tired shake of his head. "We're going as fast as we can, but it's just not fast enough."

"I can find money for overtime," Teddy offered.

"We're already working around the clock."

"How far behind are we talking about?" Teddy asked.

Bruce rubbed his eyes and sighed. "We've been at it twenty-nine days; so we only have nineteen left. After that, the Pad needs thirteen days to mount it on the booster. We're at least two weeks behind."

"Is that as far behind as you're going to get?" Teddy asked, writing a note on his papers. "Or will you slip more?"

Bruce shrugged. "If we don't have any more problems, it'll be two weeks late. But we always have problems."

"Give me a number," Teddy said.

"Fifteen days," Bruce responded. "If we had

another fifteen days, I'm sure we could get it done in time."

"All right," Teddy said, taking another note. "Let's create fifteen days."

Turning his attention to the Ares 3 flight surgeon, Teddy asked, "Dr. Keller, can we reduce Watney's food intake to make the rations last longer?"

"Sorry, but no," Keller said. "He's already at a minimal calorie count. In fact, considering the amount of physical labor he does, he's eating far less than he should. And it's only going to get worse. Soon his entire diet will be potatoes and vitamin supplements. He's been saving protein-rich rations for later use, but he'll still be malnourished."

"Once he runs out of food, how long until he starves to death?" Teddy asked.

"Presuming an ample water supply, he might last three weeks. Shorter than a typical hunger strike, but remember he'll be malnourished and thin to begin with."

Venkat raised a hand and caught their attention. "Remember, Iris is a tumbler; he might have to drive a few days to get it. And I'm guessing it's hard to control a rover when you're literally starving to death."

"He's right," Dr. Keller confirmed. "Within four days of running out of food, he'll barely be able to stand up, let alone control a rover. Plus, his mental faculties will rapidly decline. He'd have a hard time even staying awake."

"So the landing date's firm," Teddy said. "Maurice, can you get Iris on the booster in less than thirteen days?"

Maurice leaned against the wall and pinched

his chin. "Well . . . it only takes three days to actually mount it. The following ten are for testing and inspections."

"How much can you reduce those?"

"With enough overtime, I could get the mounting down to two days. That includes transport from Pasadena to Cape Canaveral. But the inspections can't be shortened. They're time-based. We do checks and rechecks with set intervals between them to see if something deforms or warps. If you shorten the intervals, you invalidate the inspections."

"How often do those inspections reveal a problem?" Teddy asked.

A silence fell over the room.

"Uh," Maurice stammered. "Are you suggesting we don't do the inspections?"

"No," said Teddy. "Right now I'm asking how often they reveal a problem."

"About one in twenty launches."

Teddy wrote that down. "And how often is the problem they find something that would have caused a mission failure?"

"I'm, uh, not sure. Maybe half the time?"

He wrote that down as well. "So if we skip inspections and testing, we have a one in forty chance of mission failure?" Teddy asked.

"That's two point five percent," Venkat said, stepping in. "Normally, that's grounds for a countdown halt. We can't take a chance like that."

"'Normally' was a long time ago," Teddy said. "Ninety-seven point five percent is better than zero. Can anyone think of a safer way to get more time?"

He scanned the room. Blank faces stared back.

"All right, then," he said, circling something on

his notes. "Speeding up the mounting process and skipping inspections buys us eleven days. If Bruce can pull a rabbit out of a hat and get done sooner, Maurice can do some inspections."

"What about the other four days?" Venkat asked.

"I'm sure Watney can stretch the food to last four extra days, malnutrition notwithstanding," Teddy said, looking to Dr. Keller.

"I—" Keller started. "I can't recommend—"

"Hang on," Teddy interrupted. He stood and straightened his blazer. "Everyone, I understand your positions. We have procedures. Skipping those procedures means risk. Risk means trouble for your department. But now isn't the time to cover our asses. We have to take risks or Mark Watney dies."

Turning to Keller, he said, "Make the food last another four days."

Keller nodded.

■ ■ ■

"RICH," said Mike.

Rich Purnell concentrated on his computer screen. His cubicle was a landfill of printouts, charts, and reference books. Empty coffee cups rested on every surface; take-out packaging littered the ground.

"Rich," Mike said, more forcefully.

Rich looked up. "Yeah?"

"What the hell are you doing?"

"Just a little side project. Something I wanted to check up on."

"Well . . . that's fine, I guess," Mike said, "but you need to do your assigned work first. I asked for those satellite adjustments two weeks ago and you still haven't done them."

"I need some supercomputer time," Rich said.

"You need supercomputer time to calculate routine satellite adjustments?"

"No, it's for this other thing I'm working on," Rich said.

"Rich, seriously. You have to do your job."

Rich thought for a moment. "Would now be a good time for a vacation?" he asked.

Mike sighed. "You know what, Rich? I think now would be an *ideal* time for you to take a vacation."

"Great!" Rich smiled. "I'll start right now."

"Sure," Mike said. "Go on home. Get some rest."

"Oh, I'm not going home," said Rich, returning to his calculations.

Mike rubbed his eyes. "Okay, whatever. About those satellite orbits . . . ?"

"I'm on vacation," Rich said without looking up.

Mike shrugged and walked away.

■ ■ ■

[08:01] WATNEY: How's my care package coming along?

[08:16] JPL: A little behind schedule, but we'll get it done. In the meantime, we want you to get back to work. We're satisfied the Hab is in good condition. Maintenance only takes you twelve hours per week. We're going to pack the rest of your time with research and experiments.

[08:31] WATNEY: Great! I'm sick of sitting on my ass. I'm going to be here for years. You may as well make use of me.

[08:47] JPL: That's what we're thinking. We'll get you a schedule as soon as the science team puts it together. It'll be mostly EVAs, geological sampling, soil tests, and weekly self-administered medical tests. Honestly, this is the best "bonus Mars time" we've had since the Opportunity lander.

[09:02] WATNEY: Opportunity never went back to Earth.

[09:17] JPL: Sorry. Bad analogy.

■ ■ ■

THE JPL Spacecraft Assembly Facility, known as the "clean room," was the little-known birthplace of the most famous spacecraft in Mars exploration history. Mariner, Viking, Spirit, Opportunity, and Curiosity, just to name a few, had all been born in this one room.

Today, the room was abuzz with activity as technicians sealed Iris into the specially designed shipping container.

The off-duty techs watched the procedure from the observation deck. They had rarely seen their homes in the last two months; a makeshift bunk room had been set up in the cafeteria. Fully a third of them would normally be asleep at this hour, but they did not want to miss this moment.

The shift leader tightened the final bolt. As he

retracted the wrench, the engineers broke into applause. Many of them were in tears.

After sixty-three days of grueling work, Iris was complete.

■ ■ ■

ANNIE TOOK the podium and adjusted the microphone. "The launch preparations are complete," she said. "Iris is ready to go. The scheduled launch is 9:14 a.m.

"Once launched, it will stay in orbit for at least three hours. During that time, Mission Control will gather exact telemetry in preparation for the trans-Mars injection burn. When that's complete, the mission will be handed off to the Ares 3 presupply team, who will monitor its progress over the following months. It will take four hundred and fourteen days to reach Mars."

"About the payload," a reporter asked, "I hear there's more than just food?"

"That's true." Annie smiled. "We allocated one hundred grams for luxury items. There are some handwritten letters from Mark's family, a note from the President, and a USB drive filled with music from all ages."

"Any disco?" someone asked.

"No disco," Annie said, as chuckles cascaded through the room.

CNN's Cathy Warner spoke up. "If this launch fails, is there any recourse for Watney?"

"There are risks to any launch," Annie said, sidestepping the question, "but we don't anticipate problems. The weather at the Cape is clear with warm temperatures. Conditions couldn't be better."

"Is there any spending limit to this rescue operation?" another reporter asked. "Some people are beginning to ask how much is too much."

"It's not about the bottom line," Annie said, prepared for the question. "It's about a human life in immediate danger. But if you want to look at it financially, consider the value of Mark Watney's extended mission. His prolonged mission and fight for survival are giving us more knowledge about Mars than the rest of the Ares program combined."

■ ■ ■

"DO YOU believe in God, Venkat?" Mitch asked.

"Sure, lots of 'em," Venkat said. "I'm Hindu."

"Ask 'em all for help with this launch."

"Will do."

Mitch stepped forward to his station in Mission Control. The room bustled with activity as the dozens of controllers each made final preparations for launch.

He put his headset on and glanced at the time readout on the giant center screen at the front of the room. He turned on his headset and said, "This is the flight director. Begin launch status check."

"Roger that, Houston" was the reply from the launch control director in Florida. "CLCDR checking all stations are manned and systems ready," he broadcast. "Give me a go/no-go for launch. Talker?"

"Go" was the response.

"Timer."

"Go," said another voice.

"QAM1."

"Go."

Resting his chin on his hands, Mitch stared at the center screen. It showed the pad video feed. The booster, amid cloudy water vapor from the cooling process, still had *EagleEye3* stenciled on the side.

"QAM2."

"Go."

"QAM3."

"Go."

Venkat leaned against the back wall. He was an administrator. His job was done. He could only watch and hope. His gaze was fixated on the far wall's displays. In his mind, he saw the numbers, the shift juggling, the outright lies and borderline crimes he'd committed to put this mission together. It would all be worthwhile, if it worked.

"FSC."

"Go."

"Prop One."

"Go."

Teddy sat in the VIP observation room behind Mission Control. His authority afforded him the very best seat: front-row center. His briefcase lay at his feet and he held a blue folder in his hands.

"Prop Two."

"Go."

"PTO."

"Go."

Annie Montrose paced in her private office next to the press room. Nine televisions mounted to the wall were each tuned to a different network; each network showed the launch pad. A glance at her computer showed foreign networks doing the same. The world was holding its breath.

"ACC."

"Go."

"LWO."

"Go."

Bruce Ng sat in the JPL cafeteria along with hundreds of engineers who had given everything they had to Iris. They watched the live feed on a projection screen. Some fidgeted, unable to find comfortable positions. Others held hands. It was 6:13 a.m. in Pasadena, yet every single employee was present.

"AFLC."

"Go."

"Guidance."

"Go."

Millions of kilometers away, the crew of *Hermes* listened as they crowded around Johanssen's station. The two-minute transmission time didn't matter. They had no way to help; there was no need to interact. Johanssen stared intently at her screen, although it displayed only the audio signal strength. Beck wrung his hands. Vogel stood motionless, his eyes fixed on the floor. Martinez prayed silently at first, then saw no reason to hide it. Commander Lewis stood apart, her arms folded across her chest.

"PTC."

"Go."

"Launch Vehicle Director."

"Go."

"Houston, this is Launch Control, we are go for launch."

"Roger," Mitch said, checking the countdown. "This is Flight, we are go for launch on schedule."

"Roger that, Houston," Launch Control said. "Launch on schedule."

Once the clock reached −00:00:15, the television networks got what they were waiting for. The timer controller began the verbal countdown. "Fifteen," she said, "fourteen . . . thirteen . . . twelve . . . eleven . . ."

Thousands had gathered at Cape Canaveral, the largest crowd ever to watch an unmanned launch. They listened to the timer controller's voice as it echoed across the grandstands.

" . . . ten . . . nine . . . eight . . . seven . . ."

Rich Purnell, entrenched in his orbital calculations, had lost track of time. He didn't notice when his coworkers migrated to the large meeting room where a TV had been set up. In the back of his mind, he thought the office was unusually quiet, but he gave it no further thought.

" . . . six . . . five . . . four . . ."

"Ignition sequence start."

" . . . three . . . two . . . one . . ."

Clamps released, the booster rose amid a plume of smoke and fire, slowly at first, then racing ever faster. The assembled crowd cheered it on its way.

" . . . and liftoff of the Iris supply probe," the timer controller said.

As the booster soared, Mitch had no time to watch the spectacle on the main screen. "Trim?" he called out.

"Trim's good, Flight" was the immediate response.

"Course?" he asked.

"On course."

"Altitude one thousand meters," someone said.

"We've reached safe-abort," another person

called out, indicating that the ship could crash harmlessly into the Atlantic Ocean if necessary.

"Altitude fifteen hundred meters."

"Pitch and roll maneuver commencing."

"Getting a little shimmy, Flight."

Mitch looked over to the ascent flight director. "Say again?"

"A slight shimmy. Onboard guidance is handling it."

"Keep an eye on it," Mitch said.

"Altitude twenty-five hundred meters."

"Pitch and roll complete, twenty-two seconds till staging."

■ ■ ■

WHEN DESIGNING Iris, JPL accounted for catastrophic landing failure. Rather than normal meal kits, most of the food was cubed protein bar material, which would still be edible even if Iris failed to deploy its tumble balloons and impacted at incredible speed.

Because Iris was an unmanned mission, there was no cap on acceleration. The contents of the probe endured forces no human could survive. But while NASA had tested the effects of extreme g-forces on protein cubes, they had not done so with a simultaneous lateral vibration. Had they been given more time, they would have.

The harmless shimmy, caused by a minor fuel mixture imbalance, rattled the payload. Iris, mounted firmly within the aeroshell atop the booster, held firm. The protein cubes inside Iris did not.

At the microscopic level, the protein cubes were solid food particles suspended in thick vegetable oil. The food particles compressed to less than half their original size, but the oil was barely affected at all. This changed the volume ratio of solid to liquid dramatically, which in turn made the aggregate act as a liquid. Known as "liquefaction," this process transformed the protein cubes from a steady solid into a flowing sludge.

Stored in a compartment that originally had no leftover space, the now-compressed sludge had room to slosh.

The shimmy also caused an imbalanced load, forcing the sludge toward the edge of its compartment. This shift in weight only aggravated the larger problem, and the shimmy grew stronger.

■ ■ ■

"SHIMMY'S GETTING violent," reported the ascent flight director.

"How violent?" Mitch said.

"More than we like," he said. "But the accelerometers caught it and calculated the new center of mass. The guidance computer is adjusting the engines' thrusts to counteract. We're still good."

"Keep me posted," Mitch said.

"Thirteen seconds till staging."

The unexpected weight shift had not spelled disaster. All systems were designed for worst-case scenarios; each did its job admirably. The ship continued toward orbit with only a minor course adjustment, implemented automatically by sophisticated software.

The first stage depleted its fuel, and the booster coasted for a fraction of a second as it jettisoned stage clamps via explosive bolts. The now-empty stage fell away from the craft as the second-stage engines prepared to ignite.

The brutal forces had disappeared. The protein sludge floated free in the container. Given two seconds, it would have re-expanded and solidified. But it was given only a quarter second.

As the second stage fired, the craft experienced a sudden jolt of immense force. No longer contending with the deadweight of the first stage, the acceleration was profound. The three hundred kilograms of sludge slammed into the back of its container. The point of impact was at the edge of Iris, nowhere near where the mass was expected to be.

Though Iris was held in place by five large bolts, the force was directed entirely to a single one. The bolt was designed to withstand immense forces; if necessary to carry the entire weight of the payload. But it was *not* designed to sustain a sudden impact from a loose three-hundred-kilogram mass.

The bolt sheared. The burden was then shifted to the remaining four bolts. The forceful impact having passed, their work was considerably easier than that of their fallen comrade.

Had the pad crew been given time to do normal inspections, they would have noticed the minor defect in one of the bolts. A defect that slightly weakened it, though it would not cause failure on a normal mission. Still, they would have swapped it out with a perfect replacement.

The off-center load presented unequal force to the four remaining bolts, the defective one bearing the brunt of it. Soon, it failed as well. From there, the other three failed in rapid succession.

Iris slipped from its supports in the aeroshell, slamming into the hull.

■ ■ ■

"WOAH!" exclaimed the ascent flight director. "Flight, we're getting a large precession!"

"What?" Mitch said as alerts beeped and lights flashed across all the consoles.

"Force on Iris is at seven g's," someone said.

"Intermittent signal loss," called another voice.

"Ascent, what's happening here?" Mitch demanded.

"All hell broke loose. It's spinning on the long axis with a seventeen-degree precession."

"How bad?"

"At least five rps, and falling off course."

"Can you get it to orbit?"

"I can't talk to it at all; signal failures left and right."

"Comm!" Mitch shot to the communications director.

"Workin' on it, Flight," was the response. "There's a problem with the onboard system."

"Getting some major g's inside, Flight."

"Ground telemetry shows it two hundred meters low of target path."

"We've lost readings on the probe, Flight."

"Entirely lost the probe?" he asked.

"Affirm, Flight. Intermittent signal from the ship, but no probe."

"Shit," Mitch said. "It shook loose in the aeroshell."

"It's dreideling, Flight."

"Can it limp to orbit?" Mitch said. "Even super-low EO? We might be able to—"

"Loss of signal, Flight."

"LOS here, too."

"Same here."

Other than the alarms, the room fell silent.

After a moment, Mitch said, "Reestablish?"

"No luck," said Comm.

"Ground?" Mitch asked.

"GC" was the reply. "Vehicle had already left visual range."

"SatCon?" Mitch asked.

"No satellite acquisition of signal."

Mitch looked forward to the main screen. It was black now, with large white letters reading "LOS."

"Flight," a voice said over the radio, "US destroyer *Stockton* reports debris falling from the sky. Source matches last known location of Iris."

Mitch put his head in his hands. "Roger," he said.

Then he uttered the words every flight director hopes never to say: "GC, Flight. Lock the doors."

It was the signal to start post-failure procedures.

From the VIP observation room, Teddy watched the despondent Mission Control Center. He took a deep breath, then let it out. He looked forlornly at the blue folder that contained his cheerful speech praising a perfect launch. He placed it in his briefcase and extracted the red folder, with the *other* speech in it.

■ ■ ■

VENKAT STARED out his office windows to the space center beyond. A space center that housed mankind's most advanced knowledge of rocketry yet had still failed to execute today's launch.

His mobile rang. His wife again. No doubt worried about him. He let it go to voice mail. He just couldn't face her. Or anyone.

A chime came from his computer. Glancing over, he saw an e-mail from JPL. A relayed message from *Pathfinder*:

[16:03] WATNEY: How'd the launch go?

CHAPTER 16

Martinez:

Dr. Shields says I need to write personal messages to each of the crew. She says it'll keep me tethered to humanity. I think it's bullshit. But hey, it's an order.

With you, I can be blunt:

If I die, I need you to check on my parents. They'll want to hear about our time on Mars firsthand. I'll need you to do that.

It won't be easy talking to a couple about their dead son. It's a lot to ask; that's why I'm asking you. I'd tell you you're my best friend and stuff, but it would be lame.

I'm not giving up. Just planning for every outcome. It's what I do.

■ ■ ■

GUO MING, director of the China National Space Administration, examined the daunting pile of paperwork at his desk. In the old days, when China wanted to launch a rocket, they just launched it. Now they were compelled by international agreements to warn other nations first.

It was a requirement, Guo Ming noted to himself, that did not apply to the United States. To be fair, the Americans publicly announced their launch schedules well in advance, so it amounted to the same thing.

He walked a fine line filling out the form: making the launch date and flight path clear, while doing everything possible to "conceal state secrets."

He snorted at the last requirement. "Ridiculous," he mumbled. The *Taiyang Shen* had no strategic or military value. It was an unmanned probe that would be in Earth orbit less than two days. After that, it would travel to a solar orbit between Mercury and Venus. It would be China's first heliology probe to orbit the sun.

Yet the State Council insisted all launches be shrouded in secrecy. Even launches with nothing to hide. This way, other nations could not infer from lack of openness which launches contained classified payloads.

A knock at the door interrupted his paperwork.

"Come," Guo Ming said, happy for the interruption.

"Good evening, sir," said Under Director Zhu Tao.

"Tao, welcome back."

"Thank you, sir. It's good to be back in Beijing."

"How were things at Jiuquan?" asked Guo Ming. "Not too cold, I hope? I'll never understand why our launch complex is in the middle of the Gobi Desert."

"It was cold, yet manageable," Zhu Tao said.

"And how are launch preparations coming along?"

"I am happy to report they are all on schedule."

"Excellent." Guo Ming smiled.

Zhu Tao sat quietly, staring at his boss.

Guo Ming looked expectantly back at him, but Zhu Tao neither stood to leave nor said anything further.

"Something else, Tao?" Guo Ming asked.

"Mmm," Zhu Tao said. "Of course, you've heard about the Iris probe?"

"Yes, I did." Guo frowned. "Terrible situation. That poor man's going to starve."

"Possibly," Zhu Tao said. "Possibly not."

Guo Ming leaned back in his chair. "What are you saying?"

"It's the *Taiyang Shen*'s booster, sir. Our engineers have run the numbers, and it has enough fuel for a Mars injection orbit. It could get there in four hundred and nineteen days."

"Are you kidding?"

"Have you ever known me to 'kid,' sir?"

Guo Ming stood and pinched his chin. Pacing, he said, "We can really send the *Taiyang Shen* to Mars?"

"No, sir," said Zhu Tao. "It's far too heavy. The massive heat shielding makes it the heaviest unmanned probe we've ever built. That's why the booster had to be so powerful. But a lighter payload could be sent all the way to Mars."

"How much mass could we send?" Guo Ming asked.

"Nine hundred and forty-one kilograms, sir."

"Hmm," Guo Ming said, "I bet NASA could work with that limitation. Why haven't they approached us?"

"Because they don't know," Zhu Tao said. "All our booster technology is classified information. The Ministry of State Security even spreads disinformation about our capabilities. This is for obvious reasons."

"So they don't *know* we can help them," Guo Ming said. "If we decide not to help, no one will know we could have."

"Correct, sir."

"For the sake of argument, let's say we decided to help. What then?"

"Time would be the enemy, sir," Zhu Tao answered. "Based on travel duration and the supplies their astronaut has remaining, any such probe would have to be launched within a month. Even then he would starve a little."

"That's right around when we planned to launch *Taiyang Shen*."

"Yes, sir. But it took them two months to build Iris, and it was so rushed it failed."

"That's their problem," Guo Ming said. "Our end would be providing the booster. We'd launch from Jiuquan; we can't ship an eight-hundred-ton rocket to Florida."

"Any agreement would hinge on the Americans reimbursing us for the booster," Zhu Tao said, "and the State Council would likely want political favors from the US government."

"Reimbursement would be pointless," Guo Ming said. "This was an expensive project, and the State Council grumbled about it all along. If they had a bulk payout for its value, they'd just keep it. We'd never get to build another one."

He clasped his hands behind his back. "And the American people may be sentimental, but their government is not. The US State Department won't trade anything major for one man's life."

"So it's hopeless?" asked Zhu Tao.

"Not hopeless," Guo Ming corrected. "Just hard. If this becomes a negotiation by diplomats, it will never be resolved. We need to keep this among scientists. Space agency to space agency. I'll get a translator and call NASA's administrator. We'll work out an agreement, then present it to our governments as a fait accompli."

"But what can they do for us?" Zhu Tao asked. "We'd be giving up a booster and effectively canceling *Taiyang Shen*."

Guo Ming smiled. "They'll give us something we can't get without them."

"And that is?"

"They'll put a Chinese astronaut on Mars."

Zhu Tao stood. "Of course." He smiled. "The Ares 5 crew hasn't even been selected yet. We'll insist on a crewman. One we get to pick and train. NASA and the US State Department would surely accept that. But will our State Council?"

Guo Ming smiled wryly. "Publicly rescue the Americans? Put a Chinese astronaut on Mars? Have the world see China as equal to the US in space? The State Council would sell their own *mothers* for that."

■ ■ ■

TEDDY LISTENED to the phone at his ear. The voice on the other end finished what it had to say, then fell silent as it awaited an answer.

He stared at nothing in particular as he processed what he'd just heard.

After a few seconds, he replied, "Yes."

■ ■ ■

Johanssen:

Your poster outsold the rest of ours combined. You're a hot chick who went to Mars. You're on dorm-room walls all over the world.

Looking like that, why are you such a nerd? And you are, you know. A serious nerd. I had to do some computer shit to get Pathfinder talking to the rover and oh my god. And I had NASA telling me what to do every step of the way.

You should try to be more cool. Wear dark glasses and a leather jacket. Carry a switchblade. Aspire to a level of coolness known only as . . . "Botanist Cool."

Did you know Commander Lewis had a chat with us men? If anyone hit on you, we'd be off the mission. I guess after a lifetime of commanding sailors, she's got an unfairly jaded view.

Anyway, the point is you're a nerd. Remind me to give you a wedgie next time I see you.

■ ■ ■

"OKAY, HERE we are again," said Bruce to the assembled heads of JPL. "You've all heard about the *Taiyang Shen*, so you know our friends in China have given us one more chance. But this time, it's going to be harder.

"*Taiyang Shen* will be ready to launch in twenty-eight days. If it launches on time, our payload will get to Mars on Sol 624, six weeks after Watney's expected to run out of food. NASA's already working on ways to stretch his supply.

"We made history when we finished Iris in sixty-three days. Now we have to do it in *twenty-eight*."

He looked across the table to the incredulous faces.

"Folks," he said, "this is going to be the most 'ghetto' spacecraft ever built. There's only one way to finish that fast: no landing system."

"Sorry, what?" Jack Trevor stammered.

Bruce nodded. "You heard me. No landing system. We'll need guidance for in-flight course adjustments. But once it gets to Mars, it's going to crash."

"That's crazy!" Jack said. "It'll be going an *insane* velocity when it hits!"

"Yep," Bruce said. "With ideal atmospheric drag, it'll impact at three hundred meters per second."

"What good will a pulverized probe do Watney?" Jack asked.

"As long as the food doesn't burn up on the way in, Watney can eat it," Bruce said.

Turning to the whiteboard, he began drawing a basic organizational chart. "I want two teams," he began.

"Team One will make the outer shell, guidance system, and thrusters. All we need is for it to get to Mars. I want the safest possible system. Aerosol propellant would be best. High-gain radio so we can talk to it, and standard satellite navigational software.

"Team Two will deal with the payload. They need to find a way to contain the food during impact. If protein bars hit sand at three hundred meters per second, they'll make protein-scented sand. We need them *edible* after impact.

"We can weigh nine hundred and forty-one kilograms. At least three hundred of that needs to be food. Get crackin'."

■ ■ ■

"UH, DR. KAPOOR?" Rich said, peeking his head into Venkat's office. "Do you have a minute?"

Venkat gestured him in. "You are . . . ?"

"Rich, Rich Purnell," he said, shuffling into the office, his arms wrapped around a sheaf of disorganized papers. "From astrodynamics."

"Nice to meet you," Venkat said. "What can I do for you, Rich?"

"I came up with something a while ago. Spent a lot of time on it." He dumped the papers on Venkat's desk. "Lemme find the summary. . . ."

Venkat stared forlornly at his once-clean desk, now strewn with scores of printouts.

"Here we go!" Rich said triumphantly, grabbing a paper. Then his expression saddened. "No, this isn't it."

"Rich," Venkat said. "Maybe you should just tell me what this is about?"

Rich looked at the mess of papers and sighed. "But I had such a cool summary. . . ."

"A summary for what?"

"How to save Watney."

"That's already in progress," Venkat said. "It's a last-ditch effort, but—"

"The *Taiyang Shen*?" Rich snorted. "That won't work. You can't make a Mars probe in a month."

"We're sure as hell going to try," Venkat said, a note of annoyance in his voice.

"Oh, sorry, am I being difficult?" Rich asked. "I'm not good with people. Sometimes I'm difficult. I wish people would just tell me. Anyway, the *Taiyang Shen* is critical. In fact, my idea won't work without it. But a Mars probe? Pfft. C'mon."

"All right," Venkat said. "What's your idea?"

Rich snatched a paper from the desk. "Here it is!" He handed it to Venkat with a childlike smile.

Venkat took the summary and skimmed it. The more he read, the wider his eyes got. "Are you sure about this?"

"Absolutely!" Rich beamed.

"Have you told anyone else?"

"Who would I tell?"

"I don't know," Venkat said. "Friends?"

"I don't have any of those."

"Okay, keep it under your hat."

"I don't wear a hat."

"It's just an expression."

"Really?" Rich said. "It's a stupid expression."

"Rich, you're being difficult."

"Ah. Thanks."

■ ■ ■

Vogel:
Being your backup has backfired.

I guess NASA figured botany and chemistry are similar because they both end in "Y." One way or another, I ended up being your backup chemist.

Remember when they made you spend a day explaining your experiments to me? It was in the middle of intense mission prep. You may have forgotten.

You started my training by buying me a beer. For breakfast. Germans are awesome.

Anyway, now that I have time to kill, NASA gave me a pile of work. And all your chemistry crap is on the list. So now I have to do boring-ass experiments with test tubes and soil and pH levels and Zzzzzzzzz . . . .

My life is now a desperate struggle for survival . . . with occasional titration.

Frankly, I suspect you're a super-villain. You're a chemist, you have a German accent, you had a base on Mars . . . what more can there be?

■ ■ ■

"WHAT THE fuck is 'Project Elrond'?" Annie asked.

"I had to make something up," Venkat said.

"So you came up with 'Elrond'?" Annie pressed.

"Because it's a secret meeting?" Mitch guessed. "The e-mail said I couldn't even tell my assistant."

"I'll explain everything once Teddy arrives," Venkat said.

"Why does 'Elrond' mean 'secret meeting'?" Annie asked.

"Are we going to make a momentous decision?" Bruge Ng asked.

"Exactly," Venkat said.

"How did you know that?" Annie asked, getting annoyed.

"Elrond," Bruce said. "The Council of Elrond. From *Lord of the Rings*. It's the meeting where they decide to destroy the One Ring."

"Jesus," Annie said. "*None* of you got laid in high school, did you?"

"Good morning," Teddy said as he walked into the conference room. Seating himself, he rested his hands on the table. "Anyone know what this meeting's about?" he asked.

"Wait," Mitch said, "*Teddy* doesn't even know?"

Venkat took a deep breath. "One of our astrodynamicists, Rich Purnell, has found a way to get *Hermes* back to Mars. The course he came up with would give *Hermes* a Mars flyby on Sol 549."

Silence.

"You shittin' us?" Annie demanded.

"Sol 549? How's that even possible?" asked Bruce. "Even Iris wouldn't have landed till Sol 588."

"Iris is a point-thrust craft," Venkat said. "*Hermes* has a constant-thrust ion engine. It's always accelerating. Also, *Hermes* has a *lot* of velocity right now. On their current Earth-intercept course, they have to decelerate for the next month just to slow down to Earth's speed."

Mitch rubbed the back of his head. "Wow . . . 549. That's thirty-five sols before Watney runs out of food. That would solve everything."

Teddy leaned forward. "Run us through it, Venkat. What would it entail?"

"Well," Venkat began, "if they did this 'Rich

Purnell Maneuver,' they'd start accelerating right away, to preserve their velocity and gain even more. They wouldn't intercept Earth at all, but would come close enough to use a gravity assist to adjust course. Around that time, they'd pick up a resupply probe with provisions for the extended trip.

"After that, they'd be on an accelerating orbit toward Mars, arriving on Sol 549. Like I said, it's a Mary *flyby*. This isn't anything like a normal Ares mission. They'll be going too fast to fall into orbit. The rest of the maneuver takes them back to Earth. They'd be home two hundred and eleven days after the flyby."

"What good is a flyby?" Bruce asked. "They don't have any way to get Watney off the surface."

"Yeah . . . ," Venkat said. "Now for the unpleasant part: Watney would have to get to the Ares 4 MAV."

"Schiaparelli!?" Mitch gaped. "That's thirty-two hundred kilometers away!"

"Three thousand, two hundred, and thirty-five kilometers to be exact," Venkat said. "It's not out of the question. He drove to *Pathfinder*'s landing site and back. That's over fifteen hundred kilometers."

"That was over flat, desert terrain," Bruce chimed in, "but the trip to Schiaparelli—"

"Suffice it to say," Venkat interrupted, "it would be very difficult and dangerous. But we have a lot of clever scientists to help him trick out the rover. Also there would be MAV modifications."

"What's wrong with the MAV?" Mitch asked.

"It's designed to get to low Mars orbit," Venkat explained. "But *Hermes* would be on a flyby, so the MAV would have to escape Mars gravity entirely to intercept."

"How?" Mitch asked.

"It'd have to lose weight . . . a *lot* of weight. I can get rooms full of people working on these problems, if we decide to do this."

"Earlier," Teddy said, "you mentioned a supply probe for *Hermes*. We have that capability?"

"Yes, with the *Taiyang Shen*," Venkat said. "We'd shoot for a near-Earth rendezvous. It's a lot easier than getting a probe to Mars, that's for sure."

"I see," Teddy said. "So we have two options on the table: Send Watney enough food to last until Ares 4, or send *Hermes* back to get him right now. Both plans require the *Taiyang Shen*, so we can only do one."

"Yes," Venkat said. "We'll have to pick one."

They all took a moment to consider.

"What about the *Hermes* crew?" Annie asked, breaking the silence. "Would they have a problem with adding . . ." She did some quick math in her head. "Five hundred and thirty-three days to their mission?"

"They wouldn't hesitate," Mitch said. "Not for a second. That's why Venkat called this meeting." He glared at Venkat. "He wants us to decide instead."

"That's right," Venkat said.

"It should be Commander Lewis's call," Mitch said.

"Pointless to even ask her," Venkat said. "*We* need to make this decision; it's a matter of life and death."

"She's the mission commander," Mitch said. "Life-and-death decisions are her damn job."

"Easy, Mitch," Teddy said.

"Bullshit," Mitch said. "You guys have done end runs around the crew every time something goes wrong. You didn't tell them Watney was still alive; now you're not telling them there's a way to save him."

"We already have a way to keep him alive," Teddy said. "We're just discussing another one."

"The crash-lander?" Mitch said. "Does anyone think that'll work? Anyone?"

"All right, Mitch," Teddy said. "You've expressed your opinion, and we've heard it. Let's move on." He turned to Venkat. "Can *Hermes* function for five hundred and thirty-three days beyond the scheduled mission end?"

"It should," Venkat said. "The crew may have to fix things here and there, but they're well trained. Remember, *Hermes* was made to do all five Ares missions. It's only halfway through its designed life span."

"It's the most expensive thing ever built," Teddy said. "We can't make another one. If something went wrong, the crew would die, and the Ares Program with them."

"Losing the crew would be a disaster," Venkat said. "But we wouldn't lose *Hermes*. We can remotely operate it. So long as the reactor and ion engines continued to work, we could bring it back."

"Space travel is dangerous," Mitch said. "We can't make this a discussion about what's safest."

"I disagree," Teddy said. "This is *absolutely* a discussion about what's safest. And about how many lives are at stake. Both plans are risky, but resupplying Watney only risks one life while the Rich Purnell Maneuver risks six."

"Consider *degree* of risk, Teddy," Venkat said. "Mitch is right. The crash-lander is high-risk. It could miss Mars, it could reenter wrong and burn up, it could crash too hard and destroy the food . . . We estimate a thirty percent chance of success."

"A near-Earth rendezvous with *Hermes* is more doable?" Teddy asked.

"Much more doable," Venkat confirmed. "With sub-second transmission delays, we can control the probe directly from Earth rather than rely on automated systems. When the time comes to dock, Major Martinez can pilot it remotely from *Hermes* with no transmission delay at all. And *Hermes* has a human crew, able to overcome any hiccups that may happen. And we don't have to do a reentry; the supplies don't have to survive a three-hundred-meters-per-second impact."

"So," Bruce offered, "we can have a high chance of killing one person, or a low chance of killing six people. Jeez. How do we even make this decision?"

"We talk about it, then Teddy makes the decision," Venkat said. "Not sure what else we can do."

"We could let Lewis—" Mitch began.

"Yeah, other than that," Venkat interrupted.

"Question," Annie said. "What am I even here for? This seems like something for you nerds to discuss."

"You need to be in the loop," Venkat said. "We're not deciding right now. We'll need to quietly research the details internally. Something might leak, and you need to be ready to dance around questions."

"How long have we got to make a decision?" Teddy asked.

"The window for starting the maneuver ends in thirty-nine hours."

"All right," Teddy said. "Everyone, we discuss this only in person or on the phone; never e-mail. And don't talk to *anyone* about this, other than the people here. The last thing we need is public opinion pressing for a risky cowboy rescue that may be impossible."

■ ■ ■

Beck:

Hey, man. How ya been?

Now that I'm in a "dire situation," I don't have to follow social rules anymore. I can be honest with everyone.

Bearing that in mind, I have to say . . . dude . . . you need to tell Johanssen how you feel. If you don't, you'll regret it forever.

I won't lie: It could end badly. I have no idea what she thinks of you. Or of anything. She's weird.

But wait till the mission's over. You're on a ship with her for another two months. Also, if you guys got up to anything while the mission was in progress, Lewis would kill you.

■ ■ ■

VENKAT, MITCH, Annie, Bruce, and Teddy met for the second time in as many days. "Project Elrond" had taken on a dark connotation throughout the Space Center, veiled in secrecy. Many people knew the name, none knew its purpose.

Speculation ran rampant. Some thought it was a completely new program in the works. Others worried it might be a move to cancel Ares 4 and 5. Most thought it was Ares 6 in the works.

"It wasn't an easy decision," Teddy said to the assembled elite. "But I've decided to go with Iris 2. No Rich Purnell Maneuver."

Mitch slammed his fist on the table.

"We'll do all we can to make it work," Bruce said.

"If it's not too much to ask," Venkat began, "what made up your mind?"

Teddy sighed. "It's a matter of risk," he said. "Iris 2 only risks one life. Rich Purnell risks all six of them. I know Rich Purnell is more likely to work, but I don't think it's six times more likely."

"You coward," Mitch said.

"Mitch . . . ," Venkat said.

"You god damned coward," Mitch continued, ignoring Venkat. "You just want to cut your losses. You're on damage control. You don't give a shit about Watney's life."

"Of course I do," Teddy replied. "And I'm sick of your infantile attitude. You can throw all the tantrums you want, but the rest of us have to be adults. This isn't a TV show; the riskier solution isn't always the best."

"Space is dangerous," Mitch snapped. "It's what we do here. If you want to play it safe all the time, go join an insurance company. And by the way, it's not even your life you're risking. The crew can make up their own minds about it."

"No, they can't," Teddy fired back. "They're too emotionally involved. Clearly, so are you. I'm not gambling five additional lives to save one. Especially when we might save him without risking them at all."

"Bullshit!" Mitch shot back as he stood from his chair. "You're just *convincing* yourself the crashlander will work so you don't have to take a risk. You're hanging him out to dry, you chickenshit son of a bitch!"

He stormed out of the room, slamming the door behind him.

After a few seconds, Venkat followed behind, saying, "I'll make sure he cools off."

Bruce slumped in his chair. "Sheesh," he said nervously. "We're scientists, for Christ's sake. What the hell!?"

Annie quietly gathered her things and placed them in her briefcase.

Teddy looked to her. "Sorry about that, Annie," he said. "What can I say? Sometimes men let testosterone take over—"

"I was hoping he'd kick your ass," she interrupted.

"What?"

"I know you care about the astronauts, but he's right. You *are* a fucking coward. If you had balls, we might be able to save Watney."

■ ■ ■

Lewis:

Hi, Commander.

Between training and our trip to Mars, I spent two years working with you. I think I know you pretty well. So I'm guessing you still blame yourself for my situation, despite my earlier e-mail asking you not to.

You were faced with an impossible scenario and made a tough decision. That's what commanders do. And your decision was right. If you'd waited any longer, the MAV would have tipped.

I'm sure you've run through all the possible outcomes in your head, so you know there's nothing you could have done differently (other than "be psychic").

You probably think losing a crewman is the worst thing that can happen. Not true. Losing the whole crew is worse. You kept that from happening.

But there's something more important we need to discuss: What is it with you and disco? I can understand the '70s TV because everyone loves hairy people with huge collars. But disco?

Disco!?

■ ■ ■

VOGEL CHECKED the position and orientation of *Hermes* against the projected path. It matched, as usual. In addition to being the mission's chemist, he was also an accomplished astrophysicist. Though his duties as navigator were laughably easy.

The computer knew the course. It knew when to angle the ship so the ion engines would be aimed correctly. And it knew the location of the ship at all times (easily calculated from the position of the sun and Earth, and knowing the exact time from an on-board atomic clock).

Barring a complete computer failure or other critical event, Vogel's vast knowledge of astrodynamics would never come into play.

After completing the check, he ran a diagnostic on the engines. They were functioning at peak. He did all this from his quarters. All onboard computers could control all ships' functions. Gone were the days of physically visiting the engines to check up on them.

Having completed his work for the day, he finally had time to read e-mail.

Sorting through the messages NASA deemed worthy to upload, he read the most interesting first and responded when necessary. His responses were cached and would be sent to Earth with Johanssen's next uplink.

A message from his wife caught his attention. Titled *"unsere kinder"* ("our children"), it contained nothing but an image attachment. He raised an eyebrow. Several things stood out at once. First, "kinder" should have been capitalized. Helena, a grammar school teacher in Bremen, was very unlikely to make that mistake. Also, to each other, they affectionately called their kids *die Affen*.

When he tried to open the image, his viewer reported that the file was unreadable.

He walked down the narrow hallway. The crew quarters stood against the outer hull of the constantly spinning ship to maximize simulated gravity. Johanssen's door was open, as usual.

"Johanssen. Good evening," Vogel said. The crew kept the same sleep schedule, and it was nearing bedtime.

"Oh, hello," Johanssen said, looking up from her computer.

"I have the computer problem," Vogel explained. "I wonder if you will help."

"Sure," she said.

"You are in the personal time," Vogel said. "Perhaps tomorrow when you are on the duty is better?"

"Now's fine," she said. "What's wrong?"

"It is a file. It is an image, but my computer cannot view."

"Where's the file?" she asked, typing on her keyboard.

"It is on my shared space. The name is 'kinder.jpg.' "

"Let's take a look," she said.

Her fingers flew over her keyboard as windows opened and closed on her screen. "Definitely a bad jpg header," she said. "Probably mangled in the download. Lemme look with a hex editor, see if we got anything at all. . . ."

After a few moments she said, "This isn't a jpeg. It's a plain ASCII text file. Looks like . . . well, I don't know what it is. Looks like a bunch of math formulae." She gestured to the screen. "Does any of this make sense to you?"

Vogel leaned in, looking at the text. *"Ja,"* he said. "It is a course maneuver for *Hermes*. It says the name is 'Rich Purnell Maneuver.' "

"What's that?" Johanssen asked.

"I have not heard of this maneuver." He looked at the tables. "It is complicated . . . very complicated. . . ."

He froze. "Sol 549!?" he exclaimed. *"Mein Gott!"*

▪▪▪

THE *HERMES* crew enjoyed their scant personal time in an area called "the Rec." Consisting of a table and barely room to seat six, it ranked low in gravity priority. Its position amidships granted it a mere 0.2 g.

Still, it was enough to keep everyone in a seat as they pondered what Vogel told them.

" . . . and then mission would conclude with Earth intercept two hundred and eleven days later," he finished up.

"Thank you, Vogel," Lewis said. She'd heard the explanation earlier when Vogel came to her, but Johanssen, Martinez, and Beck were hearing it for the first time. She gave them a moment to digest.

"Would this really work?" Martinez asked.

"Ja." Vogel nodded. "I ran the numbers. They all check out. It is brilliant course. Amazing."

"How would he get off Mars?" Martinez asked.

Lewis leaned forward. "There was more in the message," she began. "We'd have to pick up a supply near Earth, and he'd have to get to Ares 4's MAV."

"Why all the cloak and dagger?" Beck asked.

"According to the message," Lewis explained, "NASA rejected the idea. They'd rather take a big risk on Watney than a small risk on all of us. Whoever snuck it into Vogel's e-mail obviously disagreed."

"So," Martinez said, "we're talking about going directly against NASA's decision?"

"Yes," Lewis confirmed, "that's exactly what we're talking about. If we go through with the maneuver, they'll have to send the supply ship or we'll die. We have the opportunity to force their hand."

"Are we going to do it?" Johanssen asked.

They all looked to Lewis.

"I won't lie," she said. "I'd sure as hell like to. But this isn't a normal decision. This is something NASA expressly rejected. We're talking about mutiny. And that's not a word I throw around lightly."

She stood and paced slowly around the table. "We'll only do it if we all agree. And before you answer, consider the consequences. If we mess up the supply rendezvous, we die. If we mess up the Earth gravity assist, we die.

"If we do everything perfectly, we add five hundred and thirty-three days to our mission. Five hundred and thirty-three days of unplanned space travel where anything could go wrong. Maintenance will be a hassle. Something might break that we can't fix. If it's life-critical, we die."

"Sign me up!" Martinez smiled.

"Easy, cowboy," Lewis said. "You and I are military. There's a good chance we'd be court-martialed when we got home. As for the rest of you, I guarantee they'll never send you up again."

Martinez leaned against the wall, arms folded with a half grin on his face. The rest silently considered what their commander had said.

"If we do this," Vogel said, "it would be over one thousand days of space. This is enough space for a life. I do not need to return."

"Sounds like Vogel's in." Martinez grinned. "Me, too, obviously."

"Let's do it," Beck said.

"If you think it'll work," Johanssen said to Lewis, "I trust you."

"Okay," Lewis said. "If we go for it, what's involved?"

Vogel shrugged. "I plot the course and execute it," he said. "What else?"

"Remote override," Johanssen said. "It's designed to get the ship back if we all die or something. They can take over *Hermes* from Mission Control."

"But we're right here," Lewis said. "We can undo whatever they try, right?"

"Not really," Johanssen said. "Remote override takes priority over any onboard controls. It assumes there's been a disaster and the ship's control panels can't be trusted."

"Can you disable it?" Lewis asked.

"Hmm . . ." Johanssen pondered. "*Hermes* has four redundant flight computers, each connected to three redundant comm systems. If any computer gets a signal from any comm system, Mission Control can take over. We can't shut down the comms; we'd lose telemetry and guidance. We can't shut down the computers; we need them to control the ship. I'll have to disable the remote override on each system . . . . It's part of the OS; I'll have to jump over the code. . . . Yes. I can do it."

"You're sure?" Lewis asked. "You can turn it off?"

"Shouldn't be hard," Johanssen said. "It's an emergency feature, not a security program. It isn't protected against malicious code."

"Malicious code?" Beck smiled. "So . . . you'll be a hacker?"

"Yeah." Johanssen smiled back. "I guess I will."

"All right," Lewis said. "Looks like we can do it. But I don't want peer pressure forcing anyone into it. We'll wait for twenty-four hours. During that time, anyone can change their mind. Just talk to me in private or send me an e-mail. I'll call it off and never tell anyone who it was."

Lewis stayed behind as the rest filed out. Watching them leave, she saw they were smiling. All four of them. For the first time since leaving Mars, they were back to their old selves. She knew right then no one's mind would change.

They were going back to Mars.

■ ■ ■

EVERYONE KNEW Brendan Hutch would be running missions soon.

He'd risen through NASA's ranks as fast as one could in the large, inertia-bound organization. He was known as a diligent worker, and his skill and leadership qualities were plain to all his subordinates.

Brendan was in charge of Mission Control from one a.m. to nine a.m. every night. Continued excellent performance in this role would certainly net him a promotion. It had already been announced he'd be backup flight controller for Ares 4, and he had a good shot at the top job for Ares 5.

"Flight, CAPCOM," a voice said through his headset.

"Go, CAPCOM," Brendan responded. Though they were in the same room, radio protocol was observed at all times.

"Unscheduled status update from *Hermes*."

With *Hermes* ninety light-seconds away, back-and-forth voice communication was impractical. Other than media relations, *Hermes* would communicate via text until they were much closer.

"Roger," Brendan said. "Read it out."

"I . . . I don't get it, Flight," came the confused reply. "No real status, just a single sentence."

"What's it say?"

"Message reads: 'Houston, be advised: Rich Purnell is a steely-eyed missile man.'"

"What?" Brendan asked. "Who the hell is Rich Purnell?"

"Flight, Telemetry," another voice said.

"Go, Telemetry," Brendan said.

"*Hermes* is off course."

"CAPCOM, advise *Hermes* they're drifting. Telemetry, get a correction vector ready—"

"Negative, Flight," Telemetry interrupted. "It's not drift. They adjusted course. Instrumentation uplink shows a deliberate 27.812-degree rotation."

"What the hell?" Brendan stammered. "CAPCOM, ask them what the hell."

"Roger, Flight . . . message sent. Minimum reply time three minutes, four seconds."

"Telemetry, any chance this is instrumentation failure?"

"Negative, Flight. We're tracking them with SatCon. Observed position is consistent with the course change."

"CAPCOM, read your logs and see what the previous shift did. See if a massive course change was ordered and somehow nobody told us."

"Roger, Flight."

"Guidance, Flight," Brendan said.

"Go, Flight," was the reply from the guidance controller.

"Work out how long they can stay on this course before it's irreversible. At what point will they no longer be able to intercept Earth?"

"Working on that now, Flight."

"And somebody find out who the hell Rich Purnell is!"

■ ■ ■

MITCH PLOPPED down on the couch in Teddy's office. He put his feet up on the coffee table and smiled at Teddy. "You wanted to see me?"

"Why'd you do it, Mitch?" Teddy demanded.

"Do what?"

"You know damn well what I'm talking about."

"Oh, you mean the *Hermes* mutiny?" Mitch said innocently. "You know, that'd make a good movie title. *The Hermes Mutiny*. Got a nice ring to it."

"We know you did it," Teddy said sternly. "We don't know how, but we know you sent them the maneuver."

"So you don't have any proof."

Teddy glared. "No. Not yet, but we're working on it."

"Really?" Mitch said. "Is that *really* the best use of our time? I mean, we have a near-Earth resupply to plan, not to mention figuring out how to get Watney to Schiaparelli. We've got a lot on our plates."

"You're damn right we have a lot on our plates!" Teddy fumed. "After your little stunt, we're committed to this thing."

"*Alleged* stunt," Mitch said, raising a finger. "I

suppose Annie will tell the media we decided to try this risky maneuver? And she'll leave out the mutiny part?"

"Of course," Teddy said. "Otherwise we'd look like idiots."

"I guess everyone's off the hook then!" Mitch smiled. "Can't fire people for enacting NASA policy. Even Lewis is fine. What mutiny? And maybe Watney gets to live. Happy endings all around!"

"You may have killed the whole crew," Teddy countered. "Ever think of that?"

"*Whoever* gave them the maneuver," Mitch said, "only passed along information. Lewis made the decision to act on it. If she let emotion cloud her judgment, she'd be a shitty commander. And she's not a shitty commander."

"If I can ever prove it was you, I'll find a way to fire you for it," Teddy warned.

"Sure." Mitch shrugged. "But if I wasn't willing to take risks to save lives, I'd . . ." He thought for a moment. "Well, I guess I'd be you."

CHAPTER 17

LOG ENTRY: SOL 192

Holy shit!

They're coming back for me!

I don't even know how to react. I'm choked up!

And I've got a shitload of work to do before I catch that bus home.

They can't orbit. If I'm not in space when they pass by, all they can do is wave.

I have to get to Ares 4's MAV. Even NASA accepts that. And when the nannies at NASA recommend a 3200-kilometer overland drive, you know you're in trouble.

Schiaparelli, here I come!

Well . . . not right away. I still have to do the aforementioned shitload of work.

My trip to *Pathfinder* was a quick jaunt compared to the epic journey that's coming up. I got away with a lot of shortcuts because I only had to survive twenty-two sols. This time, things are different.

I averaged 80 kilometers per sol on my way to *Pathfinder*. If I do that well toward Schiaparelli, the trip'll take forty sols. Call it fifty to be safe.

But there's more to it than just travel. Once I get there, I'll need to set up camp and do a bunch of MAV modifications. NASA estimates they'll take thirty sols, forty-five to be safe. Between the trip and the MAV mods, that's ninety-five sols. Call it one hundred because ninety-five cries out to be approximated.

So I'll need to survive away from the Hab for a hundred sols.

"What about the MAV?" I hear you ask (in my fevered imagination). "Won't it have some supplies? Air and water at the very least?"

Nope. It's got dick-all.

It does have air tanks, but they're empty. An Ares mission needs lots of O_2, N_2, and water anyway. Why send more with the MAV? Easier to have the crew top off the MAV from the Hab. Fortunately for my crewmates, the mission plan had Martinez fill the MAV tanks on Sol 1.

The flyby is on Sol 549, so I'll need to leave by 449. That gives me 257 sols to get my ass in gear.

Seems like a long time, doesn't it?

In that time, I need to modify the rover to carry the "Big Three": the atmospheric regulator, the oxygenator, and the water reclaimer. All three need to be in the pressurized area, but the rover isn't big enough. All three need to be running at all times, but the rover's batteries can't handle that load for long.

The rover will also need to carry all my food, water, and solar cells, my extra battery, my tools, some spare parts, and *Pathfinder*. As my sole means of communication with NASA, *Pathfinder* gets to ride on the roof, Granny Clampett style.

I have a lot of problems to solve, but I have a lot of smart people to solve them. Pretty much the whole planet Earth.

NASA is still working on the details, but the idea is to use both rovers. One to drive around, the other to act as my cargo trailer.

I'll have to make structural changes to that trailer. And by "structural changes" I mean "cut a big hole in the hull." Then I can move the Big Three in and use Hab canvas to loosely cover the hole. It'll balloon out when I pressurize the rover, but it'll hold. How will I cut a big chunk out of a rover's hull? I'll let my lovely assistant Venkat Kapoor explain further:

> [14:38] JPL: I'm sure you're wondering how to cut a hole in the rover.
>
> Our experiments show a rock sample drill can get through the hull. Wear and tear on the bit is minimal (rocks are harder than carbon composite). You can cut holes in a line, then chisel out the remaining chunks between them.
>
> I hope you like drilling. The drill bit is 1 cm wide, the holes will be 0.5 cm apart, and the length of the total cut is 11.4 m. That's 760 holes. And each one takes 160 seconds to drill.
>
> Problem: The drills weren't designed for construction projects. They were intended for quick rock samples. The batteries only last 240 seconds. You do have two drills, but you'd still only get 3 holes done before needing to recharge. And recharging takes 41 minutes.

That's 173 hours of work, limited to 8 EVA hours per day. That's 21 days of drilling, and that's just too long. All our other ideas hinge on this cut working. If it doesn't, we need time to come up with new ones.

So we want you to wire a drill directly to Hab power.

The drill expects 28.8 V and pulls 9 amps. The only lines that can handle that are the rover recharge lines. They're 36 V, 10 amp max. Since you have two, we're comfortable with you modifying one.

We'll send you instructions on how to step down the voltage and put a new breaker in the line, but I'm sure you already know how.

I'll be playing with high-voltage power tomorrow. Can't imagine anything going wrong with that!

LOG ENTRY: SOL 193

I managed to not kill myself today, even though I was working with high voltage. Well, it's not as exciting as all that. I disconnected the line first.

As instructed, I turned a rover charging cable into a drill power source. Getting the voltage right was a simple matter of adding resistors, which my electronics kit has in abundance.

I had to make my own nine-amp breaker. I strung three three-amp breakers in parallel. There's no way for nine amps to get through that without tripping all three in rapid succession.

Then I had to rewire a drill. Pretty much the same thing I did with *Pathfinder*. Take out the battery and replace it with a power line from the Hab. But this time it was a lot easier.

Pathfinder was too big to fit through any of my airlocks, so I had to do all the rewiring outside. Ever done electronics while wearing a space suit? Pain in the ass. I even had to make a workbench out of MAV landing struts, remember?

Anyway, the drill fit in the airlock easily. It's only a meter tall, and shaped like a jackhammer. We did our rock sampling standing up, like Apollo astronauts.

Also, unlike my *Pathfinder* hatchet job, I had the full schematics of the drill. I removed the battery and attached a power line where it used to be. Then, taking the drill and its new cord outside, I connected it to the modified rover charger and fired it up.

Worked like a charm! The drill whirled away with happy abandon. Somehow, I had managed to do everything right the first try. Deep down, I thought I'd fry the drill for sure.

It wasn't even midday yet. I figured why not get a jump on drilling?

[10:07] WATNEY: Power line modifications complete. Hooked it up to a drill, and it works great. Plenty of daylight left. Send me a description of that hole you want me to cut.

[10:25] JPL: Glad to hear it. Starting on the cut sounds great. Just to be clear, these are modifications to Rover 1, which we've been calling "the trailer." Rover 2 (the one with your modifications for the trip to Pathfinder) should remain as is for now.

You'll be taking a chunk out of the roof, just in front of the airlock in the rear of the vehicle.

The hole needs to be at least 2.5 m long and the full 2 m width of the pressure vessel.

Before any cuts, draw the shape on the trailer, and position the trailer where Pathfinder's camera can see it. We'll let you know if you got it right.

[10:43] WATNEY: Roger. Take a pic at 11:30, if you haven't heard from me by then.

The rovers are made to interlock so one can tow the other. That way you can rescue your crewmates if all hell breaks loose. For that same reason, rovers can share air via hoses you connect between them. That little feature will let me share atmosphere with the trailer on my long drive.

I'd stolen the trailer's battery long ago; it had no ability to move under its own power. So I hitched it up to my awesomely modified rover and towed it into place near *Pathfinder*.

Venkat told me to "draw" the shape I plan to cut, but he neglected to mention how. It's not like I have a Sharpie that can work out on the surface. So I vandalized Martinez's bed.

The cots are basically hammocks. Lightweight string woven loosely into something that's comfortable to sleep on. Every gram counts when making stuff to send to Mars.

I unraveled Martinez's bed and took the string outside, then taped it to the trailer hull along the path I planned to cut. Yes, of course duct tape works in a near-vacuum. Duct tape works anywhere. Duct tape is magic and should be worshiped.

I can see what NASA has in mind. The rear of the trailer has an airlock that we're not going to mess with. The cut is just ahead of it and will leave plenty of space for the Big Three to stand.

I have no idea how NASA plans to power the Big Three for twenty-four and a half hours a day and still have energy left to drive. I bet they don't know, either. But they're smart; they'll work something out.

[11:49] JPL: What we can see of your planned cut looks good. We're assuming the other side is identical. You're cleared to start drilling.

[12:07] WATNEY: That's what she said.

[12:25] JPL: Seriously, Mark? Seriously?

First, I depressurized the trailer. Call me crazy, but I didn't want the drill explosively launched at my face.

Then I had to pick somewhere to start. I thought it'd be easiest to start on the side. I was wrong.

The roof would have been better. The side was a hassle because I had to hold the drill parallel to the ground. This isn't your dad's Black & Decker we're talking about. It's a meter long and only safe to hold by the handles.

Getting it to bite was nasty. I pressed it against the hull and turned it on, but it wandered all over the place. So I got my trusty hammer and screwdriver. With a few taps, I made a small chip in the carbon composite.

That gave the bit a place to seat, so I could keep drilling in one place. As NASA predicted, it took about two and a half minutes to get all the way through.

I followed the same procedure for the second hole and it went much smoother. After the third hole, the drill's overheat light came on.

The poor drill wasn't designed to operate constantly for so long. Fortunately, it sensed the overheat and warned me. So I leaned it against the workbench for a few minutes, and it cooled down. One thing you can say about Mars: It's *really* cold. The thin atmosphere doesn't conduct heat very well, but it cools everything, eventually.

I had already removed the drill's cowling (the power cord needed a way in). A pleasant side effect is the drill cools even faster. Though I'll have to clean it thoroughly every few hours as dust accumulates.

By 17:00, when the sun began to set, I had drilled seventy-five holes. A good start, but there's still tons to do. Eventually (probably tomorrow) I'll have to start drilling holes that I can't reach from the ground. For that I'll need something to stand on.

I can't use my "workbench." It's got *Pathfinder* on it, and the last thing I'm going to do is mess with that. But I've got three more MAV landing struts. I'm sure I can make a ramp or something.

Anyway, that's all stuff for tomorrow. Tonight is about eating a *full* ration for dinner.

Awww yeah. That's right. I'm either getting rescued on Sol 549 or I'm dying. That means I have thirty-five sols of extra food. I can indulge once in a while.

LOG ENTRY: SOL 194

I average a hole every 3.5 minutes. That includes the occasional breather to let the drill cool off.

I learned this by spending all damn day drilling.

After eight hours of dull, physically intense work, I had 137 holes to show for it.

It turned out to be easy to deal with places I couldn't reach. I didn't need to modify a landing strut after all. I just had to get something to stand on. I used a geological sample container (also known as "a box").

Before I was in contact with NASA, I would have worked more than eight hours. I can stay out for ten before even dipping into "emergency" air. But NASA's got a lot of nervous Nellies who don't want me out longer than spec.

With today's work, I'm about one-fourth of the way through the whole cut. At least, one-fourth of the way through the drilling. Then I'll have 759 little chunks to chisel out. And I'm not sure how well carbon composite is going to take to that. But NASA'll do it a thousand times back on Earth and tell me the best way to get it done.

Anyway, at this rate, it'll take four more sols of (boring-ass) work to finish the drilling.

I've actually exhausted Lewis's supply of shitty seventies TV. And I've read all of Johanssen's mystery books.

I've already rifled through other crewmates' stuff to find entertainment. But all of Vogel's stuff is in German, Beck brought nothing but medical journals, and Martinez didn't bring anything.

I got really bored, so I decided to pick a theme song!

Something appropriate. And naturally, it should be something from Lewis's godawful seventies collection. It wouldn't be right any other way.

There are plenty of great candidates: "Life on Mars?" by David Bowie, "Rocket Man" by

Elton John, "Alone Again (Naturally)" by Gilbert O'Sullivan.

But I settled on *"Stayin' Alive"* by the Bee Gees.

LOG ENTRY: SOL 195

Another day, another bunch of holes: 145 this time (I'm getting better). I'm halfway done. This is getting really old.

But at least I have encouraging messages from Venkat to cheer me on!

[17:12] WATNEY: 145 holes today. 357 total.

[17:31] JPL: We thought you'd have more done by now.

Dick.

Anyway, I'm still bored at night. I guess that's a good thing. Nothing's wrong with the Hab. There's a plan to save me, and the physical labor is making me sleep wonderfully.

I miss tending the potatoes. The Hab isn't the same without them.

There's still soil everywhere. No point in lugging it back outside. Lacking anything better to do, I ran some tests on it. Amazingly, some of the bacteria survived. The population is strong and growing. That's pretty impressive, when you consider it was exposed to near-vacuum and subarctic temperatures for over twenty-four hours.

My guess is pockets of ice formed around some of the bacteria, leaving a bubble of survivable pressure inside, and the cold wasn't quite enough to kill them. With hundreds of millions of bacteria, it only takes one survivor to stave off extinction.

Life is amazingly tenacious. They don't want to die any more than I do.

LOG ENTRY: SOL 196

I fucked up.

I fucked up big-time. I made a mistake that might kill me.

I started my EVA around 08:45, same as always. I got my hammer and screwdriver and started chipping the trailer's hull. It's a pain in the ass to make a chip before each drilling, so I make all the day's chips in a single go.

After chipping out 150 divots (hey, I'm an optimist), I got to work.

It was the same as yesterday and the day before. Drill through, relocate. Drill through, relocate. Drill through a third time, then set the drill aside to cool. Repeat that process over and over till lunchtime.

At 12:00, I took a break. Back in the Hab, I enjoyed a nice lunch and played some chess against the computer (it kicked my ass). Then back out for the day's second EVA.

At 13:30 my ruination occurred, though I didn't realize it at the time.

The worst moments in life are heralded by small observations. The tiny lump on your side that wasn't there before. Coming home to your wife and seeing two wineglasses in the sink. Anytime you hear "We interrupt this program . . ."

For me, it was when the drill didn't start.

Only three minutes earlier, it was working fine. I had finished a hole and set the drill aside to cool. Same as always.

But when I tried to get back to work, it was dead. The power light wouldn't even come on.

I wasn't worried. If all else failed, I had another drill. It would take a few hours to wire it up, but that's hardly a concern.

The power light being off meant there was probably something wrong with the line. A quick glance at the airlock window showed the lights were on in the Hab. So there were no systemic power problems. I checked my new breakers, and sure enough, all three had tripped.

I guess the drill pulled a little too much amperage. No big deal. I reset the breakers and got back to work. The drill fired right up, and I was back to making holes.

Doesn't seem like a big deal, right? I certainly didn't think so at the time.

I finished my day at 17:00 after drilling 131 holes. Not as good as yesterday, but I lost some time to the drill malfunction.

I reported my progress.

[17:08] WATNEY: 131 holes today. 488 total. Minor drill issue; it tripped the breakers. There may be an intermittent short in the drill, probably in the attachment point of the power line. Might need to redo it.

Earth and Mars are just over eighteen light-minutes apart now. Usually, NASA responds within twenty-five minutes. Remember, I do all my communication from Rover 2, which relays everything through *Pathfinder*. I can't just lounge in the Hab awaiting a reply; I have to stay in the rover until they acknowledge the message.

[17:38] WATNEY: Have received no reply. Last message sent 30 minutes ago. Please acknowledge.

I waited another thirty minutes. Still no reply. Fear started to take root.

Back when JPL's Nerd Brigade hacked the rover and *Pathfinder* to be a poor man's IM client, they sent me a cheat sheet for troubleshooting. I executed the first instruction:

[18:09] WATNEY: system_command: STATUS

[18:09] SYSTEM: Last message sent 00h31m ago. Last message received 26h17m ago. Last ping reply from probe received 04h24m ago. WARNING: 52 unanswered pings.

Pathfinder was no longer talking to the rover. It had stopped answering pings four hours and twenty-four minutes ago. Some quick math told me that was around 13:30 today.

The same time the drill died.

I tried not to panic. The troubleshooting sheet has a list of things to try if communication is lost. They are (in order):

1. Confirm power still flowing to *Pathfinder*.
2. Reboot rover.
3. Reboot *Pathfinder* by disconnecting/reconnecting power.
4. Install rover's comm software on the other rover's computer, try from there.
5. If both rovers fail, problem is likely with *Pathfinder*. Check connections very closely. Clean *Pathfinder* of Martian dust.
6. Spell message in Morse code with rocks, in-

clude things attempted. Problem may be recoverable with remote update of *Pathfinder*.

I only got as far as step 1. I checked *Pathfinder*'s connections and the negative lead was no longer attached.

I was elated! What a relief! With a smile on my face, I fetched my electronics kit and prepared to reattach the lead. I pulled it out of the probe to give it a good cleaning (as best I could with the gloves of my space suit) and noticed something strange. The insulation had melted.

I pondered this development. Melted insulation usually means a short. More current than the wire could handle had passed through. But the bare portion of the wire wasn't black or even singed, and the positive lead's insulation wasn't melted at all.

Then, one by one, the horrible realities of Mars came into play. The wire wouldn't be burned or singed. That's a result of oxidization. And there's no oxygen in the air. There likely was a short after all. But with the positive lead being unaffected, the power must have come from somewhere else. . . .

And the drill's breaker tripped around the same time. . . .

Oh . . . shit . . .

The internal electronics for *Pathfinder* included a ground lead to the hull. This way it could not build up a static charge in Martian weather conditions (no water and frequent sandblasting can make impressive static charge).

The hull sat on Panel A, one of four sides of the tetrahedron which brought *Pathfinder* to Mars. The other three sides are still in Ares Vallis where I left them.

Between Panel A and the workbench were the Mylar balloons *Pathfinder* had used to tumble-land. I had shredded many of them to transport it, but a lot of material remained—enough to reach around Panel A and be in contact with the hull. I should mention that Mylar is conductive.

At 13:30, I leaned the drill against the workbench. The drill's cowling was off to make room for the power line. The workbench is metal. If the drill leaned against the workbench just right, it could make a metal-to-metal connection.

And that's exactly what had happened.

Power traveled from the drill line's positive lead, through the workbench, through the Mylar, through *Pathfinder*'s hull, through a bunch of extremely sensitive and irreplaceable electronics, and out the negative lead of *Pathfinder*'s power line.

Pathfinder operates on 50 milliamps. It got *9000* milliamps, which plowed through the delicate electronics, frying everything along the way. The breakers tripped, but it was too late.

Pathfinder's dead. I've lost the ability to contact Earth.

I'm on my own.

CHAPTER 18

LOG ENTRY: SOL 197

Sigh . . .

Just once I'd like something to go as planned, ya know?

Mars keeps trying to kill me.

Well . . . Mars didn't electrocute *Pathfinder*. So I'll amend that:

Mars and my stupidity keep trying to kill me.

Okay, enough self-pity. I'm not doomed. Things will just be harder than planned. I have all I need to survive. And *Hermes* is still on the way.

I spelled out a Morse code message using rocks. "PF FRIED WITH 9 AMPS. DEAD FOREVER. PLAN UNCHANGED. WILL GET TO MAV."

If I can get to the Ares 4 MAV, I'll be set. But having lost contact with NASA, I have to design my own Great Martian Winnebago to get there.

For the time being, I've stopped all work on it.

I don't want to continue without a plan. I'm sure NASA had all kinds of ideas, but now I have to come up with one on my own.

As I mentioned, the Big Three (atmospheric regulator, oxygenator, and water reclaimer) are critical components. I worked around them for my trip to *Pathfinder*. I used CO_2 filters to regulate the atmosphere, and brought enough oxygen and water for the whole trip. That won't work this time. I need the Big Three.

Problem is, they soak up a lot of power, and they have to run all day long. The rover batteries have 18 kilowatt-hours of juice. The oxygenator *alone* uses 44.1 kilowatt-hours per sol. See my problem?

You know what? "Kilowatt-hours per sol" is a pain in the ass to say. I'm gonna invent a new scientific unit name. One kilowatt-hour per sol is . . . it can be anything . . . um . . . I suck at this . . . I'll call it a "pirate-ninja."

All told, the Big Three need 69.2 pirate-ninjas, most of that going to the oxygenator and the atmospheric regulator. (The water reclaimer only needs 3.6 of that.)

There'll be cutbacks.

The easiest cutback is the water reclaimer. I have 620 liters of water (I had a lot more before the Hab blew up). I need only three liters of water per sol, so my supply will last 206 sols. There's only 100 sols after I leave and before I'm picked up (or die in the attempt).

Conclusion: I don't need the water reclaimer at all. I'll drink as needed and dump my waste outdoors. Yeah, that's right, Mars, I'm gonna piss and shit on you. That's what you get for trying to kill me all the time.

There. I saved myself 3.6 pirate-ninjas.

LOG ENTRY: SOL 198

I've had a breakthrough with the oxygenator!

I spent most of the day looking at the specs. It heats CO_2 to 900°C, then passes it over a zirconia electrolysis cell to yank the carbon atoms off. Heating the gas is what takes most of the energy. Why is that important? Because I'm just one guy and the oxygenator was made for six. One-sixth the quantity of CO_2 means one-sixth the energy to heat it.

The *spec* says it draws 44.1 pirate-ninjas, but all this time it's only been using 7.35 because of the reduced load. Now we're getting somewhere!

Then there's the matter of the atmospheric regulator. The regulator samples the air, figures out what's wrong with it, and corrects the problem. Too much CO_2? Take it out. Not enough O_2? Add some. Without it, the oxygenator is worthless. The CO_2 needs to be separated in order to be processed.

The regulator analyzes the air with spectroscopy, then separates the gasses by supercooling them. Different elements turn to liquid at different temperatures. On Earth, supercooling this much air would take ridiculous amounts of energy. But (as I'm acutely aware) this isn't Earth.

Here on Mars, supercooling is done by pumping air to a component outside the Hab. The air quickly cools to the outdoor temperature, which ranges from −150°C to 0°C. When it's warm, additional refrigeration is used, but cold days can turn air to liquid for free. The real energy cost comes from heating it back up. If it came back to the Hab unheated, I'd freeze to death.

"But wait!" You're thinking, "Mars's atmosphere isn't liquid. Why does the Hab's air condense?"

The Hab's atmosphere is over 100 times as dense, so it turns to liquid at much higher temperatures. The regulator gets the best of both worlds. Literally. Side note: Mars's atmosphere *does* condense at the poles. In fact, it solidifies into dry ice.

Problem: The regulator takes 21.5 pirate-ninjas. Even adding some of the Hab's power cells would barely power the regulator for a sol, let alone give me enough juice to drive.

More thinking is required.

LOG ENTRY: SOL 199

I've got it. I know how to power the oxygenator and atmospheric regulator.

The problem with small pressure vessels is CO_2 toxicity. You can have all the oxygen in the world, but once the CO_2 gets above 1 percent, you'll start to get drowsy. At 2 percent, it's like being drunk. At 5 percent, it's hard to stay conscious. Eight percent will eventually kill you. Staying alive isn't about oxygen, it's about getting rid of CO_2.

That means I need the regulator. But I don't need the oxygenator all the time. I just need to get CO_2 out of the air and back-fill with oxygen. I have 50 liters of liquid oxygen in two 25-liter tanks here in the Hab. That's 50,000 liters in gaseous form, enough to last 85 days. Not enough to see me through to rescue, but a hell of a lot.

The regulator can separate the CO_2 and store it in a tank, and it can add oxygen to my air from my oxygen tanks as needed. When I run low on oxygen, I can camp out for a day and use *all* my power to run the oxygenator on the stored CO_2. That way, the oxygenator's power consumption doesn't eat up my driving juice.

So I'll run the regulator all the time, but only run the oxygenator on days I dedicate to using it.

Now, on to the next problem. After the regulator freezes the CO_2 out, the oxygen and nitrogen are still gasses, but they're −75°C. If the regulator fed that back to my air without reheating it, I'd be a Popsicle within hours. Most of the regulator's power goes to heating the return air so that doesn't happen.

But I have a better way to heat it up. Something NASA wouldn't consider on their most homicidal day.

The RTG!

Yes, the RTG. You may remember it from my exciting trip to *Pathfinder.* A lovely lump of plutonium so radioactive it gives off 1500 watts of heat, which it uses to harvest 100 watts of electricity. So what happens to the other 1400 watts? It gets radiated out as heat.

On the trip to *Pathfinder,* I had to actually remove insulation from the rover to vent excess heat from the damn thing. I'll be taping that back in place because I'll need that heat to warm up the return air from the regulator.

I ran the numbers. The regulator uses 790 watts to constantly reheat air. The RTG's 1400 watts is more than equal to the task, as well as keeping the rover a reasonable temperature.

To test, I shut down the heaters in the regulator and noted its power consumption. After a few minutes, I turned them right back on again. Jesus Christ that return air was cold. But I got the data I wanted.

With heating, the regulator needs 21.5 pirate-ninjas. Without it . . . (drumroll) 1 pirate-ninja. That's right, almost *all* of the power was going to heat.

As with most of life's problems, this one can be solved by a box of *pure radiation*.

I spent the rest of the day double-checking my numbers and running more tests. It all checks out. I can do this.

LOG ENTRY: SOL 200

I hauled rocks today.

I needed to know what kind of power efficiency the rover/trailer will get. On the way to *Pathfinder*, I got 80 kilometers from 18 kilowatt-hours. This time, the load will be a lot heavier. I'll be towing the trailer and all the other shit.

I backed the rover up to the trailer and attached the tow clamps. Easy enough.

The trailer has been depressurized for some time now (there's a couple of hundred little holes in it, after all), so I opened both airlock doors to have a straight shot at the interior. Then I threw a bunch of rocks in.

I had to guess at the weight. The heaviest thing I'll bring with me is the water. 620 kilograms' worth. My freeze-dried potatoes will add another 200 kilograms. I'll probably have more solar cells than before, and maybe a battery from the Hab. Plus the atmospheric regulator and oxygenator, of course. Rather than weigh all that shit, I took a guess and called it 1200 kilograms.

Half a cubic meter of basalt weighs about that much (more or less). After two hours of brutal labor, during which I whined a lot, I got it all loaded in.

Then, with both batteries fully charged, I drove circles around the Hab until I drained them both.

With a blistering top speed of 25 kph, it's not an action-packed thrill ride. But I was impressed it could maintain that speed with all the extra weight. The rover has spectacular torque.

But physical law is a pushy little shit, and it exacted revenge for the additional weight. I only got 57 kilometers before I was out of juice.

That was 57 kilometers on level ground, without having to power the regulator (which won't take much with the heater off). Call it 50 kilometers per day to be safe. At that rate it would take 64 days to get to Schiaparelli.

But that's just the travel time.

Every now and then, I'll need to break for a day and let the oxygenator use all the power. How often? After a bunch of math I worked out that my 18-pirate-ninja budget can power the oxygenator enough to make about 2.5 sols of O_2. I'd have to stop every two to three sols to reclaim oxygen. My sixty-four-sol trip would become ninety-two!

That's too long. I'll tear my own head off if I have to live in the rover that long.

Anyway, I'm exhausted from lifting rocks and whining about lifting rocks. I think I pulled something in my back. Gonna take it easy the rest of today.

LOG ENTRY: SOL 201

Yeah, I definitely pulled something in my back. I woke up in agony.

So I took a break from rover planning. Instead, I spent the day taking drugs and playing with radiation.

First, I loaded up on Vicodin for my back. Hooray for Beck's medical supplies!

Then I drove out to the RTG. It was right where I left it, in a hole four kilometers away. Only an idiot would keep that thing near the Hab. So anyway, I brought it back to the Hab.

Either it'll kill me or it won't. A lot of work went into making sure it doesn't break. If I can't trust NASA, who can I trust? (For now I'll forget that NASA told us to bury it far away.)

I stored it on the roof of the rover for the trip back. That puppy really spews heat.

I have some flexible plastic tubing intended for minor water reclaimer repairs. After bringing the RTG into the Hab, I *very carefully* glued some tubing around the heat baffles. Using a funnel made from a piece of paper, I ran water through the tubing, letting it drain into a sample container.

Sure enough, the water heated up. That's not really a surprise, but it's nice to see thermodynamics being well behaved.

There's one tricky bit: The atmospheric regulator doesn't run constantly. The freeze-separation speed is driven by the weather outside. So the returning frigid air doesn't come as a steady flow. And the RTG generates a constant, predictable heat. It can't "ramp up" its output.

So I'll heat water with the RTG to create a heat reservoir, then I'll make the return air bubble through it. That way I don't have to worry about when the air comes in. And I won't have to deal with sudden temperature changes in the rover.

When the Vicodin wore off, my back hurt even

more than before. I'm going to need to take it easy. I can't just pop pills forever. So I'm taking a few days off from heavy labor. To that end, I made a little invention just for me. . . .

I took Johanssen's cot and cut out the hammock. Then I draped spare Hab canvas over the frame, making a pit inside the cot, with extra canvas around the edges. Once I weighed down the excess canvas with rocks, I had a water-tight bathtub!

It only took 100 liters to fill the shallow tub.

Then, I stole the pump from the water reclaimer. (I can go quite a while without the water reclaimer operating.) I hooked it up to my RTG water heater and put both the input and output lines into the tub.

Yes, I know this is ridiculous, but I hadn't had a bath since Earth, and my back hurts. Besides, I'm going to spend 100 sols with the RTG anyway. A few more won't hurt. That's my bullshit rationalization and I'm sticking with it.

It took two hours to heat the water to 37°C. Once it did, I shut off the pump and got in. Oh man! All I can say is "Ahhhhhh."

Why the *hell* didn't I think of this before?

LOG ENTRY: SOL 207

I spent the last week recovering from back problems. The pain wasn't bad, but there aren't any chiropractors on Mars, so I wasn't taking chances.

I took hot baths twice a day, lay in my bunk a lot, and watched shitty seventies TV. I've already seen Lewis's entire collection, but I didn't have much else to do. I was reduced to watching reruns.

I got a lot of thinking done.

I can make everything better by having more solar panels. The fourteen panels I took to *Pathfinder* provided the 18 kilowatt-hours that the batteries could store. When traveling, I stowed the panels on the roof. The trailer gives me room to store another seven (half of its roof will be missing because of the hole I'm cutting in it).

This trip's power needs will be driven by the oxygenator. It all comes down to how much power I can give that greedy little bastard in a single sol. I want to minimize how often I have days with no travel. The more juice I can give the oxygenator, the more oxygen it'll liberate, and the longer I can go between those "air sols."

Let's get greedy. Let's say I can find a home for fourteen more panels instead of seven. Not sure how to do that, but let's say I can. That would give me thirty-six pirate-ninjas to work with, which would net me five sols of oxygen per air sol. I'd only have to stop once per five sols. That's much more reasonable.

Plus, if I can arrange battery storage for the extra power, I could drive 100 kilometers per sol! Easier said than done, though. That extra 18 kilowatt-hours of storage will be tough. I'll have to take two of the Hab's 9-kilowatt-hour fuel cells and load them onto the rover or trailer. They aren't like the rover's batteries; they're not small or portable. They're light enough, but they're pretty big. I may have to attach them to the outside hull, and that would eat into my solar cell storage.

One hundred kilometers per sol is pretty optimistic. But let's say I could make 90 kilometers per sol, stopping every fifth sol to reclaim oxygen. I'd get there in forty-five sols. That would be sweet!

In other news, it occurred to me that NASA is probably shitting bricks. They're watching me with satellites and haven't seen me come out of the Hab for six days. With my back better, it was time to drop them a line.

I headed out for an EVA. This time, being very careful while lugging rocks around, I spelled out a Morse code message: "INJURED BACK. BETTER NOW. CONTINUING ROVER MODS."

That was enough physical labor for today. I don't want to overdo it.

Think I'll have a bath.

LOG ENTRY: SOL 208

Today, it was time to experiment with the panels.

First, I put the Hab on low-power mode: no internal lights, all nonessential systems offline, all internal heating suspended. I'd be outside most of the day anyway.

Then I detached twenty-eight panels from the solar farm and dragged them to the rover. I spent four hours stacking them this way and that. The poor rover looked like the Beverly Hillbillies truck. Nothing I did worked.

The only way to get all twenty-eight on the roof was to make stacks so high they'd fall off the first time I turned. If I lashed them together, they'd fall off as a unit. If I found a way to attach them perfectly to the rover, the rover would tip. I didn't even bother to test. It was obvious by looking, and I didn't want to break anything.

I haven't removed the chunk of hull from the trailer yet. Half the holes are drilled, but I'm not committed to anything. If I left it in place, I could have four stacks of seven cells. That would work fine; it's just two rovers' worth of what I did for the trip to *Pathfinder*.

Problem is I need that opening. The regulator has to be in the pressurized area and it's too big to fit in the unmodified rover. Plus which, the oxygenator needs to be in a pressurized area while operating. I'll only need it every five sols, but what would I do on that sol? No, the hole has to be there.

As it is, I'll be able to stow twenty-one panels. I need homes for the other seven. There's only one place they can go: the sides of the rover and trailer.

One of my earlier modifications was "saddlebags" draped over the rover. One side held the extra battery (stolen from what is now the trailer), while the other side was full of rocks as counterweight.

I won't need the bags this time around. I can return the second battery to the trailer from whence it came. In fact, it'll save me the hassle of the mid-drive EVA I had to do every day to swap cables. When the rovers are linked up, they share resources, including electricity.

I went ahead and reinstalled the trailer's battery. It took me two hours, but it's out of the way now. I removed the saddlebags and set them aside. They may be handy down the line. If I've learned one thing from my stay at Club Mars, it's that *everything* can be useful.

I had liberated the sides of the rover and the trailer. After staring at them for a while, I had my solution.

I'll make L-brackets that stick out from the undercarriages, with the hooks facing up. Two brackets per side to make a shelf. I can set panels on the shelves and lean them against the rover. Then I'll lash them to the hull with homemade rope.

There'll be four "shelves" total; two on the rover and two on the trailer. If the brackets stick out far enough to accommodate two panels, I could store eight additional panels that way. That would give me one more panel than I'd even planned for.

I'll make those brackets and install them tomorrow. I would have done it today, but it got dark and I got lazy.

LOG ENTRY: SOL 209

Cold night last night. The solar cells were still detached from the farm, so I had to leave the Hab in low-power mode. I did turn the heat back on (I'm not insane), but I set the internal temperature to 1°C to conserve power. Waking up to frigid weather felt surprisingly nostalgic. I grew up in Chicago, after all.

But nostalgia only lasts so long. I vowed to complete the brackets today, so I can return the panels to the farm. Then I can turn the damn heat back on.

I headed out to the MAV's landing strut array to scavenge metal for the shelves. Most of the MAV is made from composite, but the struts had to absorb the shock of landing. Metal was the way to go.

I brought a strut into the Hab to save myself the hassle of working in an EVA suit. It was a triangular lattice of metal strips held together with bolts. I disassembled it.

Shaping the brackets involved a hammer and . . . well, that's it, actually. Making an L doesn't take a lot of precision.

I needed holes where the bolts would pass through. Fortunately, my *Pathfinder*-murdering drill made short work of that task.

I was worried it would be hard to attach the brackets to the rover's undercarriage, but it ended up being simple. The undercarriage comes right off. After some drilling and bolting, I got the brackets attached to it and then mounted it back on the rover. I repeated the process for the trailer. Important note—the undercarriage is not part of the pressure vessel. The holes I drilled won't let my air out.

I tested the brackets by hitting them with rocks. This kind of sophistication is what we interplanetary scientists are known for.

After convincing myself the brackets wouldn't break at the first sign of use, I tested the new arrangement. Two stacks of seven solar cells on the roof of the rover; another seven on the trailer, then two per shelf. They all fit.

After lashing the cells in place, I took a little drive. I did some basic acceleration and deceleration, turned in increasingly tight circles, and even did a power-stop. The cells didn't budge.

Twenty-eight solar cells, baby! And room for one extra!

After some well-earned fist-pumping, I unloaded the cells and dragged them back to the farm. No Chicago morning for me tomorrow.

LOG ENTRY: SOL 211

I am smiling a great smile. The smile of a man who fucked with his car and *didn't break it.*

I spent today removing unnecessary crap from

the rover and trailer. I was pretty damn aggressive about it, too. Space inside the pressure vessels is at a premium. The more crap I clear out of the rover, the more space there is for me. The more crap I clear out of the trailer, the more supplies I can store in it, and the less I have to store in the rover.

First off: Each vehicle had a bench for passengers. Bye!

Next: There's no reason for the trailer to have life support. The oxygen tanks, nitrogen tanks, CO_2 filter assembly . . . all unnecessary. It'll be sharing air with the rover (which has its own copy of each of those), and it'll be carrying the regulator and oxygenator. Between the Hab components and the rover, I'll have two redundant life support systems. That's plenty.

Then I yanked the driver's seat and control panel out of the trailer. The linkup with the rover is physical. The trailer doesn't do anything but get dragged along and fed air. It doesn't need controls or brains. However, I did salvage its computer. It's small and light, so I'll bring it with me. If something goes wrong with the rover's computer en route, I'll have a spare.

The trailer had tons more space now. It was time for experimentation.

The Hab has twelve 9-kilowatt-hour batteries. They're bulky and awkward. Over two meters tall, a half meter wide, and three-quarters of a meter thick. Making them bigger makes them take less mass per kilowatt hour of storage. Yeah, it's counterintuitive. But once NASA figured out they could increase volume to decrease mass, they were all over it. Mass is the expensive part about sending things to Mars.

I detached two of them. As long as I return

them before the end of the day, things should be fine. The Hab mostly uses the batteries at night.

With both of the trailer's airlock doors open I was able to get the first battery in. After playing real-life Tetris for a while I found a way to get the first battery out of the way enough to let the second battery in. Together, they eat up the whole front half of the trailer. If I hadn't cleared the useless shit out earlier today, I'd never have gotten them both in.

The trailer's battery is in the undercarriage, but the main power line runs through the pressure vessel, so I was able to wire the Hab batteries directly in (no small feat in the damn EVA suit).

A system check from the rover showed I had done the wiring correctly.

This may all seem minor, but it's awesome. It means I can have twenty-nine solar cells and 36 kilowatt-hours of storage. I'll be able to do my 100 kilometers per day after all.

Four days out of five, anyway.

According to my calendar, the *Hermes* resupply probe is being launched from China in two days (if there were no delays). If that screws up, the whole crew will be in deep shit. I'm more nervous about that than anything else.

I've been in mortal danger for months; I'm kind of used to it now. But I'm nervous again. Dying would suck, but my crewmates dying would be way worse. And I won't find out how the launch went till I get to Schiaparelli.

Good luck, guys.

CHAPTER 19

"HEY, MELISSA . . . ," said Robert. "Am I getting through? Can you see me?"

"Loud and clear, babe," said Commander Lewis. "The video link is solid."

"They say I have five minutes," Robert said.

"Better than nothing," Lewis said. Floating in her quarters, she gently touched the bulkhead to stop drifting. "It's nice to see you in real-time for a change."

"Yeah." Robert smiled. "I can hardly notice the delay. I gotta say, I wish you were coming home."

Lewis sighed. "Me, too, babe."

"Don't get me wrong," Robert quickly added. "I understand why you're doing all this. Still, from a selfish point of view, I miss my wife. Hey, are you floating?"

"Huh?" Lewis said. "Oh, yeah. The ship isn't spinning right now. No centripetal gravity."

"Why not?"

"Because we're docking with the *Taiyang Shen* in a few days. We can't spin while we dock with things."

"I see," said Robert. "So how are things up on the ship? Anyone giving you shit?"

"No." Lewis shook her head. "They're a good crew; I'm lucky to have them."

"Oh hey!" Robert said. "I found a great addition to our collection!"

"Oh? What'd you get?"

"An original-production eight-track of *Abba's Greatest Hits*. Still in the original packaging."

Lewis widened her eyes. "Seriously? A 1976 or one of the reprints?"

"1976 all the way."

"Wow! Good find!"

"I know, right!?"

■ ■ ■

WITH A final shudder, the jetliner came to a stop at the gate.

"Oh gods," said Venkat, massaging his neck. "That was the longest flight I've ever been on."

"Mm," said Teddy, rubbing his eyes.

"At least we don't have to go to Jiuquan till tomorrow," Venkat moaned. "Fourteen and a half hours of flying is enough for one day."

"Don't get too comfortable," Teddy said. "We still have to go through customs, and we'll probably have to fill out a bunch of forms because we're U.S. government officials. . . . It's gonna be hours before we sleep."

"Craaaap."

Gathering their carry-on luggage, they trudged off the plane with the rest of the weary travelers.

Beijing Capital International Airport's Terminal 3 echoed with the cacophony common to huge air terminals. Venkat and Teddy moved toward the long immigration line as the Chinese citizens from their flight split off to go to a simpler point-of-entry process.

As Venkat took his place in line, Teddy filed in behind him and scanned the terminal for a convenience store. Any form of caffeine would be welcome.

"Excuse me, gentlemen," came a voice from beside them.

They turned to see a young Chinese man wearing jeans and a polo shirt. "My name is Su Bin Bao," he said in perfect English. "I am an employee of the China National Space Administration. I will be your guide and translator during your stay in the People's Republic of China."

"Nice to meet you, Mr. Su," Teddy said. "I'm Teddy Sanders, and this is Dr. Venkat Kapoor."

"We need sleep," Venkat said immediately. "Just as soon as we get through customs, please get us to our hotel."

"I can do better than that, Dr. Kapoor." Su smiled. "You are official guests of the People's Republic of China. You have been preauthorized to bypass customs. I can take you to your hotel immediately."

"I love you," Venkat said.

"Tell the People's Republic of China we said thanks," Teddy added.

"I'll pass that along." Su Bin smiled.

■ ■ ■

"HELENA, MY LOVE," Vogel said to his wife. "*I trust you are well?*"

"*Yes,*" she said. "*I'm fine. But I do miss you.*"

"*Sorry.*"

"*Can't be helped.*" She shrugged.

"*How are our monkeys?*"

"*The children are fine.*" She smiled. "*Eliza has a crush on a new boy in her class, and Victor has been named goalkeeper for his high school's team.*"

"*Excellent!*" Vogel said. "*I hear you are at Mission Control. Was NASA unable to pipe the signal to Bremen?*"

"*They could have,*" she said. "*But it was easier for them to bring me to Houston. A free vacation to the United States. Who am I to turn that down?*"

"*Well played. And how is my mother?*"

"*As well as can be expected,*" Helena said. "*She has her good days and bad days. She did not recognize me on my last visit. In a way, it's a blessing. She doesn't have to worry about you like I do.*"

"*She hasn't worsened?*" he asked.

"*No, she's about the same as when you left. The doctors are sure she'll still be here when you return.*"

"*Good,*" he said. "*I was worried I'd seen her for the last time.*"

"*Alex,*" Helena said, "*will you be safe?*"

"*As safe as we can be,*" he said. "*The ship is in perfect condition, and after receiving the* Taiyang Shen, *we will have all the supplies we need for the remainder of the journey.*"

"*Be careful.*"

"*I will, my love,*" Vogel promised.

■ ■ ■

"WELCOME TO JIUQUAN," Guo Ming said. *"I hope your flight was smooth?"*

Su Bin translated Guo Ming's words as Teddy took the second-best seat in the observation room. He looked through the glass to Jiuquan's Mission Control Center. It was remarkably similar to Houston's, though Teddy couldn't read any of the Chinese text on the big screens.

"Yes, thank you," Teddy said. "The hospitality of your people has been wonderful. The private jet you arranged to bring us here was a nice touch."

"My people have enjoyed working with your advance team," Guo Ming said. *"The last month has been very interesting. Attaching an American probe to a Chinese booster. I believe this is the first time it's ever been done."*

"It just goes to show," Teddy said. "Love of science is universal across all cultures."

Guo Ming nodded. *"My people have especially commented on the work ethic of your man, Mitch Henderson. He is very dedicated."*

"He's a pain in the ass," Teddy said.

Su Bin paused before translating but pressed on.

Guo Ming laughed. *"You can say that,"* he said. *"I cannot."*

▪▪▪

"SO EXPLAIN it again," Beck's sister Amy said. "Why do you have to do an EVA?"

"I probably don't," Beck explained. "I just need to be ready to."

"Why?"

"In case the probe can't dock with us. If something goes wrong, it'll be my job to go out and grab it."

"Can't you just move *Hermes* to dock with it?"

"No way," Beck said. "*Hermes* is *huge*. It's not made for fine maneuvering control."

"Why does it have to be you?"

"'Cause I'm the EVA specialist."

"But I thought you were the doctor."

"I am," Beck said. "Everyone has multiple roles. I'm the doctor, the biologist, and the EVA specialist. Commander Lewis is our geologist. Johanssen is the sysop and reactor tech. And so on."

"How about that good-looking guy . . . Martinez?" Amy asked. "What does he do?"

"He pilots the MDV and MAV," Beck said. "He's also married with a kid, you lecherous homewrecker."

"Ah well. How about Watney? What did he do?"

"He's our botanist and engineer. And don't talk about him in the past tense."

"Engineer? Like Scotty?"

"Kind of," Beck said. "He fixes stuff."

"I bet that's coming in handy now."

"Yeah, no shit."

■ ■ ■

THE CHINESE had arranged a small conference room for the Americans to work in. The cramped conditions were luxurious by Jiuquan standards. Venkat was working on budget spreadsheets when Mitch came in, so he was glad for the interruption.

"They're a weird bunch, these Chinese nerds," Mitch said, collapsing into a chair. "But they make a good booster."

"Good," Venkat said. "How's the linkage between the booster and our probe?"

"It all checks out," Mitch said. "JPL followed the specs perfectly. It fits like a glove."

"Any concerns or reservations?" Venkat asked.

"Yeah. I'm concerned about what I ate last night. I think it had an eyeball in it."

"I'm sure there wasn't an eyeball."

"The engineers here made it for me special," Mitch said.

"There may have been an eyeball," Venkat said. "They hate you."

"Why?"

"'Cause you're a dick, Mitch," Venkat said. "A total dick. To everyone."

"Fair enough. So long as the probe gets to *Hermes*, they can burn me in effigy for all I care."

■ ■ ■

"WAVE TO DADDY!" Marissa said, waving David's hand at the camera. "Wave to Daddy!"

"He's too young to know what's going on," Martinez said.

"Just think of the playground cred he'll have later in life," she said. " 'My dad went to Mars. What's your dad do?' "

"Yes, I'm pretty awesome," he agreed.

Marissa continued to wave David's hand at the camera. David was more interested in his other hand, which was actively engaged in picking his nose.

"So," Martinez said, "you're pissed."

"You can tell?" Marissa asked. "I tried to hide it."

"We've been together since we were fifteen. I know when you're pissed."

"You volunteered to extend the mission five hundred and thirty-three days," she said, "asshole."

"Yeah," Martinez said. "I figured that'd be the reason."

"Your son will be in kindergarten when you get back. He won't have any memories of you."

"I know," Martinez said.

"I have to wait another five hundred and thirty-three days to get laid!"

"So do I," he said defensively.

"I have to worry about you that whole time," she added.

"Yeah," he said. "Sorry."

She took a deep breath. "We'll get past it."

"We'll get past it," he agreed.

▪ ▪ ▪

"WELCOME TO CNN's *Mark Watney Report*. Today, we have the director of Mars operations, Venkat Kapoor. He's speaking to us live via satellite from China. Dr. Kapoor, thank you for joining us."

"Happy to do it," Venkat said.

"So, Dr. Kapoor, tell us about the *Taiyang Shen*. Why go to China to launch a probe? Why not launch it from the US?"

"*Hermes* isn't going to orbit Earth," Venkat

said. "It's just passing by on its way to Mars. And its velocity is *huge*. We need a booster capable of not only escaping Earth's gravity but matching *Hermes*'s current velocity. Only the *Taiyang Shen* has enough power to do that."

"Tell us about the probe itself."

"It was a rush job," Venkat said. "JPL only had thirty days to put it together. They had to be as safe and efficient as they could. It's basically a shell full of food and other supplies. It has a standard satellite thruster package for maneuvering, but that's it."

"And that's enough to fly to *Hermes*?"

"The *Taiyang Shen* will send it to *Hermes*. The thrusters are for fine control and docking. And JPL didn't have time to make a guidance system. So it'll be remote-controlled by a human pilot."

"Who will be controlling it?" Cathy asked.

"The Ares 3 pilot, Major Rick Martinez. As the probe approaches *Hermes*, he'll take over and guide it to the docking port."

"And what if there's a problem?"

"*Hermes* will have their EVA specialist, Dr. Chris Beck, suited up and ready the whole time. If necessary, he will literally grab the probe with his hands and drag it to the docking port."

"Sounds kind of unscientific." Cathy laughed.

"You want unscientific?" Venkat smiled. "If the probe can't attach to the docking port for some reason, Beck will open the probe and carry its contents to the airlock."

"Like bringing in the groceries?" Cathy asked.

"Exactly like that," Venkat said. "And we estimate it would take four trips back and forth. But that's all an edge case. We don't anticipate any problems with the docking process."

"Sounds like you're covering all your bases." Cathy smiled.

"We have to," Venkat said. "If they don't get those supplies . . . Well, they need those supplies."

"Thanks for taking the time to answer our questions," Cathy said.

"Always a pleasure, Cathy."

■ ■ ■

JOHANSSEN'S FATHER fidgeted in the chair, unsure what to say. After a moment, he pulled a handkerchief from his pocket and mopped sweat from his balding head.

"What if the probe doesn't get to you?" he asked.

"Try not to think about that," Johanssen said.

"Your mother is so worried she couldn't even come."

"I'm sorry," Johanssen mumbled, looking down.

"She can't eat, she can't sleep, she feels sick all the time. I'm not much better. How can they make you do this?"

"They're not 'making' me do it, Dad. I volunteered."

"Why would you do that to your mother?" he demanded.

"Sorry," Johanssen mumbled. "Watney's my crewmate. I can't just let him die."

He sighed. "I wish we'd raised you to be more selfish."

She chuckled quietly.

"How did I end up in this situation? I'm the district sales manager of a napkin factory. Why is my daughter in space?"

Johanssen shrugged.

"You were always scientifically minded," he said. "It was great! Straight-A student. Hanging around nerdy guys too scared to try anything. No wild side at all. You were every father's dream daughter."

"Thanks, Dad, I—"

"But then you got on a giant bomb that blasted you to Mars. And I mean that literally."

"Technically," she corrected, "the booster only took me into orbit. It was the nuclear-powered ion engine that took me to Mars."

"Oh, much better!"

"Dad, I'll be all right. Tell Mom I'll be all right."

"What good will that do?" he said. "She's going to be tied up in knots until you're back home."

"I know," Johanssen mumbled. "But . . ."

"What? But what?"

"I won't die. I really won't. Even if everything goes wrong."

"What do you mean?"

Johanssen furrowed her brow. "Just tell Mom I won't die."

"How? I don't understand."

"I don't want to get into the how," Johanssen said.

"Look," he said, leaning toward the camera, "I've always respected your privacy and independence. I never tried to pry into your life, never tried to control you. I've been really good about that, right?"

"Yeah."

"So in exchange for a lifetime of staying out of your business, let me nose in just this once. What are you not telling me?"

She fell silent for several seconds. Finally, she said, "They have a plan."

"Who?"

"They always have a plan," she said. "They work out everything in advance."

"What plan?"

"They picked me to survive. I'm youngest. I have the skills necessary to get home alive. And I'm the smallest and need the least food."

"What happens if the probe fails, Beth?" her father asked.

"Everyone would die but me," she said. "They'd all take pills and die. They'll do it right away so they don't use up any food. Commander Lewis picked me to be the survivor. She told me about it yesterday. I don't think NASA knows about it."

"And the supplies would last until you got back to Earth?"

"No," she said. "We have enough food left to feed six people for a month. If I was the only one, it would last six months. With a reduced diet I could stretch it to nine. But it'll be seventeen months before I get back."

"So how would you survive?"

"The supplies wouldn't be the only source of food," she said.

He widened his eyes. "Oh . . . oh my god . . ."

"Just tell Mom the supplies would last, okay?"

■ ■ ■

AMERICAN AND Chinese engineers cheered together at Jiuquan Mission Control.

The main screen showed *Taiyang Shen*'s contrail

wafting in the chilly Gobi sky. The ship, no longer visible to the naked eye, pressed onward toward orbit. Its deafening roar dwindled to a distant rumbling thunder.

"Perfect launch," Venkat exclaimed.

"Of course," said Zhu Tao.

"You guys really came through for us," Venkat said. "And we're grateful!"

"Naturally."

"And hey, you guys get a seat on Ares 5. Everyone wins."

"Mmm."

Venkat looked at Zhu Tao sideways. "You don't seem too happy."

"I spent four years working on *Taiyang Shen*," he said. "So did countless other researchers, scientists, and engineers. Everyone poured their souls into construction while I waged a constant political battle to maintain funding.

"In the end, we built a beautiful probe. The largest, sturdiest unmanned probe in history. And now it's sitting in a warehouse. It'll never fly. The State Council won't fund another booster like that."

He turned to Venkat. "It could have been a lasting legacy of scientific research. Now it's a delivery run. We'll get a Chinese astronaut on Mars, but what science will he bring back that some other astronaut couldn't have? This operation is a net loss for mankind's knowledge."

"Well," Venkat said cautiously, "it's a net gain for Mark Watney."

"Mmm," Zhu Tao said.

■■■

"DISTANCE 61 meters, velocity 2.3 meters per second," Johanssen said.

"No problem," Martinez said, his eyes glued to his screens. One showed the camera feed from Docking Port A, the other a constant feed of the probe's telemetry.

Lewis floated behind Johanssen's and Martinez's stations.

Beck's voice came over the radio. "Visual contact." He stood in Airlock 3 (via magnetic boots), fully suited up with the outer door open. The bulky SAFER unit on his back would allow him free motion in space should the need arise. An attached tether led to a spool on the wall.

"Vogel," Lewis said into her headset. "You in position?"

Vogel stood in the still-pressurized Airlock 2, suited up save his helmet. "*Ja*, in position and ready," he replied. He was the emergency EVA if Beck needed rescue.

"All right, Martinez," Lewis said. "Bring it in."

"Aye, Commander."

"Distance 43 meters, velocity 2.3 meters per second," Johanssen called out.

"All stats nominal," Martinez reported.

"Slight rotation in the probe," Johanssen said. "Relative rotational velocity is 0.05 revolutions per second."

"Anything under 0.3 is fine," Martinez said. "The capture system can deal with it."

"Probe is well within manual recovery range," Beck reported.

"Copy," Lewis said.

"Distance 22 meters, velocity 2.3 meters per second," Johanssen said. "Angle is good."

"Slowing her down a little," Martinez said, sending instructions to the probe.

"Velocity 1.8 . . . 1.3 . . . ," Johanssen reported. "0.9 . . . stable at 0.9 meters per second."

"Range?" Martinez asked.

"Twelve meters," Johanssen replied. "Velocity steady at 0.9 meters per second."

"Angle?"

"Angle is good."

"Then we're in line for auto-capture," Martinez said. "Come to Papa."

The probe drifted gently to the docking port. Its capture boom, a long metal triangle, entered the port's funnel, scraping slightly along the edge. Once it reached the port's retractor mechanism, the automated system clamped onto the boom and pulled it in, aligning and orienting the probe automatically. After several loud clanks echoed through the ship, the computer reported success.

"Docking complete," Martinez said.

"Seal is tight," Johanssen said.

"Beck," Lewis said, "your services won't be needed."

"Roger that, Commander," Beck said. "Closing airlock."

"Vogel, return to interior," she ordered.

"Copy, Commander," he said.

"Airlock pressure to one hundred percent," Beck reported. "Reentering ship. . . . I'm back in."

"Also inside," Vogel said.

Lewis pressed a button on her headset. "Houst— er . . . Jiuquan, probe docking complete. No complications."

Mitch's voice came over the comm. "Glad to hear it, *Hermes*. Report status of all supplies once you get them aboard and inspected."

"Roger, Jiuquan," Lewis said.

Taking off her headset, she turned to Martinez and Johanssen. "Unload the probe and stow the supplies. I'm going to help Beck and Vogel de-suit."

Martinez and Johanssen floated down the hall toward Docking Port A.

"So," he said, "who would you have eaten first?"

She glared at him.

"'Cause I think I'd be tastiest," he continued, flexing his arm. "Look at that. Good solid muscle there."

"You're not funny."

"I'm free-range, you know. Corn-fed."

She shook her head and accelerated down the hall.

"Come on! I thought you liked Mexican!"

"Not listening," she called back.

CHAPTER 20

LOG ENTRY: SOL 376

I'm finally done with the rover modifications!

The tricky part was figuring out how to maintain life support. Everything else was just work. A *lot* of work.

I haven't been good at keeping the log up to date, so here's a recap:

First I had to finish drilling holes with the *Pathfinder*-murderin' drill. Then I chiseled out a billion little chunks between the holes. Okay, it was 759 but it felt like a billion.

Then I had one big hole in the trailer. I filed down the edges to keep them from being too sharp.

Remember the pop-tents? I cut the bottom out of one and the remaining canvas was the right size and shape. I used seal-strips to attach it to the inside of the trailer. After pressurizing and sealing up leaks as I found them, I had a nice big balloon bulging out of the trailer. The pressurized area is easily big enough to fit the oxygenator and atmospheric regulator.

One hitch: I need to put the AREC outside. The imaginatively named "atmospheric regulator external component" is how the regulator freeze-separates air. Why sink a bunch of energy into freezing stuff when you have incredibly cold temperatures right outside?

The regulator pumps air to the AREC to let Mars freeze it. It does this along a tube that runs through a valve in the Hab's wall. The return air comes back through another tube just like it.

Getting the tubing through the balloon canvas wasn't too hard. I have several spare valve patches. Basically they're ten-by-ten-centimeter patches of Hab canvas with a valve in the middle. Why do I have these? Consider what would happen on a normal mission if the regulator valve broke. They'd have to scrub the whole mission. Easier to send spares.

The AREC is fairly small. I made a shelf for it just under the solar panel shelves. Now everything's ready for when I eventually move the regulator and AREC over.

There's still a lot to do.

I'm not in any hurry; I've been taking it slow. One four-hour EVA per day spent on work, the rest of the time to relax in the Hab. Plus, I'll take a day off every now and then, especially if my back hurts. I can't afford to injure myself now.

I'll try to be better about this log. Now that I might actually get rescued, people will probably read it. I'll be more diligent and log every day.

LOG ENTRY: SOL 380

I finished the heat reservoir.

Remember my experiments with the RTG and having a hot bath? Same principle, but I came up with an improvement: submerge the RTG. No heat will be wasted that way.

I started with a large rigid sample container (or "plastic box" to people who don't work at NASA). I ran a tube through the open top and down the inside wall. Then I coiled it in the bottom to make a spiral. I glued it in place like that and sealed the end. Using my smallest drill bit, I put dozens of little holes in the coil. The idea is for the freezing return air from the regulator to pass through the water as a bunch of little bubbles. The increased surface area will get the heat into the air better.

Then I got a medium flexible sample container ("Ziploc bag") and tried to seal the RTG in it. But the RTG has an irregular shape, and I couldn't get all the air out of the bag. I can't allow any air in there. Instead of heat going to the water, some would get stored in the air, which could superheat and melt the bag.

I tried a bunch of times, but there was always an air pocket I couldn't get out. I was getting pretty frustrated until I remembered I have an airlock.

Suiting up, I went to Airlock 2 and depressurized to a full vacuum. I plopped the RTG in the bag and closed it. Perfect vacuum seal.

Next came some testing. I put the bagged RTG at the bottom of the container and filled it with water. It holds twenty liters, and the RTG quickly heated it. It was gaining a degree per minute. I let it go until it was a good 40°C. Then I hooked up the regulator's return air line to my contraption and watched the results.

It worked great! The air bubbled through, just like I'd hoped. Even better, the bubbles agitated the water, which distributed the heat evenly.

I let it run for an hour, and the Hab started to get cold. The RTG's heat can't keep up with the total loss from the Hab's impressive surface area. Not a problem. I've already established it's plenty to keep the rover warm.

I reattached the return air line to the regulator and things got back to normal.

LOG ENTRY: SOL 381

I've been thinking about laws on Mars.

Yeah, I know, it's a stupid thing to think about, but I have a lot of free time.

There's an international treaty saying no country can lay claim to anything that's not on Earth. And by another treaty, if you're not in any country's territory, maritime law applies.

So Mars is "international waters."

NASA is an American nonmilitary organization, and it owns the Hab. So while I'm in the Hab, American law applies. As soon as I step outside, I'm in international waters. Then when I get in the rover, I'm back to American law.

Here's the cool part: I will eventually go to Schiaparelli and commandeer the Ares 4 lander. Nobody explicitly gave me permission to do this, and they can't until I'm aboard Ares 4 and operating the comm system. After I board Ares 4, before talking to NASA, I will take control of a craft in international waters without permission.

That makes me a pirate!
A space pirate!

LOG ENTRY: SOL 383

You may be wondering what else I do with my free time. I spend a lot of it sitting around on my lazy ass watching TV. But so do you, so don't judge.

Also, I plan my trip.

Pathfinder was a cake run. Flat, level ground all the way. The only problem was navigating. But the trip to Schiaparelli will mean going over massive elevation changes.

I have a rough satellite map of the whole planet. It doesn't have much detail, but I'm lucky to have it at all. NASA didn't expect me to wander 3200 kilometers from the Hab.

Acidalia Planitia (where I am) has a relatively low elevation. So does Schiaparelli. But between them it goes up and down by 10 kilometers. There's going to be a lot of dangerous driving.

Things will be smooth while I'm in Acidalia, but that's only the first 650 kilometers. After that comes the crater-riddled terrain of Arabia Terra.

I do have one thing going for me. And I swear it's a gift from God. For some geological reason, there's a valley called Mawrth Vallis that's *perfectly* placed.

Millions of years ago it was a river. Now it's a valley that juts into the brutal terrain of Arabia, almost directly toward Schiaparelli. It's much gentler terrain than the rest of Arabia Terra, and the far end looks like a smooth ascent out of the valley.

Between Acidalia and Mawrth Vallis I'll get 1350 kilometers of relatively easy terrain.

The other 1850 kilometers . . . well, that won't be so nice. Especially when I have to descend into Schiaparelli itself. Ugh.

Anyway. Mawrth Vallis. Awesome.

LOG ENTRY: SOL 385

The worst part of the *Pathfinder* trip was being trapped in the rover. I had to live in a cramped environment that was full of junk and reeked of body odor. Same as my college days.

Rim shot!

Seriously though, it sucked. It was twenty-two sols of abject misery.

I plan to leave for Schiaparelli 100 sols before my rescue (or death), and I swear to God I'll rip my own face off if I have to live in the rover for that long.

I need a place to stay where I can stand up and take a few steps without hitting things. And no, being outside in a goddamn EVA suit doesn't count. I need personal space, not 50 kilograms of clothing.

So today, I started making a tent. Somewhere I can relax while the batteries recharge; somewhere I can lie down comfortably while sleeping.

I recently sacrificed one of my two pop-tents to be the trailer balloon, but the other is in perfect shape. Even better, it has an attachment for the rover's airlock. Before I made it a potato farm, its original purpose was to be a lifeboat for the rover.

I could attach the pop-tent to either vehicle's airlock. I'm going with the rover instead of the trailer. The rover has the computer and controls. If I need to know the status of anything (like life support or how well the battery is charging), I'll need access. This way, I'll be able to walk right in. No EVA.

Also, while traveling, I'll keep the tent folded up in the rover. In an emergency, I can get to it fast.

The pop-tent is the basis of my "bedroom," but not the whole thing. The tent's not very big; not much more space than the rover. But it has the airlock attachment so it's a great place to start. My plan is to double the floor area and double the height. That'll give me a nice big space to relax in.

For the floor, I'll use the original flooring material from the two pop-tents. If I didn't, my bedroom would become a big hamster ball because Hab canvas is flexible. When you fill it with pressure, it wants to become a sphere. That's not a useful shape.

To combat this, the Hab and pop-tents have special flooring material. It unfolds as a bunch of little segments that won't open beyond 180 degrees, so it remains flat.

The pop-tent base is a hexagon. I have another base left over from what is now the trailer balloon. When I'm done, the bedroom will be two adjacent hexes with walls around them and a crude ceiling.

It's gonna take a lot of glue to make this happen.

LOG ENTRY: SOL 387

The pop-tent is 1.2 meters tall. It's not made for comfort. It's made for astronauts to cower in while their crewmates rescue them. I want two meters. I want to be able to stand! I don't think that's too much to ask.

On paper, it's not hard to do. I just need to cut canvas pieces to the right shapes, seal them together, then seal them to the existing canvas and flooring.

But that's a lot of canvas. I started this mission with six square meters and I've used up most of that. Mostly on sealing the breach from when the Hab blew up.

God damn Airlock 1.

Anyway, my bedroom will take 30 square meters of the stuff. Way the hell more than I have left. Fortunately, I have an alternate supply of Hab canvas: the Hab.

Problem is (follow me closely here, the science is pretty complicated), if I cut a hole in the Hab, the air won't stay inside anymore.

I'll have to depressurize the Hab, cut chunks out, and put it back together (smaller). I spent today figuring out the exact sizes and shapes of canvas I'll need. I need to not fuck this up, so I triple-checked everything. I even made a model out of paper.

The Hab is a dome. If I take canvas from near the floor, I can pull the remaining canvas down and reseal it. The Hab will become a lopsided dome, but that shouldn't matter. As long as it holds pressure. I only need it to last another sixty-two sols.

I drew the shapes on the wall with a Sharpie. Then I spent a long time re-measuring them and making sure, over and over, that they were right.

That was all I did today. Might not seem like much, but the math and design work took all day. Now it's time for dinner.

I've been eating potatoes for weeks. Theoretically, with my three-quarter ration plan, I should still be eating food packs. But three-quarter ration is hard to maintain, so now I'm eating potatoes.

I have enough to last till launch, so I won't starve. But I'm pretty damn sick of potatoes. Also, they have a lot of fiber, so . . . let's just say it's good I'm the only guy on this planet.

I saved five meal packs for special occasions. I wrote their names on each one. I get to eat "Departure" the day I leave for Schiaparelli. I'll eat "Halfway" when I reach the 1600-kilometer mark, and "Arrival" when I get there.

The fourth one is "Survived Something That Should Have Killed Me" because some fucking thing will happen, I just know it. I don't know what it'll be, but it'll happen. The rover will break down, or I'll come down with fatal hemorrhoids, or I'll run into hostile Martians, or some shit. When I do (if I live), I get to eat that meal pack.

The fifth one is reserved for the day I launch. It's labeled "Last Meal."

Maybe that's not such a good name.

LOG ENTRY: SOL 388

I started the day with a potato. I washed it down with some Martian coffee. That's my name for "hot water with a caffeine pill dissolved in it." I ran out of real coffee months ago.

My first order of business was a careful inventory of the Hab. I needed to root out anything that would have a problem with losing atmospheric pressure. Of course, everything in the Hab had a crash course in depressurization a few months back. But this time would be controlled, and I might as well do it right.

The main thing is the water. I lost 300 liters to sublimation when the Hab blew up. This time, that won't happen. I drained the water reclaimer and sealed all the tanks.

The rest was just collecting knickknacks and dumping them in Airlock 3. Anything I could think of that doesn't do well in a near-vacuum. All the pens, vitamin bottles (probably not necessary but I'm not taking chances), medical supplies, etc.

Then I did a controlled shutdown of the Hab. The critical components are designed to survive a vacuum. Hab depress is one of the many scenarios NASA accounted for. One system at a time, I cleanly shut them all down, ending with the main computer itself.

I suited up and depressurized the Hab. Last time, the canvas collapsed and made a mess of everything. That's not supposed to happen. The dome of the Hab is mostly supported by air pressure, but there are flexible reinforcing poles across the inside to hold up the canvas. It's how the Hab was assembled in the first place.

I watched as the canvas gently settled onto the poles. To confirm the depressurization, I opened both doors of Airlock 2. I left Airlock 3 alone. It maintained pressure for its cargo of random crap.

Then I cut shit up!

I'm not a materials engineer; my design for the bedroom isn't elegant. It's just a six-meter perimeter and a ceiling. No, it won't have right angles and corners (pressure vessels don't like those). It'll balloon out to a more round shape.

Anyway, it means I only needed to cut two big-ass strips of canvas. One for the walls and one for the ceiling.

After mangling the Hab, I pulled the remaining

canvas down to the flooring and resealed it. Ever set up a camping tent? From the inside? While wearing a suit of armor? It was a pain in the ass.

I repressurized to one-twentieth of an atmosphere to see if it could hold pressure.

Ha ha ha! Of course it couldn't! Leaks galore. Time to find them.

On Earth, tiny particles get attached to water or wear down to nothing. On Mars, they just hang around. The top layer of sand is like talcum powder. I went outside with a bag and scraped along the surface. I got some normal sand, but plenty of powder, too.

I had the Hab maintain the one-twentieth atmosphere, backfilling as air leaked out. Then I "puffed" the bag to get the smallest particles to float around. They were quickly drawn to where the leaks were. As I found each leak, I spot-sealed it with resin.

It took hours, but I finally got a good seal. I'll tell ya, the Hab looks pretty "ghetto" now. One whole side of it is lower than the rest. I'll have to hunch down when I'm over there.

I pressurized to a full atmosphere and waited an hour. No leaks.

It's been a long, physically taxing day. I'm totally exhausted but I can't sleep. Every sound scares the shit out of me. Is that the Hab popping? No? Okay. . . . What was that!? Oh, nothing? Okay. . . .

It's a terrible thing to have my life depend on my half-assed handiwork.

Time to get a sleeping pill from the medical supplies.

LOG ENTRY: SOL 389

What the hell is in those sleeping pills!? It's the middle of the day.

After two cups of Martian coffee, I woke up a little. I won't be taking another one of those pills. It's not like I have to go to work in the morning.

Anyway, as you can tell from how not dead I am, the Hab stayed sealed overnight. The seal is solid. Ugly as hell, but solid.

Today's task was the bedroom.

Assembling the bedroom was way easier than resealing the Hab. Because this time, I didn't have to wear an EVA suit. I made the whole thing inside the Hab. Why not? It's just canvas. I can roll it up and take it out an airlock when I'm done.

First, I did some surgery on the remaining pop-tent. I needed to keep the rover–airlock connector and surrounding canvas. The rest of the canvas had to go. Why hack off most of the canvas only to replace it with more canvas? Seams.

NASA is good at making things. I am not. The dangerous part of this structure won't be the canvas. It'll be the seams. And I get less total seam length by not trying to use the existing pop-tent canvas.

After hacking away most of the remaining tent, I seal-stripped the two pop-tent floors together. Then I sealed the new canvas pieces into place.

It was so much easier without the EVA suit on. So much easier!

Then I had to test it. Again, I did it in the Hab. I brought an EVA suit into the tent with me and closed the mini-airlock door. Then I fired up the

EVA suit, leaving the helmet off. I told it to bump the pressure up to 1.2 atm.

It took a little while to bring it up to par, and I had to disable some alarms on the suit. ("Hey, I'm pretty sure the helmet's not on!"). It depleted most of the N_2 tank but was finally able to bring up the pressure.

Then I sat around and waited. I breathed; the suit regulated the air. All was well. I watched the suit readouts carefully to see if it had to replace any "lost" air. After an hour with no noticeable change, I declared the first test a success.

I rolled up the whole thing (wadded up, really) and took it out to the rover.

You know, I suit up a lot these days. I bet that's another record I hold. A typical Martian astronaut does, what, forty EVAs? I've done several hundred.

Once I brought the bedroom to the rover, I attached it to the airlock from the inside. Then I pulled the release to let it loose. I was still wearing my EVA suit, because I'm not an idiot.

The bedroom fired out and filled in three seconds. The open airlock hatchway led directly to it, and it appeared to be holding pressure.

Just like before, I let it sit for an hour. And just like before, it worked great. Unlike the Hab canvas resealing, I got this one right on the first try. Mostly because I didn't have to do it with a damn EVA suit on.

Originally, I planned to let my bedroom sit overnight and check on it in the morning. But I ran into a problem: I can't get out if I do that. The rover has only one airlock, and the bedroom was attached to it. There was no way for me to get out without detaching the bedroom, and no way to attach and pressurize the bedroom without being inside the rover.

It's a little scary. The first time I test the thing overnight will be with me in it. But that'll be later. I've done enough today.

LOG ENTRY: SOL 390

I have to face facts. I'm done prepping the rover. I don't "feel" like I'm done. But it's ready to go:

Food: 1692 potatoes. Vitamin pills.
Water: 620 liters.
Shelter: Rover, trailer, bedroom.
Air: Rover and trailer combined storage: 14 liters liquid O_2, 14 liters liquid N_2.
Life Support: Oxygenator and atmospheric regulator. 418 hours of use-and-discard CO_2 filters for emergencies.
Power: 36 kilowatt-hours of storage. Carrying capacity for 29 solar cells.
Heat: 1400-watt RTG. Homemade reservoir to heat regulator's return air. Electric heater in rover as a backup.
Disco: Lifetime supply.

I'm leaving here on Sol 449. That gives me fifty-nine sols to test everything and fix whatever isn't working right. Then decide what's coming with me and what's staying behind. And plot a route to Schiaparelli using a grainy satellite map. And rack my brains trying to think of anything important I forgot.

Since Sol 6 all I've wanted to do was get the hell out of here. Now the prospect of leaving the Hab behind scares the shit out of me. I need some encouragement. I need to ask myself, "What would an Apollo astronaut do?"

He'd drink three whiskey sours, drive his Corvette to the launchpad, then fly to the moon in a command module smaller than my Rover. Man those guys were cool.

CHAPTER 21

LOG ENTRY: SOL 431

I'm working out how to pack. It's harder than it sounds.

I have two pressure vessels: the rover and the trailer. They're connected by hoses, but they're also not stupid. If one loses pressure, the other will instantly seal off the shared lines.

There's a grim logic to this: If the rover breaches, I'm dead. No point in planning around that. But if the trailer breaches, I'll be fine. That means I should put everything important in the rover.

Everything that goes in the trailer has to be comfortable in near-vacuum and freezing temperatures. Not that I anticipate that, but you know. Plan for the worst.

The saddlebags I made for the *Pathfinder* trip will come in handy for food storage. I can't just store potatoes in the rover or trailer. They'd rot in the warm, pressurized environment. I'll keep some in the rover for easy access, but the rest will be outside in the giant freezer that is this planet. The trailer will be packed pretty tight. It'll have two bulky Hab batteries, the atmospheric regulator, the oxygenator, and my homemade heat reservoir. It would be more convenient to have the reservoir in the rover, but it has to be near the regulator's return air feed.

The rover will be pretty packed, too. When I'm driving, I'll keep the bedroom folded up near the airlock, ready for emergency egress. Also, I'll have the two functional EVA suits in there with me and anything that might be needed for emergency repairs: tool kits, spare parts, my nearly depleted supply of sealant, the other rover's main computer (just in case!), and all 620 glorious liters of water.

And a plastic box to serve as a toilet. One with a good lid.

■ ■ ■

"How's Watney doing?" Venkat asked.

Mindy looked up from her computer with a start. "Dr. Kapoor?"

"I hear you caught a pic of him during an EVA?"

"Uh, yeah," Mindy said, typing on her keyboard. "I noticed things would always change around 9 a.m. local time. People usually keep the same patterns, so I figured he likes to start work around then. I did some minor realignment to get seventeen pics between 9 and 9:10. He showed up in one of them."

"Good thinking. Can I see the pic?"

"Sure." She brought up the image on her screen.

Venkat peered at the blurry image. "Is this as good as it gets?"

"Well, it is a photo taken from orbit," Mindy said. "The NSA enhanced the image with the best software they have."

"Wait, what?" Venkat stammered. "The NSA?"

"Yeah, they called and offered to help out. Same software they use for enhancing spy satellite imagery."

Venkat shrugged. "It's amazing how much red tape gets cut when everyone's rooting for one man to survive." He pointed to the screen. "What's Watney doing here?"

"I think he's loading something into the rover."

"When was the last time he worked on the trailer?" Venkat asked.

"Not for a while. Why doesn't he write us notes more often?"

Venkat shrugged. "He's busy. He works most of the daylight hours, and arranging rocks to spell a message takes time and energy."

"So . . . ," Mindy said. "Why'd you come here in person? We could have done all this over e-mail."

"Actually, I came to talk to you," he said. "There's going to be a change in your responsibilities. From now on, instead of managing the satellites around Mars, your sole responsibility is watching Mark Watney."

"What?" Mindy said. "What about course corrections and alignment?"

"We'll assign that to other people," Venkat said. "From now on, your only focus is examining imagery of Ares 3."

"That's a demotion," Mindy said. "I'm an orbital engineer, and you're turning me into a glorified Peeping Tom."

"It's short-term," Venkat said. "And we'll make it up to you. Thing is, you've been doing it for months, and you're an expert at identifying elements of Ares 3 from satellite pics. We don't have anyone else who can do that."

"Why is this suddenly so important?"

"He's running out of time," Venkat said. "We don't know how far along he is on the rover modifications. But we do know he's only got sixteen sols to get them done. We need to know exactly what he's doing. I've got media outlets and senators asking for his status all the time. The President even called me a couple of times."

"But seeing his status doesn't help," Mindy said. "It's not like we can do anything about it if he falls behind. This is a pointless task."

"How long have you worked for the government?" Venkat sighed.

LOG ENTRY: SOL 434

The time has come to test this baby out.

This presents a problem. Unlike on my *Pathfinder* trip, I have to take vital life support elements out of the Hab if I'm going to do a real dry run. When you take the atmospheric regulator and oxygenator out of the Hab, you're left with . . . a tent. A big round tent that can't support life.

It's not as risky as it seems. As always, the dangerous part about life support is managing carbon dioxide. When the air gets to 1 percent CO_2, you start getting symptoms of poisoning. So I need to keep the Hab's mix below that.

The Hab's internal volume is about 120,000 liters. Breathing normally, it would take me over two days to bring the CO_2 level up to 1 percent (and I wouldn't even put a dent in the O_2 level). So it's safe to move the regulator and oxygenator over for a while.

Both are way too big to fit through the trailer airlock. Lucky for me, they came to Mars with "some assembly required." They were too big to send whole, so they're easy to dismantle.

Over several trips, I moved all of their chunks to the trailer. I brought each chunk in through the airlock, one at a time. It was a pain in the ass reassembling them inside, let me tell you. There's barely enough room for all the shit the trailer's got to hold. There wasn't much left for our intrepid hero.

Then I got the AREC. It sat outside the Hab like an AC unit might on Earth. In a way, that's what it is. I hauled it over to the trailer and lashed it to the shelf I'd made for it. Then I hooked it up to the feed lines that led through the "balloon" to the inside of the trailer's pressure vessel.

The regulator needs to send air to the AREC, then the return air needs to bubble through the heat reservoir. The regulator also needs a pressure tank to contain the CO_2 it pulls from the air.

When gutting the trailer to make room, I left one tank in place for this. It's supposed to hold oxygen, but a tank's a tank. Thank God all the air lines and valves are standardized across the mission. That's no mistake. It was a deliberate decision to make field repairs easier.

Once I had the AREC in place, I hooked the oxygenator and regulator into the trailer's power and watched them power up. I ran both through full diagnostics to confirm they were working correctly. Then I shut down the oxygenator. Remember, I'll only use it one sol out of every five.

I moved to the rover, which meant I had to do an annoying ten-meter EVA. From there, I monitored the life support situation. It's worth noting that I can't monitor the actual support equipment from the rover (it's all in the trailer), but the rover can tell me all about the air. Oxygen, CO_2, temperature, humidity, etc. Everything seemed okay.

After getting back into the EVA suit, I released a canister of CO_2 into the rover's air. I watched the rover computer have a shit fit when it saw the CO_2 spike to lethal levels. Then, over time, the levels dropped to normal. The regulator was doing its job. Good boy!

I left the equipment running when I returned to the Hab. It'll be on its own all night and I'll check it in the morning. It's not a true test, because I'm not there to breathe up the oxygen and make CO_2, but one step at a time.

LOG ENTRY: SOL 435

Last night was weird. I knew *logically* that nothing bad would happen in just one night, but it was a little unnerving to know I had no life support other than heaters. My life depended on some math I'd done earlier. If I dropped a sign or added two numbers wrong, I might never wake up.

But I did wake up, and the main computer showed the slight rise in CO_2 I had predicted. Looks like I'll live another sol.

Live Another Sol would be an awesome name for a James Bond movie.

I checked up on the rover. Everything was fine. If I don't drive it, a single charge of the batteries could keep the regulator going for over a month (with the heater off). It's a pretty good safety margin to have. If all hell breaks loose on my trip, I'll have time to fix things. I'll be limited by oxygen consumption rather than CO_2 removal, and I have plenty of oxygen.

I decided it was a good time to test the bedroom.

I got in the rover and attached the bedroom to the outer airlock door from the inside. Like I mentioned before, this is the only way to do it. Then I turned it loose on an unsuspecting Mars.

As intended, the pressure from the rover blasted the canvas outward and inflated it. After that, chaos. The sudden pressure popped the bedroom like a balloon. It quickly deflated, leaving both itself and the rover devoid of air. I was wearing my EVA suit at the time; I'm not a fucking idiot. So I get to . . .

Live Another Sol! (Starring Mark Watney as . . . probably Q. I'm no James Bond.)

I dragged the popped bedroom into the Hab and gave it a good going-over. It failed at the seam where the wall met the ceiling. Makes sense. It's a right angle in a pressure vessel. Physics hates that sort of thing.

First, I patched it up, then I cut strips of spare canvas to place over the seam. Now it has double-thickness and double sealing resin all around. Maybe that'll be enough. At this point, I'm kind of guessing. My amazing botany skills aren't much use for this.

I'll test it again tomorrow.

LOG ENTRY: SOL 436

I'm out of caffeine pills. No more Martian coffee for me.

So it took a little longer for me to wake up this morning, and I quickly developed a splitting headache. One nice thing about living in a multibillion-dollar mansion on Mars: access to pure oxygen. For some reason, a high concentration of O_2 will kill most headaches. Don't know why. Don't care. The important thing is I don't have to suffer.

I tested out the bedroom again. I suited up in the rover and released the bedroom, same as last time. But this time it held. That's great, but having seen the fragile nature of my handiwork, I wanted a good long test of the pressure seal.

After a few minutes standing around in my EVA suit, I decided to make better use of my time. I may not be able to leave the rover/bedroom universe while the bedroom is attached to the airlock, but I can stay in the rover and close the door.

Once I did that, I took off the uncomfortable EVA suit. The bedroom was on the other side of the airlock door, still fully pressurized. So I'm still running my test, but I don't have to wear the EVA suit.

I arbitrarily picked eight hours for the test duration, so I was trapped in the rover until then.

I spent my time planning the trip. There wasn't much to add to what I already knew. I'll beeline out of Acidalia Planitia to Mawrth Vallis, then follow the valley until it ends. It'll take me on a zigzag route which will dump me into Arabia Terra. After that, things get rough.

Unlike Acidalia Planitia, Arabia Terra is riddled

with craters. And each crater represents two brutal elevation changes. First down, then up. I did my best to find the shortest path around them. I'm sure I'll have to adjust the course when I'm actually driving it. No plan survives first contact with the enemy.

■ ■ ■

MITCH TOOK his seat in the conference room. The usual gang was present: Teddy, Venkat, Mitch, and Annie. But this time there was also Mindy Park, as well as a man Mitch had never seen before.

"What's up, Venk?" Mitch asked. "Why the sudden meeting?"

"We've got some developments," Venkat said. "Mindy, why don't you bring them up to date?"

"Uh, yeah," Mindy said. "Looks like Watney finished the balloon addition to the trailer. It mostly uses the design we sent him."

"Any idea how stable it is?" Teddy asked.

"Pretty stable," she said. "It's been inflated for several days with no problems. Also, he built some kind of . . . room."

"Room?" Teddy asked.

"It's made of Hab canvas, I think," Mindy explained. "It attaches to the rover's airlock. I think he cut a section out of the Hab to make it. I don't know what it's for."

Teddy turned to Venkat. "Why would he do that?"

"We think it's a workshop," Venkat said. "There'll be a lot of work to do on the MAV once he gets to Schiaparelli. It'll be easier without an

EVA suit. He probably plans to do as much as he can in that room."

"Clever," Teddy said.

"Watney's a clever guy," Mitch said. "How about getting life support in there?"

"I think he's done it," Mindy said. "He moved the AREC."

"Sorry," Annie interrupted. "What's an AREC?"

"It's the external component of the atmospheric regulator," Mindy said. "It sits outside the Hab, so I saw when it disappeared. He probably mounted it on the rover. There's no other reason to move it, so I'm guessing he's got life support online."

"Awesome," Mitch said. "Things are coming together."

"Don't celebrate yet, Mitch," Venkat said. He gestured to the newcomer. "This is Randall Carter, one of our Martian meteorologists. Randall, tell them what you told me."

Randall nodded. "Thank you, Dr. Kapoor." He turned his laptop around to show a map of Mars. "Over the past few weeks, a dust storm has been developing in Arabia Terra. Not a big deal in terms of magnitude. It won't hinder his driving at all."

"So what's the problem?" Annie asked.

"It's a low-velocity dust storm," Randall explained. "Slow winds, but fast enough to pick up very small particles on the surface and whip them into thick clouds. There are five or six of them every year. The thing is, they last for months, they cover huge sections of the planet, and they make the atmosphere thick with dust."

"I still don't see the problem," Annie said.

"Light," Randall said. "The total sunlight reaching the surface is very low in the area of the storm. Right now, it's twenty percent of normal. And Watney's rover is powered by solar panels."

"Shit," Mitch said, rubbing his eyes. "And we can't warn him."

"So he gets less power," Annie said. "Can't he just recharge longer?"

"The current plan already has him recharging all day long," Venkat explained. "With twenty percent of normal daylight, it'll take five times as long to get the same energy. It'll turn his forty-five-sol trip into two hundred and twenty-five sols. He'll miss the *Hermes* flyby."

"Can't *Hermes* wait for him?" Annie asked.

"It's a flyby," Venkat said. "*Hermes* isn't going into Martian orbit. If they did, they wouldn't be able to get back. They need their velocity for the return trajectory."

After a few moments of silence, Teddy said, "We'll just have to hope he finds a way through. We can track his progress and—"

"No, we can't," Mindy interrupted.

"We can't?" Teddy said.

She shook her head. "The satellites won't be able to see through the dust. Once he enters the affected area, we won't see anything until he comes out the other side."

"Well . . . ," Teddy said. "Shit."

LOG ENTRY: SOL 439

Before I risk my life with this contraption, I need to test it.

And not the little tests I've been doing so far. Sure, I've tested power generation, life support, the trailer bubble, and the bedroom. But I need to test all aspects of it working together.

I'm going to load it up for the long trip and drive in circles. I won't ever be more than 500 meters from the Hab, so I'll be fine if shit breaks.

I dedicated today to loading up the rover and trailer for the test. I want the weight to match what it'll be on the real trip. Plus if cargo is going to shift around or break things, I want to know about it now.

I made one concession to common sense: I left most of my water supply in the Hab. I loaded twenty liters; enough for the test but no more. There are a lot of ways I could lose pressure in this mechanical abomination I've created, and I don't want all my water to boil off if that happens.

On the real trip, I'm going to have 620 liters of water. I made up the weight difference by loading 600 kilograms of rocks in with my other supplies.

Back on Earth, universities and governments are willing to pay millions to get their hands on Mars rocks. I'm using them as ballast.

I'm doing one more little test tonight. I made sure the batteries were good and full, then disconnected the rover and trailer from Hab power. I'll be sleeping in the Hab, but I left the rover's life support on. It'll maintain the air overnight, and tomorrow I'll see how much power it ate up. I've watched the power consumption while it's attached to the Hab, and there weren't any surprises. But this'll be the true proof. I call it the "plugs-out test."

Maybe that's not the best name.

■ ■ ■

THE CREW of *Hermes* gathered in the Rec.

"Let's get through status quickly," Lewis said. "We're all behind in our science assignments. Vogel, you first."

"I repaired the bad cable on VASIMR 4," Vogel reported. "It was our last thick-gauge cable. If another such problem occurs, we will have to braid lower-gauge lines to carry the current. Also, the power output from the reactor is declining."

"Johanssen," Lewis said, "what's the deal with the reactor?"

"I had to dial it back," Johanssen said. "It's the cooling vanes. They aren't radiating heat as well as they used to. They're tarnishing."

"How can that happen?" Lewis asked. "They're outside the craft. There's nothing for them to react with."

"I think they picked up dust or small air leaks from *Hermes* itself. One way or another, they're definitely tarnishing. The tarnish is clogging the micro-lattice, and that reduces the surface area. Less surface area means less heat dissipation. So I limited the reactor enough that we weren't getting positive heat."

"Any chance of repairing the cooling vanes?"

"It's on the microscopic scale," Johanssen said. "We'd need a lab. Usually they replace the vanes after each mission."

"Will we be able to maintain engine power for the rest of the mission?"

"Yes, if the rate of tarnishing doesn't increase."

"All right, keep an eye on it. Beck, how's life support?"

"Limping," Beck said. "We've been in space way longer than it was designed to handle. There are a bunch of filters that would normally be replaced each mission. I found a way to clean them with a chemical bath I made in the lab, but it eats away at the filters themselves. We're okay right now, but who knows what'll break next?"

"We knew this would happen," Lewis said. "The design of *Hermes* assumed it would get an overhaul after each mission, but we've extended Ares 3 from 396 days to 898. Things are going to break. We've got all of NASA to help when that happens. We just need to stay on top of maintenance. Martinez, what's the deal with your bunk room?"

Martinez furrowed his brow. "It's still trying to cook me. The climate control just isn't keeping up. I think it's the tubing in the walls that brings the coolant. I can't get at it because it's built into the hull. We can use the room for storage of non-temperature-sensitive cargo, but that's about it."

"So did you move into Mark's room?"

"It's right next to mine," he said. "It has the same problem."

"Where have you been sleeping?"

"In Airlock 2. It's the only place I can be without people tripping over me."

"No good," Lewis said, shaking her head. "If one seal breaks, you die."

"I can't think of anywhere else to sleep," he said. "The ship is pretty cramped, and if I sleep in a hallway I'll be in people's way."

"Okay, from now on, sleep in Beck's room. Beck can sleep with Johanssen."

Johanssen blushed and looked down awkwardly.

"So . . . ," Beck said, "you know about that?"

"You thought I didn't?" Lewis said. "It's a small ship."

"You're not mad?"

"If it were a normal mission, I would be," Lewis said. "But we're way off-script now. Just keep it from interfering with your duties, and I'm happy."

"Million-mile-high club," Martinez said. "Nice!"

Johanssen blushed deeper and buried her face in her hands.

LOG ENTRY: SOL 444

I'm getting pretty good at this. Maybe when all this is over I could be a product tester for Mars rovers.

Things went well. I spent five sols driving in circles; I averaged 93 kilometers per sol. That's a little better than I'd expected. The terrain here is flat and smooth, so it's pretty much a best-case scenario. Once I'm going up hills and around boulders, it won't be nearly that good.

The bedroom is awesome. Large, spacious, and comfortable. On the first night, I ran into a little problem with the temperature. It was fucking cold. The rover and trailer regulate their own temperatures just fine, but things weren't hot enough in the bedroom.

Story of my life.

The rover has an electric heater that pushes air with a small fan. I don't use the heater itself for anything because the RTG provides all the heat I need, so I liberated the fan and wired it into a power line near the airlock. Once it had power, all I had to do was point it at the bedroom.

It's a low-tech solution, but it worked. There's plenty of heat, thanks to the RTG. I just needed to get it evenly spread out. For once, entropy was on my side.

I've discovered that raw potatoes are disgusting. When I'm in the Hab, I cook my taters using a small microwave. I don't have anything like that in the rover. I could easily bring the Hab's microwave into the rover and wire it in, but the energy required to cook ten potatoes a day would actually cut into my driving distance.

I fell into a routine pretty quickly. In fact, it was hauntingly familiar. I did it for twenty-two miserable sols on the *Pathfinder* trip. But this time, I had the bedroom and that makes all the difference. Instead of being cooped up in the rover, I have my own little Hab.

After waking up, I have a potato for breakfast. Then, I deflate the bedroom from the inside. It's kind of tricky, but I worked out how.

First, I put on an EVA suit. Then I close the inner airlock door, leaving the outer door (which the bedroom is attached to) open. This isolates the bedroom, with me in it, from the rest of the rover. Then I tell the airlock to depressurize. It thinks it's just pumping the air out of a small area, but it's actually deflating the whole bedroom.

Once the pressure is gone, I pull the canvas in and fold it. Then I detach it from the outer hatch and close the outer door. This is the most cramped part. I have to share the airlock with the entire folded-up bedroom while it repressurizes. Once I have pressure again, I open the inner door and more or less fall into the rover. Then I stow the bedroom and go back to the airlock for a normal egress to Mars.

It's a complicated process, but it detaches the bedroom without having to depressurize the rover cabin. Remember, the rover has all my stuff that doesn't play well with vacuum.

The next step is to gather up the solar cells I laid out the day before and stow them on the rover and trailer. Then I do a quick check on the trailer. I go in through its airlock and basically take a quick look at all the equipment. I don't even take off my EVA suit. I just want to make sure nothing's obviously wrong.

Then, back to the rover. Once inside, I take off the EVA suit and start driving. I drive for almost four hours, and then I'm out of power.

Once I park, it's back into the EVA suit for me, and out to Mars again. I lay the solar panels out and get the batteries charging.

Then I set up the bedroom. Pretty much the reverse of the sequence I use to stow it. Ultimately, it's the airlock that inflates it. In a way, the bedroom is just an extension of the airlock.

Even though it's possible, I don't rapid-inflate the bedroom. I did that to test it because I wanted to find where it'll leak. But it's not a good idea. Rapid inflation puts a lot of shock and pressure on it. It would eventually rupture. I didn't enjoy that time the Hab launched me like a cannonball. I'm not eager to repeat it.

Once the bedroom is set up again, I can take off my EVA suit and relax. I mostly watch crappy seventies TV. I'm indistinguishable from an unemployed guy for most of the day.

I followed that process for four sols, and then it was time for an "Air Day."

An Air Day turns out to be pretty much the same as any other day, but without the four-hour drive. Once I set up the solar panels, I fired up the oxygenator and let it work through the backlog of CO_2 that the regulator had stored up.

It converted all the CO_2 to oxygen and used up the day's power generation to do it.

The test was a success. I'll be ready on time.

LOG ENTRY: SOL 449

Today's the big day. I'm leaving for Schiaparelli.

The rover and trailer are all packed. They've been mostly packed since the test run. But now I even have the water aboard.

Over the last few days, I cooked all the potatoes with the Hab's microwave. It took quite a while, because the microwave can only hold four at a time. After cooking, I put them back out on the surface to freeze. Once frozen, I put them back in the rover's saddlebags. This may seem like a waste of time, but it's critical. Instead of eating raw potatoes during my trip, I'll be eating (cold) precooked potatoes. First off, they'll taste a lot better. But more important, they'll be cooked. When you cook food, the proteins break down, and the food becomes easier to digest. I'll get more calories out of it, and I need every calorie I can get my hands on.

I spent the last several days running full diagnostics on everything. The regulator, oxygenator, RTG, AREC, batteries, rover life support (in case I need a backup), solar cells, rover computer, airlocks, and everything else with a moving part or electronic component. I even checked each of the motors. Eight in all, one for each wheel, four on the rover, four on the trailer. The trailer's motors won't be powered, but it's nice to have backups.

It's all good to go. No problems that I can see.

The Hab is a shell of its former self. I've robbed it of all critical components and a big chunk of its canvas. I've looted that poor Hab for everything it could give me, and in return it's kept me alive for a year and a half. It's like the Giving Tree.

I performed the final shutdown today. The heaters, lighting, main computer, etc. All the components I didn't steal for the trip to Schiaparelli.

I could have left them on. It's not like anyone would care. But the original procedure for Sol 31 (which was supposed to be the last day of the surface mission) was to completely shut down the Hab and deflate it, because NASA didn't want a big tent full of combustible oxygen next to the MAV when it launched.

I guess I did the shutdown as an homage to the mission Ares 3 could have been. A small piece of the Sol 31 I never got to have.

Once I'd shut everything down, the interior of the Hab was eerily silent. I'd spent 449 sols listening to its heaters, vents, and fans. But now it was dead quiet. It was a creepy kind of quiet that's hard to describe. I've been away from the noises of the Hab before, but always in a rover or an EVA suit, both of which have noisy machinery of their own.

But now there was nothing. I never realized how utterly silent Mars is. It's a desert world with practically no atmosphere to convey sound. I could hear my own heartbeat.

Anyway, enough waxing philosophical.

I'm in the rover right now. (That should be obvious, with the Hab main computer offline forever.) I've got two full batteries, all systems are go, and I've got forty-five sols of driving ahead of me.

Schiaparelli or bust!

CHAPTER 22

LOG ENTRY: SOL 458

Mawrth Vallis! I'm finally here!

Actually, it's not an impressive accomplishment. I've only been traveling ten sols. But it's a good psychological milestone.

So far, the rover and my ghetto life support are working admirably. At least, as well as can be expected for equipment being used ten times longer than intended.

Today is my second Air Day (the first was five sols ago). When I put this scheme together, I figured Air Days would be godawful boring. But now I look forward to them. They're my days off.

On a normal day, I get up, fold up the bedroom, stack the solar cells, drive four hours, set up the solar cells, unfurl the bedroom, check all my equipment (especially the rover chassis and wheels), then make a Morse code status report for NASA, if I can find enough nearby rocks.

On an Air Day, I wake up and turn on the oxygenator. The solar panels are already out from the day before. Everything's ready to go. Then I chill out in the bedroom or rover. I have the whole day to myself. The bedroom gives me enough space that I don't feel cooped up, and the computer has plenty of shitty TV reruns for me to enjoy.

Technically, I entered Mawrth Vallis yesterday. But I only knew that by looking at a map. The entrance to the valley is wide enough that I couldn't see the canyon walls in either direction.

But now I'm definitely in a canyon. And the bottom is nice and flat. Exactly what I was hoping for. It's amazing; this valley wasn't made by a river slowly carving it away. It was made by a mega-flood in a single day. It would have been a hell of a thing to see.

Weird thought: I'm not in Acidalia Planitia anymore. I spent 457 sols there, almost a year and a half, and I'll never go back. I wonder if I'll be nostalgic about that later in life.

If there is a "later in life," I'll be happy to endure a little nostalgia. But for now, I just want to go home.

▪▪▪

"WELCOME BACK to CNN's *Mark Watney Report*," Cathy said to the camera. "We're speaking with our frequent guest, Dr. Venkat Kapoor. Dr. Kapoor, I guess what people want to know is, is Mark Watney doomed?"

"We hope not," Venkat responded, "but he's got a real challenge ahead of him."

"According to your latest satellite data, the dust storm in Arabia Terra isn't abating at all, and will block eighty percent of the sunlight?"

"That's correct."

"And Watney's only source of energy is his solar panels, correct?"

"Yes, that's right."

"Can his makeshift rover operate at twenty percent power?"

"We haven't found any way to make that happen, no. His life support alone takes more energy than that."

"How long until he enters the storm?"

"He's just entered Mawrth Vallis now. At his current rate of travel, he'll be at the edge of the storm on Sol 471. That's twelve days from now."

"Surely he'll see something is wrong," Cathy said. "With such low visibility, it won't take long for him to realize his solar cells will have a problem. Couldn't he just turn around at that point?"

"Unfortunately, everything's working against him," Venkat said. "The edge of the storm isn't a magic line. It's just an area where the dust gets a little more dense. It'll keep getting more and more dense as he travels onward. It'll be really subtle; every day will be slightly darker than the last. Too subtle to notice."

Venkat sighed. "He'll go hundreds of kilometers, wondering why his solar panel efficiency is going down, before he notices any visibility problems. And the storm is moving west as he moves east. He'll be too deep in to get out."

"Are we just watching a tragedy play out?" Cathy asked.

"There's always hope," Venkat said. "Maybe he'll figure it out faster than we think and turn around in time. Maybe the storm will dissipate unexpectedly. Maybe he'll find a way to keep his life support going on less energy than we thought was possible. Mark Watney is now an expert at surviving on Mars. If anyone can do it, it's him."

"Twelve days," Cathy said to the camera. "All of Earth is watching but powerless to help."

LOG ENTRY: SOL 462

Another uneventful sol. Tomorrow is an Air Day, so this is kind of my Friday night.

I'm about halfway through Mawrth Vallis now. Just as I'd hoped, the going has been easy. No major elevation changes. Hardly any obstacles. Just smooth sand with rocks smaller than half a meter.

You may be wondering how I navigate. When I went to *Pathfinder*, I watched Phobos transit the sky to figure out the east-west axis. But *Pathfinder* was an easy trip compared to this, and I had plenty of landmarks to navigate by.

I can't get away with that this time. My "map" (such as it is) consists of satellite images far too low-resolution to be of any use. I can only see major landmarks, like craters 50 kilometers across. They just never expected me to be out this far. The only reason I had high-res images of the *Pathfinder* region is because they were included for landing purposes; in case Martinez had to land way long of our target.

So this time around, I needed a reliable way to fix my position on Mars.

Latitude and longitude. That's the key. The first is easy. Ancient sailors on Earth figured that one out right away. Earth's 23.5-degree axis points at Polaris. Mars has a tilt of just over 25 degrees, so it's pointed at Deneb.

Making a sextant isn't hard. All you need is a tube to look through, a string, a weight, and something with degree markings. I made mine in under an hour.

So I go out every night with a homemade sextant and sight Deneb. It's kind of silly if you think about it. I'm in my space suit on Mars and I'm navigating with sixteenth-century tools. But hey, they work.

Longitude is a different matter. On Earth, the earliest way to work out longitude required them to know the exact time, then compare it to the sun's position in the sky. The hard part for them back then was inventing a clock that would work on a boat (pendulums don't work on boats). All the top scientific minds of the age worked on the problem.

Fortunately, I have accurate clocks. There are four computers in my immediate line of sight right now. And I have Phobos.

Because Phobos is ridiculously close to Mars, it orbits the planet in less than one Martian day. It travels west to east (unlike the sun and Deimos) and sets every eleven hours. And naturally, it moves in a very predictable pattern.

I spend thirteen hours every sol just sitting around while the solar panels charge the batteries. Phobos is guaranteed to set at least once during that time. I note the time when it does. Then I plug it into a nasty formula I worked out and I know my longitude.

So working out longitude requires Phobos to set, and working out latitude requires it to be night so I can sight Deneb. It's not a very fast system. But I only need it once a day. I work out my location when I'm parked, and account for it in the next day's travel. It's kind of a successive approximation thing. So far, I think it's been working. But who knows? I can see it now: me holding a map, scratching my head, trying to figure out how I ended up on Venus.

■ ■ ■

MINDY PARK zoomed in on the latest satellite photo with practiced ease. Watney's encampment was visible in the center, the solar cells laid out in a circular pattern as was his habit.

The workshop was inflated. Checking the time stamp on the image, she saw it was from noon local time. She quickly found the status report; Watney always placed it close to the rover when rocks were in abundance, usually to the north.

To save time, Mindy had taught herself Morse code, so she wouldn't have to look each letter up every morning. She opened an e-mail and addressed it to the ever-growing list of people who wanted Watney's daily status message.

"ON TRACK FOR SOL 494 ARRIVAL."

She frowned and added "Note: five sols until dust storm entry."

LOG ENTRY: SOL 466

Mawrth Vallis was fun while it lasted. I'm in Arabia Terra now.

I just entered the edge of it, if my latitude and longitude calculations are correct. But even without the math, it's pretty obvious the terrain is changing.

For the last two sols, I've spent almost all my time on an incline, working my way up the back wall of Mawrth Vallis. It was a gentle rise, but a constant one. I'm at a much higher altitude now. Acidalia Planitia (where the lonely Hab is hanging out) is 3000 meters below elevation zero, and Arabia Terra is 500 meters below. So I've gone up two and a half kilometers.

Want to know what elevation zero means? On Earth, it's sea level. Obviously, that won't work on Mars. So lab-coated geeks got together and decided Mars's elevation zero is wherever the air pressure is 610.5 pascals. That's about 500 meters up from where I am right now.

Now things get tricky. Back in Acidalia Planitia, if I got off course, I could just point in the right direction based on new data. Later, in Mawrth Vallis, it was impossible to screw up. I just had to follow the canyon.

Now I'm in a rougher neighborhood. The kind of neighborhood where you keep your rover doors locked and never come to a complete stop at intersections. Well, not really, but it's bad to get off course here.

Arabia Terra has large, brutal craters that I have to drive around. If I navigate poorly, I'll end up at the edge of one. I can't just drive down one side and up the other. Rising in elevation costs a ton of energy. On flat ground, I can make 90 kilometers per day. On a steep slope, I'd be lucky to get 40 kilometers. Plus, driving on a slope is dangerous. One mistake and I could roll the rover. I don't even want to think about that.

Yes, I'll eventually have to drive down into Schiaparelli. No way around that. I'll have to be really careful.

Anyway, if I end up at the edge of a crater, I'll have to backtrack to somewhere useful. And it's a damn maze of craters out here. I'll have to be on my guard, observant at all times. I'll need to navigate with landmarks as well as latitude and longitude.

My first challenge is to pass between the craters Rutherford and Trouvelot. It shouldn't be too hard. They're 100 kilometers apart. Even I can't fuck that up, right?

Right?

LOG ENTRY: SOL 468

I managed to thread the needle between Rutherford and Trouvelot nicely. Admittedly, the needle was 100 kilometers wide, but hey.

I'm now enjoying my fourth Air Day of the trip. I've been on the road for twenty sols. So far, I'm right on schedule. According to my maps, I've traveled 1440 kilometers. Not quite halfway there, but almost.

I've been gathering soil and rock samples from each place I camp. I did the same thing on my way to *Pathfinder*. But this time, I know NASA's watching me. So I'm labeling each sample by the current sol. They'll know my location a hell of a lot more accurately than I do. They can correlate the samples with their locations later.

It might be a wasted effort. The MAV isn't going to have much weight allowance when I launch. To intercept *Hermes*, it'll have to reach escape velocity, but it was only designed to get to orbit. The only way to get it going fast enough is to lose a lot of weight.

At least that jury-rigging will be NASA's job to work out, not mine. Once I get to the MAV, I'll be back in contact with them and they can tell me what modifications to make.

They'll probably say, "Thanks for gathering samples. But leave them behind. And one of your arms, too. Whichever one you like least." But on the off chance I can bring the samples, I'm gathering them.

The next few days' travel should be easy. The next major obstacle is Marth Crater. It's right in my straight-line path toward Schiaparelli. It'll cost me a hundred kilometers or so to go around, but it can't be helped. I'll try to aim for the southern edge. The closer I get to the rim the less time I'll waste going around it.

▪▪▪

"DID YOU read today's updates?" Lewis asked, pulling her meal from the microwave.

"Yeah," Martinez said, sipping his drink.

She sat across the Rec table from him and carefully opened the steaming package. She decided to let it cool a bit before eating. "Mark entered the dust storm yesterday."

"Yeah, I saw that," he said.

"We need to face the possibility that he won't make it to Schiaparelli," Lewis said. "If that happens, we need to keep morale up. We still have a long way to go before we get home."

"He was dead before," Martinez said. "It was rough on morale, but we soldiered on. Besides, he won't die."

"It's pretty bleak, Rick," Lewis said. "He's already fifty kilometers into the storm, and he'll go another ninety kilometers per sol. He'll get in too deep to recover soon."

Martinez shook his head. "He'll pull through, Commander. Have faith."

She smiled forlornly. "Rick, you know I'm not religious."

"I know," he said. "I'm not talking about faith in God, I'm talking about faith in Mark Watney. Look at all the shit Mars has thrown at him, and he's still alive. He'll survive this. I don't know how, but he will. He's a clever son of a bitch."

Lewis took a bite of her food. "I hope you're right."

"Want to bet a hundred bucks?" Martinez said with a smile.

"Of course not," Lewis said.

"Damn right." He smiled.

"I'd never bet on a crewmate dying," Lewis said. "But that doesn't mean I think he'll—"

"Blah blah blah," Martinez interrupted. "Deep down, you think he'll make it."

LOG ENTRY: SOL 473

My fifth Air Day, and things are going well. I should be skimming south of Marth Crater tomorrow. It'll get easier after that.

I'm in the middle of a bunch of craters that form a triangle. I'm calling it the Watney Triangle because after what I've been through, stuff on Mars should be named after me.

Trouvelot, Becquerel, and Marth form the points of the triangle, with five other major craters along the sides. Normally this wouldn't be a problem at all, but with my extremely rough navigation, I could easily end up at the lip of one of them and have to backtrack.

After Marth, I'll be out of the Watney Triangle (yeah, I'm liking that name more and more). Then I can beeline toward Schiaparelli with impunity. There'll still be plenty of craters in the way, but they're comparatively small, and going around them won't cost much time.

Progress has been great. Arabia Terra is certainly rockier than Acidalia Planitia, but nowhere near as bad as I'd feared. I've been able to drive over most of the rocks, and around the ones that are too big. I have 1435 kilometers left to go.

I did some research on Schiaparelli and found some good news. The best way in is right in my direct-line path. I won't have to drive the perimeter at all. And the way in is easy to find, even when you suck at navigating. The northwest rim has a smaller crater on it, and that's the landmark I'll be looking for. To the southwest of that little crater is a gentle slope into Schiaparelli Basin.

The little crater doesn't have a name. At least,

not on the maps I have. So I dub it "Entrance Crater." Because I can.

In other news, my equipment is starting to show signs of age. Not surprising, considering it's way the hell past its expiration date. For the past two sols, the batteries have taken longer to recharge. The solar cells just aren't producing as much wattage as before. It's not a big deal, I just need to charge a little longer.

LOG ENTRY: SOL 474

Well, I fucked it up.

It was bound to happen eventually. I navigated badly and ended up at the ridge of Marth Crater. Because it's 100 kilometers wide, I can't see the whole thing, so I don't know where on the circle I am.

The ridge runs perpendicular to the direction I was going. So I have no clue which way I should go. And I don't want to take the long way around if I can avoid it. Originally I wanted to go around to the south, but north is just as likely to be the best path now that I'm off course.

I'll have to wait for another Phobos transit to get my longitude, and I'll need to wait for nightfall to sight Deneb for my latitude. So I'm done driving for the day. Luckily I'd made 70 kilometers out of the 90 kilometers I usually do, so it's not too much wasted progress.

Marth isn't too steep. I could probably just drive down one side and up the other. It's big enough that I'd end up camping inside it one night. But I don't want to take unnecessary risks. Slopes are bad and should be avoided. I gave myself plenty of buffer time, so I'm going to play it safe.

I'm ending today's drive early and setting up for recharge. Probably a good idea anyway with the solar cells acting up; it'll give them more time to work. They underperformed again last night. I checked all the connections and made sure there wasn't any dust on them, but they still just aren't 100 percent.

LOG ENTRY: SOL 475

I'm in trouble.

I watched two Phobos transits yesterday and sighted Deneb last night. I worked out my location as accurately as I could, and it wasn't what I wanted to see. As far as I can tell, I hit Marth Crater dead-on.

Craaaaap.

I can go north or south. One of them will probably be better than the other, because it'll be a shorter path around the crater.

I figured I should put at least a little effort into figuring out which direction was best, so I took a little walk this morning. It was over a kilometer to the peak of the rim. That's the sort of walk people do on Earth without thinking twice, but in an EVA suit it's an ordeal.

I can't wait till I have grandchildren. "When I was younger, I had to walk to the rim of a crater. Uphill! In an EVA suit! On Mars, ya little shit! Ya hear me? Mars!"

Anyway, I got up to the rim, and damn, it's a beautiful sight. From my high vantage point, I got a stunning panorama. I figured I might be able to see the far side of Marth Crater, and maybe work out the best way around.

But I couldn't see the far side. There was a haze in the air. It's not uncommon; Mars has weather and wind and dust, after all. But it seemed hazier than it should. I'm accustomed to the wide-open expanses of Acidalia Planitia, my former prairie home.

Then it got weirder. I turned around and looked back toward the rover and trailer. Everything was where I'd left it (very few car thieves on Mars). But the view seemed a lot clearer.

I looked east across Marth again. Then west to the horizon. Then east, then west. Each turn required me to rotate my whole body, EVA suits being what they are.

Yesterday, I passed a crater. It's about 50 kilometers west of here. It's just visible on the horizon. But looking east, I can't see anywhere near that far. Marth Crater is 110 kilometers wide. With a visibility of 50 kilometers, I should at least be able to see a distinct curvature of the rim. But I can't.

At first, I didn't know what to make of it. But the lack of symmetry bothered me. And I've learned to be suspicious of everything. That's when a bunch of stuff started to dawn on me:

1. The only explanation for asymmetrical visibility is a dust storm.
2. Dust storms reduce the effectiveness of solar cells.
3. My solar cells have been slowly losing effectiveness for several sols.

From this, I concluded the following:

1. I've been in a dust storm for several sols.
2. Shit.

Not only am I in a dust storm, but it gets thicker as I approach Schiaparelli. A few hours ago, I was worried because I had to go around Marth Crater. Now I'm going to have to go around something a lot bigger.

And I have to hustle. Dust storms move. Sitting still means I'll likely get overwhelmed. But which way do I go? It's no longer an issue of trying to be efficient. If I go the wrong way this time, I'll eat dust and die.

I don't have satellite imagery. I have no way of knowing the size or shape of the storm, or its heading. Man, I'd give anything for a five-minute conversation with NASA. Now that I think of it, NASA must be shitting bricks watching this play out.

I'm on the clock. I have to figure out *how* to figure out what I need to know about the storm. And I have to do it now.

And right this second nothing comes to mind.

■ ■ ■

MINDY TRUDGED to her computer. Today's shift began at 2:10 p.m. Her schedule matched Watney's every day. She slept when he slept. Watney simply slept at night on Mars, while Mindy had to drift forty minutes forward every day, taping aluminum foil to her windows to get any sleep at all.

She brought up the most recent satellite images. She cocked an eyebrow. He had not broken camp yet. Usually he drove in the early morning, as soon as it was light enough to navigate. Then he capitalized on the midday sun to maximize recharging.

But today, he had not moved, and it was well past morning.

She checked around the rovers and the bedroom for a message. She found it in the usual place (north of the campsite). As she read the Morse code, her eyes widened.

"DUST STORM. MAKING PLAN."

Fumbling with her cell phone, she dialed Venkat's personal number.

CHAPTER 23

LOG ENTRY: SOL 476

I think I can work this out.

I'm on the very edge of a storm. I don't know its size or heading. But it's moving, and that's something I can take advantage of. I don't have to wander around exploring it. It'll come to me.

The storm is just dust in the air; it's not dangerous to the rovers. I can think of it as "percent power loss." I checked yesterday's power generation, and it was 97 percent of optimal. So right now, it's a 3 percent storm.

I need to make progress and I need to regenerate oxygen. Those are my two main goals. I use 20 percent of my overall power to reclaim oxygen (when I stop for Air Days). If I end up in an 81 percent part of the storm, I'll be in real trouble. I'll run out of oxygen even if I dedicate all available power to producing it. That's the fatal scenario.

But really, it's fatal much earlier than that. I need power to move or I'll be stranded until the storm passes or dissipates. That could be months.

The more power I generate, the more I'll have for movement. With clear skies, I dedicate 80 percent of my total power toward movement. I get 90 kilometers per sol this way. So right now, at 3 percent loss, I'm getting 2.7 kilometers less than I should.

It's okay to lose some driving distance per sol. I have plenty of time, but I can't let myself get too deep in the storm or I'll never be able to get out.

At the very least, I need to travel faster than the storm. If I can go faster, I can maneuver around it without being enveloped. So I need to find out how fast it's moving.

I can do that by sitting here for a sol. I can compare tomorrow's wattage to today's. All I have to do is make sure to compare at the same times of day. Then I'll know how fast the storm is moving, at least in terms of percent power loss.

But I need to know the shape of the storm, too.

Dust storms are big. They can be thousands of kilometers across. So when I work my way around it, I'll need to know which way to go. I'll want to move perpendicular to the storm's movement, and in whatever direction has less storm.

So here's my plan:

Right now, I can go 86 kilometers (because I couldn't get a full battery yesterday). Tomorrow, I'm going to leave a solar cell here and drive 40 kilometers due south. Then I'll drop off another solar cell and drive another 40 kilometers due south. That'll give me three points of reference across 80 kilometers.

The next day, I'll go back to collect the cells

and get the data. By comparing the wattage at the same time of day in those three locations, I'll learn the shape of the storm. If the storm is thicker to the south, I'll go north to get around it. If it's thicker north, I'll go south.

I'm hoping to go south. Schiaparelli is southeast of me. Going north would add a lot of time to my total trip.

There's one *slight* problem with my plan: I don't have any way to "record" the wattage from an abandoned solar cell. I can easily track and log wattage with the rover computer, but I need something I can drop off and leave behind. I can't just take readings as I drive along. I need readings at the same time in different places.

So I'm going to spend today working on some mad science. I have to make something that can log wattage. Something I can leave behind with a single solar cell.

Since I'm stuck here for the day anyway, I'll leave the solar cells out. I may as well get a full battery out of it.

LOG ENTRY: SOL 477

It took all day yesterday and today, but I think I'm ready to measure this storm.

I needed a way to log the time of day and the wattage of each solar cell. One of the cells would be with me, but the other two would be dropped off and left far away. And the solution was the extra EVA suit I brought along.

EVA suits have cameras recording everything they see. There's one on the right arm (or the left if the astronaut is left-handed) and another above the faceplate. A time stamp is burned into the lower left corner of the image, just like on the shaky home videos Dad used to take.

My electronics kit has several power meters. So I figured, why make my own logging system? I can just film the power meter all day long.

So that's what I set up. When I packed for this road trip, I made sure to bring all my kits and tools. Just in case I had to repair the rover en route.

First, I harvested the cameras from my spare EVA suit. I had to be careful; I didn't want to ruin the suit. It's my only spare. I extracted the cameras and the lines leading to their memory chips.

I put a power meter into a small sample container, then glued a camera to the underside of the lid. When I sealed up the container, the camera was properly recording the readout of the power meter.

For testing, I used rover power. How will my logger get power once I abandon it on the surface? It'll be attached to a two-square-meter solar cell! That'll provide plenty of power. And I put a small rechargeable battery in the container to tide it over during nighttime (again, harvested from the spare EVA suit).

The next problem was heat, or the lack thereof. As soon as I take this thing out of the rover, it'll start cooling down mighty fast. If it gets too cold, the electronics will stop working.

So I needed a heat source. And my electronics kit provided the answer: resistors. Lots and lots of them. Resistors heat up. It's what they do. The camera and the power meter only need a tiny fraction of what a solar cell can make. So the rest of the energy goes through resistors.

I made and tested two "power loggers" and

confirmed that the images were being properly recorded.

Then I had an EVA. I detached two of my solar cells and hooked them up to the power loggers. I let them log happily for an hour, then brought them back in to check the results. They worked great.

It's getting toward nightfall now. Tomorrow morning, I'll leave one power logger behind and head south.

While I was working, I left the oxygenator going (why not?). So I'm all stocked up on O_2 and good to go.

The solar cell efficiency for today was 92.5 percent. Compared to yesterday's 97 percent. This proves the storm is moving east to west, because the denser part of the storm was to the east yesterday.

So right now, the sunlight in this area is dropping by 4.5 percent per sol. If I were to stay here another sixteen sols, it would get dark enough to kill me.

Just as well I'm not going to stay here.

LOG ENTRY: SOL 478

Everything went as planned today. No hiccups. I can't tell if I'm driving deeper into the storm or out of it. It's hard to tell if the ambient light is less or more than it was yesterday. The human brain works hard to abstract that out.

I left a power logger behind when I started out. Then, after 40 kilometers' travel due south, I had a quick EVA to set up another. Now I've gone the full 80 kilometers, set up my solar cells for charging, and I'm logging the wattage.

Tomorrow, I'll have to reverse course and pick up the power loggers. It may be dangerous; I'll be driving right back into a known storm area. But the risk is worth the gain.

Also, have I mentioned I'm sick of potatoes? Because, by God, I am sick of potatoes. If I ever return to Earth, I'm going to buy a nice little home in Western Australia. Because Western Australia is on the opposite side of Earth from Idaho.

I bring it up because I dined on a meal pack today. I had saved five packs for special occasions. I ate the first of them twenty-nine sols ago when I left for Schiaparelli, but I totally forgot to eat the second when I reached the halfway point a few sols ago. So I'm enjoying my belated halfway feast.

It's probably more accurate to eat it today anyway. Who knows how long it'll take me to go around this storm? And if I end up stuck in the storm and doomed to die, I'm totally eating the other earmarked meals.

LOG ENTRY: SOL 479

Have you ever taken the wrong freeway entrance? You just need to drive to the next exit to turn around, but you hate every inch of travel because you're going away from your goal.

I felt like that all day. I'm now back where I started yesterday morning. Yuk.

Along the way, I picked up the power logger I'd left behind at the halfway point. Just now I brought in the one I'd left here yesterday.

Both loggers worked the way I'd hoped. I downloaded each of their video recordings to a laptop and advanced them to noon. Finally I had solar efficiency readings from three locations along an 80-kilometer line, all from the same time of day.

As of noon yesterday, the northernmost logger showed 12.3 percent efficiency loss, the middle one had a 9.5 percent loss, and the rover recorded a 6.4 percent loss at its southernmost location. It paints a pretty clear picture: The storm's north of me. And I already worked out it's traveling west.

So I should be able to avoid it by heading south a ways, letting it pass me to the north, then heading east again.

Finally, some good news! Southeast is what I wanted. I won't lose much time.

Sigh . . . I have to drive the same god damned path a third time tomorrow.

LOG ENTRY: SOL 480

I think I'm getting ahead of the storm.

Having traveled along Mars Highway 1 all day, I'm back at my campsite from yesterday. Tomorrow, I'll finally make real headway again. I was done driving and had the camp set up by noon. The efficiency loss here is 15.6 percent. Compared to the 17 percent loss at yesterday's camp, this means I can outrun the storm as long as I keep heading south.

Hopefully.

The storm is *probably* circular. They usually are. But I could just be driving into an alcove. If that's the case, I'm just fucking dead, okay? There's only so much I can do.

I'll know soon enough. If the storm is circular,

I should get better and better efficiency every day until I'm back to 100 percent. Once I reach 100 percent, that means I'm completely south of the storm and I can start going east again. We'll see.

If there were no storm, I'd be going directly southeast toward my goal. As it is, going only south, I'm not nearly as fast. I'm traveling 90 kilometers per day as usual, but I only get 37 kilometers closer to Schiaparelli because Pythagoras is a dick. I don't know when I'll finally clear the storm and be able to beeline to Schiaparelli again. But one thing's for sure: My plan to arrive on Sol 494 is boned.

Sol 549. That's when they come for me. If I miss it, I'll spend the rest of my very short life here. And I still have the MAV to modify before then, too.

Sheesh.

LOG ENTRY: SOL 482

Air Day. A time for relaxation and speculation.

For relaxation, I read eighty pages of Agatha Christie's *Evil Under the Sun* courtesy of Johanssen's digital book collection. I think Linda Marshall is the murderer.

As for speculation, I speculated on when the hell I'll get past this storm.

I'm still going due south every day; and still dealing with efficiency loss (though I'm keeping ahead of it). Every day of this crap I'm only getting 37 kilometers closer to the MAV instead of 90. Pissing me off.

I considered skipping the Air Day. I could go another couple of days before I ran out of oxygen, and getting away from the storm is pretty important. But I decided against it. I'm far enough ahead of the storm that I can afford one day of no movement. And I don't know if a couple more days would help. Who knows how far south the storm goes?

Well, NASA probably knows. And the news stations back on Earth are probably showing it. And there's probably a website like www.watch-mark-watney-die.com. So there's like a hundred million people or so who know exactly how far south it goes.

But I'm not one of them.

LOG ENTRY: SOL 484

Finally!

I am FINALLY past the god damned storm. Today's power regen was 100 percent. No more dust in the air. With the storm moving perpendicular to my direction of travel, it means I'm south of the southernmost point of the cloud (presuming it's a circular storm. If it's not, then fuck).

Starting tomorrow, I can go directly toward Schiaparelli. Which is good, 'cause I lost a lot of time. I went 540 kilometers due south while avoiding that storm. I'm catastrophically off course.

Mind you, it hasn't been that bad. I'm well into Terra Meridiani now, and the driving is a little easier here than the rugged, ass-kicking terrain of Arabia Terra. Schiaparelli is almost due east, and if my sextant and Phobos calculations are correct, I've got another 1030 kilometers to get there.

Accounting for Air Days and presuming 90 kilometers of travel per sol, I should arrive on Sol

498. Not too bad, really. The Nearly-Mark-Killin' storm only ended up delaying me by four sols.

I'll still have forty-four sols to do whatever MAV modifications NASA has in mind.

LOG ENTRY: SOL 487

I have an interesting opportunity here. And by "opportunity" I mean *Opportunity.*

I got pushed so far off course, I'm actually not far from the Mars exploration rover *Opportunity.* It's about 300 kilometers away. I could get there in about four sols.

Damn it's tempting. If I could get *Opportunity*'s radio working, I'd be in touch with humanity again. NASA would continually tell me my exact position and best course, warn me if another storm was on its way, and generally be there watching over me.

But if I'm being honest, that's not the real reason I'm interested. I'm sick of being on my own, damn it! Once I got *Pathfinder* working, I got used to talking to Earth. All that went away because I leaned a drill against the wrong table, and now I'm alone again. I could end that in just four sols.

But it's an irrational, stupid thought. I'm only eleven sols away from the MAV. Why go out of my way to dig up another broken-ass rover to use as a makeshift radio when I'll have a brand-new, fully functional communications system within a couple of weeks?

So, while it's really tempting that I'm within striking range of another rover (man, we really littered this planet with them, didn't we?), it's not the smart move.

Besides, I've defiled enough future historical sites for now.

LOG ENTRY: SOL 492

I need to put some thought into the bedroom.

Right now, I can only have it set up when I'm inside the rover. It attaches to the airlock, so I can't get out if it's there. During my road trip that doesn't matter, because I have to furl it every day anyway. But once I get to the MAV, I won't have to drive around anymore. Each decompress/recompress of the bedroom stresses the seams (I learned that lesson the hard way when the Hab blew up), so it's best if I can find a way to leave it out.

Holy shit. I just realized I actually believe I'll get to the MAV. See what I did there? I casually talked about what I'll do after I get to the MAV. Like it was nothing. No big deal. I'm just going to pop over to Schiaparelli and hang with the MAV there.

Nice.

Anyway, I don't have another airlock. I've got one on the rover and one on the trailer and that's it. They're firmly fixed in place, so it's not like I can detach one and attach it to the bedroom.

But I can seal the bedroom entirely. I don't even have to do any hatchet jobs on it. The airlock attachment point has a flap I can unroll and seal the opening with. Remember, I stole the airlock attachment from a pop-tent, which is an emergency feature for pressure loss while in the rover. It'd be pretty useless if it couldn't seal itself off.

Unfortunately, as an emergency device, it was

never intended to be reusable. The idea was that people seal themselves in the pop-tent, then the rest of the crew drives to wherever they are in the other rover and rescues them. The crew of the good rover detaches the pop-tent from the breached rover and reattaches it to theirs. Then they cut through the seal from their side to recover their crewmates.

To make sure this would always be an option, mission rules dictated no more than three people could be in a rover at once, and both rovers had to be fully functional or we couldn't use either.

So here's my brilliant plan: I won't use the bedroom as a bedroom anymore once I get to the MAV. I'll use it to house the oxygenator and atmospheric regulator. Then I'll use the trailer as my bedroom. Neat, eh?

The trailer has tons of space. I put a shitload of work into making that happen. The balloon gives plenty of headroom. Not a lot of floor space, but still lots of vertical area.

Also, the bedroom has several valve apertures in its canvas. I have the Hab's design to thank for that. The canvas I stole from it has valve apertures (triple-redundant ones, actually). NASA wanted to make sure the Hab could be refilled from the outside if necessary.

In the end, I'll have the bedroom sealed with the oxygenator and atmospheric regulator inside. It'll be attached to the trailer via hoses to share the same atmosphere, and I'll run a power line through one of the hoses. The rover will serve as storage (because I won't need to get to the driving controls anymore), and the trailer will be completely empty. Then I'll have a permanent bedroom. I'll even be able to use it as a workshop for whatever MAV modifications I need to do on parts that can fit through the trailer's airlock.

Of course, if the atmospheric regulator or oxygenator have problems, I'll need to cut into the bedroom to get to them. But I've been here 492 sols and they've worked fine the whole time, so I'll take that risk.

LOG ENTRY: SOL 497

I'll be at the entrance to Schiaparelli tomorrow!

Presuming nothing goes wrong, that is. But hey, everything else has gone smoothly this mission, right? (That was sarcasm.)

Today's an Air Day, and for once, I don't want it. I'm so close to Schiaparelli, I can taste it. I guess it would taste like sand, mostly, but that's not the point.

Of course, that won't be the end of the trip. It'll take another three sols to get from the entrance to the MAV, but hot damn! I'm almost there!

I think I can even see the rim of Schiaparelli. It's way the hell off in the distance and it might just be my imagination. It's 62 kilometers away, so if I'm seeing it, I'm only just barely seeing it.

Tomorrow, once I get to Entrance Crater, I'll turn south and enter the Schiaparelli Basin via the "Entrance Ramp." I did some back-of-the-napkin math, and the slope should be pretty safe. The elevation change from the rim to the basin is 1.5 kilometers, and the ramp is at least 45 kilometers long. That makes for a two-degree grade. No problem.

Tomorrow night, I'll sink to an all-new low!

Lemme rephrase that. . . .

Tomorrow night, I'll be at rock bottom!

No, that doesn't sound good either. . . .

Tomorrow night, I'll be in Giovanni Schiaparelli's favorite hole!

Okay, I admit I'm just playing around now.

▪ ▪ ▪

FOR MILLIONS of years, the rim of the crater had been under constant attack from wind. It eroded the rocky crest the way a river cuts through a mountain range. After eons, it finally breached the edge.

The high-pressure zone created by the wind now had an avenue to drain. The breach widened more and more with each passing millennium. As it widened, dust and sand particles carried along with the attack settled in the basin below.

Eventually, a balance point was reached. The sand had piled up high enough to be flush with the land outside the crater. It no longer built upward but outward. The slope lengthened until a new balance point was reached, one defined by the complex interactions of countless tiny particles and their ability to maintain an angled shape. Entrance Ramp had been born.

The weather brought dunes and desert terrain. Nearby crater impacts brought rocks and boulders. The shape became uneven.

Gravity did its work. The ramp compressed over time. But it did not compress evenly. Differing densities shrunk at different rates. Some areas became hard as rock while others remained as soft as talc.

While providing a small *average* slope into the

crater, the ramp itself was rugged and bitterly uneven.

On reaching Entrance Crater, the lone inhabitant of Mars turned his vehicle toward the Schiaparelli Basin. The difficult terrain of the ramp was unexpected, but it looked no worse than other terrain he routinely navigated.

He went around the smaller dunes and carefully crested the larger ones. He took care with every turn, every rise or fall in elevation, and every boulder in his path. He thought through every course and considered all alternatives.

But it wasn't enough.

The rover, while descending down a seemingly ordinary slope, drove off an invisible ridge. The dense, hard soil suddenly gave way to soft powder. With the entire surface covered by at least five centimeters of dust, there were no visual hints to the sudden change.

The rover's left front wheel sank. The sudden tilt brought the right rear wheel completely off the ground. This in turn put more weight on the left rear wheel, which slipped from its precarious purchase into the powder as well.

Before the traveler could react, the rover rolled onto its side. As it did, the solar cells neatly stacked on the roof flew off and scattered like a dropped deck of cards.

The trailer, attached to the rover with a tow clamp, was dragged along. The torsion on the clamp snapped the strong composite like a brittle twig. The hoses connecting the two vehicles also snapped. The trailer plunged headlong into the soft soil and flipped over on to its balloon-roof, shuddering to an abrupt halt.

The rover was not so lucky. It continued tumbling down the hill, bouncing the traveler around like clothes in a dryer. After twenty meters, the soft powder gave way to more solid sand and the rover shuddered to a halt.

It had come to rest on its side. The valves leading to the now-missing hoses had detected the sudden pressure drop and closed. The pressure seal was not breached.

The traveler was alive, for now.

CHAPTER 24

THE DEPARTMENT heads stared at the satellite image on the projection screen.

"Jesus," Mitch said. "What the hell happened?"

"The rover's on its side," Mindy said, pointing to the screen. "The trailer's upside down. Those rectangles scattered around are solar cells."

Venkat put a hand on his chin. "Do we have any information on the state of the rover pressure vessel?"

"Nothing obvious," Mindy said.

"Any signs of Watney doing something after the accident? An EVA maybe?"

"No EVA," Mindy said. "The weather's clear. If he'd come out, there'd be visible footsteps."

"Is this the entire crash site?" Bruce Ng asked.

"I think so," Mindy said. "Up toward the top of the photo, which is north, there are ordinary wheel tracks. Right here," she pointed to a large disturbance in the soil, "is where I think things went wrong. Judging by where that ditch is, I'd say the rover rolled and slid from there. You can see the trench it left behind. The trailer flipped forward onto its roof."

"I'm not saying everything's okay," Bruce said, "but I don't think it's as bad as it looks."

"Go on," Venkat said.

"The rover's designed to handle a roll," Bruce explained. "And if there'd been pressure loss, there'd be a starburst pattern in the sand. I don't see anything like that."

"Watney may still be hurt inside," Mitch said. "He could have banged his head or broken an arm or something."

"Sure," Bruce said. "I'm just saying the rover is probably okay."

"When was this taken?"

Mindy checked her watch. "We got it seventeen minutes ago. We'll get another pic in nine minutes when MGS4's orbit brings it into view."

"First thing he'll do is an EVA to assess damage," Venkat said. "Mindy, keep us posted on any changes."

LOG ENTRY: SOL 498

Hmm.

Yeah.

Things didn't go well on the descent into Schiaparelli Basin. To give you some indication of how unwell they went, I'm reaching up to the computer to type this. Because it's still mounted near the control panel, and the rover is on its side.

I got bounced around a lot, but I'm a well-honed machine in times of crisis. As soon as the rover toppled, I curled into a ball and cowered. That's the kind of action hero I am.

It worked, too. 'Cause I'm not hurt.

The pressure vessel is intact, so that's a plus. The valves that lead to the trailer hoses are shut. Probably means the hoses disconnected. And that means the trailer junction snapped. Wonderful.

Looking around the interior here, I don't think anything is broken. The water tanks stayed sealed. There aren't any visible leaks in the air tanks. The bedroom came unfolded, and it's all over the place, but it's just canvas, so it can't have gotten too hurt.

The driving controls are okay, and the nav computer is telling me the rover is at an "unacceptably dangerous tilt." Thanks, Nav!

So I rolled. That's not the end of the world. I'm alive and the rover's fine. I'm more worried about the solar cells I probably rolled over. Also, since the trailer detached, there's a good chance it's fucked up, too. The balloon roof it has isn't exactly durable. If it popped, the shit inside will have been flung out in all directions and I'll have to go find it. That's my critical life support.

Speaking of life support, the rover switched over to the local tanks when the valves shut. Good boy, Rover! Here's a Scooby Snack.

I've got twenty liters of oxygen (enough to keep me breathing for forty days), but without the regulator (which is in the trailer) I'm back to chemical CO_2 absorption. I have 312 hours of filters left. Plus I have another 171 hours of EVA suit CO_2 filters as well. All told, that gives me 483 hours, which is close to twenty sols. So I have time to get things working again.

I'm really damn close to the MAV now. About

220 kilometers. I'm not going to let something like this stop me from getting there. And I don't need everything to work at top form anymore. I just need the rover to work for 220 more kilometers and the life support to work for fifty-one more sols. That's it.

Time to suit up and look for the trailer.

LOG ENTRY: SOL 498 (2)

I had an EVA and things aren't too bad. Mind you, they're not good.

I trashed three solar cells. They're under the rover and cracked all to hell. They might still be able to piss out a few watts, but I'm not holding out much hope. Luckily, I did come into this with one extra solar cell. I needed twenty-eight for my daily operations and I brought twenty-nine (fourteen on the rover's roof, seven on the trailer's roof, and eight on the makeshift shelves I installed on the sides of both vehicles).

I tried pushing the rover over, but I wasn't strong enough. I'll need to rig something to get a leverage advantage. Other than being on its side, I don't see any real problems.

Well, that's not true. The tow hook is ruined beyond repair. Half of it ripped clean off. Fortunately, the trailer also has a tow hook, so I have a spare.

The trailer's in a precarious situation. It's upside down and sitting on the inflated roof. I'm not sure which god smiled down on me and kept that balloon from popping, but I'm grateful. My first priority will be righting it. The longer it puts weight on that balloon, the larger the chances it'll pop.

While I was out, I collected the twenty-six solar

cells that aren't under the rover and set them up to recharge my batteries. May as well, right?

So right now, I have a few problems to tackle: First, I need to right the trailer. Or at least get the weight off the balloon. Next, I need to right the rover. Finally, I need to replace the rover's tow hook with the one on the trailer.

Also, I should spell out a message for NASA. They're probably worried.

▪▪▪

MINDY READ the Morse code aloud. "ROLLED. FIXING NOW."

"What? That's it?" Venkat said over the phone.

"That's all he said," she reported, cradling the phone as she typed out an e-mail to the list of interested parties.

"Just three words? Nothing about his physical health? His equipment? His supplies?"

"You got me," she said. "He left a detailed status report. I just decided to lie for no reason."

"Funny," Venkat said. "Be a smart-ass to a guy seven levels above you at your company. See how that works out."

"Oh no," Mindy said. "I might lose my job as an interplanetary voyeur? I guess I'd have to use my master's degree for something else."

"I remember when you were shy."

"I'm space paparazzi now. The attitude comes with the job."

"Yeah, yeah," Venkat said. "Just send the e-mail."

"Already sent."

LOG ENTRY: SOL 499

I had a busy day today, and I got a lot done.

I started out pretty sore. I had to sleep on the wall of the rover. The bedroom won't work when the airlock is facing up. I did get to use the bedroom, somewhat. I folded it up and used it as a bed.

Anyway, suffice it to say, the wall of the rover wasn't made for sleeping on. But after a morning potato and Vicodin, I was feeling much better.

At first I figured my top priority was the trailer. Then I changed my mind. After taking a good look at it, I decided I'd never be able to right it by myself. I'd need the rover.

So today was focused on getting the rover righted.

I brought all my tools along on this trip, figuring I'd need them for the MAV modifications. And along with them I brought cabling. Once I get set up at the MAV, my solar cells and batteries will be in a fixed position. I don't want to move the rover around every time I use a drill on the far side of the MAV. So I brought all the electrical cabling I could fit.

Good thing, too. Because it doubles as rope.

I dug up my longest cable. It's the same one I used to power the drill that destroyed *Pathfinder*. I call it my "lucky cable."

I plugged one end into the battery and the other into the infamous sample drill, then walked off with the drill to find solid ground. Once I found it, I kept going until I'd gone as far as the electrical line would reach. I drove a one-meter bit half a meter into a rock, unplugged the power line, and tied it around the base of the bit.

Then I went back to the rover and tied off the cord to the roof-rack bar on the high side. Now I had a long, taut line running perpendicular to the rover.

I walked to the middle of the cord and pulled it laterally. The leverage advantage on the rover was huge. I only hoped it wouldn't break the drill bit before it tipped the rover.

I backed away, pulling the line more and more. Something had to give, and it wasn't going to be me. I had Archimedes on my side. The rover finally tipped.

It fell onto its wheels, kicking up a large cloud of soft dust. It was a silent affair. I was far enough away that the thin atmosphere had no hope of carrying the sound to me.

I untied the power line, liberated the drill bit, and returned to the rover. I gave it a full system's check. That's a boring-as-hell task, but I had to do it.

Every system and subsystem was working correctly. JPL did a damn good job making these rovers. If I get back to Earth, I'm buying Bruce Ng a beer. Though I guess I should buy all the JPL guys a beer.

Beers for everyone if I get back to Earth.

Anyway, with the rover back on its wheels it was time to work on the trailer. Problem is, I ran out of daylight. Remember, I'm in a crater.

I had gotten part of the way down the Ramp when I rolled the rover. And the Ramp is up against the western edge of the crater. So the sun sets really early from my point of view. I'm in the shadow of the western wall. And that royally sucks.

Mars is not Earth. It doesn't have a thick atmosphere to bend light and carry particles that reflect light around corners. It's damn near a vacuum here. Once the sun isn't visible, I'm in the dark. Phobos gives me some moonlight, but not enough to work with. Deimos is a little piece of crap that's no good to anyone.

I hate to leave the trailer sitting on its balloon for another night, but there's not much else I can do. I figure it's survived a whole day like that. It's probably stable for now.

And hey, with the rover righted, I get to use the bedroom again! It's the simple things in life that matter.

LOG ENTRY: SOL 500

When I woke up this morning, the trailer hadn't popped yet. So that was a good start.

The trailer was a bigger challenge than the rover. I only had to tip the rover. I'd need to completely flip the trailer. That requires a lot more force than yesterday's little leverage trick.

The first step was to drive the rover to near the trailer. Then came the digging.

Oh God, the digging.

The trailer was upside down, with its nose pointed downhill. I decided the best way to right it was to take advantage of the slope and roll the trailer over its nose. Basically to make it do a somersault to land on its wheels.

I can make this happen by tying off the cable to the rear of the trailer and towing with the rover.

But if I tried that without digging a hole first, the trailer would just slide along the ground. I needed it to tip up. I needed a hole for the nose to fall into.

So I dug a hole. A hole one meter across, three meters wide, and one meter deep. It took me four miserable hours of hard labor, but I got it done.

I hopped in the rover and drove it downhill, dragging the trailer with me. As I'd hoped, the trailer nosed into the hole and tipped up. From there, it fell onto its wheels with a huge plume of dust.

Then I sat for a moment, dumbstruck that my plan had actually worked.

And now I'm out of daylight again. I can't wait to get out of this damn shadow. All I need is one day of driving toward the MAV and I'll be away from the wall. But for now it's another early night.

I'll spend tonight without the trailer to manage my life support. It may be righted, but I have no idea if the shit inside still works. The rover still has ample supplies for me.

I'll spend the rest of the evening enjoying a potato. And by "enjoying" I mean "hating so much I want to kill people."

LOG ENTRY: SOL 501

I started the day with some nothin' tea. Nothin' tea is easy to make. First, get some hot water, then add nothin'. I experimented with potato skin tea a few weeks ago. The less said about that the better.

I ventured into the trailer today. Not an easy task. It's pretty cramped in there; I had to leave my EVA suit in the airlock.

The first thing I noticed was that it was really

hot inside. It took me a few minutes to work out why.

The atmospheric regulator was still in perfect working order, but it had nothing to do. Without being connected to the rover, it no longer had my CO_2 production to deal with. The atmosphere in the trailer was perfect—why change anything?

With no regulation necessary, the air was not being pumped out to the AREC for freeze-separation. And thus it wasn't coming back in as a liquid in need of heating.

But remember, the RTG gives off heat all the time. You can't stop it. So the heat just built up. Eventually, things reached a balance point where the heat bled through the hull as fast as the RTG could add it. If you're curious, that balance point was a sweltering 41°C.

I did a full diagnostic on the regulator and the oxygenator, and I'm happy to report both are working perfectly.

The RTG's water tank was empty, which is no surprise. It has an open top, not intended to be turned upside down. The floor of the trailer has a lot of puddled water that took me quite a while to sop up with my jumpsuit. I topped the tank off with some more water from a sealed container that I'd stored in the trailer earlier. Remember, I need that water to have something for the returning air to bubble through. That's my heating system.

But all things considered, it was good news. The critical components are working fine, and both vehicles are back on their wheels.

The hoses that connected the rover and trailer were designed well, and released without breaking. I simply snapped them back into place and the vehicles were sharing life support again.

The one remaining thing to fix was the tow hook. It was absolutely ruined. It took the full force of the crash. But as I suspected, the trailer's tow hook was unscathed. So I transferred it to the rover and reconnected the two vehicles for travel.

All told, that little fender bender cost me four sols. But now I'm back in action!

Sort of.

What if I run into another powder pit? I got lucky this time. Next time I might not get off so easy. I need a way to know if the ground in front of me is safe. At least for the duration of my time on the Ramp. Once I'm in the Schiaparelli Basin proper, I can count on the normal sandy terrain I'm used to.

If I could have anything, it would be a radio to ask NASA the safe path down the Ramp. Well, if I could have *anything,* it would be for the green-skinned yet beautiful Queen of Mars to rescue me so she can learn more about this Earth thing called "lovemaking."

It's been a long time since I've seen a woman. Just sayin'.

Anyway, to ensure I don't crash again, I'll—Seriously . . . no women in like, years. I don't ask for much. Believe me, even back on Earth a botanist/mechanical engineer doesn't exactly have ladies lined up at the door. But still, c'mon.

Anyway. I'll drive slower. Like . . . a crawl. That should give me enough time to react if one wheel starts to sink. Also, the lower speed will give me more torque, making it less likely I'll lose traction.

Up till now I've been driving 25 kph, so I'm

going to cut that to 5 kph. I'm still toward the top of the Ramp, but the whole thing is only 45 kilometers. I can take my time and get safely to the bottom in about eight hours.

I'll do it tomorrow. I'm already out of daylight again today. That's another bonus: Once I clear the ramp, I can start beelining toward the MAV, which will take me away from the crater wall. I'll be back to enjoying the entire day's sunlight instead of just half of it.

If I get back to Earth, I'll be famous, right? A fearless astronaut who beat all the odds, right? I bet women like that.

More motivation to stay alive.

■ ■ ■

"So, it looks like he's fixed everything," Mindy explained. "And his message today was 'ALL BETTER NOW,' so I guess he's got everything working."

She surveyed the smiling faces in the meeting room.

"Awesome," Mitch said.

"Great news." Bruce's voice came in through the speakerphone.

Venkat leaned forward to the phone. "How are the MAV modification plans coming, Bruce? Is JPL going to have that procedure soon?"

"We're working around the clock on it," Bruce said. "We're past most of the big hurdles. Working out the details now."

"Good, good," Venkat said. "Any surprises I should know about?"

"Um . . . ," Bruce said. "Yeah, a few. This might not be the best venue for it. I'll be back in Houston with the procedure in a day or two. We can go through it then."

"Ominous," Venkat said. "But okay, we'll pick it up later."

"Can I spread the word?" Annie asked. "It'd be nice to see something other than the rover crash site on the news tonight."

"Definitely," Venkat said. "It'll be nice to have some good news for a change. Mindy, how long until he gets to the MAV?"

"At his usual rate of 90 kilometers per sol," Mindy said, "he should get there on Sol 504. Sol 505 if he takes his time. He always drives in the early morning, finishing around noon." She checked an application on her laptop. "Noon on Sol 504 will be 11:41 a.m. this Wednesday here in Houston. Noon on Sol 505 will be 12:21 p.m. on Thursday."

"Mitch, who's handling Ares 4 MAV communications?"

"The Ares 3 Mission Control team," Mitch replied. "It'll be in Control Room 2."

"I assume you'll be there?"

"Bet your ass I'll be there."

"So will I."

LOG ENTRY: SOL 502

Every Thanksgiving, my family used to drive from Chicago to Sandusky, an eight-hour drive. It's where Mom's sister lived. Dad always drove, and he was the slowest, most cautious driver who ever took the wheel.

Seriously. He drove like he was taking a driver's test. Never exceeded the speed limit, always had his hands at ten and two, adjusted mirrors before each outing, you name it.

It was infuriating. We'd be on the freeway, cars blowing by left and right. Some of them would blare their horns because, honestly, driving the speed limit makes you a road hazard. I wanted to get out and push.

I felt that way all damn day today. Five kph is literally a walking pace. And I drove that speed for eight hours.

But the slow speed ensured that I wouldn't fall into any more powder pits along the way. And of course I didn't encounter any. I could have driven full speed and had no problems. But better safe than sorry.

The good news is I'm off the Ramp. I camped out as soon as the terrain flattened out. I've already overdone my driving time for the day. I could go further, I still have 15 percent battery power or so, but I want to get as much daylight on my solar cells as I can.

I'm in the Schiaparelli Basin at last! Far from the crater wall, too. I get a full day of sunlight every day from now on.

I decided it was time for a very special occasion. I ate the meal pack labeled "Survived Something That Should Have Killed Me." Oh my god, I forgot how good real food tastes.

With luck, I'll get to eat "Arrival" in a few sols.

LOG ENTRY: SOL 503

I didn't get as much recharge as I usually would yesterday. Because of my extended driving time, I only got up to 70 percent before night fell. So today's driving was abbreviated.

I got 63 kilometers before I had to camp out again. But I don't even mind. Because I'm only 148 kilometers from the MAV. That means I'll get there the sol after tomorrow.

Holy hell, I'm really going to make it!

LOG ENTRY: SOL 504

Holy shit, this is awesome! Holy shit! Holy shit!

Okay calm. Calm.

I made 90 kilometers today. By my estimate, I'm 50 kilometers from the MAV. I should get there sometime tomorrow. I'm excited about that, but here's what I'm really stoked about: I caught a blip from the MAV!

NASA has the MAV broadcasting the Ares 3 Hab homing signal. Why wouldn't they? It makes perfect sense. The MAV is a sleek, perfectly functional machine, ready to do what it's told. And they have it pretending to be the Ares 3 Hab, so my rover will see the signal and tell me where it is.

That is an *exceptionally* good idea! I won't have to wander around looking for the thing. I'm going straight to it.

I only caught a blip. I'll get more as I get closer. It's strange to think that a sand dune will stop me from hearing what the MAV has to say when it can talk to Earth no problem. The MAV has three redundant methods of communicating with Earth, but they're all extremely directed and are designed for line-of-sight communication. And there aren't any sand dunes between it and Earth when they talk.

Somehow they messed with things to make a radial signal, however weak it may be. And I heard it!

My message for the day was "GOT BEACON SIGNAL." If I'd had enough rocks, I would have added, "AWESOME IDEA!!!" But it's a really sandy area.

▪▪▪

THE MAV waited in southwestern Schiaparelli. It stood an impressive twenty-seven meters tall, its conical body gleaming in the midday sun.

The rover crested a nearby dune with the trailer in tow. It slowed for a few moments, then continued toward the ship at top speed. It came to a stop twenty meters away.

There it remained for ten minutes while the astronaut inside suited up.

He stumbled excitedly out of the airlock, falling to the ground then scrambling to his feet. Beholding the MAV, he gestured to it with both arms, as if in disbelief.

He leaped into the air several times, arms held high with fists clenched. Then he knelt on one knee and fist-pumped repeatedly.

Running to the spacecraft, he hugged Landing Strut B. After a few moments, he broke off the embrace to perform another round of leaping celebrations.

Now fatigued, the astronaut stood with arms akimbo, looking up at the sleek lines of the engineering marvel before him.

Climbing the ladder on the landing stage, he reached the ascent stage and entered the airlock. He sealed the door behind him.

CHAPTER 25

LOG ENTRY: SOL 505

I finally made it! I'm at the MAV!

Well, right this second, I'm back in the rover. I did go into the MAV to do a systems check and boot-up. I had to keep my EVA suit on the whole time because there's no life support in there just yet.

It's going through a self-check right now, and I'm feeding it oxygen and nitrogen with hoses from the rover. This is all part of the MAV's design. It doesn't bring air along. Why would it? That's a needless weight when you'll have a Hab full of air right next door.

I'm guessing folks at NASA are popping champagne right now and sending me lots of messages. I'll read them in a bit. First things first: Get the MAV some life support. Then I'll be able to work inside comfortably.

And then I'll have a boring conversation with NASA. Well, the content may be interesting, but the fourteen-minute transmission time between here and Earth will be a bit dull.

■ ■ ■

[13:07] HOUSTON: Congratulations from all of us here at Mission Control! Well done! What's your status?

[13:21] MAV: Thanks! No health or physical problems. The rover and trailer are getting pretty worn out, but still functional. Oxygenator and regulator both working fine. I didn't bring the water reclaimer. Just brought the water. Plenty of potatoes left. I'm good to last till 549.

[13:36] HOUSTON: Glad to hear it. Hermes is still on track for a Sol 549 flyby. As you know, the MAV will need to lose some weight to make the intercept. We're going to get you those procedures within the day. How much water do you have? What did you do with urine?

[13:50] MAV: I have 550 liters of remaining water. I've been dumping urine outside along the way.

[14:05] HOUSTON: Preserve all water. Don't do any more urine dumps. Store it somewhere. Turn the rover's radio on and leave it on. We can contact it through the MAV.

■ ■ ■

BRUCE TRUDGED into Venkat's office and unceremoniously plopped down in a chair. He dropped his briefcase and let his arms hang limp.

"Have a good flight?" Venkat asked.

"I only have a passing memory of what sleep is," Bruce said.

"So is it ready?" Venkat asked.

"Yes, it's ready. But you're not going to like it."

"Go on."

Bruce steeled himself and stood, picking up his briefcase. He pulled a booklet from it. "Bear in mind, this is the end result of thousands of hours of work, testing, and lateral thinking by all the best guys at JPL."

"I'm sure it was hard to trim down a ship that's already designed to be as light as possible," Venkat said.

Bruce slid the booklet across the desk to Venkat. "The problem is the intercept velocity. The MAV is designed to get to low Mars orbit, which only requires 4.1 kps. But the *Hermes* flyby will be at 5.8 kps."

Venkat flipped through the pages. "Care to summarize?"

"First, we're going to add fuel. The MAV makes its own fuel from the Martian atmosphere, but it's limited by how much hydrogen it has. It brought enough to make 19,397 kilograms of fuel, as it was designed to do. If we can give it more hydrogen, it can make more."

"How much more?"

"For every kilogram of hydrogen, it can make thirteen kilograms of fuel. Watney has five hundred and fifty liters of water. We'll have him electrolyze it to get sixty kilograms of hydrogen." Bruce reached over the desk and flipped a few pages, pointing to a diagram. "The fuel plant can make seven hundred and eighty kilograms of fuel from that."

"If he electrolyzes his water, what'll he drink?"

"He only needs fifty liters for the time he has left. And a human body only borrows water. We'll have him electrolyze his urine, too. We need all the hydrogen we can get our hands on."

"I see. And what does seven hundred and eighty kilograms of fuel buy us?" Venkat asked.

"It buys us 300 kilograms of payload. It's all about fuel versus payload. The MAV's launch weight is over 12,600 kilograms. Even with the bonus fuel, we'll need to get that down to 7,300 kilograms. So the rest of this booklet is how to remove over 5,000 kilograms from the ship."

Venkat leaned back. "Walk me through it."

Bruce pulled another copy of the booklet from his briefcase. "There were some gimmes right off the bat. The design presumes five hundred kilograms of Martian soil and rock samples. Obviously we won't do that. Also, there's just one passenger instead of six. That saves five hundred kilograms when you consider their weight plus their suits and gear. And we can lose the other five acceleration chairs. And of course, we'll remove all nonessential gear—the med kit, tool kit, internal harnessing, straps, and anything else that isn't nailed down. And some stuff that is.

"Next up," he continued. "We're ditching all life support. The tanks, pumps, heaters, air lines, CO_2 absorption system, even the insulation on the inner side of the hull. We don't need it. We'll have Watney wear his EVA suit for the whole trip."

"Won't that make it awkward for him to use the controls?" Venkat asked.

"He won't be using them," Bruce said. "Major Martinez will pilot the MAV remotely from *Hermes*. It's already designed for remote piloting. It was remotely landed, after all."

"What if something goes wrong?" Venkat asked.

"Martinez is the best trained pilot," Bruce said. "If there is an emergency, he's the guy you want controlling the ship."

"Hmm," Venkat said cautiously. "We've never had a manned ship controlled remotely before. But okay, go on."

"Since Watney won't be flying the ship," Bruce continued, "he won't need the controls. We'll ditch the control panels and all the power and data lines that lead to them."

"Wow," Venkat said. "We're really gutting this thing."

"I'm just getting started," Bruce said. "The power needs will be dramatically reduced now that life support is gone, so we'll dump three of the five batteries and the auxiliary power system. The orbital maneuvering system has three redundant thrusters. We'll get rid of those. Also, the secondary and tertiary comm systems can go."

"Wait, what?" Venkat said, shocked. "You're going to have a remote-controlled ascent with no backup comm systems?"

"No point," Bruce said. "If the comm system goes out during ascent, the time it takes to reacquire will be too long to do any good. The backups don't help us."

"This is getting really risky, Bruce."

Bruce sighed. "I know. There's just no other way. And I'm not even to the nasty stuff yet."

Venkat rubbed his forehead. "By all means, tell me the nasty stuff."

"We'll remove the nose airlock, the windows, and Hull Panel Nineteen."

Venkat blinked. "You're taking the front of the ship off?"

"Sure," Bruce said. "The nose airlock alone is four hundred kilograms. The windows are pretty damn heavy, too. And they're connected by Hull Panel Nineteen, so may as well take that, too."

"So he's going to launch with a big hole in the front of the ship?"

"We'll have him cover it with Hab canvas."

"Hab canvas? For a launch to orbit!?"

Bruce shrugged. "The hull's mostly there to keep the air in. Mars's atmosphere is so thin you don't need a lot of streamlining. By the time the ship's going fast enough for air resistance to matter, it'll be high enough that there's practically no air. We've run all the simulations. Should be good."

"You're sending him to space under a tarp."

"Pretty much, yeah."

"Like a hastily loaded pickup truck."

"Yeah. Can I go on?"

"Sure, can't wait."

"We'll also have him remove the back panel of the pressure vessel. It's the only other panel he can remove with the tools on hand. Also, we're getting rid of the auxiliary fuel pump. Sad to see it go, but it weighs too much for its usefulness. And we're nixing a Stage One engine."

"An engine?"

"Yeah. The Stage One booster works fine if one engine goes out. It'll save us a huge amount of weight. Only during the Stage One ascent, but still. Pretty good fuel savings."

Bruce fell silent.

"That it?" Venkat asked.

"Yeah."

Venkat sighed. "You've removed most of the safety backups. What's this do to the estimated odds of failure?"

"It's about four percent."

"Jesus Christ," Venkat said. "Normally we'd never even consider something that risky."

"It's all we've got, Venk," Bruce said. "We've tested it all out and run simulations galore. We should be okay if everything works the way it's supposed to."

"Yeah. Great," Venkat said.

■ ■ ■

[08:41] MAV: You fucking kidding me?

[09:55] HOUSTON: Admittedly, they are very invasive modifications, but they have to be done. The procedure doc we sent has instructions for carrying out each of these steps with tools you have on hand. Also, you'll need to start electrolyzing water to get the hydrogen for the fuel plant. We'll send you procedures for that shortly.

[09:09] MAV: You're sending me into space in a convertible.

[09:24] HOUSTON: There will be Hab canvas covering the holes. It will provide enough aerodynamics in Mars's atmosphere.

[09:38] MAV: So it's a ragtop. Much better.

LOG ENTRY: SOL 506

On the way here, in my copious free time, I designed a "workshop." I figured I'd need space to work on stuff without having to wear an EVA suit. I devised a brilliant plan whereby the current bedroom would become the new home of the regulator and the oxygenator, and the now-empty trailer would become my workshop.

It's a stupid idea, and I'm not doing it.

All I need is a pressurized area that I can work in. I somehow convinced myself that the bedroom wasn't an option because it's a hassle to get stuff into it. But it won't be that bad.

It attaches to the rover airlock, so the getting stuff in is going to be annoying. Bring the stuff into the rover, attach the bedroom to the airlock from the inside, inflate it, bring the stuff into the bedroom. I'll also have to empty the bedroom of all tools and equipment to fold it up any time I need to do an EVA.

So yeah, it'll be annoying, but all it costs me is time. And I'm actually doing well on that front. I have forty-three more sols before *Hermes* flies by. And looking at the procedure NASA has in mind for the modifications, I can take advantage of the MAV itself as a workspace.

The lunatics at NASA have me doing all kinds of rape to the MAV, but I don't have to open the hull till the end. So the first thing I'll do is clear out a bunch of clutter, like chairs and control panels and the like. Once they're out, I'll have a lot of room in there to work.

But I didn't do anything to the soon-to-be-mutilated MAV today. Today was all about system checks. Now that I'm back in contact with NASA, I have to go back to being all "safety first." Strangely, NASA doesn't have total faith in my kludged-together rover or my method of piling everything into the trailer. They had me do a full systems check on every single component.

Everything's still working fine, though it's wearing down. The regulator and the oxygenator are at less-than-peak efficiency (to say the least), and the trailer leaks some air every day. Not enough to cause problems, but it's not a perfect seal. NASA's pretty uncomfortable with it, but we don't have any other options.

Then, they had me run a full diagnostic on the MAV. That's in much better shape. Everything's sleek and pristine and perfectly functional. I'd almost forgotten what new hardware even looks like.

Pity I'm going to tear it apart.

■ ■ ■

"YOU KILLED Watney," Lewis said.

"Yeah," Martinez said, scowling at his monitor. The words "Collision with Terrain" blinked accusingly.

"I pulled a nasty trick on him," Johanssen said. "I gave him a malfunctioning altitude readout and made Engine Three cut out too early. It's a deadly combination."

"Shouldn't have been a mission failure," Martinez said. "I should have noticed the readout was wrong. It was way off."

"Don't sweat it," Lewis said. "That's why we drill."

"Aye, Commander," Martinez said. He furrowed his brow and frowned at the screen.

Lewis waited for him to snap out of it. When he didn't, she put a hand on his shoulder.

"Don't beat yourself up," she said. "They only gave you two days of remote launch training. It was only supposed to happen if we aborted before landing; a cut-our-losses scenario where we'd launch the MAV to act as a satellite. It wasn't mission-critical so they didn't drill you too hard on it. Now that Mark's life depends on it, you've got three weeks to get it right, and I have no doubt you can do it."

"Aye, Commander," Martinez said, softening his scowl.

"Resetting the sim," Johanssen said. "Anything specific you want to try?"

"Surprise me," Martinez said.

Lewis left the control room and made her way to the reactor. As she climbed "up" the ladder to the center of the ship, the centripetal force on her diminished to zero. Vogel looked up from a computer console. "Commander?"

"How are the engines?" she asked, grabbing a wall-mounted handle to stay attached to the slowly turning room.

"All working within tolerance," Vogel said. "I am now doing a diagnostic on the reactor. I am thinking that Johanssen is busy with the launching training. So perhaps I do this diagnostic for her."

"Good idea," Lewis said. "And how's our course?"

"All is well," Vogel said. "No adjustments necessary. We are still on track to planned trajectory within four meters."

"Keep me posted if anything changes."

"*Ja*, Commander."

Floating to the other side of the core, Lewis took the other ladder out, again gaining gravity as she went "down." She made her way to the Airlock 2 ready room.

Beck held a coil of metal wire in one hand and a pair of work gloves in the other. "Heya, Commander. What's up?"

"I'd like to know your plan for recovering Mark."

"Easy enough if the intercept is good," Beck said. "I just finished attaching all the tethers we have into one long line. It's two hundred and fourteen meters long. I'll have the MMU pack on, so moving around will be easy. I can get going up to around ten meters per second safely. Any more, and I risk breaking the tether if I can't stop in time."

"Once you get to Mark, how fast a relative velocity can you handle?"

"I can grab the MAV easily at five meters per second. Ten meters per second is kind of like jumping onto a moving train. Anything more than that and I might miss."

"So, including the MMU safe speed, we need to get the ship within twenty meters per second of his velocity."

"And the intercept has to be within two hundred and fourteen meters," Beck said. "Pretty narrow margin of error."

"We've got a lot of leeway," Lewis said. "The launch will be fifty-two minutes before the intercept, and it takes twelve minutes. As soon as Mark's

S2 engine cuts out, we'll know our intercept point and velocity. If we don't like it, we'll have forty minutes to correct. Our engine's two millimeters per second may not seem like much, but in forty minutes it can move us up to 5.7 kilometers."

"Good," Beck said. "And two hundred and fourteen meters isn't a hard limit, per se."

"Yes it is," Lewis said.

"Nah," Beck said. "I know I'm not supposed to go untethered, but without my leash I could get way out there—"

"Not an option," Lewis said.

"But we could double or even triple our safe intercept range—"

"We're done talking about this," Lewis said sharply.

"Aye, Commander."

LOG ENTRY: SOL 526

There aren't many people who can say they've vandalized a three-billion-dollar spacecraft, but I'm one of them.

I've been pulling critical hardware out of the MAV left and right. It's nice to know that my launch to orbit won't have any pesky backup systems weighing me down.

First thing I did was remove the small stuff. Then came the things I could disassemble, like the crew seats, several of the backup systems, and the control panels.

I'm not improvising anything. I'm following a script sent by NASA, which was set up to make things as easy as possible. Sometimes I miss the days when I made all the decisions myself. Then I shake it off and remember I'm infinitely better off with a bunch of geniuses deciding what I do than I am making shit up as I go along.

Periodically, I suit up, crawl into the airlock with as much junk as I can fit, and dump it outside. The area around the MAV looks like the set of *Sanford and Son*.

I learned about *Sanford and Son* from Lewis's collection. Seriously, that woman needs to see someone about her seventies problem.

LOG ENTRY: SOL 529

I'm turning water into rocket fuel.

It's easier than you'd think.

Separating hydrogen and oxygen only requires a couple of electrodes and some current. The problem is collecting the hydrogen. I don't have any equipment for pulling hydrogen out of the air. The atmospheric regulator doesn't even know how. The last time I had to get hydrogen out of the air (back when I turned the Hab into a bomb) I burned it to turn it into water. Obviously that would be counterproductive.

But NASA thought everything through and gave me a process. First, I disconnected the rover and trailer from each other. Then, while wearing my EVA suit, I depressurized the trailer and back-filled it with pure oxygen at one-fourth of an atmosphere. Then I opened a plastic box full of water and put a couple of electrodes in. That's why I needed the atmosphere. Without it, the water would just boil immediately and I'd be hanging around in a steamy atmosphere.

The electrolysis separated the hydrogen and

oxygen from each other. Now the trailer was full of even more oxygen and also hydrogen. Pretty dangerous, actually.

Then I fired up the atmospheric regulator. I know I just said it doesn't recognize hydrogen, but it *does* know how to yank oxygen out of the air. I broke all the safeties and set it to pull 100 percent of the oxygen out. After it was done, all that was left in the trailer was hydrogen. That's why I started out with an atmosphere of pure oxygen, so the regulator could separate it later.

Then I cycled the rover's airlock with the inner door open. The airlock thought it was evacuating itself, but it was actually evacuating the whole trailer. The air was stored in the airlock's holding tank. And there you have it, a tank of pure hydrogen.

I carried the airlock's holding tank to the MAV and transferred the contents to the MAV's hydrogen tanks. I've said this many times before, but: Hurray for standardized valve systems!

Finally, I fired up the fuel plant, and it got to work making the additional fuel I'd need.

I'll need to go through this process several more times as the launch date approaches. I'm even going to electrolyze my urine. That'll make for a pleasant smell in the trailer.

If I survive this, I'll tell people I was pissing rocket fuel.

■ ■ ■

[19:22] JOHANSSEN: Hello, Mark.

[19:23] MAV: Johanssen!? Holy crap! They finally letting you talk to me directly?

[19:24] JOHANSSEN: Yes, NASA gave the OK for direct communication an hour ago. We're only 35 light-seconds apart, so we can talk in near-real time. I just set up the system and I'm testing it out.

[19:24] MAV: What took them so long to let us talk?

[19:25] JOHANSSEN: The psych team was worried about personality conflicts.

[19:25] MAV: What? Just 'cause you guys abandoned me on a godforsaken planet with no chance of survival?

[19:26] JOHANSSEN: Funny. Don't make that kind of joke with Lewis.

[19:27] MAV: Roger. So uh . . . thanks for coming back to get me.

[19:27] JOHANSSEN: It's the least we could do. How is the MAV retrofit going?

[19:28] MAV: So far, so good. NASA put a lot of thought into the procedures. They work. That's not to say they're easy. I spent the last 3 days removing Hull Panel 19 and the front window. Even in Mars-g they're heavy motherfuckers.

[19:29] JOHANSSEN: When we pick you up, I will make wild, passionate love to you. Prepare your body.

[19:29] JOHANSSEN: I didn't type that! That was Martinez! I stepped away from the console for like 10 seconds!

[19:29] MAV: I've really missed you guys.

LOG ENTRY: SOL 543

I'm . . . done?

I think I'm done.

I did everything on the list. The MAV is ready to fly. And in six sols, that's just what it'll do. I hope.

It might not launch at all. I did remove an engine, after all. I could have fucked up all sorts of things during that process. And there's no way to test the ascent stage. Once you light it, it's lit.

Everything else, however, will go through tests from now until launch. Some done by me, some done remotely by NASA. They're not telling me the failure odds, but I'm guessing they're the highest in history. Yuri Gagarin had a much more reliable and safe ship than I do.

And Soviet ships were death traps.

■ ■ ■

"ALL RIGHT," Lewis said, "tomorrow's the big day."

The crew floated in the Rec. They had halted the rotation of the ship in preparation for the upcoming operation.

"I'm ready," Martinez said. "Johanssen threw everything she could at me. I got all scenarios to orbit."

"Everything other than catastrophic failures," Johanssen corrected.

"Well yeah," Martinez said. "Kind of pointless to simulate an ascent explosion. Nothing we can do."

"Vogel," Lewis said. "How's our course?"

"It is perfect," Vogel said. "We are within one meter of projected path and two centimeters per second of projected velocity."

"Good," she said. "Beck, how about you?"

"Everything's all set up, Commander," Beck said. "The tethers are linked and spooled in Airlock 2. My suit and MMU are prepped and ready."

"Okay, the battle plan is pretty obvious," Lewis said. She grabbed a handhold on the wall to halt a slow drift she had acquired. "Martinez will fly the MAV, Johanssen will sysop the ascent. Beck and Vogel, I want you in Airlock 2 with the outer door open before the MAV even launches. You'll have to wait fifty-two minutes, but I don't want to risk any technical glitches with the airlock or your suits. Once we reach intercept, it'll be Beck's job to get Watney."

"He might be in bad shape when I get him," Beck said. "The stripped-down MAV will get up to twelve g's during the launch. He could be unconscious and may even have internal bleeding."

"Just as well you're our doctor," Lewis said. "Vogel, if all goes according to plan, you're pulling Beck and Watney back aboard with the tether. If things go wrong, you're Beck's backup."

"*Ja,*" Vogel said.

"I wish there was more we could do right now," Lewis said. "But all we have left is the wait. Your work schedules are cleared. All scientific experiments are suspended. Sleep if you can, run diagnostics on your equipment if you can't."

"We'll get him, Commander," Martinez said as the others floated out. "Twenty-four hours from now, Mark Watney will be right here in this room."

"Let's hope so, Major," Lewis said.

■ ■ ■

"FINAL CHECKS for this shift are complete," Mitch said into his headset. "Timekeeper."

"Go, Flight," said the timekeeper.

"Time until MAV launch?"

"Sixteen hours, nine minutes, forty seconds . . . mark."

"Copy that. All stations: Flight director shift change." He took his headset off and rubbed his eyes.

Brendan Hutch took the headset from him and put it on. "All stations, Flight director is now Brendan Hutch."

"Call me if anything happens," Mitch said. "If not, I'll see you tomorrow."

"Get some sleep, Boss," Brendan said.

Venkat watched from the observation booth. "Why ask the timekeeper?" he mumbled. "It's on the huge mission clock in the center screen."

"He's nervous," Annie said. "You don't often see it, but that's what Mitch Henderson looks like when he's nervous. He double- and triple-checks everything."

"Fair enough," Venkat said.

"They're camping out on the lawn, by the way," Annie said. "Reporters from all over the world. Our press rooms just don't have enough space."

"The media loves a drama." He sighed. "It'll be over tomorrow, one way or another."

"What's our role in all this?" Annie said. "If something goes wrong, what can Mission Control do?"

"Nothing," Venkat said. "Not a damned thing."

"Nothing?"

"It's all happening twelve light-minutes away. That means it takes twenty-four minutes for them to get the answer to any question they ask. The whole launch is twelve minutes long. They're on their own."

"So we're completely helpless?"

"Yes," Venkat said. "Sucks, doesn't it?"

LOG ENTRY: SOL 549

I'd be lying if I said I wasn't shitting myself. In four hours, I'm going to ride a giant explosion into orbit. This is something I've done a few times before, but never with a jury-rigged mess like this.

Right now, I'm sitting in the MAV. I'm suited up because there's a big hole in the front of the ship where the window and part of the hull used to be. I'm "awaiting launch instructions." Really, I'm just awaiting launch. I don't have any part in this. I'm just going to sit in the acceleration couch and hope for the best.

Last night, I ate my final meal pack. It's the first good meal I've had in weeks. I'm leaving forty-one potatoes behind. That's how close I came to starvation.

I carefully collected samples during my journey. But I can't bring any of them with me. So I put them in a container a few hundred meters from here. Maybe someday they'll send a probe to collect them. May as well make them easy to pick up.

This is it. There's nothing after this. There isn't even an abort procedure. Why make one? We can't delay the launch. *Hermes* can't stop and wait. No matter what, we're launching on schedule.

I face the very real possibility that I'll die today. Can't say I like it.

It wouldn't be so bad if the MAV blew up. I

wouldn't know what hit me, but if I miss the intercept, I'll just float around in space until I run out of air. I have a contingency plan for that. I'll drop the oxygen mixture to zero and breathe pure nitrogen until I suffocate. It wouldn't feel bad. The lungs don't have the ability to sense lack of oxygen. I'd just get tired, fall asleep, then die.

I still can't quite believe that this is really it. I'm really leaving. This frigid desert has been my home for a year and a half. I figured out how to survive, at least for a while, and I got used to how things worked. My terrifying struggle to stay alive became somehow routine. Get up in the morning, eat breakfast, tend my crops, fix broken stuff, eat lunch, answer e-mail, watch TV, eat dinner, go to bed. The life of a modern farmer.

Then I was a trucker, doing a long haul across the world. And finally, a construction worker, rebuilding a ship in ways no one ever considered before this. I've done a little of everything here, because I'm the only one around to do it.

That's all over now. I have no more jobs to do, and no more nature to defeat. I've had my last Martian potato. I've slept in the rover for the last time. I've left my last footprints in the dusty red sand. I'm leaving Mars today, one way or another.

About fucking time.

CHAPTER 26

THEY GATHERED.

Everywhere on Earth, they gathered.

In Trafalgar Square and Tiananmen Square and Times Square, they watched on giant screens. In offices, they huddled around computer monitors. In bars, they stared silently at the TV in the corner. In homes, they sat breathlessly on their couches, their eyes glued to the story playing out.

In Chicago, a middle-aged couple clutched each other's hands as they watched. The man held his wife gently as she rocked back and forth out of sheer terror. The NASA representative knew not to disturb them, but stood ready to answer any questions, should they ask.

"Fuel pressure green," Johanssen's voice said from a billion televisions. "Engine alignment perfect. Communications five by five. We are ready for preflight checklist, Commander."

"Copy." Lewis's voice. "CAPCOM."

"Go," Johanssen responded.

"Guidance."
"Go," Johanssen said again.
"Remote Command."
"Go," said Martinez.
"Pilot."
"Go," said Watney from the MAV.
A mild cheer coruscated through the crowds worldwide.

■ ■ ■

MITCH SAT at his station in Mission Control. The controllers monitored everything and were ready to help in any way they could, but the communication latency between *Hermes* and Earth rendered them powerless to do anything but watch.

"Telemetry," Lewis's voice said over the speakers.

"Go," Johanssen responded.

"Recovery," she continued.

"Go," said Beck from the airlock.

"Secondary Recovery."

"Go," said Vogel from beside Beck.

"Mission Control, this is *Hermes* Actual," Lewis reported. "We are go for launch and will proceed on schedule. We are T minus four minutes, ten seconds to launch . . . mark."

"Did you get that, Timekeeper?" Mitch said.

"Affirmative, Flight" was the response. "Our clocks are synched with theirs."

"Not that we can do anything," Mitch mumbled, "but at least we'll know what's supposedly happening."

■ ■ ■

"ABOUT FOUR minutes, Mark," Lewis said into her mic. "How you doing down there?"

"Eager to get up there, Commander," Watney responded.

"We're going to make that happen," Lewis said. "Remember, you'll be pulling some pretty heavy g's. It's okay to pass out. You're in Martinez's hands."

"Tell that asshole no barrel rolls."

"Copy that, MAV," Lewis said.

"Four more minutes," Martinez said, cracking his knuckles. "You ready for some flying, Beth?"

"Yeah," Johanssen said. "It'll be strange to sysop a launch and stay in zero-g the whole time."

"I hadn't thought of it that way," Martinez said, "but yeah. I'm not going to be squashed against the back of my seat. Weird."

■ ■ ■

BECK FLOATED in the airlock, tethered to a wall-mounted spool. Vogel stood beside him, his boots clamped to the floor. Both stared through the open outer door at the red planet below.

"Didn't think I'd be back here again," Beck said.

"Yes," Vogel said. "We are the first."

"First what?"

"We are the first to visit Mars twice."

"Oh yeah. Even Watney can't say that."

"He cannot."

They looked at Mars in silence for a while.

"Vogel," Beck said.

"Ja."

"If I can't reach Mark, I want you to release my tether."

"Dr. Beck," Vogel said, "the commander has said no to this."

"I know what the commander said, but if I need a few more meters, I want you to cut me loose. I have an MMU, I can get back without a tether."

"I will not do this, Dr. Beck."

"It's my own life at risk, and I say it's okay."

"You are not the commander."

Beck scowled at Vogel, but with their reflective visors down, the effect was lost.

"Fine," Beck said. "But I bet you'll change your mind if push comes to shove."

Vogel did not respond.

■■■

"T-MINUS TEN," said Johanssen, "nine . . . eight . . ."

"Main engines start," said Martinez.

". . . seven . . . six . . . five . . . Mooring clamps released . . ."

"About five seconds, Watney," Lewis said to her headset. "Hang on."

"See you in a few, Commander," Watney radioed back.

". . . four . . . three . . . two . . ."

■■■

WATNEY LAY in the acceleration couch as the MAV rumbled in anticipation of liftoff.

"Hmm," he said to nobody. "I wonder how much longer—"

The MAV launched with incredible force. More than any manned ship had accelerated in the history of space travel. Watney was shoved back into his couch so hard he couldn't even grunt.

Having anticipated this, he had placed a folded-up shirt behind his head in the helmet. As his head drove ever deeper into the makeshift cushion, the edges of his vision became blurry. He could neither breathe nor move.

Directly in his field of view, the Hab canvas patch flapped violently as the ship exponentially gained speed. Concentration became difficult, but something in the back of his mind told him that flapping was bad.

▪▪▪

"VELOCITY SEVEN hundred and forty-one meters per second," Johanssen called out. "Altitude thirteen hundred and fifty meters."

"Copy," Martinez said.

"That's low," Lewis said. "Too low."

"I know," Martinez said. "It's sluggish; fighting me. What the fuck is going on?"

"Velocity eight hundred and fifty, altitude eighteen hundred and forty-three," Johanssen said.

"I'm not getting the power I need!" Martinez said.

"Engine power at a hundred percent," Johanssen said.

"I'm telling you it's sluggish," Martinez insisted.

"Watney," Lewis said to her headset. "Watney, do you read? Can you report?"

■ ■ ■

WATNEY HEARD Lewis's voice in the distance. Like someone talking to him through a long tunnel. He vaguely wondered what she wanted. His attention was briefly drawn to the fluttering canvas ahead of him. A rip had appeared and was rapidly widening.

But then he was distracted by a bolt in one of the bulkheads. It only had five sides. He wondered why NASA decided that bolt needed five sides instead of six. It would require a special wrench to tighten or loosen.

The canvas tore even further, the tattered material flapping wildly. Through the opening, Watney saw red sky stretching out infinitely ahead. "That's nice," he thought.

As the MAV flew higher, the atmosphere grew thinner. Soon, the canvas stopped fluttering and simply stretched toward Mark. The sky shifted from red to black.

"That's nice, too," Mark thought.

As consciousness slipped away, he wondered where he could get a cool five-sided bolt like that.

■ ■ ■

"I'M GETTING more response now," Martinez said.

"Back on track with full acceleration," Johanssen said. "Must have been drag. MAV's out of the atmosphere now."

"It was like flying a cow," Martinez grumbled, his hands racing over his controls.

"Can you get him up?" Lewis asked.

"He'll get to orbit," Johanssen said, "but the intercept course may be compromised."

"Get him up first," Lewis said. "Then we'll worry about intercept."

"Copy. Main engine cutoff in fifteen seconds."

"Totally smooth now," Martinez said. "It's not fighting me at all anymore."

"Well below target altitude," Johanssen said. "Velocity is good."

"How far below?" Lewis said.

"Can't say for sure," Johanssen said. "All I have is accelerometer data. We'll need radar pings at intervals to work out his true final orbit."

"Back to automatic guidance," Martinez said.

"Main shutdown in four," Johanssen said, ". . . three . . . two . . . one . . . Shutdown."

"Confirm shutdown," Martinez said.

"Watney, you there?" Lewis said. "Watney? Watney, do you read?"

"Probably passed out, Commander," Beck said over the radio. "He pulled twelve g's on the ascent. Give him a few minutes."

"Copy," Lewis said. "Johanssen, got his orbit yet?"

"I have interval pings. Working out our intercept range and velocity . . ."

Martinez and Lewis stared at Johanssen as she brought up the intercept calculation software. Normally, orbits would be worked out by Vogel, but he was otherwise engaged. Johanssen was his backup for orbital dynamics.

"Intercept velocity will be eleven meters per second . . . ," she began.

"I can make that work," Beck said over the radio.

"Distance at intercept will be—" Johanssen stopped and choked. Shakily, she continued. "We'll be sixty-eight kilometers apart." She buried her face in her hands.

"Did she say sixty-eight *kilometers*!?" Beck said. *"Kilometers!?"*

"God damn it," Martinez whispered.

"Keep it together," Lewis said. "Work the problem. Martinez, is there any juice in the MAV?"

"Negative, Commander," Martinez responded. "They ditched the OMS system to lighten the launch weight."

"Then we'll have to go to him. Johanssen, time to intercept?"

"Thirty-nine minutes, twelve seconds," Johanssen said, trying not to quaver.

"Vogel," Lewis continued, "how far can we deflect in thirty-nine minutes with the ion engines?"

"Perhaps five kilometers," he radioed.

"Not enough," Lewis said. "Martinez, what if we point our attitude thrusters all the same direction?"

"Depends on how much fuel we want to save for attitude adjustments on the trip home."

"How much do you need?"

"I could get by with maybe twenty percent of what's left."

"All right, if you used the other eighty percent—"

"Checking," Martinez said, running the numbers on his console. "We'd get a delta-v of thirty-one meters per second."

"Johanssen," Lewis said. "Math."

"In thirty-nine minutes we'd deflect . . . ," Johanssen quickly typed, "seventy-two kilometers!"

"There we go," Lewis said. "How much fuel—"

"Use seventy-five point five percent of remaining attitude adjust fuel," Johanssen said. "That'll bring the intercept range to zero."

"Do it," Lewis said.

"Aye, Commander," Martinez said.

"Hold on," Johanssen said. "That'll get the intercept *range* to zero, but the intercept *velocity* will be forty-two meters per second."

"Then we have thirty-nine minutes to figure out how to slow down," Lewis said. "Martinez, burn the jets."

"Aye," Martinez said.

■■■

"WHOA," Annie said to Venkat. "A lot of shit just happened really fast. Explain."

Venkat strained to hear the audio feed over the murmur of the VIPs in the observation booth. Through the glass, he saw Mitch throw his hands up in frustration.

"The launch missed badly," Venkat said, looking past Mitch to the screens beyond. "The intercept distance was going to be way too big. So they're using the attitude adjusters to close the gap."

"What do attitude adjusters usually do?"

"They rotate the ship. They're not made for thrusting it. *Hermes* doesn't have quick-reaction engines. Just the slow, steady ion engines."

"So . . . problem solved?" Annie said hopefully.

"No," Venkat said. "They'll get to him, but they'll be going forty-two meters per second when they get there."

"How fast is that?" Annie asked.

"About ninety miles per hour," Venkat said. "There's no hope of Beck grabbing Watney at that speed."

"Can they use the attitude adjusters to slow down?"

"They needed a lot of velocity to close the gap in time. They used all the fuel they could spare to get going fast enough. But now they don't have enough fuel to slow down." Venkat frowned.

"So what can they do?"

"I don't know," he said. "And even if I did, I couldn't tell them in time."

"Well fuck," Annie said.

"Yeah," Venkat agreed.

■ ■ ■

"WATNEY," Lewis said "Do you read? . . . Watney?" she repeated.

"Commander," Beck radioed. "He's wearing a surface EVA suit, right?"

"Yeah."

"It should have a bio-monitor," Beck said. "And it'll be broadcasting. It's not a strong signal; it's only designed to go a couple hundred meters to the rover or Hab. But maybe we can pick it up."

"Johanssen," Lewis said.

"On it," Johanssen said. "I have to look up the frequencies in the tech specs. Gimme a second."

"Martinez," Lewis continued. "Any idea how to slow down?"

He shook his head. "I got nothin', Commander. We're just going too damn fast."

"Vogel?"

"The ion drive is simply not strong enough," Vogel replied.

"There's got to be something," Lewis said. "Something we can do. Anything."

"Got his bio-monitor data," Johanssen said. "Pulse fifty-eight, blood pressure ninety-eight over sixty-one."

"That's not bad," Beck said. "Lower than I'd like, but he's been in Mars gravity for eighteen months, so it's expected."

"Time to intercept?" Lewis asked.

"Thirty-two minutes," Johanssen replied.

■ ■ ■

BLISSFUL unconsciousness became foggy awareness which transitioned into painful reality. Watney opened his eyes, then winced at the pain in his chest.

Little remained of the canvas. Tatters floated along the edge of the hole it once covered. This granted Watney an unobstructed view of Mars from orbit. The red planet's crater-pocked surface stretched out seemingly forever, its thin atmosphere a slight blur along the edge. Only eighteen people in history had personally seen this view.

"Fuck you," he said to the planet below.

Reaching toward the controls on his arm, he

winced. Trying again, more slowly this time, he activated his radio. "MAV to *Hermes*."

"Watney!?" came the reply.

"Affirmative. That you, Commander?" Watney said.

"Affirmative. What's your status?"

"I'm on a ship with no control panel," he said. "That's as much as I can tell you."

"How do you feel?"

"My chest hurts. I think I broke a rib. How are you?"

"We're working on getting you," Lewis said. "There was a complication in the launch."

"Yeah," Watney said, looking out the hole in the ship. "The canvas didn't hold. I think it ripped early in the ascent."

"That's consistent with what we saw during the launch."

"How bad is it, Commander?" he asked.

"We were able to correct the intercept range with *Hermes*'s attitude thrusters. But there's a problem with the intercept velocity."

"How big a problem."

"Forty-two meters per second."

"Well shit."

■■■

"HEY, AT least he's okay for the moment," Martinez said.

"Beck," Lewis said, "I'm coming around to your way of thinking. How fast can you get going if you're untethered?"

"Sorry, Commander," Beck said. "I already ran

the numbers. At best I could get twenty-five meters per second. Even if I could get to forty-two, I'd need *another* forty-two to match *Hermes* when I came back."

"Copy," Lewis said.

"Hey," Watney said over the radio, "I've got an idea."

"Of course you do," Lewis said. "What do you got?"

"I could find something sharp in here and poke a hole in the glove of my EVA suit. I could use the escaping air as a thruster and fly my way to you. The source of thrust would be on my arm, so I'd be able to direct it pretty easily."

"How does he come up with this shit?" Martinez interjected.

"Hmm," Lewis said. "Could you get forty-two meters per second that way?"

"No idea," Watney said.

"I can't see you having any control if you did that," Lewis said. "You'd be eyeballing the intercept and using a thrust vector you can barely control."

"I admit it's fatally dangerous," Watney said. "But consider this: I'd get to fly around like Iron Man."

"We'll keep working on ideas," Lewis said.

"Iron Man, Commander. *Iron Man.*"

"Stand by," Lewis said.

She furrowed her brow. "Hmm . . . Maybe it's not such a bad idea. . . ."

"You kidding, Commander?" Martinez said. "It's a terrible idea. He'd shoot off into space—"

"Not the whole idea, but part of it," she said. "Using atmosphere as thrust. Martinez, get Vogel's station up and running."

"Okay," Martinez said, typing at his keyboard. The screen changed to Vogel's workstation. Martinez quickly changed the language from German to English. "It's up. What do you need?"

"Vogel's got software for calculating course offsets caused by hull breaches, right?"

"Yeah," Martinez said. "It estimates course corrections needed in the event of—"

"Yeah, yeah," Lewis said. "Fire it up. I want to know what happens if we blow the VAL."

Johanssen and Martinez looked at each other.

"Um. Yes, Commander," Martinez said.

"The vehicular airlock?" Johanssen said. "You want to . . . open it?"

"Plenty of air in the ship," Lewis said. "It'd give us a good kick."

"Ye-es . . . ," Martinez said as he brought up the software. "And it might blow the nose of the ship off in the process."

"Also, all the air would leave," Johanssen felt compelled to add.

"We'll seal the bridge and reactor room. We can let everywhere else go vacuo, but we don't want explosive decompression in here or near the reactor."

Martinez entered the scenario into the software. "I think we'll just have the same problem as Watney, but on a larger scale. We can't direct that thrust."

"We don't have to," Lewis said. "The VAL is in the nose. Escaping air would make a thrust vector through our center of mass. We just need to point the ship directly away from where we want to go."

"Okay, I have the numbers," Martinez said. "A breach at the VAL, with the bridge and reactor room sealed off, would accelerate us twenty-nine meters per second."

"We'd have a relative velocity of thirteen meters per second afterward," Johanssen supplied.

"Beck," Lewis radioed. "Have you been hearing all this?"

"Affirmative, Commander," Beck said.

"Can you do thirteen meters per second?"

"It'll be risky," Beck replied. "Thirteen to match the MAV, then another thirteen to match *Hermes*. But it's a hell of a lot better than forty-two."

"Johanssen," Lewis said. "Time to intercept?"

"Eighteen minutes, Commander."

"What kind of jolt will we feel with that breach?" Lewis asked Martinez.

"The air will take four seconds to evacuate," he said. "We'll feel a little less than one g."

"Watney," she said to her headset, "we have a plan."

"Yay! A plan!" Watney replied.

■ ■ ■

"HOUSTON," Lewis's voice rang through Mission Control. "Be advised we are going to deliberately breach the VAL to produce thrust."

"What?" Mitch said. "What!?"

"Oh . . . my god," Venkat said in the observation room.

"Fuck me raw," Annie said, getting up. "I better get to the press room. Any parting knowledge before I go?"

"They're going to breach the ship," Venkat said,

still dumbfounded. "They're going to *deliberately* breach the ship. Oh my god . . ."

"Got it," Annie said, jogging to the door.

■ ■ ■

"HOW WILL we open the airlock doors?" Martinez asked. "There's no way to open them remotely, and if anyone's nearby when it blows—"

"Right," Lewis said. "We can open one door with the other shut, but how do we open the other?"

She thought for a moment. "Vogel," she radioed. "I need you to come back in and make a bomb."

"Um. Again, please, Commander?" Vogel replied.

"A bomb," Lewis confirmed. "You're a chemist. Can you make a bomb out of stuff on board?"

"*Ja*," Vogel said. "We have flammables and pure oxygen."

"Sounds good," Lewis said.

"It is of course dangerous to set off an explosive device on a spacecraft," Vogel pointed out.

"So make it small," Lewis said. "It just needs to poke a hole in the inner airlock door. Any hole will do. If it blows the door off, that's fine. If it doesn't, the air will get out slower, but for longer. The momentum change is the same, and we'll get the acceleration we need."

"Pressurizing Airlock 2," Vogel reported. "How will we activate this bomb?"

"Johanssen?" Lewis said.

"Uh . . . ," Johanssen said. She picked up her headset and quickly put it on. "Vogel, can you run wires into it?"

"*Ja,*" Vogel said. "I will use threaded stopper with a small hole for the wires. It will have little effect on the seal."

"We could run the wire to Lighting Panel 41," Johanssen said. "It's next to the airlock, and I can turn it on and off from here."

"There's our remote trigger," Lewis said. "Johanssen, go set up the lighting panel. Vogel, get in here and make the bomb. Martinez, go close and seal the doors to the reactor room."

"Yes, Commander," Johanssen said, kicking off her seat toward the hallway.

"Commander," Martinez said, pausing at the exit, "you want me to bring back some space suits?"

"No point," Lewis said. "If the seal on the bridge doesn't hold, we'll get sucked out at close to the speed of sound. We'll be jelly with or without suits on."

"Hey, Martinez," said Beck over the radio. "Can you move my lab mice somewhere safe? They're in the bio lab. It's just one cage."

"Copy, Beck," said Martinez. "I'll move them to the reactor room."

"Are you back in yet, Vogel?" Lewis asked.

"I am just reentering now, Commander."

"Beck," Lewis said to her headset. "I'll need you back in, too. But don't take your suit off."

"Okay," Beck said. "Why?"

"We're going to have to literally blow up one of the doors," Lewis explained. "I'd rather we kill the inner one. I want the outer door unharmed, so we keep our smooth aerobraking shape."

"Makes sense," Beck responded as he floated back into the ship.

"One problem," Lewis said. "I want the outer

door locked in the fully open position with the mechanical stopper in place to keep it from being trashed by the decompress."

"You have to have someone in the airlock to do that," Beck said. "And you can't open the inner door if the outer door is locked open."

"Right," Lewis said. "So I need you to come back inside, depressurize the VAL, and lock the outer door open. Then you'll need to crawl along the hull to get back to Airlock 2."

"Copy, Commander," Beck said. "There are latch points all over the hull. I'll move my tether along, mountain climber style."

"Get to it," Lewis said. "And Vogel, you're in a hurry. You have to make the bomb, set it up, get back to Airlock 2, suit up, depressurize it, and open the outer door, so Beck can get back in when he's done."

"He's taking his suit off right now and can't reply," Beck reported, "but he heard the order."

"Watney, how you doing?" Lewis's voice said in his ear.

"Fine so far, Commander," Watney replied. "You mentioned a plan?"

"Affirmative," she said. "We're going to vent atmosphere to get thrust."

"How?"

"We're going to blow a hole in the VAL."

"What!?" Watney said. "How!?"

"Vogel's making a bomb."

"I *knew* that guy was a mad scientist!" Watney said. "I think we should just go with my Iron Man idea."

"That's too risky, and you know it," she replied.

"Thing is," Watney said, "I'm selfish. I want the memorials back home to be just for me. I don't want the rest of you losers in them. I can't let you guys blow the VAL."

"Oh," Lewis said, "well if you won't let us then— Wait . . . wait a minute . . . . I'm looking at my shoulder patch and it turns out I'm the commander. Sit tight. We're coming to get you."

"Smart-ass."

■ ■ ■

As a chemist, Vogel knew how to make a bomb. In fact, much of his training was to avoid making them by mistake.

The ship had few flammables aboard, due to the fatal danger of fire. But food, by its very nature, contained flammable hydrocarbons. Lacking time to sit down and do the math, he estimated.

Sugar has 4000 food-calories per kilogram. One food-calorie is 4184 joules. Sugar in zero-g will float and the grains will separate, maximizing surface area. In a pure-oxygen environment, 16.7 million joules will be released for every kilogram of sugar used, releasing the explosive force of eight sticks of dynamite. Such is the nature of combustion in pure oxygen.

Vogel measured the sugar carefully. He poured it into the strongest container he could find, a thick glass beaker. The strength of the container was as important as the explosive. A weak container would simply cause a fireball without much concussive force. A strong container, however, would contain the pressure until it reached true destructive potential.

He quickly drilled a hole in the beaker's stopper, then stripped a section of wire. He ran the wire through the hole.

"Sehr gefährlich," he mumbled as he poured liquid oxygen from the ship's supply into the container, then quickly screwed the stopper on. In just a few minutes, he had made a rudimentary pipe bomb.

"Sehr, sehr, gefährlich."

He floated out of the lab and made his way toward the nose of the ship.

▪▪▪

JOHANSSEN WORKED on the lighting panel as Beck floated toward the VAL.

She grabbed his arm. "Be careful crawling along the hull."

He turned to face her. "Be careful setting up the bomb."

She kissed his faceplate then looked away, embarrassed. "That was stupid. Don't tell anyone I did that."

"Don't tell anyone I liked it." Beck smiled.

He entered the airlock and sealed the inner door. After depressurizing, he opened the outer door and locked it in place. Grabbing a handrail on the hull, he pulled himself out.

Johanssen watched until he was no longer in view, then returned to the lighting panel. She had deactivated it earlier from her workstation. After pulling a length of the cable out and stripping the ends, she fiddled with a roll of electrical tape until Vogel arrived.

He showed up just a minute later, carefully

floating down the hall with the bomb held in both hands.

"I have used a single wire for igniting," he explained. "I did not want to risk two wires for a spark. It would be dangerous to us if we had static while setting up."

"How do we set it off?" Johanssen said.

"The wire must reach a high temperature. If you short power through it, that will be sufficient."

"I'll have to pin the breaker," Johanssen said, "but it'll work."

She twisted the lighting wires onto the bomb's and taped them off.

"Excuse me," Vogel said. "I have to return to Airlock 2 to let Dr. Beck back in."

"Mm," Johanssen said.

■ ■ ■

MARTINEZ FLOATED back into the bridge. "I had a few minutes, so I ran through the aerobrake lockdown checklist for the reactor room. Everything's ready for acceleration and the compartment's sealed off."

"Good thinking," Lewis said. "Prep the attitude correction."

"Roger, Commander," Martinez said, drifting to his station.

"The VAL's propped open," Beck's voice said over the comm. "Starting my traverse across the hull."

"Copy," Lewis said.

"This calculation is tricky," Martinez said. "I need to do everything backward. The VAL's in front, so the source of thrust will be exactly opposite to our engines. Our software wasn't expecting us to have an engine there. I just need to tell it we plan to thrust *toward* Mark."

"Take your time and get it right," Lewis said. "And don't execute till I give you the word. We're not spinning the ship around while Beck's out on the hull."

"Roger," he said. After a moment, he added "Okay, the adjustment's ready to execute."

"Stand by," Lewis said.

■■■

VOGEL, BACK in his suit, depressurized Airlock 2 and opened the outer door.

"'Bout time," Beck said, climbing in.

"Sorry for the delay," Vogel said. "I was required to make a bomb."

"This has been kind of a weird day," Beck said. "Commander, Vogel and I are in position."

"Copy" was Lewis's response. "Get up against the fore wall of the airlock. It's going to be about one g for four seconds. Make sure you're both tethered in."

"Copy," Beck said as he attached his tether. The two men pressed themselves against the wall.

■■■

"OKAY, MARTINEZ," Lewis said, "point us the right direction."

"Copy," said Martinez, executing the attitude adjustment.

Johanssen floated into the bridge as the adjustment was performed. The room rotated around her as she reached for a handhold. "The bomb's ready, and the breaker's jammed closed," she said. "I can set it off by remotely turning on Lighting Panel 41."

"Seal the bridge and get to your station," Lewis said.

"Copy," Johanssen said. Unstowing the emergency seal, she plugged the entrance to the bridge. With a few turns of the crank, the job was done. She returned to her station and ran a quick test. "Increasing bridge pressure to 1.03 atmospheres. . . . Pressure is steady. We have a good seal."

"Copy," Lewis said. "Time to intercept?"

"Twenty-eight seconds," Johanssen said.

"Wow," Martinez said. "We cut that pretty close."

"You ready, Johanssen?" Lewis asked.

"Yes," Johanssen said. "All I have to do is hit enter."

"Martinez, how's our angle?"

"Dead-on, Commander," Martinez reported.

"Strap in," Lewis said.

The three of them tightened the restraints of their chairs.

"Twenty seconds," Johanssen said.

■ ■ ■

TEDDY TOOK his seat in the VIP room. "What's the status?"

"Fifteen seconds till they blow the VAL," Venkat said. "Where have you been?"

"On the phone with the President," Teddy said. "Do you think this will work?"

"I have no idea," Venkat said. "I've never felt this helpless in my life."

"If it's any consolation," Teddy said, "pretty much everyone in the world feels the same way."

On the other side of the glass, Mitch paced to and fro.

▪▪▪

". . . FIVE . . . four . . . three . . . ," Johanssen said.

"Brace for acceleration," Lewis said.

". . . two . . . one . . . ," Johanssen continued. "Activating Lighting Panel 41."

She pressed enter.

Inside Vogel's bomb, the full current of the ship's internal lighting system flowed through a thin, exposed wire. It quickly reached the ignition temperature of the sugar. What would have been a minor fizzle in Earth's atmosphere became an uncontrolled conflagration in the container's pure oxygen environment. In under one hundred milliseconds, the massive combustion pressure burst the container, and the resulting explosion ripped the airlock door to shreds.

The internal air of *Hermes* rushed through the open VAL, blasting *Hermes* in the other direction.

Vogel and Beck were pressed against the wall of Airlock 2. Lewis, Martinez, and Johanssen endured the acceleration in their seats. It was not a dangerous amount of force. In fact it was less than the force of Earth's surface gravity. But it was inconsistent and jerky.

After four seconds, the shaking died down and the ship returned to weightlessness.

"Reactor room still pressurized," Martinez reported.

"Bridge seal holding," Johanssen said. "Obviously."

"Damage?" Martinez said.

"Not sure yet," Johanssen said. "I have External Camera 4 pointed along the nose. I don't see any problems with the hull near the VAL."

"Worry about that later," Lewis said. "What's our relative velocity and distance to MAV?"

Johanssen typed quickly. "We'll get within twenty-two meters and we're at twelve meters per second. We actually got better than expected thrust."

"Watney," Lewis said, "it worked. Beck's on his way."

"Score!" Watney responded.

"Beck," Lewis said, "you're up. Twelve meters per second."

"Close enough!" Beck replied.

■ ■ ■

"I'M GOING to jump out," Beck said. "Should get me another two or three meters per second."

"Understood," Vogel said, loosely gripping Beck's tether. "Good luck, Dr. Beck."

Placing his feet on the back wall, Beck coiled and leaped out of the airlock.

Once free, he got his bearings. A quick look to

his right showed him what he could not see from inside the airlock.

"I have visual!" Beck said. "I can see the MAV!"

The MAV barely resembled a spacecraft as Beck had come to know them. The once sleek lines were now a jagged mess of missing hull segments and empty anchor points where noncritical components used to be.

"Jesus, Mark, what did you *do* to that thing?"

"You should see what I did to the rover," Watney radioed back.

Beck thrust on an intercept course. He had practiced this many times. The presumption in those practice sessions was that he'd be rescuing a crewmate whose tether had broken, but the principle was the same.

"Johanssen," he said, "you got me on radar?"

"Affirmative," she replied.

"Call out my relative velocity to Mark every two seconds or so."

"Copy. Five point two meters per second."

"Hey Beck," Watney said, "the front's wide open. I'll get up there and be ready to grab at you."

"Negative," interrupted Lewis. "No untethered movement. Stay strapped to your chair until you're latched to Beck."

"Copy," Watney said.

"Three point one meters per second," Johanssen reported.

"Going to coast for a bit," Beck said. "Gotta catch up before I slow it down." He rotated himself in preparation for the next burn.

"Eleven meters to target," Johanssen said.

"Copy."

"Six meters," Johanssen said.

"Aaaaand counter-thrusting," Beck said, firing

the MMU thrusters again. The MAV loomed before him. "Velocity?" he asked.

"One point one meters per second," Johanssen said.

"Good enough," he said, reaching for the ship. "I'm drifting toward it. I think I can get my hand on some of the torn canvas. . . ."

The tattered canvas beckoned as the only handhold on the otherwise smooth ship. Beck reached, extending as best he could, and managed to grab hold.

"Contact," Beck said. Strengthening his grip, he pulled his body forward and lashed out with his other hand to grab more canvas. "Firm contact!"

"Dr. Beck," Vogel said, "we have passed closest approach point and you are now getting further away. You have one hundred and sixty-nine meters of tether left. Enough for fourteen seconds."

"Copy," Beck said.

Pulling his head to the opening, he looked inside the compartment to see Watney strapped to his chair.

"Visual on Watney!" he reported.

"Visual on Beck!" Watney reported.

"How ya doin', man?" Beck said, pulling himself into the ship.

"I . . . I just . . ." Watney said. "Give me a minute. You're the first person I've seen in eighteen months."

"We don't have a minute," Beck said, kicking off the wall. "We've got eleven seconds before we run out of tether."

Beck's course took him to the chair, where he clumsily collided with Watney. The two gripped each other's arms to keep Beck from bouncing away. "Contact with Watney!" Beck said.

"Eight seconds, Dr. Beck," Vogel radioed.

"Copy," Beck said as he hastily latched the front of his suit to the front of Watney's with tether clips. "Connected," he said.

Watney released the straps on his chair. "Restraints off."

"We're outa here," Beck said, kicking off the chair toward the opening.

The two men floated across the MAV cabin to the opening. Beck reached out his arm and pushed off the edge as they passed through.

"We're out," Beck reported.

"Five seconds," Vogel said.

"Relative velocity to *Hermes*: twelve meters per second," Johanssen said.

"Thrusting," Beck said, activating his MMU.

The two accelerated toward *Hermes* for a few seconds. Then the MMU controls on Beck's heads-up display turned red.

"That's it for the fuel," Beck said. "Velocity?"

"Five meters per second," Johanssen replied.

"Stand by," Vogel said. Throughout the process, he had been feeding tether out of the airlock. Now he gripped the ever-shrinking remainder of the rope with both hands. He didn't clamp down on it; that would pull him out of the airlock. He simply closed his hands over the tether to create friction.

Hermes was now pulling Beck and Watney along, with Vogel's use of the tether acting as a shock absorber. If Vogel used too much force, the shock of it would pull the tether free from Beck's suit clips. If he used too little, the tether would run out before they matched speeds, then jerk to a hard stop at the end, which would also rip it out of Beck's suit clips.

Vogel managed to find the balance. After a few seconds of tense, gut-feel physics, he felt the force on the tether abate.

"Velocity zero!" Johanssen reported excitedly.

"Reel 'em in, Vogel," Lewis said.

"Copy," Vogel said. Hand over hand, he slowly pulled his crewmates toward the airlock. After a few seconds, he stopped actively pulling and simply took in the line as they coasted toward him.

They floated into the airlock, and Vogel grabbed them. Beck and Watney both reached for handholds on the wall as Vogel worked his way around them and closed the outer door.

"Aboard!" Beck said.

"Airlock 2 outer door closed," Vogel said.

"Yes!" Martinez yelled.

"Copy," Lewis said.

■ ■ ■

LEWIS'S VOICE echoed across the world: "Houston, this is *Hermes* Actual. Six crew safely aboard."

The control room exploded with applause. Leaping from their seats, controllers cheered, hugged, and cried. The same scene played out all over the world, in parks, bars, civic centers, living rooms, classrooms, and offices.

The couple in Chicago clutched each other in sheer relief, then pulled the NASA representative in for a group hug.

Mitch slowly pulled off his headset and turned to face the VIP room. Through the glass, he saw various well-suited men and women cheering wildly. He looked at Venkat and let out a heavy sigh of relief.

Venkat put his head in his hands and whispered, "Thank the gods."

Teddy pulled a blue folder from his briefcase and stood. "Annie will be wanting me in the press room."

"Guess you don't need the red folder today," Venkat said.

"Honestly, I didn't make one." As he walked out he added, "Good work, Venk. Now, get them home."

LOG ENTRY: MISSION DAY 687

That "687" caught me off guard for a minute. On *Hermes*, we track time by mission days. It may be Sol 549 down on Mars, but it's Mission Day 687 up here. And you know what? It doesn't matter what time it is on Mars because *I'm not there*!

Oh my god. I'm really not on Mars anymore. I can tell because there's no gravity and there are other humans around. I'm still adjusting.

If this were a movie, everyone would have been in the airlock, and there would have been high fives all around. But it didn't pan out that way.

I broke two ribs during the MAV ascent. They were sore the whole time, but they really started screaming when Vogel pulled us into the airlock by the tether. I didn't want to distract the people who were saving my life, so I muted my mic and screamed like a little girl.

It's true, you know. In space, no one can hear you scream like a little girl.

Once they got me into Airlock 2, they opened

the inner door and I was finally aboard again. Hermes was still in vacuo, so we didn't have to cycle the airlock.

Beck told me to go limp and pushed me down the corridor toward his quarters (which serve as the ship's "sick bay" when needed).

Vogel went the other direction and closed the outer VAL door.

Once Beck and I got to his quarters, we waited for the ship to repressurize. *Hermes* had enough spare air to refill the ship two more times if needed. It'd be a pretty shitty long-range ship if it couldn't recover from a decompression.

After Johanssen gave us the all clear, Dr. Bossy-Beck made me wait while he first took off his suit, then took off mine. After he pulled my helmet off, he looked shocked. I thought maybe I had a major head wound or something, but it turns out it was the smell.

It's been a while since I washed . . . anything.

After that, it was X-rays and chest bandages while the rest of the crew checked the ship for damage.

Then came the (painful) high fives, followed by people staying as far away from my stench as possible. We had a few minutes of reunion before Beck shuttled everyone out. He gave me painkillers and told me to shower as soon as I could move my arms. So now I'm waiting for the drugs to kick in.

I think about the sheer number of people who pulled together just to save my sorry ass, and I can barely comprehend it. My crewmates sacrificed a year of their lives to come back for me. Countless people at NASA worked day and night to invent rover and MAV modifications. All of

JPL busted their asses to make a probe that was destroyed on launch. Then, instead of giving up, they made *another* probe to resupply *Hermes*. The China National Space Administration abandoned a project they'd worked on for years just to provide a booster.

The cost for my survival must have been hundreds of millions of dollars. All to save one dorky botanist. Why bother?

Well, okay. I know the answer to that. Part of it might be what I represent: progress, science, and the interplanetary future we've dreamed of for centuries. But really, they did it because every human being has a basic instinct to help each other out. It might not seem that way sometimes, but it's true.

If a hiker gets lost in the mountains, people will coordinate a search. If a train crashes, people will line up to give blood. If an earthquake levels a city, people all over the world will send emergency supplies. This is so fundamentally human that it's found in every culture without exception. Yes, there are assholes who just don't care, but they're massively outnumbered by the people who do. And because of that, I had billions of people on my side.

Pretty cool, eh?

Anyway, my ribs hurt like hell, my vision is still blurry from acceleration sickness, I'm really hungry, it'll be another 211 days before I'm back on Earth, and, apparently, I smell like a skunk took a shit on some sweat socks.

This is the happiest day of my life.

ANDY WEIR was first hired as a programmer for a national laboratory at age fifteen and has been working as a software engineer ever since. He is a lifelong space nerd and a devoted hobbyist of subjects such as relativistic physics, orbital mechanics, and the history of manned spaceflight. *The Martian* is his first novel.